SARA

THE COMPLETE SERIES

SARA

THE COMPLETE SERIES

Ernie Lindsey

ISBN-13: 9781505471489
ISBN-10: 1505471486

Sara: The Complete Series / Ernie Lindsey. – 1st ed.

Includes the following works:
SARA'S GAME
SARA'S PAST
SARA'S FEAR
and the companion novella
ONE MORE GAME

"Say, 'It's just a game,' one more time. Go on, do it. I dare you."
—*Anonymous*

SARA'S GAME

Chapter One
SARA

Sara was late again.

She plowed into her office, greeted by the overpowering scent of cologne and hair gel. Teddy Rutherford, the clichéd heir to the throne and obnoxious VP of Research & Development, sat at her desk using *her* PC to play that little game involving dogs, cats, and giant cannons. Her kids loved it, but she never saw the appeal.

As the VP of Marketing for a growing video game company in Portland, Oregon, it was her job to get their *Juggernaut* series into as many hands as possible. And since she'd been promoted to a marketing position after a decade of hundred-hour workweeks as a tester, then up to VP, LightPulse Productions had grossed more in the past eight months than over the previous five years.

Marketing came naturally to her, and nobody in the industry had seen her coming. She had been interviewed in numerous magazines, made it into the upper half of multiple Top 40 Under 40 lists, and signed a contract to write a monthly column for *Professional Mother*. All while raising twin girls and their younger brother, alone, since the day their father left for the gym and never came back.

She'd been wined and dined with some incredible offers from Fortune 500 companies, but LightPulse was her home, the house she'd helped build, and she had no intention of leaving.

Even if it meant dealing with a privileged, spoiled cretin like Teddy on a daily basis.

He said, "These guys are pure genius, aren't they? Nothing but flat animation, some bright colors, and the chance to destroy the enemy with a single click. And people play it for hours. Incredible."

He was obtrusive, annoying, and infantile: a thirty-year-old man-child who had never had his dad around growing up. Jim spent more hours at the office running LightPulse than he did at home, and his three ex-wives certainly hadn't been the right women to guide Teddy toward anything resembling a respectable human being.

But the fact that he'd been brazen enough to hack into her work account was more than an invasion. She probably would've been less offended if he'd put his hand up her shirt. She took one deep breath, then another, and tucked what she *wanted* to say back into her throat. Instead, she asked, "How'd you get into my system?"

He ignored the question. "I mean, really, look at it. I flick, it goes *boom*, pieces of wood go flying. Flick, *boom*, done. After Juggs 3 comes out,"—*that childish nickname again*, Sara thought—"we should look at going in this direction. Cut some of the staff, cut some costs. Get in good with Apple. Dad said—I mean *Jim* said—they were dying to work with us. Put something like this up on the App Store, charge a buck apiece? We can all retire and sip some boat drinks and swap wives." He winked at her.

She looked down at the heavy crystal paperweight on her desk, wondering how big the dent in the side of his head would be.

"You're trying too hard, Teddy. Now get away from my computer and out of my chair."

Teddy stood up, lifted his hands in apologetic resignation, and then squeezed her shoulder as he walked around to the other side.

God, this guy is a harassment lawsuit wearing a fake Rolex. If he ever tried that with some of the hardcore gamer girls out in The Belly, he'd be toast.

"Sorry," he said. "You shouldn't leave your password written on a sticky note. And you're late. I got bored."

"Still not okay, Little One." Being the youngest member of the executive team—and the owner's son—was more of a scarlet letter than a badge of honor, and they all knew that the nickname was the perfect way to knock a couple inches off Teddy's platform loafers whenever he got out of line. Vertically challenged (as he insisted he was, often), he had to look up a good three inches at Sara on the days he came into the office wearing unprofessional flip-flops.

He straightened the collar of his polo shirt, smoothed out his khakis, and gave a snort of disapproval, but nothing more.

Sara smirked.

Putty.

She laid her tattered and thinning leather briefcase on her desk and took her time unpacking, making Teddy wait on purpose, letting his impatience and ADHD reach a festering point. She was poking the badger, of course, but it was justifiable retribution, and he stayed silent.

And while 'guilt' wasn't a word in his vocabulary or a feeling that had ever impregnated the three brain cells he had floating around in that all-too-polished, bronzer-coated melon, she figured he was at least aware that he'd done something wrong by invading her privacy.

She sat, pulled a notepad out of her desk, and chose a pen from her cup with such slow deliberation that Teddy was almost vibrating by the time she finally said, "I can't come up with a marketing plan without a product. So tell me, why are you two months behind?"

The direct, personalized blame was enough to send Teddy into a barrage of excuses that lasted for over an hour.

. . .

By the time he was done—and by the time she had tortured him to the point where it was no longer fun—they'd worked out a plan that they could take to Jim. A few extra hours per employee on Teddy's side would get them both back on schedule in another month, and Sara would have what she needed to begin a viral marketing campaign. If everything worked out as it should, *Juggernaut 3* would demolish the success of its previous two releases, but they had to be ready. Public outcry over production delays was never a good thing, and Sara had no experience in handling the backlash. Nor did she want any.

Teddy got up, but before he could leave, Sara stopped him at the door. "Teddy," she called after him.

"What?"

"If I ever catch you on my PC again..."

It was all she needed to say. He hung his head, examined the tops of his shiny Kenneth Coles, and muttered a doleful, "Won't happen again," before he escaped the prison yard of her office.

After he walked out, her assistant, Shelley, poked her timid, dimple-cheeked face around the corner. Sara smiled and motioned for her to come in. Shelley crossed through the doorway, one halting step at a time, like she was testing the ground for landmines.

It's definitely Tuesday, Sara thought. *Same blue top, every week.*

Shelley's sense of style was somewhere in the neighborhood of *convent-chic* and *librarian-demure*. Straight hair yanked into a tight ponytail. Glasses hanging around her neck by a chain, aging her by twenty years. Plain tops, neutral slacks, and comfortable black loafers that went with everything—except for Tuesdays, when the splash of blue added life and light to her wardrobe, which must have been as uncomfortable for Shelley as coloring outside the lines in kindergarten.

Sara had never raised her voice at the poor girl, but she always approached Sara as if she would explode and send her running from the office coated in curse words and insults. Shelley was shy to the point of having trouble interacting with the outside world, but she was a brilliant marketer, and had a way with copywriting that could convince a politician to refuse campaign funding.

She worked more hours than anyone in the building, constantly refining ad copy and press releases, searching for the perfect words to tell LightPulse's story, studying the advertising giants of the past like David Ogilvy and John Caples. More than once Sara had found her asleep at her desk after pulling an all-nighter. For the past two months, the girl had been a perpetual motion machine when it came to her job, but her social life consisted of leaving her apartment on Sunday morning to brave the lines at Voodoo Doughnut and Powell's.

Sara was positive that Shelley was the smartest person in the office, and had tried to convince her of that once, but the recent San Diego State University grad had refused to accept the compliment. It had been the first and only time she had shown signs of confidence regarding something she believed in—however misguided her intent might have been, in Sara's view.

Still, her genius, under Sara's guidance, was a major factor in the success of their advertising and marketing campaigns for their last release. If and when Sara decided to move on, she planned to ask Jim to promote Shelley over some of the other, more-seasoned team members as her replacement. But, that would all depend on Shelley's ability to leave her fears behind. Sara was working on her. Slowly.

Any nudge to Shelley's delicate nature that was too forced, too forward, would tilt her in the wrong direction. Sara had seen it before, and was careful in her attempts to build up her introverted assistant's confidence.

Sara said, "How's it going, Sarge?" The shortening of Shelley's last name, Sergeant, seemed to please her the first time Sara had used it, so it stuck, and she'd been 'Sarge' ever since.

Shelley's voice came out a notch above a whisper. "Jacob's school called. They said it was urgent."

Sara tensed. The last time they'd called, he'd fallen off the monkey bars and had come home with a knot the size of a golf ball on his forehead. She said, "And you didn't forward the call? Did they say what it was about?" and knew at once that it was a little too brusque.

Shelley backed away a step, fiddling with the ruffles on her blue top. "I'm so sorry, Mrs. Winthrop. You were busy with Teddy and I knew the meeting was important and I didn't want to interrupt and—and—"

"Hey, no, it's fine. You didn't do anything wrong. Could just be another beetle stuck up his nose." *That* particular visit to the doctor caused a lot of chuckles around LightPulse, and the other employees began referring to him as 'the little bugger'. *"How's the little bugger doing? Pick any buggers out of his nose lately?"* At the age of five, boys do what boys do.

Shelley said, "The principal called this time, not the school nurse." Admitting that it was more important than a bug up the nose made Shelley take another step back, just in case.

"What? Really? Did she say what it was about?"

"No, but she was super frustrated when I wouldn't let her talk to you right away." Shelley backed up all the way to the door.

"Weird," Sara said. "I'll give her a call. Thanks for being a good gatekeeper. But," she added, "it's okay to put a principal through during a meeting. Broken bones, too. Bugs, not so much."

Shelley acknowledged the ruling with a meek grin. Once she'd retreated, Sara dialed the school, wondering what kind of trouble Jacob had gotten into that warranted a call from the principal.

. . .

"Hello, Mrs. Bennett's office, Dave speaking."

"Dave, hi, it's Sara Winthrop, Jacob's mom? My assistant said—"

"Oh thank God, I'll put you right through."

Whoa, what? What's going on?

The up-tempo blast of the on-hold music didn't help her building tension while she waited. Thirty seconds passed, a minute, two minutes. She tried to distract herself by going through her email.

Mrs. Bennett's voice came on the line. She sounded rushed, out of breath. "Mrs. Winthrop? Hello? Are you there?"

"Yes, here," Sara said, turning away from Jim's request for an all-hands meeting at 10AM out in The Belly. It was her favorite place in the building, the open-cube hub of LightPulse where she had spent so many years with the programmers and testers looking for glitches and offering suggestions on the fluidity of gameplay. "What happened? Everything okay with Jacob? Your receptionist sounded worried."

"We have a bit of a situation." The word 'situation' was loaded with unease.

"A situation?"

"Please stay calm, because we think everything is fine."

Sara sat up straight and leaned into the coming news. "You *think?* He's not hurt, is he?"

Mrs. Bennett said, "I'm sure it's nothing to worry about. It's crazy around here on the last day of school. The kindergarten classes were all outside playing hide and seek and when Mr. Blake rounded up his kids for a head count, Jacob wasn't with the rest of the group."

Sara sprang out of her chair, then tried to compose herself with a couple of deep breaths before she said, "Have you found him yet?"

The pause on the other end of the line was longer than Sara expected. "No," Mrs. Bennett said, "but we have every available adult looking. Our assistants, our teachers—even the janitor, Mr. Burns. We're positive he didn't realize that he wasn't supposed to be hiding anymore. We'll find him, but I think it's best that you come down anyway."

"I'm walking out the door right now."

Sara hung up the phone, grabbing her keys and her purse. A delicate blanket of fear enveloped her, but she tried not to let it take control. He had done this once before, months ago, when the four of them were playing hide and seek in the house. He'd climbed under a dusty green tarp down in their basement and had managed to fall asleep while she and the girls hunted for over an hour. She'd panicked and had come close to calling the police before Callie accidentally stepped on him.

Without that particular instance as a buffer, she would've been throwing people out of her way. Instead, she took a long swallow from her water bottle and then walked over to Shelley's desk to let her know what had happened and where she was going.

She heard Shelley mumbling into her headset, saying, "Yes… Oh wow, you're the second one today…Let me send you to her—wait, here she is."

Sara raised her eyebrows. "For me? Who is it?"

Shelley covered the mouthpiece, saying, "Mr. Brown? Says he's the principal at Lacey and Callie's school?"

"Him, too?" *What's up with my kids today? Sheesh.* "Okay if I take it here?"

Shelley nodded.

Sara picked up the receiver, pushed the button for Line 1, and said, "Mr. Brown? This is Sara Winthrop, Lacey and Callie's mother."

The conversation that followed left the phone dangling from its cord, and at least one blindsided coworker lying flat on his back. There may have been more. It was all so blurry.

Sara flung open the glass entryway doors and sprinted down the sidewalk toward the parking lot. The sun had broken through, evaporating the morning's rain, creating a level of humidity that made the air syrupy and hard to breathe. Added to that was the realization that without her husband, she had no one to help.

I need you, Brian. Damn it, I need you. Why aren't you here when I need you?

Two years after Brian's disappearance, she'd been able to release her grip on the anxiety and fear and panic that had plagued her for days, for weeks, for months. Over time, sleepless nights dwindled to sleepless hours, and then lessened to troubled dreams and reluctant acceptance. But now, as the soles of her flats slapped against the concrete, the idea that her children might be taken from her fueled those long-subdued emotions like a gust of wind through a forest fire.

Not again. I can't go through this again.

A flash of white under her minivan's windshield wiper caught her attention. She thought it was another flyer for the local pizza place and ripped it from the rubbery grasp, ready to crush it in her fist.

The neon-orange, bold lettering was just bright enough to stop her squeezing hand, saving the paper slip from turning into a crumbled mass.

Seven words, asking a question that created even more questions:

ARE YOU READY TO PLAY THE GAME?

Chapter Two

SARA

Sara opened the driver's side door and climbed in, numb from the tips of her toes to the top of her head. Lacey, Callie, and Jacob, all three missing and unaccounted for at their schools. And now this message, whatever it was.

Her heart strained against the wall of her chest, the rhythmic thumps pounding in her ears. She needed to be on the move. Going, going, going. But the note felt like it held a deeper, more threatening meaning than a few words asking a simple question.

She stared down at the slip of paper, reading it over and over.

Are you ready to play the game? Are you ready to play the game?
Are you ready? Are you ready? Are you...

She looked at the back side, expecting to find something else, a message saying, *Just kidding! Good luck with the release!* But no. Nothing. Only the glaring, blazing question. It had to be coincidence, didn't it? Some ill-timed, cryptic joke being played on her by one of the LightPulse staff? Surely this ominous note didn't have anything to do with the kids disappearing, did it?

Of course it does. Don't be an idiot.

But what did it mean? The game? What game?

Sara flung the note into the passenger seat. *Jesus, not right now. I have to go.*

She cranked the keys and the Sienna's hybrid engine whispered to life. Before she backed out, she took one last glance at the LightPulse office. Shelley stood outside at the front doors, watching from a distance. She waved, then gave Sara a thumbs-up as if to say, *Everything is going to be okay.*

Sara forced herself to wave back, then swung the minivan out of the parking spot, and out into the lighter mid-morning commute.

...

"Come on, *come on!*" she said, willing the stalled traffic in front of her to get the hell out of the way. The promise of a faster trip had been broken by road construction three blocks down, and she sat at a dead stop, wedged so tightly in between two cars that a pedestrian would have had trouble squeezing between the bumpers. "Move!"

She pounded the steering wheel with her palm. Flashed a look at the note beside her, where it lay limp and lifeless, but foreboding and full of questions. She shook her head. *Motherf—*

"Move!" she shouted again.

But her demands went unmet. And she sat, trapped in a line of cars, imprisoned inside her minivan with no way out and no course of action other than to wait until the universe changed its mind. She briefly thought of abandoning the van where it sat to take off running. She was in good shape. She could do it. Three miles every evening on the treadmill while the kids did their homework wasn't a guarantee of finishing a marathon, but it was enough to keep up her conditioning and ensure that her slowing metabolism wouldn't allow too many fresh pounds around her hips.

The thought of doing it, of jumping out and sprinting away, gave her a second to realize that she didn't know where she was going first. She had stomped on the gas pedal and *went*, eager to be moving, anxious to be heading toward whatever horrendous event was waiting, like a Marine running toward the sound of concealed gunfire.

How does one decide where to go first when two equally horrible things are happening at once?

She tried to weigh the options. Lacey and Callie's school was closer, but Jacob was the youngest. But was he really missing, or just hiding until someone found him?

No, obviously not the latter, not with the girls missing, too. And the note. The stupid, menacing note mocking her from two feet away.

Are you ready to play the game? Are you ready to play the game?

Mr. Brown, the principal of Whitetree Elementary where Lacey and Callie were finishing up their fifth-grade year, had said that a group of teachers had taken their classes to the small ice cream shop next to the school. It was a last day treat, and Sara recalled Shelley's reminder to sign the permission slip.

And, like the chaos of Jacob's game of hide and seek, the teachers had had trouble keeping up with everyone, both inside and outside the tight confines of the three-tabled, four-stooled room. Lacey and Callie were missing from the final headcount before they headed back to the schoo.

"Move!" Sara yelled once more as the car in front of her crept ahead. She stayed put, hoping that with a few more blessed inches, she might be able to squeeze the minivan out and go hurtling down a side street, taking the long way through the surrounding neighborhood. Distance-wise, it would be out of the way, but it was better than being stalled where she was.

From what she gathered, all three had gone missing around 9:00, while she was in her meeting with Teddy. Two separate instances, two separate locations, at the exact same time.

It was coordinated, she realized. *It had to have been.*

Which meant something bigger was going on than she'd originally thought. They had been targeted. She had been targeted. And it wasn't just a coincidence.

They've been kidnapped. Oh my God.

It was obvious, now that she had an involuntary moment to stop and think it through. Earlier she had been in such a rushed panic that she hadn't taken the time to consider the details.

Why her? Why her kids?

And who? Who would be doing this to her? To them? She tried to think of anyone who might have had any reason, and came up with nothing. There hadn't been any strange vehicles in the neighborhood lately, no ragged homeless people around their favorite park, no news reports of kidnappings that she remembered. But really, as a single parent taking care of three rambunctious children, who has time to keep track of things like whether or not the green Volvo down the street is casing the block or is nothing more than a visiting relative?

The thought brought on a rush of guilt that left her feeling like she had been punched in the stomach.

It's my fault. I should've made *the time. I should've looked closer. Should've paid more attention. But how? When?*

With Brian gone, it was all up to her. *She* was the one dealing with everything. The late-night accidents in bed. The homework. Proper nutrition. Cleaning the house, doing the laundry. Rushing to t-ball games and ballet classes. Everything, all of it, on her own, on top of a fifty-hour workweek. She fumed at Brian for being gone and leaving her to deal with everything.

It didn't matter where he was, where he had gone, what had happened. He was gone, and now the kids were, too. She was alone and, without a doubt, powerless.

She tried not to cry. It didn't work.

The car in front of her crept forward and Sara angled the minivan to the left, but it wasn't enough.

Come on, just a little bit more.

Sara felt like she was suffocating. Rolled down the window for some fresh air, closed her eyes and inhaled. The smell came tainted with the stench of city and fresh asphalt from the paving crew up ahead. She coughed, but left the window open anyway. However stained the air might be, the sense of open freedom was better than being confined in her inability to get moving.

She waited. And waited. Her panic grew to a pulsating tremor, and she wondered if she was being punished for torturing Teddy the same way earlier that morning. Karma. Bad, bad karma.

She tried to think of anything strange that had happened over the past few days, searching her memories for some looked-over clue, some inkling of an idea as to why she and the kids would be the target of a coordinated kidnapping. At least it was some sort of action, some way of being productive while she sat immobile, taking short, fearful breaths.

Sara didn't have any enemies. Sure, she'd stepped on some toes while getting LightPulse into the national spotlight, but it was business, nothing more, and there had been no hard feelings. She was well liked—more than well liked—around all of the motherhood groups and the PTA. There was one minor instance where she'd exchanged cross words with the mother of a girl who had kept picking on Lacey, but enemies?

Enemies? It was such a strong word. And it didn't fit. Anywhere.

She thought about the park again, their walks down to Miss Willow's—the gray-haired, flowerchild babysitter. Their once-a-month trip to McDonald's for sundaes and an hour in the multi-colored indoor playground. The girls loved the slides and interconnected series of tubes where they could pretend to be hamsters scurrying from one spot to the next. Jacob spent most of his time in the ball pit, burying himself under the reds, blues, and greens, and then hurtling up and out, like a dolphin at SeaWorld, screaming with joy and his hands high in the air.

Those memories caused another series of tears, and she shifted her thoughts to the times when she was by herself.

The only time she *did* have to herself lately had been extended trips to the grocery store without the children. They were well-behaved in general, but taking them into the nearby Safeway resulted in so many admonishments to 'Put that back' and 'Stop picking out junk food for snacks' that she had given up and had began shopping after work before picking them up from Miss Willow.

Sara scanned the images in her mind, and the only thing that stuck out, the only thing that felt *off*, had been during her last trip over a week ago. She'd caught a tall, good-looking guy in a white (or was it gray?) collared shirt staring at her. She remembered amazing blue eyes. Short, dark hair. Tan skin. It'd been hard to believe that he was actually *checking her out* in her rumpled slacks and untucked blouse, looking tired and unkempt after a long day at LightPulse. They had made eye contact. It lingered. He smiled. And then he moved on.

It was the first and only time since Brian's disappearance that she had allowed herself to think, 'What if?' But she'd dismissed the thought and had gone back to picking out a fresh box of organic cereal.

Again, nothing. Nothing out of the ordinary. Nothing in her mind to make her think that it would lead to this theft, this agonizing robbery of the most important things in her life.

She grabbed her purse, pulled out her cell phone to call Miss Willow, but before she had a chance to dial, the car ahead of her rolled forward once more, leaving enough room to escape.

No more than five minutes had passed, but Sara felt like an animal released from captivity. She dropped her phone back into her purse and floored it across the southbound lane, screeching through a gap in the oncoming traffic.

A red Honda missed her rear bumper by inches. The driver blared his horn as she wheeled her way onto the side street, missing a parked motorcycle by less than a foot. She overcorrected and almost sideswiped a pickup on the opposite side. Sara fought the steering wheel, whipping her arms back and forth, and straightened out the minivan's trajectory just as an approaching car squealed to a stop. The driver glared at her. Sara crept past, mouthing, "Sorry," but his dirty look suggested that the apology wasn't accepted.

On course now, and under as much control as her frazzled mental state would allow, Sara drove as fast as she dared, working her way through the middle-class neighborhood, praying she wouldn't get pulled over. Talking to an officer at this point would be a good thing, but she didn't want to risk the delay. Not until she was ready. Not until she was at Jacob's school and was absolutely *sure* that he was gone and not taking a nap in some hidden place.

She knew that the first three hours after a child went missing were the most critical ones. The fact had stuck in her mind after reviewing the literature handed out each year by the schools. By now, as she raced through the quiet streets, she guessed that forty-five minutes had passed since her children had gone missing. Possibly longer, if it had taken awhile for the teachers to notice. They could've been gone for an hour or more already.

Sara pressed down harder on the gas pedal.

Chapter Three
SARA

She didn't bother with trying to find a parking spot. The minivan lurched to a stop at the front entrance to Rosepetal Elementary. She grabbed the note, shoved it in her purse, and got out, running as soon as her feet touched the ground. She flung open the wooden door, vaulted inside, and smelled the pine-scented cleaning solution. The exact same smell that had filled the halls and rooms of her grade schools back east over thirty years ago. Some things never changed.

The halls were empty. It was a huge difference from the other times she'd been here. Even when classes were in full-swing, children and parents milled about for whatever reason. Young boys with too much energy or excitement who had been excommunicated to their own island prison outside their classrooms. A mother leading her daughter by the hand, past the artwork proudly displayed along the walls. Or a group of kindergartners trudging single-file, just like Jacob had been earlier that morning, on his way out to play hide and seek.

Play. Play...

Are you ready to play the game?

But now, inside the school walls, none of those things were present. Rosepetal appeared to have been shut down. The doors of each classroom were closed, and she wondered how long it had taken them to get to that point, how long it had taken them to decide that something was wrong.

First, she checked the principal's office, in case Mrs. Bennett was there waiting for her. It was quiet and empty, as well, except for a late-twenties guy with a goatee, hipster glasses, and a flannel shirt. The typical Portland uniform.

He glanced up at her, shot out of his seat. "Mrs. Winthrop?" he asked.

She rushed up to the counter, knocked over the stack of mail. He tried to greet her as a volley of questions flew out of her mouth. Uncontained. Unrestrained. "Are you Dave? Have you found him yet? Where is everyone? Are they all out looking? Do you guys have *any idea* where he is?"

He scratched his cheek, then ran a hand across his shaved head.

She asked, "You don't, do you?" and the realization fell from overhead like a dropped piano. "You idiots. How could you let this happen?"

Dave appeared to know that this would be coming. In a calm, apologetic tone, one that sounded like it took no offense at the accusation or insult, he said, "I'm sorry, Mrs. Winthrop. I can't even begin to imagine how hard this must be, and I won't patronize you by telling you to calm down. That would be stupid—"

"Damn right it would be stupid," she said with enough contempt to keep him planted behind his desk, where it was safe.

He nodded. He'd probably seen enough irate mothers to recognize when it was time to tuck his tail between his legs and be the beta male of the situation.

"We're wasting time. Where's Mrs. Bennett?"

"She and the rest of the available staff are in back of the school, still looking. The classroom teachers are following our standard policy. We're officially locked down. You know, in case this was something—in case there was somebody—man, that's not coming out right. In case something had happened to—"

"Dave?"

"Yes?"

"Shut up."

"Yes, ma'am."

"I want you to call the police."

"Mrs. Bennett said that wouldn't be necessary yet, not until—"

"If you don't pick up that phone and dial 9-1-1 in about three seconds, I'm coming over this counter and I'm going to rip that goddamn earring out of your head. You understand me?" It seemed like such a random thing to threaten him with, but it was the first noticeable item that stuck out as a source of pain. She surprised herself with the intensity, and apologized. Then she said, "You know that *something* you were babbling about? It's happening. My daughters are missing from their school, too, so I want you to call the police, have them send someone to Whitetree, and get someone here. Tell them I think they've been kidnapped, and it's been an hour."

She didn't wait for a response.

Sara sprinted out of the office, down the hallway, and through the doors that led to the rear playground.

. . .

Out back, some of the staff looked up into trees while some looked under parked cars on the nearby street. Others worked in pairs, walking up and down the sidewalk, calling out Jacob's name, checking the yards of homes across the way.

Sara shouted, "Jacob? Mommy's here," in a feeble attempt. "Time to come out now."

Mrs. Bennett—Wanda to those familiar enough to call her that—stood by the merry-go-round, surveying the action from her post. She was a large, imposing woman who had a stern demeanor when it came to disciplining the children and keeping the school running smoothly, but one-on-one, adult-to-adult, she was as an absolute sweetheart. Ready with a laugh, ready with a hug. She'd been Lacey and Callie's principal, too, and had even brought a tray of lasagna by a week after Brian had gone missing. Sara liked and admired her, but had to contain the urge to scream at the woman.

She knew she needed Mrs. Bennett to be focused and ready with details. Yelling at her would solve nothing. Yelling at her wouldn't improve anything.

Sara marched over to her and could see that the woman was already sweating through her light blue blouse. The rings of perspiration made a semi-circle underneath her armpits as she held up a hand to shield her eyes from the sun.

"Mrs. Bennett!" Sara said.

Please have some news. Anything good.

Mrs. Bennett waved and rushed over, meeting her halfway. "Oh, Sara," she said, holding out a hand to shake, but changed her mind at the last second and embraced her with a hug.

Sara squeezed, and could feel the warmth of the principal's body, the dewy perspiration on the woman's back. She pulled away and asked, "Any luck?" but deep down, she knew it was pointless. Not with the girls gone, too. Not with that cryptic note. *Are you ready to play the game?*

Mrs. Bennett said, "Not—not yet. We're looking as hard as we can. He *has* to be here somewhere. No child has ever gone missing on my watch, and it's not about to happen now."

"You should call them off."

Mrs. Bennett squinted at her, trying to decipher what she'd heard. "Call them off? Why?"

"Because he's been—" She had to shove the next word out of her mouth. "—kidnapped."

Mrs. Bennett scoffed, disbelieving. "What? No, don't think that way. We'll find him, I'm sure of it. My gut says we're getting close."

But Sara could tell by the sound of her voice that Mrs. Bennett was only trying to stay positive, and, on some level, she didn't believe what she was saying, either. The fact that she was being mollified bubbled up the rage boiling in her gut, but she stopped short of grabbing the principal by the shoulders and shaking her so hard her skull would flop around like a bobble-head doll.

"It's worse than you think," she said. She told Mrs. Bennett about Lacey and Callie and how they were missing, too, how they had disappeared around the same time as Jacob. She told her about the cryptic note, and what she thought it meant.

A warm breeze blew strands of hair into Sara's face. She brushed them away, tucking them behind her ear, waiting on Mrs. Bennett to process the information.

Mrs. Bennett's mouth tried to produce a response, but no words came out. Lips and jaw and tongue working overtime, producing nothing. She'd gotten stuck in an infinite loop, the same kind of bug in a programmer's code that left a game character repeating the same action over and over.

Sara fidgeted. Every second wasted was another second gone from the fading three-hour time period that had, by now, worked its way down to less than two. But the truth was that she had no idea what to do next, where to go, whom to call. Talking to the police would be a step forward, but what then? Would they take her down to the station to answer questions, offer her a cup of coffee and an empty room? What good would that do?

She could call the phone tree set up by all the parents in their neighborhood. Tell them to keep an eye out in case the kids showed up there, by some miracle. Lacey and Callie had gotten in trouble twice for switching classes. They often wore the same outfits just to be mischievous. They were clever little pranksters...something they had inherited from their father. Was it possible they'd concocted a scheme to ditch school on the last day? Could Jacob have overheard them and decided he wanted to play their game, too?

Stop grasping. They wouldn't dare *pull a stunt like that. Would they? I mean, really? Would they?*

The hamster wheel caught traction inside Mrs. Bennett's head. She said, "But who would leave that note?"

"I have no idea."

"We have to call the police, right now."

"I made Dave do it. They should be here soon."

"Good. Good," she said. She reached up, pinched the bridge of her nose. "We should've done it sooner."

"You couldn't have known."

"No, it's my responsibility. We should've called as soon as I put everybody inside on lockdown. But—but I didn't want to worry you. And I was being stupid and too pigheaded, trying to protect my own reputation. Not on my watch, right?"

Part of Sara wanted to say, *Damn right, it was on your watch*, but the other part, the half that realized that it wasn't Mrs. Bennett's fault, said, "Don't blame yourself, blame the asshole who took them."

"I should've been more proactive," she said. Mrs. Bennett looked toward the back of the school, pointed. "The police are here. You go, we'll keep looking. And tell them they can find me back here when they're ready. I'm going to take full responsibility." She gave Sara another hug.

"That's not necess—"

"I won't be able to look at myself in the mirror. It's okay, Sara, really. Go on now. He's waving you over. Use my office if you need it."

Chapter Four
SARA

"Mrs. Winthrop—"

"Sara's fine," she said. "Two less syllables." She gave a nervous chuckle and then regretted saying it. There wasn't time for meaningless comments that required explanation. She'd been using the aside to dispense with formalities and as a conversation starter for years, and it was a hard habit to break.

Don't ask what it means...just get to the questions.

The real meaning behind it was a running joke between her and Brian that had never gone away, even in her life without him. They'd had an argument one night, about a week after they were married, over the most efficient way to load the dishwasher. It'd escalated into a notch below a screaming match. Brian had said, 'Efficiency is the soul of wit, Sara,' and she'd replied, 'It's *brevity*, ding-dong. Brevity is the soul of wit, and it's more efficient, because it's two less syllables.'

From that day on, whenever an impending disagreement was about to get out of hand, one of them would say, 'Two less syllables,' and it would diffuse the situation.

Detective Jonathan Johnson grinned at her and scribbled something on his notepad. "I know we're in a hurry here, but if it makes you more comfortable, you can call me 'DJ.' You know, for Detective Johnson. Or JonJon, if you're a four-year-old boy, like my nephew."

"That helps," she lied.

"I don't know why I tell people—"

Sara interrupted. "Can we get started? Sorry, I'm sure it's— time is sort of..." Anxious, she rubbed her damp palms on her pants.

His cheeks took on a light shade of pink. "Of course, of course."

They sat across from each other in Mrs. Bennett's office, uncomfortably perched on the straight-backed, hard-as-a-church-pew chairs used by parents, or unruly students as they were dealt their punishments.

Detective Johnson, *DJ*, was younger than she had expected. Younger than she'd hoped for, and she wondered how recently he'd been promoted to his position. With her children gone, her world exploding around her, she wanted the best. Someone with experience. Someone with more successful cases filed away in the 'Solved' drawer than ones gone cold. She wanted her own Dream Team with Michael and Magic and Larry.

Instead, sitting opposite of her was a mid-thirties guy who looked like he might have earned his detective's badge within the last six months.

Christ, they sent a Boy Scout to look for my kids. Unbelievable.

DJ leaned forward. "What're your children's names?"

"Lacey and Callie. They're twins. Ten years old. And then Jacob. He's five."

"Okay," he said, taking notes. "To the best of your knowledge, when did your children go missing, Sara?"

"Best guess, around nine o'clock this morning, based on what the principals told me. You have someone at Whitetree, don't you?" She squirmed in her seat, feeling guilty that she couldn't be in both places at the same time.

The young detective scribbled again on his notepad. "We do, we do. And they're in good hands over there with Detective Barker. He's been doing this longer—"

"And you've been doing it...how long?" Her heartbeat eased up at the thought of someone with experience, but she couldn't resist asking.

DJ smiled like he knew the question was coming. No doubt he'd gotten it before. "I know I look like I just started shaving yesterday," he said, "but I've been in Missing Persons for five years. All with Detective Barker. People call him Bloodhound, so you can trust me—"

"Did you have more questions, Detective?" Sara scooted forward to the edge of her seat. "I don't mean to interrupt, but my kids? Your questions?"

"Definitely. I'm in as much of a hurry as you are, so we'll get through these double-time, okay?"

"Yes, sorry, go on."

DJ cycled through the standard inquiries about how they had gone missing, had they ever run away before, any friends or immediate family who might be involved, any babysitters with less-than-stellar pasts, any enemies she might have, any strange vehicles in the neighborhood. She answered them all, being as detailed as possible, and before she could mention the cryptic note, the next question had more of an affect on her than she anticipated.

"And their father? Where is he?"

"Gone," was all she could manage.

"Gone? As in, out of the picture gone, you're divorced gone... deceased gone?" He added the last bit with some trepidation.

"I guess not talking about it isn't an option, huh?"

"If you think he could be a person of interest, we need those details so we can explore every possible alternative."

Before she could realize how ridiculous the notion might be, the possibility of Brian being involved popped into her head.

Brian? No way...Brian?

"He wouldn't," she said.

"Ma'am?"

She didn't hear the confused question. *What if it is Brian? They never found his body and people thought they saw him…Could he be involved? Could he have come back and picked the kids up? Is he on his way to the house right now, hoping to surprise me? God, that would be a cruel way to make an entrance. And after so long. I'll kick his ass back to wherever he's been, if that's the case.*

"Sara?"

"What?" Her eyes refocused, drawing her back to the present.

"Everything okay?"

"What—what was your question?"

"Your husband?"

"Right, right. Brian," she said, taking another couple of seconds to process, then added, "He couldn't be involved, Detective. He's been missing for two years."

"Missing? Do we have a file on him?"

"Two years ago, he left for the gym one morning and never came back. You guys found his car in a grocery store parking lot across from Hollywood Bowl. Said there weren't any signs of foul play, no blood, no strange DNA. No leads whatsoever. He just vanished."

"I remember that case. That was your husband?"

"Unfortunately."

"I feel like I'm doing nothing but apologizing, but I'm sorry to hear that." DJ took the opportunity to scribble on his notepad again. Cleared his throat. "I'll take a look at the files later, but right now, we really need to focus—"

A knock at the door interrupted him. "Come in," he said.

The door opened just far enough for Dave to poke his head inside. "There's a pho—"

Sara blurted out, "Did you find him?"

Dave shook his head. "Phone call for you on line two, Mrs. Winthrop."

"For me? Who is it?"

"Didn't say. Some woman. Said she needed to speak to you. You can pick it up there at Mrs. Bennett's desk."

Sara exchanged puzzled looks with the detective. "Should I answer it?"

"Yes ma'am. Could be good news."

"I hope you're right." She stood up, rushed over to the desk. "Hello, this is Sara Winthrop."

The voice on the other end of the line wasn't female. It was deep. Electronic. Synthesized.

It said, "The game begins now. You have twenty minutes to get to the Rose Gardens. Alone. Park. Leave your keys in the ignition and the van running. Leave all personal belongings in it. You will be given further instructions. Don't tell the police where you're going. If you need proof that this is real, pay attention."

She almost fainted when she heard the single-word scream that followed.

. . .

In her van, driving, it played over and over in her mind.

"Mommy!"

The ensuing silence had signaled the end, and the beginning.

Sara had recognized Lacey's voice. She and Callie both sounded so much alike on the phone, but Lacey's voice was one note higher than her sister's. She was terrified, and in pain.

All of her children's voices took on a distinct tone whenever they were hurt. Call it a mother's bond, but she was able to tell the difference between the yelp of a stubbed toe and the wail of a broken arm across all three of them. Lacey's scream lay somewhere in between.

Sara's remorse bulged underneath the surface like a volcano moments before eruption.

She drove hard, taking every shortcut she could think of, dodging traffic, ducking across parking lots to avoid stoplights and long lines. She eased up on the gas pedal when she crossed paths with a police cruiser, and then floored it again when it was out of sight. She cursed the lack of acceleration in the hybrid, damning the peer pressure from her friends to go green.

Conservation had nothing to do with her circumstances, she knew, but she had to have some outlet for her rage or she risked exploding right there in her seat. With no idea as to who was behind this stupid game, she had nothing to focus her outbursts on, so taking it out on something she *was* aware of would have to suffice. For now.

At that point, she wasn't beyond choking the life out of whoever was doing this, but until that chance presented itself, cursing the environmentally conscious would suffice.

She took the Burnside Bridge and glanced down at the minivan's clock.

Ten minutes left. I'll never make it.

She wondered what Detective Johnson must be thinking or doing after her frenzied dash out of the office. She'd slammed down the receiver, the flush in her cheeks and flared nostrils revealing that the call wasn't the good news she'd been hoping for.

Before he'd been able to ask, she'd said, "I have to go. Do *not* follow me. But here's your first clue." She'd fished the note out of her purse and shoved it into his hands. "Find out where that came from. I'll call you when I can."

He'd tried to protest, but his words got lost in the rush of wind at her back.

And now, making her way across the bridge, she wished she'd had time to give him more information, to tell him what the voice had said, and to work out a plan so she wouldn't be driving into whatever was waiting for her in the Rose Gardens without backup.

Playing this so-called game on her own.

Sara thought about calling Miss Willow, just to hear a comforting voice, but there was no sense in frightening her and risk giving out too much information. But the voice had only said, *"Don't tell the police."* Should she risk letting someone else know?

No, not yet. Who knows what they'd do to the kids if they found out. They.

Plural. Definitely more than just the person on the phone, given the timed coordination. Which meant she was up against a *group* of people. She could handle one person if she got the chance. Possibly.

Sara played it out in her mind. A well-placed kick to the balls, or a forehead to the bridge of a nose, pouncing on him with a knee across his Adam's Apple, all of her weight pressing down. It was feasible. But a group of people? No way. She imagined standing in a circle, surrounded. Imagined throwing a punch at the nearest person and then getting swarmed by a hive of vicious, grinning henchman.

She took the exit ramp and passed a young woman, bouncing lightly by on a mid-morning run.

A woman.

Why did the fact that it was a woman jogging by click in her subconscious? What was the trigger, and why did it seem important?

Dave said a woman *was on the line for me.*

Some woman.

She had forgotten that particular detail in her rush to get moving. But was it a decoy? Had they used the voice synthesizer to disguise the person's real voice as a woman's? If it *was* a woman, that narrowed the list of possibilities by half.

The kids' pamphlets said kidnappers were likely male, friends or family, and she definitely didn't know any women capable of something like this.

She had no family in the area. They were all back in Virginia. Brian had come from a small clan of Winthrops in Washington. His parents had passed. His sister lived in Des Moines. The rest of the aunts (and uncles and female cousins) stayed in the near-perpetual drizzle of Seattle. Her friends were sweethearts with children of their own. Her assistant Shelley, her coworkers, and all the rest of the women at LightPulse were good-natured and friendly. And she hadn't gotten a hint of resentment from any of them when she had been promoted to Vice President over some of the more seasoned employees. What would be their motivation?

It couldn't be anyone she knew, could it?

Behind closed doors, Sara...

No. It wasn't possible. Nobody close. It had to be a stranger. Had to.

But what if it wasn't?

She drove up Knob Hill toward the Rose Gardens, getting closer and closer, rifling through the possibilities, checking off each woman she knew, dismissing them all for different reasons. Most would be at work, leading busy lives. Some were stay-at-home moms keeping control of toddler-induced bedlam with no time to plan a coordinated kidnapping.

That wouldn't stop any of them from making a phone call, but none of them have a reason. Not a single one of them would have any reason to do this...would they?

Chapter Five
SARA

Sara arrived at the Rose Gardens with a minute remaining on her deadline. She found a parking spot, got out, and left the keys in the ignition with the minivan running, as instructed.

She stood with her arms crossed, taking in the surroundings. She didn't know what she was looking for, but it seemed like the right thing to do. She'd only been there once before, twelve years ago. It was on her first date with Brian, and they'd come up here after lunch and a matinee showing of *Gladiator*.

It was also the place where they had shared their first kiss. If Brian *did* have anything to do with this, it would be an appropriate spot. She shoved the thought away. Creating red herrings for herself would only increase her tension, and she had to keep a clear head for what was coming.

In front of her, rose upon rose upon rose drank in the sunlight. Such a happy, peaceful existence they had, with nothing to do but sit around all day and be admired. Thousands of cars flocked here each month to admire the amazing expanse of flowers, and today was no different. The tourist season had the entire area full and the place was flooded with visitors wearing sandals over knee-high black socks and pink plastic sun visors. Milling about with their oohs and aahs, taking happy family photographs on their happy family vacations.

It was easy to be jealous.

Why such a crowded place? They wouldn't do anything here with so many people watching, would they?

She didn't have to wait long for her answer.

A white sedan with heavily tinted windows stopped in front of her. A tall man wearing a black ski mask, jeans, and a green hoodie leapt out, took two steps toward her, and thrust a piece of paper in her hand. He towered over her, but she caught a glimpse of piercing blue eyes in their fleeting connection. Then, as the white sedan pulled away, he moved past Sara and climbed into her minivan. The entire exchange lasted less than five seconds, and the likelihood of someone noticing a masked man was minimal.

He backed out, almost clipped Sara's knees.

"Wait!" she said, but stopped short of screaming for help. That might break the rules of the game, whatever they were.

The messenger drove away, slipped off the ski mask. Sara tried to get a better look, but had little luck. The only thing she saw was the side of his face. A normal ear. A normal head. The strands of hair were short and dark. It could've been anyone, and it definitely wasn't someone she recognized, as if that were possible from such a quick glimpse.

Sara looked down at the folded slip of paper in her hand. Before she opened it, revealing whatever instructions awaited, she tried to examine it for any hints. The hand it had come from had been gloved, so fingerprints were out of the question. Folded, it was about three inches wide and three inches long. Standard white, no lines, taken from a printer. A crisp crease along the edge. Nothing extra, nothing like an identifying watermark.

It was just a stupid piece of paper.

A link between her and the game. A link between her and rescuing her children.

It felt dense, like holding a brick.

Inside the single piece of paper were an infinite number of possibilities, an infinite number of outcomes. The thought reminded Sara of the instruction manual that came with the open-world, open-adventure setting of *Juggernaut 2*, in which players were presented with thousands of options as they grew their characters from basement-dwelling couch potatoes into heavily armed, alien-slaying behemoths. Hundreds of different quests were offered as ways to increase their strength and agility, to gather up bigger and stronger weapons, to live out fantasies of turning themselves into something they could never become in real life. It didn't matter where they went or what route they took to get there, as long as the main quest was completed: save Earth.

But Sara's game had a different objective, one that couldn't be outlined with fancy fonts and clear directions.

She opened the folded paper and read:

FIND SHAKESPEARE

Find Shakespeare? Really? That's it? What does that even mean, find Shakespeare?

She wasn't sure what she had been expecting, and she knew it wouldn't be easy, but this? These two words of confusing... nothingness?

Where in the hell were the *real* guidelines? It wasn't like the games she was familiar with. The games she had tested for LightPulse for months and years at a time. The games that had a distinct mission with accomplishable goals that you could mark off of a checklist. A save point where you were allowed unlimited do-overs, and could attack the game again with new knowledge about the possible outcomes.

LightPulse worked hard at creating an acceptable level of artificial intelligence for the enemy combatants, but technology only allowed so much. And in the end, the objectives were the same.

Go here, do this, pull that lever, jump over the gap, kill that two-headed, slimy, spider-like alien with saliva-coated fangs and dual laser pistols. Destroy the mothership.

Real world, Sara. Real world, different game. No easy rules. If you screw up, you can't go back to the save point and start over.

Find Shakespeare.

Two words that held no meaning to her. Did it mean that she should find a collection of his plays? Would she have to walk back to the library? She tried to remember if there were any productions going on somewhere in town, or an exhibit at a museum.

Precious seconds faded away and nothing came to mind.

They sent me here for a reason. Shakespeare. Shakespeare. Find Shakespeare. A rose by any other name...Romeo and Juliet? Is that right? Shakespeare...roses...roses...Isn't there...

A faint memory skittered across her mind. She spun around, searching, searching, and then ran into the garden entrance, down the pathway, and then stopped in front of the park map. An arrow pointed the way to the Shakespeare Garden.

. . .

From where she stood, her destination was in the back right corner of the park.

She moved. Not quite walking, not quite running. If it mattered, if it was a condition of the game, she didn't want to draw too much attention to herself. Would any of these people remember a harried woman in a rush? Doubtful. They were too wrapped up in ogling the flowers and taking pictures to see that she was one heartbeat away from frantic.

Stay calm. How does that saying about the duck go? Calm on the surface, paddling like hell underneath? If there's an endgame, you can beat it.

But why a game? That has to mean something. Okay, it has to be someone that knows you work at LightPulse. This whole game thing isn't a coincidence.

She passed the spot where Brian had first leaned in, where she had first closed her eyes. Under different circumstances, she would've stopped and taken a minute to say a little prayer for his return. But living in the past and tossing a coin into the wishing well of the future wouldn't get her any closer to recovering what she had left of him. And that was Lacey, Callie, and Jacob.

They were all that mattered.

She approached the Shakespeare Garden and slowed to a walk. The nervousness of stepping into a place that was too quiet was second nature to her after spending thousands of hours testing games. Step into a quiet, unsuspecting room looking for a reward, and enemies would inevitably attack.

But no such ambush awaited her. She stood near the entrance, and saw that the foot traffic within the Shakespeare Garden was light, and none of the flower-gazers appeared interested in her or her arrival.

Now what? Do I just wait? Should I squawk like a chicken and flap my arms, you shitheads?

Rather than making a fool of herself, she announced, "I'm here," into the open space.

A middle-aged couple nearby gave her a curious look, then an older gentleman responded with an energetic, "Congratulations!"

Smartass.

She stood in place, waiting. Waiting. Waiting long enough to think that she could've been wrong, and this wasn't the Shakespeare she was supposed to find. The muffled sound of a ringing phone came from somewhere behind her. She expected one of the men or women nearby to answer, but it kept beckoning.

Is that for me?

The sound was close. She pivoted around to look for it, saw the Shakespeare plaque on the brick wall. A bust of the great bard and a quote that read, *Of all flowers, methinks a rose is best.*

Below it sat an inconspicuous collection of twigs, leaves, and small rocks. She knelt down, rummaged through the pile and uncovered a silver, older model flip-phone.

She flipped it open, answering with a subdued, "I'm—I'm here."

"Welcome to the first level, Sara. I like to call it...*Humiliation.*"

Chapter Six
SARA

"There will be three levels. One for each child. Complete all three successfully and you *may* win."

"I *may* win?"

"That depends on whether or not your prince and princesses are in another castle." The voice giggled, and digitized, it sounded even more sinister.

Sara caught the *Super Mario* reference. It had been one of her favorite games as a child. The long hours she spent mastering it, collecting coins and squashing mushrooms, were some of the happiest memories from her youth, but also some of the most maddening. Screams of frustration, followed by flying Nintendo controllers and a broken television screen had resulted in more than one grounding and innumerable parental sanctions against playing it, but they never lasted long, because her parents couldn't resist the squeals of delight when she was winning.

She surveyed the area around her. No one was paying attention. She said, "Listen, I don't know who you are—"

"No, Sara, *you* listen."

A short silence, followed by an "*Owww!*"

Her son this time.

It made her feel dizzy.

The voice said, "Did you hear that?"

Sara ground her teeth. "Yes."

"Try to defy me again. I *dare* you."

"I won't. I—I promise. Just don't hurt him again. Please?"

"That depends on how you play the game, Sara. There are rules, and in this case, they're *not* meant to be broken. Do you understand?"

"Yes, but what—can I ask what they are?"

"You'll figure them out as you play. Be aware, mistakes are costly, and there are no breakaways in this game."

Breakaways. What did that mean? Breakaways? That's a Juggernaut term.

Sara's mind raced. This twisted chick on the other end of the line, whoever she was, was familiar enough with their flagship game to know that a 'breakaway' was a power-up bonus that allowed a player to set off a mini-bomb and obliterate everything within a city block, thus evading capture or death from an advancing army of alien spider beasts.

If it's a she.

But was the mention of it a slip-up? Or was it intentional? Was it enough to be a clue?

LightPulse prided itself on their strong female following. Just because one of them was acquainted enough with the product to use a recognizable term didn't mean a damn thing. That narrowed the possibilities down to thousands and thousands of women all across the world. Especially in Japan. The current trend in the Japanese sub-culture of gamer girls was to get tattoos of their avatars on their lower backs, and to call them insane fans was an understatement.

But it was nothing concrete. The net was too wide.

Then, a revelation opened up in her mind like a house window during a hurricane.

The breakaway feature wasn't being introduced until the *third* installment of *Juggernaut* was released. Which was still in development. Which was still under lock and key. Which was still protected by non-disclosure agreements throughout the whole company.

It's somebody from LightPulse. Holy shit, that mini-bomb idea was Teddy's!

As the blast of information shook her like she'd been hit by a mini-bomb herself, the voice interrupted her thoughts. "Now, are you ready to begin the first level?"

What Sara *wanted* to say was, 'Is that you, Teddy?' but rather than revealing what she suspected, she replied, "I obviously don't have a choice."

"You're right, you don't. Now listen closely, because the instructions for each level will only be given once. Your phone is being monitored. Do not try to make any calls. Keep it with you at all times and answer it as soon as it rings."

"Whatever you say."

"You are being watched. You are being followed. Don't try to figure out who it is, because that would be a waste of time. It could be the old man holding his wife's hand about twenty feet to your left."

Sara looked around. It was the same smartass who had said, 'Congratulations!' and she seethed at him, however unlikely it was that he was involved. Her tormentor was trying to make a point. There were unseen eyes focusing on her right now from somewhere in the vicinity. The hair on her arms stood up.

"Trust me, Sara, any attempts to deviate from the game's objectives will result in consequences that these little angels will not enjoy. I can assure you."

Sara wished there was a bench nearby. She needed to sit down. She said, "Whatever you say, I'll do it."

The voice chuckled. "If your children's lives weren't at stake, I'm sure you'd regret those words in a few minutes."

"Whatever it takes."

Whatever it takes, Teddy, you little shit. I should've beaten you over the head this morning when I had the chance.

"I like your spirit. It could save three lives today. Before I give you the instructions for this level, I will offer this: you will be given the chance to ask *one* question for each round. Call it a *bonus* round. You may ask at the beginning of the level or at the end. What is your decision?"

Sara hesitated, but the immediate question on her mind meant more now than it would later, once she was in too deep. She would have to trust that she could beat or solve whatever puzzle was presented to her without any help. "I'll ask now," she said.

"That may not be your best decision so early on in the game, but...proceed."

"Why are you doing this?"

The sustained silence from the voice allowed the other sounds around her to creep in. Birds chirped. Bees buzzed around the roses. Wind rustled the leaves above her. High heels clicked on the walkway. Somewhere behind her, a carefree tourist laughed.

"I suppose I could say, 'Because I can,' but what fun would that be? Here is my answer, Sara: you don't know what it is yet, but you've taken something from me, something very important, and this is only the beginning of my retribution."

What did I take from Teddy?

She'd talked down to him far too often, but it had never been malicious. Just enough to get her point across that she wasn't interested in him, or that she wasn't going to lie down and be a doormat just because he was the owner's son. Had she called him Little One too many times? Taken his manhood? Would that be enough of a motivator for him to kidnap her children and threaten their lives?

No. It couldn't be. Could it?

All the other seniors call him that, too. If that were the reason, he'd be targeting them, too.

Before she could stop herself, an instinctive response shot out. "What was it?"

A pause, and then another yelp of pain. This time from Callie. Sara covered her mouth to keep from screaming.

"You broke a rule, Sara. Only one question per round."

"I know. I'm sorry. Just, please, don't do that again."

"This has gone on too long. I'm getting bored," the voice said, then followed it with a drawn out sigh. "So bored, Sara. I want to play *now*."

It was almost childish. Whiny. Infantile. Just like Teddy. Sara said, "Tell me what to do."

"Oh, goodie. This will be fun. Here is your objective for the first level, Humiliation. I'll admit that it's the easiest, but aren't all first levels? I don't want to break you before you get started. Now, you must strip where you stand. Remove every last bit of clothing. Walk to the center of the Shakespeare Garden and stand perfectly still for five minutes. No matter who approaches, you must not speak to them. In that time, you must solve this riddle, which will lead you to your next destination. The riddle is this: *The scarlet trusses contain the key where East meets West.* Take the phone with you. I'll call when your five minutes are up."

The call disconnected, and the voice was gone. Sara had never felt such rage against another human being. She felt like screaming at the sky and smashing the phone under her heel. She felt like tearing down the brick wall with her bare hands. She felt like ripping the head off each rose one by one, crushing their beauty within her fists.

She was under surveillance, however, and destroying the world around her wasn't an option.

Humiliation. Okay. Okay, I can do this. For the kids.

She recited the riddle slowly. "The scarlet trusses contain the key where East meets West."

Okay, figure it out later. They're watching. Five minutes. What's the worst that could happen? I get taken down by park security? Do they have security here? They could call the cops on me. Then what? Stop analyzing! You don't have time for this!

Sara took a look around her. Some of the browsers had moved on. Some were gawking at the flowers. Others had been replaced with a new gaggle of tourists.

Do it. You don't have a choice.

She reached up and unbuttoned her blouse. Her fingers that were once quick and nimble from a decade of clicking away on a game controller were now fumbling and clumsy. The buttons resisted escaping their slots and she grew so impatient that she ripped her shirt open and sent the last two flying into the grass. She slipped off her flats, and then took another look. No one was watching, but they would be soon enough. She took off her pants, then her bra and panties.

The warmth of the sun did nothing to save her from full-body gooseflesh as a cool breeze rushed past. She tried to cover herself, but it was about as effective as using a necktie for a blanket. One arm crossed her breasts, the other went down to the spot between her thighs.

She wasn't sure how much time had passed since the call had ended, but she was certain that it hadn't counted toward her five minutes.

Move, Sara. Go. Go now. Do it!

She stepped out onto the walkway, naked, and in no way free.

. . .

Sara tiptoed over to the center of the Shakespeare Garden and stopped in the middle of the path. The men close by began to sense that something was amiss, heads swiveling in her direction. Furtive glances crawled over her skin, violating and scrutinizing her body, getting a good look at the birthmark on her left thigh, the dimple on her right butt cheek, the ever so slight pudginess of her middle that would never go away, no matter how much she ran. She felt like she was being judged. Critiqued over every tiny flaw like livestock at an auction.

At least until their wives or girlfriends noticed her, too, and began urging them to look away or move on. One man tripped and fell over his dog. A woman scolded her from a distance, yelling at her to put some clothes on.

If you only knew, lady.

The only eyes that had seen her naked body in the past two years had been her own. And before that, before the twins came along, she and Brian had taken one adventurous trip down to the Cougar Reservoir where they had skinny-dipped in the hot springs that were buried amongst the waterfalls and evergreens. That was different. That was intentional. And it didn't matter so much, because everyone else lounged around naked, too, burning incense and warming themselves in the man-made pools.

But this—this was pure, unadulterated *humiliation.*

They must think I escaped from an asylum. What did I ever do to you, Teddy, to deserve this?

Sara felt the hot bricks burning the soles of her feet and shifted to remove a piece of gravel digging into her skin. How much time had passed? How much longer did she have to wait? Thirty seconds? A minute? She wondered how long it would take someone to locate an employee and tell him about the nude crackhead over by Shakespeare.

A couple of minutes tops, then another couple of minutes to call the police. I can get through this. Quit glaring at me, asshole. Take a damn picture. Lady, I know I need to put some clothes on! Stop yelling. You're going to attract more attention! Seriously, I will punch you in your fat hamburger face if you get close enough.

A younger guy wearing a bandana, showing off tattooed arms that stuck out of his basketball jersey, turned to see what the commotion was about. "Woohoo!" he shouted, and then his girlfriend slapped his shoulder.

If humiliation is the easiest level, I don't want to know what the rest of this game is going to be like. Game. Game. Damn it, the riddle! What was it again? Scarlet trusses. The key. East meets West. Trusses. Okay, some kind of bridge. Right? A bridge? Is there a scarlet bridge around here? It has to be somewhere close, somewhere here in Portland.

Sara ran down the list of bridges that crossed the Willamette River. The Fremont. The Hawthorne. The Steel Bridge and the Morrison. Broadway and Burnside.

Scarlet. Scarlet is red. Are any of those bridges red? The Broadway Bridge is kind of red…could that be it? Yeah, but it wouldn't be that easy. He specifically said scarlet. What does scarlet have to do with any of the bridges?

Sara thought. And thought. And shifted her weight from one foot to the other as people glared and stared at her body. It was difficult to concentrate with all the turmoil going on around her. People would enter the Shakespeare Garden and pause long enough to take in the spectacle and either stand with their arms crossed and watch or rush away, covering their children's eyes.

At least you have your kids with you. You'd do the same thing. Ugh, how much time do I have left? Two minutes? Three?

A man walked up to her and stopped no more than four feet away. He smiled, and then clapped five beats. He put his hands on his hips and looked down. Sara could feel him examining her feet, looking at her chipped toenail polish. Regardless of the fact that she was completely naked, she was embarrassed by the neon pink color she had chosen over a month ago. Such a small decision to do something *fun* had resulted in a sense of self-consciousness that momentarily outweighed her nudity, even in such a public place.

I know, I know. I haven't had time to get them fixed. Now get away from me. I need to concentrate. Please. Please leave.

His gaze worked his way up her legs, over her covered crotch, across her tummy and breasts, then he looked her in the eyes. Sara didn't know whether or not he could sense her pain and unease, but his words brought on an odd sense of muted comfort. In a deep, southern drawl, he said, "I don't know what you're doing, lady, if you're plumb crazy or brave as hell, but we need more people like you in this world. This takes some balls. Bigger than mine, that's for sure."

He walked away.

Sara watched him go, wanted to beg him not to leave.

Crazy and *brave. And I'd give you a million bucks just to be wearing your baseball cap right now. What's that on the back of your hat? Is that an 'A'? Who is that? Atlanta? A big red 'A,' just like the scarlet letter. How appropriate would that be? Shame. Humiliation. I hated The Scarlet Letter. What Hawthorne put that poor woman through—oh my God.*

The Scarlet Letter. Nathaniel Hawthorne. The Hawthorne Bridge.

Wait, the bridge is green, but the railing is red. And the Hawthorne Bridge was named after some doctor…doesn't matter. That has *to be it. It's too much of a coincidence. The humiliation factor. Scarlet. That's what he had in mind. The scarlet trusses contain the key where East meets West. The key he was talking about has to be in the middle, where the bridge is raised. Where East meets West.*

She was so relieved she would've clapped too if it wouldn't have revealed her more intimate parts.

Now I just have to make it through the rest of the five minutes—

"Ma'am? Ma'am?!"

Sara saw a woman, a park employee carrying a walkie-talkie, striding toward her, stomping so hard she could've left footprints in the bricks.

Here we go. That didn't take long. Jesus, what'll happen to the kids if I'm in jail?

Lacey, Callie, and Jacob, hidden away somewhere, suffering at the hands of a madman. Begging for their mother. Wrists bound with rough rope on little arms. What would happen to them? What would he do to them if she got arrested, if she weren't able to finish the game? Surely Teddy had planned for something like this, had contingencies set up in case something went wrong. The game was his, and he wanted it played. It wouldn't be any fun if it was over before it started.

Twenty feet away, the park employee said, "I'm gonna have to ask you—"

The phone rang in Sara's hand. She flipped it open, held it up to her ear.

The voice said, "My contact tells me you're about to get in trouble. Laugh. Apologize. Tell her you lost a bet. Stay on the line."

Sara did as she was told. Forced a laugh and apologized to the approaching employee. "I'm sorry, I'm sorry. I didn't mean to cause a scene. I lost a bet."

"Leave. Now."

The woman reached for Sara's arm, but she twisted away and said, "I'm going, don't worry," and then dashed down the walkway toward her clothes. Into the phone, she said, "Okay, I'm clear."

"I heard. And I enjoyed that very much, Sara. You played well. Good game."

"Are the kids okay?"

"*Tsk, tsk, tsk*, Sara. Only one question per round. But I will let this one slide. It's a natural reaction, of course."

Sara approached the spot where she had taken off her work clothes, but instead, they had been replaced by a running outfit. *Her* running clothes and *her* running shoes.

He's been inside my house. How did he get past all the alarms?

The ultra-expensive security system had been installed after Brian's disappearance, in case whoever had taken him wasn't satisfied with just a single Winthrop in their collection. Aside from her and the children, who never remembered it anyway, the only other two people that she trusted with the code were Miss Willow and Shelley, who were allowed to drop by for extra sets of clothes for the kids or to pick up things she needed for the office.

Did you torture one of them to get the code, Teddy? Make them play your stupid game, too?

Sara couldn't imagine what it would've taken for one of her two closest confidantes to reveal that secret.

Shelley was fine this morning. Oh no, Willow!

The voice asked, "Did you solve the riddle?"

"Yes. The Hawthorne Bridge. In the center. Where East meets West."

"I knew you could do it. See? I told you this level would be easy. In front of you are your running clothes. You have forty-five minutes to reach your destination. When you find the key, the first level will be complete. Keep the phone. Await further instructions."

Sara dressed.

And then she ran.

Chapter Seven
DJ

Detective Johnson, DJ, sat hunched over his desk, reading through Brian Winthrop's file. He tried to tune out the noise around him and focus, but the rustling papers and ringing phones and near constant foot traffic between the desks hindered his attempts at complete attention. He lifted his coffee cup and swallowed the last dregs of oil refinery leftovers.

Barker, a.k.a. *Bloodhound*, peered at him from over the top of his bifocals. "You could peel paint with that stuff, JonJon. Imagine what it's doing to your insides."

DJ looked up from the file. "Again?"

"Again what?"

"Again with the JonJon."

"It's your fault, cowboy. I don't know what life's like down yonder in Texas, but 'round these here parts, you don't offer a man the noose that's gonna hang you."

"You need to work on that accent. A real Texan would whip your ass just for trying."

"You're saying you're not a real Texan?"

DJ shook his head and grinned. Similar exchanges happened at least once a day, and he'd taken the ribbing as a sign that Barker was warming up to him five years later. Up until about six months ago, the most that could be said about their relationship was 'same car, same job.' But once DJ had solved a case that had perplexed even the great and mighty Bloodhound, a microscopic seam had opened in the older detective's armor. They weren't friends, yet, but at least DJ got to see what respect looked like when viewed through a pair of binoculars.

And in truth, 'respect' wasn't the right word. He felt like he deserved it, but the way Barker treated him suggested he'd yet to earn it. Not from Barker, not from the other detectives. One day, though, they'd be looking up to him. One day.

Their three-hour window had closed thirty minutes earlier. Barker had insisted that they return to the office and review the missing husband's file because his instinct said that Brian Winthrop was the catalyst. DJ had complied without question, partly out of deference to the senior detective, and partly because he'd witnessed the accuracy of Barker's initial reactions so many times that he knew that it was as reliable as the sun rising.

Barker's main mantra—the one that had resulted in so many solved cases—was simple: *Nature gave us the tools, but not all of us know how to use them properly.*

But now, with a short file and no new leads, DJ wished he'd pressed harder to get out into the field and start looking and asking questions. Rather than digging through one of the most confounding cases the department had seen in the past ten years, according to the notes, they needed to be focusing on the present. Detective Wallace, who'd retired a year ago, was so dumbfounded by the complete disappearance of Brian Winthrop that he had left the following in his records: *"Better chance of finding Amelia Earhart."*

Barker said, "Quit looking at the clock, DJ. I know what time it is," with the tolerance of a bemused grandfather. "If you hadn't let Mrs. Winthrop go, we might have a little more to guide us."

"I told you already, she handed me the note and ran out. What was I supposed to do, tackle her in the parking lot?"

"You could've tailed her. Less chance of a lawsuit."

They had been through this at least three times already. "Like I said, she asked me not to follow her." He didn't mention that she had *ordered* him not to follow her.

"Since when do you listen to somebody who could be a suspect?"

"Since *you* taught me to trust my instincts. And she's not a suspect."

"People lie, DJ—"

"'*Even when they think they're telling the truth.*' I know that, Barker, but whatever it was, it had to do with that note and her kids. No question."

"She could be dead by now."

DJ didn't have a response for that, but he hoped it wasn't true. He looked down at his desk, at the note Sara had found on her windshield, safely contained in a plastic evidence bag.

Are you ready to play the game?

He held it up and asked, "So what do we have here? What is this?"

Barker took off his glasses, and began chewing on the earpiece. "Conundrum," he said. "It's a sign that we're dealing with something other than a run-of-the-mill kidnapper who's looking for some kind of ransom. What we have is a sociopath who's looking to toy with this woman. He's playing a game—for lack of a better word—and if it means what I think it means, he's smarter than your average wannabe who'll make mistakes."

"What do you think it means?"

"He created the game, he can change the rules. That, cowboy," he said, "does not bode well for us, nor for Mrs. Winthrop, I'm afraid."

"You think it's the husband? Is that why we're sitting here going through this useless report?"

"Patience, Speed Racer. What I *know* is that when it comes to cases like this—"

"'*Coincidences put the bad guys behind bars and keep the paychecks coming.*'" DJ huffed, and then laid the note back down on the desk.

He stared at it, thinking about the interview with Sara, and the call that came for her. "One question."

"One answer."

"You keep saying *he*, but how do we know it's not a *she*? The receptionist at the school said a woman was calling for Sara."

"*Mrs. Winthrop.* Don't get too close. Could've been an accomplice. You should know that. And besides, the statistics say the ratio is something like eight-to-one, male to female. Numbers don't—"

"'*Numbers don't lie, people do.*'"

"And the sooner you learn that, the easier my job will get. Get back to Mr. Winthrop's file. We're missing something." He leaned back, repositioned his glasses, and resumed reading. The only way he could've looked more relaxed would be with the addition of a pipe, a smoking jacket, and a pair of expensive slippers. Throw in a roaring fireplace and a mahogany bookshelf for good measure.

Sniffing down the wrong path, Bloodhound. We're wasting time.

But he let it go. With zero solid leads and an absent mother who wouldn't answer her phone, they had nowhere to rush off to. He and Barker both complained about how unhelpful the interviews were with the staff at both schools. And the babysitter, Willow Bluesong, wasn't answering his calls, either, and hadn't been home when they'd stopped by on their way back to the station.

DJ resigned himself to giving the file one more pass and decided that when he was done, he was going to LightPulse. With or without Barker.

. . .

Brian Jacob Winthrop had just turned 38 at the time of his disappearance on a Friday morning in May. He was two years older than his wife Sara, and a father to twin girls and one boy. He'd worked reasonable hours as a financial analyst for a small investment company, operating his own storefront out of the east side of Portland, which was open from 8 to 5, every weekday. He ate lunch at the sub shop next door and played softball on the weekends, when the absence of familial obligations allowed for it. Athletic center records indicated that he swam for an hour each Monday, Wednesday, and Friday, and he hadn't missed a workout on those days in five months. The week he'd missed before that was the result of a conference in San Diego, according to his wife.

He had no prior record, except for two speeding tickets. Had no outstanding debts, no mortgage, and they were financially comfortable, if not well to do, in some respects. He'd struggled to gain new customers during the recession, but invested his existing clients' money wisely. No lost money, no bad blood to be found there, either.

No gambling addictions, no transaction records from strip clubs. No reason to be involved in the shadier side of society. His wife, Sara, had admitted that they'd smoked marijuana once, on their honeymoon, and hadn't touched anything since. Drugs weren't a factor, and they rarely drank, so alcoholism and its detrimental effects weren't a likely culprit. They had disagreements over finances and obligations like most couples, but none had been recent, and nothing that would've created the need to skip town.

From what DJ gathered, the guy had been a normal husband and father, completely clean.

He remembered another one of Barker's refrains. *'Nobody's a whistle, DJ,'* which he took to mean that nobody was as *clean* as a whistle. Sometimes his partner's attempts at being a wise old sage got in the way of the actual message.

Could that be it? Was he too clean? Is that what Barker's looking at? I'm not seeing a damn thing.

DJ flipped to another page.

Winthrop had packed up his workout gear that morning, kissed his wife goodbye, and then left for the gym. That was the last time Sara had seen him, and three days later, his BMW hatchback had been located in a grocery store parking lot. There were no odd fingerprints: only his, his wife's, and those of their three children. No secondary DNA traces, no blood, no out of the ordinary hair samples. No signs of forced entry on the car. No signs of foul play whatsoever.

The only strange thing that Detective Wallace had noted was the fact that the car was so clean on the inside, and it looked like it'd been washed as recently as that day. He'd reasoned that the car of a father with three young children should be filled with cracker crumbs, errant french fries, and enough dirt to cover a baseball diamond. Wallace had checked credit card transactions for any car wash visits in an effort to set up a timeline of his whereabouts, but came up empty.

No money was ever removed from their bank accounts, and no additional pings on credit card usage had ever turned up. His side of the closet contained every bit of clothing he owned. Wherever Brian had gone, the only things that went with him were his keys, his wallet, his gym bag, and the sweat suit he was wearing when he walked out the door.

Except for a number of unreliable sightings, Brian Winthrop had evaporated.

"Barker," he said.

His partner looked up from his copy of the report.

"I got nothing. The guy's a ghost, man. *Poof*...gone."

Barker said, "You're partly right."

"How so?"

"He's gone."

"Gone where?"

"Anything in those reported sightings look fishy to you?"

"Other than the fact that they're unreliable?"

"Take another look."

DJ hated it when Barker made a point of testing him, but he played along. He checked the list again. "Outskirts of Portland, the day after they found his car. Somebody thought they saw him in Eugene after that. Grants Pass. Eureka. The last one was in San Francisco, three weeks after he disappeared. Who'd remember to be looking for some guy three weeks later?"

"And?"

"And what, Barker? Six feet tall, brown hair, brown eyes. Great, we just narrowed our options down to half the male population in the US. It could've been anybody. You say it all the time—what people see and what they think they see are two completely different things."

"We're supposed to question their reliability, JonJon. That's what we're here for, but you gotta understand that the mind makes connections," Barker said, pointing at his temple. "It's a dang complex computer. What sticks out to me—and what you should be seeing, too—is that if these sightings were real, he might've been heading *south*. Why was he hightailing it south? That means something."

DJ shoved himself up from the desk, grabbing his badge and gun. "This is pathetic," he said. "When the *real* Barker shows up, the one that doesn't make assumptions based on complete nonsense, let me know. I'm going to look for this woman's children that are missing *right now*, not some guy who vanished two years ago."

"The signs are there, DJ. It's connected somehow. Why? Why would he be going south?"

"Because that's how the news traveled, Barker. People saw his picture on television, it created an image in their brain, and then they *thought* they saw him at a gas station the next day, when in reality it was some random guy on his way to work. You keep chasing your tail. I'm going to LightPulse."

The approaching Sergeant Davis blocked DJ's dramatic exit. He said, "Barker, you and the cowboy here need to get up to the Rose Gardens. Report just came in about some crazy naked woman there that fit Sara Winthrop's description."

DJ thanked him, then said to Barker, "Well?"

"Sounds like the game's already started. Okay, you head over to her office, I'll go check out the Gardens. But this doesn't mean the mister is off the table, got it? And drop that note off at the lab on your way out, see if they can find some prints."

He nodded, and offered a curt salute.

Naked at the Rose Gardens? What kind of game are you playing, Sara?

Chapter Eight

SARA

Sara's feet pounded the pavement. She ran as fast as she dared down the hill, away from the Rose Gardens, away from her humiliation, cutting through the trees. The shortcut was more dangerous than taking the winding, looping road all the way to the bottom, but it would save her valuable time as long as she managed to keep from rolling an ankle. A sprain would be disastrous, but it was a risk she had to take.

She reached Sherwood Boulevard and found the opposite side blocked by a chain link fence, topped with barbed wire. "Shit," she said. "Son of a bitch."

She turned left and sprinted down Sherwood, controlling her breathing on a 3-2 count. Inhale on three steps, exhale on two. Inhale on three steps, exhale on two. Cars crept past and she examined each one, looking for someone that might be watching her, keeping an eye on her progress. Not a single driver gave her more than a passing glance. She risked a look over her shoulder, examining the road behind her for the white sedan with tinted windows. Her only tail was the Gray Line trolley with wooden seats and pink trim.

If the goons in the white sedan *were* trying to track her, they probably hadn't expected her to cut straight down the hill, and thus they hadn't been able to catch up yet.

She passed a parked, City of Portland work truck and then the chain link fence to her right melded into a wrought iron one, painted black. Below it, and on the other side, was one of the many reservoirs stationed around the hill. Once she reached Washington Way, she turned right onto the sidewalk and picked up her pace.

A paved walkway carved a path through the trees to her right. She wasn't sure where it went, and rather than risk an avoidable delay, she held her course through the mossy pines.

The rhythm of her breathing began to deteriorate as her lungs burned and her quads strained to keep up. A stitch crawled its way into her left side. She backed off her pace, enough to get her breathing under control fifty yards later.

I should ease up. Can't crash so soon.

No, no whining. Think about what the kids are going through. Push harder, damn it, push harder.

She increased her speed and thought about a video that Brian had shown her about a year before he had gone missing. She'd been suffering through a bout of depression for at least two months. Work wasn't going well, Jacob was going through his Terrible Twos, she wasn't sleeping, and many, many more things that she couldn't remember. A variety of factors had lined up to take their shot at pounding on her and then everything had coalesced at once after a good reaming from Jim when her team didn't make a hard deadline.

The video itself, the one Brian had dug up on YouTube, was Jim Valvano's speech from the ESPY awards, back in the early '90s. She couldn't remember all of it, other than the fact that he was dying from cancer and the message he wanted to convey. *"Don't give up. Don't ever give up."*

Those words carved themselves into her memory like a commandment on a stone tablet, and they would resurface whenever she needed them the most, just as they were doing right then. Sara could see the images of Valvano being helped up the stairs to the podium. His smile. His tuxedo. His slicked back hair. Pleading to the crowd.

Don't give up. Don't ever give up, Sara.

She picked up her pace another notch, and figured she had to be somewhere around an eight-minute mile. Her usual speed on the treadmill was around nine and a half or ten minutes, but she had always known she could do more.

Sara took another look over her shoulder.

No white car. Maybe they weren't following. Maybe she'd lost them.

She reached a junction in the road and crossed over to read the street signs. Straight ahead, the road wound back up into the trees on Lewis Clark Way, so she turned right and ran down Park Place until she reached an intersection she recognized. She made another right on Vista and headed toward Jefferson, which would lead her directly down to the park beside the Hawthorne Bridge.

I could stop, call the police. Tell Johnson where I am.

She looked down at the phone in her hand, now slippery from her sweaty palm.

Teddy said it was being monitored. I could leave it somewhere, run into a store. Should I risk it? If I'm caught…the kids…

Sara passed parked cars and shrubbery. Staircases leading up to nice homes and hand-laid rock walls. When she reached an intersection that had Kings Court on her left and Madison to her right, she realized she'd made a costly mistake.

The Vista Bridge crossed *over* Jefferson below, where she needed to be.

She stopped and looked up the incline of the bridge, dreading the uphill trudge that would lead her across it. She tried to slow her ragged breathing, wiped the sweat from her face. Cursed herself for forgetting. Every wasted second costing her, keeping her from Lacey, Callie, and Jacob.

She sprinted to the bridge's edge and looked down the hillside.

I'll break my ankle.

The phone rang in her hand, startling her so much that she almost dropped it.

"What?" she answered, and almost added, *'Teddy,'* to the end of it.

The voice said, "Why are you stopping?"

"Stopping?"

"Yes, you are stopped at the bridge on Vista, Sara, and I want to know why. You wouldn't be trying to inform someone of your... *situation*...would you?"

The creepy sensation of being *watched* hovered around her. She scanned the area and saw no white sedan, nor anyone that looked like they might be keeping tabs on her position. Looked up into the trees nearby, half expecting to see someone perched on a limb holding a camera. Instead, a squirrel twitched its tail and then scampered further up the trunk as a cyclist zipped by.

"Answer me, Sara."

"I'm just trying to figure out the quickest way. That's all."

"I sense some tension in your voice," it said. "You wouldn't be lying to me, would you?"

"No, no, I'm not. I swear."

"Because if you are, I have some pliers in my hand that haven't pinched anything in a while."

"Don't!" she screamed, scaring another passing cyclist so much she almost ran into the curb. "If you put one more motherf—"

"Careful," the voice shot back. "Remember the rules."

"You can take your rules and—I mean, damn it. Okay, your game, your rules. I'll play."

"That's a good girl. I trust you won't get any ideas?"

"No. No ideas. I'm going, I'm going."

"Good. But as a penalty for this minor infraction, I'm reducing your time. Twenty minutes remain. The clock is ticking."

Sara slammed the phone shut.

Asshole! Okay, move. Go.

Down the hill of King street, up to Main, running hard, forcing her tired legs to get one foot in front of the other, cutting through the neighborhood, making her way back to Jefferson, and then straight ahead toward the Hawthorne Bridge.

The slight decline of Jefferson increased her momentum, but it also made for an awkward running position and caused more painful heel strikes that sent shockwaves up through her shins and into her lower back.

Pain is temporary. You have no choice. For the kids.

Sara worked her way back through her past interactions with Teddy and tried to remember what she'd done to him. All the times she had called him 'Little One'. All the times they had sat in meetings together and she'd proved him wrong. All the times she had removed his hand from some part of her body with a cautioning tone.

The number of instances where he could've taken offense were endless, but was it enough? People killed for less, didn't they?

But Teddy? He's not...he's not smart *enough for something like this.*

Sara's lungs felt like they were turning themselves inside out. Her quads and calves were melting into mush, but the adrenaline allowed her to keep pushing, pushing. Pushing past the light rail stop and across intersections. Past apartment complexes and empty office buildings.

Sweat ran into her eyes and soaked her shirt so much that it hugged her skin like a wetsuit. Feet swelling, muscles straining, but she kept putting one leg in front of the other.

No, it has to be Teddy. Has to.

Was that why he'd kept her in the meeting so long that morning? So his plan would have time to work? And he mentioned the breakaway. His baby. His idea. His big contribution. One of the rare times he'd contributed something useful to a project. One of the rare times the senior staff had given him credit instead of chiding him. He had to be throwing it back in her face. Enough of a hint to say, 'See what happens? See what happens when you push too far?'

All of it was there. The admonishments, the chiding, the years of subtle insults to pop his inflated ego.

But the more she thought about it, the longer she analyzed their past, and as she sprinted toward her destination, she couldn't shake the sensation that no matter what their history might be, Teddy Rutherford was just too lazy and self-absorbed to bother with something like this.

. . .

She played an impromptu, live version of *Frogger* crossing Naito, and then made a left at Riverfront Park, angling her way up the entrance ramp to the Hawthorne. Her body ached and she was so thirsty she could've buried her head into the Willamette and chugged until she regurgitated the less-than-pristine river water.

I was so sure it was Teddy, but now—

It has to be him. He's the only one with the slightest bit of motive.

But it doesn't feel right.

When would anything like this ever seem right?

I don't know, but if it is him, I'm gonna show him what 'flick, boom, done' *really feels like.*

She passed the line of cars waiting for their turn. The exhaust fumes polluted the air around her, leaving a thick, burnt-fuel taste on her tongue. She coughed and spat, wiped the dangling saliva from her lower lip. She looked south, toward the Marquam Bridge and saw that a number of small, private yachts and boats were parked at the marina.

Teddy has his own boat. Good place to hide your children.

Too obvious.

Sara approached the center of the Hawthorne Bridge. Cars zipped past her on the rattling, clanging steel-grated deck of the bridge's center. The sound blasted its way into the side of her head, beating against her eardrums. The red paint of the hand railing hadn't been touched in years, worn away by the elements and the passage of time.

Time that slipped faster and faster away as she ran, though it had crawled like molasses back in the Shakespeare Garden.

She stopped at the middle. Doubled over, inhaling through the coffee straws her lungs had become. The breeze was cool and penetrating out over the water as it whipped past, heightening the chill of the soaked running shirt molding itself around her skin. She felt the sun on her back, then straightened up and put her hands behind her head.

Breathe. Breathe. Don't puke. I'm here, you bastard. Where East meets West. What am I supposed to be looking for? Some kind of key?

She looked at the phone in her hand, waiting for it to ring.

Are you supposed to call me? What am I supposed to do?

Sara spun in desperate circles, searching the area around her feet, across the bridge to the other side, up at the towering green trusses. She heard the roar of a hulking metal beast as a TriMet bus slouched its way by, lumbering along, kicking up dust that pelted her skin.

All the other instructions were on a piece of paper.

She twirled, hoping to see a flash of white. Some bit of guidance. Something to point her way to the next level.

I don't see anything. Nothing there. Nothing on the sidewalk. Anything wrapped around the railing? Shit. No. Empty. Is it on me somewhere? Has it been with me this whole time? No pockets in the shirt...no pockets in the shorts...nothing in the key pocket...shoes? Shoes? Damn. No. Where in the hell is the key?

She walked to the railing and leaned across it, looking for anything below, feeling the sun-warmed metal on her palms. The deep green water of the Willamette swirled along some fifty feet down. The height, coupled with dehydration and exhaustion, caused an overpowering feeling of vertigo. Sara backed away, afraid that she might topple over the edge and plunge into the river. This world, the real one, wasn't like the landscape inside the realm of *Juggernaut*, where you could bump into the outer limits of the backdrop and be stopped from going further. A trip over *this* ledge meant something she didn't want to think about.

Sara looked to her left. A streetlamp reached into the sky and she walked over to it, intending to use the metal post as a support, something to lean against while the dizzy spell passed.

Before she flopped back against it, she saw a small bulge protruding from the front side. She looked closer, and then she gasped. Right at eye level, underneath a wide, clear strip of tape, was a bronze-colored key stuck to the lamppost.

She peeled it away with harried, scrabbling fingers. Ripped the key from the tape's sticky grasp.

The phone rang.

She answered, "I found it, found the key."

"Good for you, Sara. My apologies for the delay. I was having a bit of fun with your children. Who knew they could...*bleed* so easily?"

Chapter Nine
DJ

DJ sat in a plush leather chair across from Jim Rutherford, the CEO and President of LightPulse Productions. The private office had one glass wall that offered a view of the interior machinations of the company, another was populated with promotional posters of their past releases, and, behind him, a shelved wall held a number of awards and family photographs. The windows to his right were covered with drawn shades, allowing parallel strips of sunlight to penetrate into the room. No overhead lights illuminated the area, and no desk lamps were present to give off a soft glow.

The cave-like atmosphere reminded DJ of some super villain's secret lair.

The desk was as big as a full-sized mattress and oddly empty, except for a single notepad, one pen, and a laptop. DJ expected mountains of paperwork and a ringing phone. At least a nameplate and some kitschy knickknack, like a Newton's Cradle. Instead, the sparseness of the desk gave DJ the impression that this was a man who had little time for distractions. Or, a man who made it a point to eliminate the near-constant interruptions that invariably came with running a busy, growing company like LightPulse. It was an admirable quality—one that DJ wished he had, as well.

Jim wasn't dressed like the average CEO. At least, not the ones that DJ had interacted with before. His buzz-cut salt and pepper hair complimented the plain black t-shirt he was wearing, along with jeans and sneakers that suggested he was a man who dressed however he wanted because he was in charge.

DJ thought, *Dude looks like a poor man's version of Steve Jobs.*

Jim said, "I hope you don't mind sitting in the dark, Detective. It's easier on my eyes. Too many years of working under these damn office lights. They give me headaches."

"How long have you been involved with video games, Mr. Rutherford? I was a huge fan of *Shotgun Shooter* back in the day." DJ knew he should be jumping right into his questions about Sara—he was already way behind on their timeline, after all—but buttering up the man with a miniature ego boost couldn't hurt. Like Barker said, *'Bees with honey, DJ. More bees with honey.'*

"About thirty years. I was on some of the original Atari teams, if you can believe it. So you liked *Shooter*, huh? Wow. Memories. That was back when this was a tiny shop and I was still involved in the actual programming. Blocky pixels, left to right scrolling, 2D worlds. I miss those days. Now we create these 3D masterpieces with nearly the square mileage of Portland for our players to run around in. But hell, it's what they want." Jim crossed his legs, tented his fingertips. "I've been toying with the idea of releasing a 2D throwback for nostalgia's sake, but since Sara lit the fuse under the *Juggernaut* series, we'd get creamed by the media for a stunt like that."

Eh, sounds like regret, but not enough of a motive for kidnapping. "Have you spoken to her today?"

"Not a word. I've been trying to get in touch with her since she left this morning, but she won't answer her phone."

"And you're aware that her children are missing?"

"That's the report I got from her assistant, Shelley. Such a shame. They're sweet kids, and I hope I can help. Do you have any leads yet?"

"We're working on it. How well do you know Sara—I mean, Mrs. Winthrop?"

"We're close. She's a bulldozer sometimes, but she's one of my favorites. I'm sure you can understand that I'm busy as hell trying to run this place, but I try to keep tabs on everyone here, you know. I do my best to get out into the trenches with these guys so they don't think I'm some seagull owner."

"Seagull owner?"

"Flies in, shits on everything, and then leaves."

DJ chuckled. "I think I've known a few of those." He liked the man, had a strong feeling that he wasn't a suspect, and regretted having to ask his next question. "Are you in any way involved in the disappearance of Sara Winthrop's children?" Such a pointed question obviously wouldn't get a positive answer, but it was designed to take Rutherford by surprise in order to gauge his immediate response.

"Definitely not."

The clear, definitive answer, coupled with the body language of a truth-teller, was the response DJ was looking for, in contrast to the dodging, evasive answers, and nervous tics of a person on the front-end of a lie. He asked, "And do you have any idea who might be?"

"Not in the slightest. Like I mentioned, she's an asskicker, but around here," he said, motioning toward the glass wall and the open office on the other side, "she's well liked. Respected. Some of the younger kids have a healthy dose of fear of her, but I love that about Sara. She scares the hell out of my son, Teddy, which is sorta funny, to be honest, and frankly I think he does better work because of it. Out there in the real world, though, I'm sorry to say that I don't know what people think. I can't imagine their opinions would be much different. But here in the office, she gets shit done, Detective Johnson, and we'd be lost without her."

"And you don't think that type of demeanor would be enough to create some animosity?"

"Animosity? Of course it's a possibility, but if every poor sap stuck in a cube got pissed off and kidnapped his boss's kids, there wouldn't be any children left."

"True, Mr. Rutherford, but I'm trying to establish a motive. It has to come from somewhere, and an angry employee is an obvious place to start."

"Not with the kids we have working here. They just want to play video games and have fun. Sara's like the—ah, hell, what do they call the older lady who stays at a sorority house?"

"The house mom," DJ answered, which he knew only because his wife Jessica had been an Alpha Phi at the University of Oregon. Her reluctance to leave her home state was the reason he'd said goodbye to Texas. But for her, he would have done anything.

"That's it, the house mom," Jim said. "She's either the house mom or the drill sergeant that you eventually like and respect, even after he's removed his size eleven boot from your ass."

DJ knew what he meant. Four years in the Army, two of them spent as an MP, had left him with distinct memories of that exact same boot insertion and removal. He said, "I had one of those. Believe it or not, we exchange Christmas cards. Was Sara ever in the military?"

"Not unless she was in an ROTC program while she was in school, and I don't remember anything like that on her resume. She started working here right after she got out of college and has been killing it since day one. What Sara has," Jim said, "is an inherent strength." He groaned as he stood up, massaging his lower back. He moved with a slight limp over to the window, pried open two shades, and took a long look out into the world beyond.

DJ waited. According to Barker, if you stayed silent long enough, individuals would usually offer more information than if you had asked them something directly. *People want to talk, DJ. Listening is an art. Hearing is biology.*

Still looking out the window, Jim said, "Detective?"

"Yes, sir?"

"What I'm about to tell you—" The blinds snapped shut with a metallic *chink*. "—should be used with some discretion," Jim said. He leaned against his massive expanse of a desk and crossed his arms. "Do whatever you like with it, and I completely understand that you have an investigation to conduct, but I'm asking you to keep this as contained as you can. I feel guilty for saying this, but I have a multi-million dollar business to run, and I can't risk having Sara's authority undermined if—not if, *when*—you find her children and she's able to come back to work."

There it is. There's the ruthless businessman. You're all the same. At least you made it this far.

He said, "I'll do my best, Mr. Rutherford. You've got a business to run, but I've got three missing children to find."

"I'm well aware," Jim said, pausing. He bounced a hanging foot, toe-tapping the air. "I wasn't sure I should bring this up, because I think in absolutes. Ones and zeroes. Something is, or it isn't. This information is pure speculation, got it?"

"Of course."

"I don't know why I'm telling you this." Jim shifted on the desk. Flashed a look at the ceiling, then down at the floor. His bouncing foot moved faster. "Ah, hell, what I'm trying to say is—before Sara's husband disappeared, I had a hunch that he was cheating on her."

DJ rolled his eyes. *Not you, too. The husband, the husband. I'm looking for the kids, damn you.*

"At the Christmas party—why is it always the Christmas party, huh?—anyway, Sara was talking to some of the programmers from out there in The Belly, and in the back of the room, I saw Brian walk in looking like he'd been running around the block, and about thirty seconds later, one of the waitresses came in after him, putting on some fresh lipstick."

DJ said, "Not exactly proof. And I don't see how that has anything to do with the kids being missing."

"No, it probably doesn't. Like I said, pure speculation, but where I was going with that—my mind wanders, Detective. I dream up these crazy ideas. Storylines, right? I mean, that's what I do for a living. I don't want to distract you with dreamed up scenarios, but what if it's Brian? What if he's come back for the kids?"

"It's something we'll take into consideration."

"You're not a fan of the idea, huh?"

"It's not at the top of my list, Mr. Rutherford," he said. Then another Barker-ism popped in his head: '*Acknowledge the possibilities first, but trust the facts later.*' DJ adjusted his tie, fidgeted in his seat, frustrated with the fact that Barker was rarely wrong and was leaning toward the husband-as-culprit scenario, as well. And now Rutherford hinted at the prospect. "Let's say that it *is* the husband, it *is* Brian Winthrop, and he's come back from the dead or wherever he's been, why now? What makes you think that he would come back two years later and kidnap his own children?"

Jim shrugged. "It's a plausible scenario. When we design games here, we weigh the possible against the whimsical, and if the two meet in the middle, we know we have a winner. In Sara's case, that's all I can come up with."

DJ stood, no closer to having any leads than when he'd walked into Jim Rutherford's office fifteen minutes earlier. Regardless of what the Bloodhound's instincts were telling him, he wasn't about to sit there any longer and dream up convoluted schemes with an aging gamer who lived in some fantasy world where a mass of invading aliens could be considered possible.

Whimsical—yes. Possible—not likely. They'd have a better chance of crafting the plotline for a new game with this nonsense than he would of uncovering the truth if he sat here any longer, entertaining these implausible notions. He had children to find, and he'd already wasted enough time on the inane hypothesizing of Barker and the absurd theories of Rutherford.

He said, "I appreciate your time, Mr. Rutherford. Mind if I ask your staff some questions while I'm here?"

"Be my guest. They're on strict deadlines, so please keep that in mind."

"It won't take long. Any suggestions on where to start?"

"Shelley would be your best bet. She's only been here a couple of months, but I'd say she knows Sara better than anyone in the office. Except for me."

DJ thanked him again, and moved for the door. Opened it, then stopped before he left. "One last thing, Mr. Rutherford. I'm sure you've heard it thousands of times, given your profession, but does the phrase, 'Are you ready to play the game?' have any special meaning around here?"

Rutherford's eyes popped open. "How'd you know about that?"

The reaction surprised DJ so much that he didn't have an adequate response ready. He'd tossed the question out almost as an afterthought, never intending to fully discuss that particular aspect of the case. He said, "It's a—it's a lead we're following."

"A lead? Is Teddy a suspect?"

"Your son? No. Why?"

"Did you two talk before you came in to see me?"

"I didn't. Mr. Rutherford, if you know anything—"

"I'm sure he has nothing to do with Sara's kids."

"Does that phrase have anything to do with *him*?"

"He wanted it on the title sequence in *Juggernaut 3*. The staff shot him down, told him it was too mundane. He came crying to me and then pitched a fit when I agreed with them."

DJ took a single step back inside Rutherford's office. He said, "If that's the case, I have some questions for him. Where's his office?"

"He left early this morning, around ten o'clock. Said something about a golf tournament."

"Any idea which one?"

"If I did know, Detective, I'm not sure I'd be willing to offer that information, given the circumstances."

DJ said, "And you know that impeding an investigation is a serious offense?"

"Young man, there are a lot of things I *do* know that I'm sure you don't. Unfortunately for both of us, I have no idea where Teddy might be, golfing or not."

"I'll still be asking around before I go."

Rutherford shooed him away with a dismissive hand. "Good luck."

Chapter Ten
SARA

...I didn't know they could bleed so easily.

The words clanged around inside her head. Sara bent over the hand railing and vomited a mixture of bile and breakfast into the Willamette. She retched and dry-heaved until nothing was left. Coughing and spitting, she wiped her mouth with her sweaty forearm, and cursed into the phone. "You son of a bitch. If I ever find you, if you touch my children again, I will—"

"You'll what, Sara?"

"—do whatever you've done to them a thousand times over. Do you understand me?"

"But you're there, and I'm here, and you have a game to play."

It came out before she could stop herself, but the anger, the fury inside her had reached the internal temperature of the sun. Reason, and the result of the consequences that would come, provided a gauzy barrier and her words ripped through unhindered. "You can shove this goddamn game up your ass."

"Now, now, Sara. We mustn't let things get out of hand. And by the way—" Another yelp of pain from one of her children— Lacey, this time. "—I told you not to defy me again."

"*Stop!*" she screamed. If it'd been an option, if it'd been offered as an end to the game, an end to her children's torture, she would've backed up, climbed over the railing, and flung herself into the river. "You win, okay? You win."

"We'll find out who wins when the game is over."

"I have the key, just tell me what to do and I'll do it."

"Do you want to ask your question for this round now, or later?"

She wanted to ask now. She wanted to ask Teddy why he had chosen her. Why he had picked her instead of one of the other senior managers that constantly teased him and made fun of his height and called him 'Little One'.

Why did he get her children involved? Why did he have to bind them and torture them? Why not kidnap her? Why not take her, by herself, to some abandoned warehouse where he could do whatever unmentionable things he wanted to do? If he really wanted to get revenge for whatever offenses she had committed, why drag it out with this elaborate game that had so much room for error?

Because he's a cat playing with a mouse right before it eats it. He wants *me to ask now. To make the game harder.*

"Later," she said. "I'll save it."

The disappointed answer of, "Fine," and the long silence that followed confirmed her guess.

She said, "I'm waiting."

"I'm sorry, Sara. I took a moment to feel how soft your son's hair is. It's like gossamer, isn't it?"

Her stomach churned again. She imagined Teddy standing over her son, running his sausage fingers through Jacob's hair. Saw Jacob's tear-streaked face, cringing, trying to move away but unable to because of the tight ropes or rough chains. Rather than screaming more poisonous threats, she rolled her head from side to side, stretching her neck, trying to maintain control. Made a fist, punched the lamppost hard enough for a knuckle to pop.

Think, Sara, think. He's testing you. What's he want? Obedience? Submission?

She clenched her jaw and said, "You're right."

"Soft, blonde gossamer. You may get to feel it again one day."

"Please just tell me what the next level is."

"Such impatience. I expected you to be eager, but this fire in your belly is encouraging. It should serve you well during the first half of Level Two. I like to call it...*Confusion.* Are you ready to play the game?"

"I'm ready."

And you'd better be ready, because if I ever get the chance—

The voice said, "Keep the phone. Keep the key. Continue to the eastern side of the bridge. Take the bike path exit, down to the parking lot under the bridge. Your transportation will be waiting. I'm sure you'll recognize the car. You will be given further instructions. Do you understand?"

"Yes."

"This next level will provide quite the challenge. Oh, and Sara?"

"What?"

"You're doing great...Little One."

Little One. It was more than a hint. It was a taunt, saying, 'I want you to know, come and get me.'

Such a deliberate admission. It was enough, so obvious. She could go to the police, tell them precisely who had her children. But why, why be so blatant?

Because he has your kids. And you have no idea where. He knows you won't risk it. He's in complete control.

Sara paced back and forth as a woman approached, riding a bicycle. She looked like one of the many environmentally conscious commuters around Portland who biked to and from work every day in an attempt to reduce their carbon footprint, even if it was the size of a baby's shoe. Dressed well in a pants-suit, blue backpack clinging to her shoulders, listening to something on her iPod.

I have to fight back. This might be my only chance.

Are you insane? Don't do it.

Sara made an impulse decision in the few remaining feet before the biker was upon her. She ran, looking back, trying to match the woman's speed.

When they were side by side, the woman flicked at look at her, then refocused on the bike path ahead.

Sara said, "Can you help me?"

The biker removed her right ear bud. "I'm sorry?"

"Can you slow down a little?"

"What's up?" she asked, easing up her pace.

"My phone is dead," Sara said, wheezing, plodding along the hard concrete. "Would you mind making a call for me? Or can I use your phone? It'll only take me a second."

The woman shook her head. "I'm sorry. I can't."

"If you could call for me—I really need help—you don't have to do it now, just when you get a chance."

"That's not—"

"All I need you to do is call Detective Johnson at the police department. Tell him the game is real, and it's Teddy Rutherford at LightPulse."

"I can't do that, Sara."

Sara ran into an invisible wall, screeching to a halt.

Oh no.

The biker pedaled faster, shouting over her shoulder, "That's not how the game is played."

. . .

Damn it.

How many rules had she broken? How many offenses had she committed with that ridiculous, ill-conceived stunt? How long would it take before the woman told Teddy what she'd done? And what would he do to the kids as a result?

Sara sprinted, chasing after the woman for the remaining half of the bridge, but it was a useless waste of energy. She was on a bike, moving too fast, and had gone out of sight by the time Sara reached the opposite shore. She stopped under the overpass.

So stupid. What did I just do? Who else is watching? It could be anyone.

An older couple strolled past, holding hands, laughing. They smiled at her, said hello. Or were they checking on her, making sure she was playing the game as she should? They kept walking. Sara waited on them to reverse their course, follow her. Check in with Teddy, report that she was on schedule. Paranoia billowed in her mind like a gathering thundercloud. Dark and threatening, voluminous, ready to pour down and soak her last remaining sense of composure.

They never looked back.

She wrapped her arms around her body, doubled over, and cried. Wind blew at her back, scattering the teardrops before they reached the concrete. She thought about Brian and the way he had pulled her in close whenever she was sad or having a bad day. Thought about how she used to lay her head on his shoulder, listening to the bass reverberate in his chest as he told her she'd be fine, that he was there for her, and that she had nothing to worry about. If he was still here, would any of this be happening? Would she be at the office right now, answering emails, making calls, reviewing Shelley's latest copywriting masterwork?

Tell me it'll be okay, Brian. Tell me it'll be okay.

She heard the squeal of brakes as a car slowed to a stop beside her. The driver called out, "Hey, you need some help?"

Sara stood and waved him off. "I'm fine," she lied. "Bad knee. Hurts to run."

"Go see a doctor," he said, pulling away as a honk from another car urged him on.

She remembered Teddy was tracking her with the phone. He'd be able to see that she'd sprinted to the far edge of the Hawthorne and stopped.

Move, Sara. Move before he calls. Move before the son of a bitch hurts the kids again.

She walked, exhausted from the run, exhausted from the spent emotional energy, up to the bike path exit, and then down toward the Eastbank Esplanade.

The white sedan waited for her in the parking lot. The sight of it gave her a foreboding sense of dread as black as its tinted windows. What waited inside? Who waited inside? The woman from the bicycle? The man who had driven away in her minivan? The person who had dropped him off back at the gardens?

How many are involved? Three? Three at the least?

She scrambled over the fence, stepped around the bushes, and then walked over to the white sedan. Hesitated at the rear door, yanked it open. Climbed inside. The soft *shunk* of rubber on rubber as the door sealed shut was as loud as a prison cell clanging shut.

The interior of the car was dark from the window tint. Front and rear seats separated by a metal grating, like a police cruiser. The air was thick and difficult to breathe, permeated by the scent of stale cigarette smoke and the lemon-shaped air freshener that dangled from the rear view mirror. The driver, a male, wore a baseball cap pulled low, wraparound shades, and a jacket with the collar up, revealing nothing more than a sliver of his tanned cheek and the pointy tip of his nose.

To her left sat a small, brown paper bag. "Is that for me?"

The driver offered one slow nod.

Sara placed the bag in her lap, almost afraid to open it, but she relented. Inside was a bottle of water, an apple, a small box, and a familiar white slip of paper. She pulled it out and read:

KEYS OPEN LOCKS. LOCKS OPEN CAGES.
24 HOURS. IF YOU THINK HARD,
THE ANSWER WILL COME.

Confusion. I'm supposed to lock myself up for twenty-four hours. What am I supposed to think about for twenty-four hours? And the kids? Just sitting there waiting for me. I'm so sorry, guys. So sorry that Mommy got you into this.

The driver started the car. Drove out of the lot.

Sara reached into the bag and removed the small, square container, examining it as they pulled onto the street, heading east. Charcoal gray, hinged on the back side. A jewelry box. She held it up to her ear and shook. Something rattled inside.

She held her fingers to the lid, waiting, not knowing what to expect. Perhaps some clue, something to help her remember, something to remind her of what she was supposed to think about for the next twenty-four hours.

Twenty-four hours. It seemed impossible. Undoable. But that was what he wanted. The torture of being helpless. The torture of making her sit idly, locked in a cage, unable to do anything. Waiting while he controlled the game, controlled her fate, controlled her children's fates. How afraid they must be without their mother, hoping she would save them soon, not knowing why they were trapped in a room with a stranger, not knowing why she hadn't come yet.

The guilt was settling in already, and she wasn't even inside the cage yet.

She looked down at the box, her hands poised, ready to open it.

Did you take this from my house, too, Teddy? What did you find in there to torture me with?

She squeezed, pried the lid back, then slammed it shut when she saw the object inside.

Chapter Eleven
DJ

DJ marched out of Jim Rutherford's office.

What had started out as a pleasant, helpful conversation had disintegrated into a muddled mess, turning his mood foul. But it left him with two leads. The husband theory had its structure built on sand and speculation, while Rutherford's son, Teddy, had just become the prime suspect. The exact phrase match, coupled with his convenient disappearance to an unknown golf tournament, was enough to pursue.

Yet it wasn't as concrete as he would've liked, because it was missing motive, and he wanted a measure of reassurance before he issued an APB for the guy and brought him in for questioning. He didn't want to risk a lawsuit if Teddy Rutherford were standing on the 18th fairway over at Riverside or Heron Lakes.

He called the station, asked them to check up on golf tournaments in the area. "Call me if you find any. Call me faster if you don't."

DJ approached the nearest employee, a scrappy looking kid with a greasy, unwashed mop and pimpled skin. He went into Barker's version of 'steamroller mode': a tactic he used to overpower and intimidate someone that might offer more information when confronted with a bigger presence. *Bees with honey, DJ, but piss and vinegar when necessary.*

DJ said, "Name and rank, soldier."

The kid looked up from his laptop. "I'm sorry?"

"I said name and rank, soldier."

"My rank?"

Doesn't work on the clueless, Barker. He said, "Forget it. What's your name?"

"Jeremy. And you're...?"

"Detective Johnson," he said, flashing his badge. "Where can I find Sara Winthrop's assistant?"

Jeremy recoiled. He gave a simple, "Whoa," and added, "Not sure. I think she's gone for the day."

"Gone?"

"Yeah. Pretty sure."

"How sure is pretty sure?"

"Well, I mean, very, I guess."

"You guess?"

He pointed toward the front door. "I heard her tell somebody over there that she'd see them tomorrow."

"You *heard?* Did you actually *see* her leave?"

"Kinda."

"Kinda?" *What's he hiding?* "Come on, you either did or you didn't—which is it?"

"I did."

"And you're positive?"

"Positive," Jeremy said, and then added with some reluctance, "She's got a tight body. I checked out her ass when she left. So yes, I saw her leave. You got me. Guilty as charged."

Jesus. He's just embarrassed. "Not exactly a crime, Skippy. When was this?"

"Ten-ish," he said, pausing to think. "Wait, yeah, ten o'clock. She and Teddy both left right before the group meeting."

DJ put his hands on his hips, examined him for any signs of malfeasance. No twitching, no avoided eye contact, no hint of deception in his body language. He seemed legit. A goofy dork who happened to be admiring an untouchable ass from a distance. Right place, right time.

So the girl who knows the most about Sara and the guy who has a connection to the note are both gone, and they left around the same time. Coincidence?

Jeremy said, "Anything else? I'm kinda behind here, dude."

"You said you heard her say she'd see somebody tomorrow? Any idea who she was talking to?"

"There's like, forty-five people here. Best guess would be Sara."

DJ sighed. "Not likely." Dead end. Not that observant when he wasn't checking out somebody's ass. "What do you know about Mrs. Winthrop?"

"Is she in trouble?"

"Not with us. How would you describe her?"

Jeremy thought for a second, said, "About five-eight. Brown hair, brown eyes—"

"Not physically. Her personality. She get along with people here? Any reason to think someone might hold a grudge?"

"Not that I know of. She's kinda like a bowl of ice cream. Cold but sweet at the same time."

"A bowl of ice cream, huh? You come up with that all by yourself?"

"I write some of the creative storylines for our games. Keeps me thinking in metaphors."

"Sounds like a fun job. And Teddy Rutherford? What kind of dessert is he?"

"Um…a sugar cookie?"

"How so?"

Jeremy looked around, wary of prying ears. "Promise you won't tell him I said this?"

"Promise."

With a hint of a smile, he said, "He *thinks* he's delicious, but in reality, he's just small and boring."

...

DJ drove away from LightPulse, wondering where he should go next. Maybe catch up with Barker, see if he had gotten anything solid from the witnesses at the Rose Gardens, let him know about Teddy Rutherford and the absent assistant. Question Sara's friends and neighbors, which they should've been doing hours ago, instead of wasting precious minutes on half-cocked theories about Brian Winthrop.

Damn. We're blowing this one. Big time.

The remainder of his conversations with some of the other employees proved to be as insignificant as Jeremy's sugar cookie. The general impression of Sara around the office was exactly as Jim Rutherford had described. She was fierce but encouraging, down to earth but revered. They had witnessed her heated encounters with Teddy, but it was nothing more than putting him in his place, like the rest of their management did on a daily basis.

The ones that had interacted with her outside the office talked about how great she was with her children and how well she'd coped when her husband disappeared. DJ sensed that the hat she wore at LightPulse was completely different than the one she wore at home, which wasn't unusual for anyone juggling a high-profile career and family life.

And from what he got based on their answers, Teddy was universally disliked around the office but either knew and didn't care, or floated along in this oblivious state of being God's gift to humanity. A Napoleon complex wasn't enough to make the guy a suspect, but his connection to Sara's note and the timing of his absence was, and it was close enough to make DJ suspicious.

But what about his dad? He knew where the phrase came from. Is he involved?

Jim Rutherford was a remote possibility, but he had too much to lose and too little to gain from kidnapping the children of his shining star.

"Don't chase, DJ," he said. "Stay focused."

His cell rang. He whipped into the nearest parking lot, stopped and answered. "Johnson."

"Got some info on those golf tournaments, JonJon."

"Seriously, Davis? You, too?"

A chuckle, followed by, "Too easy, DJ. Couldn't resist."

"Whatever. The tournaments?"

"Bupkis. None scheduled until the weekend."

That's a game-changer. "What do you have on Teddy Rutherford?" he asked, then spelled out the last name for clarification.

"Hold on a sec."

DJ heard the clacking of a keyboard as Sergeant Davis pulled up the information. While he waited, he asked, "Barker check in yet?"

"Yep. Said he tried your cell. Wants you to call him ASAP. Okay...Theodore Alan Rutherford, last known address...1848 Graystone. Wow. Guy must have a gold-plated toilet seat."

"Any priors?"

"Two. Nothing major. One speeding ticket and one assault, six years ago. Looks like it might've been a bar fight."

"Send a car over to his house."

"Want us to bring him in?"

The phrase match, no golf tournaments. It was the best he had. "If he's there. If not, start looking."

He called Barker next.

Barker answered with a perturbed, "Where the hell have you been?"

"LightPulse. Asking around. I think we may have something."

"Good. I didn't come up with much here. Some of the witnesses said they saw a naked woman. Said she threw on some clothes and hightailed it down the hill."

"On foot?"

"Like she was in a big damn hurry to get somewhere. But hell, who wouldn't be if they'd been standing around naked in front of a hundred strangers?"

"Right. Sara left the school in a hybrid Sienna. Beige, I think. Any sign of it?"

"Damn, cowboy, you might've mentioned that. Had a lady tell me she recognized the naked woman from the parking lot. Light brown minivan, she said, but it ain't there now. Not where she said it was."

"If she left on foot and didn't come back to get it, where'd it go?"

"Better yet, who took it?"

"Get somebody on it, then meet me at 1848 Graystone. Davis has somebody on the way, but I think you and I need to go have a look."

"Residential? You got a possible?"

"Heavy on the possible, but no motive yet."

"Anything to do with the husband?"

No, Barker. Jesus, would you give it up?

"Negative. Teddy Rutherford, son of the LightPulse CEO. See you in fifteen. I'll explain later."

. . .

By the time DJ got to Teddy Rutherford's home near Portland Heights, Barker was already waiting on him, leaning on the side of his car, admiring the house from a distance. DJ parked behind him.

Barker whistled as he walked up. "What do you think? Million five? How do people afford this shit?"

"Spending his daddy's dollars certainly doesn't hurt." DJ looked up to the house, taking in the spectacle. His shoebox-sized home could easily fit inside three times. Modern design with lots of straight lines and boxy edges. Gray exterior with white trim.

A cobblestone walkway led up to a sky blue door. Lush, vibrant landscaping made it look like the house was hiding within a jungle rather than being a place where a person might lay his head down at night. A huge, three-paneled picture window took up a good portion of the left side of the facing wall, and on the opposite side of the front door, a smattering of rectangular windows formed a wavelike pattern.

Barker said, "I get dizzy looking at it. Makes me think of those flashing cartoons that give kids seizures. Would you live in something like this?"

"If I had *your* salary, I might."

"My salary couldn't rent a room in that thing, cowboy." He angled sideways to face DJ. "What's the deal here? Uniforms left about five minutes ago. Nobody home."

"Damn. It's never easy, is it?"

"You'll learn one of these days."

"And I'm sure you'll take credit for it when I do."

DJ recounted the details of his LightPulse visit. The shitty meeting with Jim Rutherford. The connection to Teddy and the note. The golf tournament. The *lack* of golf tournaments. The unaccounted for assistant and her coincidental departure. The teasing that Teddy Rutherford may or may not have taken offense to. "The lead is there," he said, "but I don't feel like it's enough for motive."

Barker said, "What we feel and what we can reason—"

"*'Do not sleep in the same bed together.'* I know, Barker. I know."

"I wish you'd stop interrupting me."

"I don't need to. Your ramblings are ground into my brain."

"One of these days I might surprise you with something you've never heard before."

"When you do, I'll be all ears."

Barker tapped a cigarette out of his soft pack. Lit it with a one-handed *click* and strike of his Zippo, then took a long drag, slowly exhaling, letting the billowing smoke get lost in the breeze. "What now, cowboy? We've got a missing woman, her missing children, a missing husband, a missing suspect, a missing assistant."

"Don't forget the missing babysitter. The Bluesong woman."

"Seems to me like we're doing the exact opposite of our jobs. Losing people instead of finding them. I'm not sure I've ever gone this far in the wrong direction."

DJ decided against reminding his partner of all the time they'd wasted that morning chasing puffs of smoke that dissipated faster than the filth coming out of his lungs. "We're here. We might as well take a look around."

Barker stood quietly, smoking his cigarette, staring at the house.

"Well?" DJ said.

"Hold your horses. I'm pondering."

"Pondering what, Barker? We have to do—" DJ stopped mid-sentence as the front door swung open.

The young woman that stumbled out of the doorway and lurched toward them was naked from the waist down, with one strap of white cloth around her left wrist and one on her right ankle. Ripped purple t-shirt. What looked to be a ball gag dangled like a sadistic necklace. Her legs were covered in cuts and bruises that were so prominent, DJ could see them and her black eye from fifteen yards away.

Barker choked on his cigarette smoke, coughed hard.

DJ said, "Holy shit." He sprinted toward her, shouting back, "Call 9-1-1, Barker. Now!"

"Help me," she said, and then collapsed on the walkway.

Chapter Twelve
SARA

Sara opened the small box again as the driver headed east in the direction of Gresham and Powell Valley. She had to be sure that what she saw wasn't a trick of her imagination. Could it be the exhaustion? Was she hallucinating? It was possible. She was empty. Physically to the point of collapsing. Mentally to the point of seeing things that just couldn't be.

The object inside was a relic of history come to life. It was a memory that had manifested itself into a tangible form. It was the dead rising.

Sara peered inside and immediately regretted looking. It sat motionless, right where it was thirty seconds earlier, daring her to pick it up and *feel* what was really there.

Brian's wedding ring. It's not possible.

She reached into the box and pinched the ring, pulled it out and examined it in the light. The thick band of hammered tungsten felt cool on her fingertips. The tinted windows made it harder to see, but it *looked* like Brian's. She held it by the outside, tilting it this way and that until she was able to get a better glimpse of the interior. She didn't want it to be true, but it was.

The inscription read:

Forever Yours – SLW

A storm surge of emotions—anger and frustration and hope—rushed over her body, plowing their way through like a ten-foot-high wall of water over shoreline streets. It tore what remained of her stability to splinters, ripping it from the foundation, grinding it into shards of unrecognizable flotsam before it retreated and dragged her sanity with it.

She inhaled as deep as her constricted lungs would allow and let loose a banshee scream toward the front of the car. The driver ducked and swerved. She pounded the metal grating between them with her fists, rattling the cage. She wrapped her fingers through the holes and shook and shook and shook, pulling and pulling, trying to rip it free so she could claw at the driver's eyes, wrap her fingers around his neck until he couldn't breathe, or reach inside his chest and rip out his beating heart.

When he didn't turn around, when he didn't acknowledge her, when he did nothing more than click on his blinker to make a left turn, it unleashed a level of fury so deep that Sara began to feel cramps forming in the arches of her feet. She screamed. She raged. She pounded the metal grating until her knuckles bled. She shouted, "Who are you? Why are you doing this? Where did you get my husband's ring?"

On and on she went, screaming every question she could think of, every question that had plagued her since early that morning. She knew her temper tantrum that had escalated into a full-bore Hiroshima explosion was against whatever rules Teddy had dreamed up, but she was past containing herself. All the emotions she'd swallowed and hidden away for the past two years, all the anxiety and stress and fear that she'd kept buried so the kids wouldn't see, everything, all of it, detonated there in that car, leveling the walls she'd built around her psyche.

Sara screamed until her throat was raw and her vocal chords burned. Every muscle in her body ached from the vehement expulsion of her wrath and she went limp, flopping back onto the seat when no more words would come.

She looked down at Brian's ring in her open palm. The aftershocks of pain sent tremors vibrating through her hand and she could feel her pulse throbbing through the fluid in her swollen knuckles.

What did you do to him?

She tried one last time with the driver, this stoic courier delivering his pathetic, distraught package. "Where did Teddy find this?"

Nothing.

So many questions. No answers. Did the ring mean that Brian was still alive? Or worse, did it mean the opposite? What possible link could there be between Teddy and Brian?

Her chauffeur, the stone statue in the front seat, pulled over to the side. Sara sat up straight, tried to figure out where they were, but didn't recognize the area. Somewhere east of Portland proper, but not quite to Gresham yet. The driver reached up and worked a green strip of cloth through one of the openings in the grate.

"What's that for?"

His one word response was, "Blindfold."

Indignant, she said, "I'm not wearing that."

"Blindfold."

"No."

"Blindfold."

She clenched her jaws. "I said no."

The driver reached down, grabbed something from the seat beside him. He held up what was left of Jacob's Tyrannosaurus Rex t-shirt, the one he'd worn to school that morning. The one he'd worn so much the color had begun to fade. "Blindfold."

"If you hurt him—"

"Blindfold."

She ripped the green strip of fabric from its metal grasp. "If you've done something to him or my girls…if I get out of this goddamn game alive, and if I ever, *ever* find out who you are, you better pray to God there's another wall between us, because I'll be coming for you. Do you understand me?"

"Blindfold."

Sara wrapped the cloth around her head, covering her eyes, turning out the lights on a world that was already dark. She shifted the material around until she found a thinning spot on the old t-shirt, allowing her just enough sight to make out shapes in the sunlight.

What good will it do me? "Done," she said.

She heard him shuffling around, heard the familiar clicking of fingers on a keypad. Silence. More clicking.

"What're you doing? Did you hear me? I said I'm done."

The car began to move again. The driver turned on the radio. Classical music blared from the speakers, drowning out every other sound.

I can't hear where we're going, asshole. The blindfold is enough.

But with limited sight, her other senses took over, amplified themselves. She felt the rough material of the car's seat on the back of her legs. The throbbing in her swollen hands. The weight of the key in one, and the ring in the other. She felt the vibration of the tires rolling across decaying roads. Every pothole felt like they were falling. Every incline, a roller coaster climbing toward its apex. Tasted the remnants of vomit. She remembered the apple and bottle of water.

Save it. Might be all you'll get.

I hope they're feeding the kids. They didn't eat much this morning. Oh God, why didn't I make them finish their breakfast?

Breathe…breathe…breathe…

Everything will be fine.

Sara repeated the mantra in her mind, even said it aloud a number of times, but it didn't help. No matter how much she tried to convince herself that the ending of the game would be a happy one, no matter how many alternate ending scenarios that she came up with, the feeling that something bad would happen wouldn't go away.

Sliding into depression was an understatement. She careened downward, headlong, toward the awaiting and inevitable bottom.

Thought about how rare truly happy endings were out in the real world. You got handed the results and you had to acknowledge them and move on, regardless of the outcome or circumstances.

. . .

She had no idea how long they'd been driving. Twenty minutes? Half an hour? Surely they were out of the city, but for all she knew, they could've doubled back. It was too hard to make out where they'd gone with the fleeting glimpses through the material, but it wasn't worth risking a peek. If the driver saw her do it, one call to Teddy might result in more pain for her children.

As the car rattled and bounced along, Sara got the feeling that they were no longer on a paved road. The vibrations were different. More rugged and unforgiving. Wherever he was taking her, and however long it had been, it was far from where she wanted to be.

Which was on her porch, in her rocking chair, watching the kids play a game of freeze tag in their postage stamp of a backyard. Or in their living room, putting together a puzzle after dinner. Lying between the twins, reading them a bedtime story as her little boy dozed across the hall, mouth open, slobbering on his favorite pillow.

We just did that yesterday. Seems like a year ago. I miss them so much.
She slipped Brian's ring over her left thumb.
I miss you too, sweetheart. What happened that day? Where did you go? How did Teddy get your ring?

The radio went silent. The driver made a lurching left turn that slung Sara sideways and then he slammed on the brakes, pitching her forward into the grating. Without the benefit of vision, it was impossible to tell when she needed to brace herself.

"Ouch," she said, rubbing the impact spot on her forehead. "How about a little warning, asshole?"

"Sorry," he said, shutting off the car.

"Did you just apologize to me?"

"Yes."

"Why?"

Five seconds passed. Ten. He shifted in the front seat. Fingers tapped on the steering wheel. Not being able to see his reaction unnerved her.

He said, "Guilt."

"Guilt? Guilt for the knot on my head or guilt for what you're doing?"

"Both."

"So you *are* human."

Another long silence, then a dejected, "Sometimes."

With her heightened sense of hearing, Sara picked up on the regret in his tone. She wondered if nudging it along would help. She needed an ally. "Why're you doing this?"

"Because."

"Because? *Because?* What kind of answer is that? What if it were your children? Do you have kids?"

Tap, tap, tapping on the steering wheel. "One."

"Honestly? And you're doing this to me?"

"Sorry," he said. It came out laced with frustration, and she didn't want to push him too far in the wrong direction.

"Boy or girl?" she asked.

"Boy."

"How old?"

"Eight."

"It's a good age. I remember when my girls were eight. We had so much fun together playing dress up and watching Disney together. They're twins, though. Quite a handful. My son, he's five. Typical boy, you know? Dirt and lizards and monster trucks. What's your son's na—"

"Quiet."

She was getting through. She could feel it.

Delicate, Sara. Don't go too far. Push too hard and he'll turn on you.

She said, "It's okay. You don't have to tell me. I don't need to know." She leaned forward, softened her voice. "Aren't little boys the best? What's your favorite thing about him?"

"Smile."

"Don't you love that mischievous grin they get? Mine has the cutest dimples. And he has this thing he does—"

"Enough," the driver said.

Sara heard his car door open and the warning chime of the keys in the ignition. "Wait," she said. "I'm sorry. Don't—"

Her door opened and then a rough, gloved hand wrapped around her upper arm. He squeezed, hard, dragging her out of the car. He was strong, and for an instant she was airborne before she hit the ground, face-first, getting a mouthful of dirt, busting her bottom lip on a rock. She spat out a mixture of earth and blood. She tried to get to her feet, felt a foot on her ribs, shoving her back down.

"Stay," he said.

She complied, rolled onto her back, hands up in submission.

She listened to him walk away, heard both car doors slam shut, and then receding footsteps.

I can run.

You have no idea where you are. He has a car. You'll never make it.

And Teddy might punish the kids.

Might?

Sara ran her tongue across her lip, felt the swelling. More blood leaked into her mouth. She swallowed, afraid to move. Afraid he would hurt her if she disobeyed.

The sun warmed her face, and from above came the sounds of rustling leaves as the trees creaked and swayed in the wind. Somewhere nearby, a stream crawled its way across some rocks. A bird chirped.

You went too far. You had him.

He said he felt guilty.

Guilt can turn on you.

She heard the approaching sounds of heavy boots on gravel. She lay still.

What if I surprised him? Kicked the bastard in the nuts?

Then what? What if he has a gun? If you're dead, what happens then?

What if I got the gun from him? Forced him to take me to the kids?

He may not know where they are. Bad, bad idea. Too many things could go wrong.

I can do it. I'm sure I—

Her scheming ended when felt a hand in her hair, tugging her up from the ground. It hurt, but she refused to scream, refused to show any more signs of pain.

Sara heard what sounded like the crackling of a paper bag, then felt him shove it into her hand.

"Go," he said, whipping her around, shoving at her back.

He led her along, tightening the grip on her upper arm. She tripped over something, felt like a root, and he lifted her upright. They trudged downhill, then up again, tree limbs scraping her skin. A ragged, broken limb gouged a chunk out of her thigh. Blood trickled down her leg.

"Faster," he said.

The voice rained down from above, miles and miles above her head. She tried to remember how tall the guy was at the Rose Gardens, the one who had taken her van. She had no way of knowing until he removed the blindfold, but her sixth sense *felt* that he was the same man.

Tall. Dark hair. Blue eyes.

The thought sparked a memory from earlier in the day.

The guy. The tall one in the grocery store? Was he following me? Was that why he was checking me out?

Should I ask if that was him? Throw him off? He won't expect me to remember.

He pulled her to the right, leading her in a different direction. She took a chance, saying, "It's such a shame."

"What?"

"You seemed nice in the grocery store."

He didn't respond, but the faint, halting hitch in his step was enough.

Chapter Thirteen

DJ

DJ and Barker stood in front of the Rutherford home, watching the paramedics load the young woman into the back of the ambulance. They drove away with instructions for the doctor to call as soon as she was stable and coherent. DJ had tried to talk to her while Barker was inside, tried to ask her what had happened, but her delusional ramblings had made no sense.

He said, "I don't know, Barker. She was out of it. Kept saying something about how this woman told her she'd be okay."

"A *woman?*"

"She kept repeating, 'She said I'd be okay.' Over and over. *She* said she'd be okay. Nothing about a *he.* Nothing about Rutherford."

"And?"

"And what, Barker? You don't find that strange?"

"That I do, cowboy, but from the looks of her, I doubt that girl could tell you what day it is."

"Doesn't make any sense, that's all I'm saying. You find anything in the house?"

"Possible signs of forced entry on the back door. Single chair down in the basement. I figure that's where she was being kept. Managed to get herself loose. Other than that, the place is clean. Nothing like a weird torture room or crazy sex toys. From the looks of it, dude has more money to spend than he has sense. You should've seen the size of the boob tube."

"Forced entry on the back door, you said?"

"Wasn't much. Closed. Not locked, but it didn't look like somebody beat it in with a sledgehammer. More like it'd been pried open with a screwdriver. Figured Dumbo locked himself out at some point."

DJ looked at the house. Something didn't feel right. "What're we missing here? Where's the disconnect?"

"The disconnect?"

"We got a suspect in one kidnapping keeping another vic in his basement," DJ said. He pinched his earlobe, thinking. "But then there's a possible forced entry and the girl mentioning a *she*."

Barker studied him. "I ain't following."

"What if she was planted here?"

Barker laughed. "God almighty, DJ. And you say I come up with some cockamamie ideas."

"I'm assuming you've heard of the word 'hypothetical' before."

"Look here, cowboy, when I say explore the possibilities, I don't mean for you to put Elmore Leonard to shame with your plotlines."

"Then what's your theory?"

"Whoever *she* is," Barker said, "she partnered up with Rutherford. Conned our vic with some sweet words, brought her back here."

"Still doesn't feel right."

"Occam's Razor. Simplest explanation."

DJ put his hands behind his head. "Say we disregard my left field idea, make it a non-factor for now...if Rutherford and this mystery woman are working together, there has to be at least a third person, maybe more, right? He was at the LightPulse office until ten o'clock, and the Winthrop kids went missing around nine at separate locations. So while he was at the office, the rest of his team was out doing his dirty work."

"Now you're getting somewhere. And who knows how long that poor gal was down in the basement."

"But why, though? We don't have a ransom note. We've got a random woman in her twenties and three kids of a coworker. What're they doing?"

"I told you earlier we were dealing with a sociopath. Now it might be two. And if they ain't trying to ransom, what they're doing," Barker said, "is collecting trophies."

Trophies, DJ thought. *That would tie in with the idea of making Sara play a game.*

"Horseshoes and hand grenades, but it's all we've got," he said. "And I hate to ask, but where's the husband in all this? You give up on him?"

Barker shook his head. "Not yet. If he ain't the main course, he's a side dish."

"You think he could be the third?"

"Hell, I've seen stranger things. C'mon, let's get back to the station, see if that young lady was reported. Hospital might have an ID on her by the time we get back, and if there's a connection between her and Mrs. Winthrop or Captain Ugly House here, we'll get a better lead on the kids."

. . .

DJ found Barker coming out of the bathroom, tucking in his shirt. He said, "Hospital got an ID on the girl. Anna Townsend," and handed over her thin file. "Woke up long enough to give a name and then passed back out."

"Can we go talk to her?"

"Doc said to give it a couple of hours."

"What's her story?"

"Anna Townsend…also known as Stardust."

"Stardust?" Barker asked, flipping the folder open. "She a stripper?"

"Works the poles at this new club called Ladyfingers."

"Heard of it. Never been."

"Sure," DJ said, dragging the word out.

Barker ignored him. "What do we got here...one prior...driving under the influence. Twenty-one years old. Let me guess, paying for college?"

"Nope. Not your average stereotype. Get this...according to her *husband,* they're happily married with a one-year-old son."

"No shit? They got an open relationship or something?"

"Sounded as secure as Fort Knox. High school sweethearts. Said she started stripping to help pay the bills once he lost his job. Money is too good for her to quit, so he's a stay-at-home dad."

"I'll be damned. So why didn't he report her missing?"

"I had to pry it out, but he said that she doesn't get off work until around three in the morning. Once in a while, if some guy flashes big dollars, she'll go home with him for a private show. No sex, just extra money, and she'll get back around six or seven. He was worried because she wasn't answering her cell, but knew we wouldn't do anything until she'd been gone for twenty-four hours."

Barker pushed his glasses up to his forehead, rubbed the bridge of his nose. "I'm spitballing here, but I doubt there'll be a link between a stripper and Mrs. Winthrop."

"But," DJ said, "a stripper and a guy with money—that's a no-brainer."

"Let's go have a Q and A. One of the other girls might be able to give us some info on where she went last night."

DJ agreed, but couldn't escape the feeling that they were getting further and further away from Sara's children, regardless of whether or not they were heading in the right direction by chasing down Teddy Rutherford and his mystery-woman partner.

It keeps getting deeper and deeper, he thought.

Twenty minutes later, they walked into the Ladyfingers Gentleman's Club, Portland's latest addition to the growing cadre of strip joints that gave the city a higher per capita rate of naked dancer locations than Sin City itself. Some were prominent and popular; others were tucked away on side streets with little more than pink neon signs promising *LIVE NUDE GIRLS*. The market had yet to saturate, and doubtfully never would. If the world ran out of men (and women) willing to pay for the chance to see a woman in her birthday suit, it would be the end of times.

DJ had only been a paying customer once, a couple years back, for a friend's bachelor party. The experience was awkward. He'd found it difficult to look them in the eye, difficult to stare at the parts he was supposed to be looking at, difficult to figure out what to do with his hands during a private dance that had set him back fifty bucks.

He and Barker had been a couple of times for on-the-job visits and it was easier to feel in control and not under the spell the strippers seemed to cast over every person desperately waving a single, hoping to get a closer glimpse.

And Ladyfingers was even more acceptable when the doors had just been unlocked and the stages were empty.

They stopped a couple of feet inside the doorway. No patrons yet, no bartender, no girls.

The same smell that came with every strip club hung in the air. Evaporated alcohol, girl sweat, and cheap perfume. It was thick and cloying. DJ knew it would get stuck in his clothes and made him think about having to do laundry. He glanced around at the dark walls, the mirrors, the strobe lights hanging overhead. Rows of liquor bottles stood at attention behind the bar. Across from it, the main stage perched three feet above the floor with a signature, shiny pole in the middle. Tables and chairs stretched all the way to the back of the room where two smaller stages occupied each side.

He said, "I still haven't figured out why these damn places make me so uncomfortable."

"It's because you're not human," Barker said.

"True, but at least I don't put dinner on the table for half the strippers in town."

"The ex ain't coming back, and I'm not getting any better looking, JonJon."

"I know it used to take months to paint a naked woman back in your day, but you've heard of the internet, right?"

Barker examined him, head to toe, squinting at DJ's face, at his ear.

"What're you doing?" DJ asked.

"Looking for your mute button."

A bartender emerged from the swinging doors to their left, her tattooed arms straining to hold onto the three cases of beer. She noticed them, said, "No tits for another hour, guys. Can I get you a drink?" She lifted the beer cases up, sat them down heavily on the bar. The bottles clinked around inside.

DJ and Barker walked over, showed their badges. Barker said, "No thank you, ma'am. On duty. Detectives Barker and Johnson."

She said, "And the cherry is popped."

"The cherry?" DJ said.

"Been open a month. You're not the first cops we've had in here, but you're the first that were on duty." She opened one of the cases and began restocking the cooler.

Barker said, "I'm sure we won't be the last, either. Mind if I ask your name?"

"Mildred," she said, tearing open another box.

"Is that right? That purple mohawk don't exactly scream such an old fashioned name."

"Blame my grandmother."

Barker chuckled. "Don't be ashamed of it. My dear ol' gran was a Mildred, too."

DJ shot a quick look at him, wondered if he was lying. Remembered Barker saying, '*Butter can go on both sides of the toast, cowboy.*'

Mildred finished up the third box, leaned over the bar toward them. "Not trying to be a douche, but I got shit to do, man. What's up?"

DJ said, "You have a dancer here who goes by Stardust?"

"Anna. She's a good one."

"And were you working last night?"

"I own the place, Detective. I'm here every night. Something happen to her?"

Barker said, "*Something* happened, but we'd like to find out what."

"Oh, shit. She's not dead, is she?" Mildred stood up straight, looking from Barker to DJ, Barker to DJ.

"She's alive, but she won't be back to work for some time," Barker said.

DJ asked, "Did you know she was going home with customers after hours? Doing private shows?"

"It's against my rules, but some of the girls do it. I can't stop whatever happens once their shifts are over."

"Was Mrs. Townsend paying extra attention to anyone in here last night? Short guy, about this tall. Probably flashing bills with a couple extra zeros."

"She was," Mildred said. "But not a dude. Some girl. They were down at the end of the bar, flirting with each other for half the night."

DJ waffled his curious glance between Barker and Mildred. "Can you describe her?"

"Straight brown hair, shoulder length. Great smile. Nice body. At least what I saw of it. I remember thinking that if she threw on a bunch of makeup and some glitter, she could go onstage."

"Any chance she paid with a credit card?"

"Nah. She had two Cosmos, paid cash for both."

"Good memory," Barker said.

Mildred picked up a rag, swiped at some crumbs. "It's what we do. You work behind a bar long enough, you learn to pay attention to the big tippers."

"Can you think of anything out of the ordinary about her?" DJ asked. "Anything we could identify her with? Tattoos, unusual birthmarks?"

"Um...no, just naturally pretty. Around the same age as Anna. Low-cut blouse. Good rack, like she'd had them done, you know?" She focused on the countertop like she was staring into her memory. "Other than that...oh yeah, a necklace with these diamonds that looked like two letters sort of intertwined together. Might've been initials."

DJ said, "You remember that?"

"With cleavage like hers, who wouldn't be looking right there?"

Barker said, "Can you remember what they were?"

"My memory's not *that* good."

"Take a guess," DJ said. "Anything helps."

"Shit...okay...D. I'd say one of them was a D."

Barker said, "One last question, Miss Mildred. Did Anna leave with her?"

"She was here until around two-thirty. Anna left a few minutes past three. After that, who knows?"

"Thanks for your time," Barker said. "Might see you again one of these days."

"First drink is on the house."

Back on the sidewalk, heading for Barker's car, DJ said, "How many boxes of Cracker Jacks do we have to open before there's a *good* prize inside?"

"Preaching to the choir, DJ. Preaching to the choir. Now hit that mute button I was looking for. The Bloodhound here needs to think a minute."

They walked the last two blocks in silence.

Downtown Portland could get hot and crowded in the middle of summer with so many people walking and shopping, sitting outside to eat. These days, it seemed like any shop with a front door and a couple of chairs handy would set up a table and offer something *al fresco*. A cup of coffee, a scone, a glass of wine and some cheese. It was fun when he and Jessica actually had a chance to get downtown and pass a lazy Saturday together, but when he was in a hurry and on a mission to get somewhere with no destination, navigating the window-shopping horde was a nightmare.

Jesus, it's three o'clock on a Tuesday. Why are you people not at work?

He needed to talk, needed to get his mind off the crowds and the people in his way before he started shoving somebody. He said, "We can peg both of them back there between 2:30 and 3:00. Confirms the *she* that Anna was talking about. I don't think we got much else out of that, do you?"

"Not a whole lot, but don't forget, today's suspect was brought to you by the letter *D*."

DJ was already tense and the possibility of Barker chasing another set of empty leads ratcheted his agitation higher. He threw his hands into the air. "Barker, that could've been anything," he said. "Bigger net, bigger waste."

"I wouldn't say it was *entirely* a waste. I might get a free drink out of it."

"Would you stop for a minute? Seriously. We're blowing this whole freaking thing. We got more questions being thrown at us than Alex Trebek, and you're happy about a free drink? Where's Teddy Rutherford? Who's the mystery woman? Where's Sara Winthrop?"

Barker said, "They're all having drinks together, laughing at a couple of dumbass cops."

"You're kidding, right?"

"I'm just saying—"

"Rein it in, man. You're chasing. Forget the necklace, forget the husband, forget your damn pride for one single minute and *focus*."

Barker stopped in the middle of the sidewalk. "I'm chasing because I'm lost, Jon. For the past twenty years, I've found people using breadcrumbs no bigger than a speck of dust. But this one, this case...until we find Rutherford or figure out who the girl is...I'm running on empty."

The regret in his voice was genuine, and for the first time ever, DJ felt sorry for the man. It was like watching his favorite quarterback make it to the Super Bowl and throw one bad pass after another.

After five years of looking up to Barker, it seemed weird to be the one on the consoling end of things, but DJ tried anyway. He said, "Then that's what we'll focus on. We haven't lost yet, Barker. We can't win them all, but our game, and Sara's game, they're not over yet."

Barker's cell phone rang. "Barker...uh-huh...she is? Right... okay, we'll be there in couple."

"Hospital?"

"Stardust is awake. She's ready to talk."

Chapter Fourteen
SARA

Sara walked with her hands held out in front, trying to block the limbs from smacking her in the face.

On the slim chance that she could possibly identify him, she'd tried a more conversational approach, hoping to coax out more information. She asked questions about her husband and where the ring had come from. If he knew Brian and had he ever met him before. If he had any details about his disappearance. She asked what he liked to read, what the last movie was that he'd seen. What his favorite cereal was, what his *son's* favorite cereal was. Anything to spark a reaction, but she was ignored and had been given more yanks or tugs or shoves each time she'd asked a question. When he'd pushed too hard and she'd fallen, losing a layer of skin from both knees, she gave up and let him guide her.

They'd been hiking uphill and down, twisting left and right, and the sounds of exertion were evident in her captor's labored breathing.

The bastard's out of shape. If I knew where to go, I could run.

Just play the game. You can't win that way.

She'd been without sight for so long that she could almost get a picture of their surroundings using her hearing. Somewhere deep in the woods. She could smell damp earth and pine trees. The stream's gurgling had faded a while back, so they were steadily moving away from it, farther into the forest, higher into whatever hill they might be climbing. The ground leveled out, and the surface changed underneath her feet, became softer and more malleable.

Is that grass? Pine needles? That's a new smell...what is that? Smells like a wet campfire.

The last time she'd been camping was on their fifth anniversary, the weekend the twins were conceived. Too much red wine had resulted in risqué sex out in the open, under the stars, and the next morning, she wasn't sure the fun had been worth the raging hangover. It'd rained in the middle of the night and the smell of the smoldering, soaked campfire had made her roiling stomach worse.

To test the echoes nearby, she raised her voice and asked, "Where are we?" The sound bounced off something big and solid in front of her.

Her guide said, "Cabin."

"Whose?"

"Nobody's."

"Does Nobody mind that you're using his cabin to hold a woman hostage?"

"Abandoned."

"Perfect. Abandoned cabin, middle of the woods. Mother of three with a desperate loser being controlled by a psychopath. I think I've seen this on Lifetime."

"Step."

"What?"

"Step."

Her foot caught on something and she tripped forward, realizing he meant *steps*. She lifted her leg, tested the area ahead, and placed her foot down. Pushed herself up, and felt for the next one. The wood sagged in the middle and creaked under her weight. "How many?"

"Three."

Up she went. With both feet safely on the porch, she said, "This might be easier if you said more than one word at a time."

"Unlikely."

She felt a hand on her back, pushing her forward. Heard the metallic screech of rusted hinges as a door swung open. She walked through and felt the cooler temperature inside on her skin. Smelled the musty scent of age and interior dampness of something that had been shuttered and neglected for far too long.

The door slammed shut.

He said, "Blindfold."

She took it off, relieved to have the use of her eyes again, but they hurt from the sudden rush of light pouring in through the cracked and broken windows. They cast their glow on an old wood stove squatting in the corner. She looked around the open room, saw a table with a single chair, an empty shelf. A decrepit bed with metal railings, a sagging mattress, and a sleeping bag. A red cooler, the kind used for picnics and long trips.

Is this my cage? I can do this. Twenty-four hours.

"I'm staying here?" she asked, looking around and up at him. He towered over her, dressed all in black, the familiar ski mask taking place of the baseball cap and sunglasses. Ice blue eyes stared back at her.

"There," he said, pointing to a door in the back of the room.

"What's in there?"

"Cage."

"And what's all this stuff? Sleeping bag, cooler. You're staying here with me?"

"Observation."

"So this is it, huh?"

She angled her head upward, stepped closer to him. Aggressive, but contained.

Be strong, Sara.

She said, "If you are who I *think* you are, understand one thing, you big bastard. I've seen your face, and if things don't go well for me, this place will look like a five star resort compared to where you're going. I hope your son doesn't mind talking to his daddy behind a glass wall. Got me?"

His eyes narrowed. "Understood."

Control. For the first time in hours, control. At least a little bit. Enough to give her a renewed feeling of hope.

But what if he's lying? Trying to throw you off? This level is supposed to be about confusion, isn't it? He probably doesn't have a son. For God's sake, use your head. This isn't supposed to be easy.

Shut up. It's all you've got. Ask him something about Teddy. Scare him some more.

"Can I ask you one more question?" Sara thought she heard a muffled huff of exasperation through the ski mask.

"Another?"

"How much is he paying you?"

"He?"

"Teddy. Your boss, my shit-for-brains coworker. The guy who has my kids. How much is he paying you?"

His first response that contained more than a single word might as well have been a fist in the center of her chest.

"Not a *he*."

He pulled a black, cloth sack from his pocket and, as she tried to comprehend, shoved it over her head before she could stop him. He grabbed her by the neck, his large hand wrapping halfway around it as he forced her toward the back of the room.

Sara could hear the door opening, then he shoved her inside. The door slammed. He struck a match and a *whoosh* of flames followed. He removed the hood and she shielded her eyes from the light of a hissing gas lantern as they readjusted. A large dog cage sat in front of her, partially covered with a black blanket.

And sitting behind it, along one of the windowless walls, was an unconscious, bound and gagged man.

In the soft burn of the lantern, it wasn't difficult to make out the shirtless, miniature form of Teddy Rutherford.

...

Everything that Sara had anticipated, everything that she thought she knew, imploded like an old building brought to the ground with a bevy of well-placed explosives.

"*Teddy!*" she said. "What's he doing here?"

"Waiting," said the tall man.

"Waiting for what?"

"Pain," he said, motioning toward the table.

Beside the lantern were four objects she hadn't noticed before. A blowtorch, a knife, a set of clipping shears, and a cleaver.

If Teddy's here, then who has the kids? Who've I been talking to this whole time?

What if Teddy wants you to think he's being tortured?

Teddy slowly lifted his head. Sara watched him blink and then his eyes went wide as he focused on her. He mumbled a surprised, "Sara! Sara!" through the gag, then added something that sounded like, "Help me!"

Her notion that this was part of Teddy's plan disappeared as the tall man walked over, pivoted, and swung a bowling ball fist into his jaw. The crunch was sickening as Teddy's head whipped to the side and then flopped down to his chest, the blow knocking him unconscious.

"Why?" she said. She didn't know what to think, how to feel. Her emotions were bundled up with the promised confusion and tossed into the well of her consciousness. Switching to pity after so many hours of focusing her rage on Teddy was...difficult.

But she did.

As much as she detested him back in the real world, seeing his slumped, limp body straining against the ropes set her bottom lip to quivering. He was sleazy, offensive, and deceitful, but whatever sins he committed on the rest of humanity weren't deserving of this. Why was he here? What purpose did it serve to torture Teddy in front of her?

Confusion, Sara. Distraction. She wants you to know that you were wrong.

Who?! Who is SHE?!

Someone at the office. She knew I'd think it was him. He's the obvious choice.

The tall man said, "In," as he pointed toward the cage.

Sara looked down, saw the padlock on the cage's door.

Keys open locks, locks open cages. She wants me to cage myself. Why? What does that prove?

Control. She can make you do whatever she wants.

"I'm not getting in that thing," she said.

"Expected." The tall man grabbed the blowtorch, ignited it, and shoved the flame at Teddy's bare shoulder. His skin seared and the sudden shock of pain brought him back to life.

His muffled scream clawed at Sara's eardrums. She dropped the paper bag, covered her ears, tried to block the sound of his wailing. "Enough!" she said. "I'll get in, I'll get in. No more, okay?"

Seconds later, she sat inside the cage, the door open in front of her, padlock dangling from it.

"Key," the tall man said.

She flung it at his legs.

He closed the cage door with a clank and a rattle, snapped the padlock shut with a click.

The black blanket covered half the cage, making it darker inside, blocking her view of Teddy. The metal rungs dug into her skin, pressing through her running shorts and into her thighs, her buttocks. She tested the distance of the sides, the top, each of them a half an arm's length away. It gave her room to move, to turn around if she needed.

Sara had never been claustrophobic, but the feeling of confinement overpowered her mind as it crawled its way over her body, sending her breathing into short, ragged bursts. Her chest hurt from straining to get enough oxygen. Fingertips tingled. Dizzy. The floor tilted underneath.

The tall man said, "Calm."

Teddy whimpered behind her, inhaling heavily through his draining nose, exhaling around the slobber-soaked rag.

Sara dumped the contents of the paper bag onto the cage's floor. The water bottle bounced. The apple rolled and settled. The jewelry box landed with a *thunk* and came to rest against her foot. She kicked it away, held the bag up to her mouth and breathed. Inhaling, exhaling, inflating the bag with air, sucking it back into her lungs.

Inhaling. Exhaling. Inhaling. Exhaling. Bringing herself to a controlled cadence.

Tempered normality returned. The tall man knelt down, shoved a familiar slip of paper through the bars.

"Instructions," he said.

She snatched it from his hand, held it around to read in the light.

SECOND HALF OF LEVEL 2 – SELF-PRESERVATION
HIS PAIN = YOUR COMFORT
REMEMBER – 24 HOURS
IF YOU THINK HARD, THE ANSWER WILL COME.

His pain equals my comfort? God, this is insane. If I get hungry? Thirsty? If I have to pee? Torture Teddy, get rewarded.

She wants to see how selfish you are.

The tall man rattled the door. "Understood?" he asked, returning her earlier threat, returning to control.

"Yes," she said. "But she won't break me."

He nodded and slid another slip of paper through the cage.

This one read:

SO PREDICTABLE
HIS PAIN = YOUR CLUES
SOLVE THIS RIDDLE AND THE FIRST ONE IS FREE
WHAT IS GREATER THAN GOD, MORE
EVIL THAN THE DEVIL?
THE POOR HAVE IT. THE RICH NEED IT.
AND IF YOU EAT IT, YOU WILL DIE.

Sara almost laughed with relief. Sometimes luck aligns with the universe.

Two weeks earlier, Lacey had come home from school with the exact same riddle and had flaunted it at her for hours. She had been tired and cranky after another day of dealing with Teddy's inadequacies and Jim's demands. She'd wanted to relax and unwind, to forget about the day, and Lacey's teasing had been so relentless that Sara had almost sent her to her room. The threat had worked well enough for her daughter to apologize and give her the answer.

Sara wadded up the slip of paper and threw it at the cage wall, toward the tall man's face. He didn't flinch. She said, "The answer is *nothing*."

"Quick." He slid yet another slip of paper into the cage.

CONGRATULATIONS. YOUR FIRST CLUE:
WHY DO I HAVE BRIAN'S WEDDING RING?
LITTLE ONE'S PAIN = MORE CLUES
LITTLE ONE'S PAIN = YOUR COMFORT
HOW MUCH DO YOU WANT TO KNOW?

Little One…she knows his nickname.

When she finished reading, she peered through the bars, glared at the tall man. "Are you done?"

"Temporarily," he said, sliding the black blanket over the cage, covering her in darkness, wrapping her in a shroud of solitary confinement. The only thing that penetrated her square tomb was the steady sound of Teddy's erratic, panicked breathing.

Chapter Fifteen

DJ

DJ walked beside Barker down the hospital hallway, passing busy nurses and a couple of doctors who had their noses buried in clipboards. He had mixed feelings about the place. Spend enough time interviewing victims, you got to see every aspect of the darker side of humanity and what people are capable of doing to one another. But, on the opposite end of the spectrum, it also offered the prospect of seeing the power of human strength, resolve, and will. How hospitals managed to be simultaneously uplifting and demoralizing was as much of a mystery as the one they were trying to solve.

They located Room 323 and walked in, finding Anna lying in bed, a nurse hunched over her, checking her pulse. The nurse pushed her patient's hair back from her face, and told them to keep it short—doctor's orders. They agreed, then waited until she left to approach their only lead in a case that was falling apart faster than a house of cards.

Anna tried to smile, croaked out a raspy, "Hi," and then cringed when she tried to readjust herself upward.

DJ held up a hand, urging her back down. "No need to get up. Save your energy."

"Thanks," she said, voice dry and hoarse.

DJ looked at the swollen and bruised face. Lips puffy, eyes black. Long scrape down her cheek. He could see her former beauty underneath all the destruction. Felt his stomach fill up with pity and anger.

Barker said, "Getting along okay? Full recovery?"

"Something like that."

"Your husband knows you're here?"

"On his way. He didn't want Hank to see me like this, so he's dropping him off at my mom's house."

"Good idea," DJ said.

"Hank's a great name," Barker added. "Strong."

"My grandfather's name. So, I guess you want to know how I got—how I got so pretty, huh?"

DJ pulled a seat up beside the bed, sat down face to face with her. "Just a few questions, if you're up for it."

Barker leaned against the windowsill, crossed his arms. "Can you remember what happened?"

"She said her name was Deana."

Barker said to DJ, "D on the necklace?" then to Anna, "Did she give you a last name?"

"No. Didn't say much about herself. She asked me a lot of stuff, though."

"Personal questions?"

"Just stuff about stripping and if I liked it. Where I got my outfits, what my family thought. I didn't tell her I was married with a kid. Gotta keep the fantasy alive. I'm not bi, like some of the other dancers are, so I wasn't really into her, you know? But she kept flirting with me and I figured I'd play along, get some extra tips out of it. No harm in that, right? Money is money."

"Understandable. We spoke with Mildred, got a physical description. Anything stand out to you? Anything identifiable? Any chance you remember the necklace she was wearing?"

Dead end, Barker. Let it go. Just a necklace.

Anna shook her head. "Necklace? No, but she was attractive. About my age. Oh, she had one blue eye and one brown eye. Like that actress. I can't remember her name."

"Different colored eyes? You mean like two different colors of contacts?" Barker asked, scribbling something down on his notepad.

DJ said, "I think it's a disease."

"Let's check into that. Now, Mrs. Townsend, we were informed that you and some of the other girls offer, uh, offer...*after hours* dances. Is that true?"

Anna tried to roll over to face Barker, but the depth of her pain was evident. She winced and flopped onto her back. "If I say yes, will I get in trouble?"

"That hospital bed says you're free from judgment, the way I see it."

"Same here," DJ said. "It's important that we know the truth. This woman could be involved in another case we're investigating, and we need to know exactly what happened."

He watched the physical discomfort morph into mental anguish on her face. Eyes leaking tears. Her bottom lip, swollen and split-skinned, began to quiver. She inhaled deeply, tried to fight it.

"You have to understand—this whole thing—it's not easy for me. For us. My husband, he's been out of work for over a year. He and my son mean everything to me, and no matter how hard I try to keep my chin up and say, 'It pays the bills,' I hate it. Every second of it. But you wouldn't believe how much some of these pricks will pay to have you all to themselves."

A knock at the door interrupted them. The nurse poked her head in, reminded them to keep it short, and was gone as quickly as she had appeared.

"She's right," DJ said. "You need your rest, so let's fast forward a little bit. She offered you money for a private dance back at her home?"

"Ten *thousand* dollars, Detective."

Barker whistled.

"She showed me the roll of bills. Flipped through so that I could see it was really filled with hundreds. I couldn't say no."

DJ sat back. It was all a ruse, of course, but the amount was staggering, and it was easy to see how a young mother with an unemployed husband could get sucked in by the promises. "And then what happened? Mildred mentioned the woman left around two-thirty and you at three o'clock. Did you meet her somewhere?"

"Out in front of the club. She was waiting in her car."

"Any chance you remember what it was?"

"Some hybrid. Blue. Look, I want you to know that we're broke and desperate, and I realize how dangerous it is, but believe me, Detective, I'm usually *very* careful when I go somewhere for a private dance. I don't *ever* get into a car with someone and *always* follow them to their house."

"What was different this time?"

"The amount." She put a hand on her forehead. "Nobody had ever offered that much before. And she seemed nice enough...but don't they all? She insisted it would be okay. Over and over again. And I thought I'd lose the money if I didn't. Look where it got me. Look at my face. What was I thinking?"

Barker moved away from the window, walked over and took her hand in his. "Young lady," he said, "at my advanced age, I've learned some things, and one of them is this...beating yourself up won't do you any good. Don't make a bad situation worse."

"It's my fault," she said, wiping her eyes with her free hand.

"You were looking out for your family, and that's just as good of a reason as any. Blame the bastards that did this, not yourself. And I don't want to hear another peep out of you about it being your fault. Sound good to you?"

She nodded.

"That said, we need to hear what happened before they kick us out of here. You want a little payback, give us some details."

"It's so not like me, but I got into the car with her, we drove about a block, and then I felt a hand grab me from behind and somebody shove a rag over my mouth."

DJ said to Barker, "Chloroform."

"Yep."

"I tried to fight it, but I woke up half-naked in this basement. Ball gag shoved in my mouth. I could barely breathe. She was standing over me, smiling. Had a guy with her."

DJ thought, *Rutherford?* The silent look from Barker suggested he was thinking the same thing. DJ said, "Short guy? What did he look like?"

"No, super tall. Like, massive. Had a mask on."

Damn...but at least it confirms a third person. "Have you ever heard the name Teddy Rutherford?"

"No."

"Thought not. Sorry for interrupting. Then what happened?"

"She leaned over—and it's fuzzy—but I think she said something like, 'If you make a sound, you'll never see your family again.' I was so scared at that point, but I had no idea what was coming. This is the part I'll never forget. The rest is blurry, but I remember this exactly. She said, 'It's a shame we have to damage such a beautiful thing,' then she looks at the guy and goes, 'Don't leave her alive.' She left, and he started punching and punching and punching. His fists felt like cinderblocks. But I'm still here, so either he didn't listen, or he didn't hit me hard enough."

DJ shuddered. After years of working cases and seeing the worst of the human condition, making himself immune to such reactions remained impossible, and in truth, he hoped he never lost it, unlike Barker. The cantankerous veteran was able to let it slide off like rain on a slicker, and his display of sympathy with Anna was a rare one, but DJ used the emotional connection as a reminder that this was more than a paycheck.

Anna, as young as she was, had plenty of good decades in front of her, and she would have to live with that haunting memory for the rest of her life. He reached over, patted her arm. "Get some rest," he said. "You've been a big help."

"Hang on," Barker said. "How'd you get free?"

"That's the weird part. When I woke up, the ropes were untied."

"Huh. Interesting…"

. . .

DJ and Barker exited and walked down the hallway. Seconds later, a younger guy, clean-cut and in a hurry, rushed past them in the direction of her room.

Barker said, "Reckon that was the husband?"

"Yeah," DJ said. "Poor bastard's in for a shock, huh?"

"No doubt in my mind that girl ain't ever going back to stripping again. She's lucky to be alive."

They stepped into the elevator, waited on the door to close. DJ asked, "Why *is* she still alive? Why leave a witness? Why would he untie her?"

"Hell if I know. Guilty conscience? Dissention in the ranks?"

"Your guess is as good as mine. But we do need to check out the blue eye, brown eye thing."

"Haystack, needle. Needle, haystack."

"No more than Sara's husband and that damn necklace. It's all we've got to go on, Barker." The elevator chimed, signaling the ground floor. They stepped out, stopping in the hallway. DJ put his hands on his hips, defiant. "And who was it that suggested the idea that she might have been planted in Rutherford's basement?"

Barker snorted, said, "I suppose it would be the same dingle-berry who's asking the question. Just because she woke up in his basement and Rutherford wasn't in the room doesn't mean he didn't know she was there. He could've been upstairs."

"It doesn't make any *sense*, Barker. If he's working with the necklace girl and the goon, collecting trophies or whatever, why not show up for the fun? What's the purpose?"

"Does it *have* to have a purpose? We're dealing with a couple of freaks, JonJon. We can profile all the hell we want, but if you try to read a psychopath's mind—"

"'*You'd have a better chance reading tea leaves in a blender.*' I know. I know."

"But, you're right, Captain Interruption, her screwed up eyes are the only solid thing we have to go on, so where do you suggest we start?"

DJ had been thinking about this from the moment Anna had mentioned it. He told Barker that they had to go with the closest connections. Sara and Teddy Rutherford both worked together at LightPulse. They had to consider the possibility that he had an accomplice there. It was a stretch, but they had to start narrowing down the possibilities somewhere. Medical records were protected by both Federal and State laws, and they didn't have enough solid evidence for a subpoena. "But," he said, "we can check photo IDs, look at criminal records. See if anybody pointed out mismatched eyes in their reports."

It'd be easy enough to take the list of employees and examine them across the board.

"Good idea," Barker admitted. "And if we come up with *nada*?"

"What're the chances that she'd use her own car to drive off with someone she planned to kidnap and murder? We check the rental companies for a blue hybrid. Narrow that list down to all the women that have rented one in the past few days."

Barker reached up, slapped DJ on the shoulder. Smiled.

"What?"

"I might've taught you a thing or two over the years, cowboy. You're wet behind the ears, but at least you're standing up for what you think is right. For once."

"Was that a compliment?"

"Don't let your head swell up. I don't have enough wisdom to fill it." Barker's cell rang. "Barker...yeah...at the hospital... What?...Where?...Okay, we're on it." He hung up, shook his head.

DJ raised an eyebrow.

Barker said, "Damn, I thought it couldn't get any stranger. They found Rutherford's car."

"And no Rutherford?"

"No Rutherford, but plenty of bloodstains."

Chapter Sixteen
SARA

Sara tried to straighten her legs. The cage closed in; the metal bars formed the sides of a coffin. The absence of light was so complete that she could have been buried alive, under mounds and mountains of dirt, under roots and worms, under rocks and a thick gravestone. The only reminder that she was indeed alive was Teddy whimpering and shuffling behind her. Outside the cage, but inside his own prison. Inches and miles away.

Hours had passed. Or was it minutes? Time doesn't stand still in a vacuum, but in the absence of everything else, it loses all form, becomes elusive and teasing. Taunting with its childish game of 'catch me if you can'.

Sara shifted to one side, rubbed the skin on her behind, massaging out the deep crevices left by the thin, metal wiring. Toes numb. Back aching from being hunched over for so long. Neck stiff and throbbing. She could smell the dried sweat on her running clothes. Felt guilty for wanting the luxury of a shower when the world around her was covered in physical and emotional blackness.

Sara pawed the cage floor and found the bottle of water. Took a small sip, rationing what remained. Partly as preservation, partly as a preventative. The tingling sensation in her bladder wasn't going away, no matter how hard she tried to direct her thoughts elsewhere. She refused to allow her abductor the satisfaction of torturing Teddy to get what she wanted. She would piss on the floor inside her cage before she would give in.

I won't let them win, she thought. *I won't.*

Sara twisted Brian's ring around her thumb, feeling the sweat between skin and metal.

Why...why...his wedding ring...his ring...oh my God...she knows what happened to him...she knows...

How? Unless she kidnapped him, too? Stole him from me. Took him away.

She knows...maybe he...maybe he was having—

No. Don't think like that. He wouldn't.

Would he? An affair?

Not Brian. He wouldn't...there were never any signs...I never suspected anything...

You know that's not true...

...the receipt...

Teddy moaned behind her, followed by the dull scrape of wood on wood as the chair legs scratched against the floor. Then, silence. Nothing more. Back to the darkened depths of her solitude.

She took a small sip of water, just enough to wet her tongue.

Brian...what did you do?

The receipt, the one that had fallen out of the book he'd been reading on his trip to San Diego. Two meals at a restaurant. A bottle of wine.

Brian never drank wine...hated it. Hated the taste. It made him sick.

At the time, she hadn't questioned it. Business trip. Colleagues with a taste for expensive Bordeaux. Trying to woo a new client at a conference. It meant nothing. Less than nothing. An innocuous drink with someone who had money to invest. Choked it down with a smile to earn a hefty commission.

But was that it? Was that all?

She thought back to all the connections she'd made earlier in the day, back when she'd thought it might've been a woman, back when she thought it might've been someone inside LightPulse. The mention of a breakaway, the mini-bomb idea that led her to believe it was Teddy.

A woman at the office...was Brian having an affair with one of the girls at work?

No, couldn't be. He was in San Diego.

They could've met him there. Was anyone on vacation then? Anyone missing from the office?

I can't remember...so long ago...

Sara's stomach churned. The realization of a deeper truth to his disappearance took her breath away, tightened its grip around her lungs. Made her head swim, made her dizzy. She rubbed her eyes, wiped a tear from her cheek.

What did I do, Brian? Was it me? Did you not love me anymore?

The betrayal. The anguish. The pain. It was too much. All those years of loving a man who would dare to take another woman to bed. Had it been going on for some time? Or was it a single act of indiscretion? Too much wine? Promises to do all the things between the covers that they had grown too tired and bored and busy to do? Their relationship had *seemed* great. To her. To her family. To everyone who complimented them. To her friends, who admitted to jealousy over the emotional connection they had.

It was true that their sex life had faded to once or twice a month. Brief encounters when they had enough energy to squeeze it in after long days, after the kids had gone to bed. It was the typical scenario of many busy marriages, something they'd discussed and were excited to fix, but he'd gone missing before they'd had the chance.

Went missing, or left intentionally for another woman?

She wanted to run away, leave, disappear. Evaporate into a fine mist and escape the cage walls. But, she was trapped, contained, forced to deal with her regret and sorrow with no way out.

Sara drew her knees up to her chest, buried her face in her arms. *Damn you, Brian. Who was it? Who was she?*

Someone at the office...which one? Who was there two years ago when he disappeared? Me. Susan. She wouldn't...Kara and Sandra in R&D. Mandy at the front desk. She was cute. Her? Jenny in Accounting. Not his type. What was the office manager's name, the one who retired...Janet... Janet? Too old.

Six of them. All gone. All moved on to different places in their lives. New jobs, higher paying jobs. Motherhood. From what she'd heard, they were all living in Portland, except for Janet, who'd moved to Key West.

This woman knows about stuff in the new Juggernaut...all the women who used to be there are gone, so if he was cheating...she's been hired since he disappeared...

Why do that? Why get so close to me if she was sleeping with my husband?

Keep tabs on me? Make sure I wasn't getting closer to finding him?

Such a stretch. Somebody could be breaking the NDA, passing along info.

Lots of new faces...Shelley and Amy and Wendy and Shay and Christina...

Was it possible? Could any of the women who were there now be the one who had destroyed her life? Damaged her children's lives? Still so many questions, still no closer to a reasonable answer. The possibilities were endless. So were the motivation and reasoning. It didn't make any sense. None of it.

And what if she was completely off? What if Brian hadn't been having an affair, and the woman was some psycho targeting her family for some unknown reason? She had access to confidential LightPulse information, but it didn't mean she was actually *inside* the company. And it could be one of the men, a partner, passing along details. What if they had murdered Brian, taken his ring, kept it all this time in order to torture her, toy with her, make her play a game? Was it a game of life and death? Was that really what was going on?

I need to know more. Teddy...his pain...more clues...

No, don't. You can figure this out.

How? I know nothing. One...two...three...seven...eight. Eight other women in the office. It could be any one of them. And if it's one of the guys... how many women do they know? It's impossible. Why does she have Brian's wedding ring? No idea. None whatsoever. Affair? Maybe. Kidnapped him and took it? Murdered him and took it? Why me? Why now? Why two years later?

I could ask Teddy...what if he saw her face?

She clambered around inside the cage, felt the metal bars digging into her knees. She thought about tugging at the blanket, slipping it off so she could see him, but that would be against the rules. Breaking them would result in another phone call, another scream from one of her children in pain because she refused to obey.

"Teddy," she whispered. "*Teddy*. Wake up."

Sara cocked an ear, listened over her shoulder. Tried to hear any movement coming from the other room. Earlier, who knows how long ago, she'd heard the tall man moving around, followed by the front door slamming. Was he gone? Sitting on the front porch? Taking a leak out in the woods?

I need to pee...almost hurts...

"Teddy? Can you hear me?"

She heard him inhale, imagined him waking up, opening his eyes. Panic setting in as he realized that it wasn't a dream, that he was tied to a chair in a pitch black room. He mumbled her name through the gag. It came out as a question, testing the space in front of him, like he was unsure if her voice was truly there.

"I'm here, Teddy, I'm here. Keep your voice down, okay?"

His response was muffled and wet. "Okay."

"Are you in pain?"

"A lot."

"I'm sorry. Listen to me. Listen. Everything will be okay. We'll get out of here. I'll get you out, I promise."

"What's…what's going on?"

She could tell it was difficult for him to speak, difficult to push his words around the cloth binding his mouth open. "Someone's playing a game with me."

"A game?"

"A bad one. They have my kids."

"What?"

"They've been kidnapped." She scooted close to the cage wall, wrapped her fingers through the bars and whispered, "How'd you get here? Did he bring you?"

"The guy…him."

"Not so loud, okay? He's working with some woman, any idea who?"

"No. A voice…on a phone."

"What did she say?"

"Said I…said I deserved this. For being…a pig."

"I think it's somebody at the office."

"Said I'm…motivation."

"Motivation? Teddy, focus. Who's doing this?"

"Don't know."

"Anything at all. Think. Guess."

"Don't know."

"Teddy, please. Say the first name that comes to your mind."

The seconds ticked by. He was silent for so long, Sara thought he might've passed out again. Finally, he mumbled, "Maybe—maybe it's—"

The door crashed open, slamming against the wall hard enough for Sara to feel the vibrations through the floor. Thundering footsteps, followed by, "Quiet!" The voice echoed off the walls as Sara screamed, pushing herself up against the far side of the cage, away from him. Light from the open door penetrated the black cloth enough to illuminate the interior. She could see her hands shaking.

The sickening *thuds* of fists on flesh replaced the noise of her gasping. It sounded like someone with a sledgehammer beating a dead animal carcass.

Teddy coughed and gagged. Moaned. She was almost relieved that she couldn't see what was happening to him, but the images in her mind were just as bad.

One, two, three more punches, and then it stopped.

The black cloth whipped open and the tall man knelt down in front of her.

"Don't hurt him again," she begged.

"Penalty," he said, slipping another note through the cage.

Sara grabbed it. Hands unsteady, paper flapping like a wounded dove. She didn't want to read it, terrified of what it might contain. What penalty had she brought upon herself? What had she done by breaking a rule? If it was for her, she'd take it. She would take the punishment.

Not the kids...not the kids...don't hurt them anymore...I'll play...

Fingers trembling and uncooperative, she fumbled the note open.

THE PENALTY IS SEVERE. NO MORE CLUES.
NO QUESTION FOR THIS ROUND.
AND NOW YOU MUST CHOOSE YOUR PATH:
1. HE DIES – YOUR CHILDREN ARE SAFE
AND YOUR CAGE TIME ENDS
2. HE LIVES – I'LL REVEAL WHO I AM BUT
THERE MAY BE CONSEQUENCES

One simple choice that changed the game completely. Sara dropped the note to the cage floor. It was easy. The first option was clear: order Teddy's death and the kids would be fine. The ambiguity of the second choice left her wondering. It didn't say anything about harming Lacey, Callie, and Jacob, just that she would reveal her identity.

She won't do anything to hurt them. The game is over if she does.

I can't risk it. I can't. It's not—it's not even a choice.

She'd read about questions like these before. Psychological tests designed to assess compassion. A passenger train is speeding down the tracks, a single person in its path. Derail the train to save one man and risk countless lives, or run him over and save everyone on board? The problem with the question was the lack of guarantee that anyone would die in the first option.

But this...this was different. There were no alternatives.

She would have to play God. Choose when and where someone died. The remainder of her days would be spent wondering what might've happened if she had picked the second option, but the regret would pale in comparison to what she'd feel if she had read too far into it and something happened to her babies.

The tall man said, "Choose."

"Give me a minute."

She listened to Teddy's breathing.

He was clueless. His fate contained in a simple slip of paper. No idea that he was about to die. *Had* to die. If he knew what the note said, would he offer himself as a sacrifice? Would he say, 'Do it, save them,' or would he be the same self-centered, egotistical brat that he'd always been? Could he, for once, let go of his self-absorption and care about another person? She'd heard stories of soldiers jumping on hand grenades, surrendering their lives to save others. That level of personal disregard was almost incomprehensible. She would do it for the children. Would Teddy? If he knew what was at stake, would he make that choice?

He wouldn't. He would come up with an excuse. Run if he could. Forcing away her pity didn't make the decision any easier. But, she only had one to make.

She kicked the cage, close to the tall man's face, surprising him. Watched him fall backwards, landing on his ass. "Number one," she said.

He grunted, groaned, crawled back to his feet. Grabbed the cage and shook it. His only form of retaliation.

Sara thought about kicking his fingers, smashing them against the bars.

He pulled a handgun from his waistband, screwed a silencer into the barrel. Pointed it at her head.

She lifted her arms, knowing the fleshy shield would do no good, but it was a natural reaction.

"Watch," he said, throwing the blanket off the cage, revealing the room.

Teddy was a crumpled mass, bloodier and covered with extra bruises. His body purple and limp. Unconscious, unaware of his impending death.

The tall man lifted his gun, pointed, and paused.

Paused.

Paused.

Paused.

Sara screamed, "Don't—" as he pulled the trigger.

Chapter Seventeen
DJ

DJ sat at his desk, going over a list of LightPulse's female employees while Barker went to check out Rutherford's car for any evidence. The initial feedback had been discouraging, but the Bloodhound was on a trail, and there was no convincing him otherwise.

There were nine women at LightPulse, including Sara, and he'd turned up nothing significant on the first five. Mostly clean, a traffic ticket or two, one instance of a Minor in Possession. Young women fresh out of college. Still in party-mode, first real job, first real paycheck. None of them fit the profile of what he was looking for, but then again, did a sociopath ever reveal her true nature? And since Oregon didn't list eye color on driver's licenses, he examined their ID photos, enhancing them for clarity as much as possible, trying to discern different-colored irises. Considering any one of them could've been wearing contacts to hide that fact, he could almost hear Barker over his shoulder, telling him how pointless it was. Yammering on with some proverb that he'd heard hundreds of times over the years.

What I need, he thought, *is an outlier. Something that stands out.*

The next two proved to be as unrewarding as the rest. Grandmothers in their sixties. He didn't bother going through their information. It was unlikely either of them could be misconstrued as an attractive twenty-something with a possible boob job like the Ladyfingers bartender had suggested.

The last employee didn't come up in his Oregon DMV search. He checked the spelling of her name again. *Hmm...still driving with an out of state license, are we? How long have you been here? A couple of months...where are you from...where are you from...California.*

There you are, Shelley. Shelley Ann Sergeant. Formerly of San Diego... registered a tan SUV...California driver's license says your eyes are...green.

"Shit." DJ hurled his mouse at the nearby wall, the cheap plastic shattering into a dozen pieces. Heads whipped around, examined him, and then went back to their calls and case files. Amongst the cluttered desks, with keyboards clacking and phones ringing, frustrated outbursts were common enough that nobody paid much attention. As long as you didn't hurt anyone in the process, you got it out, you moved on. Standard norm for a group of people chasing wisps of information, trying to put jigsaw puzzles together in the dark.

Regardless, it'd been a long time since he'd had an outburst like that, and the embarrassment of losing his composure left his cheeks flushed. He crawled across the floor, scooped up the remnants and tossed them in the trashcan. Put his back against the wall.

We screwed up. Chased too many shitty leads. I'm wrong, Barker's been wrong about everything.

Sergeant Davis ambled up to DJ's desk, tossed a file down. "Judge denied your request, JonJon, not enough circumstantial to search the car rentals. Better luck next time, huh?"

DJ stared at the ceiling and beat the back of his head against the wall as Davis waddled away.

He called Barker, hoping he'd made some progress.

"Go for Barker."

"Any luck?"

"Waitress across the street saw a tall guy park the car sometime this morning. Said he left and never came back."

"Tall guy, huh? Think it's the same one?"

"Has to be. Too convenient."

"Can she identify him?"

"Dressed in black, dark hair. That's about it. Sent some blood samples back. Hope we'll be able to identify Rutherford from it, but we've got another clog in the drainpipes."

"What's that?"

"Found two receipts from yesterday in the center console. Guess where the first one's from?"

"Where?"

"No, really. Guess."

"Barker."

"Ladyfingers, for eighty-four dollars."

"Damn it. I was sure he—"

"Hold up now, don't get your panties in a wad. Time-stamped at eight-fifteen, so he was there, but considering the amount of blood in his car and the second receipt, I'm about to give in and say you were right."

"About what?"

"About Rutherford not being involved with Miss Stardust. Not directly, anyway. Ladyfingers is a connection, but the second one is from Hotel Llewellyn. Our boy may not have been home last night."

"Easier to frame somebody when they're not home."

"Doesn't mean he wasn't removing himself from the situation."

"If the connection's there, it's there, but I won't say I told you so about him not being involved."

"Wild ass guesses don't make you a genius, cowboy, but your instincts are getting better."

"Wouldn't worry about me being a genius. Came up empty on the heterochromia."

"The what?"

"The different colored eyes thing. None of the women at LightPulse have it, from what I can tell."

"Hate to break it to you, but I didn't figure she'd be that close to home. Where are you with the rental records?"

"Denied. Not enough evidence."

"No shit? I figured Carson would be all over this one. He's usually Quick Draw McGraw when it comes to missing kids."

"Guess it takes more than a stripper in a hospital bed. So, what's next?"

"Face time, JonJon. Ask questions. No more chasing ghosts. Gotta pound the ground before this one gets too far away from us."

"Like it hasn't already."

"Finish this one for me. When one door closes..."

"Another one opens?"

"No. You kick that son of a bitch off its hinges. Now get your chin off your chest, put your helmet on, and get back out there for the second half, got me?"

"Got it, coach."

"Back to the basics, DJ. I'm sticking with the car and the giant for now. Check for witnesses around the schools, check the babysitter—hell, check garbage cans. Check out anybody who's tweaked your whodunit instinct. We're missing something simple, I can feel it."

"Will do." DJ hung up, thinking, *If it were simple, Barker, we'd have figured it out already.*

...

DJ took out a notepad and began to draw a mind map of everything he knew about the case. Sara Winthrop and her three missing children were at the center of it all. The outward lines connected to Teddy Rutherford, Jim Rutherford, her assistant, Shelley, and the seven other women who worked at LightPulse. Willow Bluesong, the babysitter who hadn't been home when they'd stopped by. Reluctantly, he added Brian Winthrop, but only because he knew

Barker would've demanded that he be included. He added the schools, their principals, the ice cream shop. The tall man, the mystery woman. Ladyfingers and Stardust. By the time he was finished, it looked like a never-before-seen constellation and sparked no new sense of direction.

He came up with a reason to draw an X over each person and place on the chart. Jim Rutherford had behaved oddly because he was trying to protect his son. Teddy Rutherford was either missing or dead. They knew almost nothing about the tall man or the mystery woman, except that they were working together. The schools had already told them everything they knew. He wrote 'Ghost' underneath Brian Winthrop's name and 'Collateral' under Anna Townsend's.

He crossed out everyone with good reason.

Everyone except Willow Bluesong and Shelley Sergeant.

He decided to start with them, and if neither one could provide anything fresh, he'd move on to friends and family. Beyond that—as much as he hated the idea, and Barker loathed it because it made him feel inadequate—they would have to get the press involved.

The last they'd heard of Sara Winthrop, she was on foot, running away from the Rose Gardens. If she were still playing this game—

Are you ready to play the game?

—and if she were still racing around Portland, surely someone would've spotted a distraught and harried woman. They'd have to get pictures of her and her kids on the news, issue an alert.

It felt good to be going in a concrete direction, regardless of the fact that he had no idea where it was heading. The case hadn't gotten away from them yet, not completely, and he left for Willow Bluesong's house, excited that something tangible might be on the horizon.

She wasn't what he had expected.

"Mrs. Bluesong?" he asked when she answered the door.

"Yes?" she said, pushing her waist-length, graying braids over her shoulder. "Miss, actually," she added, smoothing down her tie-dyed dress.

The hesitant smile and ratty Birkenstocks screamed innocence, and DJ had to remind himself not to assume. *Ass out of you and me.* "Detective Johnson, ma'am."

She smiled. "And I'm Miss Willow, *sir.*"

"Mind if I ask you a few questions?"

"What's this about?"

"Sara Winthrop."

Her smile disappeared, her hand rushing up to cover her gaping mouth. "Is she okay?"

"May I come in?"

"She's not dead, is she?"

"Not that we—we're trying to—I think it's best that we sit down."

"How'd it happen?" She fell against the doorjamb.

"I'm sorry—I didn't mean—she's not dead...that we know of. Missing. She and her children."

"That you *know of?* What does that mean?"

He sighed. It never got any easier. A couple of wrong words and the message drifted like a rudderless boat. "We're assessing the facts. If you could give me five or ten minutes, I could use your help."

"But is she okay?"

"I—we don't know yet. But whatever you can offer—"

"I just saw her this morning. Oh God, okay. Come in, come in." She pushed the door open further and motioned him inside.

DJ stepped across the threshold, greeted by incense blended with the scent of freshly baked chocolate chip cookies. He followed her down the hallway, shoes squeaking on the hardwood floor. Dusty picture frames sat on dustier shelves. Miss Willow in her younger days, smiling beside a thin, scraggly man with a hippie mane and a

ZZ Top beard. No children, except for the couple of recent photos where she posed beside Sara's kids, all of their smiles beaming. At a park, one perched above the other on a slide. Another with her balancing opposite them on a seesaw.

She led him into the living room, offered him tea and cookies as he sat on the brown, forest-print couch. He declined. She insisted.

And a couple of minutes later, DJ bit into one of the best chocolate chip cookies he'd ever tasted.

Miss Willow sat on the edge of her recliner, sipping her tea. "How—how serious is this, Detective?"

DJ sat the plate of cookies down on the coffee table, licked his fingers. "Unfortunately, we're treating it as a multiple kidnapping and a missing person, at least for now."

"Kidnapping? What happened?"

"Like I said, we're assessing the situation. As of right now, all four of them are missing. Under—we think under different circumstances."

"That's horrible."

"You said you saw Mrs. Winthrop and her children this morning?"

"She stopped by before she took them to school."

"And she sounded okay to you? Mention anything bothering her?"

She shook her head, blew cool air over the tea. "She was rushed. Who isn't with three kids? Don't get me wrong, I love the three of them like they're my own, but they're a handful."

"She was rushed?"

"Late for a meeting. Said something about Teddy, this coworker she doesn't like. That's not out of the ordinary. And...what else... we talked about plans for this evening."

"Plans?"

"She was supposed to drop the kids off and then meet with another reporter. She's so busy these days. Magazines calling all the time. She manages it well, but I can tell it's getting to her."

"She's in magazines? What kind?" *Public spotlight, somebody's jealous?*

"Oh, those business ones. I can't keep up anymore."

"So she's successful?"

"Overnight, more or less. Within the past six months."

"Interesting. Crossed paths with anyone in that timeframe?"

Miss Willow sat her mug down on the table. "I know what you're getting at, Detective, but no, not that I know of. She can be—how do I say this—she can be a bit bullheaded at times. In my mind, though, it's all a part of the game."

Whoa...the game...are you ready to play the game? Did she slip up? No, not her. Can't be involved. What would Barker say? Something about fish and worms, probably.

DJ took a chance. Dangled the bait to see how she would react. He said, "Are you ready to play the game?"

She squinted at him, shook her head. "Pardon?"

Clueless. "Sorry, you reminded me of something my partner says. He rambles a lot."

"Oh."

"What do you mean by part of the game?"

"Nothing, really, just a figure of speech. She's mentioned stepping on some toes before, that's all. From what I remember, it wasn't anything that called for...oh, what's the word I'm looking for?"

"Retaliation?"

"Retaliation, that's it. She's a good woman, Detective Johnson. If she's—if she's okay, I can't imagine what she's going through. First her husband, and now this? What's the world coming to?" Miss Willow stared out the window. "When my husband passed, I didn't leave the house for months. But Sara's strong. Smart, too. So smart. I've never had any doubts about her."

"Right." DJ tapped his pen on the notepad. As pleasant as the woman was, he was wasting time. She was no more involved with the situation than any of the other worthless dead ends. "Couple more questions and I'll be on my way."

She kept her eyes locked on the world outside. "It would seem I'm free for the evening. Stay as long as you'd like."

"You mentioned her husband. How'd you feel about him?" He didn't want to ask any more pointless questions, but he knew that Barker would send him back if he failed to ask everything.

"Never met him. Sara and I didn't meet until after he was gone. The way she talked about him, the man was a saint."

"I'm sure it was hard on her."

"Not was. *Is.*"

"Definitely. Definitely." DJ took one last look at his notepad to see if he'd missed anything, reading over his mind map scribbles. *Nothing there...nothing there...she wouldn't know about Ladyfingers... let's see...* "Shelley Sergeant," he said. "Familiar with her?"

Miss Willow whipped her head around. "*That* girl?"

The vehemence in her voice made DJ sit up straighter. "What's—"

"Have you ever met someone who makes your skin crawl so much, you don't want to be in the same room with them?"

"All the time." For him, the sensation was another day at the office.

She said, "Wolf in sheep's clothing."

"What makes you say that?"

"I won't let her in my house anymore. Bad energy. Acts like a mouse to your face, but you watch her when she thinks nobody's looking. She wears this diamond necklace with the letters 'S.D.' I couldn't tell you what they really stand for, but in my mind, it might as well be *She-Devil.*"

DJ's notepad fell to the floor. *The necklace...*

Chapter Eighteen

SARA

Sara pulled her hands away from her ears. The screams she heard weren't her own. Muted and muffled, they were coming from somewhere else within the room.

She glanced up, saw the tall man pointing the gun at Teddy. Silent. Motionless.

Flicked her head around.

Teddy's eyes bulged. He strained against his ropes, wailing through the fabric stretched across his mouth. He was alive. No fresh wounds. No bullet holes that she could see. A wet patch darkened the center of his khakis.

Sara reached down, felt the dryness of her running shorts. Somehow, she'd maintained control of her own bladder.

The tall man let the gun drop to his side, flopped down on the floor next to Sara's cage, and removed his ski mask. His dark, disheveled hair was twisted and tangled with a number of sprigs standing at attention.

Him. I can't believe I was right.

He shook his head, saying, "I couldn't...I couldn't do it."

Teddy's howls subsided to whimpers of relief.

Sara scooted to the cage wall, rested her forehead against the cool metal, staring at him. *What now? If he doesn't...the kids...*"Look at me," she said. "If you don't—my children—what'll happen to them?"

The same face, the one from the grocery store, contorted with regret. The corners of his mouth curving downward. Eyes wide, uncertain. "I—I don't know."

"Can you lie? Can you tell her you did it?"

"She'll know. She always knows."

"What's your name?"

"I can't—"

"What's your *name?*"

He slapped the gun barrel against his palm, looked out the door, then back to Sara. Wavered. "Michael."

"Michael, okay. I didn't want you to, I didn't, but my kids—what'll happen if you don't?"

"She'll come up with something."

"She who?"

"It was supposed to be simple."

"You mean the game?"

"I never thought I—God, how could I let myself—I always said no kids. No kids, ever." He growled in frustration, then slung the handgun upward and fired three shots into the ceiling.

The soft, dull *pop*s filled the room as Sara recoiled. She felt no pity for him, but sensed an opening. "Help me," she said. "Help me before she does something."

"She won't."

"How do you know?"

"Because they're not the endgame—you are."

Damn you, give me some clear answers. "Please," she said, "tell me what's going on."

"You should've figured it out by now."

Sara slapped the cage, felt the stinging in her palm. "Who *are* you people? If you're not going to help, at least let me out. I promise you, with every ounce of truth I have in me, that if you let me out of here, I won't say a word."

"I'm not stupid, Sara, if I let you—"

"Teddy won't, either, will you?"

Teddy looked up at the sound of his name, shook his head. "Nothing," he mumbled through the rag. "Never saw you."

"Not that easy," Michael said.

"It is," Sara said. "I promise. You'll never see us again. Let me out. Please, let me out."

"You don't know my sister, don't know what she's like. Your husband didn't, either. At least not until he tried to leave her."

Sara's chest tightened. The inside of the cage felt smaller.

Oh, God…Brian…you didn't—you were…so it's true. I can't believe it.

"He was clueless. Tried to leave. He wanted to go home, wanted to get away. See if he could patch things up, you know?"

"Was that what she meant when she said I'd taken something from her? Because he wanted to come home?"

The crack in his dam widened. "More or less. Brian tried. The guilt ate at him all the time. He'd come to me, ask me what he should do, but what was I supposed to tell him? What he was doing was wrong, I absolutely know that, and I'm sorry for what you've had to go through, but how're you supposed to tell somebody that there *is no* escape? You can't look a guy in the face and say, 'If you leave, you're dead.' He wouldn't have believed me. Oh no, not my sweet, innocent little sister. She's too cute, too shy. Nobody knows what she's capable of. Nobody. There's something black inside her, something dark, and I can't do it anymore. No matter what I do for her, no matter how far I go to protect her or help her, there's no way to make up for the things that made her this way. I'm done, I'm done, I'm done."

What Sara wanted to say was, *Don't give me your bullshit sob story. I don't care what happened to either of you, and both of you can burn, for all I care.* But she was afraid he would leave her locked up, and she and Teddy would begin the slow, agonizing wait, biding their time in the godforsaken cabin until Death knocked at the door. And, as

Sara listened to him talk, she struggled with the realization that a revelation was coming. One that she didn't want to hear, but had no ability to prevent herself from asking.

"Did you—did you kill him, Michael?"

Michael hung his head. "It was her. I just do the before and after. Wasn't ever able to cross that line like she can. But your husband, he definitely had some heart. I don't know how he lasted as long as he did. Too long. I couldn't watch anymore."

Sara fell back against the cage, removed Brian's ring from her thumb, twisted it between her fingers. Let it drop to the cage floor. It bounced, rattled about, and disappeared through the bars.

The tears wouldn't come.

There was hurt. There was an aching buried further down than whatever shallow grave contained Brian's body, but the brief respite of having some closure was enough to contain the sorrow. Mourning would come later, if she ever had another minute to herself, if she made it through this alive, if the day ever came when she would have the chance to look back and grieve. And if she were to have that opportunity, she had to play smart. Win him over.

She watched him scoot around, lean his head against the wall. He closed his eyes. Sara waved a hand at Teddy, catching his attention. She mouthed, "It'll be okay."

Teddy blinked twice.

I almost got him killed. How will I ever look at him again without thinking about that?

You won't. You owe him.

I wonder if he knows I had to choose…

Maybe, but will he care if you get him out of here?

If I explain what the note said…

Later. You still have to get out of this.

"Michael?"

"Yes?"

"What happened to your sister?"

"Long story."

"Well, you have a captive audience."

"How do you still have a sense of humor?"

"It's the only thing I have left."

"Good point."

"Your sister?"

"I know what you're doing."

"I'm curious."

"And a terrible liar."

"Was she abused?"

"You could say that."

"What would *you* say?"

"I wouldn't say anything. The past is the past." He climbed to his knees, lit the lantern, and sat back down.

The new light in the room revealed the extent of Teddy's bruising, the snot draining from his nostrils. The wet patch between his legs had expanded to cover his crotch and the inside of his thighs.

Sara gawked at Teddy.

Michael said, "He can take a punch."

"Do you like hurting people?"

"Enough with the therapy session, Sara."

"I'm trying to understand."

"You wouldn't. You wouldn't. The things I had to watch them do to her..."

"Who, Michael? Who did those things?"

"You really want to know what happened? You really want to know why you're in a cage?"

"I can—"

"You can't *anything*, Sara. There's no helping her. Believe me, I've tried."

"What happened?"

Michael stood up, walked into the main room. She heard him rummaging around in the cooler, heard the sounds of ice clattering about. He came back with a beer, twisted off the cap, and drained the bottle. Pivoted, and hurled it out the door. The glass shattered. He said, "She—she has issues."

"Who doesn't?"

"Not like this. Not most people. Our dad—he left when we were kids. We never knew why. No reason. One day he stood up from the dinner table and walked out the door. Never saw him again. I didn't mind so much. He was strict. Mean. Drunk all the time, but my sister loved him like nothing else in the world. So when he left, it ruined her. Abandonment issues. Doesn't like people leaving her. That's why she does what she does when they try to leave. Melodrama, right? Like some bad TV show, like you said. But then Mom...she took a bunch of pills about a week later. We wound up in this foster home—God, I shouldn't be telling you this. She wouldn't like it."

"If you need to talk, talk. She'll never know."

Michael paced back and forth. "They made us call them Mother and Father. She *hated* them, and they knew it, too. Our dad was a cupcake compared to them. And you want to know what made it worse? They adored me. I don't know why, maybe because I listened. Obeyed. They gave me anything I asked for, and Mother—Mother put her in a cage whenever she misbehaved. An actual cage, Sara.

"Locked her in a cage in a windowless bedroom, and she'd make her play these sadistic games to get out. I know it damaged her at first, but after a while—when she got older—I think she *enjoyed* it, and I swear she'd get thrown in there on purpose. I wish that I'd been able to do something sooner. Father didn't do a damn thing, and I couldn't do a damn thing to help her because I was too scared—what could I do? But your—your husband—he tried to leave, and now she's taking it out on you. You see? You wanted to know, you wanted to know. See how it all fits together now? Do you? Huh? *Do you?* The game, the cage, torturing a mother? It was bad before, but this, it's too much. I'm done. No more."

Too far, Sara. Bring him back.

"Let's talk about something else, something better. Do you really have a little boy?"

"You got what you wanted to hear."

"I'm serious. I want to know, really. You've got a son?"

"Had."

"Had? What happened?"

"He's gone."

"Did your sister—"

"God, no," he interrupted. "He's with his mother."

"Do you see him much?"

"Never."

"Why?"

"She gave me a choice. No sister or no wife. When I told her I *had* no choice, she left. Haven't seen her or William since."

"Where are they?"

"No clue."

"Haven't you ever tried to find them?"

"That wouldn't be a good idea. She wouldn't like it."

"Your wife or your sister?"

"Sister."

"She has that much control over you?"

"I owe it to her."

"No you don't. You said so yourself, you're done. Take your life back."

"It's not that easy."

"It *can* be. You have my permission."

"I don't need your permission, Sara. What I need is for that little black cloud to be gone."

"She owns you."

"Owns? I guess that's the right word." He went quiet. The whispering lantern drowned out everything else in the room until he spoke again. "I think of her as another organ. Something inside me that a doctor's never seen before, like this thing that only lets my heart beat when she's ready to allow it."

"What if she's your appendix?"

"My appendix?"

"Something you could live without."

"It doesn't work that way."

"But what if it did?" Sara tried to stretch. Every muscle was cramping and aching again. "What if you could disappear?"

"She found me in Chicago. She found me in Atlanta. She found me in San Diego. I don't know how, but she always does. She finds me, draws me in again, and I have no control over it. She said if I tried to hide from her one more time...game over." He leaned against the wall, slid down to the floor.

The resignation in his voice, the defeated tone of it, gave Sara new hope. He'd tried and failed on his own, but if he had help, if he really wanted out...

She said, "It might be game over for you, but not for me. Let me out, let me fight back. I'll fight with you, or even *for* you. You can be free. If you won't try, at least let me. Give me a chance."

"I can't. She'll never forgive me."

"Please, Michael. I want my kids to have a good life."

He said, "I wanted a good life. She wanted a good life."

"I know you did. We all do, but there's nothing I can do to change that. My kids still have a chance."

He rubbed a shaky hand across his face. Slapped the gun barrel against his palm again. *Slap...slap...slap*, like a ticking clock. "You'll have to get past Samson first."

"Samson?"

"The one who took your son this morning."

"Who is he?"

"Doesn't matter."

"Is he an ex-boyfriend or something?"

"I told you it doesn't matt—Jesus, you're stubborn. He stayed with us for a while. With Mother and Father. Just a *beast* of a kid, even back then."

"And she has control over him, too? Like you?"

"Unconditional."

"But how?"

"I can't tell you this stuff, Sara. She wouldn't like it."

"Come on, it's okay. I won't say anything."

Michael punched his thigh, forced a few sharp breaths in and out, and then scratched his head with the silencer's rim. "He'd only been there for a couple of days before it started."

"What started?"

"The bullying. He zeroed in on her. Hounded her constantly. No mercy, day after day. I look back now and think that Mother probably put him up to it. Whenever my sister would try to fight him, *bam*, straight in the cage. That went on for a while, and then one day, he shot me in the thigh with a BB gun. Bully the little girl all you want, but no, you hurt Mother's favorite? You're done for. I think she had him locked up for week, maybe longer. You should've seen him. I mean, he barely fit. So he's in there, and my sister, she goes in and she says, 'I can get you out, but you have to do whatever I say, forever and ever. Pinky swear.' Calculating, you know? Even when she was twelve. I think he was already broken at that point, but he didn't say a word, he just slipped his pinky finger out and wrapped it around hers. The next day, she threw a handful of spaghetti at Mother's face, and that was the end of it. He's been under her thumb since. Asks her how high before she even tells him to jump."

It was sad, in a way, but Sara couldn't make herself care about the pathetic bastard that had taken her little boy. "Does she have anyone else?"

"That she controls? No. She can manipulate anyone to get whatever she wants, but we're the only two…we're the only two—"

"Only two what?"

Michael sighed. "Slaves."

"What about the woman on the bike, on the bridge?"

"Some drama student she hired. Told her we were playing a practical joke—this game—and all she had to do was follow you and report whatever she saw."

"You weren't worried she would go to the police?"

"It was risky, but you give somebody just enough detail, they'll believe anything is harmless."

"I asked her for help."

His surprise was visible. "You did? We never thought—"

"She said that wasn't how the game was played."

Michael nodded. "Enough to spook you, let you know you were being watched. She's out of the picture, though. Played her part and now she's gone. But Samson—it's impossible. He won't let anything happen."

"I'll figure it out. I can do it. You have to let me try."

"You won't win."

"You can't win if you don't play. Give me a chance. Give my kids a chance. Think about your little boy. You'd fight for him, wouldn't you?"

Seconds passed. A minute. Sara waited and watched him. *Slap... slap...slap.* Whatever was going on inside his mind had left his face blank. She didn't dare say anything else, didn't want to ruin her chances by pushing too far.

Another minute passed before he shoved himself away from the wall, crawled over to her. He took the key out of his pocket and reached for the lock. Hesitated, then jammed it in and twisted.

The sound of the lock clattering to the floor was the most liberating thing Sara had ever heard. She scrambled out, nearly falling over when she tried to stand on her weak, throbbing legs.

He stood up beside her.

She flinched when he took her hand, but relaxed when he put the set of car keys in her palm, closing her fingers around them. "Take these," he said. "She's in my basement. The kids, too." He recited his address and then made Sara repeat it back to him.

"Got it," she said.

"When you go in, the basement door is to the left, just past the living room, but you're going to need somebody with you. She'll know something's up if she only hears one person walking upstairs."

"You're not coming?"

"I can't...I should—I have other plans."

She didn't know what he meant by that, and didn't dare to ask. She pointed at Teddy, who'd passed out during their conversation. "What about him?"

Michael looked over his shoulder at the crumpled and beaten body. "He was supposed to be the scapegoat."

"I mean, can I take him with me?"

"There's no use for him now. He can go, but you're carrying him." He untied Teddy, slung the soaking gag to the floor. Brought him close, draped his arm over Sara. He shoved his cell phone into her hand. "Her number is in there. Look under 'Sis'. You'll have service about a mile down the road, but *don't* call, don't you dare call, or you'll never see them again. Send a text. Say, 'Penalty enforced, ready for level three.' She'll think it's me and give you instructions. You really want to know how to beat her? Play your own game. She'll never expect it."

"How?"

"You said you can figure it out. Now go, before I change my mind."

"Can't you just tell me what—"

"—I said go—"

"—the third level is supposed to be?"

Michael said, "No. She wouldn't—"

"I don't care if she likes it or not. Help me...please."

He exhaled, stepped back, and glanced down at his feet. "You'll get one more call from her on your phone. Then at the house, I'm supposed to bring you down to the basement and give you another note. Instructions like all the rest, and she's going to be tied up too, just to throw you off."

"That's it?"

"She mentioned puzzles, one for each of your kids, but she changes things at the last minute. I never know what she'll do until the end. In your case, the only thing that's certain is the outcome."

"What's the outcome?"

"You're dead and your kids are in a foster home. Same thing that happened to us."

"Dead? But she said—"

"You think what she *says* matters to her? You can't win. Not her game."

"Then what should I do?"

"I told you, play your own game, and that's all I can give you. Go. Go. *Go*," he shouted.

Sara nodded, aware that she was close to going back in the cage if she didn't get moving.

She used her hips and shoulders to pull Teddy along, shuffling through the cabin, struggling under his limp body. He could manage a step or two, follow it with a stumble. "You can do it," she whispered. "We're free."

They were halfway through the yard before Michael called out to her. "Sara," he said.

She heaved Teddy around.

He stood on the front porch, gun at his side.

Please don't...please don't shoot...

"Whatever you do," he said, "don't tell her I let you go. She wouldn't—she wouldn't like it."

"I promise." *Still trying to make her happy. Still her slave, aren't you?*

Sara bent and lifted Teddy higher, making her way through the yard, careful not to slip on the bed of pine needles.

The wind was calm. Trees stood tall and motionless overhead. Through the serenity of the peaceful forest, she heard the puff of air escaping a silencer, followed by the *thump* of a mass falling on wood.

She didn't look back.

Chapter Nineteen

DJ

DJ cursed at the rush hour traffic on I-5. He hadn't seen it this bad in ages. Radio reports indicated a three-car pileup. One overturned, serious injuries, paramedics en route.

I should've known better, he thought. It was always a gamble, even when he wasn't in a hurry. Fight the bumper-to-bumper exodus back to the suburbs on the interstate, or march from stoplight to stoplight like all the other zombies on the streets who were trying to get home.

Barker hadn't answered his multiple calls, so he sat in line, creeping ahead, inch by excruciating inch, using the delay to think, to analyze.

At the mention of the necklace, he'd rushed out of Willow Bluesong's house without thought as to where he was going or what he should do next. His first reaction was to be on the move, in a hurry to get somewhere, and now, sitting at a complete standstill, the lapse in judgment had cost him.

Lights and siren. Just get out of this mess. But go where?

Shelley Sergeant's place was the obvious choice, however unlikely it was that she would be home. But was she involved? Really? Her California DMV records had said her eyes were green. Not mismatched. Not brown and blue.

Wait...I didn't check her history...what if it was...

The Mazda in front of him managed to move forward, and DJ eased up on the brakes, coasted along with it. He called the station, got Davis on the line, asked him to check up on Shelley Sergeant with explicit instructions to look for anything out of the ordinary about her eyes.

He waited. He hoped. He crawled another two feet.

His cell rang, caller ID revealing it was Barker. He answered, "It's about time."

"Easy, JonJon, I got enough of that from my ex-wife. Looks like you were tapping that speed dial button with a jackhammer. You got something?"

"That necklace. The one the bartender mentioned."

"I thought you'd given up on that one."

"It's a stretch, but—"

"We live and die by coincidence, cowboy. What've you got?"

"Shelley Ann Sergeant. Sara Winthrop's assistant."

"She told you whose it was?"

"No," he said, rolling forward, "I think she was *wearing* it."

"What? How'd you find that out?"

"The Bluesong woman."

"The babysitter?"

"I figured I'd start the ground-pounding with her. Hit the high spots and then work my way out. Good thing I did. Anyway, you should've seen the look on her face when I mentioned the Sergeant girl."

"Could've chewed through leather, huh?"

"Fireballs out of her eyes. Here's the thing: she says that Sergeant wears this necklace with the letters 'S.D.' on it. Said she thinks it stands for 'She-Devil'."

"No kidding. She got that eye disease thing you were so hell-bent on?"

"Davis is checking up on it. She's from Cali, driver's license says her eyes are green, though."

"Liars lie. Whereabouts down south? You've got him looking for priors, don't you?"

"Yep. Last known address was...holy shit."

"What?"

"San Diego...S.D. Too much of a stretch?"

"I've seen less break a case wide open, so let's run with it. Bartender said the letters were—what was the word she used? Intertwined?"

"Right. Could it be a logo?"

"Possible. What has an S.D. on it down there? You know, for a symbol? Sports team?"

"The Chargers?"

"Lightning bolt, JonJon. You don't watch much football, do you?"

DJ ignored the jab. "The Padres? They have an S.D. on their caps, don't they?"

"That they do, but it doesn't give us much to go on. Check the colleges, too. Who's in the area? UCSD?"

"UCSD and San Diego State, that I know of."

"They use an S.D. for anything?"

"Texas, Barker. The only thing I know is orange and horns."

"Have Davis check into it when he gets back to you."

"On my list. Any news from your end?"

"Blood and hair samples off to the lab. Hunch says Rutherford, of course. But get this, cowboy, they dusted and found a full hand-print on the window. Clean as fresh underwear. Big one, too."

"Amateur or not, he wouldn't be that stupid, would he?"

"The man walked away from a bloody car in broad daylight with a perfect handprint on the inside of the windshield. Either he's a damn idiot—"

"Or he *wanted* to get caught."

"Right as rain. I'm heading back to the station to check on the results. Where are you?"

"Sitting in traffic on I-5."

"What in the hell for, son? You're wasting time in the—"

DJ heard a beep over Barker's voice. "Hang on, Davis is on the other line." He clicked over. "Tell me you've got something?"

Davis said, "Did you figure this out, or did Barker?"

"The eye thing? Me—why?"

"Sounds like one of his left field theories. He must be rubbing off on you, JonJon."

Come on, any respect? Ever? "I'll be sure to let him know. What'd you find?"

"Car accident last year. Shelley Ann Sergeant of San Diego cited for reckless driving. Driver indicated that she wasn't wearing her contacts...officer noted a discrepancy between the stated eye color on the license and the actual eye color...doesn't say what kind... no citation for providing false information. Cute girl. He probably took it easy on her."

DJ felt a rush of blood surge through his head as he looked for an opening in the blockade of cars to his right. A rig to his left hauling a load of timber. Trapped. An ambulance screamed by on the shoulder, heading for the accident. He flicked on his lights, his siren, began angling himself to the right, forcing his way between an SUV and a furniture-delivery truck. "Good work, Davis. I need a couple more things. Find out where she went to school—"

"One step ahead of you. Graduated from San Diego State University. Smart cookie. GPA up somewhere around the moon."

"You near a computer?"

"I can be, one sec."

"Look up the symbol for their sports team."

"Their sports team? Which one?"

"Doesn't matter. Football. Look up pictures of the football helmet. Tell me what you see." A horn blared and DJ flicked a look over his shoulder, expecting to see a pissed off driver with the gall to honk at a policeman, but instead, a woman had stopped and was waving him over, giving him room to get by.

"Um…looks like…red, black letters…says 'Aztecs'…another one with 'S.D.' on it, sort of wrapped together."

"Bingo. Move, dammit!"

"What're you doing?"

"Sorry. Stuck in traffic. Damn idiots won't get out of my way. I need an address. Portland current."

"Let's see…121 Blaylock Avenue."

"Thanks, Davis," he said. He made it to the shoulder, clicked over to Barker, hit the gas. The engine roared, pushed him back in his seat. "You there?"

"Thumb-twiddling. Davis got anything?"

"Forget the samples and the prints. Sergeant's place, as quick as you can." He recited the address, shot down the nearest exit ramp, and hung up before Barker had a chance to balk.

. . .

He made up time by ducking down side streets. Lights and siren off, but going too fast for the residential area. He almost clipped a cyclist as he barged past a stop sign, swerving around a woman backing out of her driveway. As long as he was careful, the dangers here were minimal compared to navigating the impossible traffic on Lombard Street, over where the pizza shops and bars and laundries kept a steady stream of customers zipping in and out of every gap they could wedge a car into.

DJ took a right onto Blaylock, and cruised to a stop two houses down from the Sergeant residence. Cut off the engine, surveyed the area while he waited on Barker. If his partner managed to fight his way through rush-hour traffic, sirens blazing, it would take him at least twenty to thirty minutes.

That's too long...too long. But I should wait.

What if she has Sara in there right now? The kids, too. Ten minutes, Barker.

Cars were parked up and down either side of the street. A plump jogger lugged her body down the sidewalk, her running clothes soaked through to the skin. Lights illuminated living rooms, dining rooms. He imagined families inside sitting down for dinner or parents leaning over algebra books, trying to help out a teenager, but getting just as confused as their children. It made him think of Jessica and the home-cooked meal he'd be missing. Again. She didn't mind. At least, she said she didn't. She never complained, never asked questions. Simply kissed him and made him promise to come home safe. Every single morning, the same routine.

And so far, he'd kept his promises. The closest he'd come to a body bag was a domestic dispute six weeks in as a patrolman. The pop of a 9mm and the subsequent explosion of a brick, inches above his head. Way too close, and he'd frozen in place, unable to *make* his body react.

That was the thing. You never knew when it was your turn. Poke your head through a door, find out what a bullet tastes like. He had a recurring nightmare about it being something simple, like a routine stop to ask a couple of questions.

In the dream, he walked into the same building every time: a beat down, rundown, decrepit tire shop. A red Mustang, late '60s model, sat with its hood up and a mechanic's legs sticking out from underneath. He'd think about how the legs looked like the Wicked Witch of the West's after the house had fallen on her. He'd walk up, poke his head under the hood, looking at all the parts, examining how they fit together, worked together, admiring how clean they were, how spotless. Then he'd twist his head around, noticing the grinning face of the mechanic looking up at him. He could see the 9mm pointed at his head and then would watch as the knife-shaped blast of fire escaped the barrel. He'd hear the *crack*, and then stare at the bullet careening toward him in slow motion.

Always waking up before it hit.

Always.

He understood the symbolism, understood what his brain was trying to work out. Or at least he thought he did. It mirrored his life. The questions, the curiosity, snooping around under the hood, trying to figure out how the criminal mind worked. The fear of getting caught by surprise, of not being able to react in time.

All justified and reasonable. Both his fears and Jessica's. He debated on whether to call her, let her know he'd be late. Decided against it, sent her a text instead, telling her it was going to be a long night, and to keep the bed warm for him.

She replied right away. Told him she loved him and missed him, and to be safe.

He smiled, checked the time. Twelve minutes had passed, and still no Barker.

He thought about Shelley, tried to scrutinize her profile. Atypical of what he knew and was accustomed to. Early twenties female, highly intelligent. Worked as close to Sara Winthrop as anybody could get. No real connection to the children yet, but it was close enough to matter. If she *was* involved with the kids, why go through all the trouble with the stripper? To frame Teddy Rutherford? Could be. From the way the people at the office talked about him, he was the obvious fall guy.

But what in the hell would a pretty little girl from San Diego have against her boss? Has to be something big to take it this far...pretty little girl...San Diego...

San Diego...San Diego...

Something blipped on the radar in his mind. Something else about San Diego. Something from earlier in the day. Something he'd read.

Where else did I see that? Barker...Barker...the station...Sara's husband...reading his report...San Diego...

Brian Winthrop had made a trip to San Diego just months before he had gone missing.

And the connection is...?

He tried to play out the scenario in his head.

Brian Winthrop takes a trip to San Diego...he meets Sergeant some-how...she's working the bar at the hotel...couple of drinks...roll in the hay with a younger woman...thinks he's in love...flies home, can't stop thinking about her...disappears like a coward...leaves a wife and three little kids behind...

Promising. Happened often—more frequently than innocent wives and families deserved.

But if that were the case, it didn't explain what Sergeant was doing in Portland, working side by side with Sara, kidnapping her children.

He knew what Barker would say: 'Only God and walls know why people do what they do.'

He checked his watch again. Twenty minutes.

Can't wait anymore.

He opened his car door, stepped out into the street. Slowly made his way down the sidewalk.

Dreading this part. Dreading the approach.

And then he was saved from doing it alone with the slam of a car door and a loud whisper of, "DJ, hold up."

Barker trotted down the street toward him.

DJ, relieved, said, "About damn time. What took you so long?"

"Had to stop and get you a fresh pair of panties," Barker said, patting him on the back. "She home?"

"Doesn't look like it. You think we've got enough for probable cause?"

"Wouldn't bet my paycheck on it, but I'm going with 'ready, fire, aim' on this one. I think you've earned the right to kick the door open this time. Have at it, JonJon."

DJ nodded and headed up the steps. Tried not to think about looking under the hood of a Mustang.

Chapter Twenty
SARA

Sara dumped Teddy into the car, lifting his legs and helping him inside. He managed to shut the door on his own, then collapsed back onto the seat.

Before getting in, she opened up the most recent texts on Michael's phone, the ones to Sis, and read through. They had started that morning.

Michael says: Packages secure. No trouble.
Sis says: Good. Samson confirms.
Michael says: Napoleon?
Sis says: Convinced him. Meet Samson as discussed. Lose the car.
Michael says: Enough time for Mother Goose?
Sis says: Yes. Stick to the plan.

Sara could see that some time had passed between that and the next series.

Michael says: Took care of car. Barely made it. She's coming.
Sis says: Stop texting, idiot. CALL ME!

And then another break, followed by a series that must have occurred while she had been blindfolded in the back seat.

Michael says: On way to cabin. Mother Goose out of control.

Sis says: OMG, are you driving and texting?

Michael says: Yes drvng. Not sure abt this. Kids?

Sis says: They're ok. Do NOT text back. Drive.

Michael says: MG and Napo no prob,
but kids? Too much. Can't do.

Sis says: You can and you WILL. If she
gets out of line, use the penalty.

Michael says: ok you right. Jus dont hurt kids. Plaes.

Sis says: You will not order me, understand?

Michael says: Sry my fault.

Sis says: Mother would not approve of this disobedience.

Michael says: I no. Sry. But ples no pain for kids, okay?

Michael says: Sis?

Michael says: Sis?

Michael says: Sis?

The conversation ended there. Sara felt a cool chill ripple across her skin.

Michael had been struggling with abducting her children the whole time.

Sara got in the car, checked on Teddy, felt for a pulse. He was out cold, beaten and bruised, sitting in his own piss-stained pants. Dried blood was caked around his nose, and his eyes were as purple as plums, his lips swollen. The gag had chafed the skin around the edges of his mouth. Bruises the size of eggplants were on his ribs and chest.

His breathing was slow, unsteady. He needed water, and she wished she'd remembered to bring the rest of her bottle.

He'd gotten the worst of it. His pain, his torture, was physical. Hers had been mental. He would eventually recover with the proper care. If he survived. She needed to get him to a hospital.

Sara cranked the ignition and sped down the gravel road. Trees and rocks and leaves and the stream flying by. She had no idea where she was, where she was going, or how far away she was from the city and her children. She remembered that they had originally been heading east. It *felt* east.

The sun, where's the sun? There. That way. West.

She checked the phone signal.

Searching...searching...searching...

And, just like Michael had said before he unlocked his own cage with a well-placed bullet, the familiar connection bars appeared about a mile from the cabin. She pulled over at the next wide spot along the shoulder and sat staring at the keypad. Once she sent the message, the game would resume, and she would be on her own again, trying to figure out how to turn the tables on a psychopath.

Where would I start? My own game?

She'll think I'm Michael...I can use that...misdirection...surprise her like they're doing in the Juggernaut storyline...the ally is the villain...

Or...throw her off...tell her I screwed up...the game is over...make her think I'm dead...

There's no game without me...if I'm dead, she'll have no use for the kids...bad idea.

Sara thumbed out: 'Penalty enforced. Ready for level three,' then took a deep breath, her finger hovering over the 'Send' button.

Get it over with. Quit stalling.

She pressed it, and waited.

Teddy inhaled deeply, opened his eyes into two slits. "Why'd you stop?" He tried to sit up. Winced. Grunted. And then fell back onto the seat.

"We'll go soon," Sara said. "Waiting on something. Hopefully it won't take long, then we'll get you some help."

"I'm fine."

"Teddy, you don't have to do that."

"My right arm is completely numb, and my heart feels like it's beating funny, but other than that—when did I piss myself?" he said, noticing the drying stain on his crotch.

"Earlier, when you thought he was going to shoot you."

"What a dick. Who *was* that guy?"

"Doesn't matter."

"The hell it doesn't, we need to tell the cops."

"He's dead, Teddy."

"Dead? Good. He deserved it."

"He had...problems."

"You think?"

Sara could understand the sarcasm, after what he'd been through. "It's not an excuse, I know, but he wasn't really—he wasn't in control of himself, if that makes any sense."

"You're defending him?"

"Not...he was...I felt—I felt sorry for him."

"C'mon, Sara. Really?"

"How much do you remember? Any idea whatsoever how you got here? *Why* you're here?" She checked the phone. No response. *What's taking you so long?*

"You saw me, didn't you? I wasn't exactly coherent."

"But what do you *remember*? You were going to tell me who you thought the woman on the phone might be, right before he—"

"Beat me half to death? Honestly, I don't have a clue. Shelley and I left the office about ten o'clock this morning—"

"Shelley? You left *with* Shelley? For what?"

He angled away from her, sucked in air through his teeth, put a hand on his ribs.

"Teddy?"

"Something stupid. I should've known better. Anyway, I got in my car, and woke up in that cabin." He rubbed his eyes. "Can we go now? Those trees are getting blurry."

Sara checked the screen. Still nothing. She checked the clock, bit her lip, checked the clock again. "Couple more minutes, then we'll go."

"Fine. Two minutes."

"Shelley?" She didn't know why, but the mention of Shelley's name stuck out at her. Intuition, something odd, inexplicable. Strange for her to be leaving *with* Teddy, like he'd said. Shelley despised him as much as everyone else in the office. Had confided to her behind a locked door that he'd been hitting on her. Said he was disgusting. Distinctly remembered her calling him a pig.

Pig...pig...Teddy said the voice told him he deserved it for being a pig. No...Shelley? Not a chance.

She repeated it again. "Shelley?"

"For God's sake, Sara, leave it alone."

"Teddy," she said, her voice rising. "Whoever's doing this has my kids—do you remember me telling you that? Do you? If you know something, if you have any idea about what's going on and something happens to them because you didn't tell me, I will *not* hesitate to bring your scrawny little ass back up here and finish what they started. Got me? Now, why were you leaving with Shelley?"

"Okay, okay, calm down. It's embarrassing, that's all."

"And?"

"She said—she came into my office after you left, said she was leaving early and wanted to know if I'd come have an early lunch with her."

"That's it? You left to go have lunch?"

"I thought she wanted—you know how I am—the way she said it...I hadn't been laid in about a week. Figured it was worth a shot."

Sara rolled her eyes. "And you didn't see anything out of the ordinary—"

Michael's cell chimed, saving Teddy from her scolding.

Sara glanced down at the screen.

Sis says: Good. Sorry for the delay. Napping.
Sis says: She chose #1? You're not driving, are you?

Sara said, "Hang on, here she is."

"Who?"

"*Ssshhh*, let me think." *What would he do? What would he say?*

Michael says: Sry. Drivn slo.

Sis says: PULL OVER RIGHT NOW.

Sara held up a finger to Teddy, counted to twenty in silence.

Michael says: #1 yes Teddy taken care of.

Sis says: No names! How many times do I have to tell you?

Sis says: Wait

Sis says: How do you know his name?

Sara gasped. "Shit." *Don't do anything to the kids…don't hurt them.*
Teddy said, "What happened?"

"I might've screwed up." *Think!*

Michael says: Heard Mother Goose say it.

Sis says: Okay. Anyway, good job. You MIGHT
get a reward if it goes well. =)

Sara didn't know how to respond. She'd recovered from the misstep, but what would a man under the spell of his psychopathic sister say to that?

Michael says: I've been good. Please?

Sis says: IF you're good.

Michael says: Back in a sec. Mother Goose losing it.

She said to Teddy, "That was close."

"What was?"

"Hush. I need to think."

Michael says: Ok, back. Crazy woman. Backhand worked.

Michael says: What kind of reward?

Sis says: Leave some for me. That's MY job.

Sis says: Reward? Let's see...

Sis says: Should I wear red lace or black lace? ;-)

The phone almost fell out of Sara's hands. What else had he kept hidden from her?

Michael says: Red!

Michael says: Please.

Sis says: MAYBE. Get Mother Goose here fast.

Sis says: Can't take much more crying.

"Time to go," she said. "Let's get you to the hospital." *And me back to the kids. I'm coming guys, I'm coming. Hang on a little longer. Mommy's coming.*

Sara started the car, pulled back onto the gravel road.

"What was that all about? The texting."

"Talking to her about what to do next."

"You're texting the kidnapper?"

"She thinks I'm her brother. The one at the cabin."

"Can I help?"

"You can't even stand up on your own. I'll drop you off at the first emergency room we can find."

"You don't have time for that."

"No, I don't, but—"

"Just get me into the city, drop me off at a gas station somewhere. I'll be fine."

"Teddy, no."

"Sara, yes. Conversation over—your kids are more important. That's it, *no mas*, end of story."

For as long as Sara could remember, it was the first sign of humanity, the first sign of caring for another human being other than himself, that she had ever seen from Teddy. It was unfortunate that it took something like the last six hours for it to emerge.

Sara choked back the lump in her throat. *I asked for him to die.*

She said, "I'm sorry."

"For what?"

"Everything."

"Those weren't *your* fists."

"It's more complicated than that."

"Honestly, I don't want to know. Just stop calling me Little One and we're good."

"Done." *But, I can't ever tell you how one-sided that deal actually is.*

. . .

Thirty minutes later, Sara pulled up in front of a well-lit Chinese restaurant on the eastern side of Portland. Lights aglow, parking lot filled with cars. She was nervous, anxious, ready to be moving, ready to get back to her children, ready to face the inevitable, but feeling torn, feeling guilty, feeling like she owed Teddy at least another few seconds. She told him to be careful, and to check in with her in a couple of days.

"Unless—" she said, "unless you see me on the news."

"Don't do that," he said. "Don't. Whoever she is, she has no idea who she's dealing with."

Sara shook her head. "I'm—I don't know."

"You want to know the difference between us?"

"The difference?"

"Self-awareness. I *know* people hate me, and it doesn't bother me. I get it. I can see why, and I don't care. I get a kick out of seeing how far I can push people, but you? You're clueless when it comes to understanding just how much people respect you. There's a reason for it. And I can promise you this…if I see you on the news, it'll have some headline like," he said, using his hand to swipe across an invisible marquee, "*Badass Chick Thwarts Kidnapper.*"

"I wouldn't bet on it."

Teddy shrugged, opened the door, dragged himself out, one arm around his ribs. He took a step, said, "Sara?" and then leaned into the car. "Eight o'clock, Monday morning. Got some good ideas for Juggs 3 that I wanted to run past you."

He closed the door and limped away, shuffling toward the restaurant.

She envied his confidence in her.

The diners stared at him out the window. Confused, pointing. A man stood up and cupped his hands against the tinted glass, hoping to get a better look. Teddy waved at them and lurched toward the front entrance. Waved like he was the homecoming queen, perched atop the highest spot on a parade float. She couldn't see his face, but she imagined him smiling, loving every second of the abject attention.

She watched him go, looking after him with a little less disgust, but not exactly admiration, realizing that her arch-nemesis, the virus that had plagued her for so many years, might, on some planet, actually be likable.

Teddy made it to the doorway before he collapsed. A waiter emerged, cautious.

Go, before somebody calls the police.

Foot to gas, acceleration pushing her against the seat. She was gone, leaving Teddy behind, hurtling forward through a sea of tail-lights and neon signs. Knowing where she was going, but driving blindly into the coming storm.

Chapter Twenty-One

DJ

DJ approached the front door of 121 Blaylock, gun drawn and held ready at his side. The shades were closed and he kept a watchful eye for any subtle movements. When he was certain it was clear, he motioned for Barker to join him. Satisfied they were out of the line of fire, he risked a peek through the decorative, paned window above his head.

"Anything?" Barker whispered.

"Empty."

"Nobody home?"

"No, I mean *empty* empty. No furniture that I can see. Nothing."

"What? You sure this is the right address?"

"On file. Should we bother knocking?"

"Try the doorknob first."

DJ reached down, grabbed the cool, brass metal. Twisted to the left, heard the latch click, followed by the groaning of corroded hinges.

Barker said, "Saved us a grand entrance. Careful, now."

They crossed the threshold. DJ first, Barker following. Hunched over, intent, all senses redlined, waiting for an ambush. The shallow Berber carpet gave them the advantage of silence as they crept.

Backs to walls, shuffling from one spot to the next. Every door open, every room void of any signs of habitation. No toothbrush, no shower curtains. Spotless kitchen counters, spotless refrigerator, two empty ice trays in the freezer.

A single cup sat next to the sink. Blue and plastic. Bone dry.

They relaxed, holstered their weapons. DJ scratched the back of his neck, let out a huff of air.

Hands on his hips, Barker said, "As empty as my cold bed at night, cowboy. Now what? Any more bright ones?"

"I thought for sure…"

"Not your fault. Gotta go with what they give you."

"We should check for prints on the cup."

"Hospitals aren't this clean, but we might as well. I got a couple baggies in the car. Poke around some. I'll be back in a minute."

DJ stepped around the kitchen counter and into the living room. Pockmarks, dings and scrapes populated the walls. Typical of a rental, like his own place when he and Jessica had moved in together. She said they gave a place character, showed signs of life. He had complained about the previous tenants' lack of respect.

He bent down, examined the carpet closer. No indentations from couch legs or tables.

Nobody's been here for months. Fake address. Where's she staying?

They could track down the owner, ask if a Shelley Ann Sergeant had ever been here, or had ever signed a rental agreement. But with a fake address given to the DMV, more than likely she would've been smart enough to use a fake name. Fake bank account.

She'd used her real name at LightPulse. They'd have a real address on file, wouldn't they?

She wouldn't be that stupid. That's probably not her real name, either.

So she leaves Sara's husband down south, moves up here, somehow gets a job working for her. Bides her time for a couple months…watches patterns… figures out schedules…snatches the kids…takes them back to San Diego… Winthrop has his kids back…everybody lives happily ever after.

It's missing something.

Damn it. The note.

He heard the front door open, moved his hand closer to his pistol. "Barker?"

"Hand off the go-boom, JonJon. Just me," Barker said as he popped around the corner, shaking the baggie open. "Got an APB out on our girl. Doubt it'll do any good."

"She hasn't gone anywhere yet."

"What makes you say that?"

"The note, Barker. The one from this morning."

"Meaning what?"

"For starters, I'd say you were right about the husband," DJ said, then went on to explain his theory about what happened to Brian Winthrop, and the possible reason that Shelley Sergeant was in Portland. He watched Barker nod, watched the flickers of comprehension light up his eyes, listened to him grunt his agreement.

When he'd finished, Barker said, "You keep this up, I might be able to retire earlier than I thought."

"Don't buy your plane ticket yet. We've got the who, and the what. The how is shaky, but the where and why…zip, zilch, zero. Can't figure out what this game has to do with anything."

Barker scooped the cup into the baggie, zipped it shut. He said, "Sounds to me like she's out for revenge of some sorts. Maybe our buddy Brian talked too much about the wifey. Miss Shelley can't take it, comes up here to take care of business."

DJ crossed his arms. "Why not go after her directly? Why get the kids involved?"

"She could've knifed her in a parking lot somewhere, but what fun would that be? She's hell-bent on revenge, she'd want to make it last, hit her where it hurts the most."

"Sometimes your mind scares me."

Barker tapped the side of his head. "The more you think like them, the easier they are to catch."

"Then where do we go from here?"

"JonJon, I'm afraid I'm done chasing my tail for the night. Sleep on it, and we'll start fresh in the morning."

. . .

But DJ knew he *wouldn't* be able to sleep on it. Sure, he could go home, flop down on the couch, or eat a lukewarm meal while Jessica read or watched another home improvement show. Then, as always, when something about a case was bothering him, the inevitable tossing and turning would lead to an hour at his desk, surfing the internet at 4AM, or checking the refrigerator to see if something new had manifested itself out of the cold ether. He'd crawl back into bed for another round of choppy, broken sleep, then eventually relent and head out to the garage for a quick 5K on the treadmill before the sun came up.

Instead of heading for home, as Barker had done, he made laps up and down Lombard Street, thinking, analyzing, trying to figure out where Shelley could've taken the kids. He read the street signs, the same ones over and over. Stopped for a cup of coffee at 7-11, chatted with the clerk for a couple of minutes about how they thought the Timbers were doing. Got back in his unmarked sedan, resumed the slow march toward more unanswered questions.

What kind of game was she playing? A literal game? Figurative? Back at the school, Sara had taken a phone call, and had rushed out in a panic. Someone matching her description had been spotted naked in the Rose Gardens, and then there were reports of her running away.

This person was toying with Sara. Had to be. Playing with her, testing her, seeing how far she would go to save her children. Humiliating her because she could. Her game, her rules.

If Sara was running away, where was she going? On to the next demeaning episode that Shelley had devised? There were no reports or sightings of Sara since that morning. She could be anywhere.

The kids could be anywhere. Tens of thousands of buildings and homes. Hidden away while Shelley got her revenge on a woman who had been nothing more than a victim of an unfaithful husband who couldn't keep his dick in his pants.

She could be dead by now. All four of them. They'd be found in the morning by some unlucky janitor making his early rounds, or a hiker who had taken a shortcut through the woods and managed to stumble across their bodies.

Don't think like that. There's still time.

How many cases went unsolved each year? How many times did a child go missing from a playground and never came home?

No matter what the number might be, he refused to add to that total.

Not them. Not this time. Barker will come up with something.

And what happens when Barker's gone? One of these days, you're not going to have the luxury of his intuition. One of these days, you'll have to think for yourself.

His ringing cell phone was a welcome interruption. "Johnson."

"JonJon, got a call for you."

"Davis? What're you still doing at the station?"

"Keeping you in a job. You want me to patch her through or take a message?"

"Who is it?"

"Said she's Sara Winthrop."

She's alive... "Put her through." He waited for the line to click over and said, "Sara? You okay? Find your kids?" *Please say yes...*

"I know where they are, but I could use some help."

"With what? Where are you? What's going on?"

"I'll tell you when you get here. Right now, I need an extra set of footsteps. Come alone, because I think that's the only way it'll work."

Chapter Twenty-Two
SARA

Sara sat on a park bench within sight of Michael's home. It was in a neighborhood that she'd never been to before, full of houses in various stages of disrepair. Missing shingles, sagging porches. Yards that hadn't been mowed in days, if not weeks. Trash littered the sidewalk. Shoes dangled from power lines.

If he'd been telling the truth, her children were inside, bound and gagged, crying, suffering, wondering why their mother hadn't come for them yet, wondering who this horrible stranger was who had been terrorizing them all day.

I'm coming, guys. Mommy's coming, but I have to be careful. Just a little longer.

She had wrestled with the decision to get Detective Johnson involved, but as Michael had said, Sis would be expecting two sets of footsteps if she really *were* hiding in the basement with Lacey, Callie, and Jacob.

Her heartbeat hammered in her chest. The ache to see their little faces again had grown to an overwhelming urge to *move, go, now*, but it clashed with the need to stay smart, stay focused, and play the game how Sis wanted it played. One wrong move, one subtle slip, and she may never see them again, whether alive, or— God forbid—dead.

Roughly forty-five minutes had passed since their last communication and Sara was no closer to coming up with her own game to play. If she had a clearer head, maybe, but the minutes were ticking away. Sis would be expecting a call or a text, or something, to let her know that the third level was about to start.

Misdirection, she thought. *That's my only play here. I don't have time to come up with my own game.*

She thought about all the times she'd hunkered around the large table in the LightPulse meeting room with a group of their sharpest minds brainstorming, plotting, hashing out ideas, trying to come up with a plethora of hazardous situations to throw at the laser gun-wielding heroes of *Juggernaut*. Given that luxury, with a notepad full of ideas and a corps of experts guiding her, outsmarting the villainess would've been simpler. Not guaranteed, but manageable. At least she'd have a shot.

But now, alone on the park bench, mind racing, no matter what form of trickery or deception she came up with, it all led to the ultimate consequence that she feared most.

Something terrible that she would be powerless to stop.

The only path that made any sense was playing the final level with advanced knowledge of what she was going into. She had the information Michael had given her, but needed more.

She needed her very own cheat code.

Like back in the glory days of Nintendo games, when you could enter a set of keystrokes on the controller and gain extra lives. Game programmers did it before then, and they were still doing it. The LightPulse guys held contests to see who could come up with the most creative way to hide something within *Juggernaut*, and to this day, some of the winners had never been found.

That's my advantage. Her game becomes my game.

She opened the text window on Michael's phone.

Be smart, but play dumb.

Michael says: Stupid traffic. Sitting at a dead stop. Accident.
Michael says: Mother Goose tried to convince me to turn on you.

The reply came swiftly.

Sis says: Surprised it took her this long.
Sis says: How far away?
Michael says: Couple of miles. Be there soon. Kids okay?
Sis says: YES, Michael. Don't start that shit again.

Sara stared at the keypad. *How do I get her to tell me what's coming?
What would he say?*

Michael says: Just want to make sure they'll be safe.
Michael says: Tell me about this level
again. Did you change anything?
Michael says: Can't call. She's listening.
Sis says: You KNOW what the plan is.
Sis says: You disgust me.
Michael says: Sorry. Don't want to disappoint you.
Sis says: Too late for that.
Sis says: But sometimes I worry Mother hit you too hard.
Sis says: That hammer must have damaged your memory.
Michael says: It did. I remember some of it.
Michael says: Traffic moving soon. Please remind.
Sis says: Jesus, you're hopeless. Read this, get
here fast. DO NOT text and drive.
Michael says: Ok.
Sis says: Bring her down to the basement. I'll be tied up, too.
Sis says: You and Samson take the kids and leave.
DO NOT forget to loosen my knot.
Sis says: Samson is no longer needed, got it? Kids, your choice.
Sis says: The rest is up to me. Can't wait to see the look on her face.

Sis says: Betrayed by her sweet little assistant. So much fun.

Sara stared the final text, hands shaking. The butterflies in her stomach thrashed around like they were on fire.

It had been Shelley all along. She had suspected, guessed, changed her mind, and then back again, but now she had confirmation of the voice's identity.

Everything made sense—a woman, someone inside LightPulse—coaxing Teddy out of the office, and even earlier, back further, back to her interview, wooing Sara with all the facts she knew about her, all the research she'd done, her insistence that she only wanted to work with the best. The now-empty compliments of Sara's skill at her profession. It embarrassed Sara to realize how shallow she'd been. The flattery had worked. She'd hired Shelley a week later.

Next came the offers to run errands for her, pick up the kids, visit her house, babysit. Work herculean hours to impress her, to win her trust. Every single move made over the past couple of months designed to get as close as she possibly could to Sara, to be involved with her, learn about her, get *inside* her. To get revenge on the other woman because Brian wanted to leave.

The betrayer had become the betrayed.

The level of duplicity was incomprehensible.

Sara blamed herself for not seeing through it, for allowing Shelley into her life, for welcoming the evil into her home with open arms.

I couldn't have known. She was flawless.

The other phone rang beside her.

Be careful. You don't know anything.

She answered, "Hello?"

"There you are, Sara. I've been told that you misbehaved, that you had a difficult decision to make during the last level." The familiar, digitized, apathetic voice rolling lazily through the words.

"Can I talk to them?"

"When I'm ready. How'd it feel?"

"How did what feel?"

"Choosing whether someone lives or dies. You may get to make that choice again when you get here. Welcome to Level Three. I like to call it...*Consequences.*"

"You can call it a hot dog eating contest, for all I care. I'm sick of this bullshit." She was pushing the limits, she knew, but the vitriol was expected, and she hoped she hadn't pushed too far. Maintaining her façade might not be possible if she heard another yelp of pain.

"Now, now, Sara. These outbursts will not be tolerated. Don't forget who's in control of the situation."

If you only knew, Shelley.

"Can we please get this over with? Just tell me what to do."

"Your companion will deliver you to the proper location. Then, and only then, will the rules of the final level be revealed. But, before I go, you do have a question left for this round. Pity you lost your chance during the last level. It may have been helpful, but you'll never know now, will you? For this round, the same rules apply. You may ask at the beginning or at the end. However, asking at the end may only be possible if you're still...*alive.*"

She pretended to stammer, to think it over. "I'll—I think I should ask—no, I'll save it."

I don't know what it'll be, but you better believe you won't see it coming.

"What a shame, Sara. Such a...such a waste. I was prepared to tell you the truth about whatever you might ask. But now that you've chosen, we must proceed."

She knew it wouldn't be allowed, but she asked anyway, to keep the ruse going. "Can I talk to them now?"

"I'm afraid not, Sara. Not part of the rules, but it does remind me that I haven't heard a scream in a while. I must admit, my ears do miss that beautiful sound. We'll see you soon enough. Maybe I'll let you listen along with me, and I hope you're ready for this," the voice said, then hung up.

Sara stood, walked to the nearest trashcan, and slung the phone in with the rest of the garbage.

I hope you're ready for me, *Shelley.*

. . .

While she waited for DJ, a young couple pushed a stroller past Sara on the sidewalk. Early thirties, probably their first child, one happy family on their way to years of laughter and smiles and more babies. Soccer games, gold stars, high school graduation, college diploma, and then bundles of grandchildren they could spoil rotten.

It reminded her of the early days with Brian. The plans they'd made, all the fun they'd had picking out matching outfits for Lacey and Callie, listening to the same princess cartoon relentlessly playing on repeat until the DVD gave out and stopped working. Brian had joked that the thing waved the white flag on its own and said something about how all DVDs go to heaven, except for that one, because it deserved its own special place in Hell for the hell it'd put them through.

And then their little baby boy had come along and the cycle started anew. More onesies, thrilled relatives, a fresh coat of blue paint on a study converted into a new bedroom. Brian couldn't have been happier. He brought home a baseball glove and model trains that wouldn't be put to use for years. Toy fire engines, plastic swords, and building blocks that had to be put away because the pieces were too small. Brian was still outnumbered, but he'd been thrilled to have another male on his side after living in a home dominated by estrogen.

Brian.

Goddamned Brian.

Two wasted years of pining for him, allowing her emotions to wither, refusing to go on blind dates arranged by her friends, checking the internet *every single morning* to see if any news had popped up overnight, consoling her babies with repeated refrains of 'Daddy's not coming home tonight, he might tomorrow,' after the bouts of depression and putting on a good face for everyone around her, after surviving on hope and good memories alone, it'd come to this.

This.

That one singular moment where she decided to say a silent goodbye to him. She looked up at the sky, grown darker now in the late evening. Sun setting, ready to bring light and life to another spot in the world.

Brian, if what he told me is true, and you didn't make it, if you're—if you're dead…I'm—I'm sorry. What you did was wrong, but you didn't deserve to die for it. That's—I can't imagine what she did to you and I don't want to, but you didn't deserve to die. I waited for you. Waited and waited and waited. It took me six months before I could go to bed without crying myself to sleep. Six months!

Did you really try to come back? What would you have said if you had come home? Would you have told the truth? Would you? Would the lies have eaten away at you while I went on, clueless and happy that the love of my life had gone through hell to get back to me?

I was a good wife, I know I was. We had a good family. We were happy, weren't we? Damn you. Do you know how hard it's been? Did you think about what I was going through while you were lying in bed beside her? Did you? God. I hate sounding so pathetic. But I have a right to be selfish. After this, after what you did, I have the right. I do. You put us in this spot. You did it. Our babies are in that house with the psycho you left me for. You did it. You did this.

And you know what? It's time to move on. I think I'm ready. One of these days, maybe I'll forgive you. Maybe I'll put on a black dress and I'll get you a gravestone and I'll lay down flowers. I will. But for now, you see that rolling down my cheek? That's the last one.

This is your fault…and you don't get any more of my tears, Brian.

Chapter Twenty-Three
SARA & DJ

Sara watched the young detective approach from a half a block away. Shirt untucked, tie loosened, sport coat hanging limp over slumped shoulders. He looked like he'd aged ten years since that morning.

He recognized her, gave a quick wave, and picked up his pace. A mixture of concern and relief in his eyes.

When he got within a couple of steps, she said, "You're alone?"

"I am. Man, you look like—I mean, good to see you're alive. We thought you were—"

"Dead? It's not over yet."

"I've got a badge and a gun. They're usually good for something. So whose house are we going into?"

She gave him the shortened version. The game, the Rose Gardens, the run through the city, the phone calls, Michael and the cabin. She told him about Teddy, but not about sentencing him to die, nor about the remorse.

DJ said, "Spent half the day looking for him. We thought *he* did it."

"I did, too. She was trying to frame him."

"Shelley Sergeant?"

Sara took a step closer, lowered her voice and said, "You figured it out?"

"I wasn't sure. Lots of guesswork, nothing solid. What's your plan?"

"Let's go. I'll tell you on the way."

Sara and DJ trotted up the street. She explained what was going on inside, what she expected, what Shelley expected, and what the final level might hold. They stopped at a neighbor's hedge fence, ducking behind it.

DJ whispered, "I'm not letting you go down there by yourself. Not an option."

"With all due respect, Detective…*my* kids, *my* choice."

"At least let me—"

"Just be ready, okay? Hurry." Sara darted around the hedge and up to the front porch with DJ trailing, muttering about bad ideas and no respect.

They climbed the five steps, passing dead plants in cracked pots, avoiding the broken slat in front of the entrance. Sara felt like a criminal, an intruder, sneaking into Michael's former home.

She pushed the front door open, stepping into foreign territory. Held up a hand to DJ, whispering, "Step hard. He was huge."

DJ mouthed, "How?"

"Try to sound—I don't know—try to sound big. Stomp, but don't be obvious."

"This is ridiculous. Let me go in first."

Sara stabbed a finger toward the floor. "I said *no*. You go in with guns blazing and my kids are dead, you hear me? Stay upstairs and let me handle this."

"But I'm supposed—" DJ stopped, lifted his hands, let them fall. Hung his head. "I don't agree with this, not at all, but I'll stay out of the way. For now, at least."

"Good. Now pretend like you're pushing me. Make it sound real."

DJ stomped forward and shoved Sara.

She stumbled, hit the floor, and whispered, "Do it again," and then got to her feet.

DJ stomped another couple of steps, helped her up, shoved again. Harder this time.

Sara tripped, reached out, and knocked a vase from a table. It crashed and shattered as she fell to her hands and knees. She yelled, "Okay, I'm going," and gave him a thumbs-up.

He urged her ahead. Stomped on the shards, heard them crunch under his heel.

Sara scuttled around the broken ceramic and over to the basement door, looked back at DJ, watched him press his lips together. Waiting, waiting.

He closed his eyes, tugged hard on his tie. "Go," he whispered. "Be careful. If anything happens, I'm coming down."

She reached for the doorknob, pulled herself up. Took one last look at DJ, mouthed, "Not until I call for you." Twisted the handle, and let the door swing open, screeching like a coffin lid as it went. Ominous. Foreboding.

She planted a foot on the creaky first step, paused, and stepped again.

Heartbeat quickening, ears going dull like her head was veiled in cotton, the temperature change of the chilly, musty basement prickling her skin. She plodded downward.

Down, down, down, until she reached the final level.

. . .

She smelled the familiar but foreign scent of laundry detergent first, then squinted to temper the sharp light of a single, bare bulb overhead as she moved into the open space. A low ceiling, an arm's length away, pressed down from above. On her left, an antique china cabinet sat against a naked cinderblock wall. To her right, the washer and dryer crouched in an open alcove, their dingy white paint visible in the shadows. Behind her, three shelves, nearly empty, held a shovel, a tarp, and a spool of rope. Instruments of a quick, secretive disposal.

I know what those are for, Sara thought.

Not what, who.

It's so quiet in here. Where are the kids?

Where's Shelley? Did Michael lie? Damn him, did he lie to me?

He said she changes things at the last minute.

He said the only thing that's certain is the outcome.

And, finally, three large wooden boxes sat in the middle of the basement floor, painted black—splotchy, like a rush job from a spray can. Sara took a step closer to get a better look as her eyes adjusted to the awkward lighting.

Each box was a carbon copy of the others, containing an LED display with **05:00** glowing bright red on what appeared to be a door, sealed at the edges by a thin strip of rubber. On their tops, silver cylinders wired to metallic containers, along with clear tubing that coiled around, disappearing inside. In front of that, green buttons the size of a quarter.

The only difference Sara could see were the stenciled, gray numbers below each LED display.

The first box: 42

The second box: 91

The third box: 18

Sara stood, frozen, as the hazy confusion melted away. The numbers were meaningless, but with Lacey, Callie and Jacob nowhere in sight, the boxes could only mean one thing:

Three boxes, three children.

"No. Please, no." Sara, nearly frantic, raised her voice and said, "Are you guys in there?"

She rushed toward the boxes and in the half-second before she reached them, instinct and a sixth sense registered movement coming from the alcove. Before she could look, a wrecking ball slammed into her ribs. Her neck whipped sideways, smashing her ear against her shoulder. Her feet came off the ground, she was airborne, and then her attacker speared her into the unforgiving concrete floor.

They rolled together, bodies smashing against the china cabinet, glass doors exploding.

Sara tried to move, felt a piercing stab in her side. Broken bone? Knife?

Dizzy, dazed, glass digging into her arms, she lifted her head and saw the behemoth scrambling to his feet.

She heard Shelley's voice say, "Upstairs, Samson. Go. Kill whoever it is, then find Michael."

She saw a hand extending toward him, the flash of light on metal, and watched his thick fingers closing around the butt of a handgun. He moved fast for his size. He darted across the floor and then thundered up the stairs.

Sara tried to sit up, but the dizziness and throbbing pain pushed her back down.

Shelley knelt over her.

Face to face, Shelley smiled. "Almost, Sara. You almost had me. Something felt *off* about the way he was texting. He always asks for *black* lace, and that comment about the hammer? Total lie. Mother never did a thing to him."

Sara heard shouting overhead. Two gunshots popped a second apart, followed by a single *thud*.

Next came the sounds of unsteady footsteps clunking down the stairs.

Please be DJ. Oh God, please be DJ.

And then *boom, boom, boom* as DJ tumbled down and crashed against the wall. Left arm broken and twisted behind his back, blood pouring out of the bullet hole in his chest, staining his shirt. He spat out a mouthful of blood and saliva, then said, "Police," and collapsed into a lump.

His chest rose and fell, rose and fell.

Shelley smirked. "Everybody dies in the end, huh? Samson. You. Your little angels. Brian. Especially Brian, because he *deserved* it. You want to know why he left? You were *boring*, Sara. Exact words.

Boring." Shelley wrapped her hands around Sara's neck and shook. "And that made it so much worse when he tried to leave *me*—for *you*—you, stupid, *boring* bi—"

Sara mustered what strength she had left and swung at Shelley's head.

Shelley blocked it, grabbed Sara's arm, used her leverage to pull backward.

The glass dug into Sara's back, sliced through shirt and skin as Shelley dragged her across the floor, depositing her in front of the boxes.

Shelley used her knees to pin down Sara's arms, slapping her across one cheek and backhanding her across the other. She grabbed Sara's shirt, twisted the material, and yanked her up, growling into her face, "Where's my brother? Where's Michael? What did you do to him? Tell me!" growing louder and louder with each vile word.

Shelley lifted her hand and balled up her fist.

Gasping, Sara said, "Dead. He's dead."

Shelley punched hard and fast.

Sara's nose shattered with a sharp *crack*. The room went white, and in a brief pause, she felt Shelley adjust her weight, and through watery eyes, she saw her former assistant reaching for something in her pocket, and then the pressing interrogation resumed.

"Did you kill him?" Shelley said, jaws clenched, teeth grinding. "Answer me. Did you kill him?"

Sara gagged on the waterfall of blood in her throat. Tried to swallow it, choking and coughing. She said, "No, he shot—he shot himself."

"Liar," Shelley screamed. She swung at Sara's head again, leaning into the motion, putting everything she had behind it.

Sara was ready this time. She squirmed out of the way and felt the blow grazing against her temple.

Shelley's fist pounded into the concrete.

Sara heard the bones crunching next to her ear.

Shelley howled, leaning backward, cradling her hand.

It was just far enough. Sara swung her legs up, wrapped them around Shelley's neck, and yanked.

The body followed the head. Shelley went tumbling backward.

Sara twisted and rolled with the momentum, tightening her leg-lock on Shelley's throat, squeezing her thighs together, choking her. Shelley flailed and kicked, hammering on Sara's legs with weakening fists.

Sara clenched tighter and tighter, waiting until no more strength remained in the punches. She released her grip and clambered around, straddling Shelley, pounding a fist into her jaw, her teeth, the side of her head. Pounding, pounding, pounding.

She grabbed Shelley by the ears, leaned down, and pulled the slobber-drenched face closer to her own. Blood dripped from Sara's broken nose, splattering on Shelley's cheeks, running into stunned and groggy eyes. "What did you do with them?"

Shelley smiled and said, "You kill me, they die."

"No," Sara said. "You don't *get* to die."

"Good, because I want to watch."

"Watch what?"

Shelley motioned toward the boxes with her eyes. "Look."

The red LED numbers ticked slowly down.

04:05...04:04...04:03...

"What's happening? What's the timer for?"

Shelley hissed like steam escaping from a leaky pipe. "Hydrogen cyanide. Once it releases, they'll have less than a minute."

Sara dug her fingernails into Shelley's ears and shook hard. "Michael said *I'm* the endgame, not them."

"Michael never made the rules."

"How could you do this? They adored you. They're little. So little. Get them out of there, right now. You hear me? Right now."

"But the game's not over, Sara. Here's a hint. They're in one box, all together. No kicking, no screaming—I made sure of that."

03:43...03:42...03:41...

"Pick the wrong one, the gas releases automatically. Last clue, in my right pocket."

Sara's lip quivered. She popped Shelley's head against the concrete, just enough to stun her, then shot over to the shelf, grabbed the rope, and tied her hands and feet together in a frenzied rush.

03:15...03:14...03:13...

Shelley slurred, "Better hurry. Tick, tock, tick, tock, tick... tick...tick..."

Sara reached into Shelley's pocket and pulled out the final godforsaken piece of paper.

She read:

CHOOSE THE PROPER ORDER
10-21-7-7-5-18-14-1-21-20

The proper order? What does that mean? Do I reorder those numbers? One...five...seven...seven...ten...no, that doesn't get me anything. Is it a phone number?

Area code? Area code...Jesus, what's the area code here? Five-oh-three! There's a one...five...zero...no three.

Damn it. I don't—what is this? I don't even know where to start.

Sara read the numbers again, looked up at the time ticking away.

02:49...02:48...02:47...

Under three minutes and counting, disappearing so quickly.

Sara walked over to the boxes and paced back and forth in front of them.

From the floor, Shelley screamed, "Tick...tock...tick...tock!"

Sara ignored her. Allowing the distraction would only waste more time.

Okay, stop, calm down. Think...breathe. The numbers, the numbers. What if they—maybe they're separate from the words? Maybe it's supposed to throw you off?

Add them together? What if it matches a box number? Ten plus twenty-one, thirty-one. Plus fourteen is forty-five, plus five is fifty...plus eighteen...plus fourteen...one hundred twenty-four total. Doesn't match. Shit...divided by three...three into twelve is four...three into four is one... forty-one and...and something.

She faced the first box, thinking she had it. Tears and panic blurred her vision as she saw the *42* painted on the front. She screamed at the ceiling.

02:20...02:19...02:18...

Lightheaded, Sara sat down on the floor, wiped her eyes.

Shelley giggled and said, "You added and divided, didn't you? I *knew* you'd do that. God, you're so predictable. Maybe that's why Brian said you were boring. So predictable."

Again, Sara tried to ignore her, but it wasn't so easy this time. It didn't matter why Brian left. Not anymore.

Or did it?

Shelley was so obsessed with him...did the numbers have anything to do with Brian?

Did he ever say I was boring to my face? Like out loud? Did I ever do anything that he thought was boring? He hated those cooking shows I watched all the time. He laughed at me when I tried to learn how to knit. What else...maybe it was—no, never boring. What was boring?

She scanned her memory for their daily and weekly rituals. Get up, shower, go to work, pick up the kids, eat dinner. The usual stuff. Normal family life. Never boring.

01:45...01:44...01:43...

He played softball on Saturdays. Sometimes they got a babysitter and went to the movies on Saturday nights. Date nights. Routine, but not boring, at least not to her.

And on Sundays...

Sunday mornings! First the crossword and then that other word game—the cipher. The one he said was...boring. Could it be a cipher?

Sara crawled to her knees.

01:27...01:26...01:25...

She held the note up, read the numbers again.

You can do this. Easy, just like the one in the paper. The two sevens repeat. Same letter. Which letters double-up? B...S...T...D...so many of them. Big word, big word. Ten letters. The two sevens repeat...what if—do they match the alphabet?

A-one, B-two, C-three...four...six...G-seven. G, G.

I got it. Holy shit, that's it.

She was so relieved that she shouted the word. "Juggernaut!"

Shelley kicked at the floor and strained against the rope, erupting in a barrage of curses.

01:05...01:04...01:03...

Shelley said, "Forget it, you'll never get the rest."

Sara glanced at the numbers on the boxes.

Choose the proper order. Do I put them in order? Eighteen, forty-two, ninety-one. Right, left, middle. Nothing. That means nothing. Choose the proper order. Juggernaut. Are they connected? Do the numbers mean anything in Juggernaut?

Forty-two? Wasn't that the number of hidden missions? Wait...no... that was forty the last time I checked. Anything? Anything at all?

Move on. Come back.

Sara moved to the next box.

Ninety-one. I can't—nothing. Ninety-one? Ninety seconds in a power round. Close...not exact...doesn't have anything to do with an order of something...

This is impossible!

Stop, you can do this. Try the next one.

Sara moved to the third and final box.

00:37...00:36...00:35...

She paused, tried to subdue her desperate breathing.

It has to be this one.

Make sure! Think first. Think, Sara.

Eighteen. Eighteen in Juggernaut. Why does that—I should know this—so familiar. Why can't I think? Damn it. Concentrate. The new storyline...new aliens...attacking Earth from a new solar system...attacking from—yes!

She glared at the LED display. Time had sped up.

00:22...00:21...00:20...

Sara wiped the blood from her nose with a shaky hand.

Attacking from Planet 18...that weird writer kid with a crush on Shelley...

Jeremy...he named it Araneae...didn't he say the aliens looked like spiders?

What was the word he used? Taxonomy, right?

Taxonomy...grade school...

Grade school...biology class...taxonomy...

Mr. Walker at the blackboard...

King Philip Came Over....

Kingdom, phylum, class...

Order.

Choose the proper order.

Planet 18.

She remembered asking Jeremy, *"Why Araneae?"*

"Taxonomy, Mrs. Winthrop. It's the Order for spiders."

The countdown careened toward 00:00.

00:09...00:08...00:07...

Positive she was right, *had to be right,* Sara inhaled deeply, steadied her frenetic hand, and slapped the green button of Box 18...and waited.

00:05...00:04...00:03...

The timer stopped. The door popped open.

Shelley screamed and thrashed.

And inside the box sat Lacey, Callie, and Jacob. Alive and unharmed, but bound and gagged. All three exploded into garbled shouts of "Mommy!" through the white cloth across their mouths.

Sara collapsed to the floor. She crawled over to them, tears and blood mixing, dripping and splattering on the concrete as she went.

Sobbing, she untied their legs, their hands, removed their gags, apologizing over and over for not finding them sooner, for what Shelley had done to them. They hugged and cried together until no more tears would come.

She stood, pulling her children with her in a wide arc around Shelley, turning them away, shielding them from where DJ lay on the floor.

At the bottom of the stairs, she urged them upward. "Wait at the top. Do *not* go any further. Mommy will be right there, she just needs to talk to Shelley for a second, okay? Remember those monkeys we saw? See no evil, hear no evil? Yeah? You do? That's what I want you to do. Pretend you're all three monkeys at the same time. Close your eyes, cover your ears. I'll be right there. I promise. And when I'm done, we'll go home for some ice cream."

They protested, she insisted, and reluctantly, they climbed the stairs and sat on the landing, eyes and ears covered. So good, so trusting. Waiting patiently.

She checked on DJ. Still breathing, barely. She found an old rag, pressed it against his chest, told him to hold it there, if he could, then dug around in his pockets until she found his cell phone. Dialed 9-1-1 and reported an officer down. "You saved us," she said. "We'd be dead without you. All four of us. They're on their way. They'll save you."

She hated to leave him like that, but help was coming, and Shelley waited.

Sara walked over, straddled Shelley and knelt down, leaning over her defeated foe.

Shelley said, "You'll never get rid of me."

"You sure about that?"

"Get used to looking over your shoulder."

"Michael, he told me about your foster home. They did some bad stuff to you, but before that, you were somebody's little girl once. Somebody's sweet little baby. Look at you now. Such—such *evil*. And you may have turned Michael, but at least he had a soul."

"He was weak."

Sara grabbed Shelley by the sides of her head. "No, he was human. You're a monster, and I don't give a fuck about the messed up shit you had to deal with, but those are *my* kids. Do you understand me? You fucked with the wrong woman," she said, thrashing Shelley's head around. "How *dare* you. I hope you burn in Hell."

Shelley grinned. "When I get there, I'll tell Brian you said hello."

Sara tightened her grip. "End of Level Three, right? Before I came in here, you told me I had one last question. Well, here it is, bitch. Are you ready to play *my* game? I like to call it...*Resolution*."

She slammed the back of Shelley's skull into the floor once, twice, three times, knocking her unconscious.

Sara fell over. Exhausted. Relieved.

Knowing she'd done it.

Knowing her children were going to be okay.

Knowing she'd won...the game.

Epilogue

Sara struggled with letting the kids out of her sight, even months later. Like most children, time passed differently for them, and the events of that day were a distant and lightly scarred memory. Something they referred to as 'Remember that time?' while Sara dreamed of dying in a cage beside Teddy's lifeless body, night after night. At the office, she was a frazzled mess in a well-pressed business suit. The only things on Lacey, Callie, and Jacob's minds were the inevitable end of summer break and the return to school in a week. She dreaded sending them back to where it had all started and had entertained the idea of homeschooling.

But life had to go on. She kept reminding herself that she'd succeeded, but peace of mind was not a prize that she had won.

The only thing that gave her comfort was a single news article regarding an incident at Coffee Creek, a female correctional facility nearby. It was vague, hinting at what happened to those who committed crimes against children. It was easy to assume that many of those women were mothers themselves and hadn't taken kindly to the new inmate. No names were given in the article, but Sara had a good idea of whom the victim might've been.

Miss Willow became a bigger part of their world, often staying over and holding Sara's hand at three o'clock in the morning, talking, and watching wisps of steam rise from chamomile tea. These impromptu therapy sessions helped Sara sleep through the remainder of the night.

Sometimes.

Sara knew that someday she would emerge from the cocoon of regret and self-doubt as a stronger, take-no-shit person, but for now, the recovery process was doing its job, albeit slowly. But it was better than sitting in a padded room, bound in a straightjacket.

She'd started referring to Jacob as "Jake," creating the nickname in an attempt to disassociate him from the memory of his father's betrayal. Some days, it worked. Some days, it seemed silly to try. So many of his facial features—his smile, the dimples in his cheeks—were all carbon copies of his dad's, making it difficult to forget and move on. One day.

Teddy, bless his narcissistic, egotistical heart, had returned to his normal self around LightPulse. Offending everyone in proximity, pushing the limits of acceptability, causing two of their strongest employees to quit. He'd stared Death in the face, and had come away from it with a renewed, invigorated sense of being untouchable. Jim had called Sara into his office one afternoon, asking for her counsel on how he should go about firing his own son. She'd talked him out of it, and, as far as she was concerned, she and Teddy were an inch closer to being even.

Besides, when they were on the private side of closed office doors, he treated her with the reverence and respect that had been missing from their professional relationship for so many years. He said 'yes, ma'am' and 'no, ma'am'. Liked to call her B.C., short for 'Badass Chick'. She'd stopped calling him 'Little One' as promised, and encouraged the rest of the senior staff to do the same. Yet another fraction closer to making up for playing God with his life.

And then, on a wet Saturday in September, she loaded the kids into the minivan, stopped to pick up Miss Willow, and drove to the cemetery.

Sara parked and stepped into the drizzly, gray morning, leaving them behind. The light rain sprinkled her face as she zipped her jacket higher to block the wind, holding the bouquet of lilies and baby's breath close to her chest. She trudged up the grassy hillside, breeze lifting the hem of her black dress, passing simple plaques with nothing more than a last name jammed into the muddy ground. Markers with elaborate designs carved into the granite. Ornate cherub statues placed by those with enough money, or enough care, to do so.

So much death buried around her. Such little time they all had. How many broken hearts were out there in the world while their loved ones rested peacefully underneath her feet?

She stopped at the gravestone she'd come to see, which was nestled amongst a group of plain gray rectangles with simple designs and simpler lettering. Sara swiped her rain soaked hair from her face, stared at the name carved into the rock. Knelt down close to it.

"You were a good man," she said, "and it wasn't supposed to happen like this. But how often do things turn out like they should, you know? Happy endings aren't always happy for everyone. I think about you a lot. I wonder about what you'd be doing, where you'd be right now. You're here because of me, and—and I haven't figured out how to deal with that yet, but I'll keep coming back until I do, I promise. Maybe after that, too. See you next week, okay?"

She laid the flowers down at the base of the granite block, read the words as she had so many times before.

DET. JONATHAN JOHNSON
"LOVED AND RESPECTED"
1977-2012

Sara stood, traced her fingers across the top of the gravestone, and walked down the hillside, back to her family.

Back to where they were close.

Close…and safe.

. . .

End of Book #1

SARA'S PAST

Chapter One

Detective Emerson Barker was *not* happy.

He marched across the playground, enduring yet another sprinkling, foggy afternoon in Portland, Oregon. You'd think the gods would allow the weekends to be nice, if nothing else, but at least the changing leaves gave some color to the drab, dreary gray.

As he approached the squealing children, he thought about his former partner, a memory that would never fade.

Detective Jonathan Johnson, DJ, JonJon, had taken a bullet trying to protect the woman that Barker now trudged toward. It had been honorable of DJ, trading his life for this small family, but damn, one life lost was one too many.

Barker thought, *It's been what, well over a year already? Time don't wait for the dead to come back, but we still miss you, cowboy.*

He stepped in a puddle, splashing sandy, dirty water onto his slacks, making his left shoe soggy and cold. "Son of a—" He caught the last word, wrenched it back, realizing he was within earshot of Sara Winthrop and her children. The twins, Lacey and Callie, and Jacob, her son, who was unfortunate enough to have not one, but two older sisters to torment him.

Over the past year, Barker had occasionally checked in on the Winthrops, making sure they were mentally sound and had gotten their lives nudged in the right direction again. Surviving the kidnapping, beating that crazy girl, Shelley Sergeant, at her own game—it'd been rougher on Sara than the kids.

Although, since he'd last checked maybe two months ago, she seemed to be settling into something that could resemble normality. Finally.

Which is exactly why he was so red-faced pissed regarding his current assignment. But, as they say, bullshit rolls downhill, and he was left with the task of asking Sara Winthrop to come out of retirement, so to speak. As he approached Sara but before he greeted her, his last thought was of Donald Timms, the pristine jerk from the FBI, and how he wished he'd told the self-righteous dickwad where he could shove it back in the captain's office that morning.

. . .

Sara moved from child to child to child, pushing them on the swings, laughing and avoiding the shoe-scuffed, rain-filled crevices below each one. "Watch your feet," she said. "The sharks might nibble on your toes."

The mist had evolved into a drizzle, and Barker angled his umbrella against the wind, blocking the cool shards of precipitation prickling his cheeks. He said, "You do know it's raining, right?"

Sara jumped, yelped, and covered her mouth. She said, "Barker. Jesus, you scared the sh—you scared the *crap* out of me."

Still jumpy, Barker thought. *That'll probably never go away. Not completely.*

"Sorry about that. I know better."

Sara forced an awkward smile and nodded. "You should."

"Went by your house. Miss Willow said I could find you down here." The wind kicked up and brought with it heavier, fatter drops of rain. Barker shuddered and turned his back to the onslaught. "Never stops, does it? Can we go over to that shelter? I'd like to talk to you about something."

"Sure. Kids? Come on, it's raining too much, let's follow Mr. Bloodhound over to the shelter, okay?" Like most Portland children who were used to it, the rain was just another aspect of typical northwestern weather to ignore, and they protested. Sara insisted and off they went, running, with the twins in the lead and Jacob quickly catching up.

Barker took a longer, steadier look at Sara. A few more streaks of gray in her hair—brought on by stress, most likely—and the darkness under her eyes had deepened a shade or two. "You sleeping much?" He held his umbrella over her head as they walked.

"Yeah. A little here and there. Why?"

"Just checking." Of course he wasn't going to say anything about her appearance. It'd only taken him three ex-wives to learn that lesson.

Sara crossed her arms, tucked her hands into the warmth of her armpits, and leaned further into him under the umbrella. "I look like hell, don't I?"

Barker smirked. "Objection, Your Honor. Leading the witness."

Sara chuckled. It was good to hear that laugh. He wondered how much of that had gone on around the Winthrop household lately. A wild guess said not much on Sara's part.

Settling back into normal didn't mean that memories disappeared. But, post-trauma, she was about as good as she could be, he reckoned. She was surviving, and that coupled with time was all it took a strong person like her to hand the past an ass whooping with an eight-pound sledgehammer.

When they reached the shelter Sara sent the kids off to the other side, told them to use their imaginations and play a game that didn't involve torturing Jacob. She said to Barker, "If that poor boy makes it through high school, I'll be surprised. Do you have sisters?" They sat down on a picnic bench where the wood was faded, gray like the sky, and speckled with pigeon droppings.

Barker shook out his umbrella and pulled it closed. "One older," he said. "Name was Beth and the sweetest woman I ever knew. Well, not when she was younger. Growing up, I'd've been lucky to have your two running the show. They're cupcakes compared to how my sister was way back then. Once we got older, every time I'd go visit and see that bubbly smile, I couldn't help but think that wasn't the girl I grew up with."

"Do you see her much?"

"Nah, she passed about three years ago. Brain tumor took her way too early."

Sara nodded. "It's always too early with something like that."

"Right."

"So what's up, Mr. Bloodhound? Still coming around to make sure I'm sane?" She leaned back, looking past his shoulders. "Jacob, no hanging from the rafters, please!"

"But Mom—"

"I said *no*, and how did you even manage to get up there?"

"Just let me—"

"Down. Now."

Barker watched in amusement as Jacob dropped to a picnic table and hopped down to the concrete flooring. He'd never had children of his own, and seeing other folks deal with theirs made him both regret and applaud his decision. "He's a handful, huh?"

"You want him?" Sara asked. "No charge."

"I'm good, thanks." Barker pulled a cinnamon-flavored toothpick from the breast pocket of his suit coat and tucked it into the corner of his mouth. He'd given up smoking six months ago and so far, so good. Except for that morning. It would've been the perfect sendoff to spark up and blow a plume of smoke in Donald Timms's face.

"Still quit?" Sara asked.

"Yup. I ran two miles yesterday, too."

"Good for you."

"Let me rephrase. I shuffled and coughed up a lung for two miles. Anyway," Barker said, getting up from the picnic table, groaning as he went, feeling the soreness in unused muscles. Tomorrow would be hell. He sighed, put his hands in the pockets of his slacks, and shook his head. He stared out across the playground through the sheets of rain, looking at the tree line across the open soccer field. "Sara, I don't want to do this."

"Do what?" She squinted at him with that questioning look that was a mixture of confusion and get-to-the-point.

"We have...uh...we have a situation, and the suits...well, they wanted me to ask you for help. And I told 'em, I said, no sir, she's been through enough already and I'm not dragging her into something like this. I mean, it's big, like national security big, and there's this guy from the FBI named Donald Timms and he's got perfect hair and the whitest teeth you've ever seen. Real jerk, you know? But he's a Fed and what the Almighty says goes, at least that's the way it works in—"

"Barker...what?" Sara interrupted, slightly shaking her head.

He pinched the bridge of his nose and took a deep breath. "Right. Sorry. I ramble when I get fired up."

"Did I hear you right? Did you say the FBI wants *my* help with something that has to do with national security?"

Barker instinctively reached for a cigarette pack and grumbled when he found the empty spot where they'd been for most of his adult life. Had he quit too soon? Like his nicotine quit coach had said, "There's never a better time than yesterday."

Barker sat down again, planting his rear on the bench this time, below Sara, and looked up at her, shaking his head. "It's the damnedest thing, and I'm still not certain he's telling us the truth. He's shiftier than some of the CIA spooks I've worked with before. Regardless, something's going on, and I have no say in it whatsoever, but they sent me here because we've got history, and they thought you'd be more responsive to the idea if it came from me. Not to mention the fact that you're the expert."

"Expert at what? What idea?"

Barker could sense that she was irritated with him. Hell, he would be too, with all this gibberish, beating around the bush, and not getting to the point. Still, he couldn't come right out and say the words. He knew she'd decline, or try to, so what was the point of asking? And why was he having so much trouble putting the request out there anyway? It wasn't the fear of rejection—he *wanted* her to say no—but maybe it was the thought of bringing up the past and shredding the thin fabric of her stability.

But he could lose his job if he didn't, so the words had to come out, no matter what. Plus, if she said no to him, that wouldn't stop Donald Timms from paying her a visit and utilizing more coercive techniques. The FBI always gets their man, right?

Rather than asking straight up with no background, Barker decided to try a different tactic. "Did you hear about that bombing in London? The one about two months ago?"

"Yeah, it was awful, but what does that have to—"

Barker held up a hand, stopping her. "I'll get there in a second, okay? So, counting back, we got the bombing in London," he said, counting them on his fingers, "the one in Rio, then Beijing before that, and then Moscow. Follow me so far?"

Sara nodded.

"And if I asked you what all four of them had in common, you'd probably say, 'Four bombs exploded and killed a bunch of people,' and you'd be right, but it wouldn't be the right answer. What I'm authorized to tell you—the thing all four of these bombings have in common is—"

Sara gasped. "Cities in *Juggernaut*."

Juggernaut was her employer's top selling game, a first person shooter that had firmly established the company's position as an industry leader.

"True. But it sounds like a stretch to say that they're all connected by a video game. If the Feds only had that to go on, I'd round up every greenhorn, rookie beat cop I could find so they could tell them how stupid the idea was. Hell, I bet we could even ask Jacob and he'd laugh it off."

Sara scooted down from the picnic tabletop and sat on the bench beside Barker. She lowered her voice and had trouble hiding her laughter. "You're saying that the FBI thinks that four terrorist bombings in four random cities are somehow connected by the *Juggernaut* series? I mean, you're kidding, right? Did they hit a dead end already?"

"I know it sounds ridiculous—"

"It's *insane*, Barker."

"—but they think it's a real threat."

"Four *random* cities that just happen to be cities in a video game that I run marketing campaigns for. It's a coincidence. If you're going to count London, Beijing, Moscow, and Rio, then why not Toronto and Cairo? Or Sydney? Or...or Portland, for that matter?"

"That's the thing, Sara. Mr. Timms knows more than he's letting on. I don't know what any of it means, and it could just be a humongous coincidence, but he'd like to talk to you."

"I don't see how I could actually help him, Barker."

"My guess is the asshole wants to use you as bait."

Chapter Two

Quirk blinked and held his breath, concentrating on the two wires in his hands.

A bead of sweat ran down his forehead, arced around his eyebrow, and crawled into the corner of his eye. He cringed at the sting but tried to ignore it. The material on the table in front of him was highly volatile—some new mixture out of the Middle East that his group had managed to procure without too much effort.

After the government had shut down DarkTrade, the world's biggest black market website, and sent the owner to prison, Quirk and his cohorts had to scramble to find a replacement if they were going to stay on schedule.

Luckily, the panic had only lasted about twelve hours before a member of The Clan was able to make a connection. A few illicit transactions through untraceable currency sites, and the package arrived a week later. With all the precautions and safety measures in place by Homeland Security, it still amazed him how easily it was to get something onto U.S. soil if you knew how to do it. Or knew which people could be bribed, bought, or coerced.

With DarkTrade gone, it wasn't like the FBI or the CIA had cut the head off of the snake and that was the end. No, all they did was give rise to twenty more sites just like it, all clamoring to be the new superpower of underworld exchanges.

Drugs, information, weapons, sex…whatever level of debauchery you needed, somebody out there had it for sale. Six months ago, when they'd been prepping for Beijing, Quirk had come across a guy selling, what he claimed to be, one of Hitler's molars. The dude said he had dental records for proof. Quirk doubted the veracity of that claim, but some collector with more money than sense snatched it up for a couple million. For that kind of cash, Quirk had briefly considered yanking out one of his own with a pair of pliers. Surely one of his teeth could pass for Stalin's, couldn't it?

That kind of thinking was old habits dying hard. He didn't need to resort to desperate tactics anymore. Get in with the wrong crowd for the right reason, come with a necessary skill, and watch the decimal places in your bank account launch sideways in a hurry. He'd been careful, subdued, and fully intended to stay invisible as long as possible. No garish purchases like cars or mansions; no flashing stacks of hundreds in strip clubs; no bling…for now—just the simple things that made life a little easier, like paying the bills on time and having something healthier than microwave pizza in the freezer.

If everything went as planned—and he knew it would, because they were meticulous and undetectable—in a year he would be sipping cocktails on a yacht somewhere in the South Pacific. He wouldn't be Mark "Quirk" Ellis anymore. The new Quirk would have a completely clean identity that said he was David Davis, former stock trader that had made millions by betting the right way when the housing bubble had burst.

The Clan had connections, and thus, Quirk had connections.

He twisted the exposed wires together then wrapped a layer of black electrical tape around the mated area. He tucked it inside the casing, gently positioning it around whatever the malleable, explosive material was out of Kabul, Afghanistan, and then secured the bottom of the casing to the laptop. He exhaled a sigh of relief when he righted the device and didn't become hamburger.

Quirk had been assured that the stability was slightly better than the words "highly volatile" suggested and he was in no danger, but you couldn't be too careful when you were working with something exotic. He knew a couple of guys who'd learned that lesson the hard way.

He wiped the sweat from his forehead and trusted his sixth sense.

Good, he thought. *That should do it. Now for the test.*

Quirk turned on the laptop and watched it cycle through the normal boot sequence. He rolled his chair back a couple of inches and turned his head to the side.

As if that would make a difference.

Some self-preservation instincts can't be helped.

The screen cast a blue glow across his face and all seemed normal. It looked like a regular laptop that anyone could be using in a coffee shop while they drank their five-dollar cappuccinos.

This particular work of art could be detonated two different ways. First, by a remote cell signal, his preferred method, and second, a hands-on approach, if his superiors wanted to see a target's face before it evaporated.

They asked him to test it, which he reluctantly agreed to, and if Rocket had programmed the back end correctly, all he had to do was press Enter and then answer with a "Y" or "N" when prompted with the question, "Engage?"

Quirk reached over, held a shaky hand above the Enter button, made the sign of the cross over his chest, even though he wasn't Catholic, and lowered his finger—

An annoying ringtone blared on the table beside the lamp. Quirk cursed and backed away from the bomb, then picked up the disposable phone and spat out a greeting. "What?"

"Is this Quirk?"

He didn't recognize the voice. Only three people had the number and whoever this was, she wasn't one of them. Protocol and common sense said to hang up, but he had a feeling that that wouldn't be wise. "Who's asking?"

"Boudica."

Every muscle in Quirk's body clenched. Part nervous reaction, part fear...all valid. Boudica, leader of The Clan, named after a Celtic queen who had led a bloody uprising against the Romans a couple thousand years ago, was ruthless, emotionless, and so, so dangerous. He'd never met her in person, but Quirk was absolutely certain that he had no desire to meet Boudica in a McDonald's or a dark alley, ever.

He stammered, "Oh—*oh*, right. How did you get—I mean, who—so, uh, what's up?" Quirk shook his head and rolled his eyes.

'What's up?' Really?

"What's up," Boudica said, "is my blood pressure, Captain Quirk."

Quirk stifled a chuckle. Captain Quirk. He'd heard rumors that she had a sense of humor when she was in a good mood—which was rare, apparently—and temporarily considered making some sort of comment about the *Enterprise*, but decided against it. "We don't want that," he replied.

"No, we don't. Rocket tells me you're close. Are you still on schedule?"

"I don't mean to brag, but I'm ahead, actually. Putting on the finishing touches just now and was about to test the initiation sequence."

"Perfect, because we're moving it up a week."

Quirk nearly dropped the cell phone. He stood up and knocked his head on the low-hanging light. It danced around and sent erratic shadows flailing throughout the room. "A week? I'm not so sure that's a—I mean, we should do more testing and I don't know how well this stuff travels, and there are a lot of things that could—"

"Next Tuesday, Quirk. No questions."

He'd become a hermit over the past forty-eight hours and had stayed so secluded and detached from reality that he had trouble

remembering what day it was, if it was light outside, or if the digital time display above his desk was AM or PM. He double-checked and realized it was seven o'clock Saturday morning, which meant—
"That's way too soon. Will all the pieces be in place by then?"

"Are you questioning my judgment?

"No, honest to God, I'm not, Boudica...Miss Boudica...ma'am. Um, it's just that, well, I'm sure you remember what happened in London."

"I do. And whose fault was that?"

"Mine, sort of, but not completely, because—"

"It won't happen again, will it, Quirk?"

"No, ma'am." Quirk felt that morning's breakfast of Mountain Dew and candy corn roiling in his stomach. Bright idea at the time; he'd needed the dual-action caffeine blast and sugar rush to keep from face-planting into Kabul's finest unstable putty. But now the concoction of soda and sugar felt like syrupy acid bubbling up and melting his insides.

"I didn't think so. Now, here's what I want you to do. Crawl out of that little cave you call a workshop, shower, dress, whatever, and make yourself presentable, then I want you to meet with Cleo down at Powell's, okay?"

Quirk agreed, but wondered why she wanted them to meet in such a public place.

Boudica answered the unasked question for him. "You two Portland hipsters will blend in to the crowd there, so it'll be a perfect place to scout undetected. Flannel, skinny jeans, just look like you belong, got me? She'll brief you on the new details."

The skin on his arms prickled. "Are we doing the drop *there?*"

Before, their targets had been low-key places. Sure, they'd resulted in some casualties, but they were considered collateral damage and merely an aspect of the objective they were trying to accomplish. Regardless of what the latest scientific study reported, violent video games like the *Juggernaut* series led to an increase in violent behavior in children, and the population of Earth needed to see that on a much grander scale.

The way things worked in the world, some kid would get shot in rural Oklahoma and people would blame it on the hottest new first person shooter, which might cause it to be newsworthy for about twenty-four hours, only to be replaced by the next major headline: "Celebutante names baby girl after fruit."

However, if somebody raised the stakes to the point where it could no longer be ignored, then surely some regulatory commissions would be formed. Someone would pay attention.

Every member of The Clan, from Boudica on down to the delivery driver, Tank, was a former gamer who'd lost a close friend or family member to video game violence. The propagandists insisted the phenomenon didn't exist. They insisted that blood, guts, guns, bullets, and scattered body parts flashing across the screen and into young minds were no more harmful than watching Jerry the mouse smash Tom the cat over the head with a mallet.

Boudica cleared her throat. She was angry now, and there would be no more jokes about Captain Quirk. "I'm starting to think your commitment might not be at the level we need."

"No, no, I'm cool—"

"Cool? I don't care if you're a penguin on an iceberg. Are you in this one hundred percent or not, Quirk?"

"Yes, ma'am. All the way."

"And I don't need to send him in?"

"Him? No. God, no. Please. I wasn't questioning you or anything like that—you caught me off guard. I wasn't expecting things to escalate so quickly." And especially not right here in his backyard. Not right in the heart of downtown Portland.

The "him" she was referring to was Boudica's own version of a black-ops cleaner. In the two years The Clan had been planning and executing missions, the Spirit had been necessary only once, when a financier of theirs had threatened exposure. In their smoky back-room meetings and secret chat rooms, no one had been able to figure out why. They made no profit off their illicit behaviors. Didn't want financial gain, didn't need financial gain. Their objective was information. So why had this guy Alvarez tried to blackmail them? He had nothing to achieve.

The only suggestion that made even the slightest bit of sense was a lover's quarrel, and if Boudica had no issues with having someone eliminated that she'd shared bodily fluids with, then scraping an uncooperative Quirk off the bottom of her shoe would be a small checkmark on her list.

All Quirk and the other members need to stay loyal and subservient was one look at the gruesome pictures of Alvarez following the Spirit's work, accompanied by a message to think before they acted.

Boudica said, "*Your* job, Quirk, is to make things go *boom*. My job is to make sure people pay attention. You worry about your job, I'll worry about mine."

Quirk mumbled in agreement, but that was it. He was positive that no matter what words came out of his mouth, they'd be misconstrued and he'd wake up in the middle of the night with that familiar stranger hovering over him.

Boudica added, "Powell's at ten. You'll remember Cleo when you see her, won't you?"

"Yes," Quirk said, thinking, *How could I forget?*

Chapter Three

There weren't enough chairs in the small office to accommodate the silent, waiting crowd. For most of them, it wasn't the way they'd intended to spend their Saturday. They had better things to do than stand in an unrented office on the third floor of a downtown Portland high-rise.

The previous occupants had left behind a desk, four chairs, and a whiteboard.

Sara had asked why they didn't meet somewhere that made sense. Barker had only been able to shrug and say that it was what Timms had requested.

Sitting on the opposite side of the desk in his usual position of authority, the President, CEO, and chief motivator of LightPulse Technologies reclined in the high-backed leather chair and tented his fingertips. He brought the forefingers up to his lips and then rested his chin on the thumbs below. He appeared to be lost in thought, but Sara knew it wasn't true. Jim Rutherford was never *lost* when he was doing anything.

Whatever turned the gears inside that skull housed under a thin sheet of salt and pepper hair had to be some brilliant plan full of such devious machinations that this so-called terrorist group would be wise to tuck tail and vanish. Sara hoped so, at least. From the way the conversation had gone so far, she'd gotten the vibe that

LightPulse was more of a target than she was bait, as Barker had assumed.

Jim was dressed in his standard outfit of jeans, sneakers, and a black turtleneck, which now was more of a tribute to Steve Jobs than some subtle attempt to emulate the late tech giant.

To Jim's left, leaning against the window with his arms crossed and one leg halfway propped up on a short table, was Teddy Rutherford, Sara's former (and sometimes current) nemesis.

He was Jim's privileged son, and had also managed to survive the wrath of Shelley Sergeant and her massive, intimidating, and morose brother, Michael. But not without a few broken bones and blackened bruises that took weeks to disappear. Sara had saved Teddy's life and occasionally wondered why, especially when he was having too much fun being...well, *Teddy*.

Thank God for small miracles, because he was in a cooperative mood, which could've been due to the presence of Karen Wallace, the private investigator that Jim kept on retainer after Sara's incident. She sat to Barker's left, and Teddy didn't have to turn his head more than a couple of degrees to ogle her.

And why shouldn't he? She was tall, beautiful, highly intelligent, well spoken, had a concealed-carry permit, and didn't want a damn thing to do with his too-polished, bronzer-coated melon. Her lack of interest fueled Teddy's need to chase, however futile the possibilities.

Agent Donald Timms of the FBI, whom Sara knew nothing about, stood to the left of Karen, next to the inter-office windows that looked into an empty hallway, where doors led to other empty offices.

Timms seemed distracted and bored by having to mingle with the mortals while he briefed them of details. Underneath his professional exterior was a layer of creepiness that didn't sit right with Sara.

In reality he was probably fine, but call it a mother's intuition, whatever the case, she wasn't sure she'd leave her children alone in a room with the guy.

Six people total, five of them waiting on Jim Rutherford to say something.

Anything.

Jim leaned forward and opened his mouth, then sank back into his seat.

Timms finally spoke. "I'm sure you understand there are time considerations."

Jim flicked a dismissive glance at him, followed it with an eye roll, and said to Teddy, "Did you see this coming?"

Teddy gulped, stammered, and shrugged, reacting as if he'd been caught dipping into Daddy's liquor cabinet. "Me, no...I—this is...Sara's the one who—"

Sara uncrossed her legs, leaned forward with her elbows on her knees, and stared at Teddy. Eyebrows raised, lips pinched tightly together, head angled to one side as if to say, *Sara's the one who* what, *you little shit?*

Teddy nodded an acknowledgment. He knew better. The days of passing the blame were gone. Same team. Don't mess with the badass chick.

He continued, "There's no way that we could've predicted this. Sara and I are involved in development and marketing. How could *we* have seen it coming? And for that matter, why would any of these bombs be specifically related to LightPulse? That's all I'm asking."

"And you're asking it so clearly." Barker smirked and waggled the toothpick in his mouth.

Teddy pushed himself away from the window and reasserted his position with his hands on his hips. "You know what I mean."

"Maybe."

Timms cleared his throat. "If I may?"

Jim ignored him and said to Sara, "What're your thoughts?"

"If I may, sir?" Timms repeated.

"You may not," Jim said. Unruffled, without making eye contact, and staring at a hangnail instead, he added, "Agent Timms, I don't care if you're J. Edgar himself. You bring us here under clandestine pretenses, insinuating that my company, my games, and my employees are responsible for these atrocities...I'm not a fan of it. So I'd like to ask my associates some questions before I decide whether or not to give merit to your ludicrous claims."

"We have evidence this is related to LightPulse. The informants all say..."

Jim held up a hand and Timms let his words trail off into frustrated silence.

Sara wondered how long he'd put up with Jim's posturing before he began asserting some federal dominance. *Whose is bigger, boys? Who cares? Put them away; there are more important issues to discuss.*

"Sara?"

She looked at Barker and managed to nod and shake her head at the same time. "Detective Barker could only tell me so much, but honestly, Jim, I don't have the slightest clue. I'm sure Agent Timms can speak more to this—"

"I can, if you'll let me—"

"—but the only connection we can see at this level is the fact that they're all cities in *Juggernaut*. It could easily be the same for ProVision's *Task Force Delta* or...what's the other one, Teddy?"

"*Black Wing Fighter*. GameCon."

"Right, *BWF*."

Jim said, "Not necessarily. GameCon moved away from the global playing area with *BWF*. They didn't have the workforce to keep that exhaustive level of development up."

"Still," Sara reminded him, "London, Beijing...all the cities that have been hit were there in their previous versions."

Jim and Teddy nodded in agreement.

Karen Wallace was finally kind enough to interject and give Timms the chance to speak. As a former FBI agent herself, having left the spit-polished life of federal investigation for the more lucrative world of public enterprise, she was sympathetic to him, yet slightly pleased by the fact that he probably wasn't used to being so dismissed.

She said, "Before we get too far into the whys, I'd like to hear what Timms knows. Is that okay with you, Jim?"

Jim nodded curtly; a short, do-as-you-must resignation.

Timms dipped his chin in thanks and stepped over to the whiteboard.

He picked up a blue marker, wrote the names of the cities where the attacks had occurred, and said, "The responsible group is now saying that these attacks are to prove a point, that video games lead to violent behavior, ergo, detonations and casualties around the world. It's a bit ironic, isn't it? Blowing things up to draw attention to youth violence? Anyway, London, Rio, Beijing, Moscow...you've all been briefed on what seems like a flimsy, superficial connection to your *Juggernaut* series by the good Detective Barker here. As far as we know, that's all it is. Coincidence.

"These are major cities in the world where a lot happens, so it stands to reason that yes, it's an insubstantial correlation. If I'm familiar enough with the concept of your game; the bombings could've been in any major metropolis and it still would've made a sliver of a connection to *Juggernaut*. However, that's not what brings me here. Something definitely happened in these cities... something that ties itself to LightPulse in a roundabout way." He finished by underlining each city name and tapping the board beside them. "And, contrary to what you might believe, the FBI isn't omnipotent—"

Barker chuckled and interrupted, "Could've fooled me."

Timms said, "Despite Barker's misgivings about our capabilities, *at first*, this string of bombings looked like nothing more than the work of a random terrorist group. We figured it was the usual suspects like Al Qaeda or any number of Middle Eastern extremist groups that aren't big enough or well-funded enough to catch the public's attention. But there were dead ends all around. None of them stepped forward to take credit for the attacks, nor did we have any false claims like we typically do."

Teddy asked, "You get a lot of those?"

"More than we'd like, since the required manpower to follow up on those leads can be limited, but they usually check out fake and we overlook them like some new kid trying to make a name for himself on the playground. It was unusual, honestly, because we typically get at least one camp that sends a message from their cave in Afghanistan, but not this time."

Karen raised a hand and didn't wait for Timms to acknowledge her. "Why do you think that is?"

Timms shrugged. "We don't know. It doesn't make any sense to us, either. The only thing that our exploratory teams can assume—"

Barker said, "Ass out of you and me."

"The only thing that makes sense is that the attacks were initially too small and they figured it wasn't worth their time. If you're a tiny group trying to get attention, it doesn't make a big enough impression if all you did was blow up a GameStop and recorded no casualties. On the opposite side of that, if you're Al Qaeda, it's beneath you. See where I'm going with this? Al Qaeda is in the business of trying to upset the world balance, not trying to disintegrate a couple of Playstations. We rounded up every informant we could find that was familiar with this style of work and none of them had anything new for us. We figured we'd start with the tangibles— the concrete evidence we had to go on. The bomb maker, whoever he may be, is military trained, but his signatures aren't consistent enough for us to determine by *whose* military. We think he's a former U.S. Marine, but he could just as easily be Israeli Intelligence."

Barker said, "I thought we were friends with the Israelis?"

"And a former Marine used to bleed red, white, and blue. What's your point?"

"What's yours?"

"He's clever enough to hide his tracks well, but the traces he's left behind suggest friendly fire, Detective."

Sara stood and joined Timms at the whiteboard. "So basically what you're telling us is that you have no idea who these people are, but for some unknown reason you think their motives are tied to *our* games."

"That's…not entirely true."

"Then what *is* true, Agent Timms? Did you just pick LightPulse out of a hat, or are you going from office to office, hoping something might stick out enough for you to latch onto it? Because, believe me, you asked for *my* help specifically, but I am *not* interested in getting involved in something like this if it's nothing more than a random assumption. Not after the year I've had. I don't know if Detective Barker filled you in on my situation or not—"

"He did."

"—but I'm definitely not prepared to help you go looking for something that may not exist, especially if it's going to put my children in danger again—or Teddy, for that matter."

Teddy grinned. "Thanks, Sara."

"Mrs. Winthrop," Timms said, "you won't be in any kind of danger. That's a promise."

"Promises are broken. Can you guarantee it?"

"Fine, I guarantee that you won't be in any danger."

"Uh-huh, right," she said, not believing a word of it. "Detective Barker here thought you were up to something, so why me? Why not Jim or Teddy? I mean, I'm sorry, guys," Sara said, looking at the father and son, "I'm not trying to throw you under the bus, but you know just as much as I do about *Juggernaut*, if not more. Right?"

Timms picked up the whiteboard eraser and scrubbed away his scribbling. "Because of this." He wrote seven names on the board:

"Boudica," "Chief," "Rocket," "Quirk," "Sharkfin," "Tank," and "Cleo."

"Yeah," Sara said, "they're the names of characters in *Juggernaut*. So what? Did you read the instruction manual before you came in?"

"We've identified these seven people as members of a small organization called The Clan. From what we know, they're former gamers, hackers, and scumbags."

"And that relates to me how?"

"It took us a few weeks of digging around in the deepest corners of the internet to come up with something concrete. Using our informants, we started putting out feelers for anything related to these bombings in particular. People talk. People are always talking. They like being in the know, they like having information to share because it gives them a sense of authority. I'd say the two biggest things that have changed world history are sex and that childish sense of hoarding information."

"They like the money, too," Barker added.

"I can't confirm that money is exchanged for information, but… you know."

Teddy stepped around the office desk and sauntered to the back of the room, grinning.

Timms said, "Something funny, Mr. Rutherford?"

"I'm not saying I know this for certain," Teddy said, shrugging. "I mean…the FBI may have the brightest and sharpest people working for them that money can buy, yet they don't hold a candle to some of the hackers and gamers out there that never finished high school. I'm sure you know that and have probably tried to recruit them. I would be willing to bet my stock in LightPulse that there's some MIT graduate living in his mom's basement, chugging Red Bull and surviving on Ramen who hasn't seen the sun for days—he's out there running circles around your Ivy League robots."

"Meaning?"

Teddy glanced at Karen Wallace, smirking. Posturing. Showing off his plumage, hoping that, eventually, the mating call would work. He said, "You can't be that naïve, can you? Seriously, if you found these people through some underground network on the internet, it's only because they *wanted* you to find them. And… *and*, they probably know which analyst did it and what shoe size he wears."

Sara shrugged. "Teddy's probably right."

"Oh, we're aware," Timms said, sneering. "Which is part of the reason I'm here to talk to *you*, Mrs. Winthrop."

Chapter Four

Quirk didn't wait for the crosswalk sign to change. He ignored the bright orange hand and dashed across the street, hearing the polite *beep* of a hybrid Honda's horn, rather than a wailing honk. That was one of the many things he loved about Portland. The sheer niceness that emanated from every pore of environmentally conscious skin and oozed from every crack in the sidewalk.

Portland was so much different than his native New York City. The dreaded visits home had become fewer with more time between them as the years had passed. He hadn't been back to Long Island since his brother Alan came home from Iraq with a flag draped over the casket.

That was four years ago. Two years ago, after Alan's widow, Melissa, had packed up and moved, heartbroken, back to North Carolina, his nephew had died from a gunshot wound to the chest. Brandon had been buried on a rainy afternoon. Quirk would never forget that day.

The courts, in their infinite wisdom, had ruled it an accident, but Quirk knew better. All the signs of bullying and violence, brought on by video games, were there. All the signs were overlooked.

Brandon was twelve years old when his father died. He buried himself in online gaming to hide from the pain, because what else do teen boys do? "Feelings" are reserved for bad poetry, written to the cute girl in class who won't offer a second glance—feelings weren't meant for anyone that might actually listen and help.

Though he lived three thousand miles away, Quirk had tried to make a connection with his nephew. They spent hours online together, chatting over headsets, playing *Juggernaut*, and Quirk thought he'd reached a breakthrough.

Brandon had become more willing to open up about missing his father, but not long after, he'd complained about some kids from school that were bullying him during rounds of online gaming when Quirk wasn't there to listen in.

Six months later, during what was supposed to be a fun, live-action reenactment of *Juggernaut* organized by the same kids that were pushing him around, Brandon took a bullet to the chest and died on the way to the hospital. The shooter's excuse—"I didn't know it was loaded"—sent Brandon's murderer walking out of the courtroom a free man. Or, a free boy, rather. Quirk was positive that he was the only one to notice the subtle grin on the little prick's face.

Quirk tracked Bobby Marlowe down one night, managed to work himself into the conversation among the young gaming team-mates, and overheard the kid bragging about what he'd done. "You should've seen him," Marlowe had said. "His chest exploded like those little purple alien bastards."

No one believed Quirk. No one would listen. He never let it go. Instead it sat heavy in his stomach, the revenge gestating, waiting for the right opportunity.

Quirk knew the boy was too young, a fourteen-year-old child, but he could wait. Four more years and adulthood would come soon enough. In the meantime, dedicating his talents to The Clan's objective would help pass the time, and, hopefully, draw much-needed attention to the cause.

He stopped beneath the overhang outside of Powell's, pinched the loose material of his nylon windbreaker, and shook it, relieving it from the drops of rain. He took off his skullcap, tucked it into an open pocket, and then tried to mash down his wayward hair.

Quirk caught his reflection in the window. Full beard, brown with flecks of red and traces of blond. A couple of gray ones, too. Those had grown rampant in recent months.

He examined the rounded eyeglasses and unkempt hair. Skinny jeans that hugged the wrong parts in the wrong places and a pair of Chuck Taylors. Flannel shirt underneath the blue windbreaker.

Yeah, he thought, *I look hipster enough. Blending in, like Boudica said.*

It wasn't his style, really, especially not at thirty-eight years old and as a former bomb disposal tech for the United States Marine Corps, but hiding in plain sight with the northwestern camouflage was the easiest route. And besides, Cleo defined hipster. She would appreciate his Portland chic.

Quirk waited for a couple of minutes, anxiously pacing, debating whether to go inside or stand his ground. He checked the time on his cell. She was either late or already among the stacks of books, waiting for him. Just as he was about to turn and push through the door, he felt a hand on his arm. At the same time, he heard the voice of his daydreams. Not so much the voice, exactly, but the woman it belonged to. "Quirk?"

He turned to face her. It'd been a while, but infatuation has a way of warping time, and he remembered her features as if they'd had coffee together that morning.

She was different, but the same.

Her hair was blonde now with blue highlights, shorter—a pixie cut—and a better length and color than the pink bob that she'd had the last time they were together. The hoop in her left nostril had been replaced with a small diamond stud that matched the new addition of a diamond stud in her bottom lip. He didn't need to survey everything about her. He could've drawn a perfect portrait of her from memory, but he liked admiring what he hoped would be his one day. Maybe she liked yachts and the South Pacific.

Quirk shook his head. Had he been staring too long? "Cleo, hi. Good to see you again." He offered his hand to shake and when she took it he felt a warm glow race up his arm and down through his legs.

Those full lips. Wide brown eyes that penetrated everything they focused on. She didn't just see things; she absorbed them. The beautiful row of upper teeth flashed when she smiled and he was glad to see that the left incisor was still a little crooked. Cleo's tiny imperfections were all minor subplots of her new age narrative.

She wore black-rimmed glasses, rectangular in shape, and the color contrasted nicely against her Portland tan, which was to say, alabaster white.

The rest of her attire surprised him. The white top was button-down and collared, followed by a gray pencil skirt and what he supposed were sensible heels.

Cleo looked...professional. Mainstream.

Cleo wasn't her real name, of course. It was a call sign, just like "Quirk" and "Boudica." In real life she was Emily Armstrong, but he wasn't supposed to know that. It could be dangerous if she found out and told Boudica, but the thousand dollars he'd offered some kid on DarkTrade to dig up information had been worth every penny.

Quirk shook her hand long enough to feel the slight tug, the pulling away, that uncomfortable moment of, 'Okay, enough already.'

He said, "You look...great."

Cleo shrugged. "New job," she said. "I'm lucky I get away with the dye and the piercings."

Quirk was already aware of her new position as a bank teller for Wells Fargo. Good for her. Working as a bartender for that strip joint, Mary's, had probably paid better in tips, but the hours were horrible and bad for her health.

He thought about asking why she even bothered to work. If the money from Boudica showed up in the offshore bank account each time for her like it did for him after every successful mission, then she should already be well on her way to freedom from Corporate America and The Man. As far as he could tell, and from what he'd learned while observing her, she simply enjoyed keeping herself busy.

"Well," he said, "they're lucky to have you," earning him an odd look.

Too much, Quirk, dial it down.

To Cleo, they were practically strangers, having met once eighteen months ago in Moscow to scout their first location. Their encounter was brief, but the impression was lasting. They'd posed as a young couple on their honeymoon; they were in, they were out, a used video-game store exploded three days later, and Quirk was in love.

He coughed into his fist and held the door open for her.

She thanked him and walked inside, saying, "Sorry I'm late. I had a friend drop me off, and she wouldn't be on time for her own funeral."

Quirk chuckled and followed her into the miraculous hub of Powell's, Reading Central, one of his favorite places in the city, and in life.

Every city deserved a place brimming with as much awesomeness and goodwill as Powell's. Stories, words, and worlds were introduced to the masses like screaming babies fresh from the womb, or they were given new life, resurrected with that defibrillator known as the enjoyment of a well told tale.

The bottom floor of Powell's was the Orange Level, reminding Quirk of the now-retired terror alert chart put in place by Homeland Security after 9/11. Back then, Orange meant the risk of terrorist activity was high, and given the reason why he and Cleo were there, it fit perfectly.

Cleo reached down and took his hand, locking her fingers with his. "Just like old times," she said. All business, with not a hint of actual nostalgia. "Over here." She pulled; Quirk followed.

Saturday mornings at Powell's were a perfect time to get lost in the crowd. The place hummed with electric excitement. Shoppers carried bags of books. Some pushed carts. They sipped coffee. They browsed for hours while children raced up and down the aisles searching for their parents, begging for this book or that story.

It was one of Quirk's favorite ways to lose an entire day, and it saddened him that after the following Tuesday he might not get another chance.

Cleo tugged his hand and he trailed after her, down a row of business books that was surprisingly empty of browsers. She whispered, "Why?"

"You mean why here?"

Cleo stepped closer. Her perfume smelled like cotton candy. Quirk swooned on the inside. She said, "Why's she changing the plan, huh? Moving it up a week, picking a new place? Doesn't that seem strange to you?"

Quirk nodded. "Totally."

She glanced past his shoulder and mouthed, "Wait," and turned his body with a subtle nudge. The young woman ten feet to their right looked, found what she wanted, and left them alone again. "Okay, she's gone. So what's the deal, do you know?"

"I didn't find out until this morning."

"I mean, I'm in, all the way, but it kinda freaks me out. Doesn't it freak you out? What if somebody's onto us and she's trying to push the agenda before we're ready?"

"You think so?"

"If somebody's onto us, they could have us under surveillance right now. It could've been that chick. Or it could be that guy over there in the purple sweater."

Quirk squeezed her hand. "Don't freak, okay? We're fine. If somebody made us, like the cops or the FBI, we'd already be in cuffs."

"Or they could be giving us just enough rope to hang ourselves with."

"True. I guess the question is who're you more afraid of? The cops or Boudica?"

Cleo pulled her hand free from his, bit her bottom lip, and scratched her head. Crossing her arms under the perfect breasts that Quirk fantasized about on a nightly basis, she said, "We both know the answer to that."

"Right." He glanced away before she could notice him staring at her chest.

"Which means we should probably do our jobs."

Quirk pushed his glasses higher on his nose. "I'll go up top. Start down here and we'll make our way through, then meet back in this aisle in an hour. You remember what to look for, don't you?"

"Yeah, we're looking for places with low traffic but near something structural."

"Good, you remember. Honestly, I don't think it's going to matter much, not with this new stuff we've got. We leave the package on a shelf right here on the ground floor—it'll bring the whole place down. Better safe than sorry, and we should still check it out, so maybe you should watch the patterns of the employees more than trying to find a good drop point. Make sense?"

"I guess, but this is a little different than a few small shops on the other side of the world, Quirk. For God's sake, this is Powell's. It's an institution, and we could potentially...you know, there could be hundreds of them."

Them. Casualties.

"Do you think we could convince her to go for some other place?"

"Would you even have the balls to try?"

He shook his head.

"Then we don't have a choice."

some of the rules are meant to be bent and broken. Happens all the time."

"I'm just saying—"

"You're out of the game. Leave the FBI's business to those that are actually still employed by them, okay? Sound fair to you?"

Karen crossed her arms and looked away. Teddy moved up behind her and Sara noticed him internally debating on whether or not to put a comforting hand on the private investigator's shoulder. Wisely, he decided against it.

Jim said to Timms, "My turn to remind *you*, Agent—there are time considerations here. Get on with it, please. No need to keep beating our chests."

"I completely agree with you, sir. Now, if you'll allow me to finish before asking questions, that would be helpful. Agreed? Everyone? Detective Barker, can we agree on that small courtesy? Good."

Barker winked at Sara. She hid her smile behind a manufactured cough.

Timms continued, "Like the younger Mr. Rutherford so helpfully suggested, we knew going into this that our analysts wouldn't likely escape undetected with the information we needed. There are kids out there, fifteen, sixteen years old, that are brilliant enough to match wits with our top-notch players. It's unfortunate, but we can do nothing about it—well, except for arresting and recruiting them. So rather than trying to sneak in like a bunch of cyber-ninjas and have the whole internet community point and laugh at us like the poor chubby kid at school, we use our informants.

"Miss Wallace and Detective Barker are familiar with this method, I'm sure. You've all seen it on television. That's not to say that we don't have some associates in deep cover, but they're the exception to the rule. Anyway. Our informants found traces of chatter that originated with the most recent event in London and they

Sara stepped away from the whiteboard and returned to her
beside Barker.

Timms made her anxious on a number of different levels,
retreating to Barker's proximity felt like the comforting thing t(
At twenty years older, roughly, maybe it was some sort of prote
father-figure association. Regardless, his masculine mustache
swagger seemed to keep Timms lurking on the perimeter.

She said, "So is this a need-to-know thing, or are you act
going to tell us how I'm connected or why I need to be a part c

Timms placed the cap back on the marker and dropped i
the tray. "I hadn't planned on doing it in a room full of peor
be perfectly honest. But Barker's superiors—and yours, and, i
tunately, mine—have assured me that this level of cooperat
necessary and the only way of getting what we want."

"Cut the bullshit," Barker said. "If this is a matter of na
security and not a single one of us in here has any level of clea
then how in the hell do you expect us to cooperate or help?"

Karen added, "My clearance expired. Jim, Teddy, and Sa
never had any government clearance that I know of, and give
I remember, protocol dictates that we should—"

Timms raised his voice, speaking over Karen, "I don't ca
protocol dictates, Miss Wallace, we're in a unique situation h

managed to trace the chain of communication all the way back to the first event in Moscow."

Sara felt some disdain at the word "event," and the nonchalant usage, as if it were a party or an annual convention instead of an explosion that claimed lives.

Timms continued, "Now, again, as Teddy suggested, it appears as if they *wanted* to be found. These most recent tracks had to have been laid on purpose like Hansel and Gretel on their way to the oven. It was too sloppy. They'd been so careful and, I don't know, *hygienic* in their methods before—a group with their caliber of talent doesn't suddenly become a bunch of bumbling idiots."

"Why would they do that?" Karen asked.

"That's the billion-dollar question, isn't it? Misdirection is the most likely reason. The crumb trail shows no indication that they were in any sort of fear whatsoever that we were onto them. They communicated primarily through untraceable, disposable cell phones in short bursts to avoid any attempts at triangulation, and they used private chat rooms with such an intense system of rerouting that it froze one of our servers trying to trace them. Then, one day, *poof*, it's like they held up a flashing neon sign saying, 'Hey, we're over here!' So that tells us one of two things: either they have a mole inside and they knew we were getting close, or they rolled one of the informants."

Teddy said, "How?"

"Crime pays better than our measly stipends. This is all speculation, of course, but The Clan, which is made up of these seven individuals, they decided that they'd throw themselves out there and offer up information about their next attack, hoping to misdirect us while they went after their actual target."

"Hold on now," Barker said, scooting forward in his chair. "If these dipshits are as smart as you *say* they are, wouldn't it occur to them that it would set off a bunch of alarm bells if all of a sudden they made a huge, honking screw-up after they'd been faultless for so long?"

"Exactly, Detective. Maybe you'd make it in the FBI after all."

"Don't bet on it. Square isn't my favorite shape." Karen and Teddy laughed.

Timms ignored the barb. "We think it's a double-double misdirection."

"Is that your official term?"

"No, I came up with that all by myself, Detective, and I thought we agreed to hold questions until I was finished?"

"*We*," Barker said, pointing at the side of his head, "agreed to no such thing, but in the interest of having lunch before sundown, I'll concede."

"How generous of you."

"Don't mention it."

Getting back to the case, Timms said, "The general consensus is that one, they knew we'd pick up on the fact that this misstep was intentional. Two, the intent was to make us think there were ulterior motives behind it and convince us to look elsewhere. By blatantly telling us what their next target would be, they hoped we'd ignore the fact that they were going to blow up exactly what they told us would be the next target."

Jim said, "I'm sorry, Agent, I don't follow."

Before Timms could answer him, Teddy said, "It's like that cutaway scene in *Troll Towers* where Balthazar says he's going to punch Grogg the Cruel with his left hand, so Grogg dodges left, thinking he's coming from the right, and then Balthazar levels him with that left hook and goes, 'I told you.' Right? Remember that, Sara?"

Sara nodded. "I do, Teddy," she said, slightly bemused at the manchild's nostalgic excitement for a game that was over a decade old—one he'd helped write the storyline for back before he even officially began working for LightPulse.

"My sons played that game," Timms said, "but yes, I think that's about as close of a comparison as I can come up with. Does that work for you, Mr. Rutherford?"

Jim sighed. "I suppose. Continue."

"No, hang on," Barker said. "So you're saying that this group came right out and *told* you what their next target was going to be, hoping you'd look for something else?"

"It looks that way, yes."

"Again, I gotta ask...don't you think they'd be smart enough to know you'd figure *that* out, too?"

"Possibly, but we can go around and around with the whole, 'I know you know that I know that you know,' thing. Eventually you have to pick a direction and go."

"What did they say the target was?" Sara asked.

"The CBOE. The Chicago Board of Exchange."

"Then why're you here? Why aren't you in Chicago trying to stop them there?"

"Because it's not the actual target."

"But you said they came right out and told you what it was."

"I did."

Frustrated, Sara barely managed to contain her anger. "Then what's the goddamn target, Timms? Why are you here? Why am *I* here?"

Teddy's voice was low and somber, so different than his usual hyper tone and energy. He said, "Oh God, it's somewhere in Portland, isn't it?"

Timms nodded. He took off his suit jacket and draped it across the coat rack. He rolled up his sleeves. "The problem is, we need to figure out where."

Barker said, "We're not doing anything until you explain how you figured out that the next target was here instead of Chicago when they deliberately *said* it was there."

"That, Detective, is where the need-to-know comes in. My superiors asked for discretion and I'm ordered to comply. Of course, I could tell you—"

"—but then you'd have to kill me. Right. Fish and squirrels may fly, but that doesn't make them birds, Timms."

"Huh?"

"Never mind. Either you show the cards you're holding, or I take Mrs. Winthrop out of here. She hasn't officially agreed to anything yet, and besides, don't think I haven't noticed. You keep beating around the bush, promising to give us information, but you really haven't told us a damn thing about why you need to have her involved. So if it's all the same to you—and Sara, if you'll allow me to speak for you here—pull that curtain to the side, Oz, or we walk, end of story."

Timms mulled it over. Sara wondered if he was debating on how much trouble he'd be in if he disobeyed direct orders. Barker had him by the balls. Timms knew it, and so did everyone else in the room. Five against one. They waited.

He pulled a handkerchief from his pocket and dabbing at his forehead, he said, "Fine. In the interest of saving lives...this does not leave this office. Are we understood? Especially you, Barker. If I happen to catch even the slightest hint that you're out there on Twitter blabbing secrets of the Federal Bureau of Investigation, you'll be spending what limited time you have left trying to survive in a cell with some guy who you probably put there in the first place. Are we clear?"

"Crystal. But one question..."

"What?"

"What's a Twitter?"

Everyone but Timms and Barker laughed. Barker may have been poking fun at himself, but if he was, he held the befuddled expression like a pro.

Timms put his hands on Jim's desk and leaned forward. Looking at Sara, he asked, "Do you remember a woman named Patricia Kellog?"

The name brought back a flood of memories. Junior year of high school, wanting so badly to be popular, to make a good impression on the cheerleaders at Washington High so she could join the upper echelon of coolness. Being part of the crowd that ruled the school was important back then. It meant all the awesome parties, the cutest boys, sharing the best clothes, and being worshipped by the scrubs walking the halls.

She'd changed, obviously. Growing up, growing older and wiser, realizing how idiotic but unavoidable the whole process was for a bunch of teens thrown together, coming into themselves, trying to figure out their place in life.

Patricia Kellog. Patty. Batty Patty. Patty the Fatty.

Old regrets hit the hardest.

Sara had plenty of them—she wasn't perfect. Who was? Yet the one that she'd subconsciously worked so hard to bury in her mind was that night at the homecoming game. Sara hadn't done the actual deed, but she was guilty of laughing to look cool while on the inside she had pleaded for them to stop. The incident was enough to change her opinions about what it took to wear the crown of supreme popularity, and she moved on. There were better ways to live her life.

Sara said, "She left high school during our junior year. I haven't seen her since. The last I heard, she spent some time in a mental hospital."

And I never got the chance to apologize, she thought. *We were dumb, cruel kids.*

"Right," Timms said, "and her former psychiatrists informed me that her stay wasn't a pleasant one." He pointed at the whiteboard. "See that name up there on the top of the list?"

"Boudica?"

"Meet Patty Kellog."

Chapter Six

With their recon complete, Quirk and Cleo found each other in the business section again. Rather, Quirk spotted Cleo first and took his time on the approach. Her pencil skirt stopped just below the knee and when she turned away, unaware of him, pretending to browse books on a different shelf, he noticed that it zipped in the back, all the way up to her waist. The short gap between the zipper and the hem provided a tiny glimpse into the unknown that resided above, and he had to shake his mind free of the lustful images that followed.

Job first, Quirk. White picket fence later. This is for Brandon, not your libido.

He stopped at the entrance of the aisle and cleared his throat.

Cleo turned, smiled, melted his heart, and walked toward him. "Hey," she said.

"Want some coffee?" The words were out of his mouth before he had a chance to consider the implications. To Quirk, those four syllables held a colossal amount of weight. 'Want some coffee,' in his mind, could easily be misconstrued as 'Will you marry me?'

But the fears of one are often not in the forefront of another's thoughts, and Cleo simply shook her head. "I have to get to work. Walk me there?"

Quirk's heart pitter-pattered. He would've walked across a bed of hot coals wearing gasoline-soaked shoes if she'd asked. Playing cool, he said, "Yeah, definitely. The café is too crowded anyway."

They walked through the lower level of Powell's, past the information desk, past the line of shoppers waiting to check out, up the stairs, and out the front door, pausing under the overhang. The rain had backed off, but a blanket of Portland's typical misty drizzle remained.

"Which branch?" Quirk asked, even though he already knew the answer.

"The one down on Sixth."

"You'll get soaked going back."

Cleo shrugged. "Not necessarily." She grabbed an umbrella leaning against the outer wall, smirked at him then flicked it open, stepping out onto the sidewalk.

It was risky, stealing something as innocuous as an umbrella. What if they were spotted, arrested, and questioned? A minor infraction, but that tiny butterfly beating its wings could potentially create a massive tsunami of disorder for the rest of The Clan. He and Cleo would be in the system and easily discoverable if anything went wrong after Tuesday.

What if they left traces of evidence or DNA behind? Of course, he'd look different next week. He planned to shave his beard and his head, lose the glasses and flannel, and wear a tailored suit. He'd go from Portland grunge to downtown businessman—he'd done it before and barely recognized himself—but a criminal trail left too many possibilities open.

Quirk considered snatching the umbrella away from Cleo or forcing her to return it, but...those attractive, well-toned legs, the small slit in the skirt, the way that mischievous grin beckoned him to join her when she looked back coaxed him into leaving it alone. *Forget it,* Quirk thought. *It's just an umbrella.*

Something had changed in her demeanor, too, but he couldn't place what. Was her mood lighter? Less businesslike? Friendlier?

He pulled his skullcap on and down low, almost to his eyebrows. He shoved his hands into the pockets of his skinny jeans and followed his temptress.

A wet breeze lifted the hood of his windbreaker, reminding him that it was there. He pulled it over his head and tugged on the strings. Cleo held the umbrella higher and asked if he wanted to join her underneath it. "No," he answered, "I don't want to crowd you."

"Suit yourself. So," she said, glancing back, checking the distance between them and the nearest pedestrian, "it looked pretty standard in there, right? There's no real rhyme or reason to the shift changes and they don't have anyone patrolling the floors looking for shoplifters. Not that I could see. I mean, it's possible that they have people undercover, though I doubt it. There *could've* been, but I was focused more on looking for someone that might've been looking for us, you know? I couldn't make anybody except for this old perv trying to get a peek down my blouse."

Quirk thought about asking which one it was so that he could go back to the bookstore later and punch the guy in the face. He tucked the fantasy away and said, "It seemed like just another day in Powell's to me. I worked retail some after I got back from Iraq and more than likely the shifts are staggered so they can keep the sales floor and registers covered all the time. Regardless, it's so crowded that they won't focus on some random guy leaving a package behind on a shelf."

"But on a Tuesday morning?"

"Maybe not *as* crowded."

Cleo said, "That's the plan?"

"Technically you're not supposed to know that." According to Boudica, each individual member of The Clan had his or her own job and had no knowledge of the other's activities. Terrorist cells operated the same way. The less you knew, the less you could implicate others and bring down the whole undertaking.

Quirk wondered why Boudica had chosen to pair him with Cleo twice, considering the fact that it violated the concept of individual cells. Two reasons came to mind; either Boudica felt Cleo—who was only twenty-four—needed some experienced guidance, or she was there to keep an eye on him. Why Moscow? Why Portland, but not Beijing or London? He didn't have an answer, and speculating would only distract him from the current job. Only Boudica knew the method to her madness.

Cleo grinned. *"Technically*, you're right. Here, hold this for a second." She handed him the umbrella.

Quirk took it and held it over her head, blocking the drizzle.

He didn't notice the handgun until he felt the barrel against his abs.

"Whoa, what's—"

Quirk was more burdened by the disappointment of having his dreams of a white picket fence with Cleo evaporate like the surrounding mist than he was with the possibility of a bullet wound.

Cleo: dream girl, love of his life, traitor.

"Quiet."

"What're you doing?"

"Shut up. Down here." She led him down a parking garage ramp, into a lower level. The bright yellow sign in the middle of the entry read "FULL," indicating a reduced risk of being spotted. No drivers entering, perhaps only a handful leaving after they'd finished shopping.

With more pressing things to focus on, Quirk forgot that he was holding the open umbrella, at least until he realized he could use it as a distraction.

Too risky, he thought. *I yank the umbrella down, she gets spooked and pulls the trigger on instinct. Gut shot, maybe I bleed out slowly behind one of these parked cars. No dice, Quirk.*

At the bottom of the ramp, Cleo turned right and Quirk followed. "Lose the umbrella," she said. He obeyed. He closed it then chucked it into the bed of a red pickup truck. Cleo backed away a step and flicked the barrel and her chin to the right. Following him between a gold minivan and a forest-green Subaru hatchback, she added, "Over there, behind that support pillar."

"Did I...Cleo, talk to me."

"Back there, out of sight."

Again, Quirk obeyed. He stopped in the shadows, behind the support pillar, and waddled underneath the ramp. It angled awkwardly overhead so that he had to stoop to fit. He lifted his hands, palms outward, and craned his neck to see her.

Cleo backed up to the post and surveyed left and right, either looking for unwanted company or witnesses, but Quirk suspected the latter. She widened her legs into a sturdier stance, screwed a silencer into the barrel, and aimed at his forehead.

"Cleo, don't," he pleaded.

"What's your real name?"

"Tell me what's going on, Cleo. Did I do something wrong? Is this because of London?"

"What's your real name?"

"Mark. Mark Ellis. Why?"

"The FBI likes to know these things."

"What?"

Cleo turned a corner of her mouth up into a half-grin. "Crime pays, but the government pays better when you're sleeping with an agent."

The burning knot in Quirk's stomach clenched tighter. "I thought you were part of the solution, not the problem. Why're you doing this?"

"Look, we all lost somebody and we all let Boudica convince us that fighting back this way was the right thing to do. Maybe it was, maybe it wasn't, but has it changed anything? No, it hasn't. And it never will. Once you realize that, there comes a time when you just have to get over it and move on."

"So your brother gets shot and your crusade only lasts a couple of years before you throw his memory away? And for what? Some peckerwood FBI guy and a few bucks?"

"They've been onto us for *two months*, Quirk, since you screwed up in London. They know everything about us. Where we live, where we work, what cars we drive. Then, about a month ago, I was cleaning underneath a nightstand in my bedroom and found some type of spy shit listening device stuck to the bottom of it. We were screwed, so as soon as he approached me with an offer, I said hell yeah. Cause or no cause, I'm not getting locked up for you people."

"And you had to sleep with him, too?" Quirk couldn't help himself. The betrayal, the jealousy—the emotions seemed childish and petty but he had to say something. It hurt, damn it. "He's what, paying you for sex and information? You're a whore. Don't you see that? Whoever this guy is, he's treating you like a whore, Cleo."

"Maybe so, but I'd rather be an FBI whore than somebody's bitch in prison."

Quirk shook his head. "Do you think you can pull that trigger?"

"I'm not supposed to kill you, moron. We're waiting."

"For what?"

"He's coming here as soon as he's done meeting with the woman you were supposed to murder."

"What're you talking about? That's not the plan."

"Cell individuality, Quirk, remember? You have no idea what the real plan was. Your job was to build your little firecracker and then make sure it went boom, right? You didn't know anything else, did you?"

"No."

"My job, not that it matters anymore, was to get this woman named Sara Winthrop into Powell's at ten o'clock next Tuesday.

That's it. That's all I knew, but from what I could guess, she was on Boudica's hit list like all the rest of them."

"The rest of who?"

"The people on her list."

Confused, Quirk inched toward her.

"Step back, do *not* come any closer. On the ground, now."

Quirk dropped and felt the cold concrete through his jeans.

"Scoot back into the corner."

"Okay, okay, Jesus. I'm here." The shadows were deep and dark underneath the ramp. He shuffled farther back and felt his hand brush against something hard and loose.

"Stay there." Cleo fidgeted, looking left and right, around the edges of the support pillar. She looked anxious, as if she were wondering what was taking her FBI lover so long.

"What list, Cleo?"

"Shut up. I've told you too much already."

"Does it matter? If I'm going to prison, what does it matter that I know?"

"Maybe he'll tell you when he gets here."

"Cleo, look at me. Look. It's fine. I'm going to prison, so what, but at least tell me that all of this wasn't for nothing, that we didn't blow up all those places for some reason other than our actual agenda."

"And what was our agenda, exactly? To help the world see that video games lead to violence? It's all bullshit and you know it. Those studies prove nothing." Cleo checked her wristwatch. "Don't move. I really don't want to shoot you."

"I'm cool," he said, but he wasn't. He was far from cool. He reached to the side, pawing the concrete flooring, and found what his hand had brushed against. It was hard and jagged. Without looking away from her, he read it with his fingers, feeling a clump of cement about the size of a softball.

Cleo reached into her handbag and pulled out a cell phone. She dialed, waited, and said, "Where are you? I'm here, right now. He's not going anywhere…Well, are you coming? How long? Fine, hurry. We're too exposed. I'm afraid someone—"

A loud *kachunk* echoed throughout the lower floor as a stairway door opened nearby. It was sudden enough, and unexpected enough, to distract Cleo. Spooked and reacting on instinct, she turned toward the noise, then back to her captive. "No—"

Quirk watched as the chunk of concrete hurtled toward her in slow motion.

Perfect aim, perfect luck.

It crashed into the side of her head. The gun fired, the silencer muffling the sound as the bullet ricocheted off the ceiling and the floor.

Cleo dropped to the ground, unconscious.

Quirk scrambled to his feet and shuffled over to her, staying low behind the minivan. He picked up her handgun. It was still warm from the heat of her palm.

He aimed, choked back the regret, and fired two shots into her chest.

Then he ran.

Chapter Seven

Patty Kellog leaned over the coffee mug and inhaled the fresh, steaming scent. Bold, black, and strong enough for the spoon to stand up straight, just the way she liked it. She clucked her tongue and thought about how her visit here would lead to such a waste of a perfectly good explosives specialist.

She stirred the contents, ensuring the poison was mixed in well, secured the plastic lid again, and waited on Quirk and Cleo to join her in the café of Powell's. She'd spied them from a distance, climbing up and down the stairs, and as long as Cleo stuck to the plan, Quirk wouldn't be the liability she thought he was.

Patty checked the clock behind the barista counter. How much longer? Ten minutes? Fifteen? She'd told Cleo to allow him to take the lead, but if he wanted to take over an hour for their supposed "recon" mission at Powell's, then she was to convince him she was thirsty and wanted something from the café. Once there, she was to excuse herself, and then Patty—or Boudica, rather—would make her acquaintance. It would go something like, "Quirk? We haven't officially met, but I think we should talk about your...upcoming job. Here's a coffee for you. Walk with me."

Three days later, the slow-acting toxins would take their toll and The Clan would begin the process of finding a new guy that liked to make things explode.

Patty watched the entrance, getting her hopes up and being let down every time some new person walked through. Her impatience grew as she bounced a leg and checked the wall clock again.

Was it too much of a risk changing the plans like she did? Melinda Wilkes had originally been next on the list, but her sudden job transfer from Chicago to Paris left too many puzzle pieces in too many different places. She'd scrambled, reorganized, and was pleased to see that it wouldn't be too much of an effort to take care of Sara Winthrop while she still had all of her resources in the U.S.

Boudica mumbled, "Damn it, where are you?"

She stood, holding both coffees, and was so agitated that she absentmindedly took a sip from one. A brief moment of panic made her hands unsteady, and she relaxed. The coffee in her right hand, from which she'd sipped, had the small blue checkmark of safety. One more look at the clock.

A barista shouted, "Caramel latte for Amanda! Amanda?"

Boudica cursed and slung both cups into the nearest trashcan.

Cleo was fifteen minutes late. Had she told Quirk about the plan?

Something had been off with that girl for the past two months, and this had been her chance at redemption. Boudica considered the fact that maybe she should've purchased *two* coffees with room for something other than cream.

Last chance, Cleo, she thought. *If you're out, game's over.*

Patty tucked the Boudica persona away and became just another patron browsing the multitude of shelves at Powell's. She took the stairs up to the top floor and worked her way down through each level. Cleo and Quirk were nowhere to be found. Why had the girl changed her mind? Why wouldn't she deliver Quirk like she'd been asked to do? Perhaps whatever had been off about her recently had finally buried its claws deep into that shaky psyche and Cleo had been turned.

It had to be the FBI, and Cleo had to be The Clan's leak.

Six months ago, when Boudica and the others had discovered that the FBI was closing in on their little operation, they had begun deliberately feeding them false information. Creating fake accounts, fake conversations, fake trails that had been manipulated to look legitimate, all the way back to before that first explosion in Moscow. They concocted a whole storyline, and from what she could tell, it had worked, up to a point.

The gambit with Chicago had been risky, blatantly leaking information about their next target, daring the Feds to catch them. The plan was to let the day pass, allow them to feel like they'd been successful in its prevention then strike when the threat no longer appeared credible.

And then Melinda had moved. Change of internal plans, but they kept the ruse going in the underground, smoke-filled caves of the hidden internet. The play was supposedly still on. The actual target was gone, but the FBI wasn't aware of it. From what they suspected to be true, the CBOE was the next location on The Clan's list.

It was perfect, actually. They'd have all their attention directed toward Chicago while The Clan slipped quietly away to their new objective in Portland.

Finish the job in the Rose City, escape to Paris where Melinda would be eliminated, and then quietly purge the remaining members of The Clan. No traces, no trails, no way of ever revealing who'd been a part of the group that had caused so much chaos around the world.

Boudica learned through Chief, her man on the inside, that the FBI had uncovered the truth behind the new plan for Portland, but hadn't officially let on in their communications. From what she'd gathered, the FBI's ploy was to leave a task force in Chicago, as if they were still waiting on things to proceed as intended, and then send a smaller team to Portland to intercept them.

She'd traced and retraced every single step The Clan had made for the past couple of months, trying to find out where and how they'd screwed up. There were no missteps whatsoever. She was painstaking in her review and didn't sleep for two days. They were clean. There had been no mistakes.

Which could only mean one thing. Someone in their group had betrayed them.

Originally, she'd suspected Quirk. After things hadn't gone as planned in London, she'd ridden him hard, perhaps too hard, and maybe it'd been too much. He seemed to be the most likely culprit, the easiest choice. Cleo was off, too, but it hadn't made Boudica suspicious enough to waste the young woman's talents as a thief and forger.

Not until today. If Cleo had revealed the truth to Quirk—whether it was regarding Boudica's plans to dispose of him or whether she'd made it known that she was an FBI informant—now there would be two problems that needed solving.

The question was, where were they?

Boudica left Powell's and headed up the street with no particular destination in mind—at least not until she'd determined where her two miscreants had gone. She removed her disposable cell from her handbag and dialed a number she'd only had to use once before.

When he answered, Boudica said, "Spirit?"

"Yes."

"Were you able to get that tracking chip into Cleo's burner?"

"I don't know what that is." His voice was flat and sterile. The Spirit was an ancient ex-KGB agent—a relic from the Cold War, tossed aside when newer, faster, younger recruits were brought in. He was old back then. Now he didn't just have one foot in the grave, he was standing with the grass at waist level.

However, he hadn't lost his touch, and from what Boudica had heard before she hired him, he was as proficient as he had been in 1983. The Spirit had certainly performed quality work when it came time to take care of Alvarez.

"Her *burner*. The disposable cell phone she had. You know, the thing where you push a few buttons, it goes *beep-beep-beep* and sends a signal up into outer space and then you get to talk to somebody else?"

"Yes. Of course."

"Did you or did you not get the tracking chip installed?"

"Dimitri says it is so."

"Good. Where is she?"

"One moment."

Boudica listened to him bark instructions in Russian, and then heard a keyboard clattering in the background. It was risky allowing him to work with a partner, because there was always too many variables exposed, but he needed help with the current technology. The Spirit was an old-school, cloak-and-dagger agent, used to working in shadows and lies, too outdated to learn new tricks. His philosophy was why bother wasting the time when he might die in his sleep that night? Boudica suspected that if she were to hand him an iPod, he wouldn't know what to do with it.

She waited, growing impatient, as the Spirit and his partner muttered to themselves in the background. "Anything?"

He coughed into the receiver. "She's in a parking garage. Downtown Portland."

"Really? Where?" He gave her the address. "That's two blocks from here. Is she on the move?"

"No, she's stationary."

"How long has she been there?" Boudica asked. "Maybe I can catch her."

The Spirit mumbled something in Russian. It sounded like he was speaking around a mouthful of marbles, drunk on cheap potato vodka. "Tracking software says…Dimitri? Dimitri says two minutes. Two minutes, no movement."

Boudica hung up, used her sleeves to wipe the disposable phone free of prints, snapped it in half, and then dropped it into a nearby recycling container.

She cut left across the street, walking fast and hoping she would make it to the parking garage in time to catch Cleo. She readjusted her handbag on her shoulder and felt the weight of her compact 9mm shifting inside.

Chapter Eight

Sara leaned forward in her seat and pointed at the whiteboard. She said, "You're kidding me, right?"

Timms shook his head. "No, ma'am."

Sara almost laughed. "Little Patty Kellog is this *Boudica* person? She's the leader of some group of international terrorists?"

"Yes."

"There's no way."

"Why not?"

"There's absolutely no way that the timid, goofy girl who grew up down the street from me is behind all this. It's not possible. I went to high school with her, for God's sake."

Timms shrugged. "I graduated with Michael Jordan. What's your point?"

Teddy, who'd apparently grown bored with the conversation that didn't revolve around him, perked up. "Whoa, Michael Jordan? Is that true?"

"I sat behind him in algebra."

"Cool."

"It is *now*, yeah, but the point I'm trying to make to *you*," he said, turning to Sara, "is that it's not *probable* that people from our past can become what they are, but it's not *impossible*. Honestly, I never thought Mike's jump shot was all that great."

Jim tapped a finger on his desk. "Agent Timms, is this going anywhere?"

Barker agreed, adding, "Who, where, what, and why, Timms. Get on with it."

"You want the shortened version?"

"That would've been nice an hour ago."

Timms grabbed a red marker, popped the top off, and wrote, "SARA WINTHROP" in big, bold letters. He underlined her name twice and then circled it. "There's your target."

Sara swallowed hard with a mixture of disbelief and fear. This seriously couldn't be happening again, could it? She felt lightheaded and confused. "*Me?* Why?"

"We're piecing that together. Do the names Melinda Wilkes, Julie Harland, Rebecca Carter, Lucy Marris, and Colleen Bishop mean anything to you?"

The muddled images in Sara's mind, like an out-of-focus photograph from the past, slowly began to sharpen. Dull forms became recognizable objects. She could see the shapes of realization gaining some clarity. Perturbed, she said, "If you know those names, then you already know they mean something to me."

"Yes, but what?"

"We all graduated together and we sort of have…something."

"I'm aware. In part, at least."

"If you know all of this, then why—oh God, are they targets, too?"

"*Were* targets. Four of them are already dead, Mrs. Winthrop."

"No." The word slipped softly from her lips. She hadn't been friends with them—not exactly—but they'd been the upper-echelon clique that Sara had so desperately wanted to be a part of all those years ago. It sat heavy on her heart knowing those women were now gone.

She was surprised she hadn't heard anything about it from friends or family, but she'd long ago given up Facebook, and in a metro area the size of northern Virginia, where she had grown up, people disappeared easily among the masses. She hadn't spoken to some of her classmates in over twenty years and hadn't bothered with the latest reunion.

Timms crossed his arms and moved closer to Sara. Barker kept his legs extended as a barrier. Timms stopped but didn't step over them. "All true, I'm afraid. Julie Harland was on vacation in Moscow. Rebecca Carter taught English classes in Beijing. Lucy Marris was a fashion photographer on assignment in Rio. And Colleen Bishop was in London for her great-grandfather's funeral."

"What about Melinda?"

"We believe she was the intended target in Chicago."

"Are you protecting her?"

"From a distance. She's in Paris."

Barker scoffed, "That's quite the distance."

"We have a team on the ground there. She'll be fine."

Sara said, "I don't understand. I thought you said that all these bombings were tied to video game violence."

"They are, in an approximate way, and I'll explain all of that in a minute, but from what we know, it was a cover-up for the real mission objectives. So what I want to know, Mrs. Winthrop, is how the six of you women are connected to Patty Kellog other than the fact that you all went to the same high school."

"How did you learn about that?"

"Standard procedure. We cross-referenced all the victims to see if they had anything in common."

"Right." Sara stood and went to the window, staring down to the street three stories below. With her back turned to them, partly in shame, partly in regret, she said, "It was the homecoming football game—"

Timms's cell phone chimed on his belt clip and he said, "Hold that thought, Mrs. Winthrop." He checked the caller ID. "Yeah, I need to take this." He stepped to a far corner of the office. He kept his voice low, but not low enough to hide his side of the conversation. "What? I'm at LightPulse. Are you in the nest yet? Is he secure? Good…I'll be there. Two minutes, tops. What was that noise? Emily? Emily? Answer me."

Timms turned back to face the room with everyone focused intently on him. His eyes were wide. His left hand shook as he tugged an earlobe. "That was…a colleague of mine. I should've been gone five minutes ago. Listen to me. You all need to do exactly what I say, because there's no time for questions—"

Teddy being, well, *Teddy*, interrupted him. "Who was that?"

Timms inhaled deeply. It didn't change the bright red color of his cheeks. "We're in play. I don't know what just happened, but I need all of you to listen. Mr. Rutherford, sir, you and Teddy— LightPulse—you're free and clear. Go home, stay safe, and cover for Sara on Monday morning."

Sara said, "Cover for me? What does—"

Teddy held his hands up. "Whoa, *no*, wait. Don't shove me out of this."

Timms scrambled over to Karen Wallace. "Can you help?"

Nodding, Karen said, "I'm all yours."

Timms rubbed his face. "Do you still have friends in the FBI?"

"A few."

"Okay, here's what I need. Use whatever connections you still have, okay? I'd put in some calls for you but I don't have the time. What I need is for you to try to find a man named Vadim Bariskov."

"The *Spirit*?"

Clearly her knowledge surprised Timms. "You know Bariskov?"

"Stories, that's all."

"Find him if you can. We think he's still in Portland. Last known movement, as of this morning, was a rental car that visited the Rose Gardens. White sedan. He was with his partner. He may still be there, he may not."

Sara shivered at the memories. The first level of Shelley Sergeant's game had been to stand nude among the roses, being humiliated while onlookers gawked and pointed.

"On it." Karen stood. "What happens when we find him?"

"Monitor him, nothing more. Do not engage, but absolutely do not lose him. I'll be in touch."

"Maybe easier said than done."

Teddy said, "I can help. Karen, seriously, let me come with you."

Karen rolled her eyes, looked to Jim for approval, and through some miracle on Teddy's desperate, puppy-dog behalf, she relented. "Stay out of the way." Karen left the office, and Teddy floated out behind her on smiles and imaginary rainbows.

Timms said, "Barker, I want you to take Mrs. Winthrop back to her house. Don't rush, don't act panicked in case her home is under Clan surveillance that we haven't picked up on yet, but get her and the children out of there and to a safe place. Listen to me: that's imperative, okay? We need to keep this trap alive as long as we can. Mrs. Winthrop, we have people on your street and they would've alerted me to any activity, so your family is safe. Don't worry, don't panic, just get them out of there. Let me know when you're secure. And Barker, no matter what, keep her protected."

"Done," Barker agreed.

Timms shook his hand in a show of genuine concern, grabbed his suit jacket, and darted out the door.

The silence in the room was overbearing as Jim, Sara, and Barker all stared at each other in the wake of such frantic, hasty exits. Sara said to Barker, "Should we go?"

"Get your coat. Mr. Rutherford, you'll be okay?"

"Always, Detective. If you need a place, my house has a panic room."

"Thank you, Jim," Sara said.

"You're welcome, now *go*."

...

Sara slammed the unmarked sedan's door closed and latched her seatbelt.

How could something like this be happening again? She couldn't believe it, couldn't wrap her mind around it. It was unfathomable.

"You really think they're safe, like he said?"

"Cops and Feds mix about as well as oil and water, but yeah, I believe him."

"Jesus. Can we hurry without acting like we know something's up?"

Barker tried to relieve her tension. "You're a hot mess, you know that?" He chuckled and playfully patted her shoulder. Barker started the car, whipped it out of the parking space, and then launched into the stream of traffic.

"I can't take much more of this." Sara pinched the bridge of her nose. She practiced breathing as he drove, counting her patterns, relaxing, relaxing. "Can I ask you something?"

"Go for it."

"I'm a good soul, right?"

"Of course. Why?"

"I don't know. These past couple of years, it just seems like trouble is looking for me on purpose. Whom did I piss off for that to happen?"

"Well, if the universe ain't on your side, you've got me, at least."

"Thanks." Sara smiled. "Still doesn't explain why."

"I don't know. Does 'shit happens' work as an explanation?"

"Not in the slightest."

The traffic moved well for a Saturday morning, but not well enough. He almost turned on his police lights then pulled his hand away. Like Timms had said, if they were under Clan surveillance, it might alert them that something was wrong and would put Sara's children, and Miss Willow, in danger. In fact, he realized, he probably shouldn't have peeled out of the parking lot like he had.

Sara said, "Can't you go faster?"

"Not if we want to keep the cover on. If they're watching, they'll know. Best bet is to play it cool and stay calm. Don't forget, Timms said he had people watching your place. They're safe."

Sara shook her head and leaned against the door. She put a shaky hand on her forehead, sheltering her eyes. "How am I supposed to stay calm when somebody wants to kill me *again*?"

"I know, I'm sorry, but it's—"

"Do you? Do you know?"

"Sara, I'm a cop. I wake up every day wondering if any number of guys I put away twenty years ago will show up on my doorstep the moment they get out of prison, so yeah, I know what it's like."

"I'm—yeah, sorry. It's just that—I mean, my God, why me?"

"It's like you're getting picked for jury duty over and over again." Barker signaled, checked his mirrors, and ducked into the left lane. He found a gap in traffic and turned into a residential neighborhood where the traffic was lighter.

Sara tried to calm herself with a joke. "Jury duty? I'll take the death threats." She looked around at the familiar homes. She passed this area every weekday on her way into the office, and she thought back to the day she found the note on her minivan. It wasn't far from here that she'd sped through another neighborhood, nearly catching air off of speed bumps in a mad rush to get to Jacob's school. It was almost as if fate, or coincidence, were unintentionally recreating the scene.

She called home and when Miss Willow answered, she was relieved to learn that the kids were fine, happily eating snacks and watching *Cars* for the five hundredth time that week. Sara offered little in the way of details, but insisted that Miss Willow get herself and the children ready to leave for a few days.

Barker listened to her say, "I'll explain when we get there, just pack their overnight bags. Yeah, you should probably come with us...We're hoping for fifteen minutes. Twenty at the most."

When Sara hung up, he asked, "Freak her out?"

"Not really. She's so calm. Thank God she's been around the house since they put Shelley away, because she's been my rock, for sure."

Barker honked his horn at a jogger who'd drifted dangerously close to the center of the street. The guy jumped, pulled an earbud from his left ear, waved, and then moved over to the sidewalk. "Idiot," Barker said. "These people running around here with their iPads and the music turned up too loud."

Sara chuckled. "They're called iPods. An iPad is like an oversized iPhone."

"How about this? *I* don't care."

"*Sure* you don't."

"Do you use that Twitter thing with an iPod?"

"You're joking, right?"

Barker grinned. "I got a smile out of you, at least. Relax, Sara, we'll be fine. We'll get you and the kids and Willow somewhere safe, you'll camp out for a few days until we're all clear, then you'll go back to normal."

Sara leaned back into the car seat and pulled her jacket tighter around her chest. "What's normal these days? Our lives in danger? More death threats?"

"This'll be the last one, I promise."

"I hope you're right."

"I know I'm right. And besides, I may bust the dude's chops a little bit, but I can tell Timms knows what he's doing, so take some deep breaths and try to be calm. I'm not trying to patronize you, because you know the deal, but have some faith in the system. Unlike that business with the Sergeant girl, we're ahead of the game this time."

"Really?" she said.

"What?"

"Ahead of *the game*? Pun intended?"

"What? Uh—right. Sorry. That was...punintentional. Get it? Pun and unintentional?"

"Oh, I get it."

Barker chuckled. "Everything will be okay, Sara. Trust me."

She nodded without believing it. "Okay."

"Now, do you mind telling me what in the hell you did to this Kellog woman twenty years ago?"

Sara laid her head back against the headrest and closed her eyes. She didn't want to remember. She'd tried so hard to forget.

Chapter Nine

Patty Kellog gently opened the heavy metal door in the northeastern corner of the parking garage, trying to prevent any echoing noise. She tiptoed into the lower level, peeking left and right, looking for Cleo...and maybe Quirk. Chances were if Cleo had informed Quirk of the plan to poison him the guy was long gone. But why was Cleo here in the parking garage, not moving?

It made no sense. According to the Spirit she'd been stationary for two minutes, and it had taken Patty at least five to speedwalk here. She'd dialed him again with a spare disposable phone, learned that Cleo hadn't moved, and again tossed the device in the trash.

Was Cleo on the phone with the FBI, spilling details of The Clan's operations? Was that why she hadn't moved? No, she'd likely done that already, plus, the FBI wouldn't risk leaving her alone. They'd pick her up, bring her in, and ask questions in the comfort of an interrogation room.

Was she sitting in a car with Quirk, revealing particulars? That didn't work, either. She could've explained everything necessary on the walk here from Powell's.

Next best guess was...Cleo was dead. She'd told Quirk, he'd led her away, and then he'd murdered her in the seclusion of the parked cars. It was quiet down below. Plenty of cars, trucks, and vans for cover. Secluded and convenient.

Until the door slammed behind her. The *kachunk* reverberated around the walls. Patty jumped, cursed, and ducked behind a blue Jeep Wrangler. She listened for the sound of a starting car, but what followed instead surprised her.

That unmistakable sound.

The chuff of a bullet through a silencer not too far away.

A thump that sounded like a mass falling against the side of a car.

And then two more muffled pops.

Patty tried to piece it together in her mind. The sound of the door shutting had surprised someone. The first shot was possibly a reaction to the distraction. The dull sound of something falling against a vehicle—a body falling—was it Cleo? Was it Quirk? Then, the two additional pops.

Chuff-chuff through the silencer.

A double-tap to the chest. Had to be.

Who was it? Cleo had been stationary for so long. Had Quirk taken her captive, demanding answers? Possibly. Three shots total. The double-tap was a decisive end, so at least one of her two problems were taken care of, and she hoped that the first shot, the reaction to the door's noise, hadn't gone errant of its target.

She had her answer—and it wasn't the one she wanted—when Quirk rounded the lower corner and sprinted up the western ramp.

Patty hesitated, trying to decide what came next. He was fast. He'd be up the ramp and onto the streets before she could catch up, if she could catch up at all. Taking care of him in broad daylight would be messy, dangerous, and stupid. There were cameras everywhere these days. Outside of shops, in ATMs, on streetlights. She'd be easily identifiable. She'd taken a big risk merely by walking the streets of Portland that morning.

The police, the FBI—whoever had access to the video surveillance tapes—could trace her movements in reverse, and who knew how far. Maybe even back to the safe house if they were able to track the route she'd driven through traffic cams.

She cursed and let him go. A couple of phone calls…he wouldn't get that far.

She stood up, checked the parking lot for any additional witnesses, and seeing none, she jogged in the direction from which Quirk had come. She paused at the western ramp and looked up, ensuring he was out of sight, and continued.

Moving in a crouch from car to car, inspecting the space between each of them, she finally found what she was looking for about twenty yards away, closer to the eastern entrance.

Cleo lay between a minivan and a green Subaru. Face up, eyes lifeless, with two bullet holes in the center of her chest.

In a way, Patty was disappointed, because one, she would've enjoyed taking care of Cleo herself, and two, she also wouldn't have the privilege of torturing her for more information. Questions like what had she told Quirk? Was she working for the FBI officially? How much did they know? And if she had turned traitor, had she told Sara Winthrop the truth about Patty's identity already? That would be unfortunate and make the situation difficult, but not impossible. Problems could easily be surpassed as long as you knew whom to pay.

Patty stared at the blood on Cleo's white top. If she looked at it from the right angle, the blotting looked like a pair of butterfly wings. It was almost pretty.

She needed to move. Now. Security cameras had likely captured Quirk and Cleo entering, and then Patty entering not long after. They would have video evidence of Quirk leaving, but not Cleo.

What to do, what to do? she thought. *Steal a car?*

Was that the best option? Perhaps not. The owner would report it stolen. The police would have verifiable video evidence. At some point, they would put the sequences together and the footage might show up in the media with a byline such as, "Authorities seek man in blue windbreaker and woman in white jacket as possible murder suspects."

Patty shook her head and put her hands on her hips. "Shit." She knew she should've thought it through, but she'd been so frustrated and intent on finding Cleo that she hadn't assessed the ramifications of being out in the open. However, there had been no way of knowing that Quirk would murder Cleo and leave her in a bind. She'd now become a suspect merely by circumstance. She ran her fingers through her hair and backed away from Cleo's body.

The sounds of hurried footsteps caught her attention. She glanced to the right.

A man in a dark blue suit with a matching tie ran toward her. He looked official. Authoritative. His face seemed familiar, like perhaps they'd crossed paths recently, or perhaps she'd seen a picture of—Jesus, it was Donald Timms. FBI. The agent that her informant had warned her about, the one that had gotten too close.

Think, Patty. Think.

She screamed, "Over here, hurry! Oh my God, she's been shot. Somebody shot this woman!"

He shouted back, "Is she alive? Is she?" as his footsteps pounded, descending the ramp. He pulled his firearm from its holster. "Stay right there. Don't move. Answer me, is she alive?"

Patty held up her hands. "I don't know. I can't tell. I don't think so."

"Did you see anything?"

"No."

Timms reached her, sweating and pale. He looked down at Cleo's body.

Patty watched his face. She saw a flicker of pain and regret flash in his expression and then he returned to stoic business. "Ma'am," he said, showing his ID, "Agent Timms with the FBI—do you have a cell phone?"

"No, no, I don't."

He unclipped his from his belt holster and dialed a number, then tried to keep one eye on Patty while he kneeled to examine Cleo's body. He said into the phone, "It's Timms. Confirmed. Cleo is down, repeat, Cleo is down. No pulse. Get them here, now. I don't know the exact address, hang on." Timms turned to face her. "What's the address here?"

Patty forced her bottom lip to quiver, pretending. "I don't know."

"What street are we on?"

"I don't know, I can't think! Sixth, maybe?"

"Sixth and something," he said into the phone. "There's a furniture store across from us. Just get here." He flicked a look over his shoulder at Patty and lowered the gun. "Did you hear anything? See anything? Was she with anyone?"

"I found her like that, I swear. Please don't—I was just trying to get to my car, and, and..." Patty forced herself into mock panic and shortened breaths. She fanned her face and stumbled.

"Okay, okay, I believe you. You're not in any trouble."

Timms turned away from her and focused on Cleo.

Wait, Patty thought, *he called her Cleo. He knows. He definitely knows.*

He bent over, examining the wounds in her chest.

Patty moved without a sound.

Timms froze as Patty pressed the silencer of her 9mm against his skull just behind his left ear. "Fuck. Boudica?" he said.

"Nice meeting you in person, Timms."

"Somebody's had some work done."

"The best cheekbones money can buy."

She squeezed the trigger. Red sprayed onto Cleo's white shirt as Timms fell on top of her.

Patty tucked the gun into her handbag and tried to decide what to do next. Avoiding any security cameras was imperative. She removed her jacket, thought about throwing it out, and then put it back on again. On a normal day, a jacket in a trashcan would hardly arouse suspicion, but with two dead bodies, one of them a Federal agent's, and the possibility of her image on the surveillance tapes, they would take the jacket as evidence, run DNA tests, and she'd be made.

She'd spent a lot of money trying to have her identity erased physically and electronically along with every paper trail imaginable, but one could never be sure what potential problems were out there.

Patty turned and went back to the stairwell where she'd descended earlier. She pulled on a pair of gloves, opened the door, wiped the interior handle, and then took the stairs in twos. At the ground level floor, she scanned the area around her, looking for people near their cars, and seeing none, she ran straight, slipping between a Suburban and a white Volkswagen Beetle. With a slight jump, she landed on top of the dividing wall, slung her legs across, and then dropped to the sidewalk.

An elderly gentleman walking a large Greyhound startled her. Smiling, he said, "I wish I was still that limber," and continued past. Patty paused, hesitated with her hand around the 9mm's grip, and then decided to let him live. She hoped it wouldn't cost her.

She walked briskly, with her head down, into the rain.

With Timms and Cleo eliminated, two of her potential problems were gone. The fact that Timms was now dead wouldn't stop the FBI, however, and it was simply a matter of how long before the next in line would take his place in resuming the hunt for The Clan. Conservatively, it could take them twelve hours to get up to speed, but more than likely it would be a lot less. So much depended on how good Timms had been about sharing information. The reports she'd gotten suggested he was a loner and a bit of a maverick, so there was a chance that providence was on her side.

Patty muttered, "Now what?" and kept walking. She took her jacket off, turned it inside out, and put it back on, blue side out. She pulled a baby blue knitted cap from her bag and tugged it over her head. The police and the Feds wouldn't be anywhere near searching for a blonde woman in a white jacket yet, but her minimal disguise might prevent the other pedestrians from identifying her later.

If Timms knew Cleo by her codename, Patty thought, *and recognized me by mine, then he definitely had inside information on the Sara Winthrop objective.*

If that was true, where was she now?

Every bit of information has a price, Sara. It won't be long.

However, finding Quirk was the next logical step. What did he know? What had Cleo told him? And why had he murdered her?

By the time she made it to her car back in the Powell's parking garage, she was thoroughly drenched and annoyed. She hated Portland, mostly because of the weather. Sun, drizzle, pouring rain, all in a five-minute span. Rinse and repeat. She longed for the somewhat stable climate of northern Virginia where she had grown up. At least there, the four distinct seasons gave you some kind of warning.

She got into her rental—a small, four-door Chevrolet—started the engine, and waited on the heater to warm up as she plotted her next move.

If I were Quirk, where would I go? God, too many places to count.

"Come on, warm up already." She slapped the vent, pointing the chilly air away from her face.

She took her third disposable phone of the day from the glove box and called the Spirit again.

"Yes?"

"It's me. Yesterday you said that was a negative on Quirk's tracer, right?"

"Unfortunately, yes. He never left his home and Dimitri was unable to—"

"Never mind. It's too late now, anyway. That little wench Cleo was the leak."

"Would you like me to…take out the trash?"

"No need. Quirk did it for us. Timms is out of play, too."

"Interesting."

"Yeah." Patty sighed and watched a young couple, maybe in their late twenties, as they pushed a stroller over to their mini-van. Some days, she thought a normal life would've been nice. Possibilities were just that…possible. She said, "We might have a little snag."

"Why is this?"

"There's a chance that Cleo leaked our plans to Quirk, too, and I need to find him before he can turn himself in and cut a deal."

"Indeed. I would think so."

"I have no idea where he could've gone. Any ideas?" She listened to the old Russian breathing heavily into the receiver.

He said, "Considering the fact that there's exotic explosive material in his basement—a bomb with his fingerprints all over it—if it were me, I'd go home first. Of course, he could conceivably go to the nearest FBI office, but it's been my experience that the first natural reaction is to cover the trails you've left behind."

Patty smiled. "Makes sense to me. Good thinking."

"Boudica?"

"What?"

"Do what you must, but think twice before you waste unparalleled talent."

"Yeah, well, that depends on what he knows or whom he's going to tell. Let's…"

"Yes?"

"Let's get Plan B moving."

"I'm not sure that's the—"

"Plan B." Patty hung up, started the car, and programmed the GPS for directions to Quirk's home.

Chapter Ten

By the third stoplight, Karen Wallace had already thought of six ways she could get rid of Teddy Rutherford, and nearly all of them involved time in prison as a consequence. She'd agreed to let him come along because his father paid well and she couldn't risk losing her only steady client.

Going out on her own *was* quite lucrative, when she was able to find the proper work, but occasionally she longed for the security of a stable job.

Maybe once the dust settled with this case, she'd have a sit-down with Donald Timms and pick his brain about the current state of affairs back in the FBI offices. She'd been nudged out after threatening a sexual harassment lawsuit against one of her superiors, and according to her exit handler, she was wise to take the severance.

The *bribe*.

She'd had a solid case and knew she would've caused some serious waves, but she wouldn't have won, no matter how clear-cut the details were.

So she'd gotten as far away as possible, used the money to start her own private investigation service, and, like Sara had told her numerous times, she'd left behind one harassment lawsuit to encounter one waiting to happen in the form of Teddy Rutherford.

He was harmless, more or less, but goddamn annoying no matter how you looked at it. The guy didn't understand the word no. Dealing with Teddy was like trying to train a puppy not to shit on the carpet, but no matter how many times you shoved his nose in the pile of crap, he just didn't get it.

Thankfully, her interactions with him were few and far between. Jim had her come into the office a couple of times per month to brief him on routine checks regarding Sara's life outside of work. Was anyone following her? No. Was the security system on her house fully functional? Yes. Did you replace the batteries in the—yes, yes, and yes.

The same questions, every second and fourth Tuesday.

The same parrying of Teddy's advances, every second and fourth Tuesday.

In the passenger's seat, taking up valuable oxygen, was Teddy, fidgeting and unable to stop talking long enough for her to think. He turned the radio dial, changing the station from the soft classical that Karen preferred. She slapped his hand away and pushed a preset channel button, returning the channel to the proper station. A piece by Chopin lilted through the car as Teddy rubbed his hand and said, "You *want* to listen to this?"

Karen clenched her teeth together, molar grinding molar. "Yes. My car, my radio. I'm sorry if classical is too highbrow for you."

"No, I mean, I'm cool with it…it's just that Chopin was too much of a sissy. He didn't really attack the composition the way he could've, you know? Whenever I listen to him, I picture the guy holding a tiny cupcake and drinking tea with his pinkie held out."

Dumbfounded, Karen said, "I'm sorry, what did you just say?"

"Chopin…he's a weakling. If I'm going to invest my time in a composer, I want the guy eating a raw steak with his bare hands. I don't want him…I don't know, *dainty*, I guess."

Karen couldn't stop herself from smiling. "Okay, who are you and what have you done with Teddy Rutherford?"

"Huh?"

"Nothing, never mind. I have some CDs there in the center console. Whom would you prefer? Beethoven?"

"*Pffft.* That old queen?"

One animated double take later, Karen asked, "You're kidding, right?"

Teddy laughed. "Yeah. Beethoven's fine," he said, pulling out the zipped-up case of CDs. As he flipped through them, he asked, "So that's crazy about Sara, huh?"

"That poor woman has been through way too much already. Her husband disappeared and was murdered, that insane girl kidnapped her kids and made her play that horrible game, and now this? These past three or four years have been trying for her. I don't know how she seems so..."

"Stable?"

"I was going to say 'together,' but stable works, too."

"There's a difference between seeming and being." Teddy slipped a Beethoven collection into the CD player. He said, "The Fifth or the Seventh?"

"Seventh," Karen answered. She checked her mirrors and merged onto the entrance ramp for I-5.

"Good choice." Teddy adjusted the volume to a reasonable level and asked, "Sara's strong, man. After that game she played, I started calling her Badass Chick. She's the B.C. Saved my life."

"I'm aware, Teddy." She was curious about Teddy's experience in the cabin, but she didn't have time for the distraction. Finding Vadim Bariskov had to be at the forefront of her thoughts.

"And what was up with meeting in that empty office, huh? Did you do weird shit like that when you were in the FBI? What was the point?"

"Total guess, but it sounded like he needed to be in the vicinity of something."

"Like what?"

"You heard him. Wherever he needed to be was nearby because he said he could be there in two minutes. Maybe he was just trying to juggle too much at once."

"He seemed pretty freaked out when he left," Teddy said. He stayed silent for a while, watching the windshield wipers swish back and forth. "I should probably tell you that we think you're doing a great job before I bring this up, so, yeah, you're doing awesome, but can I ask you something?"

"And...here it comes." Karen slipped her car between a limousine and a logging truck like a sheet of paper between the building blocks of the Great Pyramid.

"What's coming?"

"I think I know what you're going to say."

Teddy felt his right hand cramping then realized his knuckles had gone white as his fingers wrapped around the door handle. If he'd known Karen drove this poorly, he might've reconsidered his courtship ritual. "So Dad...uh, I mean *Jim* is paying you to have Sara's back, right? I'm not...I mean, man, I think you're fantastic, I really do, but—"

"How'd I miss this?"

"Yeah. You get paid to be one hundred percent on top of Sara, looking out for her."

"I'm surprised no one asked me back in that office. Believe me, I was sitting there gnawing on the inside of my cheek the whole time just waiting for it, and dreading it if it did come up, because honestly, I don't have an answer."

Teddy studied her for a moment, allowing his crush to resurface. He admired her long neck. Graceful fingers. High cheekbones. She was everything he wasn't. Tall, attractive, thin. She had angles. He was round. He'd gained weight since encountering the darker side of humanity. He blamed the dreams.

People liked Karen. He adored her. He didn't want to accuse her of shoddy work. Crush or no crush—infatuation in its purest form—Sara and her children were honorary members of the Rutherford family, and if it meant firing this beautiful angel that drove like a drunk Dario Franchitti at the Indy 500, then so be it, if it came to that.

Teddy turned the radio off. Beethoven could wait. "How could you *not* have an answer, Karen? You've practically lived inside Sara's head for the past year and a half. How does something this big slip past you?"

Karen pursed her lips and tapped an index finger on the steering wheel. "I don't know. I've looked at every bit of her history, her present, and her future—anything that I could find that would possibly indicate the potential for trouble. She gave me full access. Said her children and their safety were more important than her privacy. I missed it. God, I don't know how, but I missed it. This Patricia Kellog, she wasn't even on the radar. It had to have been something that Sara kept hidden from me."

"She's always been private," Teddy agreed, "but after that craziness with Shelley, she wrapped this sort of…emotional *shroud* around herself for the longest time. She put on a good show, but seriously, I mean, we were worried about her. Like, her sanity." He leaned over and lowered his voice, as if someone were eavesdropping. "Don't you dare tell her I said this, but that was part of the reason I started calling her 'Badass Chick.' She needed the confidence boost."

"I'm sure she appreciated it."

"Maybe. The genesis of the whole thing was when Brian disappeared, but she held up really well for those two years. After Shelley, though, man, she tried to put up a good front and it took my dad about three months before he was able to convince her we needed to hire someone like you."

Karen nodded and changed lanes without looking. Teddy winced. She said, "Yeah, those first few rounds of interviews didn't go that well—you know, where I was trying to dig into her background. She admitted later that she didn't feel like she needed me there and definitely didn't *want* me there. Totally pulling the badass routine on me. Then I showed up one Saturday morning—Miss Willow was out with the kids somewhere—and I found Sara on her couch, wrapped up in a blanket and crying into a cup of coffee and bourbon."

"What happened?"

"Nightmare about her kids being back in the boxes again, only this time she didn't solve the puzzle in time."

"Harsh."

"Yeah. That's when she opened up."

"But never anything about Patty Kellog?"

"Not a word."

"What if we go looking for her instead of this Russian dude? She's the leader, right? She's the one with the grudge who wants to kill Sara, so why in the hell are we looking for Baryshnikov?"

"Vadim Bariskov."

"Same thing."

"If you say so."

"I'm serious."

"No, Patty Kellog and whatever happens with her is up to Timms. He's good, he's got the manpower he needs, and he'll be on top of it. If we find Bariskov and keep an eye on him, he might lead us to her anyway."

"Fine." Teddy crossed his arms and leaned against the door, staring out the window.

"I know you're worried about her, but seriously, our job is just as important."

"Okay."

Karen actually signaled, gave a quick peek over her shoulder, cut across two lanes of traffic, and barreled down the exit ramp.

Once he'd released his death grip on the door handle and could breathe properly, Teddy asked, "Where are we going?"

"To look for Bariskov."

"I know that, Karen—*where* are we looking?"

"A couple of spots I know of. Places where the Russian immigrants like to hang out."

"Like what?"

"Churches. A local market."

Teddy shrugged. "Your call."

"You have a better idea?"

"We can go to those places if you really don't want to find Bariskov."

Karen waffled between reminding him who was the actual private detective and to shut the hell up. She decided to let him speak, give his opinion, and *then* put him in his place. "Okay, hotshot," she said. "Where do you suggest?"

"There's a bar downtown called Firebrand. There's a backroom poker game going on there twenty-four hours a day. Bunch of ex-Russian mafia guys who basically sit around and pass the same thousand bucks through the pot all day long, or until some poor sucker gets invited to the game and they take everything he has."

"Bullshit. Seriously?"

"Why would I make that up?"

"How do you know about this?"

"Maybe three years ago...yeah, actually, I remember it was back in 2010, we'd started development on this game called *Red Mob*—"

"You were designing a game based on the Russian mafia?"

"*Were*, yeah. Anyway, my dad wanted me to do some field research or whatever to help this kid Jeremy with writing the plot line and backstory."

"*You?*"

"I know, right?" Teddy chuckled. "It was probably easier than writing me out of his will. It took me a few days of going to the worst bars I could find, staying out all night, asking questions, playing nice with these godawful East European hookers—"

"Right, you *had* to do that."

"No, I'm serious. You would've been proud, because my detective skills were awesome. There was this one blonde girl, maybe twenty-one at the most, who had the most amazing set of...whoa, you know, that's not important—"

"Thank you."

"Right. Her name was Irina and after I'd bought her a few drinks, I started asking around because she...I don't know, she just looked like she'd seen the wrong side of the tracks. Turns out, all it took was for me to get about five shots of vodka in her and she wouldn't shut up. Two minutes of asking questions, suddenly I've got the hookup that I've been looking for. Irina's grandfather was this big-time arms dealer back in the early eighties and was something like a general in the Russian mob. When I told her what I was doing for LightPulse, she practically dragged me into the poker room."

"No way."

"I was scared shitless, to be honest. There were maybe six guys there, like, these big, massive Russian guys, all smoking cigars and wearing tracksuits. Super-stereotypes. I guess you could picture Malkovich in *Rounders* as Teddy KGB. Actually, now that I think about it, back when I was in college, my fraternity brothers used to call me Teddy KGB because I was so good at Hold 'em and my name is—"

"Stay on target, Teddy."

"Oh, right, sorry. Go left here."

Karen waited on the light to change, and followed Teddy's directions.

He continued, "So Irina dragged me into this room, rattled off something in Russian, smiled, and then left me alone with six of the scariest looking dudes ever. I didn't even get a chance to introduce myself before one of them pointed at an empty chair and said in this thick Russian accent, 'Five hundred buy-in.' And I'm like, 'I don't have any money on me,' and he's all, 'No problem. We give good credit. Interest rate is two fingers per week,' and made this motion like he's sawing with a knife. I think I peed myself a little before he started laughing. Take a right here."

"Oh my God, I'm actually kind of impressed."

"Yeah. It wasn't smart."

"What did you do?"

"What could I do? I sat down. The guy said to me, 'I kid, but seriously, five hundred, two fingers per week,' and then started laughing again. Second scariest night of my life, but it's a damn close second to that day in the cabin."

"So you hung out and played poker with the Russian mafia."

"Yep."

"And you made it out alive, apparently."

"They respected me. At least I think they did. You know, mutual poker talent respect. I was up about ten grand before Ivan— he's the fingers guy—said, 'Okay, Smurfboy, you buy answers with that money.'"

Karen giggled. "Smurfboy?"

"Laugh it up, Wallace. I'm used to it."

"Sorry. Then what happened?"

"Nothing much, really. I asked questions, got invited back a couple of times, heard some cool stories, and made a few friends. If I ever get into serious trouble, I know who to call—let's put it that way. Oh, and Ivan wanted me to marry Irina, believe it or not."

Karen pulled up to an intersection. "Which way?" Teddy pointed right and she added with a sarcastic grin, "Marry her? How'd you pass that up?"

Teddy touched her arm—she didn't pull away—and he said with mock sincerity, "I told him I couldn't, because I was waiting for you."

"Please." Karen laughed and turned into a parking garage. Maybe Teddy was bearable. Not entirely acceptable, but tolerable. "What happened with the game? I don't remember ever hearing about this *Red Mob* thing from Sara."

"Eh, my dad scrapped it when *Juggernaut* really took off, thanks to Sara. Ivan called me at least once a month for two years, asking about it. I haven't heard from him since July. Hopefully he's not pissed at me for never getting his life story into the market."

Karen parked and they got out of the car.

Teddy pointed and said, "It's down this way about two blocks."

"We can get in to speak to him, right? What happens if he's pissed at you?"

"Hell if I know, but I hope it doesn't cost me a few fingers."

Chapter Eleven

Quirk ran until his chest, lungs, and heart begged for relief.

He paused outside a gluten-free bakery and thought about going inside for a bottle of water. Would it be worth the risk? Most likely his image was all over a series of video surveillance cameras that could trace his path from the parking garage to where he stood now, bent at the waist, heaving and sucking wind. He used to be in such good shape. Back in the Marines he could run miles carrying a fifty-pound rucksack through mountainous terrain and having a conversation as if he were hanging out on a friend's couch.

Now, he wasn't so sure he could sputter the word *help* before collapsing on the ground. He'd come roughly a mile from the parking garage where he'd fired two bullets into Cleo's chest. He could feel the physical—and emotional—weight of her 9mm in his messenger bag.

Quirk glanced around, saw minimal cars and foot traffic, then ducked down a side alley. He took off his windbreaker, his skullcap, and his glasses, then threw them all in a trash bin loaded with the previous day's gluten-free cookies and pastries. Ridding himself of the clothing articles was a minor attempt at disguising his appearance should anyone check the nearby cameras, but the smallest things could help throw the authorities off his trail.

He debated for a moment, and then Cleo's firearm went in, too, after he scrubbed it free of prints as well as he could.

Quirk went into the bakery, grabbed a bottle of water from the cooler, and paid for it. He kept his face pointed away from the woman behind the counter. Ounce of prevention and all that. Was it necessary? Maybe, but maybe not, since it would be a number of days before some sketch artist's rendering of his face was all over the news. He thanked her, she smiled, and he left. Incident-free, but for how long?

Quirk walked slowly until he'd downed the bottle then picked up his pace. He hadn't been thinking clearly as he left the parking garage, and he wondered how much attention he'd drawn to himself by *running* through the streets of downtown Portland not dressed for exercise.

Stupid, he thought. *You know better than that.*

His only solace was that the police wouldn't be on his trail yet. It could be hours before Cleo's body was discovered, hours before the detectives conducted their routine checks, and hours before they reviewed the video feeds and saw him sprinting away. There would be plenty of time to get home, grab some things, and get gone. He only needed a few hours to get an adequate head start.

The exit plan had always been the same. Shave his beard, shave his head, ditch the Portland uniform, and pick up the reserve car, the rusty Camry, and drive. There was a man in northern Washington who had a private plane; they'd take a short trip up to Alaska, and then he'd be on a flight out of Anchorage with his fake identity.

With any luck, the cops, the Feds, whoever, would've shut down the escape routes from the local airports and train stations, but they wouldn't have anticipated his departure from somewhere as far away as Anchorage.

The trick was to go, get on the move, and never look back.

The money he'd earned was untouchable, untraceable, and would be waiting for him once he got to Shanghai. It would work. He knew it would.

By this time next week, he'd be on a small yacht, sipping drinks, relaxing, and hopefully watching some beautiful woman skinny-dip in the sky-blue water.

Quirk wished he'd thought to park his car somewhere away from Powell's. He could use it right now. From his current spot, it was at least three miles back to his home. Walking would take too long. Running would attract attention—no need to make that mistake again.

He raised his hand, waved down a cab, and prayed that the driver was unobservant.

. . .

The cabbie knew some of the better shortcuts and they made good time. Outside of Quirk's home, there were no police or federal agents waiting for him, which was a great sign.

He ascended his front steps slowly, stepping over the fourth one that always creaked under his weight, and stopping on the porch, he turned and scanned the streets. No unusual cars. No delivery trucks or service vans that could accommodate a couple of FBI guys with a parabolic mic and bottles of stakeout urine tucked in an empty cooler.

So far, so good.

Then the first weird thing happened.

The front door of his house was unlocked. Quirk hesitated before pushing it open. He remembered locking it before he left. Right? He had, hadn't he? Key in, pull the door tighter against the doorjamb to align the latch, and twist. It was the same routine every time.

He frowned. Maybe he had forgotten. He'd been in a hurry and was obsessing over getting to see Cleo again. The traitor. Damn her.

Quirk closed his eyes and inhaled. Time's wasting. There were no other options. He'd gather up some things, make up his mind about the laptop bomb in his basement, and then place the call. *Things got hot, get the plane gassed up.* That call.

He pushed the door open, took two steps inside, and smelled an unfamiliar scent. Perfume, maybe. No—laundry detergent? That after-scent of fabric softener that clings to clean clothes? It wasn't his. He didn't use fabric softener. His skin itched when he did.

Quirk stopped and stood motionless, listening, trying to make his breathing as silent as possible, positive the intruder could hear his heartbeat pounding. The house was old and creaky. The hard-wood floors swelled and flexed in the humidity, changing with the temperature fluctuations of Portland's weather. This fact was both a benefit and a disadvantage.

He regretted tossing Cleo's handgun in with the other refuse. The three weapons he owned—a 9mm, a .45, and a .22 revolver—were all downstairs, along with his fake IDs, his fake passport, and his small stack of get-the-hell-out money.

Downstairs. So far away. Wouldn't it have made more sense to keep them stashed by the door in prep for a hasty exit? Too late now.

Quirk wondered if he was being paranoid, if his senses were all redlining because he'd murdered a fellow...what was she? Fellow murderer? Fellow terrorist? Both? He was on edge, nothing more. That was it. He'd forgotten the door because he'd been thinking about Cleo, and the fabric softener smell could've been coming from the partially open window. Mrs. Lewis, the next-door neighbor, was doing laundry. That made the most sense, didn't it?

He took a deep breath, felt the muscles in his shoulders release, and got halfway to the basement door before a woman pivoted into the living room from where she'd been hiding in the hall.

Gun raised, urging him to stay calm.

Quirk had never seen this woman before, but he knew who she had to be.

The only question remaining was why she was in his house and not directing the mission's objectives from, well, from wherever the hell she called the shots. He imagined Boudica like a Bond villain, hiding in her impenetrable fortress high in the mountains of some tropical island only accessible by helicopter or private jet.

"Easy, Quirk," she said. "Go back and shut that door. We have a lot to talk about." She stepped around his pile of dirty laundry on the floor.

The sound of her voice confirmed it. "Boudica?"

"Over to the couch." She flicked the gun barrel to her left, nudging him. "Hands up where I can see them."

"How long have you been here?"

"Sit. Now."

"Okay." Quirk scooted around the coffee table and lowered himself onto his favorite thrift-store purchase. He'd gotten the couch years ago for twenty bucks, and it had held up well through so many moves. If Boudica shot him, he wondered how the blood-stains would look against the brown material. Probably no different than all the beer, coffee, and chocolate milk stains that blended in with the rest of the pattern.

Boudica said, "I've been here long enough to reconsider killing you."

"Reconsider? Does that mean you'd been *thinking* about it?"

"I'm pretty sure that's how the dictionary defines it, genius."

"No, I mean—why?"

"Doesn't matter. It's a moot point now, anyway. One question for you." She moved in front of the television. "Did you kill Cleo?"

"I—uh—I'm not…"

Boudica took a step closer. "I'm not going to kill you. Not yet anyway, but I know she turned, okay? So what I want to know is if *you* killed her specifically, or if you were with someone else. What I'm asking is did someone else kill her and you escaped, or did you have an accomplice? What happened back there in the garage?"

"Oh God, was that you? When the door opened?"

"Answer the question, Quirk."

"It was me! Okay? Me, I did it. She was working with the FBI and she had me trapped down there, waiting on some guy to show up. She'd turned and I think she was going to get us all arrested or something, or maybe try to get me to be an informant. Something, God, I don't know, but I heard the door to the stairs open and it distracted her just long enough for me to hit her with a chunk of concrete. She went down, I got her gun, *pop-pop,* and she's done. I did you a favor."

"I know you did."

"So does that mean you're still going to kill me?"

"I'm assessing the situation, Quirk."

"That's not...that's not reassuring."

"It wasn't meant to be. You still owe me for London."

"I said I was sorry—"

"*Sorry?*" Boudica laughed. "We're wanted by governments all across the world for international terrorism, Quirk. You don't get to say sorry when you screw up."

"But we did what we wanted to do, didn't we? The guy that owned the game shop, we got him. I thought that's what this whole thing was about. We're proving a point to the world."

"Maybe, but it was too messy, way too messy. Anyway, he wasn't the actual target—"

"He wasn't?"

"Shut up. I'm talking. You, and your brilliant idea to leave the bomb in the actual shop, instead of the second floor of the hotel like I'd asked, almost missed the woman I really wanted. You're lucky she died in the hospital."

"Who was she?" Quirk shook his head. This was the first he'd heard of an alternate mission objective. Bomb the hell out of White's Used Games in London and then wait on the media to discover their information packets in which The Clan claimed responsibility for all the previous attacks, and their written statement regarding the fact that video game violence was a preventable evil.

"Doesn't matter, not to you, anyway. The point is you've stayed loyal, unlike that pixie with a couple of holes in her chest. Nice grouping, by the way."

"Thanks."

"I have Dimitri monitoring the police radio bands. He'll let me know when the bodies have been discovered."

"Who's Dimitri? And did you say *bodies*? Plural?"

"He's the Spirit's...protégé, for lack of a better word and yes, *bodies*. Cleo and the FBI agent handling her."

In more ways than one, Quirk thought. "You got him?"

"He showed up a couple of minutes after you ran up the ramp and disappeared. I'm surprised he didn't see you on his way in."

"I'm sorry."

"Say sorry again and I'll put a bullet between your eyes. What we have to do now is figure out how to finish this screwed-up mess as quickly as we can and then disappear. We're both on video feeds all over downtown Portland and I'd guess that we have less than twenty-four hours before our pictures are on the six o'clock news."

Reluctantly Quirk agreed, feeling the daydreams of blue water and an ocean breeze fading away. At least he wasn't going to die on his couch. Not for a while. "So what do we do?"

"You and I have to find a woman named Sara Winthrop—"

That's the woman that Cleo mentioned.

"—and the Spirit is proceeding with Plan B."

"What's that?"

"Remember the first device you built and gave to Rocket two weeks ago?"

"Yeah."

"*Boom.*"

Chapter Twelve

Sara gnawed on a knuckle, a nervous habit she'd picked up since Shelley's game. The pain reminded her to stay alert and focused. She said, "What was up with Timms back in the office, huh? What made him freak out like that?"

"Somebody messed up his coffee order. Don't change the subject."

"I'm not. I'm wondering if we should be worried about the kids and Miss Willow. Obviously something went wrong."

"I'm sure whatever it was is completely unrelated to your children. The man said it himself, they've got people watching. Don't borrow trouble."

Sara sighed. They were finally moving after at least a thirty-minute delay trying to get across the Burnside Bridge.

Out the window of Barker's car, she watched the world go by. Trees, houses, a pizza joint, a laundry, a convenience store, more houses. Happy little homes where nice families were tucked away inside, cozy and warm, riding out the messy, wet autumn season. Pretty soon the temperature would dip enough to create nasty sheets of ice everywhere. She dreaded the dreary winter.

Maybe the answer was to leave Portland.

Jim had discussed the prospect of opening a satellite office back east. He'd been looking to expand and from the numbers they'd drawn up, moving into a new office and signing a long-term lease made more sense than recruiting and relocation costs.

Brian's remaining family up in Seattle would cause a ruckus about not being able to see the children on a regular basis, but after what he'd put her through, she had every right to make her world her own. The kids would enjoy more opportunities to visit Grandma and Grandpa's farm down in southwest Virginia. The laundry list of benefits was too long to list.

What was holding her in Portland? Nothing.

"Sara?" Barker said.

"Huh?"

"Where'd you go?"

"Virginia."

"Nice there. Got some family in that area."

"I was thinking that once this is over maybe I should take the kids and move back home." She turned to him, watched for his reaction. She had no solid ties to Barker other than a distant friendship and their mutual loss of JonJon, whom Sara didn't even know that well to begin with, but she enjoyed his visits, valued his opinion, and wanted to gauge his response.

The corners of his mouth turned down, not in a frown, but as if he were considering it. He offered a small nod. "Maybe so, but I can't keep an eye on you from three thousand miles away."

"You'd manage to do it somehow." She grinned at him. "Besides, it's just a thought. Jim's been considering an office somewhere back east. We need the talent, but mostly I think it's posturing."

"How so?"

"More offices, we look bigger and more attractive to investors. He's been thinking about going public again."

"Interesting. Does any of *that* have anything to do with this situation? Possibly competitive companies?"

"No. No way. I doubt anybody outside of Jim, Teddy, and I has any clue."

"Good, then stop avoiding the present issue and tell me more about this Boutique, or Bouquet, or Boudica…Crazy Lady, whatever the hell her name is."

"Right, I was hoping you'd forgotten."

"Trust me, young lady, the ol' Bloodhound has still got his wits firing on all cylinders."

Sara watched a maroon Toyota merge in front of them. They eased up to a stoplight.

"I'm waiting."

Sara closed her eyes. "Twenty years ago—was 1993 twenty years ago already? How'd that happen? We were in high school and it was my junior year, and it was the homecoming football game. Every year we played the town just south of us—I mean, God, that rivalry has been going on since my grandparents were in high school. I think we were up by something like four touchdowns at that point, so this group of girls I was trying to hang out with—"

Barker honked his horn. The driver noticed the green light and moved. Barker said, "Wait, *trying* to hang out?"

"It was more like they were evaluating me so they could see if I was cool enough to be a part of their group. Did you ever see *Mean Girls*?"

"No, but I'm divorced from three of them."

Sara laughed. "It's a movie, Barker. You should get out more."

"Did you pass their test?"

Sara's bottom lip quivered. She tried to contain it. "Not after homecoming night. I didn't want anything to do with them."

It had been unseasonably warm that fall, and Sara and the ultra-cool clique of popular girls were strutting around the stadium in their shortest shorts and tank tops, teasing all the high school boys who wanted them but couldn't have them, while the ones the girls wanted were down on the field in sweaty uniforms and tight football pants. Was that what they were called? Football pants? She couldn't remember. Regardless, Troy Thomas was down there, the all-state wide receiver, and through whatever witchcraft the other girls had conjured up, he'd asked her to the dance.

Even back then Sara thought that Julie Harland—the self-appointed leader and master manipulator—had arranged it as a test. Do well with Troy, impress him, maybe offer him an awkward handjob in the back of his Jeep, and she might get accepted as one of the elite. Fail, and it was back to the bottom of the totem pole. There's nothing quite like the pure nastiness behind a teenage girl with a motive.

Sara explained this to Barker, and he nodded knowingly, mumbling something about how none of his ex-wives had grown out of that stage.

Sara said, "It was so warm that night, and like I said, we were already up by so many points that we'd lost interest, and that's not to say we gave a shit about the points anyway, but it was sort of an unwritten rule that we were supposed to keep up with who scored and how, just so we could impress the players later…Anyway, we all walked over to the concession stand on the far side of the field to get popsicles.

"We were standing in line, and like the usual teenage brats, we were gossiping about whoever and whatever, making fun of anybody that wasn't as cool as us. Well, let me rephrase that—they were being jerks, and I was the yes-girl. Don't give me that look, Barker, it's the truth. It made me uncomfortable how…*nasty* they were, and by that time I was already having second thoughts."

"You must've been a rare breed," Barker said.

"Why do you say that?"

"A teenage girl that's waffling over morality versus being popular? I mean, damn, I was never a teenage girl—"

"Are you sure?"

"Don't let my yearbook picture fool you, but what I'm saying is, wouldn't most of them sell their soul to the devil to win the popularity contest?"

"I think some of them do. But yeah, I was having morality issues already."

"See? There's your proof that you're a good soul. You knew the difference back when you were supposed to ignore it for the sake of the wrong kind of attention."

"Not exactly."

"Uh-oh."

"Well, there was Troy to think about. He was so cute and I absolutely didn't want to give up that opportunity, at least not until after the dance, you know? I'd already made up my mind that I was going to go as far as I wanted to with him without going all the way."

"I don't need to hear those details."

"Don't worry—we didn't even go to the dance together, and I heard that he raped a cheerleader in college a couple of years later, so it's a good thing."

"Jesus, yeah. You dodged a bullet. Why didn't you go to the dance?"

"After what happened at the game, I threatened to tell somebody and they told me if I said a word, they'd make my life hell."

"What happened at the game? What'd you do?"

"You mean what *didn't* I do."

Sara recounted how they'd been waiting in line for popsicles and ice cream cones, laughing at some girl for her choice in shoes, when Lucy had spotted Patty Kellog walking behind the opposing team's bleachers. Lucy had pointed and said, "Hey, where do you think Batty Patty is going?"

The four of them had watched as the overweight, frumpy girl ducked out of sight.

Julie had said, "There's nothing back there, let's go see what she's doing."

And so they had gone. They'd hurried, ignoring the catcalls from horny high school boys and darting past the cute nerds who were too shy to speak. They'd darted past the parents who'd snuck off to the end of the stadium to add a shot of Jim Beam to their fountain sodas, and then, when they'd reached the end of the bleach-ers, they'd stopped and poked their head around the back side. The opposing team's fans were stomping the metal seats above, cheering and screaming, however hopeless the situation on the field might've been. Sara and the clique couldn't hear a thing aside from the thun-derous roar over their heads.

They hadn't been able to see much, either, since the bleach-ers backed up close to an abandoned factory building about twenty yards away. It blocked the light emanating from Sara's hometown on the other side, and the stadium lights barely penetrated back there.

Barker turned left onto Ellery Road. Sara's house was only a few blocks and a couple of turns away. He said, "Sounds like where we used to go for first base when I was a teenager. Of course, back then we were playing England as the away team."

Sara didn't laugh.

He looked over and saw her wipe at the corner of an eye.

She said, "Julie spotted Patty first and started running toward her, so we all followed like good little lemmings. Poor Patty, she never heard us coming."

"What was she doing? Drinking? Drugs?"

"No—she...you got any tissues in here?" Barker opened the center console and pulled one free of its box. Sara took it, blew her nose, and continued. "She had her shorts down around her ankles and she was squatting on one of the support beams. At first I thought maybe the line for the girl's bathroom was too long, you know? We did it all the time. Sneak off, pee wherever you can. But nope, Patty was...God, I can't even say it out loud. The closer we got, we finally realized she was...she was masturbating."

Surprised, Barker jerked the wheel a little. "*No.* Out in public like that? Why?"

"I have no idea. She wasn't really as off in the head as everyone thought she was—I'd talked to her a few times, like during classes and whatever, and she always seemed a little...misunderstood, I

guess. The only thing I can think of is that maybe she was just testing her boundaries for the thrill of it. Does that make sense? Like
maybe how people try to have sex in an airplane bathroom."

"So she was more or less joining the Mile High Club by herself
underneath the bleachers."

"Right."

"I'm afraid to ask what happened next."

"And I'm embarrassed to tell you."

"You know what, I think I've heard enough. I can get the gist of
where it's going, but please tell me you weren't a part of it."

"I've kept this buried for so long, Barker. I never told Brian
about it, I've never mentioned it to a therapist...that's how deep
it's stayed."

"Now you want to tell *me* to get it off your chest?"

"That's part of it, but maybe it'll help you and Timms understand what's going on inside Patty Kellog's head."

Barker took his eyes off the road and stared at Sara. He could see
the shame and pain twisting her features. "I'd rather you tell it to a
profiler, but okay. Shoot."

Sara told him about how they'd stopped roughly ten feet from
Patty and watched her, and it was then that they had realized what
she was doing. Julie had turned to them with a disgusted face and
mouthed, "Oh my God." She'd pulled Rebecca, Lucy, Melinda,
and Colleen closer, leaving Sara behind, saying to her, "You stand
guard."

The four of them had climbed through the bleacher supports,
surprised Patty by grabbing her arms, and held her down. She
screamed, but no one could hear with the deafening noise overhead,
thousands of feet pounding the metal structure above. Julie had
flashed a look at Sara—

"It was so *malevolent*," Sara said. "I pretended to laugh because
I was honest-to-God scared of her by then. It really hit me how
horrible she was. Then the worst part happened, as if it could get

any worse. The four of them held that poor girl down and forced her to finish. Lucy was a photographer for the school newspaper and they threatened to take pictures of her and post them all around the school if she didn't."

"Hold on—they forced her to finish masturbating?"

Sara couldn't contain her tears any longer. She whimpered, "Yes."

"Why?"

"Julie kept saying, 'It's your punishment, you dirty whore,' over and over."

"I—uh—wow, I don't even have words for that."

"Who's a good soul now, huh?"

"Come on, you didn't do it. We've all got skeletons we aren't proud of."

"I didn't do it, but I didn't stop it either. Maybe we all deserve what we get after they did that to her."

Barker turned onto Sara's street and saw her place five houses down. He slowed, creeping along, delaying their arrival so they could finish their conversation. "Listen to me, Sara, you don't deserve shit. I know you. You're a good woman. You're a fantastic mother. Your shell might be a little hard, but you're soft on the inside and I know it. Even if karma exists, and even if it's a bitch, you've already paid, you hear me?"

"Have I? Really? Have I paid enough?"

"The way I see it, yeah."

"I don't know." Sara blew her nose. "Tell me something. Do you think some people are born evil?"

"Possibly."

"Then which is worse, somebody who's born evil, or somebody who becomes evil because they were made that way?"

Barker shook his head. "I've been in this job for a long time, Sara. I've seen the horrible stuff people can do, and I still don't have an answer for that. I don't know if anyone does."

Sara shook her head, her mind refusing to let go of that distant regret. "What if I haven't paid enough, Barker? I didn't stop them and I should've. What if the universe or karma decided that I haven't bled enough for my sins?"

"Sara, stop." Barker parked in front of her house. The lights were on inside. The glow of the television seeped through the thin curtains.

Sara watched the front door, waiting on Jacob or the girls to come running out to greet them.

Barker said, "The past ain't what it used to be. You're a good soul, and you wanna know how I know?"

Sara sniffled. "Yes."

"You're still crying about it twenty years later. If you had evil in your heart, you wouldn't care...you'd be laughing about it, not sitting here regretting what you should've done. End of story, young lady. Now, let's go inside and see your kids. You look at their cute little faces and see those smiles because they're so excited to see you, then you can tell me whether or not you've paid enough, okay?"

Sara nodded.

Barker squeezed her hand.

They got out and started across the street.

The force of the deafening explosion lifted them into the air and threw them back against the side of the car.

Chapter Thirteen

Teddy led Karen into Firebrand not knowing what to expect. He hadn't been there in months, but from what he could see it didn't matter, because the place hadn't changed. It had a rather unique western theme in that there were murals of cowboys on the walls, dressed in their rustic open-range gear. Wide-brimmed hats, boots with spurs, and long dusters that stretched down to their ankles. It could be seen as normal if all the cowboys weren't cartoonish aliens with green skin, wide, round eyes, and snaggletooth smiles.

Alien cowboys herding alien-looking cattle, having gunfights with Native Americans, or sitting around campfires.

Teddy had often thought about asking Ivan, the owner, where in the hell he'd gotten his inspiration, but knowing Ivan, it was nothing more than his odd, eclectic Russian taste. A touch of the weird, just because.

There were cactus plants and the swinging double doors of a saloon. Pistols and holsters hung behind the bar. Teddy remembered that the last time he'd been there, they'd served him a sarsaparilla float. As if every night wasn't western-themed, Thursday nights were specifically designated Western Night, and the ladies got free drinks if they came to the bar dressed as cowgirls. Which, of course, meant it was Teddy's favorite night to visit Ivan and hear more stories of his time with the Red Mob.

Now, on Saturday at around noon, the place was close to empty except for the lone man at the bar eating peanuts and watching soccer on the flat-screen that hung above the rows and rows of liquor bottles.

Teddy pointed to the man and told Karen, "That's Ivan's brother, Oleg. He wrestled for Mother Russia in the Olympics. They called him The Bear."

Impressed, Karen nodded and said, "He looks like he could eat one for breakfast."

"Don't be surprised if he spits out a claw. That dude scares the crap out of me."

Oleg turned, saw Teddy, and gave a quick flick of his chin to say hello.

Teddy whispered, "He doesn't like me that much."

"Why?"

"You've met me, right? Do most people need a reason?"

"You're not so bad."

"Right."

A young blonde woman emerged from a doorway to the right of the bar. She was tall and thin with a sparkling smile and bright blue eyes that could be seen across the room. She wiped her hands on a rag, asked Oleg if he wanted another round, and then spotted Teddy and Karen standing near the doorway. "Howdy, stranger!"

To Teddy, hearing a western twang coupled with a Russian accent was impossibly cute. "Hey, Irina."

He hadn't seen her in months. She looked fantastic. She had a brighter glow to her skin and she'd put on a couple of healthy, much-needed pounds. He imagined that if she were to lift her shirt, he wouldn't be able to play her ribs like a xylophone. The last time he'd talked to her, she was close to getting her braces removed—he waited on her to smile again—yes, perfection. White and straight, giving her a look that suggested professional tennis star instead of meth addict.

Maybe Ivan had the right idea. Now that she'd straightened herself out, worked a proper job, got off whatever drugs she'd been addicted to back when they first met, he could see the possibilities. But then, there was the woman standing next to him—

Karen cleared her throat.

Teddy blinked and refocused on the present. "Right, Karen, this is Irina, she's Ivan's granddaughter."

"Hi, Irina."

"Howdy."

Teddy smirked as they moved over to the bar. "What's with the accent?"

"It's a new thing, y'all. Grandpa says it gives the place more flavor, so I gotta talk like a sweet lil' cowgirl while I'm working."

Oleg grunted. "Is bullshit. Disgrace to our homeland."

Irina giggled and threw the wet bar towel at him. "The Bear is grouchy this morning. Y'all want a drink?"

"No, thank you," Karen said. "We're sort of in a rush."

"You sure? On the house."

Teddy said, "We can't. We're actually looking for someone and wanted to know if we could speak to Ivan for a couple of minutes."

"Sure thing, sweetheart, y'all come on back. I hope you remember how to play cards."

"Oh, I haven't forgotten."

Karen flashed a look at Teddy. "We don't have time for that."

"We may not have a choice."

As they left the main bar, where the air smelled like stale beer and cleaning solution with subtle undertones of western leather, they crossed into the backroom and stepped into a murky haze where the cigar smoke hung nearly impenetrable over the heads of six men sitting around a table.

Irina, dropping the accent but speaking in English as a courtesy to Teddy and Karen, said, "Grandpa, look who's here—your favorite son."

Karen leaned over and whispered in Teddy's ear, "Favorite son?"

"Son-in-law." Teddy took a closer look at Ivan once they'd reached the perimeter of the table. The fluorescent bulb overhead broke through the thick fog of cigar smoke. Ivan didn't look so well. His hair was uncombed. He'd lost weight. His skin looked sallow and saggy around his cheeks and eyes. The oxygen tubes, extending from the tank to his left, hung across his ears, but the tips lay limply at his chest instead of in his nose where they belonged.

Teddy's heart ached. He'd never gotten over his healthy fear of the old man, but the relic drooping in his chair was not the terrifying brute he'd once been. And so quickly. Six months? If that?

Irina scolded Ivan for not having the oxygen tubes inserted into his nostrils. She fussed around him, fixed his hair, and helped him guide them in. "All this smoke in here, Grandpa, you shouldn't do this anymore."

Pride has a way of trumping sickness.

A year ago Ivan would've chased Irina out of the room, swatting her with a rolled up newspaper for speaking to him like that in front of his friends and partners. Instead, he smiled warmly at her, patted her cheek, and asked for another cup of green tea. Irina said to Teddy, "Keep an eye on him," and then left them alone.

"Ivan," Teddy said, "you look like hell. Did one of these jokers beat you up?" He patted Andrei on the shoulder, the man who used to be Ivan's former bodyguard back during the Cold War. Andrei took his hand, squeezed, and shook.

Ivan croaked, "My boy. Come see me," and waved Teddy over.

Teddy eased around the table, shook Ivan's hand, and then allowed the old man to pull him down for a hug.

"Who's your friend?"

"This is Karen Wallace. She's—" Teddy hesitated, unsure of how the group would react to a former FBI agent and current private investigator amongst them. "She's a friend of mine."

Karen smiled, waved, said hello, and kept her distance.

Ivan winked at Karen. "Not a girlfriend, I hope. You know, Teddy, my Irina is still single."

"She looks amazing."

"Thank you. All for you. Let me know when you're ready. Anyway, anyway, where are my manners—we need to introduce your friend. Karen Wallace, say hello to Andrei, Viktor, Boris, Yefim, and Nikolai. The best Mother Russia had to offer, and now the worst Uncle Sam has seen."

Karen stepped forward, waved, and responded with smiles as a chorus of greetings filled the room in broken English.

Ivan said, "You have time for a game? We could use some fresh meat in the pot. Three fingers over prime rate, as always." He laughed, and so did his comrades.

Boris, the white-haired, decrepit flower-shop owner and former hitman, said, "Ivan, please. He takes all our cash. I'm short on rent this month. Go away, Smurfboy. You're not welcome." He laughed too, as did the others.

Teddy put his hands in his pockets. "Unfortunately, as much as I'd love to steal your lunch money, Boris, we don't have time."

Irina returned, carrying a steaming mug of green tea. The string was twisted around the handle. Teddy recalled teaching her that trick. She smiled at him as she set the tea in front of Ivan.

Teddy felt a warm pull in his stomach when she bent over. What was that? Longing? He returned her smile and made up his mind to come back and visit her soon.

Should he? Why not?

Karen was out of his league and he knew it. And Irina was too, for that matter, but at least she didn't grimace whenever he walked into a room. He'd been working with his therapist on reading and processing social cues. Sara had mentioned recently that he'd shown some progress around the office, but he couldn't tell if she was telling the truth or falsely encouraging him.

"Actually," he said, "we're here to ask you for a small favor, Ivan."

"For my favorite son, anything. What do you need? Come, sit. Sit. Andrei, make some room for my boy." Andrei scooted to the side and pulled another chair around for Teddy to sit. "Join us, Karen Wallace. We're not such rude old men like we seem—we'll make room."

"No, thank you. I'll stand."

Ivan nodded. "You're young, one day you'll sit." He returned his attention to Teddy. "Tell Ivan what he can do for you, Smurfboy."

"We're looking for someone." Teddy watched as Karen stepped closer, arms crossed, waiting to get involved, if necessary. Or perhaps she was ready to shut him up if he said too much. He'd been working on that, too. "It's sort of a long shot and I don't know if you would even have the slightest clue who this guy might be…he's a Russian here in the States now, and we think he has some business here in Portland."

"And you think just because we're Russian, we know this man?"

"I…uh…well, the thing is, Ivan, he's sort of…we think he does *underground* work, if you know what I mean." Teddy swallowed hard. He hoped that he'd managed to convey his point without offending anyone. Ivan would be fine, he was sure of it, but Viktor and Nikolai could be temperamental.

Ivan raised his chin. "Mmm-hmm." He reached down to his side and twisted the valve of the oxygen tank, turning it off.

Karen added, "I think what Teddy means is—"

Ivan held up a hand. "I know what he means," he said, then faced Karen. "My apologies for interrupting. I get annoyed when I learn of comrades doing *underground* work, as Teddy says, without coming to see me first."

"He's extremely dangerous."

"And we're not?"

Teddy sensed the need to step in before Karen dug her hole any deeper. Former FBI, private investigator, whatever authoritative, mental mode she was currently in wouldn't hold up against the bravado of the retired Russian mafia. Teddy wanted to say, "Finesse, Karen. Be a ballerina, not a bulldozer." He'd heard Detective Barker say that a while back. Barker wouldn't mind if he used it.

Instead, he told Ivan, "A friend of ours is in trouble. Do you remember me telling you about Sara, the woman that works with me?"

"I do. She had the kidnapping game with her kids."

"Right, her."

"She's doing well?"

"No, not actually. She's—"

"Again with this woman? What now?"

"I wish we could tell you, but I think the official phrase is… Karen, help me out here."

"We're not at liberty to say."

"Yeah, that."

Boris laughed. "Fuck your liberty."

"Boris!" Ivan snapped. "Respect the guests, please."

Boris hung his head and offered a small, apologetic wave. "Joking, joking."

"Who is this man, Teddy? Tell me his name."

"Karen will have to confirm it for sure, but as far as I know, it's Vadim Bariskov," Teddy said, tensing when the men around him flinched. They knew the name, it seemed, and weren't too excited by the fact. "He also goes by—"

Ivan pounded the table with his fist. Poker chips bounced and drink glasses rattled. Andrei's soda toppled over. Ivan said, "The Spirit. Andrei, did you know this man was in town?"

Andrei stuttered, "N-n-no."

"Did anyone?"

The other four men muttered a combination of responses in Russian and mixed English, all amounting to, "We had no idea."

Teddy said, "So I guess you know him."

Ivan took a sip of his green tea and nodded. "Yes. Ex-KGB. Caused me years of trouble. I would rip out his heart and feed it to Andrei if we ever crossed paths again."

"Then maybe we can do something about that. We're kind of in a rush, and it's important so we can help Sara. Would you have any idea how we can find him?"

Ivan drummed his fingers on the table.

Teddy couldn't tell if it was anger, fear, or something else in the old Russian's eyes.

Ivan said, "You don't find the Spirit. The Spirit finds you."

Chapter Fourteen

Quirk drove the dark blue Honda while Boudica called the remainder of the group. Most of them were stationed around Portland in various locations, waiting to execute additional stages of her plans. She'd mentioned that Plan B was in effect because Cleo's betrayal to the FBI had left her with no choice. Quirk had no idea what Plan A had been, much less what the details of Plan B were. His only task had been to build the bombs and deliver them to Rocket when necessary, and when asked.

Boudica's first phone call was to Chief, whom Quirk had met once to finalize a minor detail, without her knowledge. She said, "How in the hell did you miss it, Chief? Cleo was the—Jesus, it sounds so stupid when I say it out loud, but she was the double agent, playing both sides. Listen to me, do not let it happen again, or I will personally fly to D.C. and I will slit your throat while you sit there in your little cubicle. I don't care if it's the FBI headquarters or not, do you hear me? If you miss something like that again, I'm going to march straight down Pennsylvania Avenue, through those front doors, and I will find you. Don't apologize; it's too late. Find out what Timms did with Sara Winthrop and call me back as soon as you know something. Then, if you've managed to do that without screwing up, get me everything you can on Melinda Wilkes in Paris. Do you need to ask when? I wanted it yesterday."

Her second phone call was to Sharkfin. Quirk had never met her before, but from some of the minor details he'd gathered from Cleo she was the "gatherer" of the group, for lack of a better term. Passports, IDs, flight information, and FBI movements were only some of the things she was responsible for. Sharkfin had been the one to find the exotic explosive material after DarkTrade's demise. Boudica said to her, "We've moved on to Plan B. I don't have time to explain everything, but let's just say that your shares are only getting split five ways now. We need a brand new set of everything for all of us. IDs, driver's licenses—U.S. and French both—new tickets to Paris. Everything. We're new people. Yes, that's right...all except for Cleo."

The sound of her name sent an uncomfortable tremor through Quirk's stomach.

He regretted what had happened to her, what he'd done to her—he couldn't make an obsession that had held strong for nearly two years disappear in an afternoon, not completely...Yet she'd betrayed them. She was going to turn him in to the FBI.

Boudica brought up an excellent point. Their pay would only be split five ways.

Quirk signaled, drove up the entrance ramp to the interstate. *Five ways*, he thought. *More for me, less for turncoats.*

Third, she called Rocket. "How'd it go? Are you there now? Jesus, don't get too close, idiot. What if they spot you? I'm sure it's beautiful, psycho, but if you get caught standing around admiring your work, you just remember what happens if they're able to get information out of you. Oh, it'll be worse than that. Listen, do me a favor and get out of there before it comes to that, okay? All right, I'll check in later. Whoa, what? She's there now? She saw it happen? Don't you think that's the first thing you should've told me? What's she's doing right now? You're kidding. Sometimes the universe aligns, huh? Damn it, I can't believe I'm missing that. Rocket? Hey, stay back. I said stay back. Keep your distance. I'll call Tank and let him take care of it. I said forget it. Don't let Sara Winthrop out of your sight, and if she's escorted away before Tank gets there, pay attention to which vehicle. He'll be in touch."

Boudica slapped the burner shut and shook her head. "Did *you* tell me to hire Rocket?"

"No." Quirk checked the mirrors. "He was…I think Cleo knew him. His brother was the one who died—"

"I don't care. But Cleo, that explains it. Anyway, it sounds like Plan B is going well so far, despite the fact that Rocket is in the crowd, staring at her house from across the street. Moron. The good news is, I think—well, I hope—he's too stupid to reveal much of anything important."

"Right. What *is* Plan B, exactly?" Quirk drove, not knowing where to go. At the moment, all he needed to do was keep the Honda between the lines. He risked a look at Boudica, paranoid that eye contact with her might turn him to stone like Medusa.

Now that he'd gotten a little closer to the woman in charge and had gotten a peek behind the curtain, he wasn't so sure what the main plan had been after all. The irony wasn't lost on him; blowing up buildings, and people, to prove the point that video games caused violence and that it was a preventable issue, but the more he listened to Boudica, the more he thought there were hidden motives behind her methods.

Boudica tapped the cheap cell phone against her knee, staring at him. She brushed a strand of wavy brunette hair out of her face and tucked it behind an ear. "You do realize I should kill you just for asking, don't you? Or have you totally forgotten that the left hand isn't supposed to know what the right hand is doing?"

"No, I was curious, that's all. I mean, it'd be nice to know if one of my creations did what it was supposed to do. Like your kid getting a word right in the spelling bee. Just…never mind. I won't ask again. Lips are sealed, you can forget I even brought it up."

"Quirk?"

"Huh?"

"Shut up."

"Yes, ma'am."

"Keep driving while I call Tank, then maybe we'll talk. Can you do that much?"

"Yes, ma'am."

Boudica dialed yet another number, and Quirk once again listened to her side of the conversation. "Tank, change of plans. I know you're as clueless as the dingleberry sitting here beside me, but we've got Plan B in effect. There's always been a Plan B. Yes. If you think you can—quiet, or I'll have to give the Spirit a call."

Boudica covered the mouthpiece with her hand and said to Quirk, "What's with you people? I feel like a goddamn kindergarten teacher trying to keep you whiny brats under control."

Then, to Tank, she added, "Yes, Tank, I *understand* it's not good when plans change, but since we don't live inside a TV show, circumstances adjust themselves accordingly. So here's what I need you to do: get over to what's left of Sara Winthrop's house and monitor the situation from a distance. Don't let Rocket see you or he'll probably wet his pants like an overexcited Chihuahua. Yeah, he's there—only engage if you can't locate Sara Winthrop. If Rocket can keep himself out of handcuffs, he'll be keeping an eye on her. If she's still there when you arrive, hang tight, and once she's escorted away, give it some distance, and then you intercept. Got it? They'll probably need the manpower there to take care of the bodies inside or to scan the area, so more than likely she'll be in an ambulance with minimal supervision, if any at all. Call me once you have her secure."

Boudica hung up, rolled down the window, and paused before tossing the disposable out onto the highway. "I should probably keep this. I don't have any spares until we meet up with Sharkfin again."

"Is that where we're going?"

"No. We're killing time until Tank can get that bitch to the drop point. Then, if I haven't killed you yet, maybe we can have a little fun together, huh?"

"If that's what you want, yeah." Quirk realized those options were likely the best he was going to get. Dying, or having fun watching…whatever it was that Boudica planned to do to this woman.

She reached over and ran the back of her knuckles down his cheek, caressing his jawline, then tugging his beard gently, playfully.

Quirk realized he'd misunderstood her definition of "fun." What in the hell was she doing?

"You've earned yourself a few more days, I guess. There's Paris to take care of, and then…who knows? Besides," Boudica said, sliding her fingers over to his ear, softly stroking the lobe. "We have some time to kill."

Quirk flinched. "Uh, wh-what do you—"

"Relax," she said, leaning over to him, putting her hand on his thigh. She eased it up toward his crotch, digging in with her fingernails at the same time. "Doesn't all of this turn you on? So close to being caught, always right on the edge of destruction. Tell me… *Mark*…what's your fantasy?"

He could feel her warm breath on his neck. Her hand slid closer to the flaccid lump in his pants. Boudica was attractive—much more attractive than he'd expected, and under normal circumstances, these advances would be welcome. But, she was also terrifying in a demented, sadistic, lady-terrorist sort of way, which helped keep the unwanted erection under control.

"Oh, uh, fantasies, fantasies—I don't really have any. So you, um, you like being caught? That's yours?" He fidgeted and tried to turn away from her teeth on his earlobe. He eased up on the gas pedal. Eighty-five miles per hour wasn't the safest or the most intelligent speed.

Boudica cupped his crotch and squeezed, traced her fingers up, and then tugged at his zipper. "So close to being caught," she said.

"The chance is always *right there*." She slid a hand underneath his shirt and pinched a nipple.

Quirk winced.

She asked, "Have you ever been caught?"

"Caught doing what?"

"Come on," she purred, "don't make me say it."

Quirk cringed. He was rarely lost. He'd always been a quick thinker, a particularly useful skill that had gotten him out of many groundings in high school, had saved his ass from a drill instructor's wrath more times than he could count, and had saved his life at least three times in Iraq. This situation with Boudica, however, was an entirely different monster altogether, and he was utterly clueless about how to proceed. Give in and entertain her lustful insanity or reject her and risk...what? A bullet to the head?

Some unfortunate hiker or hunter would discover his body in a few days, sitting lifeless and decomposing in the driver's seat of a blue Honda.

On the other hand, if he could make it out of this alive, he had a lot to look forward to, especially the twenty-footer he'd be sailing on in three months at the most.

Boudica was insane, yeah, but who was he to judge? The bombs he'd made for her had killed a dozen people around the world already, with many more on the horizon, and from the sound of it, there'd been more within the past hour.

He tried to convince himself that he could endure long enough to survive.

I'm crazy, he thought. *She's crazy. She's goddamn scary but still, she's hot, right? In that demented dominatrix way, at least? I could do it. I could do this. There's gotta be worse things than sex to stay alive. Stop it. Stop trying to talk yourself into this. Think of something.*

Boudica suckled his earlobe and pulled at it with her teeth. "I told you not to make me say it. Have you been caught before? I got caught once. Do you want me to tell you about—" The disposable phone buzzed in her lap.

She shoved herself away from him, frustrated, and snapped the phone open. "What?"

Quirk loosened his grip on the steering wheel. His fingers ached.

"Are you sure?" she asked. "Okay, good work, Rocket. Let Tank know. Yes, you're done. See you in Paris. It's in France. I'm sure you can get French fries. Goodbye, Rocket." She slammed the phone closed, threw it in the floorboard, and punched the glove compartment. Three deep breaths later, she said, "If he wasn't so good at what he does, I'd kill him myself, just to keep him from contaminating the gene pool. God help us if that guy ever breeds."

Quirk forced a laugh. He expected her to say, "Where were we?"

Instead, she gave him instructions to Coffee Creek Correctional Facility. Simple, calm, and authoritative, as if her hand hadn't been down his pants thirty seconds ago.

Yeah. Crazy.

"Why there?" he asked.

"We're going to see someone who didn't finish her job. By that time, Tank should have Sara Winthrop where we want her."

Chapter Fifteen

Sara opened her eyes. She was confused, groggy, and the muffled hum in her ears drowned out everything except the high-pitched ringing. Her head hurt, as did her back and sides. She was on the ground. Why was she on the ground?

There was a muffled pounding in her head. Was that her heartbeat? Next came the dulled voice of someone beside her. Words shouted through thick walls. Who was that?

What happened?

A piece of flaming wood fell at her side. She studied it, uncomprehending.

Fire. That's fire. Move away. Move.

Wait, that's Barker's car. Fire in the middle of the street. Wood on fire.

The voice came again. "Sara? Sara, are you okay?" Clearer than before, but masked as if filtered through a pillow.

Hands on her back, her shoulders, twisting her tenderly. "You're bleeding. Can you hear me?"

She turned her head. Pain arced through her neck and her vision muddled. When it cleared, she could see Barker kneeling at her side. A trickle of blood ran down his forehead. A piece of ash landed on his mustache as he touched her cheek and checked her eyes. He repeated, "Can you hear me?"

Sara nodded and tried to get up.

Barker urged her to stay down.

"I—I need to…what? Barker?"

Screaming. She could hear screaming in the distance. The thick shroud over her hearing slowly dissipated as she tried to regain her bearings. More flaming wood behind Barker. Shards of glass glinting on the blacktop like stars in the street.

Motion. Movement. People running, shouting for help.

Barker said, "It's going to be okay. We've got help coming. I'm sure…I'm sure there's some hope."

Hope? Why hope? What did Barker mean by that? Dizzy, Sara sat upright and glanced around her. Glass in the street. Flaming wood. A singed teddy bear, ripped, with stuffing protruding from a spot where a leg had been. A purple teddy bear with a white heart on its chest. *That's—is that—?*

"Lacey!" Sara tried to stand again and Barker grabbed her arm.

"Sara, don't. You're hurt. We need to—"

She tried to sling his arm away. "My kids. Where are—get off me. Barker, let go. Let go of me now!" She wrenched free of his grasp and stumbled when she tried to stand. She fell against his car and paused, allowing her vision to clear, feeling something warm creep down the bridge of her nose and into her right eye. Blood. She wiped it away and inhaled, centering herself.

Once the dizziness passed, she saw the unfathomable destruction.

Her home was a smoldering pile of rubble. Gone. All of it. Disintegrated into a mass of burning siding, shredded shingles, and splintered, smoking wood. There were pieces of her history laying everywhere. In the yard, in the street, on top of cars. Where once had been a life, however broken it may have seemed at times, now resided an empty spot. A hole in her heart. There, and then not there.

Were those sirens?

She screamed, "No!" and tried to run toward it. Barker grabbed her, held her back. She kicked, fought, and tried to break free.

Screaming the names of her children. They'd been inside. The three of them with Miss Willow, waiting on her to get home. She should've been in there. She should've been with them. She should've disappeared into a red mist along with them. Her life, her family. Everything she had to live for.

Gone.

The unbearable agony sent her to the ground, emotions exploding within. Detonations of anger, loss, and regret tore her insides apart, pulling so hard that she was unable to cry. Her mouth hung open, lips pulling down at the corners, stretching into an image of wretched misery.

Why? Why, God, why?

Barker sat beside her, wrapped his arms around her shoulders and pulled close. It was all he had to offer.

Sara's shoulders heaved as the sobs finally broke free. She clenched Barker's shirt and pulled, burying her face into his chest. She let go. She let the flood of tears come.

Barker stroked her hair. He waited.

The sirens approached. Fire, medical, police.

"It's not your fault," he said, gently rocking her. "There's no—"

Sara let go and slammed her fist into his chest, not from anger, but misery.

"I'm sorry, Sara."

"They're gone."

"Don't say that. Not yet." He looked at the fiery remains of the home. Maybe they were—there was always the possibility—

Sara pulled away from him and rolled onto her side. She shoved the nearest piece of flaming wood to the side. She could taste blood on her tongue, that metallic taste of a wound—emotional and physical alike. The ragged, rough edges of the blacktop dug into her cheek. She held her sides and curled into a ball, listening to the wailing sirens, the screaming, the sounds of her broken, shattered home settling...the sounds of her life ending.

Barker stood. "There's the ambulance. Can you walk? Never mind, stay there. You might have a concussion. Hey, over here! Hurry! Over here, now, damn you!" Approaching footsteps followed. "She's got a serious laceration to the head. Maybe a concussion. Over here, yeah. Sara? Do you have any nausea?"

Sara looked up to see the young paramedic leaning over her, who said, "Ma'am, can you see me okay? Hearing?" Sara told him she wanted to be left alone. "I'm sure you do, but I need to check on you anyway, okay? Follow this light for me."

Sara followed his penlight with her eyes.

"Looks like you hit your head pretty hard, but your speech is okay. No nausea? Confusion?"

"I'm fine," she said again. Physically, yes, but mentally...life would never be the same.

She heard Barker say, "That wound on her head is deep. She'll probably need stitches."

"Looks like it, yeah. Hold this here, if you don't mind."

Sara felt pressure on the side of her head. Something soft. Gauze, maybe. Barker's hand held it there. She should've been in pain. She could feel nothing but an overwhelming numbness. She stared straight ahead while the paramedic tried to treat her remaining injuries as she lay on her side.

In front of her and underneath Tom Jessup's car, the neighbor to her right, she noticed one of Jacob's shoes—the ones with lights in the soles that he'd begged and pleaded for over the summer. The explosion had damaged whatever machinations were inside the soft rubber, and she watched as the lights blinked from red, to blue, to green, to orange, and back to red. The cycle repeated like runway lights guiding an airplane in, safely delivering its passengers.

She felt the despair, the loss, somewhere deep inside, but the numbness and disbelief jammed it back down.

She heard Barker tell the paramedic, "We need to keep an eye on her, okay? That was *her* house. Her...her..." Sara could sense that Barker was having trouble with the reality, too.

She finished the sentence for him. "My family was in there."

The paramedic said, "Is anyone in the house?"

Barker stopped him. "Jesus, Mary, and Joseph. Sara. Sara, get up. Can you get up?" She turned an eye up to Barker standing overhead, but nothing more. She made no effort. He stared at something, a small smile arcing upward at the corners of his lips. "Help me get her to her feet."

Numb. Dazed. Lost. Hands hooked under her armpits. There was a sense of lifting while gravity and pain tried their best to pull her back down.

Barker said, "Look, Sara," and pointed toward the back of the gathering crowd.

"What?" she mumbled. "What am I—Willow!"

Miss Willow looked up. Her eyes went wide. Fear dissolved into relief on her face. She began shoving her way through the crowd, saying, "Excuse me! Can we get through? We need to see that woman, please."

We. That one simple word sent Sara's world into heartening mixture of gratitude and staggering joy. She stumbled around the front of Barker's car, lurching toward them as he grabbed an arm, helping her regain her balance.

Miss Willow broke through the crowd of onlookers. Jacob was in front of her. Lacey and Callie followed at her sides, each holding a hand.

Lacey and Callie shouted in unison, "Mama!"

Jacob was next with a relieved, "Mommy!"

Sara fell to her knees. She pulled all three of them in close, hugging them as if she would never let go.

She heard Barker say, "It don't happen often, but once in a while there's a goddamn miracle when you need it."

"Oh my God," Sara said, "I thought you were…Mommy thought—" She couldn't say the words. Not out loud. Saying the words out loud might make it real, it might take them away. "Where *were* you guys?"

"At the park," Jacob answered.

Sara looked up at Miss Willow, whose words came out in a nervous, shaky, rambling rush. "I have to tell you something, and it's going to sound crazy, but about fifteen minutes ago, someone called the house. I didn't recognize the number on the caller ID, but I answered it anyway because sometimes you get calls from those gaming magazine reporters and I figured it was easier to tell them not right now than to leave you to deal with it and, and—"

"Willow, what're you talking about?"

"Someone, I don't know who—he sounded older and like maybe he was…I can't even tell you what, it was so weird—but he said… he told us that we needed to leave the house, that you'd requested somebody from the police department to come by and run a sweep for bugs and it would be better if we were out of the way. He said you told him."

"And he didn't say who he was?"

Barker said, "Whoa, somebody warned you?"

Miss Willow nodded. "I almost didn't listen to him. It sounded so peculiar but maybe it was intuition or God or who knows, but he said we needed to leave the house, that it was a…I think he said 'necessary precaution,' and he said you'd requested him to call."

"And he didn't identify himself?" Barker asked, trying to confirm.

Sara added, "Think, Willow, did he?"

"No, not that I remember. Sara, who would…I'm sorry, I'm so sorry."

Barker said, "Stay right here. I'll get somebody working on the phone records right now. Be back in a sec. Donaldson? Hey,

Donaldson!" Barker moved away, walking toward a uniformed officer talking on his CB.

Sara chewed on the inside of her bottom lip. Who would call and tip off her family before blowing up her home? Was it a warning? Maybe it was a shot fired across the bow, telling her, "Look what we can do."

She shook her head. It mattered, but not right now. Her family was alive, safe, and standing in front of her.

Sara stood. She pulled Miss Willow and the children into a hug. "It's okay. Barker will figure it out. The only thing that matters is that you guys weren't in there. I thought I lost you all." She hugged Willow tighter then bent over and kissed the twins, then Jacob on top of the head. She glanced over at Barker and saw him smiling. The paramedic started to say something as he pointed at her head, but Barker shooed him away.

Some of the bystanders nearby had overheard and observed their little reunion and converged, asking if that was Sara's house and what happened and thank the Good Lord above that no one had been inside. Sara smiled and nodded, saying thank you but overwhelmed by the attention. She moved back a step and pulled her group along as well.

Barker returned and moved in front of them, urging the crowd to give them room, telling the throng of onlookers that they were now contaminating a crime scene and needed to back away, they needed to watch their step, and not to trample anything that might look like evidence. He called over some uniformed policemen and urged them into crowd control. "Rope if off, too," he said. "I want everything within the damage zone cordoned off, got it?"

"Yes, sir," one of the policemen said.

Barker marched toward Sara, all business now, transitioning into detective mode. "We'll get a look at the phone records as soon as possible."

"Good."

"Meanwhile we need to get you guys out of here, but not until they've finished checking you out. That paramedic needs to fix you up, then we'll go."

"We need to get out of here, right now."

"We will, I promise, but you're hurt and I need to brief some of the others. I need a few minutes, that's all. Besides, this is probably the safest place for you at the moment. Look at all this firepower."

"Kids, stay next to me, please," Sara said, motioning for her children to come closer. "Maybe you're right. Goddamn it. That was our *home*, Barker. And look at the neighbors' homes. Somebody needs to tell them, too. Seriously, I have to apologize whenever they get here. Their places are ruined because of me."

"Not because of you. Blame it on whoever built that bomb, you hear me? There'll be plenty of time later for apologies but at the moment, you need fixing, and then you need to be gone."

Barker marched toward an ambulance with open doors. Sara followed with her family close behind, saying, "I changed my mind, Barker. I think we should go."

"Trust me, we're safer here for the time being. Just keep the kids away from the wreckage."

"Sara," Miss Willow said, "who would do such a thing? What's going on? Did that Sergeant girl get out of prison?"

Sara shook her head. "I'll explain later."

Lacey said, "Look! My bear," and moved toward the smoldering, ragged mess of stuffing and purple material on the street.

"Leave it." Sara pulled at her arm.

"But she's mine."

"Mr. Bloodhound needs it for evidence, okay? You have to leave it there. We'll get you another one."

Jacob asked, "Is our stuff still in there, Mom?"

Mom? Not Mommy, Sara thought. *When did that start?*

"Not anymore, honey. Nothing that's worth saving."

Barker touched her shoulder. "Sara."

"Yeah?"

"Let him do his job."

The paramedic looked closely at her wound.

Sara glanced around. They were at the ambulance already. How hard had she hit her head?

Barker added, "We'll get you guys out of here soon, okay? Somewhere safe."

"Where is safe? If they can get to my home, what's to say they can't find me anywhere else, huh?"

"I'll have some of the men take you down to the station. Full escort. You'll be fine."

"That's what you said on the way over here."

"I...I know. We couldn't have seen this coming."

"What if they ambush us on the way to the station? Then where do we go? Or, supposing we make it, how long are we supposed to stay? Maybe you can have the chief bring in a decorator and cozy up one of the cells for us."

Barker reached for a cigarette and grumbled when he found a container of cinnamon toothpicks. He pulled one free and stuck it in his mouth, chewing on it, grinding it between his teeth. "I understand it's not the best option—"

"Jim's house," Sara said. "Remember? He mentioned the panic room."

"That's probably designed for short-term use, Sara. We'll do everything we can to find this group of assholes—sorry, kids—this group of *jerks* and keep y'all safe, but I can't promise it'll happen today, or even tomorrow. I need to find Timms and brief him, then we need to start pulling things together here. We'll get going as soon as possible."

The paramedic tried to get her to lie down. She shoved him away.

"Stop for a second, please?" she said, then to Barker, "We're not going anywhere without you. I don't care what has to happen, just get us to Jim's house and put us in a big metal bunker until this is over with. I don't trust anyone else except for you and him. Teddy, too, I guess, but who knows what he's doing with Karen."

"Okay, if that's the way you want it. I'll have a convoy escort you to Jim's—"

"*No*, you're coming too. Not without you. Not an option."

"Sara, I can't leave. We need to get started on the investigation."

"Take us and come back, or we'll hide in the back of one of those cruisers until you're ready to go."

Barker considered it for a moment. He pulled the toothpick from his mouth and flicked it on the ground. He paused a moment, thinking, watching the commotion of officers, firefighters, and medics working their hardest. "Okay, but here's the deal: You let Skippy here fix you up, and get these kids and Willow in the back of that ambulance and out of sight."

"Thank you."

"Hold on now. I'm not done yet. When he's finished, I want all five of you to get in my car and wait. Stay low, lock the doors, and don't speak to anyone. Let me talk to a couple of guys here and I'll be right back."

"How long?"

"I don't know, but I can't just walk away. Not yet. Not after this."

. . .

Thirty minutes later, Sara, Miss Willow, and the children climbed into Barker's car and waited. At least she thought it had been thirty minutes. Whether it was the emotional shock of thinking her family had died or the blow to her head, things seemed off. Time and distance were fuzzy.

Sara pushed a button on his radio. The LED display told her an hour had passed. She wondered if she should have the paramedic check her for a concussion again. It was easy to get lost in the chaos.

As they sat waiting on Barker, Sara noticed two men on the edge of the crowd. They appeared to be quietly arguing, and then both of them turned to stare at her in unison.

Chapter Sixteen

Teddy and Karen Wallace sat at a coffee shop three blocks away from Firebrand. Irina had begged him to stay for a drink and he'd almost obliged, but there were more pressing matters at hand. He did, however, promise that he'd be back later that evening and would take her out for a nightcap once her shift ended at ten o'clock.

They'd been there for over an hour. He hated the inaction but they were stuck, and Karen said that a hot cup of coffee always helped clear her thoughts.

Teddy thought that what she meant was a bottomless pot, quiche, and pie. For the past fifteen minutes he'd watched her jot notes down onto a small yellow pad that she'd pulled from the inside pocket of her suit coat. He admitted to himself that while he'd had a crush on her since the day his father had hired her to keep an eye on Sara, his mind, and libido, were now drifting elsewhere.

Irina looked amazing now that she'd gotten herself together. In a strange, roundabout way, down in that place where some thoughts are better left alone, he realized that if someone hadn't threatened Sara's life for a second time, he may never have gone back to Firebrand or crossed paths with Irina again, so this unfortunate situation had some silver lining to it.

And, best of all, now that he could simply admire Karen Wallace for what she was—a strong, beautiful, intelligent partner, rather than an object of desire—it might make their working relationship more efficient.

Right? He wondered if he should mention that to her. Would she appreciate it?

What would his therapist say? Or better yet, what kind of advice would *Sara* give him? She always told it to him straight, whereas sometimes he could sense that his therapist, Dr. Alan Hanks, might be telling him what he wanted to hear. Jim had likely paid the white-haired old kook too well to fit dear little Teddy into his packed schedule. Gotta keep those checks coming, Doc.

Teddy turned it over in his mind.

He could envision Dr. Hanks saying, "Teddy, my boy, the truth is always best, even when it's a lie." Or maybe that was Detective Barker, who was not his biggest fan and had a tendency to spread misinformation just to watch him squirm.

Sara would say, "Teddy, seriously…do you honestly think that Karen Wallace gives a crap about you? Has she sent you any signals of affection whatsoever?" Harsh, true, but Sara had a way of being able to read people like he couldn't.

Was the Sara in his mind right? Did Karen Wallace give a shit? Probably not.

He took a bite of a cranberry orange scone, grimaced, and said, "Ugh. Why would someone eat this on purpose?"

Without looking up from her notes, Karen smirked and said, "You ordered it."

"Well, yeah, because I thought it sounded good. That tastes like somebody sprayed fruity air freshener on a biscuit."

That got a sympathetic laugh from her.

Teddy washed the last of the bite down with a gulp of chocolate milk. It didn't improve the taste in his mouth at all. Impatient, he said, "Shouldn't we be doing something productive?"

"I am. I'm recreating the scene back at the bar with your posse. Sometimes it helps me to draw a better mental picture if I try to visualize what I might not have seen while I was looking at it."

"Uh...what?" Teddy grabbed her fork and cut away a chunk of her spinach and cheddar quiche.

"What're you doing?"

"Having a bite?"

Karen rolled her eyes and yanked the fork from his hand.

Rude, Teddy thought as she slid her plate out of his reach.

"Pay attention, you might learn something."

"Okay."

"This is what I do. Actually, let me back up a bit." Karen took a sip of her coffee. "Our brains are processing so much—okay, maybe not yours—"

"Hey!"

Karen chuckled. "Kidding. Anyway, our brains process so much that we're not consciously aware of every bit of it, right? I don't know the exact science behind it, but we'd short circuit if we were aware of everything that our brains are processing and taking in at the same time. Make sense? You look confused."

"That's because I am."

"Try it this way. While you're sitting there with a piece of scone on your cheek, you might be looking at me at the same time, and you're aware of seeing me, and you may also be aware of the sensation of something stuck to your cheek, which is when most polite people would take the hint to wipe food off of their faces."

"You're saying I'm aware I have food on my face?"

"You do, but that's not the point."

Teddy swiped at his cheek.

"Other side. Good. Got it."

"I still don't get it, and what does this have to do with Ivan and the guys?"

"The thing I'm trying to get you to see is that even though you see me, you feel the food, and maybe the weight of the fork in your hand, *that's* what you're consciously aware of, but at the same time, your brain is also processing the man in the far corner reading his newspaper. He came in about twenty minutes after we did. His hat is a bit off to one side. You might also be hearing the construction sounds going on outside. You can hear the jackhammer way off in the distance, but it's not really processing because you're focused on what's in front of you. Just because you're not paying attention to it doesn't mean that it's not happening. You might also miss the smell of the waitress's perfume—"

"Oh, no, I got that. Patchouli makes my eyes water."

"Good, that's a start. Anyway, so what I try to do is go into this sort of zone where I recreate the setting in my head and try to pluck out what I might've missed the first time."

"You mean like when you watch *Fight Club* over and over to pick up on all the spots in the film where Tyler Durden is spliced into a scene?"

"Something like that, yeah. Just think of it as watching a movie over and over and you notice new details each time."

"Got it. That was probably easier than what you were trying to describe."

"Next time I'll start with the caveman explanation first."

It was Teddy's turn to roll his eyes. Half in jest, half offended. He thought, *I wouldn't want to be with someone who treats me like something stuck to the bottom of a shoe anyway, so, uh,* your *loss, Karen.* "Whatever," he said. "So what did your subconscious pick up on back there at the bar? I've known Ivan for years and I don't really think he'd be hiding anything from me."

"He's an ex-Russian mafia boss, Teddy. He'd probably sell Irina to the highest bidder if it came to that. Who, by the way, has the serious hots for you, if you couldn't tell."

"I know. She looks great. Really cleaned herself up." He wasn't interested in talking about Irina, though, because Sara's safety was more important. You know, at least until about ten o'clock that night, and by then she'd be okay and totally out of danger, wouldn't she? It'd be cool to hang out with Irina *then*, right? Teddy asked, "Do you think Ivan was hiding something from us?"

Karen shook her head and scanned her notes again. "Not him. He might've been right when he said that the Spirit finds you, but that other guy, Viktor, I'm pretty sure I saw him shake his head when Ivan mentioned it."

Teddy cocked his head and tried to replay the scene in his mind, the way Karen had. "Wait, yeah, now that you mention it...he shook his head and took a sip of whiskey right after that, didn't he?"

"Nice! Yeah, and it looked to me like he was trying to hide it. Viktor knows something. He may not know exactly where the Spirit is, but he's got information."

"So do you want to go back there to talk to him?"

Karen shook her head. "Not a chance he'd reveal anything in front of Ivan or his comrades. He'd lose the trust they've all worked on for fifty years. But...we could stake it out and wait on him to go home. He's gotta go home at some point, doesn't he?"

Teddy fiddled with the saltshaker between his fingers. "I've seen that guy pull all-nighters, sometimes two or three days in a row. He and Ivan, and Andrei, are superhuman once they get a good game of Hold 'em running. We could be waiting until next week."

"Damn."

"I couldn't hang with them. They were brutal. "

"What if...Yeah, maybe that'd work. How close is your girlfriend to the rest of those guys?"

"Who? Irina?"

"Yeah."

"Very." Teddy faked a horrible Russian accent. "In Mother Russia, family is strong like bull, even when not family."

"You're ridiculous."

"I know."

"What if she's more into *you* than her grandfather's old cronies? Love tears families apart sometimes. I saw the way she looked at you."

"Maybe, but what're we talking about here?"

"All I want you to do is call Irina and ask her to keep an eye on Viktor. Try to eavesdrop on any phone conversations he might have if she's around. Oh, and especially if he leaves. You said he rarely leaves if they're on a bender, right? It'd be awfully convenient if he left right after we did."

"We left, what, an hour and ten minutes ago? What if he's already gone?"

Karen considered the possibility. "Nah, if Viktor's got anything to hide about an enemy of Ivan's, then he won't risk making a move so soon. He'd have to make it look natural."

"Good point."

"But you should probably call soon, just in case."

"You think it's safe to now?"

"Go for it."

Teddy got up from the table and walked to the far corner of the café, dialing Firebrand's number as he went. Irina picked up immediately, answering in her cute, Russian cowgirl accent. Teddy whispered, asking her not to reveal anything in case Oleg remained at the bar. Close by, he noticed the elderly gentlemen give him an obvious glance. It wasn't much, but enough to insinuate, "You're too close. Move."

Personal space…yet another concept he and his therapist were working on. What was the standard etiquette for U.S. citizens? Something like three feet? Was that what Dr. Hanks had said? In European countries it was more like inches.

Regardless, Teddy smiled at the man and moved twelve inches away while he relayed his instructions to Irina.

As Karen had surmised, Irina was thrilled to help Teddy, saying, "He's my least favorite, so y'all do whatever you need to, *compadre.*"

He said goodbye, and considered asking Irina to keep using the cowgirl accent when they were out later. That might be fun.

Karen finished her last bite of quiche as Teddy sat down with a huge grin. She asked, "Are we good to go?"

"I could hear her smiling through the phone, so yeah, she's in."

"Did you tell her why? You didn't say a word about me being a P.I., did you? Because we don't know how well that would fly with—"

Teddy put his hand across the table and patted her arm. *"Chill,* dude. I'm not the idiot everyone thinks I am, okay?"

She grinned. "I'll take that under consideration. So was Viktor still there?"

"As far as she knew, yeah. There's a back entrance that she can't quite keep an eye on, but she said that ninety percent of the time he'll leave through the front so he can grab a beer for the road."

"Upstanding citizen."

"Well, he's not Mother Theresa. She's supposed to call if he leaves anytime soon, but if it starts getting busy, which it likely will around five o'clock, we're on our own."

"Good enough."

"So what's next? Do we keep following leads or go ask around at the places you were talking about earlier? What's the plan?"

"Teddy, put the caffeine away. We wait."

"For what?"

"I know you think I have some sort of exciting job filled with binoculars and lasers and shootouts, but a huge part of being a private investigator is sitting, and waiting, and observing. It's a slow process sometimes. I've waited *days* to capture the right photograph. I sit in my car and drink coffee at all hours of the night, hoping that some guy's wife will leave her lover's apartment so I can take a picture and go home. It can be mind numbing, but when all you have is a flimsy lead and a strong hunch, you ride it out until the option is gone."

"Yeah, but Sara may not have days for us to wait. What if we're totally off about Viktor and he wasn't subconsciously signaling that he knew something about the Spirit, huh? We need to be proactive, not reactive."

"How, Teddy? Where do you suggest we go?"

"Your places—the churches, the markets, whatever, the ones where you said you knew some of the Russian immigrants. What if somebody there knows him?"

"First, that was a long shot because I didn't know where else to start. Second, if any of them knows where he is, there's a good chance that they'd be too terrified of him to say anything, or, if he's family, they'll keep their mouths shut to protect him. You brought us to the right place, Teddy. Thank God you had this weird little connection, because otherwise we'd be spinning in circles and chasing dead or fake leads. I know you're worried about Sara, but our best bet is to wait a while. Who knows, maybe Viktor sent a text message when we weren't looking and the Spirit will find *us*, just like Ivan said."

"I'm not sure Viktor knows what a text is. He's still struggling with the fact that phones don't hang on walls anymore. But really, do we want this Spirit guy to find us? What if he's...dangerous?"

"Then you'll be able to tell Irina about how brave you were."

Teddy heard an unfamiliar voice over his shoulder. "I'm too old to be dangerous. Move over so I can sit."

Teddy felt the gun barrel placed discreetly against his side before Karen spotted it.

Chapter Seventeen

Quirk sat with Boudica in the visitors' room of the Coffee Creek Correctional Facility.

It smelled like old perfume, bad coffee, and despair.

On their side of the glass, families gathered around telephones attached to stalls and talked to their loved—and incarcerated—ones on the other side. Some smiled, some laughed, all regretted that things had to be this way. A mother consoled her daughter, who, admittedly, looked good in the orange jumpsuit. Quirk noticed that it really brought out the shine in her greasy, uncombed blonde hair.

The mother was saying something about a boy named Brayden and how much he'd grown over the past year, and that he loved preschool. The daughter put her hand on the thick glass and tried to fight back the tears. She didn't succeed.

Being there, standing inside a prison, wasn't the best idea, in his opinion, but according to the woman controlling his every move, hiding in plain sight was clearly a preferable option. "You cover your ass well enough, you can stay as free as long as you like. Just don't get your picture on the boob tube, because that's when it all goes downhill. This way," she'd said as they walked inside the prison visitors' entrance, "you get to breathe. I'd rather live as a criminal outside than hide in some dungeon a free woman."

It made sense, Quirk thought, as he stood there with her await-ing their turn. However, what she'd failed to mention, or forgotten about, was the potential of their faces on the streetview cams around Portland. He recalled that was how they got leads on the Boston Marathon bombers. The two pricks carrying their backpacks in full view, unafraid. Regardless of what happened after Boudica's planned event, he hoped he wouldn't see himself on the nightly news sprint-ing away from the parking garage, ready to piss his pants.

Boudica said, "There she comes," and pointed at a young woman. "A friend of Sara Winthrop's."

To Quirk, her wink and mischievous smile suggested that the word "friend" was far from accurate.

The guard led them to an empty stall and was kind enough to pull out the seat for Boudica. He called her ma'am, and Quirk thought, *If the guy only knew.*

The young woman across from them, sitting with her ankles and wrists chained together, looked haggard, hardened, and empty.

She'd been beautiful at some point in the past. Quirk could see it…at least on one side of her face. On the other side, her cheek was ragged and mottled, faded red valleys carved into it as a result of scarring and poor stitching. The missing upper half of her left ear had the distinct shape of a bite mark, the way a surfboard looks when a hungry shark gets a mouthful of fiberglass and leg.

The scarring extended down to her neck on the left side and tracing perpendicular across that was another, thinner scar that went from beneath one ear, around her throat, and up to the other ear.

She wore an eye patch, too, and Quirk had no desire to see what was behind it.

The young woman picked up the phone, held it to her ear, and waited.

Boudica said, "Hi, Shelley," holding the phone so that Quirk could hear as well.

"Who are you?" she asked with no hint of care, or emotion, or actual curiosity, almost as if she were on autopilot. Her voice was ragged and raspy. "I'm not doing any more interviews, if that's what you're here for. Actually, here's a quote for you—Sara Winthrop can go die in a fire. I don't care anymore."

Boudica had refused to reveal her little surprise as they'd driven to Coffee Creek, and now that they were here, with Shelley sitting in front of them, Quirk felt the fog of confusion lift. Sara Winthrop, their—or *Boudica's*—intended target, had survived and saved her children from a horrific, sadistic kidnapping. It'd been all over the news a year and a half ago. He remembered now.

Boudica said, "We're friends of yours."

"I don't know you."

"Not now, but you will."

Shelley laughed. "You think so, huh?"

Quirk remembered more as Boudica made small talk about the food and the showers.

A detective had died trying to help and then there were follow-up stories about how the female inmates of Coffee Creek, many of them mothers themselves, had responded to the new inmate—one who'd dared to use children in her evil plans. There'd been a small riot; the warden barely contained it and saved an inmate's life. The warden, when it was all over, had said something to the effect of, "She's alive, but from the looks of it, she'll wish she was dead."

He remembered. Why, he didn't know, but he remembered. It was big news back then. A Portland mother, fighting back against her attackers and winning—what wasn't there to love about that story? And then the villainess got her comeuppance in prison at the hands of a horde of angry mothers—he remembered thinking that off camera the news anchors were probably high fiving and saluting the retribution.

Unbelievable. This was the young woman that had started the job, and now Boudica wanted to finish it for her.

And Sara Winthrop—the target—why her? Quirk remembered admiring the woman for her resolve, watching the story on the news as he assembled their first bomb meant for Moscow.

As he sat listening to Boudica and this young woman, a feeling rose within him—a notion that the façade Boudica presented regarding their cause was false, that what they were fighting was a *personal* war for *her*, not to spread awareness of the severity of video game violence.

What had Boudica said earlier? That the *real* target in London had been someone outside of the video game shop? Was Sara the real target behind their planned bombing in Portland? What about Beijing, Rio, and Moscow? Had he and Cleo, Tank and Rocket, Chief and Sharkfin…had they all been led astray by this woman?

If so, what would he do about it?

Anything? Did he have a choice?

If Boudica had been betraying them for close to eighteen months now, did it matter if he kept his mouth shut for a couple more, long enough to finish here, to finish in Paris, and be done? Maybe it didn't. Maybe it did. All this sweat, stress, and fear—Cleo's death, the FBI's involvement, all those people hurt by the bombs he'd built…was it all for nothing? A worthless waste of time?

Not necessarily. Even if Boudica had tricked their little team into congregating under false pretenses, even if she'd been fighting for something different, people were talking. The media had begun to take notice, especially after the destruction in London. After The Clan had claimed London and voiced their reason behind it, various experts had been asked to offer their opinions on shows like Anderson Cooper's and Nancy Grace's. Some for, some against. Some saying there was no correlation whatsoever and that there were studies to prove it. Quirk knew better. All those studies denouncing the connections, they didn't mean a damn thing. He knew they were wrong. He'd seen it firsthand and—

"Quirk?"

He blinked and refocused. Boudica smiled at him. "What?" he said.

"I was just telling Shelley here what a caring person you are and how you helped put that poor, sick dog out of its misery."

Quirk dipped his eyebrows and cocked an ear toward her. "Dog?"

"Cleo was such a good dog, wasn't she? Such a shame that we had to help her cross over."

He felt a corner of his upper lip turn up in disgust, but decided he needed to play along. For now. Boudica knew too much about him. His plans, his hopes, his movements. If he pissed her off, the Spirit might show up sooner than expected. Quirk said, "Yeah, damn shame. Pretty dog, too."

Also, he had assumed that Boudica wouldn't allow him to live beyond their final objective, thus the contingency plans he had in place. In theory, he could leave tomorrow. What was keeping him? Why not disappear now before she had a chance to suspect something was wrong? She'd already had her suspicions anyway; what was there to say that she wouldn't send in the Spirit simply for posterity?

And as much as he hated to acknowledge the fact about himself, greed was an identifiable culprit for his delay. He'd already saved enough to send his former sister-in-law, Melissa, a sizeable safety net—anonymously donated by a shell charity he would establish, of course—which left him with barely what he needed to disappear.

The fact was, when it came to money used to start a new life as someone else, more was always better.

He need the funds and *had* a cause to fight for, even if Boudica was deceitfully fighting for something else.

Stay. Endure. Escape.

Three simple steps, no more, no less, bridged by building one more bomb, supposing that was all Boudica had in mind. Was the one in his basement meant for Sara Winthrop now, as it had been

before? She'd told him about the detonation at the Winthrops'
house and Sara's survival, and he knew it wouldn't be long before
the bomb technicians and forensics teams would be piecing together
the puzzle of his contraption.

He'd worked hard on not having any defining signature as a
bomb maker, to remain a chameleon, but still, if they were good
enough, there would always be the chance of him making a mistake.
He had confidence in his abilities, but the universe often squashed
confidence like an egg under an anvil.

Boudica said to Shelley, "You're probably wondering why we're
here."

So am I, Quirk thought. He hadn't entirely been listening the
whole time, but up to that point, it merely seemed like Boudica had
ran into a distant friend at a cocktail party.

Shelley said, "I mean, yeah, hey, it's fun talking to you and all,
even though I have no clue who you are, but as soon as I walk out
of here, it's time for my daily abuse in the showers. Give me a real
reason to walk in there with a smile on my face."

"First," Boudica whispered as she leaned closer to the window,
"we're going to finish what you started. I know you tried, and you
got damn close, but I'm glad you didn't, because you would've
fucked up what I've been planning for the past twenty years. I want
the pleasure of watching Sara Winthrop burn."

Shelley drummed her fingers on the table and offered a limp
smile. "More power to you. Send me a postcard when you're done."

The guard at the door behind them raised his voice. "Hands and
heads where I can see them, please. Thank you."

Boudica leaned back away from the window. Still whispering, but so quietly she was almost mouthing the words, she added,
"Second, I like you. I like your spirit. You've got some spunk, but
you're minor league, honey. How much longer you got in here?"

Shelley shrugged. "After time off for good behavior, I might get
out in time to buy my own casket."

"What if I told you there were strings to pull?"

"I'd say keep dreaming."

"And if I were serious?"

"I'd ask you to give me some of whatever you're smoking."

"Two years. You stay patient for two more years. Sit in there like a good little girl should, but you take that time to let all that anger build up inside you. Poke it, stab it, make it bleed. You look hollow, Shelley. Fill yourself up with every bit of rage you can imagine. Don't waste it on Sara Winthrop. That's my job. Two years should be enough to get you close to detonation. After that, you come work for me. We'll make the world afraid of us."

Quirk watched as Shelley listened. She took it in, but Quirk couldn't be sure that she was buying it. If she was, then the quiet way in which she received it was nearly as disturbing as if she'd jumped on the table and shouted, "Hallelujah!"

So they were on a recruiting mission, huh? That's what this was about.

Did Boudica intend for Shelley Sergeant to replace Cleo in The Clan?

Hell, why not? There were worse ideas. He wasn't so sure that letting Shelley Sergeant fester in prison for two more years, before she somehow magically freed her, was the best idea, but then again, he wouldn't be around to find out. Physically. As in, on the other side of the world. Not "wouldn't be around" meaning "dead."

Quirk felt a bead of sweat trickle down his side. It was cold against his skin.

He shivered.

Could've been the sweat.

Could've been the insane grin that passed across Shelley Sergeant's lips when Boudica told her that the world wouldn't be ready for them.

Either way, he was thankful that she was on the other side of the bars for another two years.

Chapter Eighteen

Sara cautiously kept an eye on the two unfamiliar men while she waited on Barker. In the backseat, her children were scrunched in along with Miss Willow. The mom instinct took over, and she questioned the safety of no child seats in the back of Barker's unmarked sedan. Safety first, but it seemed nearly inconsequential considering the fact that their home had been reduced to smoldering rubble in a murderous attempt.

Who had called her house and warned Miss Willow? And my God, what if she hadn't answered the phone in order to heed the warning? Sara thought about the possibility of having to identify her family by their remains, gagged on the bile in the back of her throat, and then swallowed the vile taste.

She listened to the kids bicker in the back seat, clambering over one another to get a better view of their destroyed home. To them it was this massive, unbelievable occurrence, almost *cool* in a way. Explosions, smoke, fire, ambulances, police, sirens and lights, it certainly didn't happen every day, and it certainly didn't happen on their street. They'd mentioned the loss of a few things, like toys and clothes. Jacob felt sad about his goldfish, but otherwise, it was mostly, "Look how far that water is spraying!" and, "Did you see that policeman's gun?" and, "Those fire trucks sure are big!"

The final question, the innocent one that sent Sara reeling—as if the rest of it hadn't—was a simple, "Mom, when we get a new place, can I have my own room?"

Sara snapped. "Lacey, stop it. Our house is still burning, and you're already talking about the next one."

"I just wanted—"

"*No*, not right now." Sara leaned forward, elbows on her knees, and rested her head in her hands. They smelled like dirty asphalt. Disgusting, but it was better than looking at her ruined past outside the car windows. In a way, though, maybe Lacey had the right idea.

She was free to look ahead to the future.

That house had held plenty of good memories, but a lot of bad ones were associated with it as well. She'd lost keepsakes and photo albums. First locks of hair and bronzed baby shoes. Her old wedding dress that had meant something long before Brian had disappeared. The mugs that her grandmother had given her were likely gone, as were the two-hundred-year-old picture frames that had been handed down as wedding gifts through her family.

All of her past, obliterated, except for some minor, salvageable items.

The absence of the house didn't eradicate the bad memories, but it surely couldn't hurt to finally be free of the place where she'd spent so many agonizing nights. That house had been associated with Brian's disappearance—two years of holding her breath and waiting. Shelley Sergeant had been inside as well, tainting what good energy remained. There were days and nights spent inside those walls, dealing with all the post-trauma things after she'd rescued her children.

It was rather morbid to think of it this way, because she had been so close to losing everything, again, but if Patty Kellog was behind this, then maybe she'd inadvertently done Sara a favor. The evil wench had wiped part of the slate clean.

Barker interrupted her train of thought when he climbed in the car. He ran his fingers through his wet white hair. "I've been here twenty years," he said, "and I don't think I'll ever get used to this rain. Anyway, they're treating it as an attempted homicide, of course, along with a whole other host of options—basically whatever they can pile on if they catch who did it."

"Well, we *know* who, right?"

"They still have to go through the process, but I gave them a heads-up about our meeting with Timms. I had to fight them for it, but I got clearance to get you and the young 'uns to a safe place—Jim's, like you said—but they'll have to come by later for some questioning."

"Just get us away from here. I'm sick of looking at it."

Barker nodded, said something encouraging to the kids and Miss Willow, and then gave Sara a pitiful look.

"What?"

"Nothing."

"What, Barker?"

"I'm sorry, that's all. This is—it's almost too much, even for me. Before you say it, I know...I've still got a home to go to and people aren't trying to murder me, at least not today, but you've got heart, and I want you to keep it that way. Don't let shit like this—sorry, kids—don't let crap like this get you down. Those aren't the most comforting words—"

"Barker! My house exploded!"

"I'm not good at this stuff, Sara, but you know what I mean, don't you?"

He was trying, and Sara couldn't fault him for that. She slumped in her seat, annoyed but thankful for his pitiable attempt. "I shouldn't have yelled at you. I'm...This is insane. Can we get out of here? Now? Please?"

"Yes, ma'am." His cell phone rang on his belt before he could turn the ignition key. The noise reminded Sara of the old one in the house where she grew up with the yellow linoleum and paneled walls. She expected to glance down and see a 1980s rotary dial phone strapped to his hip. He checked the ID and said, "Hang on a sec, let me see what this is all about."

Sara leaned over the front seat and shushed the kids, whispering for them to get buckled in as best as they could. Miss Willow sat in the middle with the twins to her right and Jacob to her left. She couldn't stop staring at the house and shaking her head.

Beside Sara, Barker mumbled, "Uh-huh, right…no…that's a damn shame. Who's on it? Good, good. Wait, who was the girl?"

Sara said to Miss Willow, "You okay?"

"No," she answered, trying to hold back a sob. "I just keep thinking about what might've happened if I hadn't answered the phone. I mean, I don't know whether it was luck, chance, or fate. We were so close to…I can't even say it."

Sara reached over the seat. "Here, give me your hand." Miss Willow lifted a shaky hand and Sara took it, squeezing. "We can't mold the past to fit the future, Willow, and all we can do is shake our fist at the sky or hold up our hands in praise. Either way, you made the right choice. It doesn't matter what influenced it. You did it, and here we are. You saved their lives."

Miss Willow managed a grin and pushed a loose strand of long gray hair behind her ear. She dabbed at her nose with a tissue. "I suppose."

Sara squeezed her hand once more and returned her attention to Barker. He continued to ask questions for another five minutes, seemingly growing more and more agitated as time passed. He hung up and sat staring blankly out the window at her house. He chewed a cinnamon toothpick like he was angry at it, grabbed the tip, and then slung it to the floorboard of his car.

"Everything okay?" Sara asked. With so much going on around them outside of Barker's sedan, where they were securely ensconced inside their little realm of safety, she wondered what could've possibly upset him that much. There were sirens and shouts from patrolmen urging the crowd to back away. Firemen spraying fat streams onto the smoldering ruins. It looked like a couple of plain-clothes detectives had arrived in addition to the medical examiner. Oh, and now the news vans with their antennas and beautiful reporters with their perfectly coiffed hair and false sincerity. Wonderful.

And still the two men stealing occasional glances at her remained in the crowd. Was it enough to be afraid of them, or were they curious because someone had told them it was her home sitting over there like a burning trash heap?

"What happened?" she asked.

"Remember how Timms blasted out of LightPulse like a cat with its tail on fire?"

"Yeah."

Barker lowered his voice and leaned closer to Sara, motioning for her to come nearer with his hand. "I can't say it in front of the kids."

"Is he okay?" she whispered.

"They're zipping up the body bag right now."

Sara gasped and recoiled. From the backseat, Miss Willow asked what was going on. "Nothing, Willow—just keep them distracted, please?" To Barker, she said, "What—was it an accident?"

Barker started the car, turned up the radio, and then deftly maneuvered through the sea of emergency vehicles. "Not unless he tripped and fell onto a bullet moving faster than the speed of sound."

Sara risked a peek to her right and watched the unfamiliar men pretend to ignore her exit. Gawkers? Ambulance chasers? Was that it? Were they lawyers looking for a quick scheme? That actually made sense. Satisfied they were harmless, she said, "Timms was *murdered?*"

"Yep, looks that way. They found him in the bottom floor of a parking garage." They were in the clear now, driving past rows of houses with distant neighbors standing on their porches, hiding under umbrellas or overhangs, watching the commotion down the street. "Initially, they were suspecting murder-suicide because there's another body there with him but no weapon. Young woman. One of the patrol boys recognized her, and from the way it sounds, they think it might've been that Emily gal that he was on the phone with before he left. They've got some FBI jerkoffs there now trying to take over the scene and everybody's jockeying for position, but murder's at the state level, not federal. I'm sure they'll figure out how to wrestle it away from the locals somehow."

"So who was Emily?"

"Are you ready for this?"

"No, but go ahead."

"Tolson—he's a good guy, I think you'd like him—Tolson managed to get some info from one of the squares. Guy tells him that Timms had been working with this young lady, trying to bring down a clan...only the guy doesn't know it's actually called *The Clan*, right? Word was, Timms had been bragging about turning and burning the poor thing."

Sara checked her rearview mirror, gut instinct insisting that she needed to be cautious. She wasn't sure if she'd even be able to identify someone following them regardless. In the backseat, Miss Willow was doing a perfect job entertaining the kids with I-Spy. Sara said, "I don't know what that means."

"Right. Um, well, he'd turned her, as in, she was a member of Kellog's Clan that had turned snitch—"

"Whoa, that's how he knew so much about Patty and her history with the bombings."

"Exactly."

"And what does burning her mean?"

"It's stupid."

"What? Tell me."

"Turn and burn…trust me, this is all speculation, because I've never actually used or been privy to the term myself, but 'turn and burn' means to flip the contact and then sleep with her."

"You're serious? How does 'burn' mean sex with a witness?"

"Use a rubber…burn rubber…burn. Turn and burn."

"I don't—forget it. I don't want to know. So Timms is sleeping with someone that was part of Patty Kellog's Clan—"

"Cleo, I think it was."

"Cleo, and he's pumping her for information—oh God, I didn't mean it like that—that was horrible. He manages to get her to reveal plans about Chicago and Portland…and about Paris. Patty blatantly told the FBI that her next target was Chicago, but turning Cleo was how he knew that *I'm* the target *here*, instead."

"Sounds about right, Detective Winthrop."

"So why were Cleo and Timms meeting in the sub-level of a garage downtown?"

"I wouldn't put money on it, but maybe they got together to burn rubber."

Sara scoffed. "Not after the way he sprinted out of the office. You saw how freaked out he was."

"That's why I wouldn't put money on it. Remember what he said in Jim's office when he took that call? *Cleo*, I'm assuming, had somebody else held hostage, for lack of a better term, and Timms was late for their rendezvous. Something happened on the other end of that phone call, because he didn't get panicked until he couldn't get a response from her."

"That's right," Sara said. "Turn here." She knew that Barker had a vague idea about how to get to Jim Rutherford's house up in the hills of Portland, but his quick signal and taking the curve on two wheels showed a lack of recollection. "So what does that tell us?"

"The way I see it, Cleo has somebody she wants Timms to meet, maybe another informant, who knows. Timms is late to their meetup because he took too long swinging his pecker in our faces, he gets the call, and then panics when something happens—that *something*, I'm guessing, is their mystery guest escaping or fighting back against Cleo. Timms gets to the rally point, sees Cleo dead or dying, and then gets whacked when his back is turned."

Sara said, "Left here and go up about three blocks, then another right," then asked, "So do we think it's the mystery guest that shot both of them? Wait, were they both *shot?*"

Barker nodded. "Double-tap to the female vic's chest, one behind Timms's left ear, and *no*, actually, they don't think it was the same weapon. Tolson said they appear to be two different types of entry and exit wounds, but that doesn't mean that our mystery person didn't have two different weapons on him."

"How do we know it was a him?"

"We don't, but statistically, violence this…well…*violent* is relegated to the male of the species."

"You *do* remember Shelley Sergeant, right?" Sara noticed Jim's street sailing past out the window. "You missed it, Barker. We should've made a right on Bellingham."

"I wouldn't say I missed it," he said, looking in the rearview mirror. "I'm taking the scenic route."

"Why? We need to get to Jim's."

"We will, but first I want to see if our friend back there thinks he's going to the same place."

"Who?"

"Blue Dodge Ram, the one with the camper top about three cars back. He's been with us since about two blocks from your house. Not that I'm entirely suspicious…just being cautious, that's all."

Sara's stomach churned. She realized he had a reason to be wary.

Chapter Nineteen

Teddy whimpered. It was subtle and emasculating, but it was there, and he prayed that neither the old man nor Karen had heard it. If the old man was the Spirit, he didn't want to show fear. Could bad guys smell fear like dogs? Teddy hoped not.

Plus, he wanted Karen to know he could be brave.

Before the insanity with Shelly Sergeant and nearly losing his life at the hands of her brother, Michael, he'd been confident and poised. He'd never met a stranger. Granted, according to Sara, and Dr. Hanks, this self-assuredness had the tendency to be overbearing and annoying to stranger, friend, and coworker alike, but that was Teddy Rutherford.

Capital T, Capital R.

To the outside world, he was fairly close to being the pre-Shelley Teddy that everyone loved and adored. Or, well, tolerated and accepted. But on the inside, he'd been a quivering mess for months.

It had begun with the dream. Night after night. He was back in the cabin, and instead of Sara inside the cage, he was trapped within the small, metallic walls.

Naked, chained, and helpless, but not fearful. Not yet.

Candles burned. A sweet smell like fresh doughnuts wafted through the room.

Michael, the monstrous creature, was nowhere to be seen. Instead, Shelley Sergeant sat outside his cage. Beautiful, smiling, and also nude, with her hands crossed neatly in her lap. She seemed shy, almost. He sat patiently, longingly staring at her perfect breasts—perfection that only nature can provide. Flawless skin. Hair up. He could feel the warmth growing between his legs. And then...

It was the same dream. Always. He thought they were involved in some sort of freaky sub-dom sex game, like, "Oh, the dog cage would be fun, let's try that," or, "Okay, sweetie, it's your turn to get in this time."

Every night, in every dream, Shelley's smile would disappear and be replaced by rows of stalactite and stalagmite fangs dripping with saliva. Her eyes would disappear only to be replaced by empty sockets of the darkest depths of blackness. She would stand and reveal the glory of her perfect body and he would feel himself getting aroused in spite of his fear and her hideous face.

Next came the torture. Hot pokers pulled from the flaming fireplace. Cattle prods. Spears. Anything that Shelley the she-beast could find to jab, burn, and cut him with while he was trapped inside that godawful cage. He'd cry out, and in the final moments of his life the door to the cabin would swing open, casting a bright, warm light inside.

But he always woke up. He never got to learn whether he lived or died.

Dr. Hanks suggested that he was possibly dealing with some post-traumatic stress while his brain worked through the issues. In time, and with the proper medication, the dreams would stop. Or, on the other hand, his subconscious issues could merely signify that he was feeling trapped in life and his career and the horrible nightmare was how his mind chose to process the external information.

Teddy feared that it was a premonition that someday Shelley would come back to finish what she started. Now, however, if things continued on their current path, someone, this Boudica person, would beat her to the finale.

The dream, if it *was* a moment of precognitive foresight, never mentioned the fact that he might die after having had a cranberry orange scone as his final meal.

He hated being weak, but with a gun at his side, did he have an option?

To his left the old man coughed, removed a white handkerchief from a jacket pocket, and blew his nose, then coughed again. Teddy squirmed uneasily in his seat. He wasn't sure how steady those feeble hands were. One hearty cough, a twitchy finger, and wind would whistle through his insides.

Karen noticed the small, snub-nosed pistol in his hand. She said, "Hey, why don't you put that away? We're all friends here, right?"

"No."

She said, "What's your name?"

Come on, Karen, Teddy thought, yo*u know exactly who it is. You don't find the Spirit, the Spirit finds you.* Teddy shifted in his seat again. The barrel dug deeper into his side.

"Vadim Bariskov, madam, also known as the Spirit. Also known as The Red Death, or, here in your homeland, you may have heard another name. Does the codename 'Dark Horse' mean anything to you?"

It meant nothing to Teddy except for the fact that this schizophrenic Russian death machine could put a bullet in him using any name he wanted. He noticed that Karen leaned forward with her elbows on the table, mouth agape, with her hands on each cheek. "Some of the spooks I knew used to tell stories about Dark Horse that were just as crazy as the stories about the Spirit. You're...that's all *you*?"

Bariskov smiled, showing crooked, yellow teeth. "I am three in one. You don't need St. Peter to introduce you to the Father, Son, and Holy *Spirit*, eh? Huh?" He laughed. "I'm sitting right here in front of you. Come now, confess your sins."

"You're Dark Horse?"

Bariskov's accent disappeared. "Sweetheart, I've been playing both sides since Junior here was going poo-poo in the diaper." He squeezed Teddy's neck playfully and then pulled the gun away from his ribs. "I won't forget where this is, no? Let's talk," he said, and then tucked it inside his jacket.

Teddy said, "So are you Russian or American?"

Bariskov took a bite of Teddy's scone, chewed slowly, and swallowed. He said, in an accent that wobbled between Long Island and the Kremlin, "Am I American? Am I Russian?" Then he switched to faultless French. "*Oui*, do I come from Paris?" Texas now. "Or do I come from Dallas, y'all?" His final accent, which seemed to be the one with which he was most familiar, was the original Russian, overlaid with a number of years living in the States. "Does not matter, Mr. Rutherford. I come, I go. I am the Spirit. I walk through a wall in Portland, I show up in Sweden. It's all the same to me. He pays me, she pays me. Today she pays me to kill him, tomorrow she dies because he paid more. All the same."

Karen appeared to be in awe, but slightly fearful. Teddy assumed that the Spirit—or The Red Death, or Dark Horse, or whoever this guy claimed to be—had a mythical reputation within Karen's former circles. She said, "I can't believe you're sitting right here. Do you know what the bounty was on your head?"

"One million, or so I've heard. Small potatoes, my dear. If you're looking to claim it, consider sparing an old man's life, eh? Huh? I can tell you how to find five more criminals worth just as much if that's what you're after."

Karen shook her head. "No, no, that's not what I meant. I mean, you're...*here*," she said, shoving her mug to the side. "No one back in my old office would ever believe me."

Bariskov winked. "I'd rather not test that theory. So, my friends," he said, ruffling Teddy's hair, "Viktor tells me you're interested in finding the Spirit. Well, now you have him. What's on your mind?"

Teddy had no doubt that Bariskov could eliminate everyone in the café with a flick of his highly trained assassin's wrist, which was probably why Karen had kept her distance and had kept her hands visible. That made sense. She knew him and knew what he was capable of, while Teddy could do nothing but ponder why this fabled international assassin was chatting with them like Grandpa out for coffee.

Teddy slid the cranberry orange scone remnants in front of Bariskov. A peace offering. A steak to appease the hungry lion. And, if the old man actually enjoyed it, it could be called a bribe. As long as it kept Bariskov smiling, that was all that mattered.

Karen said, "I'm Karen Wallace and this is Teddy Rutherford."

"You shouldn't have done that."

Teddy nervously nudged himself away from Bariskov, looking at him sideways, asking, "W-w-why? Why shouldn't she have done that?"

"Names beget death. Always true, Teddy Rutherford. Always true."

"How solid is *always*?"

Bariskov slapped the table and howled with laughter, which then disintegrated into an epic coughing fit. He removed the white hankie from a pocket then hacked into it until the blotchy colors of his face matched the color of the cranberries on the plate.

Teddy offered him some water. Bariskov refused. Instead he removed a flask from his jacket, took a long swig, and tucked it away.

Bariskov said, "Apologies. I'm not the—how do you say—the war machine I once was. Now I'm lucky if I can piss without it feeling like fire in my dick."

Teddy wondered if that bit of information was necessary, but he wasn't about to question it.

Karen said, "We're working a case for a friend of ours and we think you might be associated with it in some small way." Karen lifted her left arm, flashing him her 9mm held in her right hand flat against the table.

Holy shit, Teddy thought. *When did that get there?*

The move surprised Bariskov, as well. He nodded. "Twenty years ago, if you pulled that on the Spirit, you would be dead before your finger touched the trigger."

Karen didn't budge.

Teddy said, "Look, maybe we should just—"

"Teddy?"

"What?"

"Quiet, please." She never broke eye contact with Bariskov.

"Yes, ma'am."

Bariskov said, "Come now, put that away. It's not necessary. I came because Viktor called and said you're looking for the Spirit, and that the woman is pretty, so I should come. Also, as a favor to him because he likes Teddy. But Viktor and I will need to have a small discussion, because Viktor said nothing about guns and danger."

Karen smirked. "Bullshit. You haven't survived this long by being an idiot. You knew you were walking into something. Why'd you come?"

Teddy could do nothing but watch the banter. Karen and Bariskov were used to this sort of—what was it, espionage? As much as he hated to admit it, this type of mental and verbal sparring was well out of his comfort zone.

"As a favor to Viktor, like I said."

This one Teddy could handle. "But Viktor knows you and Ivan are enemies, right? He wouldn't risk pissing off Ivan."

"My business with the great and mighty Ivan is none of your concern. It is what it is. But you—you and Karen are here for something else. What I can tell you is this: My part is finished, and because of me, Sara Winthrop's children are alive and safe."

Karen squinted and shook her head. "What does that mean?"

"Because I have gotten soft in my old age, they were not present when a place, shall we say, ceased to exist."

"What in the hell are you talking about?"

Bariskov shifted his eyes around the café. Two women carrying rolled up yoga mats, hair up in ponytails, stood at the counter. In the far corner an elderly couple sipped their coffees and read the newspaper. He leaned over the table.

Teddy could smell aftershave and a hint of peppermint coming from the Spirit.

Bariskov said, "This Boudica, she's an amateur. Harsh and dirty. Thirty years ago she would've pissed off the wrong person and would've been long dead before she ever got to where she is now. She works like a hammer beating a nail. It's crude. There's no style or finesse."

Karen said, "So?"

"I don't like her. She's a brute."

"Then why work for her?"

Bariskov rubbed this thumb and forefinger together. "Money. I like it, and she has connections that pay very, very well. But this time she went too far. I'm old and soft. I don't agree with harming children."

Teddy felt his pulse speed up and his cheeks grow warm. He said, "Whoa, what?"

Bariskov held up a wrinkled, liver-spotted hand. "Not to worry, Teddy Rutherford, I spared the family. I warned them, they got out, then I told Dimitri to go ahead. There's no need to worry now."

"Go ahead with what?" Karen asked.

"Let's just say the Winthrop house is no more."

Karen left the 9mm flat against the table, slid it around, and angled the barrel at Bariskov. "And Sara? What about her?"

"I don't know."

"Bullshit."

"On my honor, I don't know. This Boudica, she only calls to give single directions, but I believe I can find out for you."

Teddy sat upright, excited, and nudged closer to Bariskov. "Well, great, that's awesome! So what happens next? Do we just hang around and wait on you to make some phone calls?"

Neither Karen nor Bariskov acknowledged him.

Karen said, "How much do you want?"

Bariskov shook his head. "It's not how much. It's *who*."

Chapter Twenty

On the way back from Coffee Creek and their visit with the vicious-looking Shelley Sergeant, Quirk sat in the passenger's seat while Boudica navigated the rain-soaked interstate. She'd taken the keys from him in the parking lot, saying he drove like her grandmother and she didn't have the time or the patience to watch him creep along.

It was okay by him. With his hands free, there was the possibility of escape, or even taking Boudica out if the desire was strong enough.

She drove in silence while he imagined scenarios of freeing himself from her…what? Her grasp? Her control over him? Her ability to scare him into submission?

Quirk sat with his arms crossed, staring ahead, watching the spray fly up from the interstate and pepper the windshield. He knew that, ultimately, Boudica would likely attempt to kill him once their job in Paris was complete. Also, he wasn't perfectly confident that she wouldn't slit his throat or poison him within the next few hours once they'd taken care of Sara Winthrop.

Man's inherent survival instinct can be a powerful motivator.

New plan. He needed to convince Boudica he was worth keeping around, at least long enough to finish the job in Paris. After that, it was either kill or be killed. Disappearing might be an option, but he had no idea how far her tentacles could reach.

What was the best ploy? So many options, yet there was only one he kept coming back to: his lies in exchange for her truth.

He said, "You owe me."

Boudica snorted. "I'm sorry, what?"

"You owe me the truth."

She signaled, changed lanes, and turned the radio down. Good. The John Tesh tune was annoying anyway. "I don't owe you shit, Quirk, but I'm curious, so what truth are you talking about?"

"Two years ago, you started recruiting the six of us to be your... army."

"Right."

"Why us? Why this group of people who have such an obscure issue in common?"

"Is this some come-to-Jesus thing where you're having second thoughts? Because I'd say it's a bit late for that now, don't you think?"

"No, I'm curious. Why did you focus on getting people who had lost somebody the way we did?"

"You want to know the actual truth?"

"That's why I'm asking."

"I read an article about it."

"That's it?"

"Here's the funny thing: Sara Winthrop has been working for LightPulse Productions for decades—have you heard of them?"

"Yeah, they make *Juggernaut*."

"Right. So about two years ago, I'm running a job in Portland for this Somali warlord who wanted this deserter dead and buried. I'm sitting in this bar, having a drink, and in walks Sara Winthrop. I hadn't seen her since high school, but I knew exactly who she was. It brought up a lot of old memories that I'd buried but hadn't forgotten about." Quirk watched as she grew quiet for a moment, staring ahead at the rainy highway but seeing something in her mind. She continued, "I mean, I sat there and I seethed, you know?

Like I could've gotten up, walked across the room, and stabbed her in the neck with a fucking fork."

"Obviously you didn't."

"I didn't. I had other work, but I knew I could be patient. The crazy thing was, I was stuck in Portland for about a week, and she kept popping up everywhere. Different magazines, the newspaper—it was like the universe was shoving her in my face, over and over, and then one day, maybe a month later, there was this article in some gaming magazine—I don't even remember what it was called—but some teenage kid had died in North Carolina and there was this huge trial—"

Quirk cleared his throat. "Brandon's?"

"Yep. The one where they quoted you..."

"And Sara Winthrop. Oh my God, that's why her name sounded so familiar. I remembered her in the news after the kidnapping, but there was something else about her name that I couldn't place."

"You were a former enlisted Marine, you were angry, and you were easy to find. It gave me an idea. You were so pissed off after the trial, and I had this thing with Sara and a few of her high school slutbag friends that I needed to deal with. It didn't take long to figure out that hiding my true objective behind the idea of blowing shit up to attract attention to your cause was the way to go. I came up with the idea in about ten minutes, but it took me weeks to round up people with the skills that I needed who had experienced the same type of loss as you."

"So all these places around the world, everything we've done..."

"Julie, Rebecca, Lucy, Colleen...Sara's here in Portland, and Melinda is in Paris."

"Why?"

"You got what you want, which is attention for your cause, and I get what I want. Retribution."

"For what?" Quirk held back the lies he'd planned to tell. They could wait. She was opening up on her own.

Boudica took her right hand off of the steering wheel and placed it on his thigh. "Remember earlier how I was talking about getting caught?" She smiled and slid her palm farther up his leg, closer to his crotch.

Quirk felt himself stir, despite the situation. "Um, yeah."

"Well," she said, cupping the bulge, gently squeezing, "it's amazing how the mind works, isn't it? How it can take a traumatic experience from our childhood and turn it into a fetish or an insatiable desire? Like how a young girl can be sexually abused and then become a porn star because she still has the daddy issues to work out." She caressed him, softly sliding her hand up and down.

Quirk tried to make the erection disappear. He thought about knitting, baseball, and spoiled milk, anything to take his mind off of it.

Her voice was smooth. Seductive. Quirk imagined her crawling across the living room floor like a lioness stalking her prey. "They caught me doing something I wasn't supposed to be doing in a place I wasn't supposed to do it. Granted, I *like* being caught now, whether it's sex on a park bench or shoplifting a pack of gum, because that element of danger is so...*exciting*...but back then—"

She squeezed his testicles, hard, and Quirk yelped as the pain coursed into his abdomen. He grew nauseated and doubled over, moaning until she let go.

Boudica said, "Do you feel that, Quirk? Do you feel that pain that's so deep, so intense that you want to vomit just to get it outside your body?"

"Yes," he said, his voice weak and croaking.

Boudica reached under the front seat and removed a small .38 caliber revolver.

The ache in his stomach was so intense he didn't flinch when she rested the barrel against his temple.

"That's the pain they caused me that day and I spent years—*years*—trying to overcome it, but you know what? Some scars never fade. So you think I owe you the truth, Quirk? I *owe* you? Here's your truth, you pathetic bastard: I'm going to end this with or without you, and you can either join me and avenge your little rat nephew, or you can eat a bullet and spare me the indignation because I've got better shit to do."

He coughed, sputtered, and watched the trail of saliva dangling from his bottom lip. He'd intended to lie to her, to tell her that if she killed him, then he had a failsafe plan that would execute if he didn't check in—an anonymous note sent to the FBI, CIA, NSA, and every newspaper editor he could find. Would it have worked? He didn't know. Now he wasn't so sure that she'd care. She'd probably enjoy the notoriety—the potential of being caught.

"You're just going to kill me when you're done. Why should I bother?"

She laughed and shoved the .38 harder against his skull. "I could, yeah, but think about it, moron. Would I have given all that money to you for the other jobs if I were just going to end you when everything's done? What a waste that would've been. If I were going to kill you, I would've done it after Moscow, but then I'd have to start recruiting all over again. It's hard to find good help, so as long as you stick close and do what you're told for as long as I feel like telling you, then don't worry about it. Your skills for your life—how's that sound?"

"Good," he mumbled, though he didn't mean it. He'd be a free prisoner.

"I thought so. Here's the deal, Captain Quirk: we finish up with Portland and Paris, and then we take a nice, long vacation, just the two of us. Maybe you and I will go down to the South Pacific to some small island where nobody cares as long as the tourists spend their money. We'll get some sun and make love wherever we want. It'll be good to get away. After that we come back, we see about getting Shelley Sergeant some time outside, and then we work on making the real money. We have the proper talents, and I know people who need them."

Quirk's abdomen throbbed in pain, but through the hazy fog of ache deep in his belly, he was certain he'd heard her correctly. He knew Boudica was off, but had she just offered to take him somewhere in the South Pacific and relax like two honeymooners? Thirty seconds ago she'd been threatening to put a bullet in his head.

'Insane' didn't grasp the intensity of her emotional instability.

Did he have a choice?

"Sounds awesome," he said, finally able to sit up and take a normal breath.

"I thought it would. And I'm sorry I hurt you. Maybe after we're done with Sara tonight, I'll kiss it and make it better." She smiled and winked.

God help me, Quirk thought.

. . .

When they were only a couple of miles away from Portland proper, Boudica's cell rang. She answered with a sharp, "What's taking you so long?"

Quirk listened. Whatever had happened didn't sound like it was going according to plan.

She slapped the phone closed and slung it into the cup holder. "Damn it."

He'd decided to play along for the time being. Whether he was temporarily a free prisoner or a soon-to-be South Pacific sex slave to this insane terrorist, being alive and having hope was better than being six feet under. All he had to do was bide his time until the opportunity presented itself. It didn't matter if it happened in two hours, two months, or two years. Life awaited beyond Boudica's grasp, as long as he managed to *stay* alive.

"Who screwed up?" he asked.

"Tank thinks he's made. Sara left with that Sam Elliot-wannabe detective and her children. He thinks they were headed toward Jim Rutherford's house but they've been driving in circles for fifteen minutes."

"Who's Jim Rutherford?"

"Rich bastard that owns LightPulse. Sara's boss."

"Is there anything you *don't* know about her?"

"Nope."

"So if Tank thinks he's made, now what?"

"Maybe I could think of something if you'd shut up."

"If she's with a detective, won't he eventually take her back to the police station?"

"Possibly, but if they were going toward Rutherford's house to begin with, then they must've thought the station was a bad plan."

Quirk suggested, "What if we catch up with him and switch off? He drops the tail and we pick it up. If they think they've pegged him as a tail, it'll confuse the shit out of them if he just pulls into a grocery store parking lot like nothing happened, right? Or they'll think he backed off to recoup and they have an opening. So he'll duck away, we slip in while they're trying to figure out what in the hell happened, and then follow them to wherever they're going. Most likely they'll be suspicious that they're being watched, so if I were them and I thought my tail was gone, I'd get to where I was going as quick as I could."

"That actually makes sense, Quirk. Maybe you're not just a pulse with an erection like I thought."

"Thanks, I think."

She called Tank and explained the plan. She listened, then replied, "Good, I know the road. We'll be there in five minutes, tops. Call back if they change course." Boudica hung up then began dialing again. "Does your house have an alarm?"

"Yeah, but—"

"Is it armed?"

"No, we left too quickly earlier; I didn't have a chance."

"Perfect. We need to get the Spirit or Dimitri over there right now—come on, damn you, pick up—you said the laptop's ready, right?"

"It is, but we'll have to—"

Boudica held up her index finger. "Spirit? What took you so long? Right. Change of plans."

Chapter Twenty-One

Barker continued his not-so-subtle evasive driving from street to street, checking his mirrors with each turn. The kids had gotten impatient in the backseat. Jacob was close to peeing in his pants, the girls were complaining about being hungry, and Miss Willow had run out of ideas to keep them occupied.

Sara's hands shook. She had explained the situation to Barker, describing how the two unfamiliar men had been pretending like they weren't staring at her. He wanted her to see if she could get a look at the man driving the Dodge Ram, but every time he slowed down, hoping the truck would get closer, the guy backed off.

Barker had tried so many times to give Sara the chance that they'd wasted close to twenty minutes.

Twenty minutes during which Barker could've radioed for a patrol car to pull the truck over so they could make their escape. She'd suggested, but he'd resisted.

They sat at a traffic light, waiting for it to change.

"I know it's not the wisest choice," he said, "but if they know anything about you at all, they'll know which direction you were headed, especially since our tail saw us pass Rutherford's street. If we call it in and the guy gets pulled over for no reason, they'll for sure know we're onto them and they might have somebody staking out his house before we get there. They could ambush us the second we tried to get inside."

"I suppose. But who's to say he didn't call and tell them where we were headed already?"

"You've got a point, though I think we're safer knowing where he is, at least until we can figure out what to do next."

"I still think we should go to Jim's. I'll call him and tell him to open a garage door for us. We haul ass back there and get inside."

Barker flicked his eyes up to the mirror then nodded. "Okay. We'll hole up and alert the cavalry."

When the light changed from red to green, they inched forward. As Sara pulled her cell from a pocket, Barker reached over and touched her arm. "Hold up."

"Why?"

"He just pulled into McDonald's."

"What?" Sara craned her neck to see over her seat. The pickup cruised out of sight, behind the yellow, red, and beige brick building with the golden arches.

"Yep, he broke off."

"Weird," she said. "You don't think it was just some random guy going our direction, do you?"

"I doubt it. Something's up."

"Then all the more reason to get over to Jim's. Kids, Willow? You guys okay?" She nodded at the chorus of three no's and one gentle smile. "We'll be at Uncle Jim's house soon, I promise."

Barker said, "Looks like he's parking, but it's too far away for me to see who it is. You?"

"I can't tell either. Do you really think he was following us? Why would he give up like that?"

"Honestly, I'm—I don't know. Could be pulling a swap if he thinks he's made."

"Do they do that?"

"'They?'"

"Criminals. Bad guys."

"Probably, but I'm not sticking around to find out. You call Rutherford and let him know we're pulling a stunt-driver move up into that fancy garage of his."

"On it."

While Sara called to let Jim know they were on their way, Barker strained to see if anyone within the traffic behind them changed lanes when he did. While they were on a main road with bumper-to-bumper cars and rain blurring the rear window, it was nearly impossible to tell.

He turned right, heading west, back in the direction of the senior Rutherford's mansion, which wasn't too far from Teddy's place. Barker recalled standing in front of the smaller home—and it seemed funny to think of it as smaller, given its size—along with JonJon, trying to figure out what in the hell was going on with Sara Winthrop's case. DJ, dead and gone. Too soon.

His current partner, another greenhorn named Elkins, was currently on his honeymoon in Jamaica. Good guy, but no more sense than God gave a goose. Maybe he was trainable, but the jury was still out.

Barker glanced behind them. Three cars had made the same turn.

Three was three too many, but they would be easily weeded out with some random direction changes.

Sara hung up. "Jim's ready for us. Says he's got the door to the panic room open as well, in case we need to dash inside."

"I'm hoping it won't be necessary. But we do have some bogeys on our tail. I know it's a long shot, but do you recognize any of those cars behind us? Anybody that might be going Jim's way?"

Sara looked. "Nope. I see a red Jeep Cherokee, some sort of gray crossover model, and...a blue sedan. Oh, the Jeep just turned off."

"Gotcha. One down." Barker turned right down a side street, then made a left, then another quick left, heading back toward the road they were on. When he stopped at the intersection, the gray crossover vehicle and the blue sedan drove past. A middle-aged blonde woman was driving the crossover, and a woman and a younger man cruised by in the sedan. No one made eye contact through the windows, no one slowed to inspect them, and no one stopped to wait.

Barker grunted a curious, "Hmm."

"Are we clear?"

"Looks like it. I thought for sure they would've traded off if the Ram thought he was made."

"Or maybe he wasn't following us to begin with."

Barker shook his head. "I don't like it. Something's off, but we're closer to Jim's than we are to the station—"

"Barker, forget that you have a badge and a gun for just one minute, please? Now that our home is a big pile of scrap, everything I have is right here in this car with me, okay? Get us to Jim's, we'll camp out in his panic room, and then you can get back out there and start being a cop again. But right now all I want is to be out of the open and in a secure place."

Barker studied her then relented. "Okay."

"Okay?"

"Yeah. I get you. Sometimes it's hard to let go of the intuition." Barker turned onto Lawson Avenue, and then drove cautiously down the street. The crossover SUV was nowhere to be seen, and the blue sedan had disappeared as well.

When they reached Bellingham, he hesitated before making the turn, counted to three, and said, "Miss Willow, you hold on to those kids back there. This might get bumpy." He jerked the steering wheel to the left and jammed his foot down on the gas pedal. The engine roared. He caught a glimpse of Sara reaching for the handle above the door. In the backseat Jacob cheered, the twins laughed, and Miss Willow closed her eyes.

If The Clan was waiting on them and were prepped for an ambush, then they'd better have a tank or RPG launcher ready to stop the car. Short of a bullet to the head, he was getting Sara's family inside Jim Rutherford's home no matter what gauntlet they had to blaze through.

Parked cars zipped past in a blur of colors, shapes, and sizes.

He checked the speedometer. Fifty in a twenty-five. Not smart, not smart at all, but as long as one of the neighbors didn't decide to back into their path without looking, they'd be fine. He was confident behind the wheel, even on wet blacktop and narrow streets. Too many years of defensive driving classes, too many high-speed chases, gave him the necessary skills to hurtle down the crowded street untouched like a running back through a defensive line, dodging and evading contact.

Sara said, "Barker? Maybe not so fast?"

"We're fine."

"Yeah, but—"

"Relax, Sara. We're almost there and I'm not going to risk giving them a chance—"

Sara's scream was shrill, terrified. "Watch out!"

Barker glanced to the left, catching a fleeting glimpse of a blue car launching at them perpendicularly from a driveway. In that moment time slowed, creeping ahead frame by frame.

Snapshot. Car. Snapshot. Car.

It wasn't unintentional. It wasn't some distracted person backing out of their driveway. The car faced forward, launching straight at them. When his brain registered the intent, the scene before him broke through the slow-motion slideshow and sped up, barely allowing him time to react.

Barker slammed on the brakes and yanked the steering wheel sideways, angling it so that his left front quarter panel intercepted the blue sedan, reducing the brunt force.

A deafening *thud* shook the car, followed by the sounds of crunching, twisting metal. Barker's teeth knocked together as he was pitched to the left, slamming his head against the windshield. It cracked, dazing him, but he blinked, shook his head, and regained control.

Whether it was faulty engineering or a miracle of circumstance, the airbags didn't deploy, granting him continued visibility through the spider web of cracks in the front windshield.

The force of the collision drove his car to the right and they caromed off of a parked Suburban. Metal screeching. Sparks flying. Side-view mirrors ripped from doors.

Sara's children screamed in the backseat.

She turned around and shouted, asking if they were okay, were they hurt, as Barker fought the steering wheel, forcing it to the left, shoving the blue sedan away, but only for an instant.

They made another run at him.

Barker jammed on the brakes and yanked the steering wheel to the right, maneuvering between two cars, across a driveway, and into a yard. He narrowly avoided a small sapling, but a white statue of an angel exploded on impact.

He flashed a look to his left and saw that the blue sedan had a flat tire, likely from careening into one of the parked cars when he'd darted up into the yard.

Sparks flew from the rim.

"The hedge!" Sara shouted.

It was thick with tangled branches and Barker only had a second to react. Were the branches weak enough for them to barrel through? Doubtful. The bushes were tall with thick trunks. Maybe they could make it through. Maybe not.

Their left side was blocked by a white gazebo and a row of cars parked on the street.

Barker said, "Hold on, we're going through."

The yard dipped slightly down and then angled up again. Barker's sedan bounced, launched, and once airborne, it blasted through the thinner middle of the hedgerow. Leaves and branches flew as they erupted through to the other side. The car landed, slid sideways, and spun in a wide circle, digging up the yard and sending grass and mud scattering.

Barker regained control and aimed for an opening between two trees.

The blue sedan had shot past them and Barker saw an opportunity. He guided his car through the two oaks, slipping to the side and clipping the rear slightly, then felt the tires grab once they were back on the street. Brake lights flashed on the attacking car.

Barker dipped to the right, cut left, and used his left front to nudge just behind their right rear wheel, a perfectly executed PIT maneuver. The blue sedan spun around, slammed against a parked utility truck, and came to a stop.

Sara whipped around. "They're getting out."

"Good. Let 'em stay right there for a bit."

"How is everybody?" Sara asked, looking at Lacey and Callie's terrified faces. Jacob was silent, but seemed to be on the verge of a smile. Boys. Crazy car chases. If he only knew.

Lacey and Callie said they were okay. Miss Willow patted her chest above her heart and agreed.

"Almost there." She turned to Barker. "Should I call 9-1-1?"

"Let's get you guys in the house first; chances are somebody's already beat you to it."

"Right."

Barker turned into Jim Rutherford's short driveway. It angled uphill to a large, brick home with green vines and black shutters. Four tall, white columns stood regally on the front porch, accentuating the black shingles overhead. The massive three-car garage, roughly the size of Barker's home, adjoined the right side, and the far left garage door was open. Jim's forest-green Lexus had been removed and now sat off to the side, leaving the space available.

Barker expected to see Jim standing there waiting on them, but the LightPulse CEO was absent. Was it worth being concerned over? Doubtful. He'd probably seen or heard the commotion down the street and gone inside to report it.

They squeezed through the open garage door and parked. Barker got out, risked a look down the street toward the blue sedan, and saw the two attackers running up the sidewalk. Phone in hand, he backed away, dialing 9-1-1. "Detective Barker here. Get a team to 18972 Bellingham. Rutherford residence. I got two that're possibly armed. They're on foot and in pursuit of an officer and a family. One male, one female. I'll call back when we're secure."

He slapped the garage door button and heard the loud, groaning gears as the door rumbled down the tracks.

Sara, Miss Willow, and the children were standing by the entrance.

"In, now!" Barker said as he ran toward them. "Find Jim and get to the panic room."

Chapter Twenty-Two

Teddy sat impatiently in the backseat. Up ahead, Bellingham Avenue was awash in a sea of flashing lights and emergency vehicles. Police, fire, and ambulance, they all had the road blocked. To his right, the line of parked cars were scraped and battered, and a few houses down he could see yards that had been damaged and a hedgerow with a gaping hole.

Karen was too close to the car in front of them. The one behind had already nudged the bumper accidentally. They were blocked in and couldn't turn yet, not until their car crept forward to the point where an officer was directing drivers to turn around.

Teddy said, "What happened, Karen? You think my dad's okay?"

"I don't know, Teddy."

To Teddy's left, Dimitri shifted uncomfortably in his seat. He held a silver laptop case close to his chest. He hadn't spoken a word since they'd picked him up outside of a small, one-story house on the east side of the river. He smelled like bad aftershave and cigarettes.

In front of Teddy in the passenger's seat, the Spirit chewed on a coffee straw and appeared lost in thought. He hadn't said much either, and Teddy suspected that in his profession the less said, the better. Karen had insisted on the seating arrangement for safety.

Easier to keep an eye on the potential trouble that either of the Russians could cause.

Back in the café, Vadim Bariskov had made them a deal once he'd finished discussing the plans with Boudica. A deal that Teddy didn't like, not in the slightest, but if they wanted Bariskov's help, it was the only available option.

Ivan was a friend.

Sara was the closest thing he had to a sister.

It was an easy decision. She'd saved his life once before. Time to return the favor.

Teddy tapped Bariskov's shoulder as the car inched closer to the patrolman. "Aren't you scared they'll recognize you?" he asked.

"The Spirit, dear boy, is just that...a spirit. Elusive and invisible. Dimitri, on the other hand..."

Dimitri squirmed and took his hand off the laptop case long enough to nervously push his glasses higher on his nose.

Bariskov laughed. "Don't worry, Dimitri! I'll make sure you have only the best boyfriend in prison. I know people."

Dimitri's knee bounced.

Teddy sat back in his seat, slightly worried, but not officially panicked yet. They were a full block from his father's home, and he prayed that whatever had happened here wasn't a result of anything regarding Sara, or Boudica, or this insane mess.

According to Bariskov, the call from Boudica had provided a short set of instructions. Meet Dimitri at the house, pick him up, and deliver the suitcase to an address that Bariskov wouldn't reveal.

Neither Teddy nor Karen had realized where they were ultimately headed until Bariskov had pointed them down Bellingham. Teddy had protested, but Bariskov assured him that their role was limited and that he would take care of the rest. "We are only delivering this laptop," he'd said. "It has the best surveillance software. Nothing more."

Now, twenty minutes later, Teddy still didn't understand Bariskov's motivations. Every time he'd tried to ask, he'd gotten an evasive answer. Karen wasn't helping. Either she trusted the old Russian, or she was cautiously waiting to see what happened before she made a move. He had to do something. He didn't like this. Not at all.

Teddy said, "Hey, Vadim?"

"What?"

Teddy took a deep breath and pressed forward. "What's the laptop for?"

"*Again* you ask me this?"

"It's a simple question, and I can get you close to Ivan, remember?"

"Fine, fine. Dimitri can use it to access your father's security system. We transmit the signal to Boudica and she gets to keep an eye on your friend Sara if she's there with your father."

"What if she's not?"

"Then we wait."

"Honestly? That's it?"

"True story."

"You spy on my dad's house for a while, just long enough for you to help us get Boudica?"

"I think so, yes."

"You think so? Look, man, we had a deal. You help with Boudica, I get you access to Ivan. There's no 'think so' about it."

"*Teddy*," Karen said.

"What, Karen? I mean, come on, we're sitting in a goddamn car with two international criminals, about to go through a road check, and we're carrying some kind of super spy computer. I'd like to make sure this is worth it before Dimitri and I are stuck in a prison love triangle."

A bead of sweat ran down the side of Dimitri's face.

"I agree with you, but right now we need to stay calm. We don't want to look suspicious, do we? We turn around, take a couple of side streets, and we're back on track. We'll go around and come in from the west side."

"Ah..." Bariskov shook his head. "Not from what I can see. The road is blocked on the other side now, as well."

Teddy leaned up and tried to see around Bariskov's head. "What?"

Karen said to Teddy, "Is he serious?"

"Yeah, looks like it. Oh my God."

"What?"

"It looks like there are some S.W.A.T. guys sneaking up the street. Yeah, they are and they're...oh Jesus, that's my dad's house. They're in front of my dad's house."

"Are you sure?"

"Positive." Teddy lunged and wrapped an arm around Bariskov's neck and pulled him hard back into the seat. "What's happening down there?"

Bariskov sputtered and tried to pull Teddy's arm away. "I don't know," he said. "Dimitri!"

Teddy whipped his head around and stared at Dimitri, waiting on him to fight for Bariskov. Dimitri grinned and looked away.

Teddy squeezed tighter. "Tell me!"

"I don't...I can't breathe."

"Tell me!"

Nervous, looking at the officer then back at Teddy, Karen said, "You two may want to hurry."

Bariskov said, "Okay, okay. Let me breathe and I'll tell you."

Teddy grunted, gave one final squeeze, and then sat back in his seat.

"I told you, this Boudica, she's like a hammer. No style or finesse. Just punch, punch, punch, and she's impatient. Not smart."

Karen rolled down her window and smiled. "Good afternoon, Officer. What's going on down there?"

Teddy winced. What was she doing? Do not engage!

"Ma'am, please pull into this driveway behind me and find an alternate route."

"Can't we get through, just a little ways? We're right down there, at the big brick house with white columns. We're late for a meeting with Mr. Rutherford. He's expecting us."

"I'm afraid that won't be possible, ma'am. Please turn around."

"Okay, but can we get in from the other side?"

"The best I can tell you is to come back later. I'm sure he'll understand. Keep it moving, please, thank you."

Karen smiled and rolled up her window, turned the car around, and headed east on Bellingham, away from Jim Rutherford's home.

Teddy said, "What in the hell are you doing?"

"Getting his attention off of you two idiots."

"Whatever." Teddy said to Bariskov, "You weren't finished."

Bariskov smoothed down his white hair and rubbed his throat. "This hammer, she's erratic. Makes stupid decisions. I don't know how she's survived this long, but there are plenty of people who trust her, who give her money to do jobs for them."

"Then why do you work for her?"

"I told you, she pays big money."

"What happened up there, huh? What's going on at my dad's house?"

Bariskov sighed. "Teddy, Teddy, Teddy, if I knew, I would tell you. She saw an opportunity, she took it, and now, who knows? I'm just surprised she would move forward without the bomb."

"Bomb? What bomb?"

"The one in Dimitri's lap."

"Oh Jesus." Teddy pushed himself away from Dimitri as far as he could get. "That's a bomb?"

"Yes, a very powerful one, so I would not make Dimitri angry if I were you."

Dimitri winked and finally spoke. "Relax. It's very stable."

Karen said to Bariskov, "You son of a bitch."

Teddy added, "You *lying* son of a bitch."

"If I would've told you what was in there, you would've tried to stop us, and I would've had to kill you, see? This way you stay alive, you give me Ivan. All good thoughts in the Spirit's head. I think things through."

"Are you serious? How's it a good thing that you were going to blow up my father?"

"Not the plan. Well, not exactly."

"Then what was?"

"Boudica, she wanted us to bring the bomb while Sara Winthrop was trapped in your father's house. We bring the bomb, she blows up the house, game over. But, as you can see, something happened. She changed her mind; who can say why? Now we do it differently."

"Forget it. We're done here."

Karen pulled into the parking lot of an empty building. The drive-through window configuration suggested it used to be a bank. "Teddy," she said. "Try your dad. Try Sara. Maybe they're out. We don't know what's going on."

"Yeah, good idea." He fished his cell from his pocket and dialed. "No answer on Sara's cell." He hung up and dialed again. "Nothing on my dad's, either."

"Try his home number."

Teddy dialed and waited. He watched Karen in the mirror. They made eye contact and hope passed between their gaze.

A woman answered. "Is this the White Knight riding in on his horse?"

Teddy mouthed, "I think it's her."

Karen whispered, "Be careful."

"Who is this?" he asked.

"Introductions aren't necessary, Teddy. You know who I am."

"Where's my dad? Where's Sara?"

"Oh, we're all enjoying a game of Monopoly in the living room."

Teddy couldn't contain himself. "You let them go," he shouted.

The amusement was audible in her voice. "Has that ever worked in the history of hostages?"

He tried a different tactic. "What do you want?"

"Nothing, Teddy. I have everything I need right here." Teddy listened to what sounded like a yelp from Sara, and then heard his father telling him to stay away and let the police handle it. "Now, now, Jim, you know that won't work. Teddy?"

"What?"

"I had to threaten little Jacob with a bullet to get this out of him, but Daddy Dearest tells me there's a secret entrance one street over. He suggested we could leave his house that way, but I don't think I'm ready for that just yet. And besides, I got quite an interesting message from a contact of mine earlier. Let me speak to the Spirit."

Teddy handed his cell phone over the seat. "She wants to talk to you."

Bariskov looked surprised, but took the phone, cleared his throat, and said, "They were looking for *you*, but they found me instead. Do not worry, I have it under control."

Teddy and Karen exchanged glances. Dimitri tapped his foot.

Bariskov nodded. "Yes, Dimitri has it...No. No way. You've looked outside the window, haven't you? They're everywhere...And he knows where it is? Okay, give us a few minutes." Bariskov ended the call and said to Teddy, "She wants us to bring the bomb inside using your father's secret entrance."

Karen asked, "What secret entrance?"

"It's over on Elgin, one street behind my dad's place."

"He never told me about that."

"Why would he?"

"What's it for?"

"He's a rich billionaire with too many obsessive ideas. If he's paranoid enough to have a panic room, he's paranoid enough to have a way out of the house that doesn't involve the front or back doors."

"But why?"

"Can we not discuss this in front of Boris and Natasha, please?" In truth, Jim had spent a tremendous amount of money five years ago to have the escape route installed, involving numerous "donations" that weren't quite bribes, along with highly visible public support of Portland's new mayor. Jim had been convinced that with the astounding success of *Juggernaut* the threats of corporate espionage would increase and there was the potential for an attempt on his life.

Teddy had scoffed at the time and insisted his father had been reading too many Grisham novels, but after the insanity with Shelley Sergeant, however unrelated it may have been, well, now it seemed justifiable.

Karen nodded. "Fine. Then what's the plan, Bariskov?"

"Why're you asking him?"

"Forgive me if I ask the international criminal who's been doing this for fifty years what the best options are. Now, do you mind?"

Teddy said, "Go ahead," then glanced at Dimitri and rolled his eyes.

Dimitri chuckled his agreement.

Bariskov said to Karen, "Easy as cake. No...pie? Easy as pie? Teddy and I will go in this escape route. *Pop, pop*, Boudica is done, Teddy takes the credit, and I disappear. We'll discuss Ivan later, yes?"

"What about Dimitri?"

"He'll survive on his own. Unless, of course, Miss Wallace wants him dead. Eh, Dimitri? You'll behave?"

Dimitri nodded.

"Good," said Bariskov. "Teddy, bring the bomb. She'll be suspicious if we show up without it."

"I'm not touching that thing," he said, yet he knew he had to for his dad's sake, for the children, for Willow, and for Sara.

Dig deep, Teddy. Time to man up again.

Chapter Twenty-Three

Sara and Barker sat on Jim Rutherford's living room floor with their backs against a low, white wall. Behind them, stairs led down to a lower level with a small movie theater and extra bedrooms. Beyond that was another set of stairs leading to the basement.

Lacey, Callie, and Jacob, along with Miss Willow, were sequestered in the game room down the hallway where one of Patty Kellog's goons watched over them.

Jim Rutherford had been tied up and silenced with a strip of duct tape across his mouth. He sat in a chair in front of the fireplace, glasses missing, shirt ripped, with his nose bleeding and a dark bruise under his left eye.

The phrase, "Like father, like son," ran through Sara's mind as she watched him struggle to breathe while he drifted in and out of consciousness. Not too long ago, Teddy had been in that same position, trapped in the abandoned cabin to the east of Portland. Sara wondered where Karen and Teddy were. Had they found Vadim Bariskov, and would they be able to help if they had? Given the preparedness of The Clan, truthfully she expected them to be discovered floating facedown in the Willamette a few days from now.

Earlier, as they'd burst through the door leading from Jim's garage and into the massive kitchen, they'd only made it to the hallway entrance before Sara heard Barker yelp followed by a loud *thump*, and then another as he'd fallen to the floor. Sara had turned and saw a younger man holding what looked like a fully automatic weapon.

The guy was one of the two men that had been staring at her outside her home.

He had nudged Barker's ribs to make sure he was out then ordered Sara, Miss Willow, and the kids into the living room.

Thirty seconds later, a woman who had to be Patty Kellog and a younger, timid guy whom she referred to as "Quirk" had arrived through the front door, and then, two minutes after that, as Sara and her family sat on the couch, huddled together and fearful, another man had burst into the home. Sara had recognized him, too. Earlier he'd been staring at her with his partner. Was he the one driving the Dodge Ram?

Patty *resembled* the girl Sara remembered from twenty years ago, but she'd had some plastic surgery done. Higher cheekbones, a thinner nose. She'd lost weight and changed the color of her hair. Regardless, it was her. Different, but the same.

Now, Patty, Quirk, and the one they called Rocket stood with their backs to the wall, occasionally pulling at the curtains to survey the growing commotion outside. From the game room, the guy they called Tank yelled, "Three more commandos just took up spots behind that black Toyota."

"Got 'em," Rocket called back.

"I don't see any snipers yet, but that doesn't mean they aren't there."

"Roger that."

Sara said, "Patty, I think—"

"I don't care what you think." Patty moved away from the window, across the massive expanse of the living room, and stepped around the overturned couch and coffee table. She tucked her handgun into her waistband and slapped Sara hard across the cheek.

Barker and Sara were bound just like Jim, wrists and ankles cinched tightly together. Barker shouted, "That's enough!" and got a hard backhand to his jaw.

Patty shook her hand and flexed it.

Barker spat a mouthful of blood onto the white carpet.

Patty squatted low in front of Sara and shoved a finger into her face. "As soon as the Spirit gets here with the bomb…" She made an explosion noise, and then spread her arms overhead in a large arc. "We're gone and you're done. After that there's only one more of you bitches to take care of, and I hear Paris is great this time of year."

Sara shook her head. "I'm sorry, Patty. Oh my God, I am so sorry, but you can't blow up the memories."

Patty slapped Sara again.

Barker tried to lunge for her. Patty was faster. He halted with the handgun barrel against the center of his forehead. Patty clenched her teeth. "One more time. Try it. Give me a reason."

Barker sat back, fuming.

Sara tried again. "I know what they did was wrong—"

"They? They? You were *there*, Sara. You watched and did nothing. You *did* nothing, you *said* nothing, and then you had the nerve to look me in the eye when we passed each other in the hall until they took me away. Look at these. Look!" Patty showed her the scars on her wrists. "Too bad for you it didn't work, huh?"

"I'm sorry," Sara said. "That's all I can say. We were sixteen. It's been so long."

"You know what's neat about this situation, Sara? I don't really give a good goddamn what's going on outside. Let them bring in the S.W.A.T. team or whoever; I don't give a shit, because you know what's so great about it? Julie, Rebecca, Lucy, and Colleen all died without me being able to see their faces before it happened. That's my one regret. I didn't think it through. I thought as long as they got what they deserved, it was fine. But no, oh no, this is *so* much better. Watching you beg, waiting for the end to come. God, this is infinitely more satisfying and if I'd known—man, if I'd known—I would've done it so much differently with the other four. And believe me, Melinda is going to have it a lot worse than you, because now I know to drag it out and relish every...single...moment."

Jim groaned and opened his eyes. He mumbled something and then passed out once more.

Quirk, from his position by the massive picture window, said, "It looks like they want to talk. They're sending some guy up the sidewalk with a megaphone."

"Ignore them. We wait."

"But what if we—"

Patty shouted, "Quirk, do you want to make it out of here alive?"

He nodded, swallowing so hard that Sara could see him do it from across the room.

"Then shut up and trust me."

"Okay." He closed his eyes and leaned his head back against the wall.

From outside, they all heard the magnified voice of a man asking to speak to a representative.

Patty said to Sara, "You know, if you think about it, this is perfect justice. We've been doing this under the guise of a guerrilla group, trying to draw attention to the sad, sad plight of video game violence. Trust me, I have some sympathy for the poor people it happened to, but it's never hit me close to home." She chuckled. "Well, maybe that's because I was too screwed up to have a home and a family, but Quirk, the quivering pansy over there, his nephew took a bullet to the chest. Rocket's little brother tried to shoot a kid with a .22 pistol and when he missed, the target and his buddies beat him to death, all because he beat their high score.

"Tank's sister got obsessed with a game and drank a bottle of bleach when her character died. There are three others in our group—well, two now, since Cleo's gone—that had to deal with something similar. All of them, every single one, was because of *Juggernaut*. Do you have any idea how long it took me to find these people? I mean, really, it's just so damn perfect. I hadn't forgotten about you, not in the slightest, but one day I happened to catch the article about you and Shelley Sergeant. A few bright ideas later and here we are, about to blow up the house of the man responsible for six deaths and his number one accomplice. It's crazy how it all came together. We'll release a statement, the media will eat it up, and we'll be drinking French wine and finishing up with Melinda before they're done sifting through the ashes."

Sara said, "Don't you think they'll have looked at the house plans by now and seen Jim's way out of here? You think you can just sneak out the back door?"

"If they knew about it, they'd be in here already. Jim was smart, weren't you?"

Jim mumbled something and lifted his head.

Patty asked him, "How much did you pay to keep the tunnel plans out of the official records?"

Jim grunted and looked away.

"See, Sara? For all their guns and all their flashing lights, all their training and tactics, their bullets and shouting and plans, what trumps it? Huh? *Money*. Funny thing, isn't it? His money will save our asses while they're picking up pieces of yours."

The lump in Sara's throat felt like a softball as she tried to choke it down. They were done. Her children, Miss Willow, Barker, and Jim. This was it. She'd survived so much over the past four years. She'd been tough. She'd outlasted Brian's disappearance. She'd fought Shelley and won. She'd come so far, and now, all the struggle and perseverance had been for nothing. She couldn't see another way out. Patty was right. They were dead, but maybe not all of them. "Please," Sara begged. "Can you at least let my children go? They don't deserve this."

Patty glanced down the hallway, and for a moment Sara thought she was considering it. At least until Patty said, "Do the innocent ever deserve anything?"

Rocket said, "Uh, it looks like the FBI's out there now. I see the jackets, the blue ones with the yellow letters."

Patty stood, kicked Sara in the thigh, and backed away. "I'm surprised it took this long. I put a bullet in Agent Timms, what, four or five hours ago? What do you think, Detective Barker? Are Portland's finest and the FBI out there having a pissing contest over jurisdiction?"

Barker ignored her.

"Patty, I'm begging you," Sara said. "Send the kids out, send Barker and Willow and Jim out. This is between you and me."

"No."

"But why? It's my fault. Not theirs."

"It's a simple answer, Sara. I don't *want* to. I *like* watching people suffer. I like being the one in control, unlike that night under the bleachers when I didn't have a fucking choice!"

Behind them, a voice came up the stairway. It was foreign, tainted with what sounded like Russian. "Shouting, shouting, shouting. Always with the shouting, Boudica."

Patty darted around to the top of the stairs. "It's about damn time, Bariskov. What took you—what's he doing here? I thought I told you to kill him once you were in."

Sara tried to see whom Patty was referring to as an aging man in a long brown overcoat stepped into the living room carrying a silver case. He removed his hat and surveyed the madness.

Who followed was a complete surprise, and Sara never thought she'd be so happy to see the annoying, wonderful Teddy Rutherford. She didn't know why. It wasn't like Teddy would be able to do anything other than provide Patty with the encouragement to kill them all faster.

Teddy held his hands up and glanced around the room. When he saw Jim bound to the chair, he shouted, "Dad!" and moved toward him.

Patty aimed her handgun at Teddy's forehead and he froze.

The man she called Bariskov, who had to be the Spirit that Karen had referred to, surveyed the room and scoffed. "Stupid this, stupid that. You behave like a bull, Boudica, stomping through a garden, ruining everything."

"I don't pay you for advice. I pay you to do what I say, when I say it."

Bariskov frowned and shrugged. "Maybe so, but I also like to work with professionals. This—look at this mess, it's the work of an amateur."

Sara wondered what was going on. The power struggle between them seemed foreign, as if Patty hadn't expected it.

Teddy caught Sara's eye. It was brief, barely more than a flicker, but she was certain she saw a wink.

Oh God, Teddy, don't do it, she thought. *You'll get yourself killed.*

But then again, he was here. He didn't seem to be in any direct danger with Bariskov. Did he have a plan? Did *they* have a plan?

Barker must have sensed something, as well. He was subtly working his hands behind his back, trying to loosen the ropes around his wrists.

Bariskov asked, "Did you know they were coming here?"

"Yes," Patty answered.

"Then why didn't you wait?"

"What do you mean?"

"We saw the damage outside, down the street. Cars ruined, yards ruined, and now look outside—you made this mess. A bull through a garden. So tell me, why not wait? Why not handle it with style and grace?"

Patty shook her head and held out a hand. "We couldn't be sure that Rocket was in place, so I-I saw an opportunity and I took it."

Bariskov shook a finger at her like a parent admonishing a child. "Opportunity does not always create success."

Patty reached for the silver case. "I don't have time for lectures. Just give me the bomb."

Bariskov pulled it away. "Patience, child."

She held out her hand. "Now, Bariskov." Pointing at Teddy, she said, "Rocket, get over here and tie up this dumbass that was stupid enough to walk into a house full of terrorists."

Teddy said, "No thanks, I'm good," as Bariskov threw his hat into Patty's face, distracting her.

Sara held her breath and prayed.

Chapter Twenty-Four

Adrenaline pumped through Teddy's veins.

He heard only the sound of his own heartbeat.

Time moved in slowed, measured increments.

Thump-thump. Thump-thump.

He lifted his shirt, reached behind his back and removed the sub-compact 9mm that Bariskov had given him before they entered the tunnel leading to Jim's basement.

Thump-thump. Thump-thump.

He swung the gun to his left, aimed quickly, and—

. . .

Minutes earlier, Karen had dropped them off in front of a small dog park. She'd told him to be careful and asked them both if they wanted her to wait, then ordered Dimitri into the front seat where she could keep an eye on him.

"I can wait here," she insisted.

"No," Bariskov said. "You might attract attention. Dimitri will tell you where to go. Teddy will be fine with me."

She cursed, shook her head, and drove away.

Teddy had wondered if he'd ever see her again. Even worse, he wondered if he was on a death mission. Did he really have faith in Bariskov?

"Where is this tunnel…secret passage…whatever you call it?"

"There." Teddy pointed at a small brown building with a beige door, dirt-colored shingles, and a single word stenciled on the entrance: "UTILITY."

Bariskov grunted. "One would never know."

"That's the idea, isn't it? When Dad moved into his house, this neighborhood was full of all of these homes for sale because the housing bubble popped and so many people were upside down on their mortgages. There used to be two houses right here, side by side, and he had them torn down and turned into a dog park. I think that's how he got by the city building codes, you know, long enough for the administrative guys to look away."

Bariskov appeared confused. "What kind of secret is protected by machines digging a tunnel? People would see, no?"

"Wasn't an issue. The tunnel ties into the drainage system underneath. If anybody paid attention long enough to notice, they probably thought they were working on the bathrooms over there." He pointed about twenty yards to his right, then back to the falsely identified utility building. "We go in here, follow the drainage tunnels straight west until we get to the spot that cuts over and up into the entrance in my dad's basement. No big deal."

"No big deal, he says." Bariskov grinned, showing his yellow-stained teeth, and then slapped Teddy on the back. "Confident now, but wait until we get inside."

Teddy put his hands on his hips and sighed. "Yeah, about that…"

. . .

Teddy moved.

Thump-thump. Thump-thump.

Would the plan work? Would it work well enough to create a diversion? Before entering the basement, Bariskov had insisted he could handle Boudica's thugs, but offered Teddy the gun and asked if he knew how to use it. Of course he did, but he hoped it wasn't much different than the shooting range.

The man by the window turned and raised his hands. He appeared to be unarmed.

Teddy couldn't risk lives on appearances. He squeezed the trigger.

The *chuff* from the silencer sounded thick, dull, and hollow underneath the rhythmic pounding of his pulse. A red splotch appeared where he'd aimed. Was it luck? Was it skill? After so many hours of testing *Juggernaut*'s virtual weapons systems, maybe it was the latter. The guy fell back against the wall.

There was movement to Teddy's right. He pivoted and saw the woman bringing her arm up, handgun extending from it as Bariskov lunged at her.

Behind them, the second man at the window lifted his weapon. Teddy aimed, fired, and dropped him with a bullet to the forehead. Action without thought. Trusted instincts and learned abilities. The body flopped to the side.

Bariskov lowered a shoulder and drove it into the woman's chest. She flew backward, flailing her arms, trying to catch her balance. She tripped over a cushion that had fallen from one of the overturned couches. As she fell her weapon fired, the sound also muffled by a silencer.

Teddy felt something like a sledgehammer slam into his left thigh and he tumbled sideways and dropped to one knee. He screamed. To his right, Detective Barker was pushing himself up from the floor.

The woman fired again. Teddy heard the *chuff* from her silencer again, saw Bariskov spin to the side from impact, and then pitch to his left. Barker, with his ankles still tied together, launched himself awkwardly from a crouch and pounced on her, knocking her gun free. Barker lifted his head and drove it into her mouth.

She screamed and clawed the floor for her weapon. Barker drove another head butt into her temple and she went silent.

Bariskov groaned and lifted a bloody hand from his side, staring at his slick red palm.

"Is that everybody?" Teddy asked.

Barker said, "No, there's one more down the—"

Three more gunshots sounded as stuffing exploded from the couch next to Teddy's shoulder. He dropped, rolled, and looked up, hearing a fourth shot followed by a fifth.

He wondered why the place hadn't been stormed by the law enforcement outside yet. Did they even know what was happening? Every shot fired had been through a silencer. Maybe they'd heard. Maybe they'd seen through the curtains. Maybe they were waiting for the firefight to die down.

Maybe they had no idea.

Teddy rolled behind the overturned coffee table and chanced a peek over the top. The fourth man, a massive brute in a black jacket and black pants, ducked into the living room and then dropped behind the end section of the low wall. Teddy squirmed around so that the gaping mouth of the stairway entrance was in front of him. He fired the remaining rounds of his clip through the thin wall. Plaster exploded and rained down.

Teddy exhaled when he heard the dull *thud* of a body dropping.

To his left, Barker said, "He's down! He's down!"

Teddy's leg throbbed. He managed to crawl around and scramble up to his feet. Nearby, Bariskov kneeled over Sara, untying her while Barker used the ropes to hogtie the woman.

Jim's chair had overturned during the melee. Teddy hobbled over to him and found his father lying on his side, wounded and unable to get free. He'd taken a stray bullet and his shoulder was wet with blood. "Dad, you're okay."

Jim croaked, "Where'd you learn to shoot like that? You're a hero, son."

Teddy shook his head. "No, too many video games."

"Well, tell *that* to the media."

As soon as Bariskov had Sara free, she sprinted down the hallway. Teddy untied Jim, made sure he was strong enough to stand, and then followed Sara. Limping along, he found her and her children in the game room, crying, smiling, and hugging each other. Miss Willow had her arms wrapped around them all.

Teddy stopped and watched them, smiling. He wanted to join the group hug. The old Teddy would've jumped right in without thought or regard. He gave himself a mental pat on the back for resisting the impulse. His father, Sara, and Dr. Hanks would be impressed. He shifted his weight and felt the dull, throbbing ache in his leg.

Another pat on the back, he thought. *You got shot*. He mumbled, "You're a beast, Teddy."

Sara lifted her head, smiled, and said, "Did you just say that out loud?"

Teddy blinked. "Say what?"

"Did you just call yourself a beast?"

"Uh…no."

"Well, you should; you got shot!" She stood, moved swiftly, and hugged him. "And you saved our lives. I mean, my God, Teddy, that was unreal." Jacob darted over and wrapped his arms around Teddy's good leg and the twins followed. Miss Willow, who'd also never been his biggest fan, even joined them.

Sara added, "Say thanks to Uncle Teddy, kids."

Uncle Teddy. It had a nice ring to it.

. . .

Teddy heard Barker in the living room, shouting a short, alarmed burst of, "Sara! Teddy!"

"Yeah?" Sara called back.

Barker appeared in the doorway, breathless, both hands on either side of the doorjamb. "We need to go, right now."

"Why?"

He rushed into the game room and picked up Jacob. "No questions. Go, go, go," he said, urging Sara, the girls, and Miss Willow out the door. Looking back at Teddy over his shoulder, he asked, "You good? Can you move fast enough on that leg?"

"I think so. What's happening?"

"Your Russian buddy says the bomb activated and there's only about two minutes left on the timer."

"What? How?"

"Doesn't matter. He can't shut it down and we're moving."

Jim shouted down the hall, "Hurry!"

In the living room Bariskov stood at the head of the stairs, holding his hat in one hand while the other hand covered the wound in his abdomen.

"What're you waiting on?" Teddy said to Bariskov as the others rushed for the front door.

"I can't go out there."

"We have to."

"No, Teddy, I'm a free man, and I'm going to stay that way."

Barker opened the front door and walked out with one hand raised, carrying Jacob. Teddy could hear him saying, "Hostages coming out! Whoa! Whoa! Get back! Get everybody back! There's a bomb—whole place is gonna go. Move, move!"

"Okay," Teddy said to Bariskov. "You know the way out. You're the Spirit, right? You walk through a wall in Portland and show up in Sweden?"

"This is true."

"Then go. And...thank you."

Bariskov slipped his hat onto his head and pulled it low over his eyes. "Don't forget, you still have to honor your end of the deal."

Teddy shook his head. "Ivan's my friend. Giving you a head start down that tunnel makes us even, so do your thing and disappear, Casper."

Bariskov winked. "You'll see me again."

"Let's hope we're on the same side."

Teddy hobbled for the door.

Out in the yard, his father and Barker sprinted over, lifted him off his feet, and carried him, running after the retreating crowd.

They managed to duck behind an ambulance as the explosion shook the ground.

...

The next day, Sara walked into Room 343 at the hospital and found Teddy sitting up, eating ice cream from a small cup. At his bedside was a beautiful blonde woman she'd never seen before.

Teddy beamed when he saw her. "Sara!"

"Hey there, Beast."

He chuckled and rolled his eyes. "Badass Chick and the Beast. Sounds like a horrible musical."

"So true."

"This is Irina, my...um...she's a friend."

Irina smiled and stood. She shook hands with Sara, and then kissed Teddy on the forehead. "I'll be back later, okay? And my apologies, Sara, my grandfather is ill and I have to get back to Firebrand before the new manager screws something up."

When she was gone, Sara asked Teddy, "Firebrand? Isn't that where you used to go talk to those guys about Red Mob?"

"Yep."

"Wait a second, was she...was that the meth addict that had the hots for you, like, five years ago?"

"Yep."

"And she's here. For you."

"Yep."

"She looks amazing."

"I know, right? And she *wanted* to be here. For me. Can you believe it?"

Sara chuckled and pinched his cheek. "She doesn't know you very well, does she?"

"Hey."

"Joking. Chill, dude. So how're you feeling?"

"Better. These pain meds are amazing."

Sara pulled the chair closer to the bed and sat down. She leaned onto the armrests. "So you want to hear the latest? Or at least what Barker was allowed to tell me?"

"Of course."

"Do you want the good news, the bad news, or the worse news first?"

"The bad news."

"Okay. Your dad's house and everything in it basically evaporated, same as my house. So all your Little League trophies are gone."

"That's not bad news, that's horrible news."

"About the house or the trophies?"

"The trophies!"

"Figures."

"What's the good news?"

"Karen's going to be fine, and they caught that guy Dimitri trying to board a plane in PDX with a fake passport. From what Barker says, the scumbag tried to remotely detonate the bomb to wipe his criminal connections clean. He wanted out of that life entirely. Instead, he's going to prison. Out of the frying pan and into the fire, huh?"

"Jesus. Glad they caught him, but Karen—she's not hurt too badly, is she? What happened?"

"So he knocked Karen out, they ran into the ditch, the guy set the bomb to ticking and thankfully, your comrade Bariskov thought to check it. It's so unbelievable to think we were about ninety seconds away from…away from…"

"*Kaboom?*"

"Yeah."

Teddy set his ice cream down on the rollaway table and pushed the recline button on the bed controls. Sara waited while the gears groaned and lowered him. "You said there's worse news?"

"Uh-huh."

"Do I even want to hear it?" He fluffed the pillows and tried to get comfortable.

Sara stood up and went to the window. She put her hands in her pockets and stared at the world outside. What she was about to say meant more to her, her family, and her life than it did to Teddy, but it was important that he knew.

"Sara? What happened?"

"They could only identify three bodies. They found nothing but parts, mostly."

"Which three?"

"Bariskov wasn't one of them."

"And?"

Sara crossed her arms and walked across the hospital room. "Neither was Patty Kellog. They think she got out somehow."

"Oh God, so she's still out there? What're you gonna do?"

Sara took Teddy's hand in hers and held it tenderly. "I don't know. Run…hide."

"No. We can take her."

"It's the best option, Teddy. Your dad thinks so. Barker thinks so."

"You do what you gotta do, but who's going to keep me in line if you're gone?"

"We'll see you around, I'm sure." Sara bent down and kissed his forehead. "I have to run, okay? I don't feel comfortable having the kids out of my sight for too long."

"See you soon, Sara."

"Thanks for saving our lives. You take care of yourself, Beast."

Teddy smiled.

As Sara left the room, she took one last look at him and thought about how strange it was to be so *proud* of the little bastard.

. . .

End of Book #2

SARA'S FEAR

Chapter One

Sara Winthrop watched as her friend and former annoying nemesis, Teddy Rutherford, picked up the fifty-pound sack of cattle feed, lifted it over the top rung of the fence, and dumped the contents into the long, blue trough.

She'd invited him and his newlywed wife out for a short visit before their real honeymoon began. Southwest Virginia was far from a month in the Caribbean, but they'd jumped at the chance to come see her new place, thousands of miles from Portland where they'd lived and worked together.

Teddy grinned and stepped away. He motioned to the cattle grazing lazily nearby. "Come on, you four-legged milk machines. Time for dinner, or supper...or whatever the hell you guys eat here in the boondocks." He glanced over at Sara. "Did I say that right? Boondocks?"

"Boonies. Sticks. Backwoods. Same thing."

"Yonder? Is that one?"

Sara chuckled. "Nice try."

He was still getting used to the southern terms, but after his second day on Sara's farm, he'd assured her plenty of times that he had a handle on what it took to keep the place running. "What's that smell, Sara? Smells like...outside."

"You mean nature?"

"Yeah. That."

"It's manure and wet hay."

"You remember that guy Mark that used to work in the Testing Department?"

"Don't remind me."

"I think he wore the same thing as cologne."

"No, I sat across from Mark for three years. This is like roses compared to him."

Teddy shook his head as he stared at the cattle. They'd ambled over and buried their noses in the thick layer of feed. "Man, look at them eat. Takes a lot to keep a thousand pound hunk of beef mooing, huh?" Pointing to a large roan off to the side, he added, "Maybe when they're done, you can show me how to milk the big one over there."

Sara patted his back. "I doubt that bull would enjoy it, but you can try."

Teddy blushed and his wife, Irina, kissed him on the cheek. She said, "You stick to the business of games. Let Sara manage the cows, okay?"

Eight months earlier, Teddy's father, Jim Rutherford, had sold LightPulse Productions to a rival competitor for slightly over two billion dollars. Jim hadn't wanted to do it initially, but after the insanity with Patty Kellog, and the subsequent explosion of his home, he'd decided that maybe it was a sign that it was time for a change. He'd worked so hard to build LightPulse into an industry leader, and it had been difficult to give that up, but an extended vacation in Italy that turned into a transcontinental relocation and a swift marriage to the love of his life had softened the remorse.

Teddy had taken his share of the spoils and started his own company, called Red Mob Productions, that designed small, mindless games for mobile phones. He didn't *have* to work, would never *need* to work again, but he claimed that the desire for a challenge drove him to stay busy. Sara didn't know exactly how much he'd earned in the buyout and didn't care—it was simply good to see Teddy maturing and doing well for himself. So far, he'd turned a twenty-five million dollar investment into twenty-five million in profits. He'd done it in such a short amount of time that several gaming magazines called him the *wunderkind* of mobile development and thankfully, he hadn't allowed it go to his head.

Much.

Sara had asked him what she was supposed to do with a hundred copies of *Gamemaster Magazine* that featured his smiling face on the cover, to which he'd replied, "Don't worry, I have a shipment of frames coming, too. You'll figure something out."

Sara suspected that Irina kept Teddy somewhat grounded and focused. She was good *to* him and good *for* him, and Sara told the beautiful granddaughter of a former Russian mafia general as often as she could. "You're a miracle worker," she'd said the night before, which made Irina grin and lift her wine glass, replying, "May wonders never cease."

Jim had been more than generous in divvying up the profits among his long-time managers and faithful employees. Especially with Sara, who'd earned thirty-seven million for her shares in LightPulse, in addition to the extra twenty-five million that he'd given her as part of an exit package. She'd tried to insist that it was too much, that it wasn't necessary, but the elder Rutherford would hear none of it, and threatened to give her *more* if she didn't stop with the refusal attempts.

Now, with a large portion of it donated to various charities, she had roughly forty million dollars remaining. She'd invested most of it wisely, set aside college funds for the kids, and purchased fifty acres of land adjacent to her parents' farm in southwest Virginia. The rolling hills of the Appalachians were comforting and the kids had fit right in as soon as they set foot in the deep green grass.

Far away from the atrocities in Portland, Sara felt *new*, even though Patty Kellog was still out there somewhere. But so far, she

was comfortable with their position. The farmhouse was well forti-
fied and featured an unrivaled security system. They had acres of
open land in which to see approaching visitors, both good and bad
alike. Within the past week, the FBI assured her that they had a lead
on Patty and it wouldn't be long.

Things had finally stabilized.

Sara's fear, lingering in the back of her mind, was that her trou-
bles weren't really over and never would be as long as Patty and
Shelley were alive, but she knew that constant worry over *possible*
problems solved nothing.

Life had to move forward.

Exist, adapt, and embrace.

Embrace the day, embrace the people that matter.

Even her pesky, former arch-nemesis was welcome for a visit.

They'd been through so much together, so many unbelievable,
unwanted adventures, and after years and years of hating his guts,
she was proud to call him a friend. She'd saved his life. He'd saved
hers. They were even.

But Teddy was still…Teddy, even under Irina's guidance.
However, now Sara saw his over-confident nature more as endearing
quality than an annoying nuisance.

Teddy wasn't so bad as long as you knew how to corral him.

"Looks like rain," Sara said, glancing up at the encroaching
black clouds.

Teddy laughed. "You say things like that now? 'Green Acres is
the place to be,' huh?"

"Goes with the territory. We should probably get back up to
the house before it gets here." A gust of wind brought with it the
distinct smell of rain, confirming her assessment.

"I thought you moved three thousand miles away to get away
from rain."

"You know why she moved," Irina said. She patted Teddy's bottom. "To get away from *you*. Right, Sara?"

Sara winked and replied, "There's no place far enough."

"Hey, I don't *have* to be here, you know. Be nice to me. We're on our honeymoon." He tried to sound offended, but it didn't work. He shrugged and added, "Besides, how many of these hicks keep you on your toes like I do?"

Sara turned and walked up the gravel driveway toward her home. Teddy and Irina followed. She said, "Just because they live in the middle of nowhere doesn't mean they're hicks. You'd be surprised." She pointed across the gentle, undulating hills. Spring hadn't quite sprung yet, but some of the green had returned. Off in the distance, a large log home sat nestled among a cluster of maple and oak trees. "That house belongs to a heart surgeon. The one to the right—you see it, the one with the black shingles? A former senator lives there and then behind our house, up there between those pines, that's Dr. Hayton. He's one of the top oncologists in Virginia so I think he travels more than he's home."

"What about that one? The beautiful one. It looks like a painting." Irina asked, pointing to the southwest. An old brick farmhouse with a gray roof and white-columned porch looked slightly rundown. Where Irina saw beauty, Sara saw a home that could use some work. Bricks had fallen from various spots. Vines crawled up its exterior and in the driveway, a decrepit, rusty pickup sat with its tailgate down.

"That," Sara said, "is my backup plan."

"How so?" Teddy asked.

"The guy that lives there used to be a sniper in the Marines. I haven't met him yet, but his name is Randall. If anything ever goes wrong *here*," she said, pointing at the ground beneath her feet, "I know who I'm asking for help."

Teddy stopped in the middle of the driveway. "Seriously? A sniper?"

Sara nodded. "Yeah, I guess. My folks said he had some trouble a while back. Some crazy rumors about how these hitmen were trying to kill him, but around these parts, who knows. Life moves a little slower here and people need things to talk about, so the old folks like to hang around in the local restaurants, drinking coffee and telling stories. I'm not sure which they do more of, to be honest."

Teddy grinned. "People were trying to kill him?"

Irina added, "If that's true, isn't it dangerous to be so close?"

"Everything's seemed fine over there. Quiet. And like I said, it's probably just old folks gossiping. I've met his wife and little boy before. She's a bit rough around the edges but their son is an absolute sweetheart. Her sister, Mary, is a private investigator and former officer, too. I'm surrounded by good company."

"Sounds like it," Teddy said. "Do you think we could go talk to him later?"

A fat drop of rain smacked Sara on the forehead. "Maybe. Why?" She resumed her hike back up the short hill. Looking to the southwest, she could see the black clouds creeping in, blocking out the blue sky.

Teddy and Irina stayed close behind. He said, "We're doing a new first-person shooter called *Sniper One* and it's already getting major buzz. We're not even halfway through development yet and some reporters are calling it the next big thing. I mean, you should see the graphics, Sara. They're totally unreal for a smartphone."

"And what does this have to do with Randall?"

"I don't know. Research. It might be fun to sit down and talk to him, maybe pour him a beer and ask a few questions. We've hired some consultants—these former enlisted guys—so we could be solid on our accuracy, right? But all those dudes want to talk about is physics and trajectories and shit I don't understand in the slightest. What I'm looking for is the *story* behind it all. I couldn't care less if a bullet follows a certain flight path in windy conditions over a half mile on a random Tuesday in rural freakin' Afghanistan. What I want to know is…what's the story behind the target? How'd the sniper get there? Why does the dude he's shooting at...why does he have to die? Narratives. Not math and science. Remember how we used to argue over that stuff?"

Irina squeezed his hand. "Somebody dared to argue with you? I don't believe it."

"Yeah. Sara and I used to have some epic battles back in the day."

"And I always won," Sara informed Irina. "Didn't I, Little One?"

Teddy threw his head back and cackled. "Jesus, I haven't heard that in ages."

They laughed harder at Irina's confused look and explained the insulting term of endearment. "I can't say I miss those days, Teddy, but seriously, it's good to see you doing so well. And thanks for coming to visit." She put her arm around his shoulder. The gesture didn't feel quite so foreign anymore. "Being here, with my parents right over the hill...it's nice to have family so close and some peace, but we miss our friends, though, and the kids ask about you and your dad quite a bit."

"They do?"

"Once they found out you were coming, that's all they talked about." Sara climbed up the front porch steps. Teddy came next, then Irina.

Sara peeked through the living room window. Inside, Miss Willow sat reading a book. When Sara had decided to move, there was no question that the soft-spoken, flower-child babysitter was coming with them. She didn't need to ask, and neither did Miss Willow.

Sara gently rapped on the window.

Miss Willow looked up, waved, and then turned a page.

Teddy flopped down into a rocking chair. Irina took the one next to him, Sara settled into the third. She zipped her windbreaker higher as the chilly gust of wind pushed through.

Teddy said, "That's awesome to hear, Sara. Thanks for that."

"You're welcome. It's the truth. They ask about Barker, too, but I haven't talked to him in about two weeks. There for a while, right after we left, he called every other day to make sure we were fine."

Teddy planted both feet to stop the rocking chair. "Wait...you haven't heard?"

"Heard what?"

He glanced sideways at Irina, who put a hand over her mouth.

"Heard what, Teddy?"

"I thought for sure you knew and I wondered why you hadn't brought it up. Barker got shot a couple of weeks ago and he's been in the hospital since then. He'll be fine but it was kinda iffy there for a while."

Sara leaned up, hands on her knees. "Oh my God, what happened?"

"Normal follow-up on this case he was working. I can't remember what it was, but he went through a door and bam-bam, one in his side," Teddy said, pointing down near his waist, "and then another one went in right under his ribcage. Well, actually, it clipped the bone and ricocheted off. They think that's what saved his life."

"And he's going to make it?"

"Yeah, but I doubt he's going back to work. He'll live, but the bullet did quite a bit of damage when it plowed through there."

"That's *insane*. I mean, holy crap, I wondered why he hadn't called. Did you go see him in the hospital? Did they catch who did it?"

Teddy said to Irina, "Hon, see if you can find that article online. The one with the two pics, remember?"

"Which one?"

"The one with him in a uniform beside the one where he's in his hospital bed."

"Right, okay."

While Irina scanned through news articles on her phone, Teddy explained what he knew as dollops of rain began to pepper the porch roof.

Irina gasped and tapped Teddy on the shoulder. She handed her phone to him. "Look," she said.

"Did you find it?"

"No, read this."

Teddy scanned the screen, reading to himself. Sara watched his lips move. The expression on Irina's face worried her, too.

"What is it?" Sara said.

"Unbelievable."

"What? Tell me."

"They had a riot at Coffee Creek this morning."

Coffee Creek Correctional Facility was the place that Shelley Sergeant had called home for the past two years. "Let me see that." Sara reached over and snatched the phone from Teddy's hand, then read the article out loud. "Inmates escape after early morning riot. Local officials are still trying to figure out exactly what incited the riot at Coffee Creek Correctional Facility at four o'clock this morning...blah blah...unsubstantiated rumors report that witnesses heard a small explosion before the riot began...No comment... The only thing that Warden Bill Keller would confirm is that there are at least two dead and four missing who are presumed to have escaped. Authorities are advising residents not to open their doors for strangers...Identities and pictures of the escaped will be released as soon as they're confirmed...More details to follow."

Teddy said, "Sara, you don't think..."

Her hands were numb. She shook her head. "If she escaped, three thousand miles is a long way...right?"

Chapter Two

3:59AM
Wilsonville, Oregon
Coffee Creek Correctional Facility

Patty Kellog, also known as Boudica and former leader of the now defunct terrorist group called The Clan, stood to the west of the small prison. She was dressed in black, head to toe, providing perfect cover in the darkness. The three men behind her wore identical outfits matching hers. Each carried an Uzi and a shoulder strap flush with grenades. They were practically invisible under the thin tree line.

She listened to the far off rumble of an approaching train. It would give them good noise cover and a good distraction upon their approach. She shifted her balance from one foot to the next and waited for the train to come closer.

Months ago, when Patty had visited Shelley Sergeant for the first time, with her deceased bomb technician known as Quirk, she'd promised the young, sadistic talent that she would have her freedom in two years.

Plans, and motivations, changed.

There was a sense of urgency brought about by frustration and impatience, then delayed by the need to find decent men willing to work with her. It seemed as if Vadim Bariskov, the Spirit, had more pull in the international community than she realized. Although they had escaped from Jim Rutherford's home together, through the secret tunnel and seconds before the bomb detonated, she realized too late that it had been a mistake to let him live.

If she had known how quickly his loose tongue could spread misinformation, she would've slit his throat and watched his body float away through Portland's drainage system. Instead, they'd parted ways with the assurance that it was easier to escape as individuals rather than as a team.

She hadn't seen him since. The Spirit had vanished, as he was known to do. Then, when she began the laborious process of recruiting a new squad, words like "careless" and "inept" were suggested, along with phrases such as, "loose cannon" and "unpredictable, impulsive neophyte," which hindered her recruitment tactics over and over again. For months, she had traveled the world, enduring cockroach-infested motels in Thailand, sleazy bestiality bars in South America, and a moose-themed restaurant in Canada, looking, asking, and hunting for anyone willing to work with her soiled reputation. It took some work and more promises than she could keep, but she'd finally settled on the D-list assassins with her now.

Patty glanced at the three men standing nearby. They weren't the best, but they were affordable, and that would have to do. She shook her head. If she ever came across the Spirit again, retribution wouldn't be an option—it would be a guarantee.

The rumbling of the freight train grew louder. Patty held up a hand. "Hold," she said. "Just a little more." At three hundred yards, they had plenty of time.

The man closest to her, Jensen, fidgeted and moved a step nearer to the tracks. He'd expressed his concerns about her plan, chief among them the need to dart in front of a moving behemoth weighing millions of pounds.

Patty clenched her teeth. "I said *hold*."

Jensen flashed a look over his left shoulder and said, "I'm not waiting." He readjusted his grip on the Uzi and broke into a run, ducking low and beneath the single headlight.

Patty didn't vacillate. She dropped Jensen with an accurate shot to the calf. He yelped, fell, and rolled to the side, clutching his leg. He barely had a chance to get his arms up before she was on top of him. A muffled *chuff* escaped the silencer of her compact 9mm, leaving a single hole in the center of his forehead.

What a waste. He had potential, but she couldn't risk him accidentally sabotaging the mission any further. At least she hadn't paid him yet. Silver linings, they say.

She quickly tried to gauge the train's distance. Two hundred yards, easy. More than likely, the engineers hadn't seen anything from that far away. Jensen's body alongside the tracks would be nothing but a black lump and it was doubtful they'd even notice.

Crenley and Tanner crouched behind her, breathing quietly, waiting patiently.

"Orders, ma'am?" Tanner asked, with no regard to his fallen associate.

Patty looked at the rugged face covered in camo paint, studying the emotionless eyes. She thought she could grow to like this one. He had the right attitude. Beside him, Crenley spat a mouthful of tobacco juice onto Jensen's leg.

Crenley said, "He was weak," and then looked at the approaching train. "What now?"

Patty smiled. She'd made the right choice with these two. She signaled for them to follow her as they sprinted through the underbrush, hopping stray limbs and shallow crevices. She nearly rolled an ankle on a small rock but recovered well and kept moving. Patty stopped at the tracks and held up a hand. She checked her watch. "Train's early, but we need to move. You ready?"

Both nodded.

"Then keep your head down. This should be easy."

. . .

That was an hour ago.

Should.

Should've been easy.

She should've known.

Tanner screamed in the backseat, the bullet wound in his stomach bleeding slowly but sure to kill him if they didn't get help soon. Crenley swiped at the sweat on his forehead and resumed the pressure on Tanner's leaking gut.

Crenley said, "We gotta get him some help."

Patty checked the rearview mirror. "Where? Huh? Where?"

Shelley Sergeant sat in the passenger's seat, grinning, and occasionally looking out the windows. "I don't see anybody coming."

Crenley said to Patty, "He'll die if we don't."

"What the hell do you expect me to do? Maybe I should stop at 7-11 and get him a couple of cotton swabs. Would that work?"

"Kill him," Shelley suggested.

"No, don't."

Patty shook her head. "We need him. He's good."

"He'll slow us down."

Patty checked the side mirrors again. She leaned over and scanned the sky above, expecting to see a hovering helicopter with a searchlight. Nothing. Why weren't they chasing after them? Was it manpower issues? Did they alert the local police? The FBI? Coffee Creek was comprised of both minimum and medium-security populations, but it still didn't mean that they would've ignored a full-fledged escape. Especially not after Tanner tossed a grenade at a wall as a last resort.

Things had gone wrong from the start. The first guard she'd bribed appeared at the southwest corner without Shelley, insisting that it had been impossible to get her out. He got two bullets in the chest; one for his cowardice and one for his inability to perform.

Their backup plan didn't work as well as expected either. Inside the prison walls, the second bribed guard was supposed to create a distraction—a difficult task at four o'clock in the morning.

His "distraction" had turned into a riot. He'd managed to call Patty and give brief details before she heard a loud *thunk*, followed by the sound of a phone skittering across the floor.

Next came Tanner's grenade opening a hole in the wall. Smoke. Fires. Burning mattresses. Screaming women fighting, pulling hair, beating disoriented guards with batons and table legs. Blood and gunfire. Tanner screaming. Crenley returning sporadic, peppered shots.

Somehow, throughout the raging chaos of flashing red lights and drifting banks of gray smoke, Patty found Shelley Sergeant in the middle of a hallway. She stood with her arms crossed, watching the carnage and smiling like a kid at Disney World.

Patty had grabbed her, offered a simple "Remember me?" and then they'd all retreated with Shelley in tow. Maybe amongst the insanity, the guards were disoriented and trying to regain control. Maybe they hadn't yet realized that one of their inmates was missing. She tried to recall if any of the night guards—the ones that had lived—had seen them escaping through the crumbling gash in the wall.

Was it possible they hadn't been spotted? Perhaps. Perhaps not.

If the gods were on her side, and they usually were, they'd made it out cleanly and the search for the missing inmate wouldn't commence until the authorities performed a headcount.

How long did they have? A couple of hours at the most? The interior of the prison was in complete disarray, total madness, and she couldn't imagine that the prison officials would get things under control quickly enough to do a live pursuit.

At best, reports would emerge regarding a shadowy commando team, followed by Shelley's face on every news channel. There would be reporters and press conferences. Officials imploring residents to be on the lookout for a one-eyed blonde escapee. Hotlines would receive hundreds of calls.

It would happen, but not for a while.

They'd gotten lucky. They were away, clean, for the time being.

Now, hurtling along the interstate, Patty looked over at the excited blonde wearing the prison *chic* orange jumpsuit. The young woman would need to lose the eye patch, definitely. It was too identifying, too conspicuous. She might as well have had a tattoo on her face like Mike Tyson.

Crenley said, "We're losing him. Come on, do something."

Lights from an oncoming rig swept across his face in the back seat. Patty could see the anger and desperation in his bulging eyes and pursed lips. Tanner and Crenley had come as a package deal—longtime partners who'd worked hundreds of off-the-record missions together for the CIA. Black ops assignments in South America, Sudan, and North Korea, plus many more than they'd cared to mention. When Uncle Sam had sent them on their way, without pensions or acknowledgment, it had left a bitter taste. For the past five years, they'd happily worked for anyone who considered themselves an enemy of any state. Freedom fighters, guerrilla warlords, it didn't matter as long as the paycheck had enough zeroes behind it.

"Fine," Patty said, whipping the battered Ford Explorer to the right and down an exit ramp where she plowed over the stop sign and took a hard right turn. She wrenched the steering wheel to the left and dropped the SUV back onto all four tires. Up ahead, the searing lights of a McDonald's parking lot brightened everything within reach.

She careened into the lot and sped around to the back of the restaurant.

"What're you doing?" Crenley asked. "I said we need *help*, you dumb shit."

Tires squealed as she slammed on the brakes and pitched everyone forward.

Patty felt the gun barrel behind her right ear before she could shift the car into park.

Crenley growled. "Hospital. Now."

"This is so much fun." Shelley giggled and clapped.

Patty slammed the gearshift up and took her foot off the brakes. "We *do not* have time for this bullshit, Crenley. I'll make you a deal," Patty said. "Take your partner and throw him in that dumpster. Get rid of him and I'll pay you double."

"No."

"Triple and you stay on with me. I have more work coming."

Silence from the back seat. Patty could sense his indecision. Was he thinking it over? Was he weighing the possible scenarios? Bullet in her head, then one in Shelley? Then what?

She eased her 9mm across the bench-style front seat as deftly as possible until it was within Shelley's reach, calmly waving a hand back and forth to get her attention. As soon as Shelley glanced down, Patty said, "Crenley? Look at me, okay? Look. What did we agree on, huh? Fifty thousand for tonight and an escort to Virginia? I'll tell you what—make it five hundred if you stay with me through the end of this job. You might have fun with it anyway."

"Five hundred thousand? You're serious?"

"Tanner goes in the dumpster with an extra bullet, you come with us to see the rest of our mission through, and you're half a mil richer. Sound good?"

She watched his eyes darting back and forth. Crenley lowered the gun from her ear. The spot where the barrel had been on her skin stayed cool. When he looked away once more, she risked a peek and saw that Shelley was prepared.

"What do you say, Crenley? We could use your help."

Tanner moaned and mumbled something that sounded like, "Cold."

She watched in the rearview mirror as Crenley breathed deeply, huffed, and then shook his head. "I don't think I can do—"

Beside her: *chuff-chuff.*

Shelley giggled as Crenley slumped over. She leaned across the front seat and put a finishing touch on Tanner. *Chuff.* One in the forehead.

Patty liked this girl, for damn sure, more than she liked the two mediocre assassins in the back leaking blood that they'd have to clean up later.

Shelley said, "God, that felt good. It's been too long."

Chapter Three

Sara stood in the living room of her farmhouse, watching the headline ticker run along the bottom of the CNN broadcast. "Nothing new," she said, chewing on a fingernail. "Give me something." Three hours had passed and they continued to offer the same information. There was a prison riot in Oregon, two guards were dead, and four inmates were presumed missing. The last she'd heard, the local authorities were finalizing the headcount just to be sure.

All fires were out in the prison and several of the inmates had been escorted to the infirmary for injuries and the effects of smoke inhalation. Additional doctors were on site to conduct medical examinations and treatment. Any further information was pending the press conference at five o'clock eastern time.

Sara wasn't sure she could wait two more hours. The tips of her fingers would be bloody nubs by that time. Thankfully, the kids were home from their mid-week early release day, and they sat in the entertainment room with Teddy and Irina, watching something on the Disney Channel.

Miss Willow brought Sara a mug of chamomile tea. "Something to soothe your nerves, dear."

"Thanks." Sara blew into the mug and took a sip. A touch of cream, just the way she liked it. Over the past couple of years, Miss

Willow had nearly become as much of a sitter to Sara as she was the children.

"Anything?"

"Not a word," Sara said. "There's a press conference at five. Hopefully by then they'll have the headcount finished and we can see who escaped."

"Supposedly," Miss Willow reminded her. "*Unaccounted for* doesn't mean that the Sergeant girl is in an airplane and on her way here."

"Or, that's exactly what it means."

Miss Willow put her arm around Sara's waist and pulled her close. Sara rested her head against the taller woman's shoulder. It was comforting in the absence of her mother and father, who'd taken their annual Carnival cruise to the Bahamas at the perfectly wrong time. Miss Willow was an excellent security blanket and deserved every bit of credit for keeping Sara sane for the past twenty-four months, but nothing could replace the warm embrace of a concerned, caring parent.

Sara thought about how ridiculous it was to revert to some childish sense of dependency. She was in her mid-thirties, for God's sake, Mommy and Daddy wouldn't be around to protect her forever. In spite of this, it didn't change the fact that being comforted by a parent that loved you remained a good emotional stabilizer.

"Now, now," Miss Willow said. "I'm going to steal one of Barker's expressions for a second. What's the one? He says, 'Don't borrow trouble because the interest is too high.' Okay?"

Sara pulled free of the embrace and walked over to the couch. She sat, took a sip of her tea, then covered her eyes. "I know...This is so ridiculous. Why am I worrying about it?" She grunted, then answered her own question. "I'll tell you why, because she's insane enough to try something like this. I mean, Jesus, the FBI said they had a possible lead on Patty Kellog, but she's out there somewhere because they never found her body. What if the both of them are teaming up to hunt me down?"

Miss Willow rolled her eyes.

Sara chuckled. "Think about it, Willow. Huh? Am I crazy? Crap like that runs through my head in the middle of the night."

Miss Willow switched off the television, then shut the front door and locked it. Using the keypad near the door, she armed the multiple security systems; alarms beeped, LED displays flashed, and colors went from red to green. "There. Happy now?"

"It helps."

Miss Willow pointed a scolding finger at her and said, "And when are you going to change that pass code, huh? I've been telling you for months now that you can't use the same one for everything, especially one that you've been using for years. It's too dangerous."

"I know, I know. An ounce of prevention. I'll get to it." Sara sighed and nudged up to the edge of the couch. "Honestly, are we safe here?" She lowered her voice, flicking her chin toward the entertainment room. "Are the *kids* safe here?"

Teddy entered the room from the opposite direction, spooking Sara. Evidently he'd gone through the entertainment room, into the kitchen, and then popped in via the other side. She jumped. He apologized, then said, "Miss Willow's right, you know. Don't borrow trouble."

"Were you listening the whole time?"

He nodded. "Sorry. Jacob wanted a snack. Couldn't help but overhear because I spent so much damn time trying to find the candy he was asking for. What're you feeding those guys, huh? *Kale chips*? Really?"

"Mind your own," Sara said, feeling the gentle roots of a smile growing. "It has to be stuff like kale chips or Jacob will eat every sweet thing in the house."

"Right. Anyway." Teddy squeezed Sara's shoulder. "You okay?"

"I'm...no, I'm not. Not until I hear that Shelley's part of the headcount."

"You gotta trust the system, Sara. You're in Virginia for Christ's sake. Even if she did manage to get out and get away, they'll find her. She'll turn up in some roadside motel in who-knows-where Arizona. You see it on the news all the time, right? They usually find these people a few miles down the road because they were dumb enough to head back to their ex-girlfriend's house instead of making a smart decision for the first time in their lives. And keep in mind, the lack of smart decisions are what got them there in the first place."

"True, but you're forgetting one thing."

"What's that?"

"Shelley was a genius."

"And you beat her, and she's in prison. What does that tell you?"

Sara wasn't sure it told her that much. She'd been smart enough to get through the levels of Shelley's game, smart enough to figure out that insane puzzle with only a couple of seconds remaining, and smart enough to best Shelley overall, but was it a fluke? Anybody with enough deductive reasoning could've figured that out, couldn't they? Was she really smarter, and better, than Shelley? Not necessarily. "It tells me," she said, "that I got lucky. One good guess doesn't mean I'm the superhero to her supervillain."

"Come here," Teddy said, playing rough, pulling her up from the couch and hugging her. He used his knuckles to scrub her head like an annoying little brother. She laughed, twisted his nipple, and pulled away.

"You're ridiculous. Don't make me laugh, Teddy. I'm scared, I want to be pissed off."

"Sara, dude, take a deep breath. Miss Willow, will you tell her to relax? What did you tell me earlier, huh? You've got a *three hundred thousand* dollar security system on this house. Bulletproof glass. A panic room down in the basement that you modeled after Dad's, and enough cameras posted around the property to film a squirrel taking a dump. I'm sure the guy monitoring all the feeds out of here is gonna love that, by the way."

Despite her concern and her need to obsess, Sara had to admit that Teddy was right and being rational. Somewhat. She'd never tell him to his face, obviously—can't give the little bastard too much room for his head to grow—but it was nice to have him around to provide some validity to the obvious.

Rational and *Teddy* in the same breath. The world had surely turned upside down.

"Let's go have some fun," he said. "We'll relax a little bit, then come back and watch the press conference in a couple of hours, and everything will be fine, okay? Now, it sounds like the kids are done with their movie and I need to get Irina out of there before she decides she wants some of those little buggers running around the house."

Miss Willow said, "I'll go get a snack for them."

"I ate all the kale chips," Teddy said. "Not really. They went down the garbage disposal."

Sara stood and flicked his earlobe. "Jerk. Do you know how much those things actually cost when you can find them here in the country?"

"Whatever it is, I'm sure they're not worth it."

. . .

Irina had decided to stay behind and play with the children, which had given Teddy plenty of reason to complain on the way down to the neighbor's house. However, there was a hint of acquiescence in his voice. He said, "I don't know what's gotten into her lately, but that's all she talks about, Sara. Kids, babies. The other day I caught her online researching college savings funds. I'm telling you, put a thermometer in that woman's mouth and her baby fever would be up near one-oh-five."

"When did that start?"

"After her birthday two weeks ago."

"Ah." Sara nodded, knowingly. "How old? She's thirty, right? Couple of years younger than you?"

"Yeah."

"I know it's such a ridiculous cliché, but the biological clock ticks louder around that age. She's ready."

"*I'm* not."

"You sure?"

Teddy looked away to hide his grin. The rain had dissipated to a light misty drizzle. The smell of wet earth wafted up and off in the distance, just above the row of pine trees on top of Greenwood Hill, a speckle of blue sky poked through the clouds. He said, "I put on a good show, but...yeah. Maybe." He latched onto Sara's arm and squeezed softly. "Don't you dare tell her that, okay? Not yet. I'm getting there, but I don't want to start tomorrow. We've got the release of *Sniper One* coming up, I'm on the road all the time...it's a lot to handle."

"I don't know if there's every a right time, Teddy. People plan for children, I guess, but you never really know how much your world is going to turn upside down until you're right in the thick of it. Read all the books you want—get prepared, buy things that you'll never use like cute, pinkish changing table straps that hold the changing pad where it's supposed to go, but you never know until you're right there, holding that screaming baby with breast milk on your shirt and poop in your hair that you've made the right choice."

"So, you're actually trying to *encourage* me with the idea of poop in my hair?"

Sara laughed and entered the security code to open the gate at the end of her driveway. When it swung closed, she again tapped the numbers on the access panel and listened to the latches slide into place, along with the heavy metal bars that secured it to the driveway underneath it. Nothing was getting through there short of a tank. The perimeter fence could use some reinforcement, she knew, but those alterations weren't set to be made until the following month. She'd debated it for days, not wanting to ruin the aesthetics of the countryside, but, if she and the kids weren't alive to enjoy them, the eyesore wouldn't matter anyway.

Maybe. She was still…on the fence, so to speak.

Sara continued, "Brian and I weren't sure we wanted kids. Not at first. Realists like me, or you for that matter, we get so caught up in the way the world is that it's hard to imagine subjecting a child to all this crap that's on the news everyday. Brian and I were sure we'd rather keep a child safe from that by *not* having one than by having one and trying to protect it."

"So why did you?"

Sara shrugged. "Oops." She checked the winding country road for traffic and stepped across to the other side. Gravel had washed down from the Halloran's driveway up the hill, leaving a layer of loose gravel across the hardtop. In the field to their left, a collection of rocks and pebbles had gathered like a small creek bed.

"*Oops*? Lacey and Callie were…what's the plural of *oops*? Oopses? Oopsi?"

"I don't know if it matters anymore—whoa, don't step in that."

Teddy narrowly avoided a cow patty in the middle of the road, nimbly sidestepping in mid-stride.

Sara continued, "You know, it doesn't matter, to be honest. Oops or no oops, your world changes, and you go from panic so strong that you've got pee running down your leg to be the happiest you've ever been, with someone else's pee running down your leg. When it's one of those days where you've got breast milk on the ceiling and you haven't slept in twenty-four hours, you survive with a smile. It's an amazing thing, Teddy. It really is."

"Sara, come on. You know how I am."

"You've changed."

"I have?"

"Irina's changed you. You've changed yourself. And God, I'm sure that was like turning a battleship around—"

"Hey!"

"Even like, two years ago, Teddy, you know? Before that crazy stuff with Shelley, I wouldn't have trusted you to babysit a fish tank for the weekend, but now, you've made it, my boy. Welcome to adulthood."

"Against my better judgment, I'll take that as a compliment. Still doesn't mean that I'm ready for a baby even though I get to sit at the adult table."

"It'll happen when it happens. And, it'll probably make Irina feel better if you tell her that you're ready…you're just not *tomorrow* ready."

"You sure?"

"Communication, bud. That's the best path to take."

"Right." They stopped by the silver mailbox with black, stenciled lettering that read, "Blevins, Route 2 Box 742," though the "E" was missing in "Route." Teddy asked, "Did you let this guy know we were coming?"

"No. Around here, people show up on your front porch, whether you asked them to or not. My parents say it's a southern thing. It took some getting used to, but it helps when you have a surveillance system, too."

"You said this dude was an ex-sniper, though. He's not going to shoot us walking up to his house, is he?"

Sara marched up the long, winding gravel driveway. She looked over her shoulder and motioned for Teddy to follow. "*You* maybe, but I'm hoping he'll recognize me."

"And that's supposed to be comforting?"

"Yes."

Reluctantly, Teddy followed.

Chapter Four

Patty drove along the narrow, snow-covered road, creeping through the campground, searching for any brave souls willing to test their mettle against the cold, dreary Oregon winters. High in the Cascades, the white blanket was thick and wet.

Surely, some bearded hippie with his crunchy wife would be tucked back in a secluded corner. She and Shelley hadn't driven too far out, away from the McDonald's, before finding a campground sign. Although it read, "Closed for the Season," she knew that it was merely a marker, signifying that the state wouldn't maintain upkeep until the spring. It didn't prevent the diehard nature lovers from staying a few miserable nights.

Shelley rolled down her window and stuck her head out. She inhaled deeply.

"What're you doing?" Patty asked.

"That's what freedom smells like." Shelley leaned back inside the SUV and began rolling the window up. Pausing halfway, she whispered, "Stop. Stop! Over there. Look."

A green tent, small and triangular, big enough for one or two people only, sat nestled in between a heavy cluster of pine saplings that provided good cover against the wind. Natural and unnatural shelter coexisting. The tent looked old, worn down, and for a moment, Patty thought it might've been abandoned until she noticed the thin sliver of smoke drifting up from the remnants of a campfire.

Above it and hanging from a limb was an orange backpack, what looked to be a bag of food, and then another backpack next to it. Patty was hoping for a female hiker or camper, someone about Shelley's size so they could get her out of the screamingly obvious prison jumpsuit. She hoped she'd found what they were looking for because the second backpack was fluorescent pink.

The sun was up and Patty wondered how long it would be before the campers were as well. How should they play the situation? Approach while the couple slept and catch them off guard? That was the wisest choice. They were miles from civilization. Out here, there would be no one to hear them scream except the animals.

Or…should they snatch the campers, then tie them up in the back of the Explorer? Would hostages be good bargaining power or a burden and complete distraction? One never knew when she would need a human shield.

No, it wasn't worth the trouble. Hostages meant visibility. Hostages, if you didn't plan to kill them, had memories and voices. The private flight she'd booked out of the city of Bend was scheduled for nine o'clock. In three hours, she and Shelley would be on their way across the U.S. to an Appalachian mountain town called Marion, Virginia. That was the thing about private flights: unregulated and unburdened by NTSB rules, you could have a suitcase nuke in your luggage and travel from one spot to the next with less scrutiny than the guy in security busting your chops over a shaving cream can that was larger than three ounces.

From Bend, they would make one quick stop in Minnesota to refuel and then land in a regional airport close to Bristol, Tennessee. Patty had grown up in northern Virginia and had spent the early part of her life there before she had left for the home-away-from-home mental hospital, so she was familiar with Bristol. That's where her uncle Marty used to travel to watch NASCAR races. Marion, on the other hand, she remembered as being a blip on the map while they hurtled past on I-81. However, there were water towers along-side the interstate with gigantic words painted on the side that read "HOT" and "COLD" which her father thought was the funniest thing he'd ever seen.

There were times, like when she was slitting the throat of the man she loved in Prague, that she missed the life she'd once had. Vacations with her parents in Gatlinburg, Tennessee and Kitty Hawk, North Carolina, visiting with relatives in Nashville and Atlanta. Those were simpler days. She'd miss them long enough to recall slipping poison into her parents' coffee—retribution for sending her away—before she'd shake her head free of the nostalgia.

Sentimental reminiscing weakened resolve.

Close the box. Lock it. Throw it into the sun.

Watch it burn.

"I see movement," Shelley said.

Patty blinked and refocused. Drifting off like that was danger-ous. She'd have to be more careful now that she had the burgeoning talent of Shelley Sergeant riding shotgun. She liked what she'd seen so far, but the young woman was unpredictable. Space out like that again and she might find that Shelley had a knife at her throat.

The zipper on the tent slowly rose up and out poked the head of a sleepy-eyed camper.

Patty said, "You got a t-shirt on under there?"

"Yeah."

"Get rid of the orange. Pull it down to your waist."

"Why? Aren't we going to kill whoever it is anyway?"

"We don't want to spook them. Spooked people run, and I'm too tired to chase somebody through the snow out here."

"Whatever." Shelley wriggled out of the top half of her prison attire and tied the sleeves around her waist.

When the man emerged from the tent, Patty saw that his bushy beard hung a foot down from his cheeks and chin. The red, knitted skullcap sat at an awkward angle. He squinted against the morning sun and waved before climbing out.

Patty shut off the engine. They must've been an odd sight, sitting there in an idling vehicle and staring, miles from anywhere. "Roll your window down all the way. Be friendly," she said to Shelley. Then, as the man approached, she said, "Morning."

"How's it going?" His voice was cheerful with a younger pitch than what his beard suggested. The skin around his eyes was taut without a hint of crow's feet. When he was back at the tent, Patty would've guessed early forties, but up close, he was maybe twenty-one. "Can I help you guys?"

Before Patty could offer a sociable response, Shelley bluntly asked, "What's with your packs in the trees?"

Patty rolled her eyes. Shelley was too impetuous. There would have to be a discussion about that.

"Um...for the animals. You know, to keep them from trying to raid the tent. Bears mostly." He blew on his hands and rubbed them together.

"Oh. Makes sense."

"You guys looking for a place to post up?"

"Maybe," Patty said. "Is this a good area?"

The young man shoved his hands in his front pockets and shrugged. "Depends on what you're looking for, I guess. Peace and quiet? Yeah, it's awesome."

Patty smiled. "Is that what you're doing? Getting away from it all?"

He lowered his eyes to the ground. A little red crept into his cheeks as he looked back over his shoulder, toward the tent. "Not really."

"No?"

"We're...we're field researchers. Biologists, actually, looking for signs of...um...signs of Sasquatch, honestly."

Shelley laughed. "No shit? Have you found anything?"

"Maybe." The guy grinned and winked.

Behind him, Patty saw a blonde head poke out between the tent flaps. A young woman, around the same age as their new friend, looked over and then crawled out. She wore a puffy red jacket, a headband covering her ears, and what looked to be skintight ski pants. Her feet were tucked into those ugly brown boots that all the girls her age wore. Despite her choice of footwear, she was cute.

"Hi," she called over. "I'm Chrissy." She trudged through the snow and approached the Explorer.

"Right, and I'm Denny," the guy said, sticking his hand into the open window. Shelley shook it, and so did Patty.

"How long have you guys been out here?"

"Just for the night so far. We scheduled a three-day stay, but we expected more of the snow to be gone."

Chrissy kissed his cheek. "*He* did. I knew better."

"But," Denny said, glancing around at the ground, "it'll be easer to find tracks and trails in the snow. If we can handle the cold, we'll probably stay the whole time."

Patty thought about how perfect the opportunity could've been. Chrissy was roughly the size of Shelley, so there'd be clothes to change into. These two were here in the middle of nowhere, scheduled to be out long enough so that no one would come looking for them until it was too late.

But Denny had made an excellent point. Tracks would be easy to follow. They couldn't necessarily shoot them and then hide the bodies somewhere in the woods. Four sets of prints. Blood in the snow. Tire tracks that could be loosely matched to the make and model of their SUV.

Then, Chrissy said something that sealed their fates.

"The weather report said they're expecting another eight to twelve inches tonight or tomorrow, so we're thinking we might pack up and try again later in the spring. If you guys were looking to stay around here, it might be a better idea to go back down to a lower elevation where it's not so—"

Chuff. Chuff.

Two shots. Denny and Chrissy slumped and dropped to the ground.

Shelley smiled at Patty and blew across the top of the silencer like an Old West gunslinger.

Patty grabbed her arm and yanked. "Are you kidding me?"

"What? That's what you wanted, right?"

"Yes, but you *have* to start showing some control, okay? This isn't some game where you can just run around popping people and not expect there to be any consequences. I don't care how careless you are with *your* life, but if you're going to work *with* me and *for* me, we need some boundaries. Some rules. I'm not going to prison because you feel like you're free to do whatever the hell you want. Do you understand?"

Shelley scoffed and pulled her arm free. "Yes, *Mom*. And who says I'm working *for* you?"

Patty grabbed a handful of Shelley's hair and jerked her across the cab. Face to face, nearly nose touching nose, she said, "Let me be perfectly clear. I got you out of prison. I risked my ass to save yours. If it weren't for me, you'd be in there rotting with the rest of the pond scum."

"You're hurting—"

"Shut up." Patty shook her. "You are *mine*. There are no other options. You're mine, you work for me, or you're dead. Got it?"

"I guess..."

"There's no guessing. I own you. You work for me now. We're professionals, damn it, and you're going to start acting like it." Patty shoved her away.

Shelley curled up a lip and rubbed the side of her head.

"Now get your ass out here and help me clean up your stupid mess. Get that pink bag down and find some clothes. Bodies go in the tent, and then we'll see if there's anything to eat. Easy enough?"

"Yes."

"Good. Try not to shoot anything else." Patty slung open the door and stepped out into the cold. The two biologists had either been brave or stupid to tackle their project at this elevation and in this temperature; whichever one it was, they were also unlucky to have been in the wrong place at the wrong time. So it goes.

The meek shall inherit the earth?

Not when the predators have better weapons.

Patty stomped around to the right side of the Explorer while Shelley got out, stepped over the bodies, and then marched through the snow. Patty kneeled down and tried to survey the damage. She lifted the female's head, then the male's. The bullets had gone through on both. Patty wondered if there would be metal fragments and if it would be worth doing a quick scan of the snow. The answers were possibly, and probably not. By noon, they'd be so far away that it wouldn't matter.

Shelley, having retrieved the pink backpack, slinked toward the tent.

"No, hey," Patty said to her. "Bodies first. Don't get blood on whatever you're going to change into."

"I know that." Shelley slung the backpack to the tent's side, and kicked her way through the snow. "Aren't you going to help me?"

Patty considered telling her to do it her damn self, just to teach her a lesson, but their schedule did have some limitations. "You get under the arms, I'll get the legs."

Two minutes later, they'd dragged the bodies inside the tent and zipped it closed. With any luck, the two of them wouldn't be found for days.

Shelley stripped in the frigid, open air as Patty worked on burying the blood with snow, twigs, and dirt. She looked back and watched as Shelley stood silently, nude, arms extended to the side, with her head turned up to the sun. She was smiling, breathing deeply.

Strange girl, Patty thought.

She hoped she hadn't made a mistake.

Chapter Five

Sara sipped at her coffee and leaned back against the kitchen counter. She watched the interaction between the miniscule Teddy Rutherford and the massive Randall Blevins. It reminded her of that old Looney Tunes cartoon with that tiny dog, Chester, yapping in the face of the gruff bulldog, Spike.

However, Randall seemed friendlier than Spike, and happily answered Teddy's questions. Well, *happily* might've been a bit of a stretch. Randall, amused, endured her former coworker's neverending stream of inquiries about life as a sniper and what it took to spend days out in the bush, waiting and lying immobile with such patience that a snake could crawl across his neck.

"You really did that?" Teddy asked.

Randall gave a short, humble nod. "Yup. It's a story for another day, but my spotter didn't fare so well when it happened to him."

"Man, we've gotta work that into the plotline somehow."

Sara set her mug down on the counter and checked her watch. They'd been there for thirty minutes already, and she was anxious to get back and watch the news even though the press conference wouldn't start for another hour. As the two men talked, she listened to their chatter and surveyed Randall's kitchen. The Blevins abode could certainly use some updating. The linoleum was worn and discolored in spots. The flooring sagged slightly in the middle, and some of the cabinetry seemed to be out of flush. One cabinet door looked newer than the rest.

Across the counter and into the open area of the dining room, the paneling had a faded rectangle where a picture had once hung, larger than the one of Randall's family that hung there now. Like she'd mentioned to Teddy, she'd heard the rumors from her parents about the insanity that had happened at his house, but she wondered how much of it was actually true. There were signs of things that had been fixed, like the cabinet door and a new family portrait, but none of that meant that Randall had defended himself here against a multitude of dangerous assassins.

She almost interrupted to ask, wanting to dispel the rumors or give them weight, once and for all, but she didn't want to be rude. Maybe that was a tale for another day, too.

Teddy said to Randall, "Any chance you'd want to come out to Portland and sit in with our creative team? We'd love to have you and of course, we'd compensate you for your time. Like a consultant. I was telling Sara that the guys we have now, they just want to talk about angles and percentages and wind speed. We need somebody like you to put meat on the bone."

Randall tilted his baseball cap higher on his head, crossed his arms, and said, "Hell, I don't know, man. I've had a rough few months lately. I'm kinda enjoying hanging out here and relaxing, you know?"

"I get it, I do, honestly. But *Sniper One*, it's gonna be huge. Bigger than huge. Your name will be on millions of phones around the world, rolling through the credits."

Sara could tell that Randall wasn't motivated by recognition and glory the way Teddy was. It showed in the way he smirked and readjusted his stance, the way he tried to stifle a chuckle.

"That's the problem," Randall said. "I still got too many people out there that don't like the look of my name. The only way they'd be happy to see it is if the damn thing showed up in the obituaries."

Teddy, not to be defeated, said, "Yeah, okay, but how about this…You come out to Portland for a week or two and share some details and after you're gone, we'll leak the story to the gaming community. Actually, yeah, that's perfect! We'll tell them we had an anonymous source—a former Marine Corps sniper that didn't want to be identified, who gave us all these top secret details. I mean, they wouldn't be *real* top-secret details, but you get what I'm saying. They'll eat it up."

"Still seems kinda risky to me, chief. You got a reporter that's nosey enough, he'll find a way to figure it out. After the year I've had, man, it's probably best for me to lay low."

Teddy nodded as he listened. He put a finger up to his mouth. The thinker.

Randall continued, "And besides, on the surface, being a sniper sounds like some cool shit, but in reality, it's all a lot of dressing up like a pile of leaves and waiting a week to pull the trigger."

The floorboard creaked under Sara's feet as she shifted to get comfortable. From all the research she'd done as the marketing director for LightPulse Productions, in order to promote their *Juggernaut* series, she knew that Randall was merely trying to down-play the reality.

She'd interviewed some former snipers herself. Read books by the greats like Carlos Hathcock and Chris Kyle. There were amaz-ing stories of survival, dedication, and willpower that served to ensure a mission's success. Life as a sniper was more than being patient and pulling a trigger, she knew that for certain, and for Randall to seem so humble about it made her like and appreciate him even more.

Here was a former soldier that had served his country and done his duty like it was the natural order of things—not some blowhard who wanted to prove to the world what kind of chest-pounding, barbaric man he was.

Once Randall finished trying to convince Teddy that it was no big deal, Teddy took a step closer to him and said, "How does a hundred thousand dollars sound for a week of your time?"

"Teddy," Sara said, "don't badger the poor guy. Come on."

Randall smiled at her. "No worries, ma'am. Now I'm interested."

Teddy couldn't hide his excitement. "Interested enough, or should we talk about a higher number?"

"Let me think about it, okay?"

That appeared to be enough for Teddy—who reacted as if he'd gotten a solid confirmation—as he slapped his hands together then pumped his fist in the air.

Randall laughed. Sara shook her head.

"Hold your horses, chief. I'm not on an airplane just yet. How long are you in town?"

"Another three or four days as long as Sara doesn't kick me out."

Randall turned to her with one eyebrow arched.

"It's a long story," she said.

Teddy's phone buzzed on his hip. He checked the caller ID. "That's Irina. Hang on one sec, okay? Excuse me." He went across the kitchen, between Randall and Sara, then out the screen door. It slammed behind him, a clanging metal on metal noise that hurt Sara's ears.

She turned to Randall. "Thanks for humoring him."

"You used to work with him?"

"For years."

"And how in the hell did you handle that on a daily basis?" Randall was smiling as he asked. Not malicious, but exasperated.

"I know he's a bit overbearing, but that little munchkin's got a good heart. Well, *now* at least. It took me a long time to get him there."

"You two got history together?"

"We do, but not that kind. It's a story for another day."

Randall snorted and shrugged. "Right. I got plenty of those myself. Can I get you a beer? More coffee?" He moved over to the ancient refrigerator and pulled out a bottle of Budweiser.

After living in the Pacific Northwest for so long, where craft brews flowed like river water, it was almost foreign to see a domestic beer. "No, thanks," she said. "Where I come from, what you're holding is like a bottle of Evian."

Randall popped the beer cap off the bottle. "Sounds about right. Old habits. So I heard you were from Oregon. What in the hell are you doing over here?"

"Originally from northern Virginia, but how I got out there and back here is an even longer story. We'll have you and your family over one day for dinner. It'd be good to get to know each other."

And for me to find out how willing you'd be to shoot a terrorist if she showed up here, Sara thought.

"Absolutely."

Teddy flung open the screen door and said to Sara, "We should head back."

"Why?" she asked. "What's wrong?"

"Irina said they're starting the press conference early. Something about some new information that's got everyone freaking out."

"What press conference?" Randall asked.

Sara eyed Teddy, almost telepathically asking him if she should mention the details to Randall. What were the consequences? Freak out the new neighbor or make an ally? Randall had seen some crazy stuff, she knew that much, so the likelihood of her story affecting him would be minimal. She hoped. On the other hand, she didn't want her first cordial meeting with Randall to be one where she begged for his help.

Teddy lifted one corner of his mouth and stepped through the door, allowing it to close quietly behind him.

Sara said, "How much time do we have?"

"Fifteen minutes."

Randall took another sip of beer. "Everything okay?"

"No, not exactly." Sara turned her eyes up to the ceiling and took a deep breath, preparing to take the risk. "I know this is going to sound ridiculous, but my folks—do you know the Thompsons?"

"Yeah, good people."

"They told me about your military background and I've been meaning to get over here and talk to you, but it never seemed like the right time and I didn't want to be rude and...You're going to think I belong up on the hill in the mental hospital."

"Ma'am, at some point, we all belong in a padded room."

...

Sara enjoyed the way Randall kept calling her 'ma'am' even though they were close to the same age. The southern hospitality and politeness around here was an added bonus she hadn't expected. But, what surprised her more was the way that Randall had immediately offered to help if she needed it.

Her story, and Teddy's story, would take too long to explain, so he'd walked back to her house with them in order to hear it all. Plus, he wanted to listen in on the press conference to get a better idea of what she was so afraid of. His wife, Alice, had begun homeschooling their boy Jesse, and the two of them were on an overnight retreat to Roanoke with the other moms and children, so he insisted he had some time to kill.

Along the way back to Sara's house, Teddy yammered about how brave they'd been in both situations, first Shelley, then Patty, as if it would impress the weathered veteran. Randall listened politely, and agreed that Teddy was most definitely a brave soul, and from what he'd heard, Sara *deserved* to be called a badass chick.

Once they'd returned to Sara's farmhouse, the three of them sat in the entertainment room while Irina and Miss Willow took the children out back to play in the large, open yard since the rain had passed through.

Sara turned on the wall-mounted, flat screen television and changed the channel from the Cartoon Network over to CNN. They waited for a Cadillac commercial to finish, then "Breaking News" soared across the screen in white block letters against a blood red background, accompanied by the familiar notes of the CNN intro music and James Earl Jones' booming voice.

"Let me ask you something," Randall said. He moved over and sat down on the arm of the couch, close to Sara. "What makes you think this prison break has anything to do with these two women trying to kill you?"

"If I told you all the details, we'd be here until next Tuesday."

On the television, Wolf Blitzer walked toward a massive screen behind him, pointing to a map of Oregon. He said, "We're here with you live. More coming out of Oregon as we're gearing up to listen to a press conference that was moved up by an hour..."

Sara said, "The short version is, when we were held hostage in Teddy's father's house, one of her guys—"

"Guys?"

"Um...hitmen? Hired hands? I don't know what in the hell they're called, but I swear I heard him mention Shelley's name. I could've been imagining things or, you know, having some sort of traumatic flashback, but it stuck with me for some reason."

"What'd he say?"

"It wasn't to her and I only caught pieces of it, but it sounded like he said, *'Shelley, that girl in prison.'* It's not much, but believe me, the name catches my ear every time I hear it, no matter who it belongs to."

"Hmm."

"Hush," Teddy said, "here they come. Whoa, is that Barker?"

Chapter Six

Patty sat in the window seat of the small, private jet. It hadn't been cheap, but the ability to maneuver around the U.S. unhindered made the extra zeroes worth it. Back before she'd failed to do away with Sara, and chose not to continue her mission by eliminating her target in France, it had been a close call getting into the States from Mexico, and she'd made better arrangements this time.

In the life of an international terrorist, haste meant the death penalty. The question now remained, was she going to take Shelley Sergeant with her afterward? A lot of that depended on how she behaved for the rest of this adventure.

She thought of it that way: an adventure. It wasn't a task, or a chore, or a game even, as Shelley kept calling it. Sure, it was fun, but this had become a quest. The pot of gold at the end of the rainbow. Finding El Dorado, the lost city of gold. Unearthing Blackbeard's treasure.

Except this time, watching Sara Winthrop die was the ultimate prize, more valuable than money, and more rewarding.

Patty daydreamed about how she would do it while Shelley slept in the seat across the aisle. When the young woman stirred and rolled her head to the side, Patty glanced over and took a longer look at her face. Patty had forced her to remove the eye patch before they'd gotten on the plane. Surely, in a day or two, the pilots would recognize her on television as one of the women they'd flown across the country. The eye patch would be unmistakable. One of them would alert the local authorities and they'd know where to focus their efforts.

Maybe it wouldn't ruin the adventure totally, but it would definitely hinder her plans.

She examined Shelley's face closely, remembering what she'd seen of the poor girl back at Coffee Creek when she'd visited with Quirk. The gnarled, mottled skin. The purple-scarred rivulets along her cheek. The thin strip of discoloration that formed a ring around her neck. All signs of an attempt on Shelley's life. The prisoners, plenty of them mothers themselves, hadn't taken kindly to the new inmate who'd nearly succeeded in murdering Sara's children to achieve her objective.

Where they had seen a horrible, disgusting human being and tried to send her back to Hell, Patty saw the beauty in Shelley's angry and vengeful plans. She'd tried, and failed, to gouge out Sara Winthrop's heart, hitting her in the place where she knew it would hurt the most. Patty admired the effort, but scoffed at the poor execution.

She leaned closer to Shelley's face and stared at the lumpy folds where the eye had once been. They were a mixture of light pink and flesh tones. Hills and valleys where the stitches had pulled and prevented a proper healing.

Patty thought, *Maybe she should've left the eye patch on. That mess is just as obvious.*

Memorable, for certain, but would the pilots make the connection?

Possibly, though if her plans went as she expected, they'd be gone by the time either the pilot or co-pilot had seen enough to identify her. They'd land in Bristol, at Tri-Cities Regional Airport, and then they'd be gone. She already had a car waiting in the long-term lot—all they had to do was drive away.

At best, the pilots could say that Shelley's last known location was on the tarmac of TRI.

The pilot, a man named Jeff, came over the intercom and said, "Miss Wilson, we're about to begin our descent into northeast Tennessee where the temperature is a cozy sixty-one degrees with overcast skies. We could hit some turbulence, so I'd like to ask that you and your guest please return to your seats and buckle up."

The co-pilot, Smiling Dave, as he'd informed them, poked his head out of the cabin, smiling, and said, "Let us know if you need anything, and thanks for the company!"

Patty wanted to punch him on principle.

Smiling Dave waved one last time and closed the cabin door.

Beside her, Shelley moaned, stretched, and opened her eye. "What'd he say? Are we there already?"

"You've been out since we hit altitude right out of Minneapolis."

Shelley sat up and took a drink from her water bottle. "I haven't slept like that since…damn, since the night I put a bullet in Sara's husband."

"That relaxing, huh?" Patty knew what Shelley meant. She'd experienced the same feeling of satisfaction before with Sara's former classmates as each one of them evaporated in the explosion of Quirk's handiwork.

"I slept like the dead that night. No pun intended." Shelley arched her back and reached up to her missing left eye. She rubbed at the skin and felt around her forehead, then on top of her head. "Oh, yeah. Forgot."

Patty couldn't recall the last time she'd felt anything resembling sympathy, but a flicker of it traipsed through her mind as she watched Shelley turn her face away. "You can put your eye patch back on once we're away from those two." She wanted to sound reassuring, maybe even a little bit human, because that still existed somewhere inside her psyche, but the statement came out sounding more like a mother telling her child that she could have her toy back once the chores were finished.

"No," Shelley said. "I'm done hiding it. I want her to see. I want her to know I earned it."

Her. Sara. A tingle of excitement skittered across Patty's skin. Maybe Shelley Sergeant had been a good choice after all. "Good. Hold onto that fire."

The small jet bounced and rattled, then dipped when it hit an empty air pocket. Shelley yelped and flung a hand across the aisle, grabbing Patty's wrist for comfort. "God, I hate flying," she said.

Another tingle emerged in Patty, in a place she hadn't foreseen, and she allowed Shelley's hand to linger for a moment. She'd been with women before, but she'd never preferred their company. Each and every time it had been to complete an assignment for someone with deep pockets and a list of enemies. To get close enough to the drug lord in Caracas, Venezuela, she'd made love to his wife while he watched, sipping wine and smoking marijuana. She'd eliminated them both the second he tried to climb into bed.

Next had been the brilliant programmer in Barcelona, Spain. She'd hired a prostitute for show, seduced the squirrely nerd in a bar, and then killed them both on a balcony overlooking the tree-lined street of *La Rambla*.

There were others, but they weren't nearly as memorable or exciting. There was something alluring about the thrill of being nude and vulnerable in the minutes before purging a mark. It wasn't as exhilarating as her desire to be caught in the act, but it was fun nonetheless.

She'd never been mentally attracted to any of the women she'd been with. It was all part of the job, so the fact that she'd felt something with Shelley's touch was both tantalizing and surprising. Back in the Explorer, she'd been ready to slam the young woman's face into the dashboard to make a point.

But this? What was this? Desire?

And why? Was it because Shelley was damaged too? Was there some underlying connection, some universal bond between them?

That pure moment of "Hey, you're just like me, and it's us against the world," was that what it was?

Regardless, there was no room for it. Lust and attraction, emotion, they caused problems.

Patty yanked her arm away. She said, "Touch me again and I *will* cut you." The threat was empty, made more as a reassurance to herself than a warning to Shelley.

"Jesus. Whatever." Shelley pulled her arm back across the aisle. "I told you, flying freaks me out."

"There are plenty of things you should be more afraid of."

"Like what? The infamous Patty Kellog?"

"And then some."

"Uh-huh." Shelley shook her head, scoffed, and pulled a small bottle of vodka from the cabinet along the cabin wall. She twisted the cap, gulped down the contents, and reached for another. She poured the next one over a cup of ice and sat with it in her lap, sipping occasionally. "Sorry. I'm fine...I get nervous when we start bouncing around like that." As if on cue, the plane dipped, shook, and rattled some of the items in the overhead bin.

Jeff informed them over the intercom that everything was fine, but they'd need to remain seated and buckled for the duration of the trip.

Smiling Dave opened the cockpit door, smiled, and said, "Wheels down in fifteen minutes!"

He closed the door and Shelley said, "I'd like to punch him on principle."

"No shit," Patty agreed. Then, sensing that might have been a positive affirmation to the impetuous apprentice, she added, "But don't. They live. No questions."

Shelley replied, "They've seen my face...or what's left of it."

"My way or no way, remember? Too many bodies leaves a trail. It attracts attention. In fact, dead bodies attract more attention than a couple of pilots who may or *may not* make the connection if they happen to see your face on the Post Office wall a month from now. Even if these guys watch the news—even if your face is all over it, they can call in a tip, but we'll be so far gone by then that it won't make a difference."

"But—"

Patty lowered her voice and leaned across the aisle. Shifting tones now, she morphed from the den mother that snipped at heels and ears to keep young pups in line to the calm, soothing confidante that confided and consoled. Why? She didn't know, exactly. Something inside her suggested that this girl would respond better to a comforting figure, rather than a heavy hand and vitriolic reprimands. "Relax. I know you're…what…what are you? Eager? Green? Still wet behind the ears? Listen, you've got potential. Amazing potential. You remind me of myself when I was your age. I was too impulsive and ready to get back at everyone, you know? I didn't care how it happened, because all I wanted was to give the whole world a sledgehammer to the side of its head.

"It didn't take me long to figure out that doing things that way led to too many unwanted consequences. I learned to plan, to take my time, to think through my methods. Every day is a learning experience. Slitting a throat one way is preferable to another. Shoot a guy in the right spot, he doesn't bleed on the carpet so much. Whatever, you know? But you take it slow. Be methodical. Think, think, and think some more. I've been doing this for twenty years, and there are people out there, like this guy I know called The Spirit, who still acts like I'm a bull in a china shop. They say my methods are too reckless and rash, even after I've planned and it's taken six months to complete a job. Is any of this making sense to you?"

Shelley nodded and took a sip of her vodka. "I guess. You're telling me to put on my big girl panties."

Patty tucked a loose strand of hair behind Shelley's ear. "Right. Exactly. Now do me a favor and try not to kill everything that looks at you sideways. You stick with me, you listen to me, you'll learn from me. I'll teach you how to feed that nastiness that you're carrying around inside and how to earn more money than you'll ever need in five lifetimes."

"It's not about the money."

"It will be once I introduce you to the right crowd."

"So, it's like, murder for fun and profit?"

"More or less. But it's a lot more than that. You get to travel around the world, meet interesting people, then kill them. Trust me, it does more good for that damaged brain in your head than years of sitting in a psychiatrist's office. Been there, done that, watched him bleed out on a sunny Thursday afternoon. Best decision I ever made."

"They had an in-house shrink back at the prison. The guy's name was Pederson. Had bad teeth, bad hair. Smelled like he always had dog shit on the bottom of his shoes. I hated him. Hated him," Shelley said, turning her head upward for emphasis. "After he put his hand down my jumpsuit the second time, I had him on the ground with my knee in his balls and a pen held up to his jugular. He didn't do it again."

"Why didn't you do it?"

"They were serving macaroni at lunch and I didn't want to miss out."

Patty chuckled. "Good girl. That's what I'm talking about. Sacrifices for the sake of getting the job done correctly. It wasn't the right time and you recognized it. Show me more of that and maybe one of these days we'll pay Pederson a visit."

Shelley drained the last of her vodka. Glassy-eyed, she propped her chin up on her hand. "Got it, boss. So what's the plan with that whore Sara, huh? Are you gonna give me a chance to play the game?"

Chapter Seven

Sara turned up the television's volume.

Teddy asked, "Why would Barker be there? Dude looks like they dragged him out of his hospital bed."

She shushed him as Randall got up and moved around her, sat on the couch, then leaned forward to listen.

Wolf Blitzer's voice came from off camera, saying, *"We should be getting started any second now. I'm going to sit back and listen with you all as we're about to learn more details from this tragic event."*

All three watched as a man stepped up to the podium, in front of Barker, but behind the collection of microphones that sported various news channel insignias. He wore a navy blue suit with a white collared shirt underneath, accompanied by a red power tie. He had a shaved head and a standard-issue mustache resting on his upper lip that paled in comparison to Barker's. The man removed a folded sheet of paper from inside his suit jacket, cleared his throat, and donned a pair of reading glasses.

Sara wanted to scream at him, whoever he was, and tell him to hurry up. Her insides were wobbly and the burn in her lungs made it difficult to breathe. With any luck, they would report that the inmates had been captured and that Shelley Sergeant was never one of the four.

However, the presence of Barker was not a good sign. Why was he involved?

The man at the podium coughed into his fist and said, "Good afternoon, I am Agent Grady Morrow with the Federal Bureau of Investigation. Please hold all your questions until I have completed my statement and then we will open it up to further discussion. First, our hearts go out to the families of the two men slain during this event. Prison guards Warren Barnes and Donny Potter died at the scene and we mourn this tragic loss of life with their families." Morrow's voice was solemn and robotic. Sara thought it wouldn't be terribly comforting to hear those words if she'd been part of the families who'd lost loved ones.

Morrow continued, "At approximately four a.m. this morning, what appeared to be a paramilitary group of two males and one female assaulted Coffee Creek Correctional Facility. Initially these reports were denied by the warden and local law enforcement in an effort to contain informational leaks, but in conjunction with the FBI's involvement, video surveillance and further circumstances have proven this to be true. At this time, no known organization has claimed responsibility, nor do we believe it to be the work of a known terrorist group, foreign or domestic."

He cleared his throat again. The sound frayed Sara's nerves even more.

Agent Morrow continued, "This was a highly trained group of individuals and we are pursuing with intent to capture to the fullest extent of our capabilities. After superior cooperative efforts by prison officials and local law enforcement, we have determined that four inmates escaped and as of thirty minutes ago, three of them were captured ten miles from the prison. At this time, their names are being withheld."

Teddy squeezed Sara's shoulder. "Sweet! They got three of them. That's awesome, huh?"

She managed a grin. "Yeah, so far, so good."

Agent Morrow was still reading. "And due to the correctional facility's video surveillance, we have reason to believe that the inmate who remains at large is with this paramilitary group."

"Damn," Randall said. "They've got some balls to break *into* prison."

"At present, we ask that you remain cautious and aware of any suspicious activity involving two men and two women, believed to be driving a mid-1990s blue Ford Explorer with Oregon license plates. While no details are known regarding the assailants, the escaped inmate's photo has been released to all media outlets and should be appearing on your screen soon. The missing individual is Shelley Ann Sergeant, approximately five feet, four inches tall, one hundred and fifteen pounds, with blonde hair, and also known to wear an eye patch to hide injuries sustained in a prison attack two years prior."

Sara had already gotten up and moved close to the television, one arm around her ribs and a hand covering her mouth. She couldn't stand still. Her legs were rubber; knees shaky and weak. When Shelley's disfigured face flashed up on the screen, scarred and mangled with one eye covered by the black eye patch, Sara crumbled to the floor.

"I am in charge of this investigation and we will be treating this as a full-scale fugitive manhunt. I am assisted by Detective Emerson Barker of the Portland Police Department who volunteered as part of this special assignment and we can assure you that we will do everything possible to ensure your safety. If you have any information regarding the whereabouts of these individuals, call the hotline listed on your screen. We have agents standing by to take your calls and will follow all viable leads. Again, our heartfelt condolences to the families of Warren Barnes and Donny Potter. This concludes our prepared statement and we have time left for a couple of questions."

Sara shivered and pulled her knees closer to her chest.

Were she and her children, and Miss Willow, far enough away? How far was far enough?

She thought back to that day in Jim Rutherford's house. She thought about Patty Kellog and the men that were with her. All highly trained, but taken by surprise with Teddy's quick action and Vadim Bariskov's betrayal. Patty's body was not amongst the dead when they searched the house.

Was it possible that she was part of the group that attacked Coffee Creek?

God, that would be so insane. But is it possible?

While a reporter asked an innocuous question about timing and standard FBI practices, Teddy lowered himself onto the floor and scooted over next to Sara. He put his arm around her and said, "Don't worry, okay? They're three thousand miles away. She won't make it very far."

Sara fought the urge to throw up. "Teddy?"

"Huh?"

"What if it was Patty? You know, that helped her escape."

"What? *Pffft*. Not a chance. She probably crawled off into a hole and died somewhere after Dad's house blew up."

Randall asked, "Patty's the one you were telling me about, right?"

Sara nodded.

On the television, a reporter stood up and asked, "Agent Morrow, about ten minutes before the press conference began, we received reports of a murdered couple found in the Cascades. Do you think that's in any way related?"

"We are pursuing all relevant leads."

"But do you think it's related?"

"As I said, we're pursuing all relevant leads. We will follow up with another press conference as soon as we have pertinent information to share. Thank you for your time."

Sara reached up and turned the television off. The screen went black.

Randall said, "So what're you thinking? That was every bit of the bad news you were expecting, right?"

Sara nodded. Teddy shrugged.

Randall got up from the couch and walked around the coffee table. He was quiet when he moved, perhaps from years of creeping stealthily through jungles and across deserts, sneaking up on his prey.

Sara watched as he stood at the large picture window that overlooked the farm, the dilapidated barn with faded gray wood and a rusted tin roof, and the green hills beyond, scanning the open land. He pushed a curtain to the side and said, "I'm inclined to agree with Mr. Rutherford here. They're three thousand miles away and if you've ever watched any of these fugitive pursuits unfold on the nightly news, about a week from now, some big group of trigger happy feds will corner these guys in a cabin in the middle of a forest in northern California. They'll toss in a few smoke bombs, accidentally set the place on fire, and then all that's left will be a pile of toasted dipshits."

"Are you sure?"

Randall crossed his arms and shook his head. "I learned a long time ago that it's not a good idea to make guarantees. Too many variables. But more often than not, that's what happens. My guess is, your friend Shelley and this group of chowderheads will make a mistake somewhere along the way. They'll do something dumb in a gas station and the next thing you know, we're watching a live feed from a couple of different helicopters. Now, my question is, if these three folks broke into prison to get this girl out, what was their reason? Who is she? Is she important? Got money?"

"Not really." Sara pushed herself up from the floor, extended a hand to Teddy, and helped him to his feet. She walked over to the wet bar and poured herself a small scotch in a glass tumbler. And, for good measure, she poured two more for Teddy and Randall. He joined them and they stood, sipping in silence until Sara said, "Like I said earlier, she was just this brilliant young woman that came to work for me at LightPulse. My husband had left me for her and when he wanted to leave and come back to his family, she murdered him then kidnapped my kids to get back at me."

"Get back at *you?*"

"Yeah. She was jealous. And her brother almost beat Teddy into a pile of mush, too. Anyway, that's such a long story and I really don't want to talk about it. What I'm trying to say is, I have no idea if she had money to pay someone to break her out or what. The only thing I can think of is what I'd said about one of Patty Kellog's goons maybe, possibly, mentioning Shelley's name. Why? I don't know. God, I don't know anything." She downed the last of her scotch and reached for the bottle again.

"Tell me again who this Kellog woman is? I've got some connections to her kind. Maybe I've heard of her."

"Short version or long version?"

Randall checked his watch. "Alice and my boy won't be back until tomorrow, and you still got plenty of scotch left in that bottle."

Sara smiled. It was strained, but genuine. "Okay, long version." She freshened his glass, along with Teddy's, and told the story of Patty Kellog. Hinting at some parts and elaborating on others. Patty Kellog was dangerous. She was unstable. She was the former leader of a small terrorist group known as The Clan. They blew people up.

And, apparently, Patty Kellog was able to cheat death, or she only had eight of her nine lives remaining.

"If there's a connection between her and Shelley Sergeant, I have no idea what it could be. The story was all over the newspapers a couple of years ago. It's possible that Patty saw something and decided she could use a new partner."

Randall said, "Anything's possible. Y'all mentioned a security system on the way up here. What've you got?"

"Would you like to see it?"

"Of course. If I'm gonna help keep an eye on your place, it'd be nice to know what you've got already. There's stuff down there at the house that might do you some good, but if you've already got a whole system installed, I doubt my two-by-fours to nail over your windows could top it."

Teddy asked, "You've got guns, don't you?"

"That I do, T-bird. That I do. Have you shot much before?"

"Enough to know what I'm doing." Teddy winked at Sara. "You hear that? He called me T-bird."

"So that's better than Little One?"

"What do you think?" To Randall, he added, "I'm a pretty good shot. Sara can tell you."

"Every little bit helps. And speaking of that...Sara, you want me to call my sister-in-law to come have a look, too? Mary runs her own P.I. business over in town. She does good work, even though I joke around that all she does is try to figure out who's giving the mayor a little pickle tickle in the back of his BMW."

Sara was one shortened breath away from a minor panic attack, but the scotch had done some good, and it felt good to chuckle slightly at Randall's crude attempt at humor. "I knew that, actually. My folks mentioned her a while back, and yeah, if you think she's got the time." Sara caught herself. She was still getting used to the fact that she'd be able to *buy* someone's time, if it were necessary. The millions weren't going to spend themselves, and what better use than to add an extra layer of protection for her family? "You know, why don't you give her a call? Let her know that I'd like to hire her. I'll make her trip worth it."

Chapter Eight

When the Learjet landed near Bristol, Tennessee at the Tri-Cities Regional Airport and taxied to the private hangars, Patty made sure to have Shelley depart the plane first in order to keep a careful watch on her. Jeff and his co-pilot Smiling Dave stood side-by-side near the exit, and Patty hoped to prevent their harm if Shelley got jumpy.

Smiling Dave smiled and tipped an imaginary hat as Jeff said, "Thanks for flying with us today. I hope it was a pleasant one."

Shelley was tipsy from the vodka, and when she reached with a hand toward the pilot's face, Patty tensed. Instead of clawing at his eyes, Shelley patted his cheek, said thanks, then made her way down the exit stairs.

Patty nodded to them both.

"Can we help you with your luggage?" Smiling Dave asked.

"No, I got it."

"We'll be making a return trip with two more clients tomorrow morning if you're looking for a ride back. We can speak to them about splitting the costs if you're interested."

"That won't be necessary, but thank you."

"Any time you need us, ma'am, we're only a hop, skip, and short flight away."

"Good, thank you, again." *Now stop talking to me, idiot.* Patty didn't want to be rude—rude meant memorable—but she also didn't want to stand around gabbing with two individuals who might easily identify her and Shelley. Was it too late to worry about that? Did it matter? Not if her preparations stayed intact. "Which way to the terminal? We're meeting family there." She had lied, hoping to further distract the pilots from her true intent.

Jeff leaned his head out the fuselage door and pointed. "Just over there. Tri-Cities is about the size of a Wal-Mart, so I doubt you'll get lost."

Patty feigned interest, thanked them again, then descended to the tarmac where Shelley stood, wobbly from the alcohol, looking bewildered. Patty said, "What's wrong?"

"Nothing, it's just—"

"Good, then walk. Now. Quickly. Quickly. Tell me on the way."

They shuffled across the tarmac, Patty urging her to walk at a brisk pace but nothing out of the ordinary.

Shelley said, "It's weird, you know?"

"What is?"

"It's weird how you can get into this big metal tube, then you sit down and take a nap, then when you wake up, it's like you're in a different world."

"You're drunk."

"No, I'm serious." She slurred the 'serious,' further confirming Patty's assessment. "It's such a different experience from driving. When you drive somewhere, you get to see all the changes going on around you as it happens, but when you fly, it's almost like you're in a teleporter that takes a really long time."

Patty gripped Shelley's arm tighter, leading her into the Tri-Cities terminal, up the stairs, and into the lobby. They stopped long enough to purchase a large bottle of water, some ibuprofen, and a cup of coffee. In the small café, the news was playing on a flat-screen television hanging above the clerk. A man with a shaved head and a ridiculous mustache spoke in front of a herd of reporters.

Behind him stood yet another man that she was quite familiar with: Detective Emerson Barker.

Patty glanced over and into the open, light-filled lobby. Shelley slumped in a gray chair in the waiting area. With her head flopped to the side, she'd already passed out again.

The clerk said, "That'll be twelve dollars and twenty-nine cents, please."

She handed over a twenty and tried to hear what the man on television was saying. "At approximately four a.m. this morning, what appeared to be a paramilitary group of two males and one female assaulted Coffee Creek Correctional Facility."

Patty cursed to herself, took her change, and moved toward her new...what was Shelley? Employee? Henchwoman? Crony? She patted her on the cheek. "Up, up. Let's go."

Shelley snorted when she opened her eyes and groggily poured herself out of the chair and into a standing position. "Should've known better. No drinks in prison means no tolerance means I'm all kinds of drunkie poo!" She giggled and fell into Patty.

"Get control of yourself, right now, you hear me? You're making a scene, and we don't *want* a scene. The FBI is already doing a press conference about your escape, so we need to keep our heads down, okay?"

Shelley giggled again. "Yes, mommy."

Thankfully, they made it to the long-term parking lot before Shelley ran for a trashcan and vomited into it. Once Patty had her successfully contained within the car, head lolling to the side and against the window, she forced two ibuprofen into Shelley's mouth, made her drink some water to swallow the pills, and then exited the lot, heading west for I-81 in the overcast, afternoon light of northeast Tennessee.

Patty exhaled heavily and felt her muscles release some of their tension. She was confident they'd made it out unnoticed.

Sara Winthrop's house and Patty's vengeance were only sixty miles away.

But first, they had one stop to make.

. . .

Patty took the exit ramp off I-81 and headed west, through the town of Abingdon, Virginia—a neat place from what she remembered. Back when she was a girl, maybe eight years old, they'd stopped here once to see a play at the Barter Theater. It was *The Wizard of Oz*, and she saw it in her mind's eye as if she was sitting in the balcony yesterday. The Wicked Witch's face was painted green. The tall pointy hat. That howling, cackling laughter. Back when she was pulling The Clan together, she debated using Wicked Witch as a codename, but had eventually decided on Boudica since the association with the Celtic queen's history suited her mission's objective better.

Now, as they drove past an area that had sprouted considerably since she'd been there over thirty years ago, she tried to focus on the task ahead rather than what lay outside. It was nearly impossible. It'd changed so much. Shops and gas stations and fast food joints. Streetlights and so many cars. She had some pictures in her mind of what it used to be like, but apparently the town commission had contracted plenty of work to beautify the place. Restored buildings, colorful landscaping, and historical markers lined Highway 11.

She thought about how far she'd come since those days. She wasn't a little girl anymore. She was feared and respected—by some—all around the world, from London to Shanghai to Los Angeles. She'd gone from pigtails and lollipops to needles filled with poison and garrote wires.

Nostalgia? Forget it. Life didn't wait for those who dwelled in the past.

Although, seeing the Barter Theater again as she drove past brought back yet another flood of memories. Mother, Father, and Sis. Smiling and singing together in the car.

Dead now. Every one of them.

Acknowledge and move on.

Past Abingdon and further west, out into the country where the low hills and rolling farmland stretched for miles, she was able to clear her mind and think about what was to come next. She allowed Shelley to doze in the passenger's seat, head awkwardly propped against the window, as they passed mobile homes and well-kept barns. Cattle munched lazily in green fields. A shiny, black foal ran parallel to its mother, manes blowing in the wind.

She wished the blue sky would break through the clouds. Just because she was thirty miles away from murdering a small family didn't mean she couldn't appreciate the beauty of nature. A doctor doesn't ignore the glory of a morning sunrise because he has to be in surgery later that day. A CEO of a multi-national corporation wouldn't disregard the overwhelming magnificence of a Hawaii waterfall because he had an important meeting in a day or two.

Her line of work may have been inhuman, but it didn't mean that she wasn't human. Right?

Patty rolled down the window of the rented Honda and inhaled deeply. Fresh, clean earth with a hint of hay and other unrecognizable nature scents. It'd been so long since she'd stopped to smell *life*. She couldn't remember the last time. Always running from one airport to the next, taking out marks in Sydney and Buenos Aires, jumping over to Venezuela and then Thailand and Russia. It was exhausting. She actually missed being able to breathe without an elevated heart rate.

Okay, maybe the nostalgia thing wasn't so bad. Maybe after she took care of Sara Winthrop and figured out what to do with Shelley, she'd take a vacation. She deserved one.

But not here. She had a feeling that her time in the U.S. would be limited after the screwed up mess at Coffee Creek and what would happen within twenty-four hours at the Winthrop farm only a few miles north of here. With all of its technological advancements, the FBI, along with its cooperation with other government entities, had gotten so much better in recent years. Much more adept than some of the foreign countries she worked in where innocence could be purchased rather than proven.

She found the highway marker she was looking for, turned left, and felt the gravel vibrating the car as the tires rolled along the unpaved road.

Shelley groaned and lifted her head. "Where are we?"

"Southwest Virginia."

"You sure? Looks like they filmed *Hee-Haw* here."

"How's your head?"

"It feels like someone is beating me with a mallet. Where'd those ibuprofen go?"

Patty opened the center console and tossed the bottle to Shelley. "Water's down there at your feet."

Shelley popped the top, poured a number of gel capsules into her mouth, then washed them down. "Where we going?"

"To see some friends."

Shelley scoffed. "You have friends? Are they, like, real friends, or *friends* in quotation marks?"

"You'll see when we get there."

"Oh, such mystery." Shelley reached over and turned the radio on, flipping from channel to channel. "Country...Country... Gospel...Oh, hey, here's a country channel. Imagine that." She slapped the dial and the music went silent.

"How old are you?" Patty asked. She was genuinely inquiring, but the fact that Shelley was behaving like an impatient, bored teenager made her even more curious.

"Why? Am I annoying you, Mommy?"

Patty scowled as she shook her head. At the next open spot on the roadside, she whipped the steering wheel to the right and skidded to a halt. Gravel kicked up and rattled under the car. Though it'd been drizzling recently, the tires dug low enough to reach dry dirt, sending up a small plume of dust that the breeze carried away.

"Jesus, you do know my head is pounding, don't you?" Shelley said, holding her temples. "What did I do now?"

"One last time, Shelley. If you're going to be a professional, start acting like it. I'm sick of this shit already. I don't want to baby you and I don't want to mother you, but from what I learned, you were getting close to being a respectable badass before you went to prison. That shit you pulled with Sara? That game? Putting her kids in the boxes? That was some serious evil genius stuff—I want *that* Shelley back. Look, I don't know what happened in prison...

"Maybe they did some damage to your emotional *whatever*, maybe somebody made you her girlfriend, maybe you had to hide in the corner to stay alive. Whatever it was, you went backwards. You're not a child. You're not some...some silly teenager any more. You were a strong, powerful woman. I see myself in you, okay? Now that there are two of us, we'll be unstoppable, but I need you to find the real Shelley again, and I need you to do it right now, because the people we're going to see—they will slit our throats if you so much as stick out your tongue. No more of this teenage angst bullshit. Grow up. Be that *woman* again."

"Are you finished?"

"Yes."

"Thank you."

"For what?"

"My freedom. Seriously. Or whatever this is," Shelley said, motioning around the car, pointing out toward the fields. "But understand one thing—yes, you saved me, you rode in on your black horse and rescued me like a pretty little damsel in distress, or some princess up in a tower, but know this, you crazy bitch, you *do not* own me. You will never *own* me. I am dangerous, *so* dangerous, and this act you've got going on where you think I'm some little birdie under your wing...shove it up your ass. *You don't own me.* I don't owe you anything. I was fine where I was and I'm still here because I *want* to be here, and so help me God, if you ever try to pull any of that mommy shit on me again, I will eat your throat and drink your blood. Are we clear?"

Patty smiled and softly said, "There's the fire. There's the woman I want." She grabbed Shelley by the back of the head, drew her in close and mashed their lips together. She was thrilled when Shelley didn't pull away.

Chapter Nine

Sara sat at the kitchen table with Randall Blevins, drinking coffee, and holding the mug tightly in an effort to keep her hands steady. Miss Willow had coaxed Lacey, Callie, and Jacob inside, and the four of them were down in the basement watching a movie in the theater room. She'd had it installed weeks ago, and though she loathed to use it as a babysitter, the modified room with stadium seating and a projector hanging above, displaying the movie on nearly an entire wall, was a perfect place for the kids to escape when she needed some of her own downtime.

Teddy and Irina had gone for a hike in the hills behind Sara's farmhouse. She'd protested, slightly, but with Teddy's usual annoying insistence and Randall's assurance that they were safe in the woods, she'd relented. Teddy had said, "I don't know about you, but I can't sit there and twiddle my thumbs, waiting for some news. It'll drive me bonkers."

She'd made the argument that having a mild sense of cabin fever was better than death, because who knew what Patty Kellog could've set in motion already.

Before he'd walked out the door, Teddy added, "Sara, come on, dude. I honestly don't believe that Patty Kellog would be involved. That old KGB guy that was with me said she was an international terrorist. Why in the hell would she waste her time with some bush league criminal in prison? *Does not compute.* It'll be fine. Randall says so, don't you, Randall?"

Randall had nodded, and as she'd watched them walk across the back porch, the wood creaking beneath their feet, she'd hoped to God he was right.

If he wasn't, the answer was obvious. There were only two people in the world that held murderous grudges against her, and one had the resources to break the other one out of prison, simple as that.

Sara sipped her coffee while Randall read over the schematics and instructional guides associated with the home's security system. They were waiting on Randall's sister-in-law, Mary Walker, to arrive. Sara checked the wall clock—an old-fashioned cuckoo that Miss Willow had gotten Sara for her birthday—and saw that they had another fifteen minutes before Mary would arrive. As Randall read, Sara decided that fifteen minutes of silence wouldn't be possible. She was too worried, fearful, and wired from so much coffee.

"Randall?"

"Mmm?" He looked up from the blueprints where he'd been noting the locations of cameras and motion detectors.

"Did I thank you yet?"

"Yes, ma'am, and I've already lost track of how many times."

"You don't have to do this, you know. I mean, I just walked into your house and said, 'Hey, nice to meet you, wanna come help me keep an eye out for terrorists?' It was rude and presumptuous and…and I don't even have enough shitty adjectives for what it is. It's wrong and I shouldn't have done it. I shouldn't have dragged you into this."

"You sure didn't have to twist my arm an awful lot." Randall pushed the blueprints to the side and propped himself up at the elbows. "I did this for a living. I saw things you wouldn't believe out there in the jungles. I worked with, and *killed*, men that make you wake up sweating in the middle of the night. I hate to say it, because I don't want to make light of your situation, but this is small taters. Ain't no big deal, not at all, and besides…well, I wasn't a hundred percent honest with you, either."

"You weren't?"

Randall readjusted his baseball cap. Sara had noticed it was a habit of his whenever he was about to saw something he wasn't comfortable with. "Do me a favor and don't mention this to your folks, because I promised 'em I wouldn't say a doggone word…"

"My parents?"

Randall looked to his left, then his right, saying, "I, um, I already knew about part of your situation. Most of it, if you wanna know the truth. Ran into them a while back, not long after you moved to town, and we had breakfast together over at the Corner Café, the one there on Main Street. Anyway, long story short, they asked me if I'd keep watch around your property, you know, just to make sure there wasn't something funky going on over here."

"Why didn't you say something? Why didn't they?"

"I reckon they didn't want you to think they were butting in on your life."

"They're my parents for God's sake. That's what parents do."

"Look, your mom and pop were thinking more on the lines of a guardian angel. It wasn't a big deal. Hasn't been. A fella's gotta sleep now and again, but whenever I'm home, I make sure to peek over."

Sara didn't know how to feel. Thankful, in a sense, for the fact that there had been an extra set of eyes out there, competent ones, keeping her under loose surveillance. Yet, it was almost disconcerting knowing that if Randall had been doing it this whole time, and she'd been unaware, who else could be watching? She'd been so careful, but now, paranoia seemed like a valid emotion.

"I'm sorry," Randall said. "We probably should've said something."

"I can't believe you knew. That's why you were readjusting your hat so much. You were uncomfortable."

Randall grinned and leaned back in the chair. "What was I doing?"

"You mess with your hat whenever you're uncomfortable or feeling awkward."

"No shit?"

Sara broke eye contact and stared into her mug. "Yeah, it's probably a little weird that I noticed something like that, but after working for LightPulse for so many years, I pay more attention to people. We were always trying to give our characters a sense of realism, so we'd add in these movements and character quirks to make them more human. You said Jesse plays *Juggernaut*, right?"

"Plays it more than he breathes, I think."

"Have you seen much of it, like the cutaway scenes? The ones where it looks like you're watching a movie?"

"Yeah."

"There's one scene in the game where General Cragg is constantly tugging on his left earlobe. We wrote that into the game because Teddy's father, Jim, the owner, used to do that all the freakin' time. It was like his poker tell for when he was thinking something over." She couldn't be sure if Randall gave two hoots about the minor details of a video game, but it was a relief to talk about something she was familiar with.

Work. That old security blanket. The place she could hide when the fearful thoughts in her mind drifted to dark places. Taking the time off and relaxing here in Virginia, supposedly hidden, or with a low profile at the least, had been both a blessing and a curse. The downtime spent relaxing on the front porch, rocking back and forth, watching nature go by, had been invaluable. She could breath again without getting lightheaded.

On the other hand, when her parents were away, the kids were in school, and Miss Willow was out with her quilting committee, it offered too many opportunities for her thoughts to grow cloudy and fearful, wondering if she'd make the right choice by bringing her family here.

Still, the distance between her and her past had grown both physically and over time, which was more acceptable than allowing the horrible memories to soak her life like the rains of Portland she'd left behind.

"Anyway," she said. "That's all. If you play poker, you might want to take your hat off."

"Son of a gun. I wondered how those shitheads in my unit could always tell when I was bluffing." He shook his head wistfully. "All these years. I haven't touched a deck of cards in twenty years because I just thought I sucked at it."

Sara jumped when a buzzer sounded on the wall. Someone was calling up from the front gate.

"Easy," Randall said, getting up from the table. "That'd be Mary."

"How do you know?"

Randall tapped his ear. "I know what her car sounds like."

"Really?" Sara stood up, wiping her sweaty palms on her thin jacket. "They all sound the same to me."

"You go over to town, yeah, it's nothing but a rumbling of engines and tires, but out here in the sticks, it's different. You learn after a while that each sound has it's own...shit, I don't know...It's own reality, I reckon. You hear, you listen, you learn."

"Good to know," Sara said. She stepped around his massive frame—he smelled like sweet laundry detergent, which was out of place for such a gruff country-boy—and spoke with Mary through the intercom.

Moments later, Sara opened the front door and for a second, a small measure of panic rippled through her stomach. She'd been expecting someone that partially resembled Randall's wife, Alice, who was also Mary's sister. She hadn't spent too much time with her, but where Alice was taller, with bottle-blonde hair, a fake tan, and blue eyes, the woman at her doorstep was entirely different. A thick mop of wavy brunette hair, about Teddy's height with dark brown eyes, and naturally brown tones to her skin. She was pretty with a warm smile. She also leaned on a hand-carved, wooden cane.

When the woman extended her hand to introduce herself, Sara caught a glimpse of a concealed weapon inside of a leather shoulder holster.

"I'm Mary Walker. You must be Sara."

"I am." Sara's eyes remained fixated on the spot where she'd seen the firearm.

Mary must have noticed. "I can take it off if you'd like. Randall says you have kids around."

"No, no, sorry." Sara waved her in. "That was rude of me. I didn't mean—"

Mary chuckled as she shook Sara's hand. "Hey, no, don't worry about it. I know guns can freak people out. I'd wear it around my ankle, but I've already got a smaller one down there and two is just bad fashion."

From behind Sara, Randall's voice boomed into the room. "Get on in here, Mary. Just because you were born in a barn don't mean you have to keep Mrs. Winthrop's door wide open."

Mary looked past Sara's shoulder, flipped him the bird with a smile, then hobbled up and into the living room. Under her breath, she said to Sara, "You'd think he was fifteen years old some days."

"Do men ever really grow up?"

"Tell me about it."

"Thanks so much for coming over," Sara said. "I hate to spring this on you guys like this."

Mary hobbled along behind Sara, following her into the kitchen where Randall sat at the table with the security information displayed in front of him. She said, "I wouldn't say you sprung it on us. I'm guessing you found out that Randall already knew?"

"Yes."

"Yeah, well, your folks gave me a heads up as well about a week after him."

"Those sneaky little…"

Mary grabbed Randall's baseball cap and slapped him on top of the head with it. "Bro-in-law, how are you?"

"Fine until you got here," he replied, but the remark was accompanied by a heavy smirk.

Sara offered to get them drinks or something to eat—she'd learned the hospitable southern gesture; offer regardless, even if your guests recently walked out of a ten-course Thanksgiving meal. Mary declined, Randall asked for a glass of water, and then they sat around the table. Sara left the blueprints in front of him and pulled up a chair for Mary.

"So, can I officially hire you to help us out for a couple of weeks? At least until they catch the people who might be coming after me? Randall says you're definitely the best—"

"He lies a lot."

"Don't bring that up again."

"Bring up what?" Sara asked.

"Remember those long stories? That one's longer. And she'll never let me live it down."

Mary reached over with her cane and bonked Randall on the head. "I like watching him squirm, that's all."

Sara let it go. She was curious about what'd happened between them, but currently, her own past was out there hunting her down with bared fangs and razor-sharp claws. She said, "That's funny. But look, before we even get started, let me say that…I know, God, I know how unreasonable this is and believe me, I'd never ask this of…well, *strangers*…not in a million years, but I have a feeling—my fear is—this is going to turn into something that either *shouldn't* involve the local police, or it'll be too big for them to handle. I'm not saying they're not good at their jobs, but I doubt that around here, they've probably never encountered anyone like Shelley Sergeant or Patty Kellog. If you're willing, Mary, I can make it worth your while. You, too, Randall. I've got money. Too much of it, so you can name your price. Five times your normal rate. Ten times. Whatever. Your call."

She watched as Mary and Randall exchanged glances. The look that passed between them suggested something that Sara couldn't quite place.

Mary said, "Your folks moved down here, what, about twenty years ago?"

"Little less. They came here after I graduated high school and left for college. Why?"

"They're two of the sweetest people I've ever met, Sara."

"Same here," Randall added.

"They're practically family. And I always offer the family discount."

"How much?"

"We'll call it even at a bottle of Jim Beam."

"What? I can't let you do that."

"No ifs, ands, or buts, and don't argue with me, because we've got work to do."

Sara huffed, but knew she wasn't going to change their minds. "Sure, okay. If you say so."

Mary leaned up on the table and pulled the blueprints over in front of her. Seconds later, she whistled, long and high. "Would you look at that? Randall, you didn't say I'd be staking out Fort Knox."

"Better for you to make that assessment yourself. Keeps you on your toes."

Curious, Sara said, "So the system's good then?"

"*More* than good."

"Great, because really, all I did was track down the best security company I could find and throw a crap ton of money at them. Top of the line, spare no expense and whatever. I bought the place and we stayed with my parents while they were installing it, so I never completely saw everything as it was installed. All I wanted to know was what buttons to push and when. By the time they were finished, the owner of the company called me personally to say I was better protected than Tom Cruise."

"No kidding. Tom Cruise?"

"Apparently they have a lot of famous clients, but yeah, I guess that gives you a frame of reference, huh?"

"I wouldn't even need to hear that to know this is a fortress. Did you see this, Randall?" Mary pointed to a series of lines surrounding the perimeter of the house.

"I sure did."

"What're you looking at?" Sara asked.

"Oh, just the three-inch steel rods implanted along this line here with your fence and the laser beams along the top of it. I've seen this in movies, but never real life."

"Those are good, too, right?"

"You've got more than a panic room, sweetie, you've got a panic *house*."

Chapter Ten

Patty parked the car in the gravel driveway, which was pockmarked by craters of mud puddles and deep ruts from the runoff. Unlike back near the main road, where everything was slightly damp, it had rained here recently, and water dripped from the maple leaves overhead.

Her senses were still tingling from Shelley's kiss, but she tried not to let it show. Had she wanted it to happen? Yes and no. She had no time to think about it now. Analyzing it would have to come later. Shelley had pulled away, traced her thumb across Patty's bottom lip, and said nothing more. They'd ridden in silence after that.

Shelley craned her neck to see out the front window, looking up at the top level of the three-story farmhouse. "This place looks like there should be crazy people on the front porch, picking banjos."

"Don't let it fool you. The guys in there? I would *not* want to piss them off."

"Why?"

"You'll see, but let me tell you this...I've been all around the world. I've worked jobs for some scary human beings. I've *killed* some scary human beings. I've traded illegal arms and done recon work for people that would put a knife in your throat if you didn't laugh at their jokes fast enough, but honest to God, these backwoods, southwest Virginia rednecks scare me just as bad as the Mexican cartels."

"Really?"

"Take a look around, Shelley. Out here, they'd never find your body." Patty pointed around the yard's perimeter. Past the rusted swing set, past the old Chevy pickup that sat on cinderblocks, missing its tires, and past the gray-wood shed that would fall over in a strong gust of wind. "That's miles and miles of thick forest out there and these guys know all the best places to bury bodies. Trust me."

"Then why're we here?"

"We're picking up supplies." Patty opened her door and climbed out of the rental car. Her back and legs ached from the long flight and the ensuing drive, but she dared not relax long enough to stretch. "Don't say a word. You let me talk. Don't do anything but stand there and look..."

Shelley pointed at her disfigured face. "Pretty?"

"I was going to say confident, but whatever floats your boat."

Patty headed across the wet yard. The grass hadn't been mowed in a while and the dampness soaked into her shoes. She shivered against the moist chill. Her black t-shirt and gray cargo pants didn't provide much protection against the cool mountain climate.

Rain dripped from the leaves overhead. She pushed the tire swing to her side, held it for Shelley, and continued. A bright red tricycle lay overturned next to a child's sandbox peppered with cat turds and twigs. They stepped around it and kept going. Shelley cursed when she slipped on a baseball bat hidden in the grass.

They went up the creaking stairs, then across the sagging porch to the front door. Three rocking chairs sat empty to their left, and on their right, a porch swing hung from a single chain. The other had snapped and dangled, swaying in the breeze.

"Why's it so quiet?" Shelley asked, looking through the small windows beside the door.

"I don't know. I've only been here a couple of times, but normally they greet me with a shotgun in one hand and a jar of moonshine in the other."

"Are they gone? Did they know you were coming?"

"They know. I paid them too much not to know."

Patty lifted her hand to knock. After two quick raps on the door, she heard a familiar sound behind them and down in the yard. A racking shotgun, instantly recognizable.

"Hands on your heads, ladies." The voice was rough and deep with a thick Appalachian drawl.

Patty lifted her arms and locked her fingers behind her head. She risked a peek to the right to make sure Shelley was doing the same. Thankfully, her arms were up as ordered.

Patty said, "Bobby? Is that you?"

"Yes, ma'am. You carrying, Kellog?"

"No. Same rules apply, as always. Left everything in the car. You can check if you want."

"Who's your friend?"

Patty heard the voice getting closer as he stealthily approached them from the rear. "My new partner."

Partner? Really? Yeah, well, easier to explain than...whatever Shelley is.

"Since when do you roll with anybody that ain't your lap dog, huh?"

"She's good. Trust me."

"I can trust her? Well thanks so much for letting me know. Now I'm all hunky-dory comfortable with you bringing a goddamn stranger to my house." The voice was ascending the porch now. Patty considered turning around.

Too risky, she thought. *Wait for the okay.*

"I'm vouching, Bobby. Say hello to Shelley Sergeant. They call her Sarge."

"They do, huh? Sounds like an awful big name for such a little girl. Turn around, both of you. Hands right where they are."

Patty turned clockwise, and Shelley turned counter-clockwise, in slow, cautious circles until they faced Bobby.

His head rocked back and his eyebrows arched. "Whoa," he said. "The hell happened to you, girl?"

Shelley shrugged. "Bar fight."

"Jesus. Did you win?"

"You should see the other guy."

Bobby smirked and lowered his shotgun. Lowered only—the barrel remained pointing at their midsections. "She telling the truth, Sarge? I can trust you?"

Shelley added a thick drawl to her words, saying, "You sure can, sweetheart."

Bobby leaned back and examined her with a yellow-toothed grin. "Are you mockin' me, young lady?"

"I thought I was flirting."

"Good enough." To Patty, he said, "I like her, Kellog. Keep her around a while."

"I plan to." Patty hadn't seen Bobby in five years, since the job in Atlanta with that stubborn CEO that had to be forcefully removed, and the surly redneck hadn't changed at all. His hair was slicked back into a thick shell covering his scalp. The thin beard looked as scraggly as it always had, while the only noticeable difference was the fact that his neck tattoo of a scorpion seemed slightly more faded. He wore a red Harley-Davidson t-shirt, a leather vest, and blue jeans with holes at the knees, along with cowboy boots made out of some exotic hide. She was fairly sure he'd been wearing the same thing the last time they'd met.

She said, "You look good, Bobby."

"I liked your hair longer."

Patty flicked her chin over her shoulder, toward the entrance. "Is he here?"

"Pops?" Bobby clicked his tongue and shook his head. "You don't call, you don't write…"

"What happened?"

"Heart attack. Sumbitch dropped in the shower while we were all down at the Wal-Marts. I'm running the show 'round here now."

"I'm sorry for your loss."

"Me, too," Shelley added.

Arnold Davis, Bobby's father, also known as Papa Bear, was likely the meanest, most ruthless man Patty had ever met. She'd heard stories of worse individuals, but not many. Once, when she'd stopped by for a fresh supply of weaponry, she'd found the whole family in the middle of a revenge party. Out back, Papa Bear had tied an enemy to a clothesline pole and unleashed his pack of starving hounds on the unfortunate bastard. Patty hadn't been able to watch the frenzy. She'd turned her head away while Papa Bear ate a medium-rare steak and laughed with his mouth full.

When the dogs had had their fill, Papa Bear tossed the remnants into a wood chipper, along with the rest of his uneaten steak. That spectacle had been one of the worst things she'd seen and made her reconsider ever coming back. But, the Davis family had connections and sold their wares cheaply—plus, they'd go to their graves with their client list. That southern honor and dependability was something Patty could count on, knowing that the FBI or ATF, whomever, would have to bring in the National Guard to attempt a raid on the compound.

However, she didn't know if it was a good thing, or a bad thing, that Papa Bear was gone and Bobby was now in charge. She'd seen signs over the years that Bobby had the potential to be worse than his father.

"Really, Bobby," she lied, "he was a good man."

Bobby lifted a shoulder, let it drop. "Eh, well, shit happens, huh? Y'all come on in." He pushed past them and opened the front door. "Mind your dirty feet, and put your damn hands down. You look ridiculous."

Inside the old farmhouse, the smell was unbearable. Patty knew immediately that it was the stench of death. Shelley lifted her arm to cover her nose, and Patty pulled it down, shaking her head. Whatever the source, she didn't want to risk offending Bobby. She glanced around the room, looking for maybe a dead cat or dog and saw only deteriorating furniture and fast food bags littering the floor. Half-eaten cheeseburgers accompanied french fries and smeared ketchup on paper plates. The to-go soda cups littered on the coffee table had soaked through and the most recent ones had puddles of melted ice corralling the discolored bottoms.

Papa Bear, despite his hardened heart and corroded psyche, had loved tending to the variety of plants that once sat vibrant and lively around the living room. Patty remembered that each one had a name, and he'd coo at them like children while he spritzed water from a bottle. She'd been absolutely flabbergasted watching the display, then reassured of the man she knew when he held a knife against her cheek and demanded more money for the items she'd ordered.

That was what, nine years ago?

Those same plants were dry, brown, and dead, but they weren't the source of the smell.

Beside her, she could hear Shelley trying desperately not to dry heave.

As if he'd sensed their discomfort, Bobby rested the shotgun on his shoulder, turned, and said, "Don't mind the smell. Mama Bear ain't had time to bury the old man yet." And as they entered the kitchen, he added, "But you'll get around to it, won't you, Mama?"

Shelley gagged.

Patty swallowed and tried desperately to keep her composure.

Sitting at the table, or propped up, rather, was the body of Papa Bear Davis. Patty didn't have much experience with corpses, beyond being in the same room when her target became one, but she guessed he'd been there a while. It was impossible to guess how long.

To his right sat Myrtle Davis, also known as Mama Bear, and the only woman Patty had ever met that was more intense, determined, and evil than herself. But, gone was the woman that Patty respected and honored and in her place sat a nearly catatonic vessel of what had been. Myrtle's skin was sallow and sagging. The light brunette color of her hair had changed to a cloudy white. Her hand shook as she absently shoveled a forkful of scrambled eggs into her mouth.

She didn't look up, and she didn't acknowledge them when Bobby said again, "I *said*, you'll get around to it, won't you, Mama?"

When he slapped her on the back of the head, Patty felt a rush of anger warm her belly, and she had to resist fighting back for Myrtle's sake. Shelley took a quick step forward and Patty put a cautioning arm in front of her.

Shelley pursed her lips, scrunched her forehead, and mouthed, "Let me."

Patty shook her head.

Bobby leaned down and shouted, "Why don't you get up and get us something to drink, huh? Where's your manners, old woman?"

Myrtle put her fork down, stood up, and went to the refrigerator. She opened the door and stood, waiting.

"Y'all want something?" Bobby asked. "Beer? We got all kinds of pop, too."

"No, thanks," Patty said. "Maybe we could—how about you just give us what I came for and we'll get out of your hair, huh? Sound good?"

"What's your hurry, Kellog? Pops ain't gonna bother you none, not like that time he almost cut your cheek off. Remember that? Mean old codger, wasn't he? Take a load off and sit a spell."

"We're up against a timeline, Bobby. Sorry."

"Suit yourself. Beer, Mama." When Myrtle handed him the bottle, he popped the top and motioned for them to follow him down the shadowy hallway on the far side of the kitchen. "It's all down here. Y'all come take a gander."

Patty took a deep breath. It'd been so long since she'd been on this side of fear.

Shelley grabbed her hand and squeezed as they followed Bobby into the darkness.

Chapter Eleven

Sara greeted Teddy coming in from their hike as he sat down at the kitchen table with her, Randall, and Mary Walker. A moment later, Irina joined them and asked what all the schematics and blueprints were for.

Sara answered, "Randall and Mary have agreed to help out until the police manage to catch Shelley, so we're looking over the security measures that I already have in place here and trying to decide whether or not we need anything extra."

Teddy leaned up onto the table with his chin resting between his thumb and forefinger, looking over the drawings. "Something was bothering me while we were out for a walk, but I'd like to hear what you guys have been talking about first before I bring it up."

Mary said, "Well, from what we can see, she's almost completely covered. It's insane the amount of protection she has set up here, but we've noted a couple of vulnerable spots that Randall and I aren't quite comfortable with."

"Such as?"

"Mainly from overhead. The system they installed covers the perimeter so well that I doubt anyone would be able to get in here undetected. On foot, I mean. With cameras here, here, and here," she said, continuing around the diagram of Sara's property, "they'd have to be invisible to sneak through. There are regular cameras that are also accompanied by thermal cameras and over here at the gate entrance—if they manage to get *through* the gate—there's a pressure sensitive indicator built into the driveway..."

"What if they don't knock before they come in?"

"The fencing around the perimeter of the property has lasers from post to post, and then in a grid running along the top bar. Nothing is getting through or over that fence without something being triggered."

"Yeah, I know that. Sara showed me earlier, but what I meant was—you said there were vulnerabilities from above, right? Exactly what are you expecting? I'm assuming a coordinated air strike is out of the question." Teddy grinned.

Mary studied him, then glanced over to Sara. "You were right."

Teddy's smile faded. "About what?"

When everyone around the table finished chuckling, Irina bent over, put a hand on one cheek, and then kissed him on the other. "That *you*, dear husband, are a piece of work."

"Figures. Look, I'm just trying to help out."

Sara gave him a reassuring pat on the back. "We know, buddy, but I think Mary and Randall have this under control. She was a police officer for a long time and runs her own private investigation firm. They've been through quite a bit together and I trust them."

"I'm only looking out for you."

"And I understand that. But hey, what were you thinking about on your hike?"

Teddy sighed and shook his head. "Here's the thing. Going out on a limb, say that Patty Kellog is actually helping Shelley and they're on their way here. More than likely, Patty's got her own team with her, they've got all kinds of gadgets or whatever...You may be better protected than Tom Cruise, but I don't think Tommy Boy has a paramilitary terrorist group with access to high-tech toys trying to break into his compound, you know? Everything you have set up here, there are ways around it."

Randall reached over the table, with a long, massive arm that didn't need much stretching to cover the distance, and socked Teddy on the shoulder. "We know that, T-bird, so what we need to figure out is how they'd get around it. You've been around video games your whole life, designing them, helping with the stories—let's look at it this way. If you were creating a scene in *Juggernaut* where your horde of goons had to assault a fortress like this, how would you get into it?"

Teddy pulled the property schematics closer for a better look. He chewed on his bottom lip and said, "I honestly don't know. If we knew what was out there on the market right now…They could have one of those electro-magnetic pulse things to knock out your electronics, they could have something to disable the laser grid, who knows. Regardless of what they have, nothing is getting past the motion detectors short of disabling the system, so yeah, they'll have to hit hard and fast instead of sneaking onto the property. I guess like Miss Walker was saying, the vulnerabilities are from overhead. Or, below, supposing they wanted to tunnel underneath the fence."

Sara shook her head. "There's a wall of concrete that extends five feet underneath the surface."

"Christ on a corndog," Randall said. "How much did that set you back? You know, never mind, that was rude of me to ask."

"Doesn't matter," Teddy answered for her. "She can afford it. Anyway, yeah, so if tunneling is out, then all we have left is overhead."

"And how would you go about that?"

"You mean aside from the aforementioned air strike?" He flinched when Irina lifted her hand and playfully smacked his cheek. "Chill, okay? I'm kidding. Helicopter?"

"Too much noise, but *maybe*," Randall said. "Sara, you've heard them come through here before, haven't you?"

"At least two or three times a week."

Randall pointed behind him, toward the southwest, and brought his hand up, over, and pointed toward the northeast as he said, "We're right in the flight path from that big ass hospital down in Johnson City, coming and going. It wouldn't seem too out of the ordinary to have a chopper take that route and pause long enough for a commando team to repel down."

"Could be," Mary said. "Teddy's right, though, they'd likely hit hard and fast because they'll either have done their homework, or they'll assume motion sensors are a part of the package. If they came flying over disguised as a medical chopper, they could drop onto the roof before we even figured out what was going on."

Randall nodded. "True, true."

Irina raised her hand.

Teddy said, "Honey, you don't have to do that. Just ask."

"All of these plans, plans, plans—are you positive she's coming to this place? Here is what I see—forgive me for butting in, but Teddy has told me what he knows about the history with this Shelley person—"

"And Patty Kellog, too."

"Yes, her, but what I see is a bunch of planning for something that may never happen. What if this Shelley person and this Patty person, what if they have nothing to do with each other and you're worrying yourselves to death over nothing? My grandfather had a saying back in Russia: 'Don't drink the vodka before the potatoes are grown.' Does that make sense here?"

"It does, ma'am," Randall said, "but when it comes to shit like this, it ain't possible to be *too* prepared."

Sara listened to them chat back and forth, smiling at the differences between Irina's Russian accent and Randall's mountain twang. It felt good to have so many people looking out for her. It was reassuring. Her own little United Nations.

And maybe Irina was right. Maybe she'd misheard back in Jim Rutherford's house and maybe Shelley being rescued from prison didn't have anything to do with her or Patty Kellog.

Was she getting worked up over nothing?

She got her answer when Barker called a minute later.

. . .

Sara checked the caller ID while the others were chatting. "Whoa," she said, holding out her phone. "It's Barker."

Teddy said, "Nice. Maybe he's got some good news."

"I'll put it on speaker. Give me a sec." She answered. "Barker, thank God. Tell me something good."

"Hey, Sara. You okay out there?"

"No, I'm freaking out. Hold on, okay? I'm going to put you on speaker so everyone else can hear you." She pushed a button and sat the phone down in the middle of the table. "Still there?"

"Yeah."

"Good. Let me introduce everyone—"

"You got an army there?"

"Teddy and Irina, plus I have my neighbor Randall who's a former Marine sniper, and his sister-in-law Mary Walker. She used to be a police officer and now she has her own P.I. business."

"Damn. You've already assembled your own team, huh? Well, except for Teddy, right? You got him carrying water for everybody else?"

Teddy snorted. It was something between an annoyed scoff and a laugh. "I'm right here, Barker. I can hear you."

"You were meant to, bud."

Sara said, "We saw you at the press conference. Kinda freaked me out when we heard that Shelley was the one who escaped. We're here planning for the worst unless you have something good to report." Her tone was optimistic. On the inside, she was begging for anything positive.

"I'm..." Barker paused.

His tone, the elongated silence, waiting, waiting, Sara realized that he was about to crush her hopes.

"It's not looking good, Sara. The moment I found out it was Shelley that escaped, I got in touch with Agent Morrow and jumped right on this because I knew you'd want me to, and I'm afraid that what we're dealing with is bigger than what the press conference let on. At least when it comes to *you*."

"Meaning what?"

"It's—"

Sara's lungs cinched tighter. She closed her eyes and felt her skin prickle. "It's Patty Kellog, isn't it?"

"I'm afraid so."

Dizzy, Sara sat forward in her seat, rubbing her temples.

For the love of God, this can't be happening again.

Teddy asked, "How do you know that for sure?"

"This doesn't leave your house, okay? Everyone there understand that?"

A chorus of affirmative responses went around the table.

"I could potentially lose my job for even saying anything, but you need to know. Now, granted, I didn't expect an audience but I can't dangle the carrot and let it go, especially with what sounds like a good crew you got there." He cleared his throat. "Okay, here's the deal, folks. Since Patty Kellog escaped after Jim's house went boom, the FBI formed a small task force, maybe a two or three man team, but nothing big, see?

"Patty was low on the totem pole as far as international priorities go, but the suits wanted her gone, mostly because of the bullet she'd put into Timms. Anyway, these cats rounded up a couple of dudes that were former military and sent them undercover. I mean, Jesus, from what they tell me, these guys were so far under that they almost started believing the propaganda themselves. It was like a global chess match for about eight months, but the FBI managed to work these guys into Patty's good graces. Their orders were to gather intel on her movements and whatnot so they could put together a case against her. The feds were going for a prosecution, but if it'd been me, I would've had one of those gents slip a knife in between her ribs."

Randall bent over, closer to the phone. "Detective Barker?"

"Yes, sir?"

"Randall Blevins here. So what I'm hearing is, the FBI had someone in close proximity to Patty Kellog, like within breathing distance, and this bullshit at the prison *still* went down? That's what I'm hearing?"

"You'll never hear them admit to it, but they really screwed the pooch on this one. From what they could gather, these two guys—their names were Crenley and Tanner—they'd had intel on a different job. Patty had them thinking they were going after some big-time CEO up here in the northwest, sort of a corporate espionage thing. We don't know if she was onto them or if she changed her mind at the last minute. Whatever the case, evidently these guys had no clue that they were about to break into a prison to get Shelley Sergeant out. It's Morrow's assumption that they went through with it to keep from breaking cover."

"That's great," Sara said, her hope returning. "If that's the case, then they're right on top of her and we don't have anything to worry about, do we?"

"That's what I called to tell you. We have *everything* to worry about now."

"What? Why?"

"A Mickey D's employee found Tanner and Crenley in the dumpster about an hour ago. Looks like one of them might've been wounded during the prison break and maybe Patty finished him off with a single shot. The other one had two in the forehead. Dead and gone. Surveillance cameras show two women dumping the bodies but they're masked and we couldn't identify them. But, from what I've seen before, their physical builds seem to be about right for your two supervillains. Cameras show them driving off and heading east. No make on the license plates and we think, stressing the *think* here, that they're responsible for the two scientists that the reporter mentioned during the news conference. I mean, hell, we're lucky the supervisor went looking for those two so he could warn them about the incoming weather, otherwise, they might not have found the bodies for weeks."

"So what're you saying, Barker? Am I really hearing you right? Patty and Shelley are definitely together?"

"It looks to be that way."

"And you have no clue where they are now? Other than the fact that they were heading east to God-knows-where?"

"The feds are checking into a couple of hotline tips where people think they might've seen the blue Explorer. Aside from that, they're chasing tails. It's a goddamn shitshow in the office over there. I had to sneak out to call you."

"Why?"

"Morrow knows about your history with both of these ladies and in case they *are* heading your way, rather than sending in protection like I begged him to do over and over, he's adamant about holding back. If they're coming to your house, he doesn't want a bunch of suits hanging around the farm to tip them off. He'll have eyes on you from a distance—maybe satellites or a drone, something—but nobody on the ground except for a couple of guys in a car.

"He *says* he'll make a move before they can get close enough, but his goal is to take her alive somewhere between here and there. The way he sees it, they'll screw up before they get out of the state and I'm inclined to agree with him."

"We figured that much, too," Randall said, "but that still don't explain why he's not protecting Sara *here*."

"Your guess is as good as mine. Patty's got her Boudica cover spread all around the world and he wants her to snitch on some big names. Guy's got a real hard-on for making a name for himself. You know the type. He tells me I'm on a need-to-know and promises you'll be safe, but you can put a promise on a scale and see how much it weighs. Stinks to high heaven to me, but he swears they'll never get close to you."

"And I'm supposed to be reassured by that?"

"I know, I know, I'm not a fan of it either."

Sara sat back, limp and defeated. She looked around the table.

Teddy shook his head. Irina chewed a fingernail. Mary and Randall exchanged glances.

Barker added, "As shitty as that is, we don't know one hundred percent for certain that they're even coming in your direction. Tanner and Crenley had reported back a couple of times and mentioned that Patty had a ton of work lined up for them down in South America. Could be—and this is a strong possibility—she broke Shelley out so that crazy-ass girl could go work for her. We don't know that, but it seems plausible. As of thirty minutes ago, we're looking into any possible leads until something solid turns up."

Randall said, "Let me ask you something, Detective."

"Sure thing."

"Sara told me the history between 'em all...Where do you put the odds that those two are coming here to finish the job? Honestly. No bullshit."

"Honestly? I wouldn't bet against it."

Chapter Twelve

Patty walked slowly, allowing Shelley to keep her grip around her wrist.

They had followed Bobby down the dark hallway, reached a set of stairs, and descended into what felt like a cold Hell. Once they'd reached the bottom, orange lights illuminated the walls, casting a fiery glow, even though her skin prickled from the chill.

Bobby whistled as he strolled, shotgun resting lazily on his shoulder; just another day at the office for this hillbilly with too much power and not enough sense, while his father rotted upstairs and his mother slipped further into madness.

Inside her left pocket, she carried a small knife, disguised to look like a tube of lip balm. She slid her hand in and felt the cylindrical object. It wasn't much, but with enough force and enough repetition, she could easily get enough jabs into Bobby's neck to send him where his father had already gone.

The only downside to that plan was the fact that she'd been down here before, with Papa Bear, and knew that the door at the far end was equipped with an electronic security system. She'd need the code to get the door open, and Bobby was insane enough to allow her the pleasure of torturing him without ever giving it up. The way Myrtle had checked out of reality, she'd never get a response from her either.

When they reached the end and turned the corner, she learned that it wouldn't have mattered anyway.

Things had changed since she'd been down here last. An entire metal wall with a sliding door system had replaced the original metal door, which had been controlled by a six-digit entry code.

Patty had to stop herself from whistling. It was fancy and expensive for the backwoods in southwest Virginia. How much had it set them back? A million? More? To look at this family, it would never be apparent that they were worth millions themselves. They'd served as a mid-point, illegal arms dealer up and down the east coast for decades.

From what she'd been told, back in the seventies, Papa Bear had somehow wormed his way into the trade. He staged a rights grab on what entered and exited his territory, and a few dead bodies later, the Cuban drug lords in Florida and the mafia bosses in New York appeased him after their failed attempts to eliminate the pesky bastard.

The couriers that had tried to slip by undetected learned the hard way that crossing him was not a viable option. He made Vlad the Impaler look like a Sunday school teacher.

Where Papa Bear operated within some level of controlled chaos, Bobby had always been the one to serve *as* the chaos. And it was infinitely more disturbing now that he was in charge of what remained.

Patty shivered.

Bobby stepped to the side, pushed three green buttons, and waited on a panel to slide open in the wall. "Ain't that some shit?" he asked. "Watch this." He put his face up to the exposed hole and said, "Entry."

Patty listened to the sound of whirring gears. A blue stream of light emanated from the opening, traveled up Bobby's left eye, and then down.

Something inside the wall beeped twice, and Bobby repeated, "Entry."

A thinner, flat panel slid forward. He placed his hand on the black surface. Two more beeps, followed by the sounds of releasing latches, then hissing pistons, as the door slid open from the middle. It retracted into the wall's sides.

Whatever lay beyond was covered in a darkness so deep that Patty could see nothing beyond the spot where the orange hallway lights could reach.

Shelley squeezed Patty's hand once and let go, moving backward and then sidestepping behind her.

Bobby snickered. "Damn, girl, don't be scared. It's just a warehouse." Then to Patty, he added, "What do you think about that system, Kellog? That's some James Bond stuff, huh? Voice recognition, eyeball scanner, and not only does that panel check the fingerprints, it matches the oils in your skin to what it has on file. Ain't got no idea how all them contraptions works, but the goddamn President of the United States couldn't get in here."

She'd seen systems that were more impressive, especially in Eastern Europe, but she wasn't going to tell Bobby that. "It's amazing. What happened to the old door, the one with the code panel?"

"About a year ago, Daddy had a close call with the ATF and got a little paranoid. *Loco* in the *cabeza*. So, he had this system right here put in, figuring that if he ever took a ride to the big house, none of those pricks would be able to get in here to confiscate his stash." He flicked his chin toward the entryway, cradling the shotgun at chest level. "After you."

Patty could feel the hesitation in Shelley without looking at her. She had a bit of it herself, but she knew that what Bobby enjoyed more than killing people were people that gave him a lot of money. "Is it all in there?"

"Go on and see for yourself."

She took a deep breath and stepped forward. Once she'd passed the threshold, motion sensors detected her presence and bright, fluorescent bulbs flickered on overhead. She squinted against the light as it revealed row upon row of shelving, filled with boxes, pelican cases, and all forms of ammunition containers along the right hand side. On the left, weapons hung on pegs, all the way down to the end of the tunnel some fifty feet away. M-16s, sniper rifles, AK-47s, grenades attached to belts—it was a complete arsenal, enough to put some sort of deadly device in every hand of a small militia.

This time, Patty *did* whistle. The storage room had evolved since she'd been there last and she had to admit, the collection was impressive. Though it wasn't necessarily a collection, considering the fact that every item in there was on its way to somewhere else. It was backstock awaiting delivery.

Bobby pointed to a gold-plated 9mm Glock hanging close to Patty's shoulder. "You see that gorgeous sumbitch right there? Guess where that's going."

"Disney World."

"Hah, funny, but nope. That pretty little piece of jewelry is on its way down to Juarez. Carlos motherlovin' Jimenez. Can you believe it?"

Patty couldn't hide her surprise. "El Toro?"

"I call him El Caca de Toro, but not to his face." He glanced around at Shelley and grinned at her. "That means 'the bull shit' if you don't know *espanol*."

Shelley spoke for the first time since they'd entered the house. "I know what it means, *puto*."

The last word rattled Bobby. He stepped closer. "What'd you say to me?"

"Easy," Patty said, holding up a hand. "She called you a friend, that's all."

"You sure about that? Because I had a pretty little Mexican *mamacita* call me that same thing one time, only she didn't have a smile on her face. And you want to know what happened to her? I carved a smile for her. She's just like the Joker now, always grinning, ear to ear."

Patty tried to change the subject. "What're you doing with El Toro's Glock, Bobby? I thought the Juarez guys ran stuff through Albuquerque."

"He's setting up some operations with the Tarantino family in Yankee Town. Glock's a gift from one peckerwood to another. It's hanging out here for a few days like a show pony down at the county fair."

"So you're big time now, huh? Rubbing elbows with some of the worst badasses in two countries?" She was trying to butter him up. Bobby had always been hasty with the temper, but he was prone to having his ego stroked.

"You know how Daddy was. He got his business to where he wanted it and got lazy. There ain't no challenge when everybody's sucking at your teat already. I told him—I told him for years that we could do more, but no sir, he wasn't having it. I was 'bout damn sick of it, to tell you the truth, and if the heart attack hadn't gotten him, I wasn't too far from sending him down the road a ways myself."

Patty shrugged. "Don't make no never mind now, does it?" She'd heard the country slang once before, in some movie, and had always wanted to try it out. It felt strange rolling off her tongue, like the words had gotten mixed up somewhere in her throat.

Bobby grinned. "No, ma'am, it don't."

He glanced away, down toward the end of the room, and Patty thought she saw him lick his lips. Maybe they were dry. Maybe she could offer him the business end of the lip balm in her pocket. Or maybe he had something else in mind. Her intuition tingled with the latter—she could feel his intent, whatever it was.

. . .

Patty stood in front of a waist-high metal table, about the size of a hospital gurney, looking over the equipment she'd ordered months ago. Finally, it had all arrived two weeks prior—some of it bought easily on the black market, some of it custom-made—and she'd gotten the call from Bobby to come pick it up. The timing was perfect, coinciding with Shelley's escape, and Patty was thankful for it. She'd been contemplating what they could've done in the meantime.

Bobby said, "Took me a while, but it's all here. Let's tick things off the checklist to make sure it's everything you ordered."

"I trust you."

"You damn well better, but this is how I run things, though, and you'd be wise to play along."

"Gotcha."

The first item he grabbed was a pair of military-grade night vision goggles, the hands-free kind that could easily tighten around various head sizes. "Five pairs of night vision specs. Standard issue, no big deal getting those."

"We only need two sets."

"You fire some people?"

"You could say that."

"I was wondering where the rest of your crew was. The order stands, Kellog. You wanted five, you're paying for five."

Patty nodded. She'd expected that. Still, it never hurt to try. Over the years, she'd found that she could bargain with most folks if she was respectful. In a lot of countries, bargaining was customary and the selling party would get offended if you didn't try to haggle. Not here, though. Not in Papa Bear's, and now Bobby's, basement.

"Next, we got one laser doohickey. It's a…what is it? Hell if I remember what the damn thing is called. It breaks the beam without setting off an alarm, right?"

"Right."

"There you go. Next," he said, moving down the table, "you have five sets of various handguns, rifles, pistols, whatever—automatic, semi-automatic. This one right here would put a hole the size of a bowling ball through an elephant. I reckon you only need two sets, but you'll be taking all five with you, won't you?"

Patty nodded. From the corner of her eye, she could see Shelley crossing her arms and shaking her head, behind Bobby and out of his sight.

Not a word, Shelley. Just business.

Bobby moved to the last set of items on the table. Five black bodysuits, folded neatly, as if they were on display at an Old Navy. She wondered if they came that way, or if Bobby had taken the time to fold them himself. "And these sumbitches...You have any idea how hard it was to get *one* of these damn things, much less five of them in five different sizes?"

Stepping up to the table, Shelley bent over and examined them. "What're those?"

Patty picked up the top one from the pile and shook it out. It looked like a surfer's wetsuit, except that it had fingers and toes. Once on, the only open spots were thin slits across the eyes. "Ambient temperature suits. With these things, we're practically invisible to a thermal camera."

Shelley said, "I didn't even know those existed."

"You'd be surprised what's out there."

"And why do we need all of this stuff? You said so yourself, the bitch lives in a damn farmhouse in the middle of nowhere. It's not like we're breaking into the CIA building." When Patty didn't immediately agree, Shelley added, "Right?"

Patty held up one of the suits and examined it in the light. She said, "No, but it's damn close."

Chapter Thirteen

Detective Emerson Barker walked into the task force office, feeling comfortable about Sara's situation all the way over in Virginia. With three thousand miles between her and the evil women—he hoped—it seemed like she was in good hands with an ex-cop and a former Marine Corps sniper standing by. And as much as it pained him to admit it, Teddy wasn't a slouch when it came to firing a weapon either. He'd seen the effects of it back in Jim Rutherford's house; the way Teddy hit his targets with such accuracy, he effectively saved a number of lives that day, including Barker's.

He'd never admit that Teddy had done such a thing, because the dude's ego already filled up every room he walked into, but at least Barker now considered him a friend. That was a far cry from having the over-privileged, junior Rutherford labeled as a kidnapping and murder suspect before he and DJ had discovered Shelley Sergeant was the culprit way back when.

Barker stood at the entryway, watching the spry and spotless agents buzz around him, going over files, surveying maps, and generally looking clueless. He was relieved that he'd been granted the privilege of helping out, by both sets of superiors, but at the same time, he knew he was a protruding nail, just waiting for a hammer to come along. Proceed wisely, cooperate, and with any luck learn enough to keep Sara and her kids safe in the process.

He offered a mock salute as Agent Grady Morrow approached him and handed over a sheet of paper.

"What's this?" Barker asked.

"Contact list for private flight companies within a six-hour radius. Get on the horn with each one of these and see if they had anyone going east, most likely in the northeast Tennessee and southwest Virginia areas."

"Those private ones don't have to file a flight plan, do they?"

"No, but they'll have a record of who was going where."

"And you think they risked the visibility of an *airport*? Even if they don't have to go through the main terminal for a private flight, that's a damn chancy move."

"You never know, Barker. You asked to help, this is what I've got."

Barker suspected he was being handed the busy work while the actual FBI agents were out putting boots on concrete, but for once, he didn't mind. He hadn't healed completely yet, and this might be a good time to take a breath. His wounds ached. His muscles whined whenever he bent over or took a step, and if he popped another Percocet, he'd likely be in for a long snooze at his temporary desk. "All right then, Morrow, I'll get on it."

Besides, even if he *were* annoyed by being handed the shit jobs, he had a damn good idea where Kellog and Sergeant were heading, and the possibility of finding them through a scheduled private flight was more productive than interviewing a McDonald's fry cook who'd never seen a dead body before.

Last they'd heard, the blue Explorer had been heading east, over the Cascades, and there weren't many options on that side of the mountains. The small regional airport in Redmond was the likeliest place, along with an airfield about the size of a postage stamp down in Bend. Either could easily accommodate a hasty exit, but he decided to save those calls for last. In case the blue Explorer was a decoy, or the witnesses had reported the wrong vehicle, it made sense to rule out the private flights in the immediate vicinity first.

He started with Portland and came away with information regarding four different private flights, all heading toward the east coast, but none of them were landing in the proper region, and none of them carried two women, one of whom was missing an eye.

The FBI's saving grace on this one would be the fact that Shelley Sergeant had taken such an ass-whipping when she first arrived at Coffee Creek two years ago. The resulting loss of an eye left her so easily identifiable that he was certain they'd get call after call tracing her path. It hadn't happened yet, but once the news propagated throughout the internet and made its way onto the nightly reports, they'd be on her in no time.

Until then, grunt work would have to suffice.

Next, he tried Eugene and came up with nothing, then the rest of the list, checking off the smaller fields as he went one by one. Almost all of them had private flights that left that morning, and some of them even had flights heading in the proper direction, but none carried the reprehensible cargo he was looking for.

With two options remaining, he felt like he was scratching the last two spots on a lottery ticket, hoping beyond hope that the gold bar in Box A matched the gold bar in Box B. Or whatever the hell happened on scratch tickets these days.

Again, the calls to the Redmond private airports offered nothing. Same story. Eastbound private flights, but none to Virginia or Tennessee. Barker cursed and slammed the phone down. He sat back in his chair, twisted the tips of his mustache, and popped a cinnamon-flavored toothpick in his mouth. He'd gone nearly a year now without smoking, but the longing had never fully disappeared, especially when he was annoyed and needed something to occupy his mind while he processed details.

The airfield in Bend was the least likely of the two central Oregon choices, primarily because of how tiny it was. He'd been through it before a couple of times, landing there on the way to hunting and fishing trips with some wealthy buddies who'd chartered flights for the fun of it, and taking a private plane out of there didn't make much sense. Too small, too few people, too easy to peg a one-eyed woman.

A small flicker in the back of his mind caused Barker to sit upright. He said "Hold on, now," and grabbed the list of companies offering flights. He checked their websites to confirm what he'd remembered. The first two didn't even have an office there at the airfield, and the latter three did, and they were stationed in separate buildings, with one of those being nothing more than a guy with a desk.

Now that he'd taken time to process the situation...a flight out of Bend seemed more possible than not. However, four of the companies didn't have planes in their hangers that were capable of making cross-country flights. Instead, they were puddle jumpers used for flights up to Portland or Seattle, maybe even quick weekend trips over to the Oregon coast.

Barker managed to be worried and relieved at the same time. One option left room for both.

He was worried that he'd wasted so many hours of fruitless calling—who knew where Kellog and Sergeant could be—but also relieved because maybe those two weren't on their way to Sara's farm. They could be, but if they'd chosen to drive, that left a lot of miles and a lot of time to make mistakes.

With one last number to go, he called Cascade Aviation and crossed his fingers, praying he'd find them, praying that he wouldn't. Either was acceptable.

"Thank you for calling Cascade Aviation, this is Maria, how many I help you?"

"Maria, this is Detective Emerson Barker with the Portland P.D. I'd like to ask you a couple of questions if you have a moment."

"Um...sure."

He could sense the hesitation in her voice. People got it no matter how he introduced himself—friendly or gruff—and they turned inward, worried they'd done something wrong that they didn't know about, or they were worried they'd been busted for doing something they knew they shouldn't. Hence the pause, hence the hesitation, contemplating which one of their friends or family members was the tattletale.

Barker said, "Your company offers private flights, correct?"

"Yes, sir."

"We're aware that your pilots aren't required to file FAA flight plans, but I'm sure that you have a record of incoming and outgoing schedules, payment transactions…is that also correct?" He knew the answer would be yes, but it was a simple way to get Maria into a comfort zone, giving her the opportunity to relax and answer the easy questions. He did it with every witness. Boost up their confidence, then weed out the information he needed. Worked every time.

Maria said, "Oh, absolutely, Detective. We run a tight ship around here. My husband and I haven't had a single issue with our recordkeeping in the last twenty years."

"So this is your company?"

"Don and I run it together—well, when he's around. If he's not skiing, he's out on the golf course, but, what're you gonna do, huh? Men are men."

"I hear that."

"What can I help you with? I know you didn't call to listen to me jabber about my husband."

"Well, ma'am, I'd have to say you're my last shot. I've called more numbers than I can count today and I swear I've got a blister on my dialing finger. Anyway, you mind telling me which flights of yours went out today?"

"Not *flights*. Flight. We sold off most of our fleet when the economy tanked—and when I say fleet, I mean three planes—so now we just run with the one. They landed at the Tri-Cities airport a couple of hours ago."

Barker's heartbeat jack-hammered in his chest. He exploded out of the desk chair and felt his skin get warm. His fingers shook a little around the pen in his hand. "You're talking about TRI, there near Bristol?"

"That's the one."

"Son of a…Maria, couple more questions."

"Everything okay?"

"Can you tell me who was on that plane?"

"I can assure you, Detective, we don't cater to—"

"Who were the passengers, Maria?"

Barker listened to some papers rustling in the background. He scanned the room of bustling feds and spotted Morrow talking to an equally well-dressed woman off in the corner. He caught Morrow's eye and frantically waved him over.

Maria said, "Let's see here. Flight was booked and paid for by a woman named Sharon Ellison, um…two passengers, both female. Paid by credit card. One-way flight to TRI near Bristol, Tennessee."

"They checked in, right? Any chance you saw them board that plane today?"

Maria sighed, "Believe it or not, Detective, my husband was here then. The one time he actually spent more than thirty minutes in the office while I had a dentist's appointment."

"Is he there now? Can I speak to him?"

"I'd imagine he's made it to the back nine at this point. Always got his phone off during the rounds, but I'd say you can probably reach him in a couple of hours."

"No, that'll be too late." Barker tapped his pen on the desk, thinking. "What about the pilots? Did they radio in? Give you any details about their passengers?"

"They checked in a couple of times, but didn't say anything about their passengers. Not that they usually do. Let me give you their cell numbers and you can give them a call. Would that work? I'm not sure how much else I can help."

"Perfect, thank you." He jotted down the numbers, shaking in anticipation.

He wondered if he should ask her for the credit card information related to Sharon Ellison, then decided it would be a waste of time and resources. If Maria didn't want to go that far in her generosity of supplying the information he needed, the subpoena would take too long and tell them little. Supposing it *was* Patty Kellog, the credit card would be stolen, fake, or untraceable. No use in having the hapless feds around him chasing more ghosts.

Barker thanked her, hung up, and immediately dialed the pilot's cell phone.

Morrow stopped in front of Barker's desk. "You got something?"

While he listened to the ringing, Barker said to Morrow, "Private flight out of Bend landed in northeast Tennessee about two hours ago. Company confirms that two women were on board."

The voice on the other end of the line said, "Jeff speaking."

Barker introduced himself and waded through the initial round of hesitation, joking around with the pilot and co-pilot, giving them a moment to shore up their composure. He said, "Three simple questions for you and Smiling Dave."

"We're ready, sir."

"First, did you have two female passengers on your flight today?" Barker held his breath, waiting. This was it. While it was certainly possible that Kellog and Sergeant could make it back east a thousand different ways, he prayed to God that he could pinpoint their location with this one simple phone call.

"We did, definitely."

"Was one of them in her late thirties, brown hair, sort of muscular?"

"Yeah, she was. Kinda tall, too. And a little scary, actually."

Brother, you don't even know. "Excellent. Last question, and this is the most important one...was the woman with her missing her left eye?"

Barker hung up before the pilot could finish saying that she was attractive, even with a missing eye.

Chapter Fourteen

Patty loaded the supplies in the back of the rental car. She'd lost sight of Shelley, who'd been so disgusted by the smell of Papa Bear's decomposing body that she had to run around the back side of the house with her shoulders hunched and a hand over her mouth. Bobby had laughed, shaken his head, and offered to bring her a beer from the kitchen.

She took stock of everything to make sure they'd gotten it all, and her only regret was having to pay for all five sets of suits, night-vision goggles, guns and ammo. But, she could afford it, and perhaps the items might be used for future missions once she rebuilt her team.

She bent over to secure one of the Heckler & Koch 9mm semi-automatic handguns, her favorite of the bunch, and felt a presence behind her. An arm went around her stomach and another across her breasts. Something hard pressed against her backside and she immediately recognized what it was. Next came Bobby's heavy panting in her ear, followed by the pungent odor of alcohol on his breath.

"Watching you bend over like that got me all riled up, girl."

Patty slung an elbow at his ribs, felt the knife blade at her throat. "Get off me, Bobby."

"I don't think so. Not yet. I've been waiting for this for a long time. How long you been coming around here? Fifteen years? I've

been holding myself back since the day you walked through that door because Daddy said so. 'No business with pleasure,' he said, which was bullshit to me, because it ain't work if it's fun. Ain't that right?"

Patty felt a hand on the button of her jeans, ripping it free, followed by a hard, rough tug at the zipper. The blade at her neck pressed a little deeper as he grabbed her jeans at the waist and yanked them down around her thighs.

She wasn't used to this. She didn't *experience* fear, she created it. What a strange sensation. It'd been so long. She was always so cool and collected, but now here she was, feeling that sense of impending dread in her stomach.

Patty considered screaming for Shelley, but Bobby was unpredictable and demented, and she wasn't so sure that being dead would make a difference in what he wanted from her.

He pulled her away from the car, grunting in her ear as he tried to get his own jeans down. "Shut that damn trunk lid," he ordered, and Patty reluctantly obeyed. Bobby shoved her forward and she stumbled awkwardly into the car with her pants around her thighs. "Hands up in front of you."

The knife went back to her neck, and again, Patty did as she was told. She felt the blade pull across her skin ever so slightly. A warmness trickled down to her clavicle.

Bobby kicked at the insides of her feet, trying to get her legs apart.

Where are you, Shelley? Help me.

Patty whimpered and hated herself for it. She wasn't weak. This shouldn't be happening. She *made* people whimper. She'd watched grown men cry at her feet and beg for their lives. Was this retribution? Had karma finally caught up to her?

Had Shelley turned on her? Was that why she wasn't helping?

Patty strained to see the front porch through the car's rear window. A figure stood at the top of the stairs, but it wasn't Shelley.

Myrtle stood like a porch column. Motionless. Blank faced. Unmoving. Only her nightgown rippled in the breeze. She watched them from her perch. Had Bobby brought her out or had she come to enjoy the scene on her own?

Bobby laughed and pressed himself against Patty's backside. "You ready, huh? You ready? Maybe when I'm done with you, I'll go find that one-eyed troll you brought with you. I ain't never been with no Cyclops before." He yelled up to Myrtle on the porch, "Ain't that what it's called, Mama? Them one-eyed things are called a Cyclops, right?"

Through the car window, Patty watched as Myrtle slowly lifted a shaky arm with a long, crooked finger, pointing at something. Not directly at them, but to the side, and Patty didn't have time to consider what the old woman was pointing at, because she felt the pressure between her legs; not entering, but there, and soon.

Vulnerable, that's what she felt. Vulnerable, exposed, and livid. She had worked hard to create a name, a worldwide reputation, and here she was, about to be violated by a backwoods redneck that she could've taken out with her pinky. But, she'd let her guard down and stopped paying attention for just the right amount of time. She should've known better, the way he was eyeing her and Shelley down in the basement. He *had* been licking his lips. She was sure of it now.

Grinding molar to molar, she inhaled deeply and waited. And then, from behind, she heard, "Wha—" followed by a deep, throaty gurgling. The grip loosened at her waist and the knife fell away from her throat.

Next came Shelley's voice saying, "Die, hillbilly."
Thank God.

Patty rolled over on the car's trunk, pulled her jeans up, and watched as Shelley shoved the bleeding man to the ground. He gagged on his own blood, clutching his throat, and tried to gasp for air. His eyes bulged and he tried to get to this feet. Shelley laughed, threw her leg back, and delivered a perfect kick to his ribs. Patty was certain she heard bones crunch. Bobby flopped over to his side, babbling, trying to say something.

"What's that?" Shelley asked. She kneeled down beside him, the blade in her hand wet and red. "I can't hear you." She giggled. "A little louder. Come on. You can do it." Taunting him with a devilish grin.

Patty watched Shelley toying with him. She was a cat with a wounded mouse, batting it around, playing with it before finishing it off. Patty bent over and grabbed the blade by the handle, taking it from Shelley's hand. "Give me that." Without hesitation, she buried it deep into Bobby's heart, yanked it free, and then marched through the yard. Up the steps to where Myrtle stood expressionless and nearly catatonic.

Patty drew the blade back, and in the second before she struck, she swore she could see the sense of relief on the old woman's face. The blade slid between the ribcage easily, and Patty left it there when Bobby's mother fell. There would be no need for added insurance. Once would be enough, and chances were, the hag might die of the trauma before Bobby finished writhing on the ground. They were in a race to the end.

Patty spun around and found Shelley standing at the bottom of the steps with her arms crossed, wearing a smug, satisfied smile. Patty said, "What took you so long? I mean, Jesus H. Christ, he almost *raped* me. Where were you?"

Shelley dropped her arms and scowled. "That's what I get? I saved your life and you're scolding me?"

"Yeah, well, maybe you could've shown up a little bit sooner, huh?" Patty stormed down the stairs and used her shoulder to push Shelley out of the way. She made it two steps when she felt a hand on her wrist, and a pulling. With her nerves frayed, still charged on adrenaline, her instinct took over. She whipped around, grabbed Shelley's arm, bent low, pivoted, and threw her to the ground.

Shelley landed on her back, in the damp, muddy yard, and held up her hands in surrender as Patty dropped onto her, clutching the young woman's throat. There was real fear in Shelley's eyes. Submission. "Don't," she said. "I was going to hug you and say I'm sorry."

Patty paused and loosened her grip. She sat back on her haunches.

Shelly continued, "If he'd seen me coming, he would've slit your throat. It took me a minute to get around the damn house and I thought for sure the old skeleton had given me away. So yeah, I'm sorry."

Patty leaned forward and stared into the single, beautiful eye. Her anger dissipated. "Next time, don't take so long." She kissed her, full on the lips, with tempered forgiveness. It felt good. Right and safe. When she pulled away, a slim string of saliva joined their lips. "Let's get out of here."

Shelley climbed up to her feet and tried to knock some of the damp grass off her sweater. Glancing down at Bobby's lifeless body, then up to Myrtle twitching on the porch, she asked, "What about these two?"

"Let them rot like his dad." Patty spat on Bobby then wiped her mouth with the back of a hand. "Maybe we should throw them in with the hounds around back."

"Too late," Shelley said. "They're all dead. That's how I got around back without them howling and giving me away."

"Doesn't matter. The crows will get them eventually."

"Should we try to salvage more of that stuff in the basement? He had enough to start an army."

Patty considered it, then remembered his security system, plus so much of the contents in there belonged to people she didn't want to mess with. It was fine if something happened to Bobby and his clients had no way of retrieving their cache, but if they found out it was gone, and she took it, there wouldn't be enough places to hide.

"We're good," she said. "We'll only need what we have, and even that's more than enough."

They climbed in the car and when Patty backed up, they felt a satisfying thump as the tires rolled over Bobby. Killing him had multiple implications, but none that she wanted to concern herself with right now. They'd just eliminated one of the east coast's most well-known and trusted suppliers, which might ruffle some feathers, but at the same time, others might seek her out to offer thanks for knocking down the gates. It could go either way.

Regardless, it didn't matter. After their trip to Sara Winthrop's farm, she and Shelley would disappear, and there would never be a need to come this way again.

The rental car rattled and bounced down the pothole-filled driveway, splashing muddy rainwater in low, arching fantails each time the tires dipped into a crater.

Shelley took Patty's hand and interlocked her fingers. "Hey."

"What?"

"I'm really sorry it took me so long."

"Don't worry about it."

"No, I'm serious. I don't know if I've, like, seriously thanked you for getting me out of prison, and for giving me a purpose, and for giving me another chance at Sara. You've done so much for me already."

"You're welcome."

"Why'd you do it?"

"Get you out?'

"Yeah."

Patty shrugged. "There's something evil underneath the human side of you. That's a good thing, and it'll take us far."

"Like how far?"

"Around the world. Warm places. Beaches. Sunshine. The Louvre and Prague and Thailand. Wherever we want to go. We're rare in this line of work—two women that are so...ruthless, I guess.

We can bring top dollar simply because men are disgusting pigs, whether they're worth billions and sitting on a yacht off the coast of Fiji, or they're some primping coot in jolly old England. They get their rocks off knowing women are doing their work for them."

Shelley rolled her eyes. "That's not degrading at all."

"Looking at it from the outside, you could see it that way, but who's really getting the shaft when we're charging twice as much and knowing we can get away with it? We're playing with their egos, getting rich off their need to feel dominant without them even knowing we're pulling the strings. In a way, it's almost like watching porn, or strippers…who's screwing who?"

Patty stopped at the end of the driveway and waited on a rusted, rattling old pickup truck to lumber by. The driver took a look at them as he passed. Patty watched the aging farmer in his flannel jacket as he lifted a hand and waved.

Chances were, he was simply being friendly. People were like that around here. Stop to help somebody's grandmother change a flat tire along I-81, you became an honorary member of the family. Help your neighbor with his car in the snow, you'd earn a seat at Christmas dinner. On any other day, it wouldn't have been such a big deal, but due to nothing more than poor timing, he'd witnessed a rental car leaving Bobby's property, and in a day or two when the bodies were discovered, he would easily remember something odd about that day.

She and Shelley exchanged knowing looks.

Shelley said, "Is it your turn or mine?"

Patty grinned and followed the old farmer. She said, "Yours, but don't be messy."

Chapter Fifteen

Sara listened to the wind howling. The rain had moved on and in its place, a chilly breeze pushed against the side of the house, rattling windows and a piece of loose siding on the third floor. Normally, the sound was nothing more than an annoying reminder that the place needed aesthetic repairs. Now, the continuous thumping reminded her of someone knocking repeatedly. It was unnerving, made her feel like a persistent intruder wanted inside.

She poured coffee in six large mugs, along with hot chocolate in three smaller ones for Lacey, Callie, and Jacob. Everyone had moved down to the basement where Sara had a pool table, several vintage arcade games, and plenty of books and movies for entertainment. It was safer down there, away from windows and doors. With no need to get home immediately, Randall and Mary had decided to stay for a while, at least until Barker reported in with something new.

Mary's husband Jim was in Florida for a conference; Randall's wife and son, Alice and Jesse, had called to check in—they were having fun on their trip and Randall had made no mention of his current situation.

Sara added containers full of cream and sugar to the tray, marshmallows for the kids, and was ready to head downstairs when her cell rang. She checked her caller ID and held her breath with the prospect of good news. "Hey, Barker," she answered.

"Sara, where are you?"

"At home, why?"

"Everything okay there?"

His tone was harried and concerned. It worried her. "What's going on?"

"You still got your buddies there? House locked down and all that?"

"Yeah. Did you find something?" Barker sounded like he was running. "Are you chasing somebody?"

"No, heading down the tarmac. FBI authorized a flight. Morrow and I will be there as soon as we can."

"Why? What happened?"

"Patty and Shelley are there. They landed in Bristol a couple of hours ago."

Sara dropped a spoon and it clanged against the metal tray. She jumped, spooked by the crash. "Are you sure?" The spoon landed on the floor, bounced, and disappeared under the stove.

"Visual ID, that's all we have, but it has to be them. The pilots of a private flight out of Bend confirmed they carried two women matching the description."

Sara didn't want to believe it. *Refused* to believe it. "Anybody could match the description of a blonde and a brunette traveling together."

"Not when one of them only has one eye. It's Shelley, Sara. You know it and I know it."

Sara leaned against the countertop. Knees weak and shaking. She slid to the floor before she fell. "What do we do?" Her words cracked and crumbled out of her mouth. "How is this happening again, Barker?" She was strong—she'd survived both of these women already—but this was too much.

"Our best plan of—what? Hang on, Sara." She listened to him talk to someone nearby and heard the loud, sheer roar of plane engines. When he came back, he shouted, "Sorry, that was Morrow.

We're sticking to the original plan, okay? Stay there, hunker down, and make sure everything is armed. He's not putting anyone on the ground on your property, but he'll have overhead surveillance and grab them on the way in."

Frantic, Sara got up to her knees. "Tell him to get people here now, Barker. I don't care what kind of idiotic plan he's got going on. I want protection. I want people here, in my house."

Again, he spoke to someone with him, "Yeah, one sec, I'll be right there," then said to Sara, "I've tried—by God, I've *tried*, but you gotta know this cat to understand he does things one way only: his and his alone. Whatever will bring him the most pats on the back. As much as I hate to say it, I'm just along for the ride. It's not the best plan by any stretch of the imagination, but I can see where he's trying to go with it. Like I told you earlier, he thinks that with boots on the ground, there's a high chance a bullet will find its way into her skull, and he wants her alive. She'll be a goldmine if he can get her into cuffs instead of a body bag."

"I don't care what *he* wants, Barker. It's *my* family." Sara felt weak, lightheaded. "You're coming, right? How soon can you be here?"

The roar of the engines quieted as he entered the hull of the plane. "Five hours, tops."

"Oh my God, Barker, if she landed at the Tri-Cities airport two hours ago, she could be sitting on my front porch already."

"Planes only go so fast. We're doing the best we can, all right? Make sure all your buttons are pushed and doors are locked, stay away from the windows, and hang on. Morrow already has people moving into position. You'll be fine, and more than likely, you won't even know they've been captured until you get another phone call from me. Okay? Tell me that's okay, Sara."

"Okay," she said, slowly climbing to her feet. "Just hurry. Please."

Down in the basement, the look on her face gave everything away.

"Sara?" Teddy said, getting up from his chair. He held a pool cue in one hand and a beer in another. "What's wrong?"

Her hands vibrated as she sat the tray of coffee and hot chocolate down on the bar. "Barker called."

"What did he say?"

She put on a fake smile and waited until her children had swarmed around her, laughing and grabbing their cocoa. They dumped marshmallows into their mugs by the handful and scampered away. She didn't have the strength, nor the heart, to tell them not to spill it on the carpet. With two women on their way to murder her, what difference did it make if there were a few chocolate stains on the carpet? She said, "They're already here."

"Who's here?" Randall asked. "The FBI?"

"No...Shelley and Patty."

Teddy slung his pool stick onto the green felt. Balls scattered. "Are you serious?"

Sara nodded and was unable to contain herself any longer. Tears flowed. Shoulders shook. She buried her face in her hands.

Miss Willow, Irina, and Mary came to her, stroking Sara's hair, rubbing her back and pulling her in for hugs. Teddy and Randall stood by, watching, unsure of where to put their hands, or their beers. The kids cautiously stepped over and asked Uncle Teddy what was wrong with their mother. "Your mom got some bad news, guys, just go back to Pac-Man for a bit."

Minutes later, the adults stood in stunned silence, waiting to hear the rest of Sara's news once she was able to compose herself. She wiped her nose with a bar napkin and handed out the coffee. No one seemed like they wanted to take the mugs, but she needed something to keep her hands occupied. "Barker said they took a private flight and he had confirmation from two pilots that they were at Tri-Cities approximately two hours ago."

Mary said, "That's it?"

"Yep." Sara dropped a sugar cube into her coffee. Then another, and finally a third. She never sweetened her coffee. It seemed that with each *plop* of a sugar cube, as it sank to the bottom and melted, a tiny bit of rage released. It felt good to destroy something. "That's it. The pilots confirmed a brunette woman matching Patty's description, and obviously, who's going to miss a disfigured, one-eyed creature like Shelley Sergeant, huh?"

Randall moved over to the bar and leaned down, resting his massive frame on his elbows, cradling the mug. "Then I guess that means it's killing time."

Mary shushed him and lowered her voice. "Not in front of the kids."

He nodded. "Right, sorry. So I take it you don't have any weapons in the house, do you?"

Sara said no and asked Miss Willow if she wouldn't mind shuffling the kids out of the room again. Poor things had been moved around the house all day like she was rearranging furniture, but they didn't need to be involved, or corrupted, by yet another instance like this. They were strong, and durable, but how much more could they handle in their young lives before trauma set in, before irreparable damage scarred them? Worse yet, what if their harrowing childhoods led them to lives like Patty and Shelley's?

Once they were gone from the room—with Irina volunteering to help—Sara explained Morrow's plan again, what she knew of it from Barker, and then added, "I mean, *my God*, how far do we have to go to live a peaceful life, huh? I'm seriously asking. Can anyone answer that question for me? Where, where, *where?*"

Mary pushed her coffee to the side and leaned down beside Randall. She was nearly a third of his size, but she spoke with such conviction and authority that she filled the room as much as he did. Sara liked her for that. It reminded her of the old days back at LightPulse, when she was a Vice President and could take over a meeting simply by stepping through the door. Mary said, "Sara, it might sound like a good plan on paper—right here, right now—but let me tell you this: if that agent wants her for information, if he wants to dig around in her brain for all these contact points she's got around the world, and all the dirt she knows about them…she's not going away forever."

"Why? What does that mean?"

"She'll cut a deal," Randall added. "The Sergeant woman might go back to the big house out in Oregon; they'll tack a few years onto her sentence and who knows when she'll get out. Maybe ten years, maybe never. But, this Kellog lady, she's got something they want, and if they manage to catch her, it won't take her long to find out that she can bargain herself into freedom in a hurry. These days, information moves mountains *and* governments."

"So what're you suggesting? That they'll be free in a few years and this will happen all over again?"

"Can't say for certain, but people like these two, when they've got murder on their minds, it ain't likely that they'll just roll over and forget about it."

"And we'll never be able to get far enough away, will we?"

"Sara," Teddy said, "I know people. Dad knows people. Hell, you know Irina's whole damn family is tied to the Russian mob. We can get you a new identity. Papers, passports, driver's licenses, whatever you need, whatever the kids need. I'd hate to see you disappear because we think of you as family, and it'd be like me telling a sister to vanish, but I'd rather be confident that you were out there alive than six feet under because the FBI wants to know what moves the black markets in…in Laos or Shanghai, or whatever."

Sara reached into the cabinet below the bar and pulled out a bottle of Jack Daniels. "Anybody else?" Three arms went into the air. Sara added whiskey to each of their mugs, then took a long pull straight from the bottle before returning it to its rightful spot. "I'm not running, Teddy. Not if I don't have to."

"It makes sense."

"And leave my family behind? What about my parents?"

"It'll be worse if you and the kids are dead!"

"I'm sick of this shit. There has to be another way. Randall? Mary? Any ideas?"

Randall stood up straight and took a swig of the whiskey-laced coffee. He cleared his throat. "We were, uh, we were tossing some ideas around while you were upstairs."

"Like what?"

Mary said, "Before he gets riled up and excited about this, let me just say that I'm not the biggest fan of it. But, I agree with him, somewhat, even if it goes against everything we're standing here telling you."

Teddy agreed. "If we can't get you to disappear, which to me is the wisest choice, then...yeah, I'm on board with what Randall came up with."

"Tell me."

Randall pulled a stool out from the bar and sat down. He looked from Mary to Teddy and back again, then took a deep breath. "Okay, here goes, but before you tell me how mental this is, hear me out."

Chapter Sixteen

Teddy tried to reassure Irina as she stood in the doorway, crying, begging him not to go. "I'll be with Randall the whole way," he said. "He lives right over there in that old house. See it? Where the lights are on?"

Irina nodded, sniffling. "If anything happens to you—"

"It won't. I promise."

"You don't know that. You *can't* promise."

"Randall knows these hills better than the back of his hand. We'll be gone twenty minutes, tops, and then I'll come right back here to you."

"If you're not back in twenty, I'm coming to look for you, and I don't care who might be out there."

Teddy opened his mouth to counter her, but changed his mind. There was no use in arguing. As the granddaughter of Ivan, a former Russian mob boss, her determination and tenacity were just a couple of her admirable qualities, except for when they dissolved into bullheadedness and made situations challenging. He wiped a tear away with his thumb and kissed her cheek. "See you in a few, sweetheart."

Irina forced a smile.

Randall stood at the edge of the covered porch out back, waiting on him. He said, "Ready?"

"Yep, let's go."

"You don't have to come with me if you don't want to, especially if *she* don't want you to. I appreciate the offer, T-bird, but c'mon...y'all just got hitched."

Teddy leaned in and motioned for Randall to keep his voice down. "Don't give her any ideas, dude. It's the best plan and we all know it." He looked back over his shoulder at Irina and offered one last wave. Sara came to the doorway and told them to hurry.

Randall clapped Teddy on the back. "Okay, then. Stay close, stay low, and if you spot anything, even if a damn raccoon catches your eye, you point it out. God knows where those two heathens are by now—they could be sitting up there on the hill, scoping us with a thermal cam or night-vision goggles already, and we have to act like it, got me?"

"Roger that." Teddy followed Randall down the steps and into the last light of dusk. With the weather having passed by, leaving a smattering of clouds, what remained of the setting sun gave them a clean line of sight to their objective, Randall's house, but it also exposed them as targets. They chose to go on foot, rather than taking one of the cars, because they could move with more stealth once they made it to the trees surrounding the property.

Their plan was simple. A quick sprint to Randall's house to stock up on weapons and ammunition, then hunker down in Sara's home until some sign of Shelley and Patty appeared on Sara's monitoring system. There was no guarantee, but it had to happen. It was the only logical choice. Patty hadn't broken Shelley out of prison and flown across the entire United States, then landed at the closest commercial airport on a whim. Traveling, no matter the source of movement, was risky and dangerous. No, they were coming here. They were coming for a purpose.

Once the two invaders were spotted, Mary would take Sara, her children, and Miss Willow in Sara's oversized Suburban and get down the long driveway as rapidly as possible. Since Mary was trained in all styles of tactical driving and evasive maneuvers, she would be the one to get them to safety.

Teddy went over Randall's plan in his mind. Randall's hope was that the sudden escape would take Patty and Shelley by surprise. If they were dumb enough to give chase on foot, all the better. If they were smart enough to retreat, well, by then Randall would have a bead on their location. Two rapid shots from his perch on the third floor—dropping them both—and it would be game over, no matter what option they chose.

With Sara's connections, Mary's history, Randall's decorated service, and the fact that one enemy was an escaped convict and the other was a known international terrorist, Randall had said he was okay with the possibility that he might face legal action. So be it.

He'd admitted that was partly his burden—the inability to let injustice have its way with the world. He had his own family to worry about, he'd said, and in fact, he'd done dumber things in the recent past. But if he were incapable or didn't have the same level of training, he'd pray that someone would do the same for *his* family.

Teddy was glad this mighty monster was on their side. He hunched over and picked up his pace. All they had to do was make it to Randall's house, unarmed, without dying.

Sure. No problem.

Up at the fence, in the only gated doorway other than the driveway entrance, where the well-worn hiking trails led into the woods, Teddy entered Sara's PIN and they slipped through when the door swung open. He said to Randall, "Jesus, she really needs to set up a different code. She's used the same one for years. Remind me to bug her about that when we get back, okay?"

"Will do, T-bird. Now keep your head down before you get it shot off."

They scrambled up the hillside until they reached the thin forest and then broke into sporadic bursts of speed, moving from birch, to maple, to oak.

They had gone close to ten acres away from Sara's home before Randall dropped to the ground and pulled Teddy with him in the process. Thankfully, due to the recent rain, the leaves were moist and didn't make too much noise as they landed and scuttled up behind a fallen oak trunk.

Teddy managed to get, "What is it—" out of his mouth before he felt Randall's bear paw across his lips, silencing him.

Randall held up two fingers, pointed at his eyes, and then further up the hillside. He mouthed, "Two," and used his fingers to pantomime a walking motion.

Teddy mouthed back, "Is it them?"

Randall shrugged, put his fingers to his lips, and lifted his head over the trunk just enough to peek with one eye.

Teddy did the same. Far above their position, he spied two black-clad figures darting from tree to tree, moving in a northerly direction, and he assumed that they hadn't been spotted.

But were Shelley and Patty here already? Before the sun went down completely? It didn't make sense. Would they risk it?

If they were coming, and every known fact indicated that they were, he'd assumed they would wait until darkness fell. A new moon, along with sporadic cloud cover, would provide a perfect nighttime approach.

So why risk it now in the waning light of dusk?

Randall motioned for Teddy to stay low and nudged himself up again. He was intently focused while the two figures move through the forest. "That ain't them," he whispered seconds later, patting Teddy on the shoulder. "That's my reinforcements."

"Who?"

"A couple of my buddies I called up while you were in the pisser earlier. Two coon hunters named Dale and Harold, here to keep an eye on the perimeter. They're practically invisible in these woods."

"Yeah, but *you* saw them."

"That's because I know what to look for." Randall put his thumb and forefinger in his mouth and let loose with a shrill, three-note whistle. From somewhere north of their position, closer to Sara's house, came a reply. He grabbed Teddy's arm and pulled him to his feet. "Let's go."

"That's it?"

"They know what to do."

Randall moved, deftly, in a brisk jog, hopping over fallen trees and ducking around low-hanging limbs. Teddy managed to keep up, but not without some complaints over the pace or the branches that kept poking him in the eyes. Once they were near the road, Randall dropped into a cluster of rhododendrons and crawled forward.

Teddy followed. "What're we doing?"

Randall pointed, indicating the cow pasture on the opposite side. "Wide open space over there. Just making sure we're in the clear. It's another three minutes down to my front porch if we hurry, and then less than ten back before your wife comes after us."

"She won't," Teddy said. "She talks a bigger game than she plays. Although…"

"What's that?"

"Her grandpa was in the Russian mafia for a while, and I know that old dude's got connections and family all up and down the east coast. I bet if she made a couple of phone calls, we could have some of them here running backup, too. Would that make sense? Your redneck buddies and my Kremlin relatives hanging out in the woods together?"

Randall chuckled and pushed up to a crouch. "I wish we had the time for it. That'd make a helluva show on HBO. Let's move." Down the embankment he went, Teddy following, until he reached the blacktop. "Run," he said, without waiting. Arms pumping, one leg in front of the other.

Teddy knew the distance to Randall's front porch, from this point, would be less than a quarter of a mile away. Short enough, but it seemed like it was on the other side of the planet. A single light illuminated a room on the second floor of the farmhouse. It was a small thing, but Teddy thanked God for it, because the glow provided a warm beacon in the darkening night.

Teddy jogged easily beside Randall, keeping up with the taller man's long strides.

"Run much?" Randall asked, a slightly winded huff in his voice. He stayed in shape with free weights and hiking through the mountains, hunting and finding the best fishing spots. There was never any reason to be at a higher speed than amble.

"Ten miles every day," Teddy said. "Six minute miles at a normal cruising speed."

"Then we know who we're sending if someone has to run after the cops, huh?"

"Whatever it takes, man."

Directly in front of them, the trees in the bend lit up from the lights of an approaching car.

"Shit," Randall said. He looked around for a spot to hide.

"Who's that?"

"No idea, but just in case. There!" He pointed to a long, blue trough like the one he'd seen near Sara's barn. "Duck and cover, T-bird."

Randall dropped off the side of the embankment and climbed over the fence with Teddy following close behind.

The earth surrounding the trough was deep, thick mud, made that way by the herd of cattle tromping through twice daily during feeding times. He'd been through worse, and had hidden in worse things during his time as a sniper, but flopping down in mud and cow shit was never an option he'd choose on purpose. Grabbing the trough, he said, "Help me with this. Get that end."

"Whoa, what're we doing?"

"Hiding. Gotta hurry. C'mon now, grab that end."

"Under this?"

"Teddy, damn it, pull your end."

Over Randall's left shoulder, Teddy saw the headlights coming into view, watching as the cone of light swept over the trees, past the farmhouse, and through the field. They'd be visible in five... four...three...

Teddy said, "Yep, got it," and leaned with all his weight against the large, metal frame, which was just enough to help Randall topple the trough. They fell face first into the gunk as it landed with a splatter, sending mud and cow pies squishing out in all directions.

Randall listened to the approaching car and watched it through a rusted hole in the trough's bottom. He was certain they hadn't been spotted in the headlights—and he wondered if he'd overreacted—but given the current situation, being too careful wasn't possible.

Not that he knew every car in town, but he recognized most of the cars that came through this route on a regular basis. That was one of the quirks of living in a small town; a man could set his watch by the neighbors' schedules.

But this one—and it was hard to tell in the low light—this wasn't a car he recognized. Dark in color, a sedan, and maybe a newer model. Could be somebody down the road, maybe Tom Hammerly or Carter Conley, had traded in for a new one, but—

"Who is it?" Teddy whispered. "Anybody you know?"

"Can't tell. Probably nobody. Just somebody passing through."

It could've easily been true if the car hadn't stopped thirty feet away, idling in the middle of the road.

Teddy held his breath as the engine shut off.

Chapter Seventeen

Patty stopped the blue rental car in the middle of the road. "That's it right there," she said, pointing up through the field. "Sara thinks she's got her castle guarded, but everything has a way in and a way out."

Shelley craned her head around to see out of her good eye. "That's a lot of ground to cover, huh? Look at that fence...is that the one with the lasers?"

Patty shut off the engine and opened the door. "Let me show you what we're up against."

"Hey, are you nuts? Get back in the car. What if she's got cameras down here?"

"Then she'll know we're coming, but not when or where, and I like that idea."

"Uh, hello? Police? Guns?"

Patty leaned back inside the vehicle. "Would you trust me? Jesus. It's taken care of."

"How?"

Patty rolled her eyes. "Extraction point, one point three miles from here. We're in, we're out, and they'll never find us, not running through these woods."

"What if she's calling the cops right now?"

"Then we listen for sirens, Shelley. Get out of the damn car so I can show you what you need to see and then we'll go."

"Fine." Shelley climbed out and closed the door. She walked around the front of the car and hid her nose in a sleeve. "You think cows know they stink so much?"

Patty chuckled and put her arm around Shelley's waist. She pulled her close and felt her body's warmth against the cool spring air. "Okay, here's what we're up against." She explained the lasers, the heat-detecting cameras, the motion sensors, the weight triggers in the driveway, the depths to which the concrete ran under the fence, and everything else that she knew about Sara Winthrop's nearly impenetrable security system. "Finally," she said, planting a kiss on Shelley's cheek, "we don't have to worry about any cameras right here, because the four guarding the south side are all focused on the entrance since that's the primary access point. At most, she might've seen the car's headlights go by on the main road, but from right here, we could sit and stare at her house all night."

The corner of Shelley's mouth turned up. "You little shit. You had me freaking out."

"And you gotta start trusting the pro, sweetheart. Money leads to information. Always has and always will. Learn that first thing and the roads ahead are always smoother. We don't survive in this business by being brain-dead morons."

"Like Bobby?"

"Exactly, and to be perfectly honest, I'm surprised somebody hadn't offed him before us."

"So what's the plan from here?"

Patty smiled and stroked Shelley's hair. "Shock and awe sound good to you?"

. . .

Patty drove them to a spot two miles from Sara's home. It was a small garbage station bordered by a chain link fence roughly eight feet high. Normally locked, the night attendant had graciously accepted the hundred-dollar bill, weeks ago, to leave the sliding gate open on the prearranged date.

Shelley hopped out, rolled the gate to the side, and then closed it again as Patty hid the car behind the largest green disposal unit. It was roughly the size of a boxcar and hid the rented sedan well.

Even in the cool air of a spring night, the smell was putrid, and Patty couldn't imagine what it was like in the middle of summer. Spoiled milk, rotting meat, and God knows what else rampaged through her nostrils. She tried to breathe through her mouth as they stripped down. "Everything off," she said. "The closer you can get it to your skin, the better these heat-dispensing suits work."

Beside her, Shelley shivered in the cold. Patty let her eyes trail over her partner's body, admiring it, feeling the pull of longing, and wished they had more time and a spot that didn't melt flowers with its smell. Shelley's figure was nearly flawless, marred only by the scars, evidence that she had survived a brutal attack.

Patty chuckled and shook her head.

"What?" Shelley said.

"Nothing."

"Tell me."

"All those scars make you more attractive."

"Whatever."

"It's the truth. It's like you went through battle and came out a beast on the other side. I love it."

"Freak." Shelley grinned, turned around and then lifted her hair. "Here, zip me and then I'll get yours."

When they were fully dressed in their suits, nothing but their eyes showing, Patty handed over a set of night vision goggles and a sub-compact 9mm Glock that was small, powerful, and easily transportable over mildly challenging terrain. She gave Shelley two more spare magazines. "Are you ready?" she asked.

"That's it?" Shelley replied, glancing down at the smaller Glock in one hand and the magazines in another.

"Honey, if you need more than that, we'll need to rethink this partnership." Patty tucked her Heckler & Koch 9mm into an interior pocket.

"Okay, then I guess I'm ready."

"Good, let's go."

"We're leaving the car here? What about all this extra stuff?"

Patty checked her watch. "In seven minutes and forty-five seconds, it'll be gone. Two hours from now, they'll find it burning at a rest stop thirty miles south from here. The rest of our gear will be delivered to us as soon as we're ready to disappear. Any more questions?"

"Do you always think of everything?"

"I'm still alive, aren't I?"

They ran through the gate, down the road for an eighth of a mile, and then right and up into the wooded hillside. The night vision goggles made the jaunt easier to duck under clawing limbs, hop over fallen trees, and avoid twisting ankles on loose rocks. Down into a miniature valley and then up the ridgeline to the north, through the rolling hills, between springtime trees with little canopy overhead. No moon, guided by starlight and the hazy green view from their goggles.

Patty was in excellent shape, but Shelley struggled to keep up. Behind her, the young woman huffed and sucked wind, trying to maintain the pace but falling behind. "You okay?" Patty asked.

"No," was the breathless reply.

"Didn't you exercise in prison?"

"I spent that hour in the yard each day trying to stay alive, so excuse me if there wasn't time to run a few laps."

Patty stopped at the top of the ridge, giving Shelley time to catch up. "And whose fault is that?"

"Mine?" Shelley flopped onto a moss-covered log.

"Sara Winthrop's, and don't you forget it. Look at me. Look." Shelley turned her head up. "Find whatever fire you've got in your heart and use it. All that anger and rage is fuel. Do you understand me?"

"Yeah."

"Then get up. Let's go."

Running.

Running.

They spooked a small herd of deer that had bedded down for the night and kept going. Out here, so far away from another home or the lights of city streets, no one would notice panicked wildlife scattering to escape the human intruders.

Up ahead, where the trees thinned, they reached a fencerow that opened into an empty hayfield. "Here we are," Patty said, ducking low and crouching next to a large maple. "That's the back side of her land, right there. Look past that fence post at your one o'clock—see her house over there where the lights are?"

"Yeah."

"That's where we're going, but first, let me show you something." She dropped to her stomach and army-crawled over to the fence. She looked back over her shoulder and motioned for Shelley to join her, and once they were side by side, lying on the cool forest floor, Patty pointed up to the top of the post. "Can you see it?"

"See what?"

"Look right up at the top."

"It's dark and I have one eye, damn it. Just tell me what I'm looking for."

"The laser, remember? That's what this is for." Patty removed a device from her backpack and showed Shelley. "Bobby had to get this thing into the country all the way from Moscow. Mirrors on either end—right here and here—telescoping feature so it can go from post to post, and then these clamps. It breaks the beam without triggering the alarm." Patty pulled at either end, stretching it out, and then twisted a knob to secure the two pieces in place. She got to her knees and then hesitated.

Shelley asked, "Are you sure it'll work? I mean, won't it break the beam while you're trying to get it in place?"

"They told me there's a half-second delay to prevent things like those deer back there from setting it off every time one jumps across the fence. Somehow, it measures body temperature too, you know, so if a squirrel is sitting up there, that won't trigger it either."

"*They?*"

"The security company that installed it."

"Somebody told you?"

"Everybody has a price. I told you that already." Swiftly, Patty jumped to her feet, thrust the device forward, felt the clamps snap securely around the top of the post, and looked closely at the red dot shining back on itself. She waited, watching Sara's place for any sign of movement, any indication that a warning had been triggered. No floodlights came on, no wailing alarms sounded, and everything appeared quiet at the farmhouse acres away. She sighed with relief. "So far, so good."

"Now what?" Shelley asked.

"Now we wait."

"Why?"

Patty checked her watch. "Our two decoys should've been here already. Damn it, I knew I should've—" A branch snapped nearby. Patty pulled her handgun free and aimed. Shelley spun from her prone position on the ground and did the same. "Who's there?" Patty whispered.

A hushed voice came from behind a small patch of briars. "Y'all put them guns down."

Patty felt her stomach churn. She didn't recognize the voice. She increased the pressure under her trigger finger, ready to pull. She hesitated just long enough for the voice to say, "You the one they call Patty?"

"Yeah," she said. "Come out in the open so we can see you."

"All right then. It's just the two of us. No shootin', you hear?" Two large men lurched from behind the briars, hands up, showing they were safe…but maybe not unarmed.

Patty inched back, never pointing her barrel away from the closest one's chest. "What happened to Tess and Laura?"

They both wavered, and Patty noticed.

"They sent us instead. Got scared."

"And who're you?"

"Husbands. I'm Dale and this is Harold."

The one in the rear lifted his hand and said, "Ma'am."

Patty wasn't comfortable with this development. Not at all. Sure, plans change, they go astray, and you have to be prepared to make snap decisions, but this was inexcusable and she hated it when things got out of control. The two women she'd recruited at a local bar, months ago, had been strung out on meth and who knows how many other chemicals. Patty shook her head. She should've known better. All she needed was a couple of distractions, and to put her trust in two crackheads like Tess and Laura to show up on the right night at the right time, for a big payday, had probably been too much to ask.

"Are you armed?" she asked.

Dale shook his head. "No, ma'am. They said *you'd* be though, and we can see that."

"Two bullets, boys, and that's all it'll take. The scavengers will be plucking out your eyeballs before anyone finds you."

"Right as rain, ma'am. Whatever you need. And speaking of which, what the hell are we doing here?"

"They didn't tell you?"

The one called Harold lifted his broad shoulders to his ears and let them drop. "Said something about meeting this here lady on the back side of the Winthrop farm right about now. Said you'd tell us what to do."

Patty took a deep breath. It didn't feel right, but she couldn't think of a test to challenge them. Were these two goobers smart enough to deceive her, or were they dumb enough to show up for their wives, no matter what the women asked of them? "You have no idea why you're here?"

"All we know is, there's supposed to be some kind of reward."

Patty glanced over at Shelley. The young woman inhaled heavily through her nostrils, waiting, watching. Patty asked her, "You trust these two?"

"Maybe. Ask them where you met their wives."

Patty saw the two men exchange a fleeting look. "Well?"

"Down at Pickle's Bar and Grill."

The tension in her shoulders relaxed, but only slightly. He was right, yet it still didn't change the fact that she wasn't comfortable with the last minute switch. She said, "Okay. But I'm not happy about this so I'm cutting the payout in half, got it?"

"Yes, ma'am."

She took a step to the side and pointed at the fence section with the blocked laser. "Simple deal, guys. All we need you to do is cross the fence and run toward the Winthrop house. We need you to trigger the motion sensors and the thermal imaging cameras."

"That's it?"

"Yes."

"And what're you gonna be doing?"

Patty stepped an inch closer and aimed between Harold's eyes. "Ask me another question."

"Nah, I think I'm good."

"You run toward her house, then break off and get the hell out of there the second you see any indication that they're aware you're coming. Floodlights, alarms, whatever."

"That's it?"

"Yep."

Harold and Dale shrugged and started toward the fence. They approached too close to Patty. It made her wary. She put her finger back on the trigger.

Something had been tingling in the back of her mind. Something was off that she couldn't place...and then what Dale had said crossed her mind: "You the one they call Patty?"

She hadn't told Tess and Laura her name.

Dale took a darting step in her direction as she raised her gun.

Chapter Eighteen

Randall and Teddy retraced their steps carrying flashlights, several handguns, a bag full of MREs just in case they had to hunker down and ride out an assault, and a Barrett .50 caliber sniper rifle that Randall called "Goliath."

They ran as fast as they could go, carrying their cargo back up the road, because Randall had managed to overhear the two women talking once they'd gotten out of the car. The words, "Shock and awe sound good to you?" had sent chills down his spine, and once the women were gone, he and Teddy had debated on whether they should go back to the house or keep going.

In the end, they decided that the better option was arming themselves. Either they would get back in time to defend the property, or they would encounter the two women somewhere along the fence, trying to find a way inside, and Randall would easily be able to take them down with two wounding shots.

When they reached the edge of Sara's land, Randall backed up against the brick corner pillar and waited on Teddy to sidle up beside him. "Okay," he said, "stay behind me, stay smart, and stay quiet. Who knows where they went from here, but I can guaran-damn-tee you that it wasn't far, and they'll be close enough to get back on foot."

"How do you know that?"

"Because it's what I would do. If that Patty lady has had any kind of tactical training, she'll know that they'll be less visible on foot, so I'd bet my left nut they're coming in from the eastern side where the woods are the thickest. I'm hoping that Dale and Harold are in a position to keep an eye on them."

"Cool, yeah, but how will we know where your buddies are?"

"You know what a whippoorwill sounds like?"

"That's like a cousin to a Greyhound, right?"

Randall chuckled and shook his head. "Bird. Not a dog." He pursed his lips and offered a soft, lilting demonstration, enough for Teddy to hear and comprehend.

"Got it."

"You hear that, you'll know Dale and Harold have eyes on us. Drop and wait. One of them will come tell us where our two lady friends are hiding."

"Any last words of advice?"

"Yeah, keep your ass low, and your head lower. Time to rock, T-bird."

For a big man, Randall moved nimbly, gliding effortlessly back through the forest. He followed his own advice, keeping a low profile, moving from tree to tree and bush to bush in rapid spurts. If they'd had the time, he would've preferred a slower, more concealed approach, but that luxury wasn't possible. He recalled the days and weeks he'd spent in the jungles of South America or the deserts of the Middle East, remaining invisible to the enemy while he positioned himself for the perfect shot. Rain, heat, bugs, snakes, or nearly collapsing from exhaustion were never an issue. One shot, one kill, do it better next time.

He missed those days.

This was different.

How would Alice feel if she knew he was risking his life to protect strangers?

Angry, obviously. He could hear her now…"What about Jesse? What about me? You have a goddamn family to think about,

Randall. I thought you were done with stupid shit like this. After that game you played? Are you serious? We didn't think you were coming back to us. Not ever."

He understood what it must be like for her, but did she understand his need to defend against the bad guys, regardless of who they were, where they were, or what their motives might be? She never had. Not for as long as they'd been together. Yeah, participating in that damn game had been the dumbest decision he'd ever made, but he was alive, and that was all that mattered. He supposed that fighting back against the bad guys was a result of getting picked on so much growing up. He knew what it was like to be on that side of things, so whenever an opportunity arose to take down one of the bastards that was making someone else's life a living hell, then yes, sir, where should I sign?

Randall paused beside another brick pillar. Teddy flopped down beside him. Sweat poured from the little man's forehead, and Randall assumed it was from the nerves, because he wasn't even breathing hard. Randall asked, "You good?"

"You ever have to take a piss when you get nervous that's so bad, you can actually feel it sloshing around?"

"Nervous? *Pfft*. Never heard the word before."

"Figures. Why'd we stop?"

Randall flicked his chin northward. "About a hundred yards up. You see those two black masses on the ground?" Teddy peered around the edge. Randall grabbed his shoulder and pulled him back immediately. "Don't get your damn head shot off, T-bird. Just poke it out there a little."

Teddy did as he was instructed. "It's hard to tell, but I think so, yeah. What is it?"

"Dunno, but they weren't there when we came through the first time."

"Is it your buddies?"

"Let's find out." Randall puckered his lips and whistled like a whippoorwill. The three-tone chime went unanswered. He did it again, and still, no response. He grunted and handed Teddy his rucksack. "Take this a sec, would you? I'm gonna check it out with the scope."

He eased Goliath around the pillar and lowered his eye to the .50 cal's scope, then pushed the button to turn on night vision. He focused, took a deep breath, and saw what he feared had happened. "No," he said.

"What?"

"Move, move." Randall was on his feet and running before Teddy had a chance to ask why. Concern, not panic, gripped his lungs as he traversed the hillside while trying to maintain their cover.

As he approached the two black lumps, he cursed and dropped to the ground, made himself as flat as possible. Teddy joined him. They were too open, too exposed, and it wasn't smart, but as far as he could tell, they were too late.

Patty and Shelley had done their damage and were inside the property.

He army-crawled over and saw Dale's lifeless eyes staring up at the stars. Harold's, too. Both men, good men, were gone, the bullet holes in their foreheads a clear stamp that they'd met their ends too soon. "Son of a goddamn bitch," Randall said.

"Is that…"

"Yeah."

"Oh, God…I'm sorry…oh God, that sucks."

"We need to move." He felt Dale's cheek. "Still warm."

"Shouldn't we call the cops?"

"Unless you want to find everyone in the house like this, let's go. We'll make sad faces later. On second thought, can you talk and run?"

"Yeah."

"Then call the house. Let Sara know those two are on the farm already and we're coming."

"Got it."

Randall paused at the fence and examined the device the intruders had used to block the laser. Not too sophisticated, but high tech enough that the Kellog woman had to have some qualified connections and a good bankroll.

Behind him, Teddy explained the situation to Sara, then hung up. "She says they're ready. They'll be waiting for us at the door."

"Good. Now all we need to do is figure out which direction they went."

He surveyed the terrain, trying to decide which would be the safest way to get back to the others. From here, it was an open expanse of three acres straight across a hayfield to Sara's farmhouse.

They wouldn't have gone that way. Sure, they could've crossed it with ease—shortest distance between two points and all that—but even with the minimum ambient light, they would've been too out in the open. He assumed Patty was smarter than that. It was too revealing. She knew better. So, that meant they'd crossed, stayed close to the fence, and would approach from a more concealed route.

He put Goliath up to his shoulder and used the scope to examine the house. Everything appeared to be calm and quiet over there. Which was strange, now that he thought about it, because he recalled Sara mentioning that there were thermal imaging cameras stationed around the perimeter. Had the two women disabled them?

Surely, if Sara had been watching the monitors like she was supposed to, she would've seen the four people in this location and raised an alarm.

Right? So what happened?

How would the two women have known where those cameras were?

Did they have inside information?

Too many questions, too little time.

He'd paused for too long, because Teddy said, "Randall?"

He didn't see a path through the field where light boots had trampled rain-soaked hay, so he guessed his assumptions were correct. "We're going straight across. Point A to Point B, T-bird. Shortest distance."

"That seems dangerous, man. Out in the open like that? Why?"

"We're going that way because *they* didn't."

Randall scrambled over the fence. Teddy followed.

It wasn't the most concealed route, but from the looks of the entry wounds in Dale and Harold, the two women were carrying close-range, small-caliber weapons. They would want to move swiftly, quietly, and unencumbered, so the risk of a long-range rifle was minimal.

If he had a proper bead on Patty Kellog's style, she would approach with stealth, given the fact that they'd gone through the trouble of interrupting the laser. She and Shelley would rely on her skills as an assassin, rather than punching through with brute force. Cutting straight across the field managed to be the smartest and dumbest decision he and Teddy could make.

Time trumped caution.

Randall pumped his legs. His rucksack swung wildly on his back. He gripped Goliath tightly in his left hand and pulled a .45 semi-automatic pistol free from the holster at his waist. His footsteps pounded the soggy field as hay stalks rubbed against his thighs, soaking his jeans. Teddy caught up and nearly overtook him, then slowed by a half step to match his pace.

He didn't know if Teddy was smart enough to not take the position as lead runner, or if he'd simply held up so they could go together. If it was the former, he'd likely saved himself from taking a bullet first. "Zig zag," he told Teddy. "Harder to hit."

Two hundred yards and closing. Randall kept his eyes trained on the house as they angled back and forth across the open field, expecting to feel metal slugs penetrating his side at any moment.

Or, in the event of a lucky shot, he'd take one in the side of the head and never know it. He didn't want to risk looking around—somehow, in doing so, it felt like he would be jinxing the whole thing. Take a peek, welcome an open hole in his chest. He kept his head low and signaled for Teddy to cut left.

Fifty yards from the farmhouse. Almost there. The impending dread eased up slightly. They were close. "Right," he said, and angled north.

Teddy tracked him, took two steps, and then screamed in pain. At the same time, the sound of a gunshot echoed through the nearby hills.

Randall hunched over, turned, and watched as Teddy rolled, holding his shoulder. Teddy sprang back to his feet. Randall shouted, "You hit?"

"I'm okay. Go, go, go," Teddy said, pointing toward the house. "Grazed me."

They sprinted. As they dipped back and forth in a wild, angular pattern, Randall asked, "Where'd it come from?"

"Don't know. Behind, maybe."

Twenty yards away from the cover of Sara's home. Randall stopped, pivoted, and dropped to one knee. "Get inside."

"But—"

"Now, Teddy."

The two women could be anywhere. Randall lifted his .45 and before he squeezed the trigger, wet earth kicked up beside his leg. Too close. He fired once, twice, three times, the pops loud in his ears. He fired again, wildly. With acres and acres spread out in front of him, he was shooting blind.

Tool shed? Could they be in the tool shed? He fired at it, again and again, unsure if he'd hit anything. At this distance and lack of light, he couldn't be sure.

Another plume of earth kicked up to his left, even closer than the other one. Three inches from his foot, if that.

Gotta go, chief. No use. Can't tell where it's coming from.

He fired off two more shots and scrambled toward the house. Teddy crouched at the side entrance, holding the door open, frantically waving for Randall to hurry.

"Come on!" Teddy shouted.

"Get in there. I'm coming."

"Hurry."

Randall leaped over an overturned wheelbarrow and skirted a flowerbed. Thirty feet from the house and closing. Long, great strides covering yards with each new step. Almost there, two more steps, and then close to the porch—

The pain wasn't as bad as he remembered. He'd been shot before, but never in his hamstring. It was more like a sledgehammer slamming into the back of his leg. A thick, dull ache, combined with a force that pitched him forward and sent him down to the ground, rolling, and then hobbling back to his feet.

He reached the steps. Wood splintered to his right, then again.

He climbed.

He prayed.

Chapter Nineteen

From the side window of the old tool shed, Patty focused intently on Sara Winthrop's farmhouse. She waited patiently while Shelley paced back and forth, unable to stand in one place for more than five seconds. "Would you relax?" she said.

"I'm not nervous, I'm excited."

"That's fine, but Jesus, sit down before you make *me* nervous."

"Whatever." Shelley flopped down on a workbench, left leg bouncing like the needle of a sewing machine. "Can I pull the trigger?"

"What?" Patty turned to face her.

"You know, when we're ready. Let me do it."

Patty shook her head. "Sorry, hon, this one's mine. You can have all the rest, but Sara's got twenty years of messing with my brain to make up for."

Shelley stomped over to Patty and jammed a finger at the side of her own head. "I lost an eye, Patty. I'm a *monster* because of her."

Patty nodded slightly. "Yeah, there's that. Let me think about it."

"What're we gonna do first? What've you got in mind? I mean, we're here, shouldn't you tell me what your brilliant plan is?"

"Tic-Tac-Toe. Monopoly, maybe?"

"Be serious."

"You'll see." Patty returned her attention to the small window. The glass had broken out long ago, and aside from a few shards, she had a clear view into the cool night air. Down at the farmhouse, everything appeared to be normal. They'd reached her first planned destination unobserved, and now came the waiting. The two men that she and Shelley had killed troubled her. First, it meant that someone knew she and Shelley were coming. Back in Oregon, the police or the FBI had discovered where they'd gone and the information had leaked three thousand miles.

But, those two men weren't police or FBI. She'd checked for credentials and found nothing but two wallets, a can of Skoal, and some chewing tobacco. Maybe they weren't carrying identifications, but they were too far out of shape and too...country to be government stiffs.

Regardless, whoever they were, if those goons were Sara's first line of defense, patrolling the outer edges of her property, then she'd chosen poorly. However, it meant Sara was aware that she might be the target of a new attack.

First, Patty realized her plans would have to be altered. She'd had an elaborate scheme worked out wherein Sara would play yet another multi-level game, all in honor of Shelley. The babysitter would go first, then the children, and finally Sara, the idea being that she would be made to suffer through all of it, because the suffering would be infinitely worse than dying an easy death. She hated the idea of disappointing Shelley, but nothing could be done. Now there were too many unknown factors inside the Winthrop farmhouse.

Second, it meant that Sara was prepared for her and Shelley's arrival, which made the fact that no alarms had been raised yet all the more troubling. She couldn't figure it out. Maybe their equipment had worked as well as she'd hoped. They'd been invisible to the cameras; the laser hadn't alerted the security monitoring system; and so far, she saw no additional signs of law enforcement. Truly, it was strange all around.

Were the two men outside the boundary the only ones? Had they been placed there to maintain surveillance? The direction from which she and Shelley had entered was the most logical one—cover from the forest, closer to the house than other points on the compass—so it made sense that those men were in the area. Obviously they hadn't alerted anyone in the house before they approached.

It didn't make any goddamn sense. Was it a trap?

It had to be. If Sara knew she and Shelley were coming, then luring her in close enough to capture—or kill her—was the only remaining option. Otherwise, the place would be swarming with protection and they wouldn't have gotten within miles of the place.

Smart. Maybe.

Patty had the feeling they were being watched and scanned the interior of the tool shed for cameras. The place was clean. Based on the information she'd purchased, she already knew there wasn't one inside, but visual confirmation eased her sense of wariness.

Shelley said, "This isn't a 'need to know' thing, Patty. Tell me."

"Damn it, Shelley—I *don't* know, okay? Not anymore. Something doesn't feel right and I can't put a finger on what. I think they're pulling us into a trap and part of me wants to call it off. It's probably smarter for us to back out and come at her again some other time."

"What? No!"

"I'm serious. I say we walk. If you can smell the shit before you step in it, then it's time to take a different path." Patty could see the disappointment on the poor girl's face, but she hadn't made it this long in her line of work by giving in to pleading eyes.

Or eye, in Shelley's case.

No, it was best that they back out. Sara wasn't going anywhere. She would have to leave the house one day to shop for groceries, or take the kids to school, for anything, really, and they would strike then. Patty had been looking forward to taking care of business inside Sara's home where she thought she was safe and secure. Nothing would've been more satisfying than to watch the terror in her eyes as they swaggered through the front door unannounced. With the opportunity slipping away, she felt a bit of sadness in her chest, but decided that the disappointment was better than iron bars and a lumpy cot.

Shit. Time wasted. Money wasted. Eight months of prep, gone. Maybe now would be a good time for a vacation.

Well, after she had a west-coast friend eliminate her inside contact at the security company that installed Sara's system. Bill Chester, doting husband, father of three, subject to taking large bribes to flip some switches at a predetermined time, would need to be dead by morning.

Patty sighed, checked her watch, and felt two hands clamp around her throat.

Squeezing tightly, Shelley hissed, "That bitch dies tonight, and you are *not* taking this away from me." She shoved Patty up against the wall. Rusted tools with rotting wooden handles—a tobacco hatchet, a saw, and a post-hole digger—rattled where they hung. The table Patty sat on tipped back and stopped at an odd angle.

Patty fought for her breath, feeling fingers contracting around her windpipe, clawing at Shelley's arms. She looked up into a single, determined eye. Spittle flew from her mouth as she managed to get her arms under Shelley's, and using a foot against the table for leverage, she brought her hands up. She shoved and broke the hold. Then, with the other foot, her boot went to Shelley's chest, kicking, thrusting as hard as she could, driving her back.

Shelley tripped on a shovel and went down.

Patty spun around and reached for her firearm, with full intention of putting a bullet through Shelley's forehead. She'd grown attached to the girl, but there was no room in her life for complications like that; retaliate against a wrong and move on. Shelley would die in the tool shed, and Patty would mourn for a pathetic second, then get on with her life. Sara would still be here and other opportunities for retribution would arise in the future.

Her fingers closed around the pistol grip. She heard Shelley trying to get to her feet behind her.

Movement outside caught her eye. Through the window, she saw two hunched figures sprinting across the field, toward the farmhouse. For a moment she thought she was seeing ghosts—Dale and Harold come back to life to warn Sara—then she realized these were two *different* men. One much larger, one much smaller. Who were these guys? Two more sentries that had been posted?

She aimed, leading her target, and fired.

The smaller one dropped, rolled, and sprang up to his feet. He ran, holding his shoulder.

Patty felt Shelley's arm around her neck, yanking her backward. She swung an elbow, driving it into soft ribs. Shelley grunted and went down. Patty hesitated, then drove the butt of her pistol into Shelley's temple.

Knocked out, her body flopped to the side.

Back to the window, seconds later, the small man had made it to the house. The larger one was on his knee, firing wildly.

She fired and missed. Fired again and missed another time. She watched as he focused his attention on the tool shed. Shots rang out. Wood splintered outside the walls.

She ducked until he stopped firing, risked a glance, and saw him sprinting through the yard, leaping a wheelbarrow. He moved so fast for his size.

Patty fired yet again and sent the large man to the ground. As he crawled, clutching his leg, she fired again and again, missing, watching him duck and cover his head. She fired until the magazine was empty and reached for another, but the delay was enough to permit their escape.

When she looked again, the last she saw of them was the larger man limping through the door as it swung closed behind him.

She cursed and pounded a fist on the table. She clenched her teeth.

Shelley.

The girl lay on the ground, unconscious, and when Patty nudged her with a boot, she stirred, groaning softly as she tried to sit up.

Patty pushed her back down, straddled her, and held the barrel of her firearm an inch away from the tip of Shelley's nose. She grabbed a handful of Shelley's hair and yanked hard, twisting and pulling her face closer. "Stupid asshole," she said. "You—you are a stupid asshole. Give me one reason why I shouldn't pull the trigger. Just one, because I am *this close* to dropping you right here. I'll do it. I *will* do it. Understand me?"

Shelley winced. Her nostrils flared. She eyed Patty and remained silent.

"Nothing? Huh? Nothing? You *want* me to do it, don't you?"

One heartbeat, two heartbeats, three heartbeats pounded inside Patty's skull. "I'll do it," she said, but she wasn't sure that she actually would, now that she held Shelley's pitiable life in her hands. One finger, one trigger, one second, and it would be over.

Patty felt the anger roiling in her stomach. She'd never hesitated before. She'd survived by being ruthless, so what was this? Why couldn't she do it? Why couldn't she rid herself of this troublesome...*gnat*?

Was it care? Was it feeling? Was it some godforsaken emotional attachment?

"Sorry," Shelley whimpered.

And that was enough.

Patty got up and pulled Shelley to her feet, by her hair—not coddling her, she didn't deserve it—but for now she'd keep her alive. "I know how badly you want this, but so help me God, if you ever, ever do anything like that again...finger, trigger, bullet. Dead, done, gone."

Shelley nodded and brushed Patty's hand away from her hair. "I...I couldn't control myself. I don't know where it came from."

"Use it on them, *not* me."

"I know."

"You have to learn to be in charge of yourself. You don't know shit about me. You don't know the things I've done. You don't know the things I'm capable of. I'm not some little tart in prison that you can push around. I'm not one of your weakling…victims. Do you understand that *I* am death?"

"Yes."

"Good. Now while you were out, two more armed men ran into the house. Who knows how many more are in there and what kind of arsenal they have. We don't know if we're trapped in here and there are fifty scopes on us right now, we don't know anything, Shelley, and the only thing I can guarantee is that"—she checked her watch—"in about six minutes, the entire security system is going down. So let me ask you something: are you ready to die for this tonight? Are you going to be that stupid, or do we walk and come back when we know what we're up against?"

Shelley shrugged.

"We survive by being smart. It's worked for me for twenty years."

"We can be smart and still do this."

"How, huh? Explain it to me."

Shelley nodded at a gas can sitting on the floor. "We flush them out with that."

"Are you going to spit fire to ignite it?"

"Funny, but no. There are waterproof matches with that camping gear over there in the corner." Shelley pointed at a rolled up tent, four walking sticks, some outdoor chairs, and a red emergency bag full of supplies.

"Okay, but how do you plan to get to the house?"

"Like you said, when the security system goes down, they'll be distracted and panicked, right? We do it then."

"But what if someone puts a bullet in your head on the way there?"

"Think about it, Patty. You're supposed to be the smart one, aren't you? If there were more people out here, we'd be dead already, or the FBI would be dropping in with helicopters, whatever. Nobody's coming. My guess is, it's Sara, her kids, that wrinkled old babysitter, and then the two men you saw running inside."

"And both of them are wounded." She had to admit, Shelley had a point.

The fact that they weren't dead yet meant they still had a chance.

Chapter Twenty

Sara stood over Teddy and tried to keep an eye out the back window, carefully watching the tool shed, wondering how Patty and Shelley had gotten inside. Teddy had been right. For all the money she'd spent on protecting her home, her family, someone with enough motive and resources had easily been able to get inside.

After a heated exchange between the group, and at Randall's insistence and Mary's confirmation, they'd chosen not to call the police. They had a better chance of ending this thing once and for all without the added intrusion of local law enforcement. Too many rules, too many restrictions, and yet another avenue for Patty and Shelley to live another day.

Sara had agreed to it, but wondered if they'd made the right decision.

Teddy was lying on her kitchen table, bleeding from the wound in his shoulder. As he'd thought, the bullet only grazed him. Irina poured hydrogen peroxide on it and cleaned the area around the bloody mess. In the living room, Randall hadn't been quite as lucky. Mary helped with his wound. Thankfully, the bullet had passed through his thigh, but the damage would need medical attention.

When that would happen was anyone's guess.

What a mess her life had become in the span of one single day. Again. Sara fought the tears that threatened to blur her vision yet again. When would it ever stop?

Tonight. It had to be tonight.

She wanted to be with her kids. Miss Willow had them in the panic room. Shut, locked and secure. Nothing short of a nuclear bomb would be able to harm them, and Sara felt safe in knowing that if anything happened to her or the rest of the group, then her children and Miss Willow could last for days in there; plenty long enough for help to arrive.

"Does it hurt?" Sara asked Teddy.

"Yes and…ouch! Honey, don't be so rough." Irina apologized and continued dabbing with the wet rag.

"How'd they get in, Teddy?"

"Some crazy device that blocked the lasers. We found it on the way back and my God, Sara, at first we thought they were already here because two of Randall's friends are dead back there in the woods."

"What?"

"Yeah, he'd called them in to help with surveillance, but it looks like Patty and Shelley got to them before they could warn us."

"Oh no, those poor guys." Sara's lip trembled. Two more people dead because of her. Two more people dead that had been trying to help a stranger. How high would the body count go?

"It was awful," Teddy said. He winced again as Irina applied a bandage. "We started sprinting as fast as we could because we thought for sure we'd get here and you guys would be dead. I've never been so damn scared, Sara. I thought we'd lost everyone and it was our fault for being idiotic enough to leave you guys alone." He managed to lift his wounded arm, put it around Irina, and pulled her close, kissing her hard on the lips. "Thank God you're okay."

"For now," Irina said, finishing up the bandage. She helped Teddy sit up.

In the living room, Randall cursed and said, "Easy, dammit. That ain't a piece of ham back there. And y'all in there in the kitchen, keep an eye on the shed, but don't stand right in front of the windows."

Irina kept watch while Sara and Teddy followed the sound of more curses and Randall's hissing as Mary tried to stop the blood flow. She wrapped a thick layer of gauze around his leg. If they weren't in danger, the sight might've been amusing—Randall, former Marine sniper and hardened country boy, lying on his stomach with his pants around his ankles. Tighty-whities on full display.

"T-bird," he said. "Looks like you got the better end of the deal."

"Sorry about that. Thanks for saving my life."

"Shit, son, it wasn't me. As fast as those little legs of yours were moving, you probably outran the rest of the bullets. Ow, dammit. Easy, Mary."

"Don't be such a pansy," Mary said. She finished tying the tourniquet around his thigh. "All done."

Randall hobbled to his feet as he pulled his pants back up. "New plan," he said. "No sense in trying to lead them away from here with the cars. If we set one single foot outside these doors, we'll get a toe shot off, or worse yet, something else."

"You can't run anyway," Mary reminded him.

"Right. So, seems to me, the best plan is for you guys to head down to the panic room with the young'ns and wait it out until the reinforcements arrive. You said your cop buddy and the feds had people on the way, right?"

Sara nodded. "He said so, but where are they?"

"With the kind of equipment these two have, it's a good possibility they got in undetected, so surely, if they didn't trigger your Fort Knox security system, some dude sitting behind a desk up in

FBI headquarters, watching a monitored satellite feed didn't pick up on it either."

"Right. So if we all hide in the panic room and wait it out—"

"Not me. *You*."

Sara shook her head. "No way. You're not fighting this battle for me. I mean, my God, Randall, you barely know us. You too, Mary. There's plenty enough room in there for everyone to hide."

Randall shook his head. "Remember what we said earlier? You let the government get their hands on this woman, she'll walk in three to five and you'll be right back in this situation. No doubt about it. We gotta fight back, Sara. Again, that's why we said no cops. My trigger finger is getting twitchy, my damn leg hurts, and I'm gonna shoot to kill."

"Then I'm doing it with you, and you're not changing my mind. My house, my kids, my rules."

"Me too," Teddy said. "They shot me."

"I'm staying," Irina added from her spot in the kitchen. "They shot my husband. My family…we don't run from that."

Sara watched Randall waffle over this in his mind. He grunted. "Fine, but you all need to stay out of the way. Don't make yourself an easy target and don't even think about opening a door. T-bird, what I'll need you to do is stay with me. You know your way around a gun, so you'll be down here and we'll catch them on the way in. They didn't come all this way to hang out in a damn shed and then retreat. Okay by you?"

"Roger that, boss."

Randall continued, "Mary, you keep an eye on Sara and do recon from upstairs. These two ladies will get impatient soon enough and after that," he said, snapping his fingers, "shoot to kill. One and done."

Sara took a deep breath and felt her lungs tighten with anticipation. Was this really it? The final showdown? She wanted to believe Barker, that the FBI would swoop in and save them from Patty

Kellog and Shelley Sergeant, and that they would never have to worry about it again, but what Randall had said made sense. Behind closed doors, where deals were made, Patty was worth more alive than dead, regardless of whether or not she'd been trying to murder an innocent family.

Even if she tried to call Barker to let him know, would her call get through while he was on the flight?

She didn't have time to consider it. They had to move forward *now*. Randall was right. There would be no mercy for her enemies.

"Sounds like a plan," she said, "but I'm not hiding. I can shoot."

"Sara…there ain't no way I'm letting you—" He stopped mid-sentence as the lights went out. A beat later, a generator rumbled to life outside and the red glow of emergency lighting illuminated the house. "They cut the power?"

"Not from outside, no. There were too many redundancies built in."

"Then how?"

Teddy said, "The bigger question is, we've got lights, but the security system is backed up to the generator, right?"

"It's supposed to be," Sara said. "But…oh Jesus."

"What?"

"As far as I know, the systems had to be shut down internally."

Randall asked, "Meaning what?"

"The security company. She must have somebody on the inside." Sara put her hand to her forehead. "Irina, can you do me favor?"

"Of course."

"Run downstairs and check the monitors that I showed you earlier. Plus, there's a control board off to the right. Let us know if everything seems like it's on."

"Got it." Irina dashed over to the doorway leading down to the basement and disappeared around the corner.

Teddy asked, "You think Patty paid someone off?" He took Irina's place, surveying the back yard from a kitchen window.

Sara nodded.

"And we're sitting ducks?"

"Maybe."

Mary removed her pistol from its holster, grabbed Sara's arm, and pulled. "Come with me."

"What're we doing?"

"Upstairs. We need distance between you and them. You guys okay down here?"

Randall saluted Mary and Teddy copied him. Randall hobbled into the kitchen with Teddy on his heels.

From down in the basement, Irina called up. "Sara?"

"Everything okay?"

"All the monitors are out. No lights on the control board either."

Sara covered her mouth as Mary tugged on her arm. "Oh God."

Irina said, "Do you want me to come up or should I help Miss Willow with the kids?"

"Oh God, oh God, uh...please go stay with them. Do not open that door for anything, not until you hear me again, and me only. You know the code, right?"

"Yes," Irina called back, her voice trailing off as she raced to the far end of the basement.

"Will it work with the power off?" Mary asked. "Can she get in?"

"Yeah, the panic room has its own power and operates totally independent of the rest of the house. I made sure that they made it possible because I didn't want anyone being able to short the system and take control of it."

"Perfect, but we need to move, now."

Sara paused, resisting against Mary's coaxing grip. She couldn't decide whether it was more important to be with her children at the moment, locked inside the panic room where it was safe, or outside with the rest of them, fighting her own battles. If anything happened to her—and she prayed that it wouldn't—then Miss Willow would be their legal guardian. Beyond that, Teddy and Irina had offered their care.

"Should I go be with them?" she asked Mary.

"Your call. We can handle it, definitely."

"But if something happens to one of you…" Total strangers, risking their lives for her, while her children were locked inside a steel box which was a foot thick, capable of withstanding Armageddon.

Go, stay. Go, stay. Go, fight.

A deep rage welled inside her. She'd been angry before, upset and scared, but this was pure wrath—flaming snakes slithering around inside her chest.

No more. This is it. I'm sick of this shit. They've made our lives hell for too long, and I want to watch them burn.

She said to Mary, "Give me a gun."

"No, Sara, it's better that—"

"Gun, Mary."

Mary nodded. She pulled a snub-nosed .38 from her ankle holster and gave it to Sara. "You know how to use that?"

"Point and pull the trigger. How hard can it be?"

"Up you go."

Sara took the steps in twos while Mary followed, unable to climb as fast, damaged leg holding her back. Step, push with the cane, and then do it again.

Up on the second floor, Sara threw open Jacob's bedroom door. His window had the best view of the rear of the property, especially the tool shed in the distance. She put her back against the wall and eased her head around to survey the back yard.

Mary joined her on the opposite side. "See anything?"

"Nothing yet. I didn't realize that row of pine trees was in the way. I can only see half the building."

Downstairs, she heard Randall and Teddy opening two of the windows, followed by silence. They waited, listening intently, watching for Patty or Shelley to rush for the house. Sara's breathing was heavy, partly in anticipation, partly from bitter seething.

If she got the chance, she hoped she would be the one to end it. But, maybe it was better to let Randall or Mary take care of it— maybe even Teddy—as long as she got to watch. How dare these two evil beasts try to ruin her life, her children's lives, all because they held grudges for things Sara hadn't done.

She hadn't *made* Brian want to leave Shelley.

She hadn't been the one to force Patty into the mental institution. She'd been there, she'd been a witness, but she was innocent. She'd spent a lot of time in therapy to convince herself of that after Patty's last assault.

Stupid, petty, resentful motherfuckers. Come into my house. Do it. I dare you.

Downstairs, Randall raised his voice in warning. "We've got movement. One bogey moving from the northeast. No clear line, Mary. You got a shot?"

Mary took a firing position and examined the area. "No shot. Pine trees in the way."

"Find a north-facing window," he shouted. "I'm sending Teddy that way down here. Whichever one it is, looks like she's carrying a gas can."

"Not good," Mary said. "Sara, you go across the hall. Use that window, and let me know if you see her."

"Okay." Sara darted out the door in front of Mary, swinging around the top of the stairs with one hand on a banister. She flew into her master bedroom, slung back the curtains, and opened the window. One quick peek outside—she saw nothing—and then she pulled her head back in.

Sara held steady, tried to control her breathing, and looked again.

Nothing.

Two shots boomed below, trailed by Teddy's voice. "I missed! I missed! Northwest corner, Sara, hurry!"

One, two, three shots from Mary in the north-facing bathroom. "Shit!"

Sara leaned out the window and down below her, thirty feet away, stood Shelley Sergeant holding a can of gas with her back against the western side of the house.

"Got you." Sara aimed and felt the trigger moving underneath her finger.

Chapter Twenty-One

Sara squeezed the trigger harder and felt it give. The shot boomed and made her ears ring. Down below, Shelley screamed as the bullet ripped a hole in the siding, missing her head by inches. Sara fired again, and a crater opened in a cinderblock near Shelley's feet. Sara cursed and steadied her aim with both hands.

Shelley covered her head with one arm and scrambled for safety, pouring the gas along the ground as she went.

Sara fired a third time and missed yet again.

Three more steps and Shelley flung herself forward, diving underneath the front porch.

Sara screamed, "Randall!"

"You get her?"

"No, she made it under the front porch, still has the gas can with her."

"We're on it. Teddy? Come watch the back yard."

Sara listened to them changing positions downstairs; Randall's boots thumping across the hardwood floors. His steps were erratic, evidence of his wounded leg. She ran out of her bedroom, down the hall, and into the northernmost bathroom, hoping for a better angle. She could see down the edge of the porch, but there was no sign of Shelley.

Outside, in the hallway, Mary thumped along with her bum leg and cane, heading back to the first room with the view of the shed.

Sara called after her. "Mary? What do we do?"

"Stay there. Let Randall try to flush her out from downstairs. If she makes a break for it from your side, don't be shy about pulling that trigger."

"No chance of that."

"Don't forget to lead her a little. Shoot where she's going to be—whoa, movement! Movement back at the shed! Teddy, where are you?"

His calm voice traveled up the stairs. "I see her."

Pop, pop, pop.

"Missed! Damn it, she's fast!"

"Where's she going?"

"Moving toward the south side of the house."

"Sara," Mary said, "what's around there? Anything she can use for cover?"

Sara tried to remember but her mind went blank. Jesus, why couldn't she remember what was on the south side of her own house?

Empty, her mind was empty, and she couldn't recall a picture of what was—yes! "Nothing but a dogwood tree, but she can get under the front porch from that side, too."

"Get there, Teddy," Mary said.

"On it."

"Randall?...Randall?"

Sara could sense the growing panic in Mary's voice. She stuck her head out the window, craning her neck to see underneath the porch. The front screen door slammed and beneath the awning, she saw Randall's lower half, moving cautiously. She tried to whisper loudly across the hall. "I see him. He's okay."

At the south side of the house, Sara heard the sound of breaking glass, followed by the *pop, pop* of Teddy's handgun. He screamed, "Got her! Wait, no. Son of a bitch. She's moving."

Across the hallway, Mary shouted, "Sara, tell Randall to back out. Back out now!"

Sara didn't hesitate. She screamed, "Get in the house, Randall."

Shots were fired from a distance, too far away to be Randall. Underneath the awning, she watched him pitch to the side, spin, and fall. He climbed up to his hands and knees, jumped, propelling himself through the open doorway just as orange flames began to lick up from underneath the porch. She stood, mesmerized, watching how quickly the wood became engulfed, travelling down the side of the house. The fact that it had rained didn't seem to make a difference. The siding took to the flame like dry kindling in a fireplace.

Sara screamed, "Fire!" and ran for the door. She hit the top of the stairs as Mary came out of the bedroom. "Front of the house is going up."

"It's already around the back, too."

"What do we do?" she asked, descending the stairs.

"As far as we know, they're trapped under the front porch. We get to a spot where we can monitor both open ends and catch them when they come out. Porch is on fire, they'll have nowhere to go."

Sara shook her head. "Not true."

"What?"

"There's a small entrance under the porch that leads to the crawl space. It's like, maybe twenty square feet where a lot of the piping is, but they can get into the basement from there."

At the bottom of the steps, they found Teddy and Randall together in the living room, watching out the front picture window.

Sara said, "Randall, are you hurt? Did she get you?"

"I'm good, but I was about a half inch away from catching lead with my teeth. Did I hear you say they can get into the basement from under the front porch?"

"Yeah."

"So that means they're already in the house."

"Would they climb *into* a burning house?" Teddy asked.

Mary said to him, "They know we've got them covered from outside. They get into the basement, there's more room to hide."

Randall asked, "And they for sure can't get into the panic room, right?"

"Not a chance."

"And it's fireproof all around? Like if this house went up in flames, it wouldn't melt the wiring or get into the ventilation system in there, anything like that?"

"No. They're safe."

"Good." He moved toward the door leading down to the basement.

"Where are you going?" Mary asked.

"To shoot some people."

"Hang on a sec," Teddy said. "If they're inside the house, and it's burning, and then everyone is safe in the panic room, why don't we go outside and wait on them? Unless they want to die in here, they'll try to get out, won't they?"

Randall grinned. "I'll be damned, T-bird, that actually makes some sense." He put a hand on Sara's shoulder. "You got anything in this house you wanna rescue before we roast some marshmallows on it?"

There wasn't much time to think. Outside, the flames had crawled up the siding and had reached the windows. In a few seconds, their escape routes would be cut off. After Patty had blown up Sara's last home in Portland, all of their personal things that held memories had evaporated. Since they'd been here in southwest Virginia, they hadn't had much time to build a life or to create memories. They had new furniture, new rooms, new clothes, but no roots.

Sara shook her head. "Let it burn."

. . .

They went out the rear entrance. Randall led the way, followed by Mary, Teddy, then Sara. The flames were lighter in back because Shelley had only managed to get a small amount of gas on that side of the house. Randall looked left and right, checked again, and led them out. "Clear," he said.

Sara was too far away, but she swore she could feel the heat on her cheeks.

Maybe it was fear instead of fire.

Teddy said, "How do we know they're in the basement already?"

"We don't," Randall answered. "Somebody's gotta go check. Let's put a little distance between us first. Mary, you take the north side. Teddy, south, and then Sara, you get over there to that little outbuilding. What's in there?"

"Lawnmower," she answered.

"All right, get in there, and I only want you to stick your nose out if you got a shot, okay? And don't get your nose shot off in the process."

"Where are you going?"

"To check under the front porch."

"Be careful," Mary said. "Be a hero all you want, but you're going home tonight."

"Yes, ma'am. No doubt about it."

Sara watched them hug—their bond was unmistakable after what they'd been through the previous year. She'd gotten some of the details from Mary while Randall and Teddy were gone, and the pure insanity of that situation would've hardened anyone. When all of this was over, she'd be sure to sit down with Randall and exchange stories about the deadly games they'd both played.

She stood and watched the flames dance up the side of the house and a strange feeling came over her. How absurdly odd was it knowing that her children—and Miss Willow, and Irina—were inside a house that was about to become a smoldering pile of charred ash, yet they were completely safe?

Regardless of the hundreds of thousands of dollars she'd spent on a security system that Patty and Shelley had infiltrated easily, the panic room was the smartest decision she'd made concerning their safety.

She hated to watch the house go. She'd grown to love it and the property over the past few months, but maybe it was a blessing. A moment of finality, signifying the end to her fears, her past, and these godforsaken games.

Let it burn, she'd said.

Damn right.

She felt Teddy's arms around her. He said, "You be safe," and kissed the side of her forehead. She returned the embrace and told him to do the same. "And," she added, "so help me God, if you let anything happen to yourself and I have to face Irina's wrath, I will hunt you down in the afterlife and kick your scrawny little ass."

"If that happens, Irina will beat you to it."

"Time's wasting," Randall said. "Everybody ready?"

Three heads nodded in unison.

"Shoot to kill," he said. "If the feds don't know yet that these two are here, who knows when the cavalry will show up. We can't let them get their hands on Patty."

Teddy jogged south, using the row of pine trees as concealment. Mary hobbled north, pushing herself with her cane around the flowerbeds, staying low behind the snowball bushes and the cherub water fountain. Randall, who must have been high on adrenaline, moved faster than a man with a bullet hole in his leg should've been able to. He went straight for the house, cut north, holding his pistol down by his waist, and then vanished around the side. The last Sara saw of him was the vestige of his body behind the orange flames.

She took one last look at the house, sighed, and then jogged over to the outbuilding.

Inside, it smelled like oil and wet rags. She crouched and left the door open just enough to get a view of the house. She couldn't see Mary from her position, but to the south, Teddy squatted behind a lilac bush. She watched him peek through the branches, carefully observing, with his 9mm Glock up and ready.

She put a knee down on the ground to balance herself. The dirt floor felt cool through her jeans. She'd been meaning to have concrete poured, but hadn't gotten around to it. Now, as the flames engulfed her home, it seemed like such an innocuous thing to fret about. She hadn't heard any shots from Randall yet, so they had to have retreated to the basement.

How much longer would Shelley and Patty last inside? What were they doing?

Were they now doubting their decision? It hadn't been the wisest approach. Surely they'd had other plans. Perhaps another game for her and her children, but had the presence of Randall and Teddy thrown them off course?

Thank God she'd approached Randall, and then Randall had called Mary in—if it hadn't been for the two of them, everyone—she and the kids, Miss Willow, Teddy and Irina—would likely be dead.

Small miracles. Timing. Good people.

Those things saved lives.

A porch column collapsed and the overhang slumped to one side. The entirety of the exterior was nearly covered in flames and had begun to spread inside. Soon, the heat would be unbearable.

How long before one of the neighbors noticed and called the fire department. Sara knew there were no full time firemen on staff— they were all volunteers who lived in the surrounding area. What was their average response time if they had to get the call, get from their homes to the fire station, and then all the way out here on the outskirts of town? Fifteen minutes at the least, right?

Could Patty and Shelley last that long inside? Could they wait it out?

What would happen if the fire department arrived and two armed and highly dangerous murderers were still alive in her basement? What then?

Would they surrender? Would they shoot their way out?

Patty probably knew that the government would keep her alive for information. She would surrender and live to fight another day. But Shelley, that crazy girl had a death wish. Hadn't her brother Michael told her that back in the cabin, during the game, ages ago? That Shelley wasn't afraid of death? Or had that been a part of the dreams that haunted her since?

A window shattered from the heat on the second floor. Sara watched the flames overtake Jacob's curtains.

As the fire lit up the night sky, she held her breath and waited, wanting nothing more than the chance to shoot first.

Chapter Twenty-Two

Patty shoved Shelley as hard as she could, watching as the one-eyed girl sailed backward and fell into the pool table. Shelley hit with enough force that her legs lifted off the ground, sending her on top of it, scattering pool cues and balls across the green felt. "Any more genius ideas?"

Shelley groaned and rolled off the pool table, holding her lower back.

Patty marched over, grabbed her by the hair, and yanked her hard to the side. "Come here. Come look at this." She dragged a dazed Shelly over to a large metal door and then pounded on it with her fist. "You see that? Panic room. I don't know who's in there and my guess is it's her little parasites, but you know what? It doesn't matter, because we're not getting in there, and instead, we're trapped in the goddamn basement of a burning fucking house, you idiot."

Shelley tried to pull free, reaching for Patty's face.

Patty thrust her head to the side, held on, and dragged Shelley to the side and slammed her against the wall. "I don't know why I thought I might care about someone so stupid. I trusted you. I thought you were better than this, and now you've gotten us trapped down here. I don't even know how many people were up there, and they sure as hell aren't any more. Three? Four, five, ten? How many,

Shelley? If you'd listened to me, we could've walked away. We could be meeting my guy and we could be on our way out of the country, but no, I let you talk me into this reckless—God, what was I thinking, huh?" Patty clenched her jaws so tightly, her head hurt. "And then...I couldn't let you go. I had to come make sure you weren't dead. So that's my fault. Right? That's on me. What do we do now, huh? Tell me, Shelley, what's next? Do we die down here in the fire, or do we die trying to shoot our way out?"

"Let me go," Shelley whimpered, "and I'll show you something."

"It better be good." Patty released Shelley's hair, but finished with a hand to her face, and a hard shove against the wall before backing away. "Show me what?"

Shelley moved over to the control panel on the exterior of the panic room. A standard keypad, numbered zero through nine, along with alphabetized letters sat in a receding hole in the wall. "People are creatures of habit, right?"

"I suppose."

"How many different passwords do you use for all of your accounts?"

"The house is burning down, we don't have time for twenty questions."

"Seriously, how many?"

Patty shook her head and put her hands on her hips. "Three, at the most. Same password for email addresses or bank accounts, same PIN for ATMs or anything like..." The realization hit her. "No, you don't think she would..."

Shelley winked with her remaining eye. "I worked for her. I was her secretary, her lackey, her errand girl and her whipping post for so long. Do this for me, do that for me, pick up my kids, pick up my dry cleaning, can you get twenty bucks in cash out for me...same old shit, all the time, and *in* that time, you want to know how many different passwords and PINs she used? Two. Two, and that's it. The idiot kept her stupid email password written on a yellow sticky note beside her computer at work. Yeah, she was some kind of marketing genius, but she couldn't remember her own phone number or what color shirt—"

"The house is burning, the house is burning, the house is burning! Stop being The History Channel and open it up."

Shelley held a hand above the keypad and paused, her finger hovering over the first number. "What if it doesn't work?"

"Then I shoot you in the head and take my chances."

"Fair enough." She punched in the sequence, reciting the numbers as she went. "One, eight, four, eight. Her dead husband was dumb enough to use the same one, too. Here goes…" Shelley pressed the green button on the lower right side of the panel.

A set of red LED lights blinked three times in rapid succession, then went green, one by one. The door slid to the side, revealing three frightened children, Miss Willow the babysitter, and a woman that Patty had never seen before. No Sara, and neither of the two wounded men.

Miss Willow and the children recoiled when they saw Shelley standing in the doorway with a demented smile.

"Hi, guys," Shelley said as she waved. "Remember me?"

Patty had a feeling that those four words were the most frightening ones the children had ever heard. When they began to scream, she knew she was right. Patty had to laugh. She said to Shelley, "I thought panic rooms were supposed to *cure* panic, huh?"

"I know, right?"

Sara's kids squeezed as close to Miss Willow as they possibly could, wailing those annoying sirens of fear. Mouths wrenched down and to the side in terror, clinging to the old woman's sweater.

Miss Willow said, "I knew the Devil would come back one of these days."

Shelley chuckled. "Speak of her and she shall appear."

The blonde woman said, "Get away from us."

"Who're you?"

"Teddy's wife. My name is Irina."

"Sucks to be you," Patty said. "Out. All of you. Out, now!" She waved her gun, and when none of them moved, she lifted it and fired two shots into the ceiling. The children screamed and covered their ears. Miss Willow scrambled to her feet, pulling the twins with her, while the woman named Irina helped the little boy get up.

Miss Willow asked, "Is that smoke? Is the house on fire?"

Shelley laughed. "It is, and we need to get out of here now. Even the Devil gets warm in Hell."

"You...you...evil—"

Shelley grabbed the old woman's arm, pulled her close, and put the barrel of her handgun against Miss Willow's forehead. "You can die right here, or you can help us get the children outside, then you die. Choose."

"Okay, okay. I'll help, just don't hurt them. Please."

"That's what I thought."

Patty said to Irina, "You, up the stairs. Go see if the fire's blocking any of the doors."

"No."

Patty pointed her gun, pulled the trigger, and shot a hole in the floor near Irina's feet. Irina screamed and jumped backward. Patty said, "Go find us a way out, or you die right here. *We* don't need you, but they do." Patty pointed at Sara's children. "Go. And believe me, if you run, or try to come back down here with some kind of weapon, anything stupid like that, I will not think twice about pulling the trigger on one of these little beauties."

"I understand." Irina kissed Lacey, Callie, and Jacob on the head. "I'll be right back. We're gonna go find Mommy, okay?" All three nodded. Irina dashed across the basement and up to the ground floor.

Smoke drifted in from crevices and air ducts.

Patty said to Shelley, "Over to the stairs. We need to be ready."

Shelley put a hand on Miss Willow's back and shoved, then grabbed Jacob's arm and dragged him with her. Patty followed with the twins.

They congregated at the bottom of the steps as Miss Willow tried to comfort the coughing children. Above, Patty listened to the panicked footsteps as Irina ran back and forth. Maddening seconds ticked by as they waited. She'd sent Irina to go look, assuming that she would need Shelley downstairs to help her keep an eye on Miss Willow and the children, and now, that didn't seem to be the wisest option. Would Irina be selfish enough to escape and leave them behind? Would she be stupid enough to hunt for a weapon while she was up there?

I should've sent Shelley. God, what was I thinking?

Patty said, "She's got ten seconds, Shelley, then you're going after her."

"Okay."

Patty counted to herself. Something crashed against the floor overhead. Was it furniture collapsing? Were the walls caving in already?

She could feel the smoke seeping into her lungs. It burned when she breathed and tasted like ashes on her tongue. She watched as Miss Willow helped the children hold their shirts over their noses and mouths. Up the stairs and out one of the doors would be easier, but should they risk trying to escape the way she and Shelley had entered, through the crawlspace?

"Shelley," she said, "get up there."

And before her partner could move, the blonde woman appeared at the top of the stairs. "Back door, let's go!"

"Is it clear?"

"Barely." She glanced to her side and frantically waved them up. "Hurry!"

Patty and Shelley grabbed, dragged, and pulled Miss Willow and the children along, their footsteps pounding up and up to where the smoke hung thick and the orange flames enveloped the walls, the furniture, and the curtains. The heat was intense, unlike anything she'd ever felt before. When they all emerged into the living room, Patty shoved Irina and Miss Willow, and held her gun to their faces. "Lead us out."

They paused, exchanging knowing looks. They were one doorway from their deaths.

"Move," Patty said. "Die here or help us get them outside."

Irina and Miss Willow moved toward the rear of the house, hunched over beneath the layer of smoke. They stayed toward the center of the living room, avoiding the fire, and then scampered across the hallway, through the kitchen, and up to the back door.

Shelley yelped and swung her arm. She'd brushed against something and her sleeve was on fire. She slapped at it until the flames disappeared.

Irina touch the doorknob and hissed. "It's too hot," she said.

"Do something," Patty ordered.

Irina turned her shoulder and forced herself against the door. It flew outward and banged against the outside wall, sending a shower of embers floating through the air. Half of the porch's overhang had collapsed, but they had enough room to escape in the space that remained. The children coughed, cried, and followed when Miss Willow coaxed them, urging them to hurry.

Shelley grabbed Lacey, and Patty grabbed Callie, using them as human shields.

"What now?" Shelley asked.

"Once we get outside, drop those two," she said, pointing to the backs of Irina and Miss Willow, "and then make sure anyone out there knows we've got her kids. Sara, definitely."

"Got it."

They walked briskly underneath the burning overhang and out into the night, where the air was fresh, clean, and moist.

Patty lifted her weapon. Shelley lifted hers.

They each fired a single shot.

Irina dropped first. Miss Willow stumbled, took another step, and went down.

The children screamed and covered their eyes.

Patty shouted, "Sara! Tell your friends to back off, wherever they are. You shoot, they shoot, anyone shoots, your children die." She waited for a response. "Do you hear me? Where are you?"

"Here! I'm here! Don't hurt them."

Patty scanned the back yard, looking for the origin of Sara's voice. The dancing flames at her back brightened the night, giving her a mottled glimpse of Sara as she stepped out of the small building, holding her hands over her head.

"Tell your people, Sara! Tell them."

"They can hear you."

To her right, Patty heard a familiar male voice screaming, "Irina!" and when she glanced around, Teddy Rutherford sprinted toward his motionless wife. It had been a while since she'd seen such anguish, and for a single second, she paused to enjoy it. Relishing in the pain of others had always been one of her favorite things.

"I got him," Shelley said, whipping her arm to the right. She pulled the trigger.

Pop.

Teddy pitched hard to the side and went down.

So easy.

Chapter Twenty-Three

When Sara first heard the muffled shots, she assumed she had allowed her worst fears to take over her mind. They couldn't be shots, could they? No, it had to be the sound of popping timbers as the fire consumed the farmhouse. Or, maybe if Shelley and Patty were the only two inside, they were after each other, locked in a duel and turning on each other.

Sara felt her spirits rise a little. She held her breath in anticipation. Should she feel hope instead of agonizing desperation?

Another muffled pop and this time, it was unmistakable.

That was definitely a gunshot. What's going on in there?

Was that the final bullet to end one of their lives?

She imagined Patty standing over Shelley, pointing the gun at the younger woman's chest, and then firing. Better yet, perhaps one was dead and the other was badly wounded, and rather than perishing in the fire, she chose to end it all. That would be the preferable option. Both dead and gone; she and the children and Miss Willow could move on with their lives.

Finally, after all this time.

She took a moment to consider the aftermath—would they rebuild here on the farmland, or was this another infected place? Two evil souls would escape burning flesh in the basement of her home, damning the land underneath it. Contaminating the soil, destined to haunt the place for eternity where their horrible lives had ended. All that bad energy released into the world...maybe it was better that her family was far away from it.

They would sell the land and move yet again. Maybe to a tropical island. Hawaii was nice. She had the money. They could go and bring her parents with them, who had been discussing spending the remainder of their retirement in a sandy, ocean-side climate.

Even though she was watching her house burn, and her children, Miss Willow, and Irina were inside contained within that hulking steel container—they would be buried under the smoldering rubble but safe—she felt a sense of calm overcome her.

This was the end. They'd made it. Her worst fears had come true, and they had survived them.

And then, the house of optimism she'd built in her mind crumbled as Irina and Miss Willow emerged from the back door, followed by her children, and then those two wretched monsters, Patty Kellog and Shelley Sergeant.

She stifled a scream and froze in fear.

Oh my God, how did she get them out? How was it poss—the entry code. Shelley remembered. How could I be so stupid?

You thought she was in prison and three thousand miles away, that's how.

But Miss Willow had been begging you to change it for months. So stupid.

Two individual gunshots sent Irina and Miss Willow to the ground. Sara bit her lip hard enough to taste blood and an overpowering wave of nausea hit her stomach. Were they dead? She hadn't been able to tell where the shots went, but now they were lying on the ground, motionless. She'd gotten to know Irina better over the past few months, but Willow was a family member who had been a mother when Sara's own was three thousand miles away.

She stood, arm raised, pistol up and ready to come out firing when Patty screamed, "Sara! Tell your friends to back off, wherever

they are. You shoot, they shoot, anyone shoots, your children die."
She waited for a response. "Do you hear me? Where are you?"

"Here! I'm here! Don't hurt them." Sara stepped out of the
building, holding her arms over her head. Mary's .38 revolver
remained tucked in the waistband at her back.

"Tell your people, Sara! Tell them."

"They can hear you."

To Patty's right, Teddy's gut-wrenching wail of "Irina!" made
Sara pause. She watched as he sprinted at them, ignoring Patty and
Shelley, focused only on the love of his life, the woman who loved
and endured him, as she lay on the ground, either dead or dying.

For a moment, everything slowed. Sara watched Teddy as he
pumped his arms and legs, propelling himself across the yard. She
looked at Patty, fearing the worst, and then it happened...Shelley's
arm went up, fire erupted from the barrel, and Teddy stumbled and
went down.

"Stop!" Sara screamed. She tried to move. Her legs had become
hardened tree trunks and had grown roots. She was paralyzed, unable
to move, as she watched Teddy writhing on the ground.

Shelley tried to shoot again, but Patty grabbed her arm, laughed,
and said, "Let him suffer, Shell. It'll be fun watching him die trying
to save this moron." She kicked Irina's limp leg. Irina's head moved,
slightly, and it gave Sara an inkling of hope.

But Miss Willow...nothing.

Lacey, Callie, and Jacob stood where they were, looking so
afraid that they weren't able to scream. Sara thought about telling
them to run but she was afraid of what Patty's reaction might be.
Shelley's too.

Shelley had locked them in boxes before and would've murdered
them, given the chance. Patty could've easily blown them up with
two different bombs if it hadn't been for Vadim Bariskov's warning.

Sara remained silent. If she screamed for them to run, if they
managed to break free, they would be shot.

"Where are the rest of your people, Sara?"

"I don't know."

"Where are they? Get them out here where I can see them or... or...which one is this?"

"Lacey."

Patty yanked a handful of hair.

"Mommy!"

"It's okay, honey."

"Sara, get them out here or she's the first to go. Where are the rest? I saw them. *Where* are they?"

Sara yelled for Mary, then said to Patty, "She's the only one that made it out. And Teddy, too."

"Bullshit. Don't lie to me, Sara. Where's the tall one?"

Sara lied. "After—after we heard you shooting, he went back inside, trying to figure out what was happening."

"Do you want to see her brains all over the ground? Do *not* lie to me. Where is he?"

"I don't know."

"He has ten seconds. And Mary? Did you say Mary?"

Damn it, where are you, Randall? Why aren't you here? We need you. Please, God, help us.

Sara walked across the yard, slowly, step by agonizing step. They watched her with smiles on their faces as she paused within twenty feet. Behind them, the house was completely engulfed in flames that danced inside and licked around the doors, windows, and awnings.

To her right, Mary hobbled out of the shadows, limping and leaning on her cane, holding her pistol by the trigger guard. It dangled over her head from her index finger. Neither Shelley nor Patty had noticed her yet, and when they did, they whipped their weapons around, telling her to drop it and stay where she was.

"I'm sorry, Sara," Mary said.

"It's okay."

Shelley fired a single shot over Mary's head. "Get your friend out here."

"He went back inside. She's not lying."

Sara lied, "It's the truth, Patty."

Mary added, "He's an ex-Marine. Trust me, if he was still alive, you'd be dead already. I know you don't believe me, but that's the truth."

Patty and Shelley exchanged glances. Patty said, "You keep believing that."

Teddy tried to army crawl toward them, yelling "Irina," again and again.

Sara said, "Teddy, stay right there before they shoot you."

"No!"

"Please, stay."

He rolled onto his back and screamed at the sky.

In the distance, she heard the faint sound of sirens. Someone had reported the fire. But, the way the undulating noise carried through the nearby valleys, she couldn't be sure of how far away they were. Did it matter? Would they be able to get past the front security gate?

Wait, they'd disabled the system. Okay, okay, maybe the gate is open.

"What do you want?" she asked Patty and Shelley. "Haven't you done enough already? You murdered my husband, you've tried to murder my children. Our homes—you've destroyed our homes and chased me thousands of miles. If it's me—if it's *only* me, just pull the trigger and be done with it, but let them go. Let my babies go."

"What fun would that be, Sara?" Patty asked. "We've both been waiting for this for so long. We've suffered for *so* long while you got everything you wanted, didn't you? Life just keeps handing you all the good stuff while we're stuck down here in the shit—prison, murdering people for a living—it's not exactly the most exciting career path, you know. Look at you now, huh? How is it that you've escaped us twice, and things just keep getting better for you each time? Tell me how that's possible. Karma? Is it karma? You've dealt with enough shit that now the universe hands you millions upon millions of dollars while Shelley rots in her cell, afraid that one of those goons in prison will gouge out her other eye...is that it?"

"No, I don't know—please, let the kids go, you can have—"

"What? We can have the *money*, Sara? That's why you think we're doing this? This is payback. A reckoning. Yeah, maybe money can buy that for some people but what we want, what we've been waiting years for, is to watch you suffer. That's it. That's all."

"You can have that. Whatever you want. Let the kids go and I'll do whatever you want. Let them go and I'll walk into the house. I'll walk in there, I'll stand in the middle of the floor and I'll swallow fire if you want."

Shelley chuckled and said to Patty, "That's actually a pretty good idea."

"I thought so, too." Patty held the barrel of her gun to Lacey's head. "Go," she ordered, flicking her chin toward the house.

"Not until they're free." Sara didn't know if it would matter. If she walked into the house and if she stood there and consumed fire like she'd offered, Patty and Shelley absolutely would not walk away. They would finish off Teddy. They would put a bullet between Mary's eyes, and then her children.

No consciences. No witnesses. Nothing but death and another bloodbath in the small, southwestern Virginia town. The second one in two years. Massive, multiple murders...and it would be their names in the newspapers.

"Fine." Patty pushed Lacey over to Shelley. "Keep them here. I want them to watch."

Lacey, Callie, and Jacob screamed for Sara when they made eye contact. Reaching, reaching for her. Twenty feet away, but miles distant.

"Go to Mary," Sara said. "She'll keep you safe." Their screams were heartbreaking. "Please, go to Mary, okay? Do it for Mommy."

They tried to lunge for her but Shelley yanked their arms, pulling them hard, and they went, reluctantly walking over to Mary where she wrapped her arms around them. They buried their faces in her chest.

Patty said, "Make them watch or I'll put a bullet in each one of them. Right in the back of the head. Make them watch and I'll let you go."

"Liar," Mary said.

"You don't have a choice. Shelley, go—"

Mary relented. "Okay, stop. Just stop. Kids? Listen to me. Turn around and tell your mama you love her. She's being very brave for all of you."

Lacey, Callie, and Jacob turned to face her with tears pouring down their cheeks.

Lacey spoke first. "Love you, Mommy."

Then Callie. "Please don't go. I love you. Please stay."

And finally, Jacob, "Don't go in there, Mommy, please."

"It'll be okay, buddy. Mommy loves all of you so much."

It was absolutely heartbreaking, but she still had a chance.

Where is Randall? Where in God's name is he?

Patty put her arm around Shelley. "So touching, isn't it?"

"Makes me want to vomit."

"Sara, in you go. Into the house. Look's like Hell is waiting for you."

Sara nodded.

He'll come, won't he? Where is he? Where could he be? Did he really go back inside? Maybe he'd tried to crawl under the house, through the crawl-space. Would he do that? Were those shots I heard from him? Was he trying to get our attention? Oh God. No. Please no. Give me hope. Something.

"Move, Sara."

Shelley laughed and said, "Hey, if you've got any popcorn in there, throw it out here."

Sara took a step, then another. She glanced over at Teddy. He'd passed out on the ground. From pain? From loss of blood. What did it matter anymore? Or was he dead?

She stepped around the bodies of Miss Willow and Irina.

Miss Willow hadn't moved since Shelley pulled the trigger.

Irina lay on her stomach, alive, but breathing heavily. The wound at her upper shoulder had drenched her white shirt so that the top half was dark red and caked with drying blood.

With Randall nowhere in sight, she felt her last remnant of faith fade away.

Where had he gone? Had he ran away? Had he decided that he had his own family to worry about?

Would I have done the same? Would I have put my life at risk to save strangers if the kids were waiting for me at home? I don't know.

She sighed.

This was it. Patty and Shelley had won. After all these years of torture and distress, agonizing over Brian's disappearance and enduring so many sleepless nights and near-mental breakdowns, escaping from Shelley's cage, avoiding Patty's bombs, saving her family twice from these two deranged individuals, this was the end.

Game over. She'd lost.

"You win," she said to them.

Patty smirked. "It's easy when you make the rules. Get in inside. Go on, before the thing collapses."

Sara arced around, keeping space between them. Her skin grew hotter as she stepped closer and closer to the dancing flames. Her cheeks were flushed.

She stopped at the foot of the porch steps, wondering if she could really do it. If everyone was going to die anyway, would it matter if she tortured herself like this? If they were all going to die, wouldn't it make more sense to go out fighting and take a bullet instead of allowing herself to be burned alive?

It would, and she almost turned, but instead…

Maybe Mary can do something if they're distracted. One last possibility, right?

If she sacrificed herself, maybe, just maybe, Mary would be able to pull off a miracle. Certainly more unbelievable things had happened in the world.

Do it, Sara. Up the steps.

Behind her, Patty shouted, "Up, up, up! I'm gonna count to three—"

"I'm going!" Sara lifted a foot and put it down on the bottom step. The heat was nearly unbearable. She coughed from the smoke and lifted another foot, set it down.

Another step.

And then another.

Flames whooshed around the porch column beside her and she smelled burning hair. The roar of the fire, the groaning, crackling, and popping wood muffled the sound of her children crying and for that, she was thankful.

One final step and she was on the porch.

A slight gust of wind blew the flame at her face. It licked her skin and she winced in pain.

Patty was right: Hell awaited. Inside the back door, it hadn't completely overtaken the farmhouse, but it wouldn't be long. She could still see some of the furniture and the walls through the thick smoke. With any luck, she would die of smoke inhalation before the flames took her body.

"Burn!" Shelley screamed. "Burn, you bitch. Burn!"

Sara held up her arm to block a dancing tongue of fire to her right and then, directly in front of her and across the far side of the house, the front door burst inward, splintering in pieces. Flaming shards scattered throughout the living room. Embers danced.

Randall fell through the opening, landed and rolled, then sprang to his feet—shirt on fire, flames clinging to his jeans—he thundered toward her, arm outstretched, aiming at her head with his pistol. A white rag was tied across his nose and mouth.

"Sara! Down!" he roared.

Sara flailed backward and dropped.

Randall jumped over her, airborne, flying across the porch, pulling the trigger as he went.

Four deafening shots exploded above her head.

Boom, boom. Boom, boom.

He fell to the porch, landing at the head of the stairs, and rolled down.

Sara swung herself around.

She saw Patty on her back, red soaking through her shirt. Immobile.

Shelley writhed where she lay, clutching her throat. Gagging, choking.

Up above, the porch overhang gave a final groan and collapsed, giving Sara a split second to dive down the steps and land on top of Randall. He rolled with her, holding his shoulder and grimacing.

When they came to a stop on the ground, he said, "Think I broke my collarbone."

Sara didn't know whether to hug him or smack him. "What took you so long?"

"Sorry. I'd be late to my own funeral."

"Yeah, well, that possibility was too close." She climbed to her feet and darted over to her children. She flung herself down to her knees and pulled them in for a hug. Laughing, crying, and overcome with relief.

"We did it," she said. "We won."

Chapter Twenty-Four

The ambulance lights flashed across the hillside. They had been in such close proximity so many times. Red, the color of warning. Red, the color of blood.

Red, the end of another traumatic nightmare.

Sara sat on the open tailgate of a volunteer fireman's pickup, a blanket around her shoulders, a bottle of water in her hands. Behind her, Lacey, Callie, and Jacob had given in to exhaustion. They slept huddled together in a borrowed sleeping bag.

Across the way, the last remaining flames coughed and sputtered, trying to survive against the surge of a fire hose. The farmhouse was nothing more than a pile of charred, blackened, and smoldering timbers. Wisps of smoke drifted into the night sky.

Randall leaned up against the tailgate, his arm in a sling, bandages covering various spots of seared skin. Mary, bless her, had ridden to the hospital with Teddy and Irina. Both were in serious condition, but they would survive. If it hadn't been for Patty's desire to watch Teddy suffer, and Shelley's poor aim with one eye, both of her friends would likely be dead as well.

Sara watched in stunned silence as the paramedics lifted the black body bag inside the rear of an awaiting ambulance. Inside was the shell of Sara's friend and confidante, her rock and her second mother; despite their efforts to revive her, Miss Willow had already passed before the emergency personnel arrived.

Randall put an arm around Sara's shoulder. "I'm damn sorry about that."

"I've buried too many people," was all she could manage. True mourning would come later. For now, she'd already shed her tears— what remained was a fatigued absence of feeling.

A group of four FBI agents stood to their right, pointing at the house and talking in hushed voices with the local police.

"Can you believe those guys?" Randall asked. "Showing up late to the party like that, but still trying to take all the credit. Jesus H."

"They didn't scold you too much, did they?"

"Scold? Hell, they all thanked me, if you wanna know the truth. You wouldn't get them to say it under oath, but not a single one of them was on board with Morrow's plan to take Patty alive, and they all agreed that there should've been an active presence in the house. They still can't believe that Patty and Shelley got past their surveillance, and you won't hear them admit to that in public either. They're glad she's gone, though. Top secret info or not, she was a damn danger to society. Good riddance, bad rubbish, all that bullshit."

"So what's next?"

"Eh, I'll have to go in and answer some more questions. Debriefing and whatnot. I told them there wasn't much left to tell, but you know how the government is. They gotta spend time to waste more money."

"Yeah." Sara took a deep breath. She couldn't wait to see Randall give Morrow a piece of his mind when the agent in charge arrived. That would be fun to watch. As far as she knew, Barker and Morrow would be landing at Tri-Cities soon, then there would be the hour-long trek up I-81. So, at best, she would get to see Barker by two o'clock that morning. As soon as the agents saw fit to release them, she would head over to the hospital to check on Teddy and Irina.

Randall asked, "I think I already know the answer to this, but are you sticking around these parts?"

"I...maybe. Not *here* here, not on this property, but now that it's done and over with, I like it here. The country is just the right pace, it's beautiful, and the people are amazing. Seriously, where else would your neighbor fight a war for you?"

"We all fight some kind of war, Sara. The difference is whether you use emotions or bullets. Either way, it's good to have somebody down in the trenches with you."

"That's true, but you and Mary risked your lives for us. That was above and beyond. What if you'd died? What about your family?"

"All in a day's work, ma'am. Serve and protect."

"Somehow I don't think your wife would think that's an acceptable answer."

"She's used to it."

Sara took a sip of her water and pulled the blanket tighter around her shoulders. "You know, Randall, for so long, I've been running away from bad memories and such evil people. One step ahead was one more day alive and I got sick of living that way. I've wondered if God might have it out for me, or if I was Hitler in a former life and karma is just now catching up—the past two or three years have been unreal. Every time, right when we thought our lives had come out on the other side of Hell, we'd get forced right back into the fire. But for all of that, for all of the evil that we've had to endure, you and Mary showed up to help us out. That was something *good*—you guys were a *blessing*, Randall—and as crazy as it sounds, I'd gotten to the point where I thought I'd never see pure decency again. Thank you."

"Ain't no big deal."

"Stop trying to downplay this. It's a *huge* deal, and I won't ever forget it. You won't ever have to want for anything again, I can tell you that much. Money, favors...anything, you just ask."

"Sara—"

She held up a finger to shush him. "No arguments. Look, I know that sounds like I'm putting some sort of monetary value on your kindness, but it's not about the money, it's not about buying our thanks, nothing like that. Being able to give what I can when *you* need it, that's the only way I'll ever be able to repay something like this."

"I'll tell you what," Randall said, pushing himself away from the truck bed. "Let's start with you buying me a beer one of these days. We'll say a prayer for Miss Willow, and drink a cold one in honor of T-bird and Irina for being such badasses. It takes a lot to eat lead and walk away from it. So those are my terms. One beer. Deal?"

"That'll never make us even."

"Maybe not in your eyes, but let me tell you what my grandpa told me: 'Give as much as you can and only take what you need.' If *everybody* lived by those rules, maybe the world wouldn't be knee-deep in bullshit."

. . .

After they'd gotten a ride to the hospital to see Teddy and Irina, a kind nurse with gray hair and a purple uniform had allowed Sara's children to fall asleep in the room next to the wounded Rutherfords.

Irina's injuries had been worse than Teddy's and she too slept peacefully in the bed by the window. In the low light of the room, Sara could see how pale her skin was. Irina had lost a lot of blood, but according to their doctor, she'd walk out in a couple of days.

Sara sat beside Teddy's bed, holding his hand.

He said, "So Miss Willow didn't make it, huh?"

She could only shake her head in response.

"Damn shame. Such a damn shame."

"I know. It's going to be hard without her and God, I feel like I'm shredding apart on the inside, but...you know, at least the kids are safe. You're okay. Irina's okay. I'm trying to see a silver lining."

"Yeah, about that," Teddy said. "Can you tell me something?"

"Sure."

"How am I the one that's in the hospital again? Really? I mean, *really*, how? Three times now, somebody has tried to murder you and *I'm* the one with an I.V. and a hospital bill. I think I need a Winthrop clause in my insurance agreements."

It felt wrong to laugh, *so wrong*, but she did. Miss Willow was gone. Randall was wounded. Teddy and Irina had nearly died. Her children, yet again, would have another dose of trauma layered on top of everything they'd experienced. Resilient though they may be, right now, the damage would likely surface in a few years.

Her husband was dead. Detective Jonathan Johnson had died trying to protect her.

She was the root of so much death and destruction. It seemed fair to say that if a person had touched her life in some way, life would touch back, hard.

But she laughed anyway. It felt good to release the culmination of everything she'd held inside, trying to keep herself from breaking.

Teddy shook his head, smiling. "It's not *that* funny."

"I know," she said, dabbing at the corners of her eyes. "I'm sorry. It's just that—I mean…it's over. It's finally over and I'm so relieved but I feel like a tornado, you know? I can look back at these last couple of years and see the path of destruction I've left behind. I don't know why I'm laughing…I think it's because I can't cry anymore."

Teddy shook his head. "Nah, *you're* not the tornado, Sara. *Fate* is the tornado. Did you ever see that movie *Twister*? You're like that cow that gets picked up and tossed around and then the rest of us are trying to grab the cow and get it down out of the air to save its life. And then *we* end up in the hospital while the cow lands on its feet a mile away in the middle of some hayfield."

"Somehow, that actually makes sense."

"Not that you're a cow, obviously."

"Thanks for clarifying."

Irina stirred softly in her bed. Teddy tried to lean up to check on her, but the pain sent him onto his back. "Speaking of cows," he said, "are you staying here in Virginia?"

"Randall asked me the same thing. I think so. Or, at least this will be a home base, but for the moment I'm pulling the kids out of school and we're going away for a long while. Somewhere on an island with blue water, and as far away from civilization as possible. What about you guys? Still going on your honeymoon?"

"God, I hope so. We'll need the time to recoup. But, I don't know how Irina will feel about showing off a bullet wound in her bikini."

"Tell her to wear it like a badge of honor."

"Maybe I'll have a t-shirt made that says, 'I visited Sara Winthrop and all I got was this lousy scar.'"

"Fair enough."

Teddy put his arm behind his head. "Barker here yet?"

"He sent me a text and said he'll be here in a while. I'm just waiting on the showdown between Randall and that agent that's with Barker. Should be fun watching the fireworks."

"If I thought it'd change anything, I'd sue the guy right out of his suit."

"You could, but I have a feeling you can save your money. Randall has enough connections up in D.C. to have that guy scrubbing toilets in Antarctica."

"Good. Tell him to pack extra toothbrushes so he can really get into the corners."

The nurse poked her head inside the door. "Mrs. Winthrop? Your little boy's awake. He's asking for you."

Sara nodded. "Okay, tell him I'll be right there." She stood up and stretched. "Well, T-bird, looks like we survived another round together, huh?"

"No worse for wear."

"You asked me what *I'm* doing next…I know you've got the big release of your sniper game coming up, but are you guys staying in Portland after your honeymoon?"

Teddy shrugged. "We've talked about moving to Russia."

"Russia? Are you serious? Isn't it all corrupt and dangerous there?"

"It's probably safer than being around you."

Sara squeezed his hand one last time and glanced out the window.

The sun would be up in a few hours. The dawn of a new day.

Freedom under blue sky.

. . .

End of Book #3

ONE MORE GAME

Moscow, Russia
8:39AM Local Time
Weather: Overcast, Windy, Broken promises forecasted

Teddy Rutherford walked briskly with his hands in his pockets. Off to the right, a street vendor hailed him with a double-handed, "American? Come, come."

Of course he was American, and of course the guy knew it. He'd had the same conversation with Oleg every day that week.

Teddy tilted his head back, offered an exasperated groan, and watched his breath plume overhead. He approached the multi-colored cart decorated with flashy pieces of flair, knick-knacks, and dangly things that made obnoxious noises when the wind blew. Again, as he had done each time the guy wouldn't let him pass peacefully, Teddy stepped up to the open window and said, "Bit chilly for *kvass*, right?"

"*Da*. Is good though. Warms the heart on cold days."

Kvass, a fermented drink made from rye bread, was officially non-alcoholic, but Teddy figured if you drank a few gallons of it, the possibility of a buzz still wouldn't be worth the effort. He hated the stuff, even the strawberry-flavored kind.

The guy was persistent, however, and each day that Teddy had ignored him in the past made the next day's hawking that much worse. Damned if keeping a low profile wasn't an option with Oleg around. While he and Irina had come to Moscow for a break from the seemingly never-ending troubled life of his friend and former coworker, Sara Winthrop, Teddy hadn't found much peace here either.

After the trouble in Portland, Oregon, and the ensuing insanity in southwest Virginia on Sara's farm, the frozen streets of Moscow had been a welcome relief for no more than a week.

"Please, Teddy," Irina had said, her accent growing heavier now that she was back in her homeland. "My family will be more..."

"Accepting?" It was true that the aunts, uncles, cousins, grandfathers, grandmothers, and the cleaning lady had looked at him with snarled lips, upturned noses, and had muttered things he couldn't understand. To them, he was the spoiled rich kid whose daddy had sold a software company for billions.

The spoiled intruder who wouldn't share his inheritance.

Not from greed or a general lack of concern for her family's well-being, but because his own gaming company, Red Mob Productions—which also hadn't been the choicest of terms, given Irina's familial responsibilities—was consistently in the national spotlight and had a new release launching in August. If any nosy reporters ever discovered that he'd loaned money to the Russian mafia, bye-bye prestige, bye-bye venture capital. He wouldn't *need* the latter, ever, but why risk all of his own money when he could play with someone else's?

Irina's family had taken to calling him *Malyutka*, "Little One," without any foreknowledge of Sara's use of the nickname for so many years. When he called to tell her, he was positive he could hear her snort with laughter all the way across the Atlantic.

Irina had begged and begged. "Just a few small jobs. Maybe you can carry the money. It'll make you one of them, at least in spirit, and we can be happy here."

He relented a month ago. "Fine, but nothing more than delivering a few packages. Anybody finds out about this, I can't have *Gamemaster Magazine* calling me a communist. They'll trash *American Sniper* on release day and boom, the bottom falls out. I mean, yeah, *we* don't need to worry about the money, but it'll ruin the company. Think about all those people who'll lose their jobs, Irina, and I wouldn't be surprised if Randall showed up here to put me in the crosshairs himself."

Randall Blevins, the former Marine Corps sniper, whose life story the game was based on, had provided consultancy and logistical analysis during the development process. He also spit tobacco juice on Teddy's Forzieri oxfords one day when he'd grown frustrated with their lack of adherence to his advice. Great guy, short temper, deadly accurate with a rifle. Probably not the kind of gentleman who'd enjoy having his name muckraked through the crap with an accused commie bastard.

Irina's pouty lip had cemented his commitment, though, and now he found himself standing in front of the *kvass* vendor, with nearly two and a half million rubles—about seventy-five thousand dollars—screaming to be discovered in his briefcase.

The situation was the same as it had been, every day, for the past week. He hadn't asked questions. He didn't know where the money came from, didn't know where it was going—didn't *want* to know—and once it was out of his hands, it was gone from his mind. The less he knew, the better. The less he obsessed, the better his mental stability.

While Oleg happily poured a glass of blueberry *kvass*—a new flavor today, apparently—Teddy shifted his weight from left to right and squeezed harder on the briefcase handle, as if it would try to get away on its own.

Unbelievable, he thought. *I am literally worth nine hundred million dollars, I'm running a hundred million dollar software company, and here I am, a fucking mule for the Russian mafia. Does crazy stuff like this happen to other people? Sara, maybe. Seems like she'd get herself into this mess.*

A crucifix, hanging near some of the cart's knick-knacks, swayed with a gust of wind. Teddy hadn't noticed it before. He'd studied the local culture some before he and Irina had made the move; he remembered reading that there were few Catholics in Russia. A rarity.

"You're Catholic?" Teddy asked, making small talk while he waited.

"*Da*. An *autsayder*, just like you Americans. Close enough."

"*Autsayder?* Oh, outsider. Gotcha."

Oleg handed the *kvass* to Teddy, smiling as wide as the Moskva River, revealing a ragged set of gapped and yellowed teeth. But it was a good smile; warm and thrilled to be adding a few extra rubles to his pockets.

Except he refused the money when Teddy offered.

The smiled disappeared as Oleg shook his head. "*Nyet, nyet.* Important men don't pay."

"Who told you that?" Teddy asked, chuckling. "My wife telling stories about me again?"

Somberly, all joy gone from his expression, Oleg leaned over, as if revealing a secret, and replied, "A *sotrudnik* stopped by this morning." An employee.

Teddy didn't recognize many Russian words, not yet, but he'd heard this one enough from Uncle Nikita already. "Whose?"

Oleg glanced left and right, nervously. He leaned close enough for Teddy to smell some rancid aftershave that reminded him of mothballs and pine trees, and whispered, "Big Boss."

The name meant nothing to Teddy. "I don't know who that is."

"They see you."

"They? They who? When?"

"Every day is what he said. Every day you come down this street. You carry briefcase, you wear nice shoes, nice coat. You stop here for *kvass*."

"Yeah, because you call me over." Teddy could feel the warm burning of trepidation in his stomach. He'd never heard of Big Boss and it was disconcerting that he was under surveillance.

His involvement had been a bad idea from the start.

"What'd he want?"

Oleg held up his hands, palms outward, as an apology. Teddy was familiar with the pose, having used it numerous times over the years until his counselor, at Sara Winthrop's suggestion, had convinced him of the need for professional boundaries.

Oleg said, "I only sell drinks. I don't know."

"Did he say anything?" The anticipation built as Teddy surveyed the sidewalk, empty for a block in either direction. Behind Oleg's cart, an open park served as a pitch for a group of boys kicking around a soccer ball while an old man slept on a gray bench, huddled under three layers of blankets. A young mother pushed a bundled-up baby in a stroller. A photographer kneeled at an awkward angle, trying to capture a heart-wrenching portrait of the dozing homeless man.

"A note," Oleg said. "He left this for you." The *kvass* vendor produced a small white envelope from his apron and handed it to Teddy with an unsteady hand.

Teddy thought about setting the briefcase down, but risking any kind of invitation from a thief would not be wise, especially when Uncle Nikita was so intent on every ruble getting from Point A to Point B on time. Instead, he tucked it under his arm, squeezing it close to his body, while he fumbled with the envelope using gloved fingers. Finally, with the flap ripped open, he removed the letter and found a note written in Russian.

Figures.

"I can't read this, Oleg," he said, thrusting the note inside the *kvass* cart window. "What's it say?"

Oleg backed away. *"Nyet.* I can't."

Teddy shook the note impatiently. "Look, you said so yourself; I'm an important man. I'm busy, I'm in a hurry, and you're partly to blame for this. You tell me somebody's watching me and won't help me out? Read the damn note, Oleg, or you'll have more to worry about than this Big Boss guy. I know people, too, understood?"

The vendor nodded and anxiously wiped his palms on his apron.

He took the note from Teddy, unfolded it, and read silently. His face, normally pink-skinned underneath a thin layer of a dark, full beard, drained of all color as he flung the paper away.

Spooked, Teddy caught the note. Eyes wide, cautious.

Oleg reached up, grabbed the rollaway door, and yanked it downward. It rumbled on rickety tracks and got caught halfway down, impeding the process just long enough for Teddy to jam the briefcase underneath it. He shoved the disturbing note into a jacket pocket.

"Sir, please."

"What'd it say?"

"Sir, I—"

Teddy's heartbeat quickened. He raised his voice. "Oleg? Oleg, do *not* do this. You are seriously freaking me out, man, now *come on*, what's going on?"

Oleg tried to shove the briefcase out of the way. Teddy shoved back against the vendor's weight. They continued to grunt and thrust, caught in a reverse tug-of-war, until the bulk of Oleg won out. The briefcase was wrenched from Teddy's hands and fell to the ground where, thankfully, it remained closed. Teddy slammed a fist against the rollaway door. He heard a metallic latch sliding into place inside, then the cart shook as Oleg rumbled toward the cart's main door.

"Oh no you don't," Teddy said, grabbing the briefcase. He darted to his left. The cart door slammed against his shoulder. He backed up and threw himself against it.

Oleg's voice was muffled on the inside. "Please, go. I have a family."

"So do I, you bastard." Teddy stepped back and kicked near the handle. Nothing happened. "I got a wife"—he kicked the door again—"and a baby on the way."

He thought of Irina back in their luxurious apartment—by Russian standards—lying on the couch, eating imported Twinkies, because the local version didn't taste as good, resting the entire package on top of her pregnant belly. Three months to go and she was so excited she could barely stand it. Amazingly, she hadn't gained much weight, and the baby was as healthy as it could be.

They preferred to keep the sex a secret, anticipating the surprise. Plus, Irina still had the kind of body most women would dream of, even when they weren't pregnant, and it hadn't surprised Teddy at all when he'd overheard numerous, good-natured whispers of, "*suka*," behind her back. *Bitch*.

For all the trouble that his friend Sara had gotten into back home, when her children were kidnapped and when she had to fight for her life, twice, he had never quite understood the depth of her suffering, her anguish, as she and her family clung desperately to the limits of survival. Now, though, things were different. He loved Irina with every single molecule in his body, but nothing could replace the intensity of joy and care he felt for the tiny progeny growing inside her round tummy.

If anything ever happened to them…

Teddy shouted, "Oleg," and kicked the door again. He heard splintering and grew more determined. "Open up." He became aware of the inquisitive eyes staring in his direction. The boys had stopped kicking the soccer ball around and stood in a gaggle, pointing and laughing. The photographer had given up on the sleeping homeless man—who was now awake and staring at the cart—and proceeded to snap pictures of Teddy.

None of it mattered. The only thing that did was learning what the message said.

Sure, he could leave, right now, while there was some semblance of sanity remaining in the situation. Maybe he'd simply had an argument with the vendor and the onlookers wouldn't know the difference. He could take the note with him, deliver the money as scheduled, and ask the drop-off courier to translate it.

No, that wouldn't be good. He couldn't endanger Uncle Nikita's operation.

Although, if they had been following him, they likely already knew who he worked for. Wait, not for, *with*. Teddy Rutherford no longer worked *for* anyone.

He'd been warned to vary up his delivery route each day. "Americans attract attention," the family had said. "Don't give any scoundrels a chance to rob you." He wished now that he'd listened. Instead, he'd been traveling the same set of streets for two weeks because it was the shortest distance between two points and he'd been eager to get the delivery over with. He'd insisted on a month of service to the family and no more. Beyond that, he had a wealthy American business to run, to which Uncle Nikita had begrudgingly agreed, but only after Irina had won him over with her pouty lip, too.

Teddy pushed his fingers through his hair and tried a different tactic. He knocked gently on the door. "Oleg? I'm sorry, buddy. Hey, how about this? I got a hundred bucks for you. A hundred American and you tell me what it said, okay? No big deal, I walk away, you never see me again. How's that sound? I'll forget your name by tomorrow, I promise."

Which wasn't too far from the truth. Faces, yeah, he could spot Oleg on a random subway train in Manhattan twenty years from now and recognize the guy as a *kvass* vendor from the streets of Moscow, but if he wasn't wearing a nametag by next week, forget it. It made doing business tough some days, but he paid vice presidents and directors for that kind of thing.

"Oleg?" Teddy checked his wallet. "Two hundred. That's all I got." The two c-notes were left over from his last trip home. What a waste of time that'd been. Whenever another vital meeting came up, he'd save himself the scolding from Irina and video chat with his colleagues.

Teddy heard the latch clicking and his heart leapt a little. The door opened, slowly. Oleg's eyeball peeked through the crack, followed by a thumb and forefinger rubbing swiftly together. *Hand over the money*, they said.

Teddy smiled hesitantly. "*Nyet*. Not until you tell me."

"Okay, okay," Oleg said. "Give me the note."

Teddy gave it to him.

The fat-fingered hand with hairy knuckles slithered back inside the cart. The paper rustled and then, voice shaky, Oleg said, "It...It says, well, my English is—this is close."

Annoyed, Teddy ordered, "Just read it."

"My English can be close. It says: We know you, important man. We know who you work for. We don't like Americans. We don't like *rich* Americans coming here, stealing our women, invading our country. You work for Nikita, yes? You family with Nikita, yes? Big mistake, important man. You own game company? We like to play games, too. We have a game for you. Game starts at nine this morning. No police. No KGB. Only you. Win, they live. Lose, no more Mother Russia." Oleg shoved the note through the crack. "It's signed by Big Boss. Now here, get this demon away from me."

Teddy could barely lift his hand to take the ominous letter. He was lightheaded. Dizzy. The edge of his vision blurred. He couldn't tell if he was breathing or not.

Oleg snapped his fingers. "Two hundred. You said."

"What does—" Teddy cleared his throat. The lump went nowhere. "What does that mean? Game? What game?"

I came here to get away *from this. Oh God.*

"Two hundred," Oleg insisted. He slung the door open, grabbed the bills from Teddy's hand, and then slammed the door shut. The deadbolt engaged, the sound of it an exclamation point on top of a confusing, terrifying moment.

Teddy checked his wrist. He'd forgotten to wear his watch that morning.

Time, time, what's the time?

Phone, yeah.

He patted his pockets frantically, not being able to remember where he'd put it. Side pockets, back pockets. No. Jacket? Not there either. In the suit? Lapel pocket? Yes. There it was.

8:55AM.

Already? No.

"Oleg, what do I do, man? What kind of game, Oleg? How am I supposed to play a game without any rules?"

Silence from inside the cart.

"Help me, you piece of—this is—this is bullshit. I didn't come here for this. I don't play games. People don't play games with me."

Win, they live.

Lose, no more Mother Russia.

Irina. The baby.

Jesus.

Run.

. . .

Teddy sprinted, driving his legs like pistons pumping inside an engine, briefcase flapping wildly at his side while he held his cell phone to his ear with the other.

It rang and rang. "Pick up, honey. Please, pick up. Shit."

He ended the call. Almost nine o'clock, she should be at home. That's when the masseuse came by, right? Or was that ten?

He dodged *babushkas* pushing laden grocery carts, darted around old men hunkered over as they shuffled along, and nearly toppled a young, blonde woman in a skin-tight, leopard-print dress, wearing six-inch stilettos. He turned to make sure she was okay. She wobbled on the spindly heels and gave him the finger, gorgeous face screwed up into an irritated snarl.

From the chubby-faced grandmothers to the supermodels on stork-like legs, Moscow covered a full spectrum of life.

"Sorry. So sorry."

He reached the end of the block, slowed, and tried to make up his mind. Cut across traffic, stay north on the same street, and risk exposure on the same godforsaken path he'd taken every day, or try to find his way home by going a different route?

Did it matter?

Can I get there a different way? Do I know a different way?

Whatever. Just go.

He turned east, cutting across the street, zigzagging between rusting beaters and sparkling new Lada and Renault sedans. Brakes squealed. Horns honked. He recognized the buildings around him; they'd been down this way before, hunting for a small café that Irina used to visit as a child. They never found it, and from the looks of things, it had been torn down and replaced by an office building with beige-colored bricks and white columns.

Teddy passed this same building now, and knew that he was only two miles from home. Pedestrians stared at him, likely wondering what was wrong with the well-dressed businessman galloping down the sidewalk. He tried Irina again.

As he listened to the ringing, he prayed that this game hadn't already started and they'd...why wasn't she answering? Could she be on the other line?

Maybe she's talking to Sara.

The two had been spending a lot of time on the phone recently, mostly because of Irina asking Sara questions about her pregnancy and what to expect, at least in a modern day capacity. The grandmothers and aunts and cousins were full of old superstitions and homemade advice that left Teddy cringing, begging her not to listen to such nonsense.

Nine in the morning here...that's what, one o'clock on the east coast, or is it twelve?

No, forget it. Sara's in bed.

He shouted, "Irina, pick up the goddamn phone," his voice squealing with panic.

His feet pounded the sidewalk. Café tables and chairs whipped past in a blur, as did the morning walkers out for a stroll. The scent of hot tea and pastries drifted out of open windows.

Teddy found a break in traffic and turned north, hopping the median, jumping between two trees, and then up onto the curb. His lungs felt like Uncle Nikita, a huge bear of a man, was sitting on his chest. He'd found time to get some exercise here and there, but cardio had never been his thing, and now he paid for it.

A soft *click* on the line.

"Irina, thank God."

Her sleepy voice had never sounded sweeter. "Hey, I just saw that you called. My ringer was off—"

"Are you okay?" he interrupted.

"I'm fine, why?"

"Are the doors locked?"

"I think so—"

"What about the windows? The one by the fire escape?"

"Why, what's going on?"

"Is it locked, honey?" Teddy angled his body to the side and squeezed between two deliverymen pushing trolleys stacked with cardboard boxes. He caught a whiff of the same type of aftershave worn by Oleg.

"You're scaring me, *dorogaya*." Sweetheart. "Don't upset the baby. And why're you out of breath? What happened?"

"Listen to me," he said, hurtling a large planter when a woman with curly black hair stepped into his path. "Lock everything up and stay on the line with me. I'll be there in fifteen minutes, maybe less. I think this is about the—" He stopped himself, checked the passersby for any sign of prying ears, then continued, whispering through strained breathing, "I think it's about the delivery."

"What?"

"Some territory thing with a guy named Big Boss."

"Who?"

"That's what I said. He wants me to play a game."

"What kind of game?"

"Too hard to explain. I'll tell you all about it when I get there."

"Is it dangerous?"

"Keep everything locked. It'll be fine."

"Are you sure?"

"I promise, but for now, just keep talking, let me hear your voice."

"Okay." There was a moment of silence as she searched for something to say. "Did you make the delivery for Uncle Nikita?"

"God, no. Didn't have time. You and the baby…more important." The words were getting harder to push out between the suffocating exertion.

"You didn't take the money? Teddy, *dorogaya*, always take the money. Wait a second…"

"What?" A car horn honked close by. Distracted by it, Teddy nearly ran into a skateboarding teenager with black eyeliner, multiple piercings, and a tattoo of a scorpion crawling up his neck. The kid said something that sounded like a curse; Teddy didn't bother to stop and find out.

"How did you learn about this game?"

"A *kvass* vendor,"—*huff, huff*—"he gave me a note. Said the man had me under surveillance. Note was about playing a game."

"And you didn't take the money?"

"For God's sake, Irina, *no*. I didn't take the goddamn money."

"Could it be a test? You know how Uncle Nikita can be. He's testing your…your—what's the word?"

"Commitment?" Teddy felt some of the mental weight on his chest lift, but not enough to compensate for being out of shape.

Another mile to go. His legs had moved beyond aching. They were numb, lifeless trunks, powered only by will and determination. His dress shoes and thin socks had never been meant for running, and the blisters on his toes and heels screamed with each step.

"Yes, that one. Uncle Nikita is testing you and now you're late. Remember what he says all the time? 'Money, family, God, in that order.'" She giggled.

"Why're you laughing?"

"We don't have to worry about me, *Malyutka*. Seems like you might be the one in trouble."

"Damn it. Seriously?" It made sense. Uncle Nikita, with his austere white hair and gold chains, that stereotypical tracksuit and expensive Nikes, had mentioned numerous times that the deliveries *had* to be made, on time, no matter what. In fact, he rarely let Teddy forget it. Not that he ever would, and so far, the biggest obstacles had been a debilitating stomach bug, three straight days of freezing rain, and an insufferable *kvass* vendor that impeded his process on a daily basis.

Had Oleg not been diligent enough in his attempts at detaining Teddy? Was Uncle Nikita stepping it up a notch, pretending to scare him out of completing his assignment? Would he make up a stupid game like that, threatening him with a made-up story about a fake mafia guy?

Possibly, but Oleg's fear of Big Boss seemed real, didn't it?

Or maybe he was simply a damn good actor. He'd been so convincing.

And here I am, running in the wrong direction. Son of a bitch.

Irina couldn't stop giggling into his ear. "My poor baby. Welcome to the family, huh?"

Teddy slowed to a walk, then came to a stop. He bent over, inhaling heavily, then stood upright and grasped at the stitch in his side. When he could breathe again, he said, "Unreal. Un-freaking-real. I can't believe I fell for that."

"Where are you?"

He glanced around at the familiar shops. A tailor. A small market. A flower shop that doubled as an internet café. "Down near the flower shop. The one with the yellow pig on the door."

"It's…just after nine now," Irina said. "If you hurry, you can still make the drop."

"Oh my God. Okay, I'll try, but I'm wrecked. My feet are wrecked, my legs are jelly." The relief was almost enough to assuage the pain. "Do me a favor, huh?"

"Of course."

"Call your bastard uncle and tell him he won that round."

"Do you want me to call him a bastard, or..." He could hear the words pushing around the smile on her lips.

"Maybe some other time, but for now—"

"Hold on, *dorogaya*, I hear the doorbell. I'm going to let Oksana in."

Oksana, the masseuse, was five feet tall, ninety-eight pounds, with arms like drinking straws, but she had hands like vice grips and gave the best massages Teddy had ever experienced. She could be carried away by a strong gust of wind, yet after his scare, he was at least happy that Irina had someone with her while he came down from his unwelcome rush. He could make the drop and be home in an hour, and he didn't care that it would still be before noon—he had a tall glass of vodka and tonic waiting on him.

Teddy waited to say goodbye. He listened to her on the other line, humming as she walked through the apartment. Faintly, he heard the doorbell ring again.

"Coming," she said.

He almost asked her how the baby was doing. Instead, he said, "Hey, just in case, make sure you check to see who it is fir—"

"Sorry, one second, *dorogaya*, I'm just getting the door open. Hi...oh, hello?"

Teddy felt his stomach clench. "Irina? Who's there?"

"What's that? No, I'm sorry, you must have the wrong—what are you doing? No, get out of—"

Silence.

Teddy shouted, "Irina," and took two steps before he felt the prick in his neck, quick, like a bee sting. He reached for it on impulse, fingers closing around something small and cool. Metallic. In his palm, a silver dart, no bigger than an inch, with a sharp point on one end and what appeared to be green, feathered twine on the other.

"What the…"

His heartbeat thumped in his ears. The world slowed. He turned, searching for the source.

Behind him, a man in a brown leather jacket with buzz-cut, graying hair and a face like a potato tucked something into his waistband. Dark, piercing eyes that had never known humor bore down on Teddy as he wobbled, tired, aching legs growing weaker, but not from exertion, not now.

The man marched ahead, heavy boots stomping on unforgiving concrete.

He caught Teddy as he fell.

Before the blackness, while the fear for Irina raged inside the part of his mind that hadn't been overcome by the dart's poison, he heard the man say in English, "Let the games begin, important man."

. . .

Teddy opened his eyes and winced, grunting as he sat up. Glaring sunlight, emanating from somewhere in the vicinity, clawed its way through the entirety of his eyeballs and up into his pounding head. Still woozy, the world shifted underneath the—where was he?

Mattress. I'm on a bed in a…where?

To his left, a concrete wall, to his right, wide open space stretching across an empty warehouse for a hundred yards until it came to another wall. Overhead, the sunlight screamed at him through a row of windows bordering the structure, shouldering up against the rafters.

He was cold. His overcoat and his suit jacket were gone, leaving him only his shirt, tie, and slacks. Light gray socks stuck to his heels and toes where the blood had dried.

My shoes. And the briefcase. Phone. Phone? Yep, gone. Obviously.

Irina. I have to—what?

What am I supposed to do? How do I play?

He heard a distant bang and pushed himself up from the bed. Fluorescent lights flickered and turned on, one by one, down the length of the warehouse like falling dominoes. The artificial light was worse than the natural sun coming through the windows. Squinting, it took a moment to adjust.

To his left, thirty yards along the wall, a large bay door rattled open. Teddy shuffled sideways to get a better look, then paused. Were they coming to kill him? Torture him?

He put his hands up to his temples, backed up against the wall, and waited.

He'd made Irina promise that involvement with the family "business" wouldn't lead to anything like this. That's why they'd left the States—for a break from the insanity of the previous couple of years.

I should've known. Jesus H. Christ, how could I have been so stupid?

We rented an apartment a block away from Uncle Nikita's, for God's sake, why wouldn't they get me involved?

We could've gone to Costa Rica, like I said a thousand times. 'It's warm, Irina. There are palm trees, Irina. There are no tracksuit wearing Russian mafia members, Irina.'

She had said, "No, *dorogaya*, they won't bother you with it. They know the baby's coming. They wouldn't put you in danger like that, I promise. How do you say it? Cross my heart? I *promise*."

Yep. Right.

The bay door rattled fully open and shuddered to a stop, chains clanking.

Teddy held his breath and shook his head in disgust. He wanted to blame her—old habits of rarely accepting responsibility—but it was as much his fault, too. He could've said no. He could've insisted that with her family history, there was too much risk involved with Moscow, simply by taking a chance on it. He could've stood up to her. He could've said no to Uncle Nikita.

Yep. *Right.*

An engine roared outside and a beat later, a decrepit pickup launched through the bay door. The driver swung the truck around, rear wheels kicking out to the side, so that the nose faced Teddy. Behind the wheel, Potato Face waved and slammed on the gas.

Teddy froze, unable to move, as the pickup hurtled forward.

That ever-present sense of self-preservation sparked to life inside his brain. He jumped to the right as Potato Face jammed on the brakes, spun the wheel, and squealed the pickup's tires on the smooth concrete flooring. It came to a stop, having spun one hundred and eighty degrees, now facing the south end of the warehouse.

Teddy retreated timidly.

Run? Yeah, that was an option, but where? Potato Face had a truck.

Could I make it to the bay door? A different one somewhere?

Better to wait and see what he wanted. Run, maybe die simply for trying to escape.

If they wanted me dead, I'd be dead. Unless I'm the mouse and the cat is playing with me first.

Teddy lifted his arms above his head in surrender. Backing away, he asked, "Are you Big Boss?"

Potato Face laughed. "Perhaps one day," he answered, stepping around the rear of the truck. "For now, I am only Dimitri."

Bargain? Maybe I could bargain with him?

"Okay, Dimitri, you said? Listen, obviously you know who I am. I've got money. Plenty of it. Can we work something out? I don't know you, I don't know who this Big Boss guy is, and I swear, man, I didn't want anything to do with Uncle Nikita. I barely know the guy but he's my wife's…"

"Teddy, Teddy. You talk too much."

"If they do anything to her…"

"You'll what?" Dimitri chuckled, stalking him.

Teddy moved back. "She's pregnant," he pleaded. "Whatever it costs, okay? How much? How much will it take? Take me, leave her and the baby alone, whatever you want to do."

Dimitri stuck out his arm, a set of keys dangling, swinging from the end of his finger. "We're already doing what we want to do. And you're wasting time."

"I don't even know what I did to you guys, man. *Seriously*. My wife wanted to be closer to her family, that's why we moved here, and then Uncle Nikita—I have to pay my dues, whatever. All I do is pick up a briefcase and drop it off. I make a run, that's it."

"Yes, we know. You're an important man."

"Why does everyone keep saying that? No, I'm not. Not here, not back home. I'm not even in charge of my own damn house."

Dimitri jangled the keys. "The more you talk, the closer they get."

"Who?"

"Stop talking and listen."

Teddy could scarcely hear over the sound of his ragged breathing and the weak clatter of the pickup's engine, but off in the distance, the high wail of sirens carried into the warehouse. "Oh, God."

Dimitri grinned. "I don't think he can help you. Not with this game."

"What *game*, man? I don't even know what I'm playing for."

"Yes, you do."

"Irina?"

Dimitri shrugged. "Irina, the baby, maybe other things."

"You son of a bitch. Is she okay? Is. She. *Okay*?"

"For now, *da*."

The sirens grew louder. Teddy marched forward, yanked the keys from Dimitri's finger, and asked, "What other things?"

"Unlike you Americans, we have honorable blood. Big Boss, he doesn't want a war with Uncle Nikita. It's business. It's all business. It's not like the old guard where a few knives and guns could scare someone off a street corner. It's political and there's too much money to be made, even here where people fight for scraps. Wars bring attention, and nobody wants that."

"Then just back off, man. Go somewhere else. Forget this...this territory battle bullshit."

"It doesn't work that way."

"Why not?"

Dimitri winked. "Capitalism."

"Right."

"One man plays, one man wins or loses for his family. Your pregnant wife is—what's the word—incentive?"

"You evil bastards. Does Uncle Nikita know about this?"

Dimitri shrugged. "It was his idea."

"*What?*"

"Filthy American stain on the family. A traitor for a niece. Easy decision." Somewhere outside, close enough for the sound to heighten the panicked feeling in Teddy's chest, the sirens howled around the clatter of a metallic gate crashing open. "I would go if I were you. Take the truck for the first part of the game. Make your delivery."

Teddy felt his bloody socks slipping on the slick concrete floor as he withdrew to the idling pickup. "What delivery? What am I taking? Where?"

Dimitri offered another wink and a smile. "You'll figure it out."

The police, KGB, whomever it was outside were close enough for Teddy to hear tires slipping and crunching through loose gravel as he cursed Dimitri. He climbed into the pickup, popped it into first gear, and jammed his aching foot down onto the gas pedal. The truck lurched, barking its wheels as gears engaged, propelling him forward.

Which way out?

The *politsiya* were coming from the left where Dimitri had entered through the bay door.

Could he make it out in time? Doubtful.

Thick, solid concrete walls surrounded him. Not a chance in hell the flimsy pickup would be able to blast through like some ridiculous, unbelievable action movie. This was real life where physics and reality worked together like they should.

Thankfully, before he could descend into a full-tilt panic, he spotted a fresh strip of sunlight toward the eastern side of the warehouse. A bay door, one that he hadn't noticed before, slowly rose upward, providing another exit. Did Dimitri do that for him? Someone else controlling things in the warehouse?

Don't know, don't care. It's a way out.

He spun the steering wheel to the right, realigned himself on the path of escape, and tried to shove the gas pedal through the floorboard. The little engine roared as he picked up speed, hurtling across the warehouse floor. In the rearview mirror, the red and blue flashing lights of the *politsiya* appeared. Three cars in total, all of them white sedans with blue stripes down the length of the side.

As he careened closer to the bay door, dread sunk heavily into his stomach. It wouldn't be open in time. Not all the way.

Thirty feet.

Twenty feet.

Ten feet.

Forget it. I'm going.

I just hope—

He ducked.

An eardrum-shredding screech shrieked across the roof of the pickup for a half-second, then it was done. He'd made it—a close call that was way too close—but he was through, barreling down a delivery ramp and into a barren parking lot with weeds growing through the cracks in the blacktop. Relieved, he let out a gale-like breath and checked the rearview mirror. The bay door was rolling closed now and a moment later, one of the police cars slammed into it.

Lower than the pickup, it made it underneath, barely, but lost its rooftop lights in the process. The impact wrenched control from the policeman's grasp, sending the car sideways into the wall along the ramp, throwing the wheels to the left where it wedged itself in, perpendicular to the path of the two remaining cars.

Teddy slowed and turned in his seat to observe through the back window.

The second one hit the bay door hard enough to rip the bottom loose from the track, bending the cheap, thin metal and shattering the windshield. It slammed into the first car blocking its path. The third and final car plowed into the second—all three stopped in a pile of tangled metal, busted hoses, and steam pouring from underneath crumpled hoods.

Teddy took a deep breath and searched for an exit from the parking lot.

In the bed of the truck, he'd seen a cardboard box, roughly a foot square, strapped down with a set of bungee cords.

That had to be what he was delivering.

But where in the hell am I going?

. . .

A gap in the fence provided ample room for Teddy to burst through, launch across the sidewalk, and whip onto an empty street. He surveyed the area around him. Desolate buildings, empty parking lots, and broken glass windows populated an abandoned industrial area.

The overcast sky had cleared, leaving behind permeating sunlight that bolstered the throbbing in his head. Had it been the sedative in the dart? Focused now as he drove, he felt his scalp pulling taut against his skull when he squinted. He reached up and felt caked blood above his right ear. Beneath that, a sensitive knot the size of a large marble.

Damn, how'd that happen?

Each throb made it increasingly difficult to think. He checked the glove box, praying for some random painkillers, and instead of finding salvation, the only thing inside was a pink sheet of paper, folded in half—thin, flimsy paper, the kind that would be removed from a handwritten receipt book.

With no cars ahead, or behind, for at least a half mile in any direction—and no sirens wailing outside the window—Teddy eased off the gas, unfolded the receipt, and scanned it for something helpful.

Across the top was the name of a business—something in Russian that he couldn't read—followed by an address he didn't recognize. The standard lines of a receipt with scribbled markings. Whatever had been purchased, it was cheap, roughly forty dollars, and there had been only one of them according to the sectioned designated for quantities.

And then, below the indiscernible writing, something that couldn't have been clearer.

CONGRATULATIONS
21R – 13L – 7R

The combination to a lock—had to be—but was it meant for him? And where?

Teddy growled and smashed his fist against the steering wheel, the horn emitting a pathetic honk. He wasn't used to this. He'd grown up around video games his entire life. Jim Rutherford, Teddy's father, had started LightPulse Productions decades ago, back when video games weren't much more than pixelated colors scrambling around a screen. He'd built the company up—along with Teddy and Sara Winthrop's help—into an organization that made national headlines. By the time Jim had sold the company, their flagship game *Juggernaut*, and its sequels, were titans of the industry. Beautifully crafted gems with lifelike realities that created such an immersive experience, players often had to be forcibly returned to life away from the screen.

However, no matter what the games looked like, whether they were glorified blocks or next-gen reality, they all had something in common.

The games had rules. They had instructions. They had objectives.

Teddy knew how to play those games.

The red button shoots, the yellow button dodges, destroy the alien civilization before they take over Earth.

Simple.

But this…this *game*, if one could call it that, had no clear direction, no guidelines, nothing whatsoever to help. Even Sara's game, the first she had to play when her children were kidnapped, had rules and stages and levels. Rewards and punishments.

The Russian mafia had given him nothing to go on; nothing but a slip of paper and a combination to a lock that could be anywhere.

Although, the objective was clear: save Irina and his unborn child.

How?

He grabbed the steering wheel with both hands, clenched his muscles tight, and screamed between gritted teeth, shaking from head to toe. His bottom lip trembled, eyes watery, as he spun the steering wheel to the left and bounced over the curb and into the empty lot of a three-story building. Trash bags sat full and plump in front of a glass door, as if someone had cleaned out the building and then forgotten to dump the refuse. The windows were pockmarked with holes, signs of lowlifes with good aim and nothing better to do.

Teddy had never been much for God, religion, or the sanctity of church, but now seemed like the perfect time to start. He turned his eyes skyward, which meant looking at the torn-fabric roof of the pickup's cab, and screamed, "Tell me how to play, *please.*"

He waited.

And waited.

And received no direct answer.

Teddy punched the roof of the cab, causing the visor to rattle loose and flip open, followed by a black, rectangular object falling into his lap.

The cell phone came to rest between his legs and when he grabbed it, he saw a red light blinking in the upper right corner.

A text? A missed call?

He pushed the home button. Yes, a text waiting for him.

SEEK SHELTER

BOX – COMBO – REVELATION

"Yes! Thank God." He glanced upward again. "Yeah...*You.*"

With the truck in neutral and the emergency brake set, he left the engine running, just in case he needed to flee in a hurry.

He scrambled into the bed of the pickup, loosened the bungee cords around the cardboard box, and ripped the tape from the flaps. He paused. He'd heard something. Right?

Teddy held his breath and begged the pounding in his ears to quiet down.

Damn.

Sirens approached from the direction of Dimitri's warehouse. The *politsiya* must have gotten themselves mobile again—or at least one of the cars mobile enough to pursue.

Go, go, go.

He tore the box flaps all the way open. Inside, he found a small bible and a padlock that held a small silver box closed.

What the...?

"Gotcha, here we go. Twenty-one right, thirteen left, seven right," he said, spinning the dial. The *clunk* of the lock opening accentuated his minor victory. He pulled it free from the latch and dropped it into the truck bed.

Yet another note awaited him inside the silver container.

This time, written on it was nothing more than a set of numbers:

12 1-6

He shook the paper angrily and glanced over his shoulder, tension rising higher as the approaching sirens came closer. He spoke aloud to himself, as if speaking his frustration would add further weight and understanding. "Twelve, one dash six, and a bible? I—what? I don't even—wait. Box, combo, revelation. Revelation. That's at the end of the bible, right?"

Teddy snatched the small holy book from the bottom of the cardboard box. It was no bigger than one handed out by the groups back home in the States, or the kind one found in the drawer of some cheap hotel's bedside table.

He frantically thumbed through the flimsy pages. "Revelation, Revelation…Revelation. There you are."

Another check to his rear: the sirens were approaching, but no cars were in sight. He couldn't gauge how much longer he had. His heartbeat quickened, as did his breathing.

Teddy located the twelfth chapter of Revelation and read aloud, "A great sign appeared…She was pregnant and cried out in pain… An enormous red dragon with seven heads and ten horns…A male child who will rule all nations with an iron scepter…Child snatched up by God…The woman fled into the wilderness…"

Discouraged, Teddy slung the bible into the cardboard box. "What does that even mean?" he screamed, his voice echoing and dancing around the empty structures nearby. He stood and stomped the box until it was a shredded mess.

The sirens. Too close.

Move. Now. Figure it out later.

...

Teddy drove, making random lefts, rights, and u-turns until he was thoroughly lost and there were no signs of the pursuing *politsiya*.

The ancient radio display was modern enough to digitally inform him that the time was a quarter past three in the afternoon. Given the fact that he'd taken the dart to the neck around nine a.m., then woke up in the warehouse, and had spent the last hour distancing himself from all but certain time in a Russian prison, he figured he'd been out for at least five hours. Plenty enough time for whoever this Big Boss guy was to get Irina far from Moscow and into the wilderness if the words in Revelation were any clue as to what may have happened to her.

Twenty-minutes prior, he'd stopped in the parking lot of a busy market so that he could blend in, and retrieved the bible from the crushed cardboard box. He drove and read the passage again, analyzing the words, assuming that they had to mean something, otherwise the architect of the game wouldn't have pointed him in that direction.

That's what they'd always done with titles produced by LightPulse Productions, and now they did the same with his own company, Red Mob. Sure, they included red herrings, but every meaningful clue was there for a reason. Otherwise, players would never accomplish the objective, which was more than winning, it was satisfaction and the desire for more.

Some of the content in Revelation made sense. Maybe.

Briefly, he'd considered going to Uncle Nikita, because he recalled Dimitri mentioning in the warehouse that the game was the family head's idea. But, no, maybe that wasn't such a good plan. What if Uncle Nikita was the seven-headed dragon represented in the passage? He couldn't risk wasting the time to try.

Or…What if Dimitri had been lying? What if Uncle Nikita knew nothing of his situation and he could help if asked?

No, that's a dead end, too. The guy hates you. He'd laugh. He'd be happy. Blame you, tell the family it's your fault Irina was kidnapped. Forget him. Forget the family. They hate you. You're useless to them.

"Shit," he said, rubbing his forehead. He turned down an alley and parked. It was empty except for a ragged, stray dog with matted fur hobbling in the opposite direction.

He read the passage again, and again, until he could almost recite it.

Irina was obviously the pregnant woman. The passage all but shouted it with a bullhorn.

The red dragon with seven heads; that could be Big Boss talking about himself.

Iron scepter. Iron curtain. That's too coincidental to not be some reference to Mother Russia.

"Maybe one of the Lenin monuments?" he said.

It was possible, yet he recalled from his reading that there were over eighty statues of Lenin in Moscow alone. He would waste days hunting for the right one, and that was supposing a Lenin statue held his next clue.

He checked the cell phone again, as he'd done hundreds of times in the last hour, waiting for another message to come through. None had. The thing was a worthless block of plastic, glass, and circuitry. The option to dial out had been disabled and once he'd discovered that fact, he'd nearly slung it out the truck window. Now it did nothing more than tease him with false hope and possibility.

"Please," he said. "Give me *something*."

The phone vibrated in his palm, his plea to the universe answered.

The message read, "I'm safe for now, *dorogaya*. Hurry."

She was alive, but two simple words made his head swim.

For now.

He grew dizzy, nauseated. His stomach churned.

Teddy rolled down the window and vomited.

The stray dog glanced back at him, sniffed the air, and resumed his pitiful march westward.

Teddy wiped his mouth with a sleeve.

Calm down, she's fine. She's okay. She said so.

But now what?

Can I give up? Should I just give up and go to Uncle Nikita? That's what he wants, right? Who gives a shit about this turf war with Big Boss? If he's enough of a bastard to set up this heartless game by kidnapping his own niece, just to teach the rich, dumbass American a lesson, then so be it. Money. I'll give him money.

But that's what he wants, isn't it? He wants you to give up? He'd never really hurt Irina, would he? Are they all just empty threats?

"He won't hurt her," he said aloud. "Just keep playing."

Teddy covered his eyes with his hands. The fading light in the alleyway helped his pounding headache, but not much. He tried to recall everything that had happened throughout the day. Had he missed any clues? Had he overlooked something Dimitri had said?

There had been a call from a family member that morning. Irina had answered.

Nothing special. Making plans to go shopping with a cousin.

They had finished breakfast. He'd kissed her goodbye, never knowing what lay ahead, then he'd traveled on foot, as he always did for the extra bit of exercise, to pick up the briefcase from the coffee shop a block over.

He'd taken his same path down the same streets, as he had every day for the past two weeks, which wasn't wise, he knew, and he'd been stopped by Oleg, the *kvass* vendor with a crucifix hanging on his cart.

Maybe I could go find Oleg again. He could have an idea about the passages from the Revelation.

Supposedly, a *sotrudnik*, an employee of Big Boss had left the note for Teddy. Oleg's detail of the encounter had been limited. He'd offered no description of the man.

Teddy fished around in his pockets and, luckily, the folded up note from the kvass vendor was still there. Unfortunately, it was still in Russian, but he tried to recall everything that Oleg had said during the translation.

We don't like rich Americans coming here, stealing our women, invading our country.

Something distant, familiar, flickered deep in the recesses of his mind.

There was something else, wasn't there? Something before that?

We know you, important man.

"Holy shit," Teddy said, sitting upright. He glanced heavenward and added, "Sorry."

Important man. When I tried to give him money for the kvass...'Nyet, important men don't pay.'

The son of a bitch knew! He knew before I opened the envelope.

The crucifix, the passage from the bible.

The jigsaw pieces were beginning to form a border.

Teddy started the engine. The stray dog, having reached the end of the alley, jumped at the sound, darted around the corner and out of sight.

A speck of relief allowed his lungs to open wider. He breathed deeply. He had a clue, a lead...an objective.

Teddy cursed himself. He'd been warned numerous times by Irina, Uncle Nikita, and the family not to repeat the same delivery route. He'd been marked by Oleg and his cronies as an easy target.

I bet even those police cars were fake.

Big Boss, as the mythical, feared enemy of Uncle Nikita, had never existed. That's why Irina had never heard of him.

Oleg had to be Big Boss.

Had to be. Now all Teddy had to do was find the red-faced bastard.

...

The theory of Oleg-as-Big-Boss posed a significant problem.

While Teddy was relieved that he had an inkling of the game's motivations—Oleg was lying, Dimitri was lying—it meant that Uncle Nikita actually *wasn't* involved, which, in turn, meant that Irina could very well be in real danger.

Gone was the possibility of Uncle Nikita holding onto her to teach the rich, greedy American a lesson only to release her unharmed.

It also left open the possibility that the mid-tier mafia bossman would be pissed that one, Teddy had lost the seventy-five thousand dollars to some small-time encroachers, and two, his favorite niece had been kidnapped and not a single person in the building had seen anything suspicious that morning.

Teddy knew. He spent an hour at the apartment complex asking anyone he could find before he gave up and accepted the inevitable.

He needed help.

When he arrived at Uncle Nikita's, both his assumptions were correct.

Uncle Nikita had spent a decade in New York before returning to Moscow to run the family operations, thus his English was excellent. "You lost the delivery? *And* you lost your beautiful wife? What a disgrace you are, stupid *Amerikanskiy*. Idiot!" Uncle Nikita stood up from his chair. He flicked his lit cigarette at Teddy.

Too weak and mentally exhausted to react, it bounced off of Teddy's chest in a shower of sparks and landed on the purple carpet with gold-inlaid designs. He brushed the ashes away.

Uncle Nikita's office smelled like a mixture of heavy cigarette smoke, sour perfume, and girl-sweat. Teddy was familiar with the scent—too many strip club visits logged in all the gentlemanly establishments back home in Portland, Oregon.

Irina's uncle kept a stripper pole in the corner, over next to the fish tank that housed a single, bored-looking piranha. He also kept a bevy of beautiful women lounging about on beanbag chairs, in various stages of undress, mostly because he could. Teddy had learned quickly that Uncle Nikita was the kind of guy who didn't need a reason, or never had to offer an excuse.

Teddy had been here once before, and only now did he realize how much this place looked like a '70s pimp had been the lead interior designer.

Minus the monstrous flat screen television broadcasting a soccer match, the remainder of the office looked to be outdated by thirty years or more.

"Tell me, *Malyutka*," Uncle Nikita said, marching around the desk. "You tell me exactly what you plan to do about it." He shoved a stubby finger into Teddy's forehead. "My little Irina, and *you*. I should've sent you home the moment she brought you here."

"I was hoping—I mean—it's been a really rough day, man. Do you think you could—"

Uncle Nikita's face turned the color of Russia's flag. He erupted. "You think *you've* had a rough day? You son of a bitch! Your pregnant wife was *abducted*. God knows where she is and God only knows what they've done to her, you pathetic, tiny, selfish excuse for a husband. Some father you'll be. I should strangle you now and save that bloody child the pain and suffering of growing up with you as his papa. Get the hell out of my office. Go!"

The day from hell had just presented the Devil as part of the final act, pushing Teddy past reason and sanity. "That's not what I meant, you...you poor man's Hefner. Don't you *dare* judge me *or* how much I love that woman. I don't care if you think you're Vladimir Lenin reincarnated, don't you ever, ever doubt my feelings for her, got me? I've had a rough freakin' day *because* she's in danger...um...*sir*."

Teddy paused to take a breath. *Uh-oh. Did I go too far? Russian mob, Teddy, not a meeting room with a grouchy programmer.* Shaking with fear, anger, and embarrassment, Teddy backed away. "Anyway," he added, clearing his throat. "What're we gonna do about Irina?"

"Bravo. Finally, some balls on this one." Uncle Nikita smiled and gestured to his harem, "Ladies, you should come check them out, huh? Somebody found them."

"I don't think that'll be necessary."

Uncle Nikita gently slapped Teddy's cheek, somewhat friendly, only slightly menacing. "Relax. Look, just because your balls might clang when you walk now—it doesn't mean you've earned my respect. Listen to me, okay? You let me worry about Irina. You go down to your happy little spa and get your poor little feet massaged and your eyebrows plucked. Get your tan and your pedicure. In fact, here, take this with you. My treat, huh?" Uncle Nikita removed a roll of bills from his pocket, wrapped tightly by a rubber band, and tossed it to Teddy. "Get out of my sight. I'll find this wretched pig and deal with him on my own. I'll bring her home when I'm ready."

Bastard, son of a motherf—forget it.

"You win. I'm done. I give up."

"*Da.* It's for the best."

. . .

The pair of oxfords that Uncle Nikita had loaned him were too large. His feet slipped around inside them, irritating his blistered and bloody skin more than walking in his socked feet, so he removed the shoes and dropped them in a nearby trashcan.

He walked down the street, shivering, cold, shoeless, worried to the point of overwhelming nausea about Irina, and seriously pissed off.

Of course I'm not giving up, you pompous ass. Being persistent is what landed me in a therapist's chair, dude. I'm not walking away. Not like that.

His only measure of comfort was knowing that Uncle Nikita would put calls out to his generals and henchmen. Somebody in the neighborhood would know who Oleg was. It wouldn't be long now.

But damn, I'd love to find her first and then rub it in his stinking chubby face.

Teddy looked up at the waning light of the afternoon. Night would fall soon.

The park, where Oleg had duped him, was a block to the east, and Teddy thought it might be a good idea to revisit the place, think things through again. He could ask around, maybe see if anyone knew whom Oleg was and which direction he arrived from every morning.

Thinking of Oleg reminded Teddy of the pitiful excuse for a game the *kvass* vendor had designed. Poorly executed, with little instructions, and jumbled up storylines that would've led him on a random scramble around Moscow.

That was the point, I bet.

Teddy knew he was playing for Irina's life, the baby's life, but what was he supposed to do in exchange for it? Maybe if he'd figured out what Oleg was trying to tell him in the second clue, by using the passage from Revelation, it might've given him some insight.

The iron scepter, a red, seven-headed dragon? What was that all about?

Was it money? Wouldn't he have demanded that up front for a simple kidnapping and ransom?

Dimitri had said it was a territorial dispute, but what did he know? From what Teddy could tell, Uncle Nikita had been in charge, locally, for ages. No one dared challenge him.

Yeah, Dimitri had to be nothing more than a babysitter while Teddy slept off the sedative. He was likely a buddy of Oleg's, talked into helping. He didn't even know that Teddy wasn't supposed to "deliver" the package like he'd suggested.

Poor design, Oleg. Poor design. Not a good playing experience when your accomplices don't know the objectives either.

And if I find you first, I'm gonna show you how to really end a game.

Teddy jogged across the street, dodging cars, and ignored the honks of annoyed drivers. Up ahead, the *kvass* vendor's cart was gone. No surprise there.

The teenage boys, who'd been there previously kicking a soccer ball around, had also moved on, perhaps to do what hooligans do elsewhere. The photographer was gone as well.

He hadn't expected any of them to be there...except for the homeless man on the bench, the one who had been a permanent fixture along his route each morning, even before Oleg had shown up to peddle his disgusting beverages.

The man sat on his usual bench, awake, dressed in ragged clothes with multiple layers of holey jackets and a pair of jeans worn thin at the knees. His long beard stretched to the center of his chest and blanketed a gaunt face with sagging skin. The skullcap covered his head to the bottom of his earlobes.

He looked content as he fed scraps of bread to three cooing pigeons, their claws scrabbling against the concrete underneath their feet.

Bingo.

"Sir?" Teddy said, approaching cautiously. "Hello?"

The bum looked up at him with a surprising amount of life in his eyes. Teddy expected the vacant gaze of someone who'd lost his way in the world and regretted every second of it.

"Do you speak English?"

"*Nemnogo.*"

Teddy thought that meant 'a little bit' and the man confirmed it by holding his thumb and forefinger a half an inch apart.

"Can I ask you some questions?"

"*Da.* Sure."

"Mind if I sit?"

The homeless man grinned, revealing blackened, toothless gums. "Is that question?"

Teddy was in no mood for laughter, but it felt good to bring up one corner of his mouth. "What's your name?"

"Liev."

"Liev? I'm Teddy."

The homeless man nodded. He tossed another scrap of bread to a hovering pigeon. Teddy thought about how nice it was of the guy to share what was likely his dinner. He pointed to where Oleg's cart had been all week long. "You remember the *kvass* cart over there? *Kvass*? Remember?"

"*Da*. Uh, American say...*yuck*? His? *Koza mochi*."

"*Koza mochi*?"

"Goat, ah...How you say? Goat urine?"

This time, Teddy couldn't help himself. He chuckled. It felt wrong to laugh with Irina trapped somewhere. Pregnant, alone, and afraid.

"Liev, buddy, I'm in a hurry here, understand? Do you know that man with the *kvass* cart? Please say you do."

Liev frowned and shook his head. "I'm sorry, *comrade*. I do not."

"Shit. Then how about this? Do you know where he comes from each morning? I walk by here every morning making my deliveries for—" He almost said, "*For Uncle Nikita*," but that very well could've ended the conversation. "For the place where I work, right? And he's already here before me, every morning."

"*Da*. Is true."

"Right, so where does he come from?"

"I never see. I sleep."

Teddy sighed. "Really? Do you really not know or are you hoping I'll give you something for information?"

"*Nyet, comrade*. I need nothing. You need more. I have shoes."

"True. And you've honestly slept through him getting here and leaving with his cart every day?"

Liev shrugged. "The universe, she plays games."

"Tell me about it."

Teddy asked another round of questions, mostly eager to extract any possible bit of information that might help, and came away with nothing. He stood up from the bench, thanked Liev for his time, and walked away defeated with his shoulders slumped. A chilly gust of wind whipped past, carrying with it scraps of paper and dead leaves. Teddy shoved his hands in the pockets of his slacks, shielding them from the cold while he tried to think of a different approach.

He could start by canvassing the entire neighborhood. Someone had to have seen Oleg before—

His hand closed around a rumbled slip of paper. He removed it and saw that it was the receipt from the truck's glove box—the one with the business address up top.

"Liev?" he shouted, spinning around. "Liev, buddy? Got a sec?"

"*Da, comrade.*"

It was a long shot, but any little thing could be a clue at this point. "Can you translate this for me?" he asked, pointing at the top of the pink receipt, fingers shaking with anticipation. "What kind of business is this? What's it called?"

"Eh, let me see. *Da...da.* I think I know this. English, um, in English you say white. Then, not forest but—but—"

"Woods? Trees?"

"Another. Bigger."

"Shit, um, *wilderness?*"

"*Da, da.* White Wilderness then...workers, toilets. Ah, sinks?"

"Plumbers?"

"*Da.* White Wilderness Plumbers. *Plumbing.* One kilometer west, that way."

Still yet, it could mean nothing, but Teddy was so thankful that he nearly hugged the man. Instead, he said, "You're awesome.

So awesome. If there's anything I can ever do for—wait a second. Here, take this." He grabbed the thick roll of bills, given to him by Uncle Nikita, and shoved them into Liev's hand. He had no idea how much it was, but surely, it would keep the homeless man in food and perhaps the comfort of a hotel room long enough to find some rest and peace.

Before Liev could refuse, Teddy darted away, scattering the pigeons as he went.

...

White Wilderness Plumbing was a squat, two-story building with a low row of bricks along the bottom, roughly a foot high, with blue siding above that. The roof was flat, save the spinning exhaust protruding from it. A white sign with red lettering, attached to the wall by graying two-by-fours, protruded above the business's door. The second floor appeared to serve as an apartment, perhaps for the proprietor.

One thing stood out to Teddy on his approach: White *Wilderness*.

The passage from Revelation said that the pregnant woman, "fled into the wilderness to a place prepared for her by God." Only now he wondered if she'd been forcibly *taken* there. In the mind of a madman, it could easily mean the same thing.

The second thing that stood out was a one-car garage, roughly big enough to house a work van if someone greased it up and slid it in with no way to open the doors. Not surprisingly, a white work van with blue lettering, reminiscent of the *politsiya*, was parked out front. The lights were out in the plumber's shop, and up on the second floor, a single lamp burned in a window bordered by thin curtains.

Teddy scampered up to the rear of the van. His feet were so cold, they'd gone almost completely numb, but the excitement of possibly finding another clue to Irina's whereabouts left him warm on the inside.

Just like his poor toes, the hood of the engine was cold. No residual heat emitted from it whatsoever. It hadn't been moved in hours, which made Teddy think that either it had been a slow day at the office, or the owner of White Wilderness Plumbing had other, more sinister engagements.

Keeping an eye on the windows of the apartment, he tiptoed, quite painfully, over to the edge of the building. He paused and listened, hoping to hear any sign of Irina's presence. He listened to the sounds of the city, passing cars, doors slamming, and distant shouts. None of them belonged to his wife.

What if she's not here?

What if it's another red herring?

What if I took bait that wasn't meant to be bait and now she's a hundred miles away in the real woods, freezing in some cabin with that bastard unbuttoning his pants and zipping down his fly and—

Stop it. That's not helping. Find a way in. All you can do is ask.

Cautiously, and just in case, Teddy kept his back close to the wall, walking sideways, as he looked for a rear entrance, perhaps leading to a set of stairs. Something unlocked, preferably, though he wasn't above throwing that loose cinderblock by the fence through the front window if it came to that.

When he reached the northwest corner and poked his head around, he found what he was looking for: a set of three steps leading up to a beige door. From his spot on the building's side, he tried the knob, the latch disengaged, and it pulled open with a rusty creak.

Good, it's a start.

From the corner of his eye, he noticed a splotch of familiar color through the garage door window. A burgundy shade painted on a support post sat on the other side of the glass. It could've been anything, something innocuous, had it not been for the yellow, knitted sun held in place by a roofing tack.

Teddy let go of the door and stepped over to the garage. He put his fingers on the lip of the window and pulled himself up onto the balls of his feet.

"Little One" had always been an appropriate nickname, no matter how much he hated it, but it was never more evident than now as he stretched to his limits trying to see inside. He was able to get enough of a look to confirm what he suspected; the *kvass* cart sat inside.

It was all he needed to see.

"I'm coming, *dorogaya*," he whispered.

. . .

The door's squeak sounded like a banshee howl as Teddy slowly pulled it open, trying his damnedest to stay quiet. He paused, held his breath, and listened for any sounds of movement upstairs.

Nothing. Thank God.

He was unarmed, exhausted, and afraid, but the adrenaline made every discouraging factor irrelevant. He would run through a wall of bullets if it meant freeing Irina from Oleg, just like the characters in the games he'd played, designed, and sold over the years, both with his father's company and his own. Irrational, maybe, but heroism doesn't always involve measured sanity.

A bulletproof vest would be nice, though.

Teddy lifted his foot and set it down on the first step. He shifted his weight upward and shook his head when the wood groaned, again announcing his presence like a blaring doorbell.

He waited, heard no approaching footsteps, and felt safe for the moment.

Two more steps upward and still undetected. Three, four, five more quickly upward as he paused halfway. He heard faint noise, music and gunfire coming from above. A television somewhere inside the apartment masked his arrival.

Good. Anything helps.

Ten more breathless steps and he stood outside the door at the top of the stairs. Softly, he placed his ear against it and listened. The television continued to cover any sounds of life inside. What if it was all a decoy? What if he tried to bust inside and found Oleg's clueless wife or maybe a distraught mother-in-law? What if the red dragon had actually stolen Irina away to some Siberian wilderness?

I can back off, call Uncle Nikita. I beat him here, right? I found this bastard first. Well, maybe. Call in Uncle Nikita, tell him I know what's going on, give him a lead?

Hell, no. You don't have time. Man up, Malyutka. Do it yourself. Do this for Irina. He could have her in there doing God knows what to her and your baby.

Go. Do it. Now.

Teddy grasped the railing with both hands, braced his shoulder against the wall, and lifted his leg.

Goddamn, this is going to hurt.

He drove his foot into the door, inches to the right of the handle and the latch.

The thud echoed down the stairwell.

He kicked again and cried out in pain, then screamed, "Irina!"

With the third kick, the wood splintered and shattered, as did some bones in his right foot, but it swung open and he threw himself inside, staying low, falling onto the floor to reduce his size as a target. Even without the proper tactical training, Teddy knew to make himself harder to hit. He'd learned enough from video games and military consultants to be prepared for that.

He rolled once, twice, across faded yellow linoleum and stopped with his back against the refrigerator. In front of him, the empty kitchen. To his left, at the nine o'clock location, was a doorway leading into a hall. Directly to his right, another entrance.

Overhead, a deafening boom pierced his eardrums and a potted plant exploded next to the wide open door.

Twelve-gauge? Jesus.

Whoever pulled the trigger was firing blindly and in a hurry. Teddy listened for the *cha-chunk* of another shotgun round entering the chamber.

A second ticked by, then two, then three. He glanced up. Nothing—wait, there it was, the barrel poking through the entryway, into the kitchen, from perhaps a living room. Teddy could hear the television—the voices of Bruce Willis and Ving Rhames, *Pulp Fiction*—around the corner.

Inch by inch, the barrel shakily crept inward.

Teddy pulled his aching, throbbing feet closer, out of the line of sight. He had broken bones in the right one. He knew it. How much of a hindrance that would cost him remained to be seen.

He waited until he could see a chubby hand resting on the shotgun's light brown forestock, readjusted his weight as stealthily as possible, said a quick, *Please God* to himself, and then thrust upward with his good leg.

Oleg.

Teddy came up from underneath, grabbing the shotgun and pushing the barrel toward the ceiling.

The *kvass* vendor, the Big Boss faker, yelped and squeezed the trigger on instinct. The percussion deadened Teddy's right eardrum, replacing it with a high-pitched inner ear siren overlaying hissing white noise.

Oleg outweighed him by a hundred pounds easily, but with the element of surprise, Teddy was able to catch the big man on his heels, the momentum carrying him back, back, until he tripped over his own feet and fell. The shotgun clattered away and caromed off of an end table.

Teddy pounced, growling, driving his knees into Oleg's chest, and propelled himself forward and down, shattering the man's bulbous nose, knowing it would cause his eyes to water profusely.

Teddy had learned this bit of self-defense from Randall Blevins, his Marine Corps sniper buddy. A man who couldn't breathe or see was a man who would have a damn hard time fighting back.

Usually.

Oleg used his size to wrench his hips upward and throw Teddy to the side. He spat something in Russian, fist driving into Teddy's jaw as he rolled.

Oleg climbed to his feet.

Teddy saw flashes of light. Blood flooded his mouth. He tried to crawl for the shotgun. Oleg's heavy boot shattered Teddy's ribs and drove the air from his lungs. He curled up and tried to protect his body. Another boot tip delivered to the inside of his thigh. Another to his spine.

Oleg pinned Teddy's leg to the floor, boot heel on the outside of his knee. He reached down and grabbed Teddy's ankle.

He's gonna break it. No, no, no—

Oleg yanked and twisted sideways.

Teddy felt the *pop*, had never experienced pain so intense, and struggled to stay conscious.

I have to. Irina. Can't...

Oleg let go and stepped away, grinning, back facing the kitchen.

Teddy drifted, drifted, and weakly reached for the shotgun on the floor.

Oleg wiped the blood from his nose. "Such an important man, you are. Keep trying."

Teddy's fingers clawed at the dirty hardwood. "Irina," he whispered.

"Mine," Oleg said. "My toy."

Teddy looked up at the *kvass* vendor standing over him. "What?"

Oleg pointed at his chest. "Mine first."

"Irina?"

"Twenty years I wait. She returns with you, an American."

"So you were trying to get rid of me? Why didn't you just kill me and take her?" Teddy knew the attempt at distraction was useless, but he nudged himself with his good leg toward the shotgun. Of course he'd never get there in time. Of course he'd never have a chance to grab it, aim, and pull the trigger. Oleg was bigger, faster, and aside from a broken nose and a sore chest, he wasn't crippled.

"No fun that way. You play games? I play games. Confuse you for days. Lead you further and further away from my prize. Give Irina time to love me again; that way, not so sad when you're gone."

Teddy froze when he saw movement at the kitchen door, behind Oleg.

A man with stark white hair, gold chains, and a purple tracksuit, stood with a finger to his lips and handgun at his side. Teddy averted his eyes, trying not to give away Uncle Nikita's approach. "Good effort, Oleg, but you've got a lot to learn. Your objectives weren't clear, the storyline sucked, and that whole reference to the Bible is so clichéd, but you know what? It doesn't matter."

Oleg laughed. "You think so? Why?"

"Because...because I'd say it's game over, asshole."

Uncle Nikita lifted his handgun and squeezed the trigger.

...

Irina sat beside Teddy's hospital bed. The rope burns around her wrists and ankles were sore from hours of struggling against them. The baby kicked softly inside her tummy when Teddy groaned and rolled toward her, opening his eyes.

"Hey," he said.

"The baby knows your voice."

"So awesome." A sleepy smile lifted one corner of his mouth. "How long have I been out?"

"It's November."

Teddy's eyes went wide. "What?"

"Kidding. Just a couple of hours. The surgery went well. They say you'll walk fine soon. Maybe like a robot with all the metal in your leg, but nothing permanent."

"Good. You okay?"

"I'm fine, *dorogaya*. My hero. You worry about getting better."

"But he hurt you."

"Not much. Just the ropes."

"Yeah, but he had you tied to that metal bed without a mattress. If you're gonna kidnap your childhood sweetheart and keep her in your apartment, at least have the proper accommodations."

"He only wanted to love me. Old crushes die hard."

"Nah, he died pretty easily from what I saw." Teddy shifted his weight and whimpered. The painkillers weren't strong enough. "Uncle Nikita say anything? You know, about me?"

She winked. "He says you've earned a spot at the table, finally. Welcome to the family." The skin ripple along her stomach, underneath her green tank top. "Oh, Papa, did you see that?"

Teddy's insides grew fuzzy. "Amazing. You know what that makes me think?"

"What's that?"

"With everything that's happened to Sara, and Randall, and you, and me over the past couple of years, it's unreal, you know? From now on, if we play any more games, can we stick to something simple, like checkers?"

Irina nodded. She reached over and caressed Teddy's cheek. "Please, *dorogaya*. No more games. We're almost out of lives."

. . .

Dear Reader,

Thank you so much for spending your valuable free time with my fiction and I hope you've enjoyed the crazy ride along with Sara, Teddy, and the gang throughout these three novels and Teddy's novella! What began as a story I wrote on a whim has turned into a career as a novelist and I couldn't have made it here without your help.

To stay up to date on when I have new fiction available, and if you haven't already, you can head over to my site, ernielindsey. com, and join my new release mailing list where you'll get access to free copies of my work, be first in line for huge discounts on new releases, and get a chance to participate in some great giveaways.

As you've probably seen me request in the past, nothing helps a writer more than word of mouth. <u>Please consider leaving a review</u> and sharing with your friends and family on your social networks. It doesn't have to be much. Even a couple of sentences help!

If you're curious about the insanity that Randall and Mary had to go through, referenced throughout SARA'S FEAR, you can follow their story in **The White Mountain**.

Or, if that's not your cup o' tea, I have plenty more novels and short stories available and I invite you to check them out.

Again, thank you. It's been a wonderful journey so far and here's to many more books to come. I'll keep writing if you keep reading!

All best,
Ernie

Website: http://www.ernielindsey.com
Facebook: http://www.facebook.com/ErnieLindseyFiction
Twitter: http://twitter.com/Ernie_Lindsey

Made in the USA
San Bernardino, CA
05 October 2018